Road Ghosts
OMNIBUS

E. Chris Garrison

The Road Ghosts Omnibus

Four 'til Late (Book One)

Sinking Down (Book Two)

Me and the Devil (Book Three)

"Spectral Delivery" (Bonus Short Story)

Table of Contents

Four 'til Late

This novel is dedicated to Chuck Stringer (1963-2007), the best uncle and friend I could have ever asked for.

Chapter 1 - Uncle Gonzo

"Go away!" The papery voice whispered from the speaker of Brett's voice recorder. *"Go away!"*

"See, it repeats itself!" said Brett to Jimbo.

Jimbo ran a hand through his spiky blonde hair, squinting at the electronic device. "I dunno, how do you know it's a ghost?"

Brett stood up and pocketed the device. "Well, I don't know for sure, but I didn't say it, and neither did anyone else there."

"Sure sounds like it doesn't like you, whatever it is."

"Yeah, I know. It's sort of a trend," said Brett, taking his glasses off for a moment to polish them.

"Huh?"

Brett held the glasses up and peered at Jimbo through the lenses one at a time. "Oh, it's nothing. Just each ghost hunt I seem go to on lately, I get unfriendly messages like those."

Jimbo shrugged. "Fran's into that stuff. Gives me the creeps, honestly. Don't play it for Gonzo, you know he'll just laugh."

Brett rolled his eyes and checked his watch for the third time in ten minutes. "It's after ten now, where is he?"

Jimbo shrugged and didn't look up from his handheld game. "You know Uncle Gonzo, he probably had to make a liquor run first. He would have called if something happened, right?" He cursed at the video game.

"Maybe he's not coming at all, maybe he's gotten distracted by a shiny object and 'forgot' to let us know he can't make it." Brett scowled and glanced at his watch again. It hadn't changed.

Damn.

Jimbo glanced up at Brett. "Yeah? Think he'd pass on a road trip? This was *his* idea... He's spent the past month trying to talk us into it. I could be home playing Warcraft right now. My guild could use the help. I could have saved the drive up from Bloomington... Anyway, Gonzo can be flaky, but it'd take an act of God to keep him from his precious New Orleans road trip." The game bleeped and Jimbo clicked it off in disgust. He picked up his beer, sniffed the neck of the bottle, and then gulped down half.

"Yeah, I know," said Brett. "It's not just important to him, but to me too. I gotta get away for a while. Gonzo has good taste, New Orleans is an excellent destination, but to me it doesn't matter so much where we're going. Hitting the road with you guys will be just the thing I need.

"Work been shitty for you too?" asked Jimbo.

Brett nodded. "Yeah, it's been crazy busy. But I think I've just spent too much time in my own head, you know? All the stress, it's giving me nightmares."

A shrill car horn blared outside. Again, and again, each blast longer than the last. "Damn it, we wait two hours for him to show, and now we're holding *him* up?" Brett swung his backpack to his shoulder and grunted. Jimbo gulped down his beer and belched loudly, tossing the empty bottle in the trash. He grabbed the rolling bag he'd packed and velcroed the game into a side pocket. The two friends exited the townhouse, Brett locked the door, and they headed outside.

A powder blue minivan sat idling, headlights on, out in the parking lot. At first, Brett grabbed Jimbo's shoulder to hold him back. They looked at each other and turned to go back to the apartment. The shrill horn, more annoying outside, made Brett jump and turn around.

Jimbo cried, "Hey, it's Gonzo, in a *minivan*!"

Brett turned around and laughed, a short bark of a noise. "I'll be damned. Hey, Uncle Gonzo finally made it."

Inside the van sat Gonzo, a bear of a man with a ruddy face, reddish brown hair pulled back in a ponytail, and cheerful squinty eyes. "Junior, when are you gonna stop calling me 'Uncle'? It's embarrassing. I'm only a few years older than you! You're that much older than Jimbo, too, but he doesn't call you 'Uncle Brett'. Also, I'm sick of explaining that there's no relation between me and you mutants."

"Maybe I'll stop when you quit calling me 'Junior', Gonz? I turned 30 this year!" Brett grinned and walked toward the van.

Jimbo jogged up to the Grand Caravan and grinned at Gonzo. "What happened to the Z, Uncle Gonzo? Did it get a sex change and gain weight?" He giggled insanely, and then put on his best whiny Luke Skywalker imitation, "What a piece of junk!"

Brett joined him more slowly but snorted at the reference.

Gonzo smirked. "This fucker will do point five past light speed!" He cackled and smacked the roof of the van, leaning his head out the window to look back at the bulk of the vehicle as if checking to see if it was still all there. "I got it just for trips like this. Think we could have fit both your whiny asses in the Z? Liz would have to ride in my lap." He put on a look of mock disappointment. "On second thought, maybe I should have brought the Z after all." He shifted the Caravan into park, pulled the emergency brake and stepped out. He slid open the side door. "Load up, gentlemen, it's going to be a wild ride."

Brett coughed and looked dismayed. "Liz? Is she actually coming along? I thought she had to work?" He stared into the van rather than looking at either of the other two guys. His backpack stayed on his shoulder, weighing that side of him down. Glancing back at the townhouse, he took deep breath and let it out.

Jimbo tossed his bag in the back of the van. "You still hung up on her, Brett? You guys broke up two *years* ago, didn't you? Thought you were doing the platonic friends thing?"

Seeing that Brett still hadn't loaded his backpack, Gonzo shrugged and took his bag from him and tossed it through the van's open door to join Jimbo's. "Liz couldn't pass this vacation up, she got someone to work for her. We're picking her up in Memphis along the way. It'll be fine! Liz is cool, and it's not like either of you is seeing someone right now."

Brett sighed. "No, it's not that. We're good friends, we chat online all the time. She's even been up to see me a couple of times. She's just... Well, I'm not sure how actually traveling with her will go. She's such a dingbat. She can be hard to take in large doses. Do you know she's got a twenty-four-seven webcam going, like the 'JenniCam'?

She has actual fans, a fan club! From the sound of it, a bunch of them are crazier than she is."

Jimbo cut off Gonzo's reply and waved a hand to dismiss Brett. He patted the side of the Caravan. "Gonzo, dude, this van actually *has* a soccer symbol on the back. Are you kidding me? How can you be *seen* in this thing?"

"Hey, she's got room enough to camp in if we have to, and I don't have to worry about putting miles on the Z. I almost scraped off the soccer sticker, but I thought it'd be funnier to keep it. I'm calling her '*Soccer Mom*'. She'll get us there and back again at least. Don't mind the 'old people' smell. The last owner must have tried everything to make it stink less. Instead, it smells like pine-fresh ass now." Brett looked back at the townhouse one last time, sighed, and walked around to get in the front seat. "Shotgun," he said halfheartedly. Jimbo was already in the back, fishing his game out of his bag.

Gonzo closed the side door, got in the driver's seat and pulled *Soccer Mom* out of the parking lot and onto the main road. "Next stop, Memphis, baby!" He flicked on the CD player and cranked up the volume on Mojo Nixon's hyperactive version of "Viva Las Vegas." He sang along loudly. "Bright light city gonna set my soul, gonna set my soul on faaaaar!"

The van bounced down the road on questionable shock absorbers, swerving around slower vehicles. Gonzo's driving elicited a few honks and beeps until he found the on-ramp to the highway. At that point, every car on the road was playing the same game of dodge-em. The Indianapolis skyline loomed larger and larger, the glowing office windows defining their bulk, radio towers atop flashing red lights to warn off airplanes. Brett leaned his cheek against the passenger-side window and sighed yet again, his breath fogging on the glass in the cool October night.

"Liz'll be more fun than you assholes anyway. She's got her own style, her own brand of class. I think she's better at being 'one of the guys', too." Gonzo grinned over at Brett encouragingly, though Brett didn't feel it.

"Yeah, she's okay. I just don't know if I want to hear all about whatever her latest weird project is for a thousand miles. Trapped. No escape..." Brett forced a smile as he mimed loading his hand with an invisible bullet and pretended to blow his brains out, making wet sound effects as he did.

Jimbo laughed from the back seat. "Aw come on, Brett, she can't be into anything weirder than you are. What's *your* project this week? Time travel? Or are you building a better leprechaun trap?" He pitched his voice high without missing a beat in his game. "Always after me Lucky Charms, begum and begorra!" Gonzo cackled again and elbowed Brett.

Brett felt his face burn, and didn't respond until after the other two stopped laughing. Gonzo popped in a Pogues CD, which was now playing "The Sick Bed of Cuchulainn." Brett had to almost shout over it, "Well, I'm curious, that's all. There's so much out there that we don't know, or we think we do, but really don't. I guess Liz and I had that in common, except she just likes weird for weird's sake, she doesn't really ask a lot of questions. It always drove me crazy the things she'd just accept without any reason. She hasn't changed, either."

"You're right about being one of the guys," chipped in Jimbo, face glowing odd colors from the electronic screen as he punched at the game madly with his thumbs. "She's a real girl, but I've seen her win a belching contest and she's held her own with Gonzo playing quarters." Jimbo smiled, then snapped his handheld game shut. "What's she doing anyway?"

"Still in tech support, if you believe that. I couldn't do it, I really couldn't. I'd find a way to track those fuckers down and beat them to death with their own keyboards." Gonzo chuckled, "She loves telling stories about the Idiot of the Day and how she's strung them along, getting them to insult themselves with her sweet talk. I wouldn't trust her in a game of poker, that's for sure."

"Since when do you keep in such close contact with Liz? People said *I* was robbing the cradle when I dated her. You'd be older than the Standard Rule of Creepiness allows, 'Uncle Gonzo'."

Gonzo sniffed, turning off the van's brights due to the fog rising up the highway as they passed the city's downtown. "She's just a kid. We're both on that 'customers suck' Internet forum, and I've learned a whole lot more about what goes on in her head than I probably want to know. You're lucky your breakup was amicable. She's evidently got a katana and she told me how she'd eviscerate a man in just two cuts." Gonzo drew breath through his teeth in a hiss, wincing in mock agony.

Jimbo added, "I bet the katana has Hello Kitty on it, and she'd go, 'Uh oh, did I do that? Oopsie!'"

Brett turned in his seat. "Don't ever do that again, you sounded exactly like her. I'm going to have nightmares now."

Jimbo held his hand up flat, tips of his fingers touching the little O his mouth was making, eyes wide and innocent. Brett shook his head and looked forward. And screamed in unison with Gonzo. "Aaaaaaa!"

The fog solidified in front of them. The figure of a large man, standing in the middle of the road, raised its arm, palm held up as if to hold the van back through sheer force of will. The apparition glowed pure white in the van's headlights. Gonzo slammed on the brakes and threw the wheel towards the right shoulder. The Caravan skidded and its tires squealed. It was too late, but the figure burst into tatters of fog, and there was no impact other than a sort of muffled whuffing noise. Brett felt Jimbo hit the back of his seat and heard him yelp.

The van didn't fishtail much though, and Gonzo brought it to a halt on the side of the road, hazards blinking as the nighttime traffic whizzed past them.

"What? What the fuck?" said Jimbo, who was reseating himself, buckling up for the first time. "What the fuck just happened? Was there a dog in the road or something?"

Gonzo and Brett just stared at each other and couldn't speak for a moment, then both got out of the van. "I don't see a body," said Gonzo, voice shaking. "You saw it too, right, Brett?"

Brett could only nod, then walked to the front to examine the bumper. "He was there, then... he wasn't."

"Come back! What's going *on*? Body? What are you talking about?"

"It... it was a ghost," said Brett slowly, "an actual ghost!" He grinned as though he'd just won a prize. "Goddammit, I wish I'd had my camera out!"

Gonzo laughed nervously. "Camera? I think you're lucky we didn't piss ourselves. Ghost? No, it couldn't be, it was an illusion. It's late and the fog is pretty bad..."

Brett still grinned, looking at Gonzo as both took their seats again and shut the doors. "Who are you trying to convince? Me or you?"

Chapter 2 - Down the Road

Soccer Mom stayed in the right-hand lane of I-70. Gonzo gripped the wheel and looked in the rearview and side mirrors furtively. The fog flew in rags past the windshield. Other cars were passing them impatiently, though they were by now up to the posted speed limit. Stubbled cornfields rushed by on either side, punctuated with the occasional mile marker or road sign.

Brett rummaged in his backpack. He came up with a thick black paperback book, <u>Ghosts</u>, by Klaus Reisen. Keys jangled as he pulled out a penlight, sounding loud in the silent confines of the Caravan. Since conversation in the van had fallen silent, he paged through the book. He stopped here and there to read a passage, then flipped on, searching for something in particular, or scanning for some kind of answer.

After some time and miles passed, Jimbo groaned. "Well, here it comes."

Gonzo chuckled. "What, did Donkey Kong take a dump?"

"I wish," said Jimbo.

Brett put down his book. "Okay, what is it, then?"

"It's Frannie, she's texting me a bunch of crap."

Brett knew this story. "Let me guess, your girlfriend's home all alone and wishes you were too."

Gonzo sniffed the air around him. "I smell something… clingy!"

"Yeah, pretty much. She says the guild misses me in our Warcraft raids, but she's made no secret that she's not happy that I'm taking this trip without her."

Brett turned to look at Jimbo. The gamer's thumbs jabbed away at the keys of his cellphone, his face lit by the screen. Brett saw Jimbo's forehead furrow. "Why can't she let you have a fun trip with the guys? Well, and Liz too. Is that the problem?"

"No… I haven't even mentioned Liz yet."

"Can I read it later? I want to pinpoint the exact moment when she blows a fuse," said Gonzo, snickering.

"Be nice, Gonz," said Brett. "Jimbo, the sooner you tell her, the better. Gonzo's not wrong. Best to get it out of the way."

"Yeah, yeah, I'm telling her now. She's hinting that we should go to Savannah to pick her up instead of going to New Orleans," said Jimbo, clicking away at the phone.

"Fuck that," spat Gonzo. "The Big Easy's calling my name, not the Big Crazy."

"You're not helping, Gonz…" said Jimbo.

Brett sighed and looked out the front window. No fog now, just darkness and the lines of the highway. His heart began to beat faster, his stomach knotted. The van moved far too slowly for his taste, at that moment. He felt the urge to flee, to hide, to get somewhere safe. It worried Brett that he couldn't think of any reason for it. *Fran's Jimbo's problem. Is this just jitters about seeing Liz again soon? We've visited before, it's never been like this.*

After awhile, Jimbo unleashed a stream of curses.

"Now what?" asked Gonzo.

"She's giving me shit about Liz. If she wasn't jealous before, now she sure is. How can I explain to her that it isn't like that?"

"If she's going for anyone in this van," said Gonzo, "it'll be Brett."

"Don't start that again," said Brett. A spark of nervous hope sputtered inside him at the thought, but he crushed it out.

Jimbo said, "You're right, dude. Maybe I'll play up your history to Fran to calm her down."

Brett sighed. "Whatever. She just needs to get off your back. You having fun shouldn't make her miserable."

"Huh. She said she's going to bed."

Gonzo whistled along with the old blues ballad playing on the van's stereo, then said, "I hope that's that."

Jimbo said, "I have a feeling it's only the beginning."

*　　*　　*

"Welcome to Effingham!" cried Gonzo as he pulled *Soccer Mom* off the interstate. "I've been driving since I got off work, I need a break. I'm feeling a wee bit dry."

The others grunted assent, watching the empty streets of the little town go by. "Looks dead," said Brett, shutting off his penlight and marking his page. "Guess they roll the sidewalks up at nine here." He frowned as he passed an abandoned gas station, plastic bags over its pumps. "We even going to be able to fill up here?"

"Don't worry, little towns always have three things you need. A greasy little diner, a place to drink beer, and someplace to get gas. Sometimes all three in one! By the way, you might want to roll down a window." He smirked and waved a hand in front of his face. Both Brett and Jimbo lunged for the electric window switches to purge the van before taking another breath. The temperature dropped rapidly and Brett's hair whipped in front of his glasses, forcing him to tuck it back behind his ears. Obligatory groans and complaints accompanied Gonzo's cackles as they pulled up in front of a filling station with a bar attached.

"Ha! 'The Effing Hole.' That's spectacular! I think I'll get myself an Effing beer, what do you guys say? I think I need a picture of me in front of that sign as an Effing souvenir!" Gonzo didn't wait for an answer, the door slamming behind him as he approached the front door.

Brett looked at Jimbo. "We haven't even been going two hours yet!"

Jimbo shrugged and slid open the side door, following his older friend. "Hey, I could use a beer myself, and I've gotta pee anyway. Maybe they have sandwiches or fries or something?" The door slid shut with a thump. Brett sighed and trailed behind the other two.

When he entered, he found Gonzo already accepting a pitcher and three glass mugs at the bar from a leathery-looking little woman with a bandana tied around her hair. She smiled a welcome to the other two men, taking a couple of years off her tired face. She raised an eyebrow and asked Brett for his ID, and he handed it over, saying, "I'm thirty, but okay..." She looked surprised and handed it back with a "You sure don't look it, Sweetie!"

Gonzo poured the beers. "Typical pisswater, but what do you want at midnight in Effingham? They have *both* kinds of beer here... Bud *and* Bud Light!"

Brett made a face, but took the beer anyway, sipping at it sourly. Jimbo didn't seem bothered, and cheerfully took a healthy pull off of the mug. "Hey Gonzo, we gonna make it to Memphis in one run, or should we try to find a place to stay along the way?"

"Well, the plan was to go straight through, but I got a late start because of work crap, and I'm more tired than I thought already. I want to make it a bit further though, so we can spend part of the day in Memphis with our feet ten feet off of Beale. Liz says there's a Blues and Bar-B-Que Festival going on, we can't miss that!" Gonzo snapped his fingers and downed his beer in one long gulp. He paused dramatically and let out a belch that made the tavern's handful of other patrons all turn to look in irritation or amazement. Gonzo noticed this and did a little bow and flourish in his seat. The locals shook their heads and laughed, going back to their own conversations.

"Guess 'the Legend of Uncle Gonzo' will live on in this burg, passed down through for generations to come along with Paul Bunyan and Johnny Appleseed as a true American legend," snarked Brett with a smile. "Slow down there, hoss, how much of that pitcher were you planning on downing before getting behind the wheel?"

"Relax, *Junior*, this *Uncle's* beat, and I figure one of you can master the complexities of the beast that is *Soccer Mom* and get us an hour or two further along. I think there might be a state park somewhere in there, so maybe we can just camp for a few hours and head out in the morning?"

Jimbo raised his hand. "I'll just have this one beer and I can drive. The back seat's okay, but I'm less likely to get carsick up front. I'll need something to eat on top of it though."

The bartender soon arrived with a big basket of steak fries, as if in answer to Jimbo's hopeful request. She eyed Jimbo's "Jesus Saves... and takes half damage" t-shirt suspiciously, but still smiled as she laid out small plates and silverware rolled in napkins. The fries looked a bit well done, but began to disappear quickly as all three grabbed a handful to put on their own plates.

They munched and drank in silence awhile, then Brett spoke around a mouthful of fries. "So what do you think about seeing an actual ghost on the highway back there? Was that cool or what? The guys on The Spook Board will be so jealous! 'Course it'd have been better if I'd gotten a picture or better yet, video. It was a once-in-a-lifetime, that's for sure!"

Jimbo snickered.

Gonzo gave him a dirty look. "I don't know if it was a ghost or not. I don't think I believe in ghosts. Whatever it was though, it was pretty strange. Anything that can make Brett here scream like a little girl sure is worth the price of admission."

Brett protested. "Me? I seem to remember you just about going off the road, screaming your head off!"

Jimbo snorted. "You're both out of your minds. It was *fog*. It's a cliché, even. People have always been seeing things in the fog. Down in Bloomington, if you go off the main roads, out into the surrounding country, there's always fog late at night. I've delivered out to the sticks and thought I'd seen all kinds of crazy things. Nothing scarier than this one time though." He held up a finger while he drank more of his beer to wash down a French fry.

Brett and Gonzo waited.

"This one time, I was down in one of the hollows, out on Old 37, way out there. I don't think it was in our area, but it was a slow night, and the manager answered the phone and sent me out instead of having me put together boxes or rolling sticks. It was a big order too, so it was worth it in commission alone. Anyway, the fog was thick that night, and every time I went downhill after going over a rise, it was like I was plunging into a cloud bank, I'd have to slow way down to 20 or slower. I was terrified I'd get hit from behind by someone going faster who couldn't see my taillights. Luckily, it was 2am, and I had the roads to myself. I went on for a long while, it was pretty far out of town, I went up this hill and down into another pool of fog. The whole world went white from my headlights, when something loomed up in front of me. Something big!" He took another dramatic sip.

Brett and Gonzo hadn't taken a bite or a drink since Jimbo had started talking, and they continued to stare at him, drawn into his story. "I nearly died that night," Jimbo continued, "The thing reared up and I had to swerve just like Gonzo here did, just to keep from hitting it." He broke out into a grin as the others were still spellbound, waiting to hear more. "Goddamned deer almost took out my pickup."

"Asshole," said Gonzo, finishing his beer.

Brett snorted and rolled his eyes. "Man, if you'd seen what we saw earlier, you would have known it was a..."

The lights went out. Afterimages of the room swam as Brett's eyes darted around to see something, anything, in the darkness. Once his eyes started to adjust, Brett could see a few candles in colorful bowls on tables. The dim, flickering light was just enough to turn the locals into eerie silhouettes. The neon beer signs over the bar held a foxfire glow for a few seconds, then faded away. Brett found himself holding his breath. The bartender cursed.

Brett felt a hand shaking his shoulder. "Holy shit! What the fuck is that? Look at the TV!" Jimbo's hissing whisper right next to his ear made Brett jerk his head that direction, and he could feel his feet go ice cold and his breath suck in involuntarily at what he saw.

On the otherwise dead TV that hung in the corner above the back of the bar, there was a hand. It was as if someone was pressing their hand from *inside* the tube, and the pressure of the palm and fingers, was making the phosphors glow with a faint, sick, greenish light. Brett could see the lines on the palm and the creases in the joints.

Chapter 3 - Through the Night

Shortly after the lights came on, the bar patrons went on with their drinking and eating, carrying along like nothing had happened at all. There was a loud thump, and Brett jumped up and turned, only to see a second metal-tipped dart thunk into the old bristle dartboard. He saw that it'd been thrown by a scruffy, curly-headed guy in a denim jacket, who scowled at him. Brett flashed him an embarrassed smile and sat back down with his friends.

Gonzo looked past Brett at the bartender and waved. She smiled and nodded and held up a finger.

"So what was that?" said Jimbo. "You're the expert on this spooky ghostie Scooby Doo crap, aren't you? Isn't that what all the running around in graveyards after midnight with flashlights and cameras is all about? Don't you have a club or something that does that?"

Brett picked up his glass mug and swirled around the last of his beer. He tilted the pitcher, only getting a few remaining drips into the glass.

The bartender asked if he wanted a refill, but he shook his head. "Got a ways to go tonight still."

Gonzo asked if they had any Irish whiskey, and when she shook her head sadly no, he asked for a "Jack and Coke, skip the Coke and add more Jack, on the rocks." She grinned and set about getting a tumbler full of ice, measured out two shots, then pointedly looked away while it filled further up to cover the ice. She slid it to the grateful Gonzo, who began drinking it immediately.

"I don't know, I've never seen anything like it," said Brett, "Most of what I've done is ghost photography, and a bit of audio recording and analysis in supposedly haunted locations. What I've seen has been either explainable or hard to support as real evidence."

Jimbo asked, "You do this by yourself?"

Brett shook his head. "I'm not in a 'club' right now, but I have some friends I go ghost hunting with from time to time. Those groups are full of thrill-seekers and people who want attention or to feel special, so a lot of what's reported is pretty unreliable. There are some good people, and some folks genuinely interested in using good methods, but they're more exception than rule. And the clubs don't much care; they're usually run by folks who put more stock in media attention than in getting good evidence. They think 'the more, the merrier,' but really, the more people at a ghost hunt, the noisier and more chaotic it gets. Everyone ends up tripping over everyone else, and not many of the groups I've seen are organized enough to handle numbers over six in a team."

Ice clinked in Gonzo's half-drained glass as he set it down. "Yeah, who cares? What was that on the TV? Someone playing tricks here? It *is* close to Halloween, maybe it's something they do around midnight here as some kind of wacky tradition? Maybe there's a VCR in back that plays that... Might be something from one of the Poltergeist movies?"

"Think about it," said Brett, shaking his head. "The power was cut for the whole bar. Even if they have the TV and the hypothetical VCR on a circuit by themselves and cut all the other breaker switches, I didn't even see a power light on the TV when the lights were out. You can see it on now, the power button itself has a green light on it."

Jimbo poked at the pool of ketchup on his plate with one of the last of his overdone fries. "Still doesn't explain what it was. I'm thinking it wasn't a trick, since no one laughed. But no one's acting like they saw it, either."

Brett shrugged. "You know, I'm not sure about that. People often see what they want to see. They'd rather see something that makes sense to them, something that's within their view of how the world works, than to see something that'd completely upset everything they thought they knew about the world."

"I sure as hell didn't want to see it," grouched Gonzo, polishing off his Jack and crunching on some of the ice. "What's special about us that we've seen a traffic cop made of fog on I-70 and a TV that wants to play radioactive patty-cake with us? You might see Slimer every day before breakfast, but I've never seen anything like those things."

"Yeah, me either," said Jimbo, nodding. "Only ghosts I run into are in video games or D&D. Sure, Halloween is coming, but that wasn't a guy in a Scream mask, it was just plain freaky. Maybe you're haunted, Brett. Maybe you've gone into one too many graveyards or haunted basements and got ectoplasm all over you, dragging things from beyond in your wake." He laughed, but still scooted a half inch further away from Brett as though he might be contagious.

Brett shook his head and sighed. "I doubt it. I've never seen anything this... solid before. Yeah, I've seen, heard and felt some stuff I can't explain for sure, but nothing's ever really jumped out and gone 'Boo!' like that, not even in the places around the state that are listed as 'most haunted'. This stuff was better than special effects in scary movies. It was really *real,* and as much as I've been dying to have experiences like these, I'm still at a loss to explain them. Maybe I was able to look at the hand on the TV screen and not have my brain delete it out as impossible, but I can't figure why you two are different. Maybe it's from listening to me go on about the stuff I've seen in the past? But you've never really taken that seriously, so I don't know."

"Fuck it. Let's settle up and go. I just want to be in Memphis tomorrow and leave all this behind. That's what road trips are all about, leaving shit behind for a few days and breathing different air for awhile. I say we find a place to crash a bit further down the road and try to get rolling early." Gonzo eyed the last receipt the bartender had left for them, shuffled out some bills and walked toward the door without looking back. He also didn't look at the TV, which required turning three-quarters clockwise around his barstool, rather than taking the shorter path to his left.

Brett and Jimbo sat for only a couple of seconds, then headed out. Once they reached the door, Brett had to grab the set of keys that had been tossed without warning in his direction by Gonzo.

"You okay to drive?" asked Jimbo. Brett nodded. "Yeah, I'm a night owl, the beer was pretty weak, and I had about half of that basket of fries on top of it."

Gonzo pulled open the side door of the van and climbed in. He pulled the door shut, lay sideways in the back seat and shut his eyes.

Brett settled into the driver's seat and checked Gonzo's well-worn road map before buckling in. He drew a deep breath and let it out slow to cover a yawn.

Jimbo gassed up *Soccer Mom* at the automatic pump and growled, "Someone else better get the gas next time, this thing is a pig."

Once Jimbo settled into the passenger seat, Brett pulled the van out onto the street and found the exit back onto the highway.

Sooner than he expected, Brett saw a sign advertising the interchange to take them to Memphis, so he took it. The van sped through the night, Effingham giving way to scattered houses, then fields. Stands of trees were the only regular punctuation in the rural landscape. The highway paralleled a railroad track for a few miles, and *Soccer Mom* outmatched its speed just enough that the train seemed to slide slowly by in the opposite direction. They passed the engine, which whistled a lonely goodbye to them as it crossed a road and the highway diverged from the track. There weren't many other cars, though Brett took some irritable glee in flashing his brights at idiots who didn't turn their own brights down as they approached.

Gonzo's raucous snore echoed in the back of the van. Jimbo nodded off over his handheld video game, even dropping it once.

Brett turned on the CD player again, but found he didn't feel much like the cheerfully obnoxious Pogues, so he switched to another disc at random. He smiled at the Zydeco that played, and he slapped the steering wheel in time with the beat. He imagined the percussionist with a washboard vest capering around on stage during the live performance of the song. He could just about taste the gumbo and jambalaya that was waiting for him down the road in the Delta. This was more like it.

After an hour or so, Brett began to lose his second wind. Gonzo still snored away and Jimbo had long since shut his game off and slept, face pressed against the passenger side's glass.

Signs for a state recreation area caught Brett's attention, so he followed them off the highway and into the park. The entry booth to the camping area was closed and dark, but he pulled the van up anyway.

Jimbo woke up and looked blearily around him as Brett reached out the window to take a campsite reservation ticket. Brett pulled out some cash and slipped it into a self-check-in envelope, which he deposited in the night slot. He filled the ticket out and followed the map printed on it until he found an empty campsite. He pulled the brake and shut off the van.

"Gonzo's still where he passed out. I'll take the back back seats. Can you sleep up here?" Brett took Jimbo's dull nod as answer and climbed into the back, past Gonzo's inert form, and lay down in the empty furthest back seats.

Brett stretched out as best he could and closed his eyes. He saw, just for an instant, the green phosphorescent hand in his mind's eye, but even that couldn't keep him awake for long.

Chapter 4 - Breathless Visions

Brett awoke in the grey false-dawn, his eyes open only a slit; everything was a little blurry without his glasses on. He'd heard something scrabbling around behind the seats. Was something in here with them? An icy feeling stabbed through him at the thought, but he couldn't sit up.

Brett then heard the scrabbling become a kind of rough scraping, traveling up the back of his seat. *Could an animal have gotten into the van? Some kind of raccoon or possum, perhaps?* The thought didn't calm his panic, since even if it were just an animal, he still couldn't move.

The scraping sound moved on the other side of the seat, past his ear, and up toward the top. He couldn't move his head, but from where he lay he could see the window over the seat. Something, some sort of shadow, was moving back there, though he could not yet make out what it was, just that there was movement.

Silhouetted in the dishwater light that filtered in the van's rear hatch window, he saw claws or maybe fingers grasp the headrest, seeking purchase to pull up and over towards him. Brett tried to cry out to warn the others. He strained and pushed his will against his rebelling lungs, his unresponsive mouth and vocal cords. To his horror, Brett could not even consciously draw a breath, or force out a whisper, not even a squeak. In his mind, he was screaming, howling a warning, but try as he might, he could not speak or do anything to make a sound to wake up his friends, he was terrified and his heart began to pound as the terror rose up in him.

The form of a shadow loomed into the window's light now, more clearly inside the van, right behind the seats where Brett lay. Not a raccoon or an possum, it had the shape of a human head and shoulders. With the light behind it, Brett could make out no features, no colors at all, just the silhouette, as though a shadow had peeled itself off of the ground to menace him.

The form looked around the cabin of the van, searching... and Brett knew it was seeking him.

It found him. The shadow thing peered downward now, over the back of the seat. It seemed to stare at him, and Brett could feel its gaze cut right into him. Brett still could not move, paralyzed with fright or some more sinister force. He was sure the figure meant him harm, and once it was done with him, it would go after his friends too.

The shadowy form reached its gripping hand over the seat now, moving toward his face while Brett lay helpless. Maddeningly, he was still unable to move or speak. Brett could only watch it draw close, grasping his throat and squeezing, cutting off his breath. He found he could move just a little now and tried to lift his hand, but it felt like it weighed hundreds of pounds. The shadow began to whisper harsh, grating words to him that were not clear. Brett's panic gripped him as his breath was cut off entirely. He tried with all his might to cry out, to breathe, to scream!

Gonzo shook his shoulders. "Wake up! Brett, you fucker, wake up! You're yelling in your sleep! Wake up!"

Brett's eyes flew open and he stopped screaming. He drew ragged breaths, thankful to be back in control of his own body. He pushed Gonzo away and sat up. "Sorry, sorry, I thought I was being strangled..." He breathed in and out, slower now, trying to calm down and stop his heart from racing. He felt a flush come to his face as embarrassment overtook relief.

The light shone grey, the same as in his dream, but there was no dark form between him and the window. He saw only a tree branch waving up and down in the gentle morning winds, back behind the van, only a few leaves still on it. "I... I get night terrors sometimes, sleep paralysis."

Gonzo studied him a moment, then nodded. "I used to get that too when I was in college. My roommate just about killed me a couple of times for waking up yelling and swinging my fists around."

Brett grinned and nodded. "Yeah, so you know what it's like. It's awful, the worst thing in the world when it's happening."

Jimbo's bleary-eyed face appeared from around the front seat. "Sleep paralysis?"

"Sort of the opposite of sleep walking. In sleepwalking, your body doesn't suppress muscle movements you initiate in your dreams, and you go ambling around in real life like you perceive yourself doing in your dreams." Brett took a deep breath and willed himself to slow his speech down.

His friends waited, faces concerned, so Brett smiled and continued. "With sleep paralysis, you wake up partially, but your muscles are still frozen in place, your breathing still only autonomic, so you feel like something's sitting on you, holding you down, keeping you from breathing. Since it's only a partial state of waking, dreams and nightmares can be superimposed on reality too. It can be terrifying. It's one of the things that I ask about when I talk to people who claim to see ghosts just as they go to bed or just as they wake up."

Jimbo frowned. "Sounds like the weird stories my aunt Mel used to tell. She used to say she had this curse on her, something about an old hag who visited her and sat on her chest. We all thought she was crazy. She said that she'd read about others who were visited by the old hag in their sleep too, that the hag was trying to crush the life out of you, steal your air and your soul. One day when we visited her, she told us about how she'd seen a show about out of body experiences. From then on, she kept going on about astral projection and the strange visions she'd had at night. She even said her house was haunted. Sure makes for an entertaining Thanksgiving when we eat at Aunt Mel's."

Brett shook his head. "No, no, it's nothing like that. It's a medical issue, not a paranormal one at all. People love to make up stories, and some psychics seem to have a field day with this one to convince others that they've had a paranormal encounter. It makes real investigating more difficult when fantasies are more fun than reality."

"Well, you sure scared the crap out of me," said Jimbo with a sigh. "I thought something bad had happened to you." He checked the van's clock for the time. "Shit, looks like we haven't even been here four hours."

Gonzo looked out the windows. "Guess you found a state park. Good job. Last thing I remember was getting in the van at the Effing Hole and dying. Thanks for taking over, I was beat."

"I didn't last too much longer," said Brett, "I figure we only have a few more hours 'til Memphis. We're awake anyway now, let's get something to eat and get back on the road. I figure we can be on Liz's doorstep before noon at any rate. When was she expecting us, anyway?"

"I can deal with that." Gonzo retied his ponytail and straightened his jacket. "Well, gents, I have to go piss on some local trees before we go anywhere, but that plan sounds good to me. I told Liz we'd be there in the morning, so I guess we ought to give her a call or something once we're on the road again." He slid the side door open and stumbled off into the woods.

Brett rubbed his face and fumbled around until he found his glasses and put them on. He blinked at Jimbo and said, "I barely remember getting here myself. Have you seen my book?"

"You left it up here," said Jimbo, pointing at the dashboard. "What's with that <u>Ghosts</u> book, anyway? You find anything good in there about haunted televisions or hitchhiking ghosts?"

"It wasn't hitchhiking. I think it was trying to stop us, or warn us." Brett accepted the book from Jimbo as it was handed back to him. He jabbed a finger at the cover. "There are plenty of roadside ghosts in this book. Someone picks up a hitchhiker along a lonely rural road. They travel together awhile, and eventually part ways. The person in the story goes into a diner and describes who they've given a ride to, and the locals get freaked out because the hitchhiker was actually killed in a terrible accident many years ago. The person's been riding along with a ghost!"

Jimbo grinned. "Like 'Large Marge' in the Pee Wee movie?"

Brett laughed. "Exactly. Sometimes the story is reversed like that, with the person being picked up by a phantom driver. Same idea, though the details are different. When very similar stories get told like that, it makes me suspect it's just that... a good ghost story that's made better by telling it as though it really happened. And some people get convinced that it's the truth, and retell it... spreading it around."

"So it's really worthless? Why bother then?" Jimbo sounded genuinely curious.

Brett shrugged. "There are more than anecdotes in here. Klaus Reisen is one of the most respected in the field. He's been going around collecting stories, sure, that's what pays the bills, really. But he's in it for the evidence. He's worked for most of his adult life on researching and trying to verify accounts, to sort the real thing from campfire stories. It gets into psychic protection and other more questionable stuff... Klaus may be a fan of scientific methods, but he's also sure there are limits to what science can tell us in the paranormal field."

Something crashed around in the leaves outside of the open sliding door. The Caravan began to shake and rock, and Brett heard moaning. He dropped <u>Ghosts</u> with a cry and leaped outside and ran. The car horn honked and Brett glanced back to see Jimbo fumbling for the keys, eyes wild.

Their panic was brought up short by a familiar cackling laugh. Gonzo rose up from where he was rocking the van and said, "I wish I could have seen your faces! That was too funny!" Brett stalked back and glared at Gonzo for a moment, but Gonzo's grin was contagious, and though he pretended to take a swing at Gonzo, he was trying to hide a smile as he did so. Gonzo continued, "You're both getting way too serious about this shit. We were tired and we were seeing things. I'll grant they might have been weird, but I bet there's something that makes more sense than 'ghosts,' just like how sleep paralysis isn't an old hag, it's just a chemical malfunction in the body. I don't know the answer, but I'm not letting that ruin my vacation. Let's get something to eat. There's a lodge over there that says 'Country Breakfast Buffet' on it, and I plan to fill up on biscuits and gravy before hitting the road. Come on!"

Chapter 5 - Moving Along

After breakfast, *Soccer Mom* flew down the highway. The wind whistled in through a barely open window, competing with hyperactive punk music bouncing around the van's interior. The early morning sun streamed in the windows, making Gonzo squint at the road.

"Oh my God," exclaimed Jimbo, looking up from his cell phone. "Frannie is driving me crazy. If she tells me one more time that she wishes I'd road tripped to Savannah to see her instead of going with you guys to New Orleans… I swear I'll flush this cell phone at the next rest stop. She's being super clingy... You'd think I was on tour with the Swedish Bikini Team instead of your ugly asses!" He plugged the phone into the backseat power outlet with an adapter and shoved it in the seat pocket.

"Psycho hose beast on the loose!" cried Gonzo. "And here I thought the monsters wouldn't come out in the daytime! Man, Jimbo, you have got to get over your imaginary girlfriend. I mean, if you can't even fantasize right, something's wrong upstairs, if you know what I'm saying?" Gonzo twirled a finger around his right ear, the other hand still on the wheel, and he glanced in the rearview to grin at Jimbo. "Besides, the beast has a point, we're going to be traveling with Liz, the most notorious flirt east of the Mississippi."

Brett felt his face warm with the flush of unexpected anger at Gonzo's implication. "Oh she is, is she? Was she just stringing me along those years we lived together in Bloomington? Was she unfaithful even once when we were together?"

Gonzo rolled his eyes. "I'm saying she's a flirt, not a whore, Brett. You know how she is, she's fun, she's friendly, she hasn't got personal space issues, and she has a way of getting anyone to smile. I can see what you saw in her, she's a great girl, and you were damn lucky to have her for the time you did. But damn it, that was then, and now she's a free agent. She wouldn't do anything to hurt you, but she doesn't have to be a nun to spare your feelings. Chill out, or this is going to be a long trip."

Brett sighed. "Yeah, yeah, I know. It's still fresh enough for me, it's not like I've seen anyone since her. But Fran doesn't have anything to worry about, Liz isn't going to make a play for either of my best friends, especially not while we're going to be cooped up in a car together for days. If I thought that, I'd never have gotten in the van."

There was a sudden burst of eerie music from the back of the van. Electronic music, very tinny, it sounded vaguely like the theme from *Halloween*. Brett pointed, looking at Jimbo. "My phone! Could you grab it from the side pocket of my backpack?" Jimbo fumbled a moment, then obliged, tossing the phone to the front seat.

Brett caught it, fumbled, and then caught it again, glancing at the screen before putting it to his ear. "Speak of the devil," he mumbled before he hit the 'talk' button. "Hey there, Liz, we were just about to call you!" The irritation in his face smoothed out into a more relaxed smile as he talked.

"Hey there hot stuff, I was beginning to wonder whether you were off in a ditch somewhere. Gonzo get you lost or something?" Liz's perky tone said that she hadn't worried at all, and had a playful, warm feeling to it that made Brett long for the past. He had to smile, she still sounded a bit like a cartoon character.

"Nah, we got a late start, and had some weird stuff happen along the way. We'll have to tell you about it when we get there. I wouldn't deprive Gonzo of a storytelling opportunity." Brett pretended to duck as Gonzo sighed and drummed his fingers on the wheel, only the slightest hint of a smile playing around the corners of his mouth.

"Oh, I am sure our Gonzo will be in rare form tonight, assuming you actually get here before the Blues and BBQ Fest is over with. I have a story to tell you myself, it's pretty funny, really. Want me to save it for later?" Liz had laughter in her voice. Brett heard music in the background... Unless Liz had picked up a taste for rap, it sounded like *White and Nerdy* by Weird Al. Another thing he missed about her, her wildly ranging musical tastes.

Brett chuckled, "Oh we'll be there in an hour. Actually, we got an early start after a nap in the wee hours at a great little campground.

Who would have thought you could get Belgian waffles like those in the middle of a forest? We filled up on good food and coffee and are mostly awake. We'll need showers though. I've had to keep the window cracked since we got up."

"Hey now!" Gonzo yelled so that he could be heard over the phone. "I can't help it if sausage doesn't love me as much as I love it!"

Jimbo chimed in, "No more biscuits and gravy for you! Not if we want to live to tell the tale!" He moaned melodramatically.

Brett could hear the hysterically squeaky laughter bursting out of the phone's speaker... He had to pull the cell phone away from his ear until she quieted down.

"You... Ha ha ha... You guys kill me, ha ha, am I going to have to bring potpourri and incense to purge the car of evil spirits?" She dissolved into fits of giggling that were so contagious, Brett couldn't help but laugh along until tears came out of his eyes and he could hardly breathe. Even Jimbo got caught up in the laughter.

"Well, funny you should say that, but ah, that would be telling, and I don't want to spoil the story now. Let's just say that there's more than Gonzo's indigestion to purge from this van, my swee... uh, I mean, Lizzie," Brett stammered. Gonzo made a rude noise as he spluttered out a laugh he was trying to hold in. His eyes stayed fixed on the road though, and he resumed a mock poker face.

"Oh Brett, I heard that! You almost called me your Sweetie! Oh honey, you don't have to stop on my account, I miss being called your Sweetie. It was always so endearing, you always did treat me like a princess. I miss that. It'll be really good to see you. Even if I have to, ha ha ha, purge evil spirits from your van. Van? Whose van?"

Brett's breath was taken from him for a few heartbeats after Liz spoke, and he could feel, to his horror, that his face was flushing red, both due to the slip-up and Liz's teasing. "Oh Gonzo bought an old beater of a Caravan. He calls it *Soccer Mom*. It looks silly for a road trip machine. But hey, it's roomy enough, if you ignore the looks."

Gonzo yelled, "Hey, it was a great deal, and we'll save on hotel space and might not even kill each other before the trip's over since we'll have elbow room."

Liz's laughter chirped from the phone's little speaker again. "A minivan? That's hysterical! I've got to get a picture of all of you so I can post it online! Road-tripping with Soccer Mom! Soon to be a Major Motion Picture! Oh *Chico*, this is going to be great. I can't wait."

Liz hadn't called Brett *Chico* in ages. It gave him a little thrill and kept the flush on his face. "Me either, Lizzie. Anyway, we'll be there soon enough, so I'll let you go for now."

Gonzo called out, "Hey, tell Liz that Frannie thinks we're having an orgy! She thinks you're going to make us all your looooove slaves!" Gonzo made wet, smacking kissy kissy noises in the general direction of the phone, and cackled at his own joke.

Jimbo groaned and slumped down in the back seat and threw his arm over his forehead. "Man, I knew I shouldn't have said anything. Couldn't tell you're supposed to be the mature one here, Uncle Gonzo."

This was met by another rude noise from Gonzo as he peered back at Jimbo in the rearview mirror.

Brett shook his fist at Gonzo in mock anger, but grinned as peals of laughter came from the phone. "Oh yes, I'm going to work my wicked, wicked ways on you all and turn you into obedient slaves. I'll have you feed my cats for me and paint my nails, I'll make you prance around in kilts and wear party hats as you answer the door and cook my meals. Who needs sex slaves when you can have house servants? Muahahaa!" Liz was gasping for breath as she got this out, as she was helpless with laughter. "Anyway honey, get ready to serve my every whim, I'll see you soon! Love you guys!"

"You too, Lizzie. See you soon!" He hit the "end" button and stared at the phone's screen for a moment before cramming it in a pocket.

"Yeah, sure you're over her," teased Jimbo from the back, staring at the ceiling of the van. "Sounds like it's not me Frannie has to worry about Liz casting a spell on, it's you, dude."

Brett's smile faded and he stared out the window at the passing trees. "It's all history. I made a choice, and it's history."

Chapter 6 – History

Red sunlight streamed in the window of the computer room. Brett's shadow fell on the big line printer's innards as he fretted over it. It was the only time of day that sunlight shone through the windows in the computer lab, all the way to the alcove where the printer was kept. Brett wrestled with the paper that had been gobbled up by the treads of the high-speed machine, making a dense accordion of the single quarter-mile long sheet of paper coming from the box. He tore it roughly near the perforation and backed the tractor feed out irritably. That was what happened when idiots tried to print the binary, rather than the actual output. They did it several times per shift, it seemed.

"Oh my goodness," came the cartoonish voice from behind him, "It sure looks like the nasty Dalek monster is trying to swallow the lab technician whole! Exterminate! Exterminaaaaate!"

Giggles followed this, and an orange silk scarf draped around Brett's neck. He felt a gentle tugging, and heard exaggerated grunts and cries of "Help me save this brave man from the awful machine! Oh help!" Since the cries competed with attacks of giggles, no one rushed to help "save" him.

Brett was torn between irritation and amusement. He decided to just go with it and made mock strangulation sounds and pretended to be dragged from the printer bit by bit. After a few moments, he leaned far backwards and tilted his chin all the way up so that he could look up at his tormentor. The orange scarf slipped over his throat, chin, lips and nose, but stopped while covering his eyes. He saw that girl Liz through an orange mist, her face framed by her glossy black hair swinging down from behind her ears as she looked down at him. "Take me to your leader?" she squeaked, letting go of the scarf with one hand to bring her left hand up to make chattering noises and pretend to bite her nails.

Brett snorted and pushed the soft material out of his eyes and turned around to face Liz. He'd been working in this lab for work-study wages while he plugged away at his thesis. It was more distraction than help, and required some strange blocks of time, but it fit between classes conveniently enough to keep the job. Besides, it was one of the few vaguely social outlets he had, other than D&D on Friday nights and Date Night with Cheryl every Saturday night. He got to talk with wacky characters like Lizzie. Well, there was no one like Lizzie, really, just Lizzie.

"Hello," he began lamely. Liz was always so hyper, and she made him feel boring and slow by comparison. Why she came by to see him on his shifts so often was completely beyond him. Yet here she was, in her chunky boots, orange tights, orange T-shirt, and that black denim jumper he'd seen before.

She whipped the scarf around and tied it around her neck again with a flourish. "Hey there, Mister Computer Man, I think I just saved your life. That Dalek looked hungry. Just look at what it did to the paper! You can repay me with a pizza slice and a beer at Pepperoni's after you get off work? You can bring Cheryl too!"

No one can resist Lizzie's grin.

Brett smiled and shrugged. "Hmmm, I guess my life's worth that, at least. I don't know what I'd ever do without you. Cheryl's got night shift tonight, so it'd just be me. Hang on a minute and we'll discuss the details after I put this Dalek back into service." Liz nodded and flounced over to what Brett thought of as the Guest Chair at the Consultant's Desk and plopped into the seat, watching him with exaggerated round eyes, as though he were about to defuse a bomb.

Brett chuckled and managed to re-thread the tractor-feed paper into the big printer. A few students were beginning to mill around, trying not to be obvious about being impatient while waiting for their printouts. Once the paper looked right, he slammed the back of the washing machine-sized printer and stood up. He punched the button to put it back online and the thing began to scream and stutter as it pushed folds of paper into the output bin.

He made a show of smacking his hands together and acting like a conquering hero as he resumed his place at the desk. Liz cradled her chin on top of a hammock made from her interlaced fingers and batted her eyes at him. "Oh Doctor, you've saved the Earth once more from Invaders from Uranus!"

Brett laughed at that and stuck his tongue out at Liz. "Keep carrying on like that and Cheryl will get jealous, my dear."

Liz batted her eyes some more. "Maybe I should give her something to be jealous of then, if I'm going to be suspected anyway?" She winked and stared at Brett uncomfortably long. She couldn't hold it long and soon giggled and sat back and fiddled with her scarf. "I meant it about Pepperoni's though. I'm starved, and it wouldn't be right to go without you and Gonzo. Think he'll be around tonight?"

Brett hoped his face didn't look as hot as it felt. "No, I think he's got a writer's group meeting tonight, though he thought maybe we could catch the Dollar Night movie at the old Indiana Theatre later?"

Liz nodded. "I hear it's a real bomb tonight, so you know we can't miss it."

The Consultant's Phone rang, which was strange, since it was really meant for outgoing calls. Half the time, the consultants would answer with wacky responses since the number wasn't published. Brett decided to be funny and answered the phone, "Domino's! Thirty minutes or it's free!"

"Uh, Brett?" The voice was Cheryl's roommate, Kendall. *"I'm sorry to call you at work, but I have some really bad news. I don't know how to tell you this, so I'll just say it, okay? Cheryl... Well, Cheryl's dead, Brett. She hit a curb on her bike in traffic and got hit by a car just a couple hours ago. They took her to Bloomington Hospital, but there wasn't anything they could do. I'm sorry, Brett. She really loved you, you know?"*

Brett replied to Kendall, but he really didn't know what he said as he hung up the phone. He stared at the monitor in front of him and it all went blurry.

"Brett?" Liz's voice was soft and serious for a change, and he almost didn't realize it was her speaking. Her arm slipped around his shoulders, barely touching him. She felt warm, and her hair swung down to tickle his cheek. "Are you crying? What is it?"

"Her roommate. Cheryl's. She called and said she was dead. Cheryl's dead, Liz. There was an accident." Brett willed his words to come out without cracking or choking up. He was having more and more trouble seeing the words on the screen as he got out of his email and tried to log out. It took three tries before Liz reached over and shut the workstation down for him. He was horribly aware that people were noticing him crying, more and more eyes focused on him. People he saw most every day as they came in to work on projects and ask him questions. He sniffed and tried to say more, but only blubbering would come out.

Liz took him by the hand and pulled him up. She picked up his backpack for him and dragged him from the computer lab, out through the halls and outside into the warm summer evening. She sat him down on a stone bench and held him while he cried. "She's dead, Cheryl's dead, Lizzie! We were going to get married, and she's dead!" Brett was glad Liz was there to hold him in her arms, but he was acutely aware that he was making a scene and felt awful for burdening his friend this way, and out in public like this.

"Shhhh, I'm here, Brett, it's okay. You're okay. We're okay. I've got you. Oh honey, go ahead and let it out, it only gets worse if you hold it in. Cheryl loved you and this is insane and stupid, but this doesn't change all that you had together." Liz kept murmuring words she thought might comfort him in his ear, holding him fiercely tight. Tears streamed down her face as well, which struck Brett as wrong, something that shouldn't be allowed to happen. Liz was not a crying person, she was a laughing person. He hiccupped and gasped as he tried to compose himself enough speak.

"I... I'm sorry, it's just, it's just I don't know what to do now, you know? Can't picture it being real. I mean Cheryl was so strong and smart, how could something stupid like this take her down?" Brett forced himself to stop crying and wiped angrily at the tears on his face.

Liz loosened her hold on Brett and leaned back a bit to look him steadily in the eye. Her nearly black, deep brown eyes stared into his and she spoke more carefully than Brett had ever heard. "Listen to me. I'm here. I'm not going anywhere. You need to meet up with her family and it's going to be hard. I'll be with you whenever you want me to be. Just say the word, and I'll drop anything, okay?"

Brett stared back, trying not to shake, trying to seem more together than he was. He nodded. "Thank you. Thanks for pulling me out of there too. I'm going to need a friend."

Liz pulled him close again and kissed his cheek. He could smell a sweet floral scent in her hair. "You just got yourself a new roommate, buster. I'm not letting you out of my sight for awhile. I'm going back to my apartment to grab some clothes and a sleeping bag, and I'll camp out, okay?" Brett nodded and smiled faintly. "Okay. Thanks, Lizzie."

"Anything for the Man Who Saved the World, you know?" She winked, not as playful as before, but she let a little smile come to her lips, and to her eyes.

Brett let out a cough of a laugh and said, "Maybe, but you saved me first."

Chapter 7 - Crossroads

Elvis did a jig. It was a bad sign. The big 70's sunglasses ate up Gonzo's face, and the ridiculous, exaggerated fake sideburns flopped around as he bounced up and down to the music. The more Brett stared at them, the more the hairy accessories looked like Snoopy's ears. In fact, the dance started to remind him of Snoopy doing his happy dance. Gonzo had slapped the costume together at Liz's insistence, raiding local souvenir shops for components. The rhinestone T-shirt caught glints of the stage lights and almost made up for the outrageous mutton-chops. Liz had done her best with Gonzo's long hair, but it still didn't look right. He strummed a cardboard guitar and utterly failed at imitating Elvis' signature pelvic movements. So instead, since he'd had plenty to drink, and because the intermission music was peppier than the mellow blues bands, he simply had to go jig.

Liz was out on the dance floor too. She had donned black satin pajamas, black gloves, and a black ski mask and had what looked like a real katana in a sheath hanging from her belt. She was coasting in lazy circles around Gonzo's more stationary jigging, weaving in and out of the others in the crowd. She'd dance a little, then lean back on her heels and zip around on those crazy skate shoes she'd gotten. Brett had thought those were only made for kids, but Liz always said she had to go hunting in the children's sizes at times, since she was so small. She invented dance moves that reminded Brett of Tai Chi practice. This won her grins and cheers from other people in the bar. Showing off, she just missed skating into a server or two and startled a big bear of a guy who staggered onto the dance floor and fell down behind her, laughing.

Jimbo had protested having to dress up for the night out. Liz had begged and pleaded and threatened ultra-girly costumes made from her clothes, makeup and many accessories. He didn't have any other ideas, so he let her get away with it. So Jimbo sat, looking uncomfortable, at the table with Brett. He wore Liz's sluttiest red lipstick, false eyelashes, outrageous rouge on his cheeks, and excessive deep blue eye shadow that went to his eyebrows and out almost to his temples. He also sported a pink feather boa around his neck that Liz said had been given to her during last year's Race for the Cure. Liz even convinced him to slip one of her roomy hippie skirts on over his jeans and a floral blouse over his t-shirt. The guys had laughed as they watched Liz "doll him up" as she put it, but Jimbo took it with good grace.

Brett had had a few beers, but was not ready to get up and dance quite yet. He kept toying with the plastic whip Liz had dug out of a storage box (where had she gotten that?) and felt a little silly in the too-small Indiana Jones fedora. At least, he thought, Gonzo and Jimbo were there to distract attention away from him. He sat at the table and just let the loud commotion in the club wash over him.

They'd found the club on Beale Street, fulfilling one of Gonzo's mission objectives. The whole street had a single cover for all clubs that night for Blues & BBQ Fest. It was well worth the price, since each bar had another blues band playing their hearts out. Street performers sang out everything from Muddy Waters to Robert Johnson. Costumes were everywhere, because without one, cover was double. Women were angels, naughty nurses, and cowgirls. Men were pirates, vampires, Jedi masters and zombies. The Blues Brothers could be spotted here and there, and there was even a male-female pair of them, or at least Gonzo said "Elwood" looked a lot like a woman to him.

The barbecue was wonderful; each place's sample dishes seemed more tender and savory than the last. Even Gonzo was impressed with the food.

*　*　*

Liz was waiting outside to greet them as they pulled up in *Soccer Mom*. She ran out to the van, monarch butterfly wings flapping behind her, clipped to her sweater. She wore ruby-sequined Converse All-Stars. After she'd hugged them all, Jimbo asked about the wings. "What are you going as, a fairy or something?"

Liz looked puzzled for a moment, then said, "Oh these? No, I just saw them in a store and thought they'd go with the outfit! Do you like them?" She twirled so everyone could see the wings.

"That's just Liz," explained Brett. "Everything's an accessory for her. She wore cat ears years before it became popular with the anime crowd." Gonzo nodded agreement and shrugged.

Liz grinned and said, "I just think I look good in wings. Or cat ears. Or a lion's tail. It's just fun!"

She led them inside with their gear and lectured them about the importance of costumes when partying on the weekend before Halloween. They each got a shower in, and they went out souvenir shopping and spent far too long looking for a local greasy spoon diner that Gonzo had visited years beforehand. Brett wasn't convinced that where they ended up was really the place he'd been talking about on the trip down. The details didn't match, but Brett didn't argue, since he was starved by the time Gonzo decided that it was the place. It was good food, though they turned down dessert and extra side dishes so they could save room for the barbecue sampling later.

Over lunch, Brett, Gonzo and Jimbo took turns telling their sides of the stories of the ghosts they'd seen on the road and the TV screen in the bar. Jimbo had to badger Brett to tell her about his nightmare. Brett said, "Well, that doesn't count, does it? I've experienced sleep paralysis before, some nightmares accompanying it were a lot like that one. Strangulation, shadowy forms, they're all normal for that condition."

Liz was delighted with all of the stories, making little jokes and asking lots of questions. She'd always shared an interest in bizarre fringe things with Brett. She was especially excited about the glowing image of a hand on the TV, saying she was sure she had seen a photograph of something just like it in one of her books. She enthused, "You guys never told me this was going to be an *actually haunted* road trip! I'm even more psyched about going along with you now! This is going to be the best Halloween ever!" She bounced up and down in her seat, nearly dislodging the butterfly wings in the process. Her impish grin was hard to resist, and despite the groans of protest from the guys, they couldn't help smiling.

"Well, I hate to disappoint you," growled Gonzo through his grin, "but if I have my way, no more freaky shit is going to happen on this trip. Only spirits I'm dying to see are Jameson, Bushmills and Tullamore Dew. I need this road trip, work is just sucking out my soul one day at a time. If I can't go crazy and get the fuck away from the grind awhile, I'm just gonna snap. I think I'm not the only one, either." Jimbo nodded enthusiastically in agreement.

Brett shrugged, "Well, of course it's good to get away, but isn't a haunted road trip even more of an adventure? It might be more of my kind of fun than yours, but hey, it's almost Halloween, isn't it? Why not try to enjoy it if anything more happens? I plan to have my camera out, just in case, from here on." He patted the small camera case on the table.

Jimbo smirked. "It's bad enough being haunted by my girlfriend. She called earlier and was trying to talk me into getting you guys to reroute the trip so we'd end up in Georgia. Said she'd meet us in Atlanta."

Gonzo shook his head emphatically. "No way. New Orleans or bust. We all agreed on that. She'll get her turn some other time, but we're already on our way."

Jimbo held his hands palms-up. "I'm with you, man. I already told her no. She didn't take it well. She kind of had a hissy fit and hung up on me. I wonder if she's maybe losing it, you know? She's been jealous before, but wow, you'd think we were going out to strip clubs every night to bang hookers."

Liz giggled, "You know how I loves me some crack hoes. Oh baby, bring it on!" She writhed in her seat, evidently getting an invisible lap-dance.

Gonzo looked at Brett with a raised eyebrow. Brett snorted and shook his head. "As if."

*　　*　　*

Brett couldn't recall the name of the blues bar where they sat waiting for the Bluesman to come out and play. Gonzo and Brett had seen him play once before in Bloomington, and had been very impressed. When Gonzo had heard he'd be playing, he insisted on getting there early for the show. The house lights dimmed and the canned music faded away slowly. Gonzo stopped hopping around and came back to the table, refilling his glass from the pitcher. He poured what was left as evenly as he could between Brett and Jimbo's glasses. Liz zipped up to the table alarmingly fast, and Brett was sure she was going to crash into him. He reached out his hands to try to catch her, but she leaned forward and squeaked to a stop just in time.

Her eyes smiled impishly behind the mask. "Didn't see me coming, did you? No one sees the Roller-skating Ninja until it is too late. Ah ha ha ha ha! Ah ha ha ha ha!" Liz mouthed her fake laughter so that it seemed badly dubbed. She did a little curtsey and slipped into her chair, pulling her mask down to grin at the guys before sipping from her daiquiri.

A tall, lanky man stepped out on stage. He had two guitar cases, which he arranged next to the simple stool behind the standing mic. He didn't introduce himself, but just popped open one of the cases and took out an acoustic guitar and a harmonica on a wire headpiece. He set the guitar across his knees, made sure the harmonica was situated in front of his mouth, and began to sing and play a rendition of the old Robert Johnson song, "Hot Tamales."

The Bluesman thumped the guitar like a drum while he played. He stomped his feet. He punctuated verses with riffs on the harmonica. He in fact sounded like several people playing at once. He even managed a bass line on the same guitar on which he played the melody. It was impressive, but spooky.

Liz, who had pulled off her ninja mask and let her hair loose, mouthed "Oh my God!" with wide, round eyes. Brett nodded enthusiastically. He couldn't help but tap his feet in time with the music. When the first song ended, Gonzo and Jimbo were cheering and clapping.

The Bluesman didn't pause, and launched into manic, breathless versions of "Walking Blues" and "Terraplane Blues." Brett couldn't remember the last time blues music had so energized him. He began to understand the legends of early bluesmen selling their soul to the Devil to get their musical talents.

The Bluesman paused for a moment and gratefully accepted a glass of ice water from a server. He wiped the sweat from his eyes and pushed back his hair, before he put the acoustic guitar away. He opened the other case now and drew out a beautiful steel guitar. Brett thought it had a steampunk-like style about it.

"That thing should be in a museum!" hissed Gonzo across the table in a stage whisper. "Looks like a '33 at the newest!"

The Bluesman pulled out a metal tube, possibly a sawed-off steel table leg, and launched into a slide guitar riff that made the hairs on Brett's neck stand up and gave him chills even in the stuffy air of the club. The Bluesman tuned the steel guitar carefully as he played, and elicited tortured wails and eerie moans from the instrument, like a live thing.

After a minute or two, he stopped. The bar was silent. He looked up with a gleam in his eye and howled out the words to the song. It was "Cross Road Blues" and Brett felt a strange sort of dread come over him as the song's story of Faustian regret and despair unfolded. The guitar screamed out the agony of a damned soul and Brett realized that he felt like he had upon waking up in the van that morning. He felt as though he was paralyzed by the power of the man's performance, by the sound of the tortured instrument, and by the words of a long lost soul. He picked up his beer glass and took a gulp just to prove he was able to move, though it failed to break the spell. He couldn't break free of this music.

It was then that Liz looked back at Brett, turning slowly around as the song drew to a close. Her eyes got wide and she pointed behind him. Brett slowly turned to look.

Behind him, in the darkness, stood a shadow. He could not see through it, and it was only vaguely human in shape. All he could see were the absence of eyes, which should have been reflecting the stage lights. The figure should have been illuminated, but all he saw was a black outline. A moving black outline. He felt cold, ice cold even under his leather bomber jacket. The figure reached out its arm, extended a finger, and pointed at Brett. It took a step, and Brett's breath caught in his throat.

Time slowed, everything receded from Brett. He was distantly aware of the music continuing, but it was muffled almost to silence. People around him seemed almost as frozen as he, but they were all still wrapped up in the performance, spellbound. The figure slowly advanced on Brett, unnoticed even by patrons at tables that could be seen on either side behind it. His heartbeat was the loudest thing in the world, pounding in his ears. The terror rose in him again, as it had early that morning in the van. It occurred to him, *am I asleep?* But this did not feel the same as the sleep paralysis had. He could control his breathing, he could feel and smell and even move just a bit.

But not fast enough. The shadow took another step and was suddenly right in front of him, inky hands reaching out for Brett's throat before he could stop it. His neck burned with the freezing cold as the fingers formed a constricting band around his neck. He raised his own hands to fend off the attack, to loosen the tight grip on his throat. His hands met with a cold that just stole the strength from him. He wasn't sure of the shadow's substance, his hands were so quickly numb. There was resistance though, something solid was there.

His air cut off, and the darkness in the room started to grow. Brett struggled weakly, feeling his strength drain out of him so rapidly. He heard, in the unnatural silence, a harsh voice whisper to him, *Now you will be mine, and I will be done... Isn't this what you've always wanted?*

There was a cry from Liz behind him, and there was a blur of movement. Liz herself was all in black, but it was black that still reflected light around her. The shiny satin pajamas seemed like liquid as she leaped to her feet and drew the decorative sword. "No! Stop!" she yelled, and made a slashing arc with her arm that made the katana pass right through the shadow figure in a diagonal cut from the base of its neck through its opposite hip.

There was a terrible scream from the shadow as it ripped apart as though it were a black sheet hanging in the air. The halves further unraveled into tattered smoke. Brett felt the warmth of the room come back to him in a rush. The sound of the performance and the crowd around him slammed back, he could hear and feel the noise again. The lights, while still dim, brightened to their previous intensity. He gasped and stood up and stared at Liz, who also breathed hard, staring back at him. She dropped the sword with a clang and was instantly in his arms, a soft, warm little ninja, hugging him fiercely, shaking with adrenaline.

Then the music stopped and the lights came up, and the crowd roared with applause and cheers and whistles. The Bluesman accepted this gravely and bowed slightly on stage, his eyes to the floor. He packed up his guitars and harmonica and walked off the stage the same way he had come. No one seemed to have noticed the attack or even Liz's sword slash or the clatter it made when it hit the floor.

Gonzo and Jimbo turned around to look at the former lovers still embracing behind them. "Oh my God, that has got to be the worst song for you two to get romantic during. What the hell is wrong with you?" Gonzo teased, but Liz and Brett held onto each other a long moment more, and Gonzo dropped the jovial tone when he saw the pale, shaken look on Brett. "What the fuck is going on here?"

Jimbo shushed him, and said, "I felt something *bad* at the end of that song. Cold. I couldn't turn around because I didn't want to see what would be back there if I looked. Something *did* happen, didn't it?"

Liz let her arms go, but kept one arm around Brett's waist as she turned to face the others. "Yes. Something attacked Brett, some kind of nightmare shadow. Right out in the open and no one could see it but me. I, uh..." She glanced down at the katana on the floor.

"She saved my life is what she did!" said Brett, laughing with relief but not humor. "It was just like the sleep paralysis, except, well, it was real this time. I didn't think it was real this morning after I woke up, but maybe there was something going on there too. I'm the first to dismiss paranormal accounts that happen just before going to sleep or just after waking... Guys, I was awake this time."

Liz added, "I was awake too! I mean, I saw it too. You know what I mean. I wish I'd said something, guys, when you were telling your ghost stories. I told you earlier I had a story to tell too? Well, the night before you guys got here, I woke up in the wee hours, feeling like I was being watched. I looked and saw someone peeking in the window. Or some*thing* maybe. Anyway, I blinked and it was gone. I got out of bed and looked outside but I didn't see anything nearby."

"Isn't your bedroom on the second floor, Liz?" asked Brett.

"I *know*, isn't that freaky? It didn't even occur to me 'til I got back in bed that a Peeping Tom would need stilts to pull that one off. I just chalked it up to imagination at the time. But you know, my phantom stalker was just a shadow, like the one that attacked you, Brett!" She pulled herself closer to Brett, shivering.

Chapter 8 – Lights On

"Okay, enough with the boogieman crap, let's party!" said Gonzo, patting Liz and Brett on their shoulders.

"Gonz, Brett did just get attacked…" said Liz in protest.

Brett shook his head. "No, it's okay. I'm pretty shaken up, but I need to keep pushing on or I'll get overwhelmed by the heebie-jeebies, you know?"

Gonzo cackled with glee. "That's the spirit, Junior!"

Liz smiled at Brett and he felt warmer inside, and braver. Almost as brave as his words had been.

Gonzo led them down the street, looking for the next bar. A raggedy busker serenaded them. Her beat-up guitar was the perfect accompaniment to her rich but raspy voice. She asked Gonzo what he'd like to hear. He replied, "Anything by Janis Joplin," and she was delighted to fulfill his request. She launched into "Me and Bobby McGee."

They all beamed at the song choice, and Liz danced around uncontrollably. A few people on the street, also going from bar to bar, joined them, cheering the street performer on and tossing coins and bills into her open guitar case. Soon, a small crowd had gathered, some singing along with her. Brett felt far away from home, and a sense of bittersweet loss welled up as he listened to the feeling the busker put into the song. He fought the urge to go call it a night.

When the street performer was done, she cried, "Thank you!" and got another small shower of tips in her case. The four friends thanked the woman and moved on, hearing her launch into the next song. "*Oh Lord, won't you buy me, a Mercedes-Benz?*"

The raucous energy of Beale Street soon drove away lingering chills from the friends, and soon they were all laughing and goofing around. Jimbo got a few whistles for his costume from passers-by, and even though he grumbled, he still did sarcastic curtseys and waved his feather boa at them. Brett was set upon by another costumed ninja, waving plastic nun chucks menacingly. He stared stupidly at the person for a moment until Liz elbowed him and said, "Dr. Jones, do something!" Brett blinked and said, "Oh yeah!" and drew the squirt gun at his side and "shot" the ninja. The stranger's pratfall was so convincing that they had to applaud.

Gonzo was disappointed in the lack of reaction to his Elvis costume. They'd overheard a few people joke, "See? I told you he wasn't dead!" and one person had even sneered that he'd voted for the young, skinny Elvis stamp.

"Trade ya!" said Jimbo to Gonzo, plucking at his floral blouse.

Gonzo groaned and said, "No thanks, I'll take my chances as the King, baby."

Jimbo pointed at a bar called Coyote Ugly as a possible next destination, but Liz wrinkled her nose and remarked, "You know, I *was* joking about getting me some hoes earlier." Gonzo pointed further down the street. "No, no, that's it, right there, the Rum Boogie Cafe, home of Gator Gumbo!"

Jimbo made a face, but Liz echoed Gonzo's enthusiasm. "Take it from a local, you've *got* to try Gator Gumbo at least once. It's thick, it's rich, and there's no freaking way to tell what all is in it, but wow it's good stuff!"

They had to wait a bit for a table to free up, so they just hung around with drinks in hand, listening to the music playing on the PA. The staff had put on a Van Morrison CD between acts. Gonzo went on and on about how surprised he was that a band wasn't already playing, but a server came by at that point and replied, "You just missed the first band. Next one's in an hour." She pointed at a tiny round table surrounded by four barstools, and they thanked her and took seats gratefully.

Gonzo bought a round of shots of Tullamore Dew for the table, and ordered a bowl of Gator Gumbo to share. Jimbo protested that he'd already had enough ribs and pulled pork samplers and was full to bursting. Liz smirked and teased, "There's always room for gumbo! Come on, Jimbo, what are you afraid of? Don't worry about being ladylike, we all know better!"

It was hard to tell in the dim light of the Rum Boogie, under all the makeup Liz had put on him, but Brett was sure Jimbo's face was reddening a bit. Jimbo sighed, "Fine, I'll try some, but don't blame me if you see it again later."

Gonzo scooted his stool just a little further away from Jimbo, pretending to be worried that Jimbo might vomit at any moment.

Liz laughed and pulled her mask down again. "At least I can get out of the way with my ninja reflexes!" She made silly chopping motions at the air above the table with her hands, nearly spilling the bowl of gumbo that the waitress brought to their table at that moment. "Oops!"

The waitress smiled, shrugged and produced a small tray of shot glasses full of Irish whiskey, a couple of glasses of beer and a glass of water. She set this on the table and headed for the bar to pick up another order.

Everyone took his or her shot glass. Liz sniffed hers and shrugged. Brett grinned at Gonzo. Jimbo was still staring at the murky gravy-looking stew in the middle of the table. "A toast," cried Gonzo. 'I have to do this one at least once this trip. To friends and love." The others murmured a repeat of his words and clinked their little glasses together. Gonzo and Jimbo threw back the shots and made horrible faces at first. Gonzo's melted into a happy smile, and he took one of the beer glasses to wash it down.

Brett sipped, then gulped down the shot, closed his eyes, and coughed. He reached for his beer as well. Liz sipped at her shot, and when Gonzo looked expectantly at her, she rolled her eyes and downed the other half, putting the glass down in the table with a clack. She held a calm expression on her face for a few beats, but then grabbed her water glass and took a long pull on the straw, cheeks flushing pink.

Jimbo looked distressed, since he had not ordered a chaser. He sighed and grabbed a soup spoon and lifted some Gator Gumbo to his mouth. He looked at it for a moment, then slurped it down. He smiled. His voice was rough as he said, "Can't taste gator, it might as well be chicken, but mmm, it's tangy." He looked at Liz and asked, "I probably really don't want to ask what's in this, do I?" Liz giggled and shook her head.

Brett grinned, then looked puzzled. "Hey, do you hear... Pac Man?" He looked around the bar and saw no video game machines.

Jimbo blinked and reached for his pocket. "Ring tone," he mumbled. He looked at the screen and groaned. "Now what does she want?" He touched the "talk" button, held it to his ear and said, in a still-hoarse voice, "Hi Fran, what's up?" Gonzo rolled his eyes and drank more of his beer, making yapping motions with his free hand. Liz reached over and grabbed his thumb and forefinger between hers, making the yapping stop. She shot him a fierce reproachful look. Brett hid his smile behind his beer mug.

Jimbo plugged his other ear with a finger. "What's wrong, Frannie?" His annoyance faded, replaced with a tone of concern.

Brett poked Jimbo in the shoulder and tilted his head.

Jimbo replied by holding his stomach with one hand and pressing a hand to his forehead, wincing in pretend pain.

Jimbo chuckled. "Sounds like a preview of me tomorrow. Gonzo's got us doing shots of the Irish." He pointed at Brett's mug and then pointed at himself. Brett nodded, and waved to their server, who was at a table nearby. She nodded and held up a finger and continued taking the other table's order.

Jimbo's face fell as he listened to Frannie on the phone. After awhile, he said to her, "Gonzo is *not* trouble, Frannie…"

Gonzo coughed into his sleeve, amusement making his eyes twinkle.

"I'm not doing anything I don't want to do," said Jimbo in a lower tone, eyes lowered. Brett, glanced at Gonzo and Liz, as they all tried to pretend they weren't listening. Brett picked at the gumbo and sipped at his drink.

"Anyway, I'm sorry you're not feeling well, Frannie. Take some ibuprofen and some Pepto and try to get some sleep."

The waitress breezed over to their table, and Brett was relieved to have something else to do. He asked for another mug and a pitcher of beer. Liz drained her daiquiri and pointed to it, then mimed that she had an ice cream headache from drinking too fast. Gonzo elbowed Brett and pointed at the shots. Brett looked at Liz, who shook her head, and then at Jimbo, then nodded. Gonzo asked for two more shots. The waitress nodded at each of them, glanced at Jimbo, and then drifted off toward the bar.

Jimbo lowered his voice and turned away from the table, swiveling on the barstool. "Frannie, why are you doing this to me? You know there's no way I could get there, and there's nothing I could really do if I *was* there. The road trip has barely started, and we're having fun. Don't you want me to have fun? Is it so wrong that I'm doing something without you?"

Jimbo was quiet awhile as Frannie talked. Brett watched as his friend's face reddened and his brow furrowed.

Jimbo laughed without smiling and spoke louder, "You know what, Fran? It's funny, I do have Liz's lipstick on me. And if I'm dancing, I'll have to be careful that I don't get *guys* trying to pick me up." He lowered his voice again. "I'm sorry if you're sick. If it gets too bad, call 9-1-1 and have them send an ambulance. They'll be able to do something. I can't. And you know what? If I want to have fun with my friends, I will. You're not going to guilt me into having a lousy time! Goodnight, Fran. I'll talk to you tomorrow."

Jimbo shut the phone with a loud snap. He turned back around, and the others waited a moment for him to talk. "Sorry about that. She's really getting crazy on me." He looked at it a moment, then opened it, only to turn it off. "There. She'll be pissed, but she's going too far. It'll do her good to have some time to herself. Or it'll do me some good, anyway."

Liz said, "Oh Jimbo, it doesn't sound good, I'm sorry."

Gonzo coughed and finished his beer.

Brett said, "Why do you even put up with her? She's dragging you down, man." Gonzo nodded, but Liz caught Brett's eye and shook her head.

Jimbo scowled. "Sometimes I wonder that myself. You know, she all but accused me of cheating on her with Liz! Suggested I was chasing other women... She's sweet so much of the time, but she has this terrible jealous streak, it really gets old."

Liz smiled and patted his arm, "Well, you did get into my clothes, didn't you?" She winked and plucked at the material of the blouse. Brett and Gonzo snorted. "Yeah," said Gonzo, "we have seen the other woman, and she is you, Jimbo. I think it's a good look for you." He whistled at Jimbo and grinned.

Seemingly on cue, the waitress appeared at their table with another tray of drinks. "Hey now, we're a family establishment here. We have a couch in the sleazy back room for that kind of behavior. Don't make me have to come watch." She smirked as she handed out shots to Brett and Gonzo, handed a second daiquiri into Liz's outstretched hand, placed a glass in front of Jimbo, and set down the pitcher next to it. She looked around at them and nodded, "Yep, looks like you're set for now," and continued her orbit around the room without waiting for a reply.

Gonzo cackled. "I like her, she's got style," he said, eyes following the woman as she wound around the tables.

Brett nudged him, "I don't think she thinks you're her type. She'd try to fix you up with the bartender." Brett indicated the bar with a jut of his chin and a glance. Liz looked over and had to cover her mouth to hold in a laugh. The bartender was a round, red-faced man in his fifties with three days' growth of beard.

Liz giggled. "It's a love that's never fated to be, you'll just have to let him down gently, Gonzo. Someday his heart will mend..." She looked quickly back at the table, since the bartender had looked up and caught her looking at him.

"Fuckers," said Gonzo with a wry smile, raising the shot glass. "To your health, and your girlfriend's," he said, looking at Jimbo.

Jimbo snorted and filled his glass from the pitcher, raising the glass to clink with Gonzo. Brett followed suit and clinked his shot against Gonzo's. Liz was already slurping on her straw as the others toasted. She let out an "Oh!" and joined in by touching her glass to the others hastily, and they all drank up.

Despite the friendly banter and warmth brought by the food and drink, Brett couldn't help looking over his shoulder to check for shadows.

Chapter 9 - After Midnight

The friends had another couple of rounds in the Rum Boogie, then moved on down Beale. Gonzo insisted that they visit BB King's Blues Club. When they arrived, there was a line out the door. Brett complained that he didn't want to wait in line, but Gonzo planted himself at the end of the line, crossing his arms stubbornly. The others joined him, and they talked as they waited in line. After a half hour, the line moved only a few feet. "This is going to take all night," said Jimbo, peering up at the bouncer at the head of the line.

"Just enjoy the music," growled Gonzo, indicating the speakers playing music by BB King himself.

Brett rolled his eyes. "You know that's a recording, right? I think I even have this CD. That's a duet with Van Morrison. Great song, but I doubt BB King is here."

Gonzo shrugged. "He might be, later. He does play in his own club from time to time. He's known to make surprise appearances as well, no matter what the marquee says."

Liz teased, "And when he rises out of the pumpkin patch, he'll bring harmonicas and electric guitars for all the little children who he thinks are the most sincere blues fans!" She returned Gonzo's glare with an innocent smile and a flutter of her eyelashes.

The line moved soon though, and they found themselves in a packed, smoky club. Brett looked uncomfortable every time someone brushed up against him. Liz stood closer to him, which somehow seemed to calm him. Gonzo looked smugly happy, and he led them slowly along the wall. His luck continued, and he found a small table where a couple was just leaving. He offered the two chairs to Liz and Jimbo. "Ladies?" he grinned. Jimbo shrugged and took the chair. "May as well take advantage, I guess!"

Brett and Gonzo stood at the table for a bit until Gonzo managed to steal a couple of vacant chairs from nearby tables. The stage lights came up, and an elderly man walked out to the piano and sat.

"Oh my fucking God, it's The Killer!" Gonzo gasped. "Goddamn, he looks so old!"

Brett looked and blinked. "Wow, I think you're right, that might be Jerry Lee! He *is* old. I didn't know he was still playing gigs."

Jimbo said, "Hmm, I didn't know he was still even *alive*."

An unseen MC's voice boomed through the house's speakers, introducing the rock n' roll legend. The man began playing the piano. His face was impassive, but he hammered the keys with gusto, filling the room with music. He improvised awhile, then launched into "Whole Lotta Shakin'."

The friends grinned at each other in the light from the stage, and enjoyed the show. The Killer played energetically through a short set of five songs, then took a bow and was helped off the stage by a bouncer. The lights came up and the crowd started to thin. Liz stood up and stretched. "Looks like it's getting close to closing time. Let's hit the trolley before everyone else gets that idea."

Gonzo shrugged. "I guess. Think we could swing by the Rum Boogie again? I'd like to have a word with that waitress about that sleazy back room..." He grinned.

Liz put a hand on one hip and raised an eyebrow at him. "Oh there's a winning idea. Maybe there's even room in *Soccer Mom* for a fifth member of the crew? It'll be fun!"

Gonzo winked. "Afraid of losing your status as the only female? No offense, Jimbo." Jimbo stuck out his tongue at him.

Liz shrugged. "By all means." Brett just watched in amusement.

They left BB King's Blues Club and wandered past the Rum Boogie, but though Gonzo did peer in the window, he said, "Nah, not this time. We're on a mission from God, can't stop to take on passengers at this stage. Besides, she doesn't want to get mixed up with us, we're cursed, and she'd probably end up being possessed. Or maybe she's part of it, she's this vampire chick who'd... hmmmm...." Gonzo rubbed his chin in thought, then allowed his mouth to stretch into a comical leer. Brett and Jimbo pulled him along. "Let's go. We're never getting to New Orleans at this rate," Brett said.

They moved along and found a small crowd waiting at the trolley stop. They barely got a seat, and sat on the outside of the trolley. Liz had them all wave goodbye to Beale. People waved back cheerfully. They all laughed, and the trolley trundled off into darker parts of Memphis, leaving the sounds and lights of the festival behind. Liz led the way, and they had to walk quite a few blocks before they reached her rented duplex. They stumbled in the door, and Liz shushed them. "The landlady's my neighbor, so keep it down a bit. Okay, now for the sleeping arrangements. I've got blankets and pillows and two good couches." She looked at each of them, leaving her gaze on Brett, smiling very slightly, folding her hands in front of her.

"Two? Will one of us have to bring in a sleeping bag?" asked Brett, blinking at Liz. Even as he said it, her smile widened, still looking in his eyes. She shook her head slightly no.

Gonzo coughed to cover a laugh.

Jimbo elbowed him. "Come on, dumbass, does she have to get cut that sword and force you upstairs at knife-point? Don't be stupid."

Brett's eyes widened and he flushed red as he realized what was being suggested. "But... it's been a year... I mean... You know, what happens after?"

Liz just stood, looking at him and smiling a long while. The other guys laughed and wandered off to change clothes. When they were alone, she said, "I won't make you go at sword-point, but I've got room. No pressure, but the offer's there. After all that's happened, I'd sleep better with some company." Brett looked anxious, and bit his lip, so she added, "Nothing has to happen. In fact, I think I'm probably just going to pass out when my head hits the pillow. I'll go get the blankets, and if you want to get your sleeping bag and stay down here, I'll be okay."

Liz got the promised blankets and pillows and made up the two couches as beds for Gonzo and Jimbo. Jimbo looked more relaxed now that he'd washed off the makeup. Liz had actually brought a nightgown down with her, a white cotton garment covered with tiny blue flowers, which she offered to Jimbo to sleep in, keeping a straight face as she did so, but he thanked her and said he'd stick with his T-shirt and shorts. She tsked and seemed disappointed, but said goodnight and started up the stairs. She didn't look back, and Brett, who had changed as well, stood a moment in the room as the others got under the covers.

"Go on, Brett, you know you want to. It'll be cool, just no smoochy-smoochy in the back of *Soccer Mom.* We're going to want an appetite when we get to NOLA," said Gonzo sleepily. Jimbo waved him on.

Brett smiled and relaxed and went upstairs. He wasn't sure how sleepy he was, his mind racing with memories and excitement.

Liz grinned at him, standing in her bedroom doorway. "I'm glad you're here," she said. "I didn't know what it'd be like, going on this trip with you, and I don't know what's going to happen afterwards, but I'm going to enjoy this while I can." She stepped up to him and hugged him. The heat of her body embracing him made Brett's heart pound. The slick satin of her "ninja" pajamas slid against him as they embraced. She looked up and kissed him lightly on the lips, surprising him. Her eyes scanned his, searching for a reaction. He smiled and kissed her back, just as lightly. She giggled and pulled away, taking his hand to lead him into her room.

Liz's room was small, and full of plush toy animals, manga comic books, scattered CDs and a computer, which flashed slowly as it slept. Her bed was covered in a tattered old Star Wars duvet, with matching pillowcases. Darth Vader and Luke Skywalker dueled in the center of the bed as other characters looked on. A large brown corduroy fish with googly eyes lay just below one pillow.

She let go his hand and slipped under the covers, sliding over to the far side of the bed. She clutched at the fish out of habit, and peered at him with smiling eyes. She patted the sheets with a hand and looked at him silently.

Brett joined her, pulling the covers over himself. He could feel her body heat under the covers. They faced each other, lying on their sides.

"So what's this mean, Liz? Are we... I mean, isn't it going to make things weird?"

She giggled. "I wouldn't have things any other way. Weird is good. It's when things get boring that I have a problem. I know we went our separate ways years ago. I don't expect you to change your life for me now, but why can't we indulge in a bit of sexy nostalgia for a few days? Those couple of years I lived with you were some of the happiest days of my life, Brett. I don't regret coming to Memphis, but having you here sure makes it feel more like home. You're, well, *better* these days, Brett. More together, more like your old self. Just shut up and don't ask questions. We'll figure it all out after the trip's over."

It was easier for her, Brett thought, she wasn't a worrier like he was. He'd always envied her ability to live completely in the moment, not fretting over the past or dreading the future like he did all too often. "Well, I'll try. I'm glad to be here too, Liz. I've missed you too, and sometimes I think--"

Liz shushed him and held a finger to his lips, stopping him. "No, none of that. Just be here with me now, okay?" She took her finger from his lips and snuggled her head up to his shoulder, and he found himself putting his arms around her. It was so nice having her in his arms. Like she'd said, it felt like home. She even smelled like home.

It was also very thrilling, and she giggled, noticing his excitement. "Well, it feels like you really have missed me, hmm?"

Brett had to laugh and instead of answering her directly, he kissed her, a little longer this time. She responded enthusiastically, and slipped her fingers in his hair to hold him in the kiss longer. Brett was sure she could feel his heart pounding in his chest.

There was a loud hissing noise in the room that made them both sit up abruptly. It was Liz's orange tabby cat, staring at the window. Nothing was there, but there was a voice. It spoke in a whisper, seeming to come from the air right between them.

"You made your choice... Come to me... You're mine..."

Brett's blood ran like icewater at the voice. He looked at Liz, whose eyes had gone wide.

Liz jumped up out of the bed and hissed back, "No! He's not yours! I don't know who or what you are, but this is *my* house and *my* bed! Get out! You're not welcome here! Brett is my guest! Gonzo and Jimbo are my guests! I invited them, not you. *You* don't belong here!" She turned and lit a tall candle, and went around the room lighting other candles in lanterns and votives in glasses. "Lords and ladies," she intoned as Brett watched in surprise, "please keep this rude spirit at bay while we rest, please help it find peace somewhere other than here! So mote it be!"

Brett heard a gargling cry of rage, sounding like the whispering shadow had been flung from the room by a bouncer.

The chill in Brett's body drained away.

She blew out the long candle angrily put it back. Liz slipped back into bed and into Brett's arms again.

"What was that? I thought you were a Discordian these days, I thought you gave up Wicca when that coven you hung out with split up?" Brett looked in Liz's eyes as he spoke and saw the fierce anger melt away to the soft, happier one he'd seen before.

She's sexy when she's protective! This is the Lizzie I love.

She smiled back and shrugged. "I never really gave it up entirely. It fits in with how I see things. I'm a bad pagan, I don't practice all that often, and I only practice occasionally with others if they need a compass point. Discordia is fascinating to me, and yeah, it's what I'm studying for the most part now, but Wicca's still got a place in my heart." She glanced around at the candles then looked back in his eyes. "It needed to know I meant business."

Brett smiled at her. "I think chopping it in two with your sword probably got that across. That's twice you've saved me from that thing. What's it want with me, do you think?"

Liz bit her lip and lowered her eyes. "You heard what it said, Brett." She looked back up at him. "I wonder if it's her? I mean, you know."

Brett went a little cold despite the warmth of his former lover pressed up against his body. "You think I'm being haunted by Cheryl? That can't be right, she wouldn't strangle me. She wasn't psychotic, she was..." He looked at Liz, then continued, "She was a realist. There is no way she'd do this to me. She'd want me to be happy."

Liz smiled and kissed him. "Then let's be happy. I think we're safe for now."

Chapter 10 - Interlude

Brett floated in a warm glow. He opened his eyes and found that this was more literal than he would have suspected... He was nowhere special, just *here*. No points of reference, no sky, no walls, no horizon... He wasn't even standing on any surface. He was in the center of his head, in an artificial space, like a blackboard on which he could write out his thoughts.

This must be some kind of lucid dream. So can I just make anything I want happen here?

Brett decided that there should be a room, with a door and a couch, a carpeted floor. These things did appear, and Brett thought maybe they'd been there before, he just had not noticed them. He looked at the couch. Had he decided it was blue? What about the carpet? He closed his eyes. What color was it? He couldn't remember. I'd be interesting if it was black, with stars and planets and moons all over it, a shaggy version of the night sky. He opened his eyes, and the carpet looked just like he'd imagined.

This is cool.

So, in real life, I'm laying in Liz's bed with her in my arms, and it's sometime after dawn. He smiled, doing as she had asked, just being happy, trying to push out his doubts and worries. Hardest of all was forgetting the past, but he also felt the pressure of the future as a looming presence ahead of him.

He noticed a window in the room, and the grey light of a cloudy fall day streamed in through gauzy curtains like those in Liz's room. The light seemed to be dissolving the couch and the carpet, washing them out. He started to feel his control slip and moved to pull down the blinds he knew must be up there. It was dark in the room now, but everything seemed solid and steady again.

Of course, he definitely wanted to wake up to Liz in his arms, but this was a new experience to him, like the ultimate virtual reality.

How boring *was* he, using the ultimate virtual reality to make a small room? *Hmm, what would be better?*

There was a sudden knock at the door.

Brett walked over to the door, not sure what would be behind it. He reached for the doorknob. He hesitated, just touching the old dented brass knob. It rattled at his touch, ensuring that whoever, or whatever, was on the other side of the door knew he was there.

Whatever? Why would I think something like that? This is my dream, there's no boogieman here.

The Force-ghost of Yoda spoke to him from the couch. "Only what you take with you, hmm?"

Brett glared at the little Jedi Master. "Did I ask you? And what are you doing here anyway? Go away. Please."

Yoda laughed and nodded at Brett. "Hmmm! How wise must you be, to need no advice but your own. Gone I will be, but face yourself, you must." He faded from view.

Brett muttered, "Okay, definitely too many shots of Jameson last night."

The knocking came again, now louder and more insistent.

His hand tightened on the knob and turned. The latch clicked, and he pulled the door open.

"Hi! How's it going, baby?" Cheryl stood there. In spandex shorts and a Garfield T-shirt. She wore her hair pulled back into a Cubs baseball cap, her blonde ponytail flowing out of the back. Her nails were painted a coral pink, as were her lips. Her blue eyes peered at him through her owlishly large glasses. She smirked, Brett knew that look. She was always thrilled if she could catch him off guard.

She also wore her red ten-speed bicycle wrapped around her. Bent and ruined, with a broken drive chain and brake cables trailing, its rims twisted all out of shape. Bruises and scrapes covered every inch of exposed skin, and a tire track flattened her middle.

"Uh, hi. I'd say I didn't expect to see you here, but I guess some part of me must have, this being my dream and all." Brett stepped outside, and found that the room was all there was of a small red house.

It sat on a very small grassy lawn in the middle of a limitless desert. Alongside the house, an Interstate highway stretched from horizon to horizon.

"Nice place you've got here," she said, winking at him. "Got a moment for your old fiancée?" She put a hand on her hip, made a cute pouty pucker of her lips and locked her gaze to his.

Brett didn't look away, to avoid looking at the bicycle and tire track. "You know, I heard you hit your head, not that you were run over."

Cheryl bared her teeth in a wicked grin. "Well, it spells out what happened to me so much better than a split head would. Plus, it'd ruin my look, and I want to look my best for my Sweetie." She reached over and pinched his cheek and mussed his hair. "I hope you haven't forgotten about me, Lover Boy."

He shook his head. "No, it's been six years. In August. On the twelfth. Cheryl, you're dead."

She pouted, lowered her chin and peered at Brett over those huge glasses. "Aww, you're going to let a little thing like that bother you? I don't have to look like this, you know." She waved a hand and snapped her fingers, wrinkling her nose. There was a flash. Cheryl stood there without the bike, her midsection whole again, wearing a long white wedding dress. The train stretched off into the distance. It looked spectacular on her there in the desert. The Sun made every one of the dozens of crystals sewn into it glitter flashes of color. The white satin dress accented her voluptuous curves. She carried a bouquet of pure white and red roses. A veil covered her face, and he could see her lips and nails were now a rich ruby red. She reached down to pull up the gown to expose her right leg, clad in the faintest white stocking, a lacy garter around her thigh.

Cheryl grinned. "Now, now, it's bad luck for the groom to see his bride in her gown before the wedding!"

Brett looked down and saw that he now wore a tuxedo. "Damn it, Cheryl! You know I wanted this as much as you did. Do you know what it did to me when you were killed? Do you know how hard it was for me? You left me alone and broken, and I didn't know what to do anymore. "

Cheryl laughed and threw the bouquet over her shoulder, into the road. "*You* were broken? Ha! Try hitting the pavement after being knocked down by an Olds 88, sweet cheeks!" Her eyes blazed. "And you weren't alone long, were you, lover? How long did forever really last? Didn't your little fairy princess swoop down and snap you up on the very same day my brains spilled all over Indiana Avenue? How did you fit mourning in with your busy dating schedule?"

Brett tore off the tuxedo jacket and stripped down to the jeans and gamer T-shirt he decided would be underneath. "Look. Cheryl. You were dead. I was hurting. Was I supposed to turn her away? We didn't really date for six months or so after your funeral. It was strictly platonic."

Cheryl's eyes narrowed. "She moved in with you right away though! How can you call that platonic?"

"We slept in separate rooms, we had our own lives. Our separate friends became more of *our* friends, together. We made a home, and we fell in love. Is that so terrible?" Brett folded his arms.

A car whizzed behind Cheryl, but she ignored it. The bouquet bounced along in its wake for a few yards. "Is that so terrible?" she mocked. "Of course it's terrible. I died, and you moved on, and I guess your promises meant nothing."

Brett snorted. "So, let's get this straight. Because I asked you to marry me, and because you died before we did get married, you expected me to wait for death to be reunited with you for our eternal marital bliss?"

Cheryl nodded so hard her veil slipped off. "Yes! That or you could have followed me. You know you wanted to. You felt the pull of death, but you ignored it, you were held back by that flitty little usurper." Cheryl's wedding dress darkened, becoming black and brittle-looking, a death shroud.

Brett stared at her a moment, then nodded. "I admit it, I felt the pull. If it weren't for Liz, I would have taken my life."

"See? She stole you from me!" Blood began to seep from Cheryl's hair, trickling down her forehead, into one eye and on down her cheek to her chin, dripping. A rip opened in her scalp, exposing a widening crack in her skull.

Brett said, "It was my choice, to live or to die. I chose to live, and I can't believe you'd be this way to me. You were never so selfish in life. You're just a figment of my guilty mind, tormenting me for happening to be the one who lived on." A thought occurred to him. "Say, have you been haunting me in real life? Are you the strangling shadow?"

She looked startled by this. "Strangling shadow? No, you had it right the first time. I'm all about you, just like Yoda was in your little house. Whatever happens outside of your head isn't anything of my doing, or of yours."

The view changed; he was looking back at the house and himself. His head hurt terribly, and he reached up and felt something cold and wet. He looked at his hand and found it was not his hand. It was long and slender, with red fingernails, and covered in black, congealed blood. He looked down at the black dress he was wearing, and said in Cheryl's voice, "Okay, what's the idea?"

His own body smiled and put a hand on its hip in a disturbing feminine gesture. "Just thought you should see things from my point of view before I go."

She walked up to him and leaned down to kiss him, but before their lips met, the strong male hands began shaking his shoulders and the body he wore started falling apart. Bits of black dress ripped and floated away like so much charred newspaper.

"Brett, wake up! You have to choose, the choice isn't over! Wake up! Wake up!" His own face leered at him as he collapsed in a broken heap of body parts and ashes.

"Wake up!" The voice was suddenly Liz's, and his eyes flew open. He was lying in her bed, and she was straddling him, hands on his shoulders. "Oh thank gods! You were having a nightmare, *Chico*!

You woke me up crying out in your sleep. I was worried that something had possessed you for a moment there."

"Uh, no, I was arguing with myself, I think. Beating myself up over things from long ago." He forced a smile.

She smiled down at him and her hair hung down to either side of her face as she leaned to kiss him. It was a long and passionate kiss, and Brett thought to be alive is a better choice.

Chapter 11 - Road Trip

Gonzo sang loudly along with The Pogues once more as *Soccer Mom* flew down the Interstate, leaving Memphis hours behind. "Bury me at sea where no murdered ghosts can haunt me..."

Liz and Brett looked at each other and mouthed, "Oh. My. God."

Jimbo slapped at Gonzo's shoulder.

"Hey, hey there man, maybe... Sorry, I know it's sacrilegious to interrupt The Pogues, but think about what you're singing!" Jimbo punched the skip-ahead button on the CD player, causing Gonzo to glare at him and slap his hand away from the controls.

"Ha! This is better?" said Gonzo. Strains of "Turkish Song of the Damned" came out of the van's speakers. Gonzo quoted lyrics as it began, "I come old friend from Hell tonight..." He cackled and grinned.

This time Liz reached from between the front seats to punch ahead to the next song on the CD. Gonzo let out an offended "Hey! Hands off! Driver's choice!" but didn't stop her. He sighed and sang along with "Bottle of Smoke" instead.

Earlier, Liz and Brett had showered together in her little upstairs bathroom after she had woken him from his disturbing lucid dream. He hadn't told her about it right away. They had been a bit preoccupied with becoming reacquainted with each other's body, kissing and playing and consummating the reunion. It had been slow and careful at first, almost like they were stepping through a dance they each remembered a little differently. But soon their lovemaking became hungry and urgent, making up for lost time. After, the shower was of course playtime for Liz, who made Brett a shampoo Mohawk, and started splash fights.

It had taken Gonzo pounding on the bedroom door to break it up. He and Jimbo were awake and impatient. Brett and Liz reluctantly toweled off, got dressed and descended the stairs. Gonzo and Jimbo stood next to their packed bags, arms folded. Brett flashed a goofy grin at them and they rolled their eyes in unison.

Liz wore dark green exercise tights and one of Brett's green cotton dress shirts over it like a short dress, the sleeves rolled up to her elbows, and the collar unbuttoned to show a black tank top underneath. Enormous hoop earrings dangled from her ears, and her hair was held in place on top of her head with chopsticks. "Are you boys ready to go?" she'd asked with an innocent look. She spoiled the effect by winking at Brett, whose foolish grin spread even wider across his face.

"Would you two just come on? It's after noon already!" Gonzo moved towards the door with his bag. Jimbo just laughed, hoisted his own gear and followed his larger friend.

They ate at a local diner, where Brett shared an enormous omelet with Liz and Jimbo attacked chocolate chip pancakes, but Gonzo rushed them through the meal.

Now that they were rolling, Gonzo was in rare form, singing to his CDs and passing other cars as they became obstacles to their progress. He smiled and relaxed, and seemed more in his element than he had the whole trip. The grey overcast didn't bother him, he just seemed happier with every mile closer they came to New Orleans.

Jimbo groaned from the front passenger seat. "Ten messages from Fran on my cell this morning. Holy shit, I'm afraid to even listen to them."

Gonzo snorted. "Delete 'em. If she's chewing you out, she's going to have to calm down sometime, and it's not going to do you any good to hear them. If she's crying into the phone, it's only going to make you feel awful, and you don't deserve that. I say fuck her, just delete 'em."

Liz bit her lip and shook her head. "If you want to keep Fran, I'm not sure I'd do that, Jimbo. It'll just make her madder if she realizes you deleted her messages."

Brett waved his hands and mouthed "No, no no," at Liz, but she ignored him. "Just listen to a few seconds of each," she continued. "Figure out what she's trying to do. And you have to figure out what you want to do. Fix things or end them?"

Gonzo let out an exasperated sigh. "Liz, you should know better. She's already angry, she's worked herself into a tizzy of jealousy and is trying to assert her control over Jimbo. If he gives in and buys into her crazy world, he's lost already, and he might as well wrap his balls up in a little box with a ribbon on it and FedEx them to Frannie."

"Yeah? How do you know? Personal experience, maybe? Gonzo, be fair, Jimbo obviously cares about Fran or he wouldn't be tied up in knots about all this." Liz punctuated this by sticking out her tongue at Brett, who leaned back against the car door, holding his head.

Jimbo cut off Gonzo's reply. "All right, all right! I'm gonna listen to a little bit of each." He cut Gonzo off again. "But I am not letting her get to me! She's got to learn that she has to let me be myself, or there's no future for us."

The car went silent, other than the growl of the engine and the hum of the tires on the road as Jimbo turned off the CD player. "Just give me a minute."

Brett could hear the beeping of Jimbo's phone as he navigated the voicemail menu. Then he heard the sound of Frannie's voice, not the individual words, but the tone and texture. The first couple of messages were demanding and sharp, sounding like barked orders.

The next few messages, Frannie's tone changed to worry, and on into begging.

After that, it got weird.

Fran would start a message with shouting, then the tone would go low and threatening, then rise up to a shrill crescendo of anger. She'd end with talking, an echoing quality making it sound like she was speaking to someone else in the room.

"Oh shit, she's lost it now. She's fucking lost it," said Jimbo, awed. "I think I broke Frannie. Shit guys, she's threatening me. Here, listen..."

Jimbo put the cell phone on speakerphone so the whole car could hear.

"...it's out of my hands now, James, you've finally pushed me too far,"

Fran's voice was low and dangerous. *"I've kept you protected up 'til now, I've kept it simple and safe. Little scares and warnings, things that go bump in the night. But no, you went and blew me off, you ignored me! You've gone too far, and I'm pissed now! I'm not responsible for what happens next. Do you hear me, Jimmy? Do you fucking hear me, you asshole? I'm letting go the leash and there's hell to pay. I don't care what happens now, I really don't. But don't come crying to me when you can't handle it. When it comes for you. It'll be hungry, Jimmy. And I. Won't. Care!"* She hung up.

"Shit," murmured Gonzo. "Jimbo, she really is psycho."

"There's one more. I haven't listened to it yet. I'll just let it play."

"Jimmy, oh, I'm sorry. I'm so sorry. I can't stop it now, it's too late. Listen to me carefully. You've got to run. It's after you, and I... W-w-well I made it. Or brought it. Somehow. I don't know how I do it, I've always been able to do this, but I've controlled it 'til now. You just made me so hurt and angry. Why didn't you pick up? This didn't have to happen, and now even I can't stop it..." Fran sobbed and Brett could not make out the words she blubbered. Finally, she said, *"I love you, Jimmy. Always remember that. And I'm s-s-sorry."* She hung up.

Jimbo looked at the others, from Gonzo to Liz and Brett.

Gonzo spoke first. "Well, I guess that's over with. Change your numbers and you might want to stay with a friend for a while after you get back. She doesn't know exactly where we're going in New Orleans yet, because, well, we haven't planned that far ahead."

"No... I don't think she was crazy... Gonzo," replied Liz. "Well, okay, yeah, obviously she's as nutty as a pecan log, but I mean something in her voice said to me that she was genuinely afraid of something. Something she did. Something she thinks can hurt Jimbo all the way from Savannah."

Brett said, "And you think she's got some special power that makes her able to hurl fiery blood-curdling vengeance hundreds of miles away? What, like the shadow that went after me in the bar last night?"

Liz shrugged. "Yeah, sounds unlikely to me too, but do I have to remind you that we do seem to be under a curse?"

"If it's her doing it," asked Gonzo, "then why have most of the scarier bits been happening to your boyfriend back there? What's Brett ever done to her? In fact, if she was going to hate anyone enough to send a haunting after them... somehow... wouldn't it be me, the guy who started this trip that's taken her Jimmy from her for *days* at a time? Why not go directly for Jimbo himself? Doesn't make sense to me. None of it does."

Jimbo shrugged. "She does whine every other weekend when I head up to Indy to play in Brett's D&D game. So in that way, he's been a more regular source of irritation to her."

"Hey now, I didn't invite you to my games just to piss Fran off," objected Brett.

"No, it was just one of the side benefits," Gonzo finished for him, grinning at him in the rearview mirror. Liz couldn't stop a giggle from escaping before her hand covered her mouth.

Jimbo sighed. "Well, she's done this all to herself. Maybe I could have tried to calm her down more, but I really was getting tired of being pushed around from a distance. She knew this trip was a big deal for me, and all she's done since it came up was to try and talk me out of it or whine about how she's not going to be having fun while I'll be out with you guys. I don't honestly believe she can call down a curse on us. I can't explain the things that have been happening either, and it *is* a really strange coincidence. That's one of the 'charming' things about Frannie, strange things *do* happen around her. I've never known the coincidences and bizarre happenings to actually benefit her though. She always blamed whatever bad things happened to her on... Well, she blamed it on her *curse*... She felt like there were gremlins sabotaging her car, or maybe it was the fickle finger of fate that caused her to become sick and miss an exam. It's always something with her, and she's the first to say so. She wears her bad luck like a badge of honor, something that makes her special, you know?"

There was silence, then Liz replied, "Yes, I do know. She always seems to want to compete for attention, have everyone notice her, whether it's something good or bad. The poor thing felt left out. Doesn't forgive her behavior, but I guess I can understand it just a little. I've always just been more of one to take responsibility for my own luck, good or bad. It's all too easy to point at lousy circumstances and call yourself a victim, and if you do it enough, you really get to believing it. I'll say it again though, she thinks she's unleashed some kind of big nasty on us, and she sounds like she believes it's dangerous. Haven't we seen enough crazy stuff in the past few days to give it just a little thought?"

Brett shuffled through the pages of <u>Ghosts</u>, searching for something. "Hang on. This sounds vaguely familiar. Klaus Reisen talks about poltergeists here somewhere... Aha, here it is." He read from the book. "Poltergeists are the psychic manifestation of great stress and change in an individual. Great personal power is drawn forth from the aether by internal conflict and struggle. In some individuals, in particular pre-pubescent females, this can be such a strong force that it manifests as a physical, bodiless force of chaos. This chaos will often appear as loud, unexplained noises or voices, objects in the subject's domicile or vicinity being hurled across the room with dangerous force. In rarer cases, there will seem to be an intelligent, invisible attacker assaulting those near the individual, causing bites and burns and worse things. The individual at the center of a poltergeist phenomenon is usually unaware that they are the cause of the disturbance, and can often be the target of the chaotic violence. They are certainly unable to control this disturbance and their personal distress is often fed by the results of the psychic outbursts, causing a vicious feedback loop."

Gonzo coughed. "So, you think Fran's a psychic, psychotic hurricane of bitchiness? Even if we believe that author, and that's a *big* 'if' for me, she's not a tween, and we're not in her 'vicinity'. It's close, I'll give you that, but doesn't quite match."

Jimbo frowned. "Hmm, she did say the 'curse' all started, for her, when she was 9 or 10."

"I think you might be on to something," said Liz. "Maybe Reisen doesn't have all the answers, maybe he's just heard of or seen things that are similar. Maybe our Frannie is some kind of spiritual superconductor with uncontrolled wild psychic energy whirling all around her, growing more focused when she's upset?"

Jimbo said, "Maybe it's Stephen King who has the answers here. Hello, Carrie?"

Brett shrugged. "Hard to say. I thought that one phrase was interesting, 'intelligent, invisible attacker.' I guess we've been able to see this shadow thing. It does suggest a summoning, unless Reisen is saying it's controlled subconsciously and only appears intelligent as a result."

Jimbo shook his head. "This is all so crazy. Maybe we're just buying into her insanity. I think that's dangerous. Look where it got her, living in her crazy little world where some bad luck force of nature has it in for her. If we believe it, do we give it teeth?"

"That's the first sane thing anyone has said since you checked your voicemail," grumbled Gonzo. "I think we're spooked already, and here comes Frannie having a hissy fit, bringing the crazy with her to dump in our laps. I think we've got to decide whether we want to buy into that big chunk of crazy, or whether we want to just go on with our lives here in the real world. Let's let it go, okay?"

Brett sighed and shut the thick book with a thump. "Despite your skepticism, you might be on to something, Gonz. These things often do depend quite a bit on belief. In fact, maybe that's why I've been the target all along, I'm the one who's always looking for ghosts and shadow people and whatnot. I'm not a true believer, exactly, but I spend a lot of time and energy focusing on this kind of stuff. Maybe I'm an easier target?"

Liz shrugged. "I don't know, I used to be a card-carrying witch, and I'm as into the weird stuff as you are."

Brett nodded. "Yeah... You saw something in your window before we showed up. And you saw the shadow attacking at the blues club before I did. You also heard the whispering last night when I did."

"Not to mention," added Jimbo, "Fran's been jealous that Liz is along for the ride. Guess she wished it was her instead, or maybe she just doesn't trust me around other girls."

"Maybe?" Gonzo asked. "No maybe there, bud, she's a control freak, and having any kind of temptation is a threat to her."

Liz snickered. "Oh sure, that's me all right. I'm a boy-crazy she-demon whose only desire is to seduce other women's men away so I can drain them of their very souls!" As an afterthought, she added a flatly-spoken, "Muahahahaaa."

Gonzo looked at her in the rearview. "You've nabbed Brett already. But then, he pointed out he's an easy target." He grinned.

"Hey!" objected Brett. "I'm right here!"

Liz smiled a sly smile and leaned to slip her arms around Brett's shoulders. "Ah, my pretty, you're in my clutches now! There'll be no escape for you."

Brett wasn't unhappy about this. He snatched a kiss from Liz as her face came close to his. They smiled into each other's eyes.

"What did I say about that?" barked Gonzo, glancing in the rearview again. "No smoochy-smoochy in *Soccer Mom*! I don't want to spend the trip chauffeuring young ghouls in love. It's cute that you're back together or whatever, but I think Fran's provided all the drama we can stand already.

"Awww, but Uuuncle Goooonzoooo..." whined Liz, pouting until her grin made it impossible. She giggled and sat back up. Brett looked a little sad, so she reached over to take his hand in hers in the middle of the seat. He smiled at her.

Gonzo just shook his head and riffled through the CDs. He glanced down at them and then pulled out one, ejected the Pogues and replaced it. Soon the van was filled with a rising drumbeat. This led into John Fogerty's voice wailing out, "Suzie Q."

"Yay, Creedence!" enthused Liz.

Gonzo nodded sagely. "Only the finest road trip music on the planet."

"Cajun, too," mumbled Jimbo as he stared out the window, still turning his cell phone over and over in his hands.

Liz let go of Brett's hand long enough to reach across to the front seat to rest it lightly on Jimbo's shoulder. "This can't be easy for you, fighting with your girlfriend, thinking about her this way. I'm sorry, Jimbo."

Jimbo shrugged and forced a smile. "Eh, what are you gonna do? I played my part in it, made my choices. I didn't want to lose Fran, but she forced the matter, and if I had to choose between having her and having free will, I gotta do what's best for me, as selfish as that sounds."

Gonzo groaned. "Come *on*, I thought we were dropping this? *Holy shit!*" he yelled and tried to swerve as something fell off a truck full of junk ahead of *Soccer Mom*. The tires screeched as Gonzo slammed on the brakes, then came a double *bang* on the left side as they swerved into the skidding. Everyone was thrown around in their seats, and CDs and other loose objects flew around the cabin. The Caravan skidded right off the Interstate past the shoulder and down a slope into a grassy drainage ditch. It continued sliding in the grass, fishtailing towards the wooded area past the strip of grass.

Jimbo yelled, "Tree! Tree! Gonzo!" The nose of the van turned aside just in time to miss the trunk of a good-sized maple. Gonzo pumped the brakes some more and brought *Soccer Mom* to a halt. Brett groaned from the back seat.

Chapter 12 - Bad Luck

"Everyone... Is everyone okay?" asked Gonzo, his face drained of all color. He twisted in his seat to take stock of his passengers.

"Just a little shaken up, here," said Jimbo, rubbing his shoulder where the seat belt had dug into it.

"Same here," said Liz, shifting around in her seat. "Oh Brett, are you okay, *Chico*?"

Brett held his head on the left side and had his eyes squinched shut tightly. "Uh, yeah. Kinda. Smacked my head real good there. He lifted his hand to look with it. It was covered in blood. "Oh damn, I'm bleeding," Brett said, feeling far away. A trickle of blood rolled down past his eye and down his cheek. He wiped at it with his sweatshirt sleeve.

Liz unbuckled herself and grabbed napkins from her purse and pressed them to Brett's head wound. "What did you hit your head on? There's just the window there... Oh, I see..." Liz picked up Brett's bent glasses from the floor. "Looks like your glasses got rammed into your eyebrow. Let me look at that, can you turn your head this way?" Liz turned on the overhead dome light and peered at Brett's forehead. She dabbed at the blood with the napkins and bit her lip.

Gonzo unbuckled, looking into the back seat. "What happened, is he okay?"

Liz let out a deep breath. "It's just a little cut, I guess. Cuts on the head tend to bleed a lot more than anyplace else. I think that part's okay at least."

"I'm all right, it just rang my bell a bit," said Brett, taking his glasses from Liz. "Huh. Didn't break them. Maybe I can bend them back into place?" He worked on the glasses carefully as Liz dug around in her purse some more, coming up with a small white box.

"Ha, and you always said I carry too much in my purse. I've got a disinfectant wipe, antibiotic cream, and bandages in my little first aid kit!" She smiled, pushed Brett's hands and glasses into his lap and leaned over again to tend to Brett's wound.

"Hey, think he's got a concussion?" asked Jimbo, watching as Liz mopped at Brett's eyebrow with an alcohol wipe.

Liz lifted Brett's chin and looked into his eyes. "*Chico?* Look at me. How do you feel? Are you dizzy?"

Brett wet his lips and nodded as he looked back at Liz's steady gaze. Her eyes were so intense right now, he felt like consoling her, even as she was worrying about him. "I'm okay, Sweetie, really. No, not dizzy, but everything's so blurry!" She looked even more worried for half a second until he grinned.

Liz shook a fist at Brett, but she smiled. "Don't *do* that to me! You can put your glasses back on when I'm done here. Honestly!" She dabbed at the cut again, and then pressed some folded gauze against it firmly and affixed it with some adhesive tape. She used another wipe to clean the rivulet of blood off of his face, and mopped up with another napkin.

"Now that I've been properly fussed over," said Brett, sounding a bit more like himself, "could someone tell me what happened?" He held up his glasses to the light and pushed in on the hinges to straighten out the bridge a bit, then put them on his face. They sat at a slight angle on his nose, so he took them off again.

"There was a pickup ahead of us," said Gonzo. "It looked like something out of the <u>Grapes of Wrath</u>, piled high with junk. Something fell off, might have been a muffler or something else. Pretty sure it was metal, since it blew at least one of the tires, maybe two. If everyone's okay, I should get out and check the damage."

"Me too, I need to stretch a bit," said Jimbo, already opening his door. The cool October air wafted into the van, smelling of sweetly rotting leaves. Gonzo stepped out too, and they left the doors open as they paced around the outside of *Soccer Mom*.

Brett finally had his glasses fixed and looked at Liz. She still stared at him. She stole a furtive glance out the window at Gonzo, who seemed preoccupied, so she leaned in close and kissed Brett softly, then with more passion. She drew back an inch and smiled. "I'm really glad you're okay. Had me worried there for a minute, love."

Love, he thought, smiling and shivering just a little at the word coming so easily from her. "Aw, it's okay, thanks for patching me up." He touched the side of his face where the blood had been. "Hmm," he said, then shook his head.

Liz frowned. "What?"

Brett waved his hand. "It's nothing. Just thinking of that dream. Cheryl bled exactly like that, down her face like I just did. She died of a head wound."

Brett heard metal-on-metal grinding from the back of the van, along with some cursing from both Gonzo and Jimbo.

Liz glanced back and then returned her gaze to Brett and looked thoughtful, biting her lip. "Hmm is right. She hit her head a *lot* harder than you did though, Brett. What dream?"

Brett nodded. "Last night, I had a sort of lucid dream where Cheryl appeared. She... She wasn't herself. She was more like a memory mixed with guilt to make a bitter, dark version of her. She pretty much even said she was a figment of my imagination when I asked if she was haunting me. Still, in the dream, she had blood running down right here," Brett illustrated, tracing on his cheek down to his chin.

Liz shrugged. "Could be coincidence, but it's hard to discount anything as too weird at this point. I even wonder what made the junk fall off that truck."

Gonzo stuck his head in the door. "Hey look at this!" He held a mangled metal rake in his hand. "There's yer problem," he said in a nasal voice. "Fucker took out the front right tire and got wrapped around the rear tire on the same side. I'm amazed it didn't blow both of 'em. We'll have to get out the spare."

Jimbo already rummaged around in the back. "Where is it?" He lifted the rug and looked up at Gonzo.

"Underneath, Junior. It's strapped under the backside, and it's a bitch to get it out." Gonzo crouched and began to work at the fastenings.

Brett turned and popped open his door to get out. Liz reached over and grabbed his arm to stop him. "Oh no, I just fixed you up;

you're going to sit still awhile."

Brett looked exasperated. "I should help out, Lizzie."

Gonzo shook his head. "Count yourself as lucking out this time. I don't think you'd better do much for a little bit. Might need you two to get out when we get the jack ready. I don't want it shifting around when it's up."

Brett sighed and shut his door. "Oh well, I guess there are worse things."

Liz draped an arm around his shoulder and put her nose against his. "Oh, what fate could be worse than being watched over by your girlfriend? Hmmm?"

Brett gave a not-quite-audible gasp. "Hmm, so you're my *girlfriend* now, are you? I thought we were living in the now?"

She giggled and lowered her eyes for half a second, then looked up into his again. "Well, that just slipped out, to be honest, it just feels so much like it used to. But why the hell not? If we can live in the moment, then we can be a couple in this moment too."

He felt uneasy as he asked, "What about when the moment is over?"

She put a finger to his lips and shook her head. "Shhh. Don't worry about the next thing, right? There's never a guarantee of what's coming in the next moment, not even for couples celebrating their 50th anniversary. We've just got to enjoy what we have exactly right now, and let the future take care of itself. I've missed being with you terribly, *Chico*, ever since we went our separate ways. I've never mourned our relationship though, because that time can't ever be taken from us, and we didn't end in a way that changed how we felt about each other. It was just time to decide, and whether you want to think it ended at that moment, or just, I don't know, *paused* awhile, that's up to you, I guess." She touched his face and kissed him again.

Brett reached up and toyed with her soft hair a moment, then nodded. "Well, I don't know about all that, but I have to say, I'm enjoying right now while it lasts, Lizzie."

Gonzo cleared his throat, looking in through the hatch. "Yeah, okay break it up, don't make me get the hose out. Could you two nauseating lovebirds get your butts out of the van for a few? The jack's ready and the spare's in place."

Brett opened his door and hopped out. Liz slid across the seat to follow him. It was chillier out here, but not so much that they really needed coats. They stood to one side and watched Jimbo pump the jack while Gonzo worked the flat tire to see if it would turn. Once it budged, he spun the lug nuts the rest of the way off and struggled the tire off of the bolts and set it aside.

Liz fanned herself with a hand and pretended to look faint. "Oh mah, mah goodness just look at the big, strong men. Ah dew declare," she said, "Ah have never seen such displays of raw, animal masculinity!" She giggled.

Gonzo gave her a dirty look, but winked as he tried to fit the spare on. He looked back to his work, motioning Jimbo to raise the front end a little higher. "Hey, don't look at me," he mumbled, an impish smile spreading across his face. "It's Jimbo who's jacking his handy... I mean handy with a jack."

Jimbo took his hands off the jack and sighed. "Just put the tire on!"

Brett grumbled to Liz, "See, if I'd helped out, you could be mocking me along with them."

Liz wrinkled her nose. "Kiss mah grits, Brett!" She giggled and leaned in to whisper in his ear. "After this morning, do you really think I doubt your manly charms?"

Brett groaned and laughed. "Shhh! Stop it, they'll hear!" he hissed back at her. Her eyes twinkled in the sun as it came out from behind a cloud for the first time that afternoon.

Chapter 13 - Worse Luck

Jimbo lowered *Soccer Mom*, putting weight on the spare and the grass below. Brett and Liz cheered and clapped. Jimbo took a bow.

Gonzo grinned and rolled the shredded tire towards the rear of the van, lifting it to put it in the cargo area as best he could. "Okay, so it was a minor setback. We'll just find a service station and get a replacement for the spare and we'll still make it to New Orleans tonight!"

Liz looked up as she heard a sound. The noise turned out to be air brakes on a semi that had pulled off to the side on the highway above them. "Guys," she warned, "it looks like we've got company." She folded her arms and took a step toward the van. "And I've got a bad feeling."

Gonzo clapped his hands and rubbed them on his jeans as he slammed the back of the Caravan. "Yeah? What makes you think it's not just a trucker stopping to help?"

Liz just shook her head as the semi's door slammed and a lanky, leathery truck driver walked around the front of the truck. He was grinning, and his eyes were wide underneath his black Dale Earnhardt cap. He wore faded jeans and an even more faded denim jacket, buttoned up all the way. He waved at them and yelled, "Hey folks, run into some trouble?"

Brett and Jimbo looked at each other and shrugged. "Looks okay to me," Brett said under his breath to Liz, "but you go ahead and get in the car, we don't know how long this guy's been on the road, or what he wants."

Brett thought she'd argue the point, but she just nodded and let go of his hand and slipped into the back seat of *Soccer Mom*. She slid the door shut. Somehow this disturbed Brett more than her warning had. He looked back; the trucker was already hopping across the ditch and was almost to them.

Gonzo walked up to intercept the man. "Hey there buddy, thanks for stopping, we're just getting ready to get back on the road after a flat. We hit some debris in the road back there and lost control, but we're all right now."

The trucker peered past Gonzo, gazing at the van, still grinning like he'd won a prize. "All right? Oh no. No no no. No, you're not all right, son, you're in a lot of trouble. I don't think you'll be leaving here now. No, no no no no." His head swung from side to side like an unhinged screen door in a storm. "No, I don't think so."

Jimbo started towards the trucker and Gonzo, but Gonzo shook his head no, and he glanced at Brett to stop him as well. He looked back at the trucker and put out a hand to press against his chest to halt his progress. The weathervane swinging of the man's head stopped, and he slowly looked into Gonzo's face. The grin stayed, but his eyes narrowed.

"If I was you, and you know, I'm not really, but if I *was*, just for sake of argument, you know what I'd do?" The trucker didn't wait for an answer. "You know, I'd just take my hand off there, you know, if I knew what was good for me. Yeah, I think you'd best just do that, and get out of my way, I have, hmm, I have *business* to take care of here. Yeah."

Gonzo made no such move, and he lowered his voice. Brett could barely hear his reply, "You don't belong here. Just get out of here before you piss me off, you stupid fuck." Brett wasn't sure he'd ever heard a dangerous tone like that from his friend before.

The trucker laughed, or coughed, it was hard to say. "Fuck you, then." He hauled his fist back and swung at Gonzo. Gonzo jumped out of his way, taking his hand off the man's chest for a moment. The trucker continued forward. Gonzo braced himself and socked the trucker in the nose, hard.

The trucker backed up a step, blinked at Gonzo, and then stared at him. It seemed to get darker, and Brett almost looked up to see if a plane or something else was passing overhead. But it was a more general gloom that drew light from all around the general area. Brett actually felt the air abruptly chill around him. There was a sudden overwhelming stench, a miasma of death and decay that made his stomach churn and caused him to wince. He started toward Gonzo to help out, despite his friend's warning to stay back.

Liz shouted from the van, "Run, Gonzo, get away! No Brett, get away, he's not what he seems, please just run!"

Gonzo drew back his fist to take another shot at the trucker, but paused, breathing hard. He shook his head once, twice, then was down on his hands and knees, vomiting in the grass. The trucker laughed now, a dry barking laugh.

Jimbo rushed the trucker, tire iron still in his hand, and he reached him just before Brett. He swung the iron, putting all his strength into it, aimed right at the trucker's head. Brett had to dodge out of the way. The trucker didn't move, and the tire iron connected with the side of his head with a terrible wet smack. Jimbo dropped the tire iron, which rang like a tuning fork until it hit the grass a few feet away.

Jimbo stared at his hands in horror, shaking them as though something were on them. "Fucker! What the hell? What the hell *are* you? What did you just do to me?" His arms went limp, and he slumped to the ground weakly, a glazed look coming over his face. He convulsed once, then lay still.

Brett stared at his attacker. He reached for the fallen tire iron, though he wasn't sure what he would do with it, having seen what happened to Jimbo. It seemed just like it was night now, and it was getting more difficult to see the trucker, even though he stood just a few feet away. "You," said the trucker, grinning at him through the deepening gloom, "you I have business with. Both of you."

Brett fought the urge to look back to check on Liz. He thought he heard a van door open, and might have heard footsteps from behind him. He swallowed and began, "You do not belong here. You do not belong in that body. You need to leave. Leave us alone. You do not belong here, you are a nightmare, and this is not your world." Brett tried to put as much confidence in this as he could muster, doing all the things he'd read about psychic protection.

He envisioned a white light, a bubble-like force field of positive energy, surrounding him and protecting him. He wished he was sure it would work, but all he really hoped was that it would buy Liz time.

Brett advanced on the trucker, who actually had paused at his words. He stood there, still grinning, but was silent a moment. "Take your best shot," offered the thing in the trucker, patting its chest. Brett took a breath, feeling the bitter cold, and also feeling weaker and a little dizzy as he got nearer and nearer to the creature.

Brett was shoved roughly to one side, and he heard Liz shriek, "In Eris' name I bind you, and you shall be banished!" With the last word, he saw a flash of light reflected off of sharp metal, and she repeated the swing she'd made at the shadow the night before, this time connecting with the trucker's shoulder with a meaty thump. Her katana blade was lodged several inches into the man, and black blood began to pour from the wound.

The trucker continued to grin, and Liz fell to her knees, twitching the whole way as she fought the weakness coming on her. Her hands hung at a strange angle, like they were numb or broken. "Shit," she gasped, and fell on her side, half-curled up. Her face was invisible in the gloom.

Now Brett dropped the tire iron and grabbed at Liz and tried frantically to drag her away from the trucker, out of the cold and darkness and the stench. Her skin was cold to the touch, and she was rigid and shivering. "No," she whispered faintly. "Run, Brett..."

Brett couldn't leave her, and he didn't know how to harm the creature more than a tire iron to the head or a deep sword cut. He managed to start to drag Liz a few inches, then a foot. He felt his strength leaving him, and the putrid odor began to make his vision swim. Everything was going dark.

He could hear the trucker laugh, somewhere nearby, but even that sound was muted now. Brett fell. He couldn't push himself back to his feet again, so he held onto Liz's cold inert body and pushed with his feet, trying to drag them both backwards, toward the car. He couldn't move them anymore. His breath came in shallow gasps, and he looked up to see the trucker loom over them. The creature raised its hand and backhanded him. It wasn't even a particularly forceful blow, but Brett slumped over Liz's body, his last willing effort to cover her with himself in the vain hope that he could save her by doing so. Then all went dark and he lay still with the others.

Chapter 14 - Twilight

Brett found himself sitting on the side of that lonely highway in the dream desert, near his one-room red house, where he'd seen Cheryl. Where, horribly, he'd *been* Cheryl, if only briefly. He checked his clothes, and found them to be just jeans and a T-shirt, not a black dress of ashes or even the ironic tuxedo for the wedding that had never happened. He had his arms around his knees, and though the Sun beat down from directly above, it seemed dim here, and cold. He looked around him. Crows fluttered in from the sky, landing on the house, the ground, the road. Some strutted up to him curiously. There were dozens of them, cawing and flapping their wings impatiently.

"Go 'way, I'm not dead," said Brett, shooing an especially bold carrion bird with one hand. It cawed at him and fluttered back a few feet, but still it watched him. Its eyes seemed intelligent.

"Aren't you?" came Cheryl's voice from the bird's beak. "You're here, and I don't think it's your doing this time. You're on the cusp, my dear, sitting here on the border with your long lost love of your life."

Brett stared at the talking bird. "So you're a crow now? Cheryl Crow? That's very funny, even if it's not the right spelling. Going to sing me a few bars of 'A Change Would Do You Good'?"

The crow laughed her laugh. "Glad to be of service, I know how you like bad jokes. No, actually I wanted you to take this seriously, and I think that remembering me as I was just distracted too much. This is the edge of death, Brett. Your body is dying, and you've once again got the chance to step across and leave it behind and join me."

Brett shook his head. "I thought you said you were a figment of my imagination? All I have with me is what I brought?"

The crow danced around on clawed feet, head bobbing. "Oh, but that's exactly what I am. But you know I'm waiting for you over here on the other side. You tried to join me before. It was so sweet, giving it all up to follow your love into death itself. Are you still ready to take that step?"

Brett looked away, down the road. He paused a moment, then shook his head. "No, I have too much to live for. Especially now. Even then, I don't think I was actually ready, I think I was just too afraid to go on. If it weren't for Lizzie, I would have taken that coward's way out. I'm glad she saved me."

"Are you? Are you really? Oh, but that hurts." The crow didn't sound sarcastic, but its tone turned nasty. "Your one noble gesture and you deny it, and give credit for the decision to her. How typical. Well, lover, here's your big chance to do something all on your own. No one is going to save you, no one's going to take the plunge but you. You're hanging on by the tips of your fingers, and it would be so easy to just let go, slip into the warm, inviting waters that wait for you. Er, metaphorically speaking. All you really have to do is stand up and walk to the other side of the road."

Brett frowned. "All I have to do... Isn't the road an illusion too? What would crossing the road do?"

Cheryl cawed, "Well, yeah, this is all pretty sketchy when you come right down to it. You are effectively talking to yourself, or at least some subconscious part of yourself that holds all your memories of me. Know how people say, 'She will live on inside all of us' at funerals? In a way, it is literal truth. We all form mental models of the people we know, and it is what we use to run simulated conversations in their absence. I'm all your expectations of what Cheryl was. Anyway. Crossing the road would, to you, symbolize leaving life behind and passing on into death and whatever comes after."

"You don't *know* what comes after?" Brett objected, "If that's a real option, to decide to die by crossing this road, what kind of assurance do I have that *anything* happens afterwards?"

The crow fluttered up in the air and Cheryl's form coalesced into being in the middle of the road where it had been. She wore the low-cut red dress she had worn at the freshman mixer when he'd met her. She smiled and took a step back, to the shoulder of the other side. She beckoned to him, and Brett's heart raced with the dare. "Come on, Brett, there are never any guarantees in life, or after it. You think she's alive back there? I can't assure you that she is. She might well be over here with me by now. She didn't look so good when things went black for you, did she? And you're on the cusp yourself. Seems to me your odds are better over here."

Brett hadn't known Cheryl to be malicious in life, but she always was a tease, and she was always trying to get him to go past his personal limits. This was not the horrible thing that inhabited the trucker, this was just what she said she was, his memory personified. He stood up and dusted off his jeans and looked at Cheryl curiously. "How does this symbolic road-crossing work then? Some kind of bio-feedback where my heart stops if I take the steps?"

Cheryl shrugged. "Don't ask me, I just know this somehow. Maybe you know it too, subconsciously? So what's it going to be, hot stuff?" She turned her body sideways as if to continue walking away from him, but kept her eyes on him as long as she could, pausing mid-step before stepping entirely off the road.

He thought about it. He looked over his shoulder at the tiny one-roomed red house, its door still standing open. Was there anything back there for him? Was Liz gone? Were Gonzo and Jimbo dead too?

"You know, I can always die later," said Brett after a pause, still looking at the open door. "I can't go with you, not knowing how it stands in life, since I don't know if there's any way back from there. I'm sorry Cheryl, I love you and I've missed you all this time, but given the choice, I'm going back."

He looked back across the road, but Cheryl was gone already, with no trace left. Brett nodded and went to the doorway and stepped back inside, shutting the door behind him. He could hear the other crows fly away in a flurry of wings and chattery caws at the sound of the door latching.

Chapter 15 – Somewhere Else

Brett heard music. He wasn't sure what it was, but it reminded him of experimental music, some string of nonsense words to a somewhat atonal and quirky tune. He was pretty sure he'd heard it somewhere before. However, he couldn't seem to move or open his eyes just now. He ached all over, and he was cold and shivering. He breathed in dusty, oily air. The floor vibrated and rumbled ominously.

He realized that the words were being mumbled and the music was being hummed. The source moved a little, along with a scraping noise, somewhere near one of his ears. The one that was pressing against the gritty, possibly wooden, floor. The voice, he thought, sounded like someone he knew. Someone important. He knew he should know, but his head ached so badly, he couldn't do much but concentrate on keeping the room from spinning too badly.

Then he slid across the floor, as it felt like it was tilting or moving on its own. He still could not summon strength to move himself. It wasn't like the sleep paralysis though; it felt like he was drugged or too shakily exhausted to move a muscle. He did shiver and twitch as he thought about it, but it wasn't actual control.

He stopped sliding as he hit something sharp, and now he was crushed up against it by something heavy from his other side. Something... warm. The voice faltered as they collided, then cursed softly, then continued. "I wanna live," it sang, and he knew it was Liz singing the words, humming weakly when she paused singing. "I wanna live... I roll over and you're not there..."

Brett struggled to move and managed to twitch a foot just a little, tapping against something soft, possibly Liz's leg. He tried to speak, and was rewarded by a thin, unintelligible moan. It made lights in his head flash with the effort, and he had to struggle not to go unconscious again. Liz stopped singing and drew in a breath. "Brett?"

Brett tried to reply, but only groaned, perhaps a degree or two louder this time. His head failed to shatter into a thousand pieces as he felt it might.

"Brett..." she drew a breath again. "We're not..." breath, "dead! Wow..."

He would have laughed if he could at the weakly optimistic tone in her voice. He coughed and drew a deeper breath. "Lizzie," he breathed, amazed that he got it out.

He felt her move around next to him, rolling to spoon around him. She didn't put her arm around him though. He began to realize his own arms were over his head, and they felt numb. He wasn't even entirely certain whether he still had hands.

He felt her strain, and then felt a dry but warm kiss on the back of his neck. "I was..." breath, "so worried..."

Now he did laugh, but it didn't come out that way. He coughed and gasped. His eyes flew open. He was facing a large cardboard box that claimed to contain motor oil. The light was very dim, and he wasn't sure where it was coming from. The floor he lay on was rough pine wood planking, maybe a cargo pallet. There was dirt and a muddy boot print on it in his field of view. The wall looked like sheet metal with steel bracing. Everything vibrated and shook, and he realized he heard the sound of a big engine, and the sound of many tires on a highway.

"Truck," he began. "Where... are we, Lizzie?"

She breathed warmly on his neck as she spoke, her voice regaining some strength now. "Don't know. Guess the demon took us. I can't believe we're alive, Brett."

"Yeah," he breathed. He blinked and felt grit behind his eyelids. "Are Gonzo and Jimbo here?" He strained to look up, but only raised his head an inch, then it dropped with a hollow thump. The truck went around a curve, and they slid a bit back to the other side, away from the box and the wall on that side.

He heard Liz move around a bit. "I can't tell for sure. I can't see well, and I can't really sit up yet. I haven't heard them, though. I... I think my wrists and ankles are bound somehow." He heard her pause for breath, then she asked, "Think you're up to rolling over to face me, *Chico*?"

Brett wasn't at all sure he could, but said, "Anything for you,

Sweetie." He wanted to sound braver than he felt. She wiggled a bit to give him room, and he instantly missed her warmth. He took it in stages, first stretching out flat. This caused his aches to flare up and rearrange themselves around his body. He stretched as straight as he could manage, then lay there for a long moment. The truck started to shift again, going around another slight bend, and happily it was in his favor, so he took advantage of the inertia and rolled, pulling his knees in when he faced Liz to keep from continuing the roll. Liz hadn't scooted far, so he found himself suddenly nose-to-nose with her, and his knees banged into hers.

She favored him with a smile and strained to kiss the tip of his nose. He had to smile now too, and he found he was cheered quite a lot by seeing her face, watching her close her eyes as she kissed him. She opened her eyes and looked into his. He was amazed at her strength, her ability to be silly in a moment that should have them both peeing their pants in terror. He was surprised at how hopeful he felt, and was not sure whether it was due to having lived despite being so sure he was already dead, or because he could see Liz smiling at him now.

"Okay, let's see what options we've got," she said, tilting her head slightly to look towards their hands. "Looks like your hands are bound with duct tape over your head. I can't feel mine, but I'll bet that's why. Can you move your arms?" A lock of her hair fell into her eyes, and she had to blow several times to get it out of the way.

Once again, he wasn't sure whether he could do it, but with Liz asking, he thought he might. He rocked from side to side, pulling his arms down inch by inch. It felt like his shoulder muscles were on fire as they moved. He groaned before he could stop himself, and he saw the wince of sympathy cross Liz's face. He paused a moment, then repeated this sequence several times. "At least," he said during one of the pauses, "I think I'm feeling a little better. Do you think he drugged us and it's just starting to wear off?"

Liz pursed her lips as she thought about this. "Mmm, no, I don't think so. I think the demon just drained away all our energy back on the side of the highway. Okay, that's it. Now, don't laugh, but I'm going to try to tear the duct tape with my teeth, so hold still."

Brett didn't laugh as she started to work at the duct tape wound around his wrists. It was actually kind of funny, except it also made hope rise in his chest. He breathed faster, and felt his excitement at the idea of escape thrill through him. Liz gnawed and worried at the tape between his wrists for a minute or two, and then he heard a ripping noise. "Demon? You said that before. You really think it was a demon?"

Liz snorted, tape in her teeth, "Herro, cou'd it *be* anyfing e'se?"

Brett laughed, despite himself. "Good point. Just... Well, never encountered any evidence of demons being real before. Just sketchy photos and voices in recordings. But those are ghosts. If I hadn't just been through all that, I wouldn't believe it."

"Fink I've got it," she said, a strip of duct tape in her teeth. "Help me," she mumbled as she moved her head to tug at the strip. Brett wasn't sure what she meant at first, but then saw she was trying to unwind the tape, rather than bite through it. He tried to help, though it was all very clumsy, and Liz had to stop a moment to laugh and to rest. She had managed to unstick maybe a couple of inches of tape, though it had torn down the middle. She smiled at him, then went back to tugging on the strip, this time more successfully, winding around his wrists several times before the strip ripped completely off. There was still a fair bit of duct tape binding him, but it was a start.

"Augh, bleagh," sputtered Liz, making a face. "Fun fact: duct tape doesn't taste nearly as good as you'd think it would." They both laughed and started to feel a bit stronger.

Pins and needles started to prickle around Brett's wrists. "Hey, I think you loosened it enough to get some blood flowing, I'm starting to feel a bit." He pulled his arms apart as far as they'd go, and struggled at the bonds, and they did feel looser, but he was still too weak to break free. "Gah, it's not enough yet."

Suddenly, there was a loud rumble, and they began to slide again, this time in the direction Brett thought must be forward. The other contents of the truck were fastened down, but they slid around freely. The rumble deepened and the floor bounced as the wheels went over bumps or hit rough patches of pavement.

"I think we're slowing down, *Chico*, let me work on the tape again. We've got to get free before... well, before he gets another shot at us." She started working at the tape again with her teeth, and Brett began to feel her breath on his hands as feeling gradually returned. When she had a strip free, they unwound some more.

"It's a lot looser, let me give it another try," said Brett. Liz scooted back a bit, and Brett wiggled and then strained to pull his arms apart with quick jerking motions until there was a ripping sound and his arms were free. "There!" Brett cried, fumbling with partially numb fingers to pull off the remaining tape. Liz cheered after she spit the sticky strands of tape out of her mouth. Brett massaged his hands together to work the feeling back into them. "Now let's get you free."

"Not yet," said Liz. "We need help since we're still weak, and we're going to be no good with our feet bound, either. Free your own feet, I think I have an idea."

Chapter 16 - Escape

Brett did as Liz asked and struggled to a sitting position so he could reach to rip off the tape around his ankles. It was slow work at first. It was hard to see and his fingers were painfully coming back to life, but he tried to feel his way around. He finally got loose and looked at Liz. "Okay, boss, now what?" He worked at the duct tape binding her hands while she talked.

"No, no, now that you're free, we need a signal flare more than we need me free." She jutted her chin at the box Brett had been sliding into. "There's our signal flare, right there."

Brett looked at the box of motor oil. "Signal flare?" he asked dumbly. "I'm still kind of woozy I guess, but I don't get it."

She smiled. "Well, I just bet that if this truck was leaking a stream of oil, someone might take notice."

Understanding dawned on Brett. "Oh! Hey, that's brilliant, Lizzie! Hang on, I'll see what I can do." He hated leaving her tied up like this, but she had a point about time being of the essence. He crouched next to the cardboard crate. It was bound with plastic straps, but Brett knew a trick from past experience. He found where it was joined together and flipped that bit of the strap over, grabbed the tab underneath and pulled. The strap flew free with a snap, and he was able to rip the top of the cardboard open enough to expose a row of plastic bottles of motor oil. He grabbed up one bottle in each hand and worked his way toward the back of the semi trailer.

"Bad news, I don't see any sign of Jimbo or Gonzo in here. Hmm, maybe that's good news though. I hope they got away..." He pushed that thought away for now, focusing on his more immediate worries. He peered around the lower edge of the big doors. They were on a hinge, and seemed securely fastened in place. The doors didn't budge when he pushed against them, though he didn't really expect them to. He couldn't find a way to open them from inside. There was a small gap in the stripping around the doors at the very base where they met in the middle. He unscrewed the first bottle, punctured the safety seal, and turned it upside-down. Oil oozed out, and he put the neck of the bottle right into the gap and squeezed. A lot of the oil squirted to either side, but he could feel that it was working, oil was making it outside of the trailer, and most likely pouring onto the road behind them.

He squeezed out the one bottle, then opened the other and laid it on its side so it would pour more gradually into the gap. "Okay, now I'm going to get you free, Lizzie, since our signal flare is dripping out behind us." He worked his way back up to where she lay and continued the job he'd started on her wrists. It was easier going this time, now that his fingers felt back to normal, and his strength was returning more and more.

She looked up at him owlishly as he worked. "I hope this works, this would be a stupid way to die, sucked dry by a demon, sent by a jealous crazy girl."

"Hmm?" Brett was distracted as he worked at trying to tear through a couple of layers of tape. "So you think this was sent by Frannie? You know, a poltergeist I can see, but a demon? How's she done it? Why would she do it?"

Liz shrugged one shoulder. "That's the part that I don't get. I don't think she's some kind of occult demon-worshiper. I've run into a few of those, trying to pretend they were Pagans. Those people who give us a bad name. No, she's crazy, but not that flavor of crazy. At least I can't imagine it out of her. I'd say that maybe she knows someone who is, but if that's true, then the summoner must like her an awful lot to risk his or her life for Frannie. And if Frannie has that kind of devotion from someone else, why's she so crazy jealous about Jimbo going on a little road trip with friends?"

Brett tore at the tape and gave one final tug that ripped the last of it so that her wrists were free. He rubbed at her hands to warm them up and help the circulation.

"No, I can take care of that, *Chico*. You go keep the oil flowing back there. I'll get my ankles too," said Liz, smiling up at him.

He didn't know how she could always be so positive, always finding a light side to things. He was sure that without her keeping their hopes alive, he'd still be bound up, waiting for his fate, wherever the possessed trucker was taking them. He leaned down and kissed her quickly.

"What was that for?" she asked, puzzled. She wrung her hands and pulled her arms down to her side as she rolled onto her back. "Ow," she added, almost as an afterthought.

"Just for saving my life and keeping me going, even now." He shrugged. He crawled back over to the box of oil bottles and grabbed two in each hand this time. He scrambled back to the doors and saw that the bottle was nearly empty and wasn't pouring out any more. There was a growing puddle of oil near the doors now, soaking the wooden floor, but it looked like some of it was draining back through the crack under the door. He upended the open bottle and let the last bit spill out through the gap, and then tossed it aside with the first bottle. He opened one of the bottles he'd brought back with him and squeezed again to force oil out more quickly. It glugged and spurted, but Brett could just imagine the stream of oil squirting out the back of the truck. He hoped it was noticeable.

Liz soon joined him, handing him bottles of oil faster than he could pour them out the back of the truck. They kept at this awhile, slowly regaining strength as they worked. The truck bumped along, occasionally throwing them from side to side as it took a curve or braked.

"I'm guessing we're not on the Interstate anymore, from the quality of the road. I think that demon is *trying* to hit every pothole in the road," griped Brett. "I hope someone sees this soon."

Liz paused long enough to touch his shoulder. "It's all we can do, love. We can't get out of here, and I don't think we could get past the demon when he opens the doors."

"If he doesn't just drive into a lake and drown us," said Brett morosely.

"Oh Brett," reprimanded Liz, "that's no way to talk. Gonzo

was right, if we buy into being victims, that's just what we'll be. Planning to die is as good as giving up. The only thing that matters is doing what we can to survive and planning for it. Anything else that happens... well, then it happens and we can't control it. Don't give up yet."

Brett sighed and nodded. "You're right. It's just scary, and overwhelming. I keep thinking this has to be a nightmare, and that I'll wake up and laugh this off, but I know it's not. A demon? I'm one of the most open-minded people I know, and I've never believed in them. Residual hauntings, even intelligent ghosts and poltergeists, sure. I'd seen evidence of those, at least good enough to convince me, even before this crazy trip. Demonic possession though, it doesn't make sense, it doesn't fit with how I see the world at all. We can't even really tell anyone about it later, people will think we're crazy or that we're dropping acid."

Liz went back to shuttling bottles from the crate to Brett. "Well, we can tell our story to other people who've experienced this kind of thing. I know they're out there, I've read some things on the Internet that I wasn't sure I believed before. Maybe not all those stories are true, but I'm a believer now." She laughed her tinkling little laugh. "Wow, look at all that oil, are you sure you're getting it outside too? Maybe our backup plan will be that we hope Ugly Mother Trucker slips and knocks himself out when he comes for us."

Brett didn't feel it, but he laughed in response. He uncapped the next bottle and started to pour. Suddenly, they heard a siren wailing from nearby behind the semi, getting closer fast. He squeezed the oil as fast as it would go through the gap. There was a long moment where he thought the demon would just ignore the siren. Abruptly, he was thrown backwards as the truck braked hard. He and Liz tumbled backwards and hit cardboard crates. They groaned and then helped each other up to a sitting position, facing the doors.

"This is it, *Chico*! Once we stop, get ready to make some noise!" Liz looked around and found a thick cloth strap with a large buckle on it. She kneeled, bracing herself on a box. "Find something to rap on the wall with!"

Brett searched around. He almost fell again as the truck came to a full stop. The oil bottles wouldn't help. He couldn't find anything to use to make noise, so he beat his fists on the side, making a nice booming noise. Liz hammered on a steel strut with the metal buckle, and was rewarded with a loud clanging that rang throughout the trailer. They both shouted at the top of their lungs, pleading to be let out, hoping that help would come to them before the demon could act.

Brett's heart pounded in his chest as he yelled and beat the wall of the truck. Anyone outside would have to hear this terrible din. Liz was now screaming a wailing, piercing cry that brought chills even to Brett. He'd never heard such a sound come from her before. She was putting everything into it. Brett redoubled his efforts.

They both heard the bolt on the outside of the doors lift out of place. They stopped pounding and rushed toward the door. Liz held Brett back as they got up to the pool of oil, keeping him from slipping.

The door opened. On the other side was a mustached county sheriff, peering in at them with a shocked look on his face. He had an oversized flashlight that could probably double as a truncheon. "You folks all right? What's going on here?"

"The driver's crazy, he'd kidnapped us!" cried Liz.

"Well, you come on out of there, and we'll go have a talk with the driver," said the officer. Brett let Liz past him and she took the officer's hand to be let down.

A shadow appeared behind the officer, coming around the open door. The possessed trucker moved disturbingly quickly, putting hands around the sheriff's neck in an instant. The officer, caught off guard, tried to turn, flailing at the trucker with the flashlight.

Brett and Liz could not get past, and felt the cold and weakness return to them as the demon drained the life from the policeman. They fought against the cold, held on to each other for warmth and strength, but the demon's power seemed to grow even as the sheriff fell to the ground.

Liz and Brett pushed backwards with their feet, still embracing and shivering. The demon climbed into the doorway, blocking the reddish light of the setting sun, casting a long, inky shadow across the floorboards and onto the lovers.

"I was saving this for later," breathed the demon, "but I haven't got the time now. That's a shame, too, since I do love to play as long as I can make it last. Well, sometimes you have to have dessert first." Brett could no longer move, and everything was starting to get dimmer and dimmer as the demon climbed in behind them.

The possessed trucker advanced slowly on them, and Brett felt a surge of hope when it slipped a little on the oil, but it caught itself on a crate with a hand. It continued toward them, pulling out a large pocketknife. The demon opened the knife, which clicked as it locked in the open position. It reached their feet, and grabbed Liz's foot with one hand.

"Let's open you up and see what's inside, shall we, dear?" Brett looked on in horror as the knife went under Liz's running tights and began to slit the elastic material up her ankle and over her calf. He tried to struggle, but could not move. In fact, he was losing his hold on Liz as well, and they fell apart, touching only where their arms still lay under each other's body.

The knife traveled further up her leg, and Liz let out a low moaning protest, writhing feebly to get away. She barely moved an inch, and the demon grinned as her tights split on her thigh. "Now, now, lay still and maybe you'll enjoy this," purred the demon, eyes glowing red, wide with anticipation as it loomed over Liz. Brett screamed inside his head, but only a groan came out. He felt the cold pulling him down, down, deeper into darkness, and only the heat of his rage kept him from falling unconscious.

There was a blinding flash of a spark somewhere in the trailer, along with a loud crackle and the smell of ozone. Brett felt an electric tingle from where he touched Liz, and he felt her convulse slightly. The trucker spasmed and screamed, falling to the floor of the truck. It flopped around on the floorboards in an apparent seizure for a long, breathless moment, then lay still. There was a terrible wailing noise, seeming to come from everywhere, a horrible, despairing, drawn-out cry as a black mist, or smoke, rose from the trucker's crumpled body. It filled the trailer, and Brett could not draw breath for many pounding heartbeats.

Finally the pressure subsided as the oily, smoky mist burst out of the truck and streamed away. Brett felt warmth return instantly, and though still weak, he was freed of the terrible paralysis. He hugged Liz to him, and she kissed him fiercely.

"Aww, break it up you two, I'm not afraid to use this thing again if you're going to be like that." Gonzo stood in the doorway of the trailer, holding a small black object with two metal prongs on the top. He squeezed it and a fat spark arced between the contacts. He grinned and pocketed the device. "You guys okay?"

Chapter 17 – Decisions

"Gonzo!" Liz and Brett cried in unison. They disengaged from their warm embrace and clambered over to the doorway. Gonzo reached in and lifted Liz out of the trailer and set her on the ground. She hugged the large man tightly. "I don't know how you found us, but you had great timing. You have no idea how glad we are to see you!"

"Yeah, how did you find us, and where'd you get the taser?" asked Brett as he climbed down from the back of the truck by himself. He wiped his oily hands on his jeans and looked around. Behind the truck was the fallen officer's car. *Adams County Sheriff*, it said on the side of the car. Brett looked down to see the sheriff lying on the ground, eyes fluttering open. He groaned. Brett reached down a hand and helped the man up.

"What the hell is going on around here?" asked the officer weakly. He dusted himself off and squinted at Gonzo, Liz and Brett, then peered into the darkness of the semi trailer. "That guy, what was he, how did he do that?"

Gonzo shook his head. "We don't know either. It attacked us when we were changing a tire back on the Interstate. It knocked us all out with that freaky cold shit and took off with these two," he said, indicating Brett and Liz with a nod. "Took me a while to even get up, but we drove like crazy to catch up. We tried to call 911 for help, but our cell phone batteries were dead, and as long as we tailed that truck, they wouldn't even get a signal if they were plugged in with a charger. We followed when the truck pulled off on Highway 61, but had to try to stay a few car lengths behind so he wouldn't notice us tailing him."

The sheriff listened to Gonzo, nodding slowly. "I was set to catch speeders back there when I saw this truck spilling oil out the back. I pulled him over to let him know he was leaking, maybe inspect his cargo, then I heard your friends pounding and screaming and carrying on inside. I thought there'd be trouble, but I didn't know anyone could move that fast. I... I can't explain what happened, neither. It was cold, and he didn't have a good grip on me, but I couldn't breathe or fight him off all the same. Stringy old guy... Somehow everything went dark, too." The man's eyes held a haunted look as he talked about the trucker. "I thought I was dead when I blacked out. What happened after that?"

Gonzo pulled the taser out of his pocket and handed it back to the officer. "Got him with this. Can't win against something like that in a fair fight, so when I saw that on your belt, I thought it might just take it out, and I was right. About time something went right today."

"Where's Jimbo?" asked Liz, who had moved from Gonzo to put her arm around Brett's waist.

"Oh, he's back in the van, behind the police cruiser. He's still pretty freaked out by the attack, so I told him to wait in the driver's seat in case we had to make a quick getaway." Gonzo leaned over and waved so Jimbo could see they were okay.

The sheriff said, "I'd better go cuff that guy before he wakes up," and climbed into the truck. The others waited outside and heard him curse. "This guy's stone cold dead. Taser shouldn't do that. Shouldn't be cold yet, neither. Damn, he stinks too, like... This guy's not just dead, he's a day-old corpse. I'm not a doctor, but he already smells rotten. This all makes no sense. I'd better call this in, but I don't know what to tell 'em. No one's going to believe it."

He climbed out and looked over the friends standing there. "I'd like to get a statement from each of you. I'd like you all to tell me that you stopped to see if this trucker needed help and flagged me down when you found him dead."

Brett looked at Liz and then at Gonzo. All of them shrugged. "Why tell it that way?" asked Brett.

"Because that way, you all don't get suspected for murder, and that way I get to keep my job," said the sheriff slowly. "Things like that just don't happen, and the more I think about it, the less I believe it did happen. I like my version better. You seem like nice folks, and there's no need to get you all tangled up in a mess that's better left as a mystery. 'Sides, once the coroner sees that body, he's going to agree that there is no way that guy died today, maybe not even as recently as yesterday.

So I want to take your statements so you can just move on out of this county and get on with your lives."

Brett and Gonzo exchanged another look. Gonzo said slowly, "Well, if you think that's best, I don't see a need to complicate matters."

Liz said, "I mean, we're all more or less okay, medically speaking, and we can't exactly pursue a kidnapping charge against a corpse."

Brett frowned a moment, then shrugged in resignation. "I hate to lie, and it's a shame that this experience is going to go undocumented."

He felt Liz hug him to her, and he looked over as she spoke to him. "I understand how you feel, love, but it's beyond believing, especially if medical evidence shows he was dead at the time he abducted us. Plus, who is going to believe that one guy could overpower a group of four people, then subdue a sheriff all by himself? If nothing else, this man's career would be at stake if he came in with a story like that. Sometimes you have to pick your battles, you know? I m just glad we all came through that alive!"

Brett's gaze strayed down to Liz's exposed leg, and he stared at the tatters of that leg of her tights. Her skin was undamaged, but he still felt angry. "I just wish there was some way to get justice. What if that thing comes back in another body? We don't have a taser of our own. What are we going to do to stop it?"

The sheriff raised a hand to stop Brett. "Hold on there. I don't know anything about things that can do what you're talking about, never believed in 'em, and the sooner you folks get on your way, the sooner I can get back to not believing in 'em. So are we agreed on what happened?"

Gonzo and Liz nodded. Brett paused a long moment, then drew in a deep breath and let it out. He nodded.

"Good. Let's just go to my car and get this taken care of."

The officer took their stories one at a time, also taking down their contact information. Jimbo was let in on what was going on, and he was very happy to go along with the plan. When it was Brett's turn, he told the story as he was directed, reluctantly. He did make sure to give the officer his cell phone number "in case there's more to the story after the fact, I'd like you to call me." The sheriff agreed and also gave Brett his card, on which he wrote his personal cell number in return. *Aaron Marsh, Allen County Sheriff's Office*, it said.

They all shook hands with Sheriff Marsh and bid him goodbye. He stayed in his car, filling out paperwork and making calls as they left him.

Soccer Mom was a welcome sight to Brett and Liz. Liz made all the guys stay out of the van for a few minutes while she changed out of her sliced tights and into a pair of dark blue jeans. She wadded up the ruined tights and looked as though she might throw them out of the car, but ended up just stuffing them in a side pocket of her clothes bag. "I don't want to litter," she explained to Brett, "and anyway, if there's an investigation, I don't think I need to complicate it with something like this being left in the area."

Gonzo put one hand on Jimbo's shoulder, and one on Brett's, to get their attention. "Okay, let's go already. I feel like I've been given a "Get out of Jail Free" card, and I don't want to wait around 'til the cop changes his mind."

Jimbo put a hand on the van's driver's side door handle, blocking Gonzo. "Hey, I think I'd rather drive, I need something to do." He put on the red Pepperoni's ball cap he'd been wringing in his hands while they waited to have their statements taken. "Nothing like driving to distract me, you know?"

Gonzo nodded, but pushed Jimbo's arm aside and opened the door himself. "Yeah, that's why I'm going to drive. I want to put some miles between that body and us as fast as possible. If you drove, I'd be climbing the walls the whole time. Sorry." He climbed up into the seat, ignoring Jimbo's disgusted grunt.

Jimbo reluctantly took shotgun while Brett joined Liz in back. "So," began Liz, "who's up for heading back to Memphis?"

Gonzo started the engine and pulled the van out onto the highway. "No. Absolutely not. We're going on to New Orleans."

"You're kidding, right?" Brett leaned forward so he could look more directly at Gonzo. "After all that's happened, after just about dying, you want to keep on going? Are you nuts? Who knows what might happen next?"

Jimbo nodded. "Yeah, I have to agree with Brett and Liz, we've been hit with some crazy shit, and the last thing we want to do is be predictable. If Frannie somehow sent this thing after us, she thinks we're going to New Orleans, and therefore, so does it."

"I tazed its ass, and it's gone. I don't think it's coming back, and if it does, I doubt it's going to matter which destination we have in mind." Gonzo stared straight ahead at the road, weaving the van around slower cars as he sped along the bumpy stretch of road. Trees flashed by on either side. They passed a sign that declared this section of the highway to be "The Lower Mississippi Great River Road." It appeared to have a few bullet holes casually punched in it.

No one talked for a few minutes. Gonzo's jaw was clenched. Jimbo unsnapped the strap on his ball cap, then re-snapped it, then repeated the process, eyes lowered. Brett and Liz looked at each other helplessly. Brett turned and peered out the rear windows as though he could see Memphis getting further and further away. He had a cold feeling in the pit of his stomach, and a sick feeling he'd never see the place again.

After a while, Liz bit her lip and took a deep breath. "Gonzo, it does matter, I think. I was able to hold the thing off in my house, because it is a place of power for me. It is the one place in the whole world that's entirely mine, and I can keep things... even things like that... out and keep all of us safe. Please, Gonzo, let's just go back for tonight, I don't think we should be out on the road after dark more than we have to, not when we don't know what its next move will be."

Gonzo slammed a hand into the steering wheel. "God damn it! Yeah, okay, it's a badass, it kicked our asses, and it was bad. I know that we only escaped by a lucky break. Even if we go back to your apartment, what are we going to do then? We'd be okay for a few days, but then we have to split up and go home or we'll lose our jobs and lives. Don't you think it's better if we all stay together and see this thing through? New Orleans is where we set out to go, and we've beaten this thing so far. We know what it's capable of, and we know what stops it. We could get another taser and keep it with us."

Liz's forehead furrowed with worry. Brett almost didn't recognize her, so seldom had he seen her anything but cheerful and relaxed. Anger boiled up in him, hating that the demon could dim Liz's inner light.

The music of Pac Man began to play. Jimbo's cell phone, which was on the dash, plugged into the power outlet to charge, lit up and began to dance around as it vibrated.

Jimbo looked at it stupidly for a moment, then picked it up. "Jesus, it's Frannie's cell phone. What should I do?"

Liz and Gonzo answered quickly at the same time. Liz cried, "Answer!" and Gonzo shouted, "Don't do it!" Brett remained silent, looking back over his shoulder at the receding highway and darkening red-lit sky.

Jimbo held the phone in his hands for a moment, then muttered, "I'll probably regret this," and punched "speakerphone."

"Jimmy? Please be you, please?" Fran's voice was small and scared, and it sounded like she was talking over some noise.

Jimbo's thumb hovered over the "End" key, and he didn't reply to her for a long moment. His face softened and he let out a breath. "Frannie? Look, I'm sorry I didn't pick up the other night..." Her crying cut him off.

"Oh Jimmy, I was s-s-sure you'd be dead. I felt it leave me, and all my anger and hurt went with it. I felt so empty and sad after it was gone." Fran took a deep breath and Brett could still hear her choking back tears even as she calmed down. "You don't have to be sorry for anything, it was all my fault. But I'm okay now, I promise you. It's over now too, all that anger and hurt, I felt it go. I know it put you in danger, I could feel what it wanted to do, and you're okay."

Jimbo's face reddened and his eyes narrowed and he covered the receiver with his thumb and whispered to the others, "What should

I say to her?"

"Stupid bitch," growled Gonzo. "See? We're cool now, if that's all she's got."

"Jimmy? Are you still there?" When Jimbo grunted an affirmative, she went on, "Look, I think it's important that I see you, even if just for a minute, I want to hold you and make things all right."

Jimbo rolled his eyes and replied, "For the last time, Fran, we are not going to detour to Savannah, not even after being nearly killed by the last temper tantrum you had. I'm sorry, there's just no way..." Again, he was cut off by Frannie's blubbery reply.

"N-n-no, let me finish, Jimmy. I'm not going to have a tantrum now, the blackness is all gone, it's fled back to the shadows where it came from, and I can see clearly again, and I know I screwed up. Bad. I felt like I couldn't control myself, not that it's an excuse, but it was almost like it wasn't me for a day there. My blood ran cold and I couldn't push insecure, ugly thoughts from my head. It just wasn't me, and I don't want to be that person. I want to show you I'm not her. I don't want to lose you, Jimmy. I'm not expecting you to come to me. I'm already on my way to you." Fran seemed to pull herself together as she spoke, the tears held back for now, though she still sniffed.

"What?" cried Jimbo, "What do you mean? Where are you?"

"I'm already on I-10 heading west, Jimmy. I'll be in New Orleans before midnight. I want you to meet me. I don't want to lose you, but I know that you're angry. Please, just meet me one last time and let me hold you once more. If you still hate me and want me to l-l-leave you, I'll understand. You don't have to hear from me again. Just meet me, just for a few minutes, Jimmy. I feel like this has to have a better ending than this, one way or another. Can you be there by midnight too?"

Jimbo asked Fran to hang on the line a moment, and he muted his phone this time as he turned to talk to the others. "Guys, what do you think? If I tell her we'll do it, it might calm her down. I know she's crazy, but I'm really worried about her."

Gonzo snorted. "It's not our problem that she's on the road, we didn't invite her."

"Are you joking? I think we have to do this," Liz almost squeaked out her objection. "She sent that thing after us because she was so upset. If we deny her now, I'll bet she goes nuclear again."

Brett folded his arms in front of him. "Yeah? And so if Jimbo does that for her, but still dumps her? What then? Maybe he's got to take her back just to hold off the demon attacks? Maybe Fran gets anything she wants for the rest of Jimbo's life, living in fear of what lethal thing she can call up the next time he pisses her off?"

Gonzo nodded, turning the wheel to ease *Soccer Mom* around another minivan that seemed to be standing still by comparison. "That's what I say. It's literally emotional blackmail here."

Jimbo shook his head. "No, she sounds sincerely sad, and she's crying, but she's not angry. She says it all left her all at once, and she can feel that it's gone. Look, I'm as angry as any of you, probably angrier. I don't really want to see her, especially right now, but I figure it'll be better closure if I see her in person to break it off. I've got her promise that she'll leave us alone after that."

Brett spoke up now, "I think this is all the more reason to go back to Memphis. We know where she'll be, she knows where we're headed, she won't expect us to turn around, and it'd take her even longer to follow us there even if she figures it out. I can't see her getting her way, it just seems wrong to me."

Gonzo's hands gripped the wheel tightly. "Look, I'm going to New Orleans, and we can be there by midnight, and I'll take anyone who wants to go there with me. If you want to meet up with her after what's happened, that's your business, but I sure as hell wouldn't do it."

Liz shook her head. "I don't want to go back anymore. We need to see this through and end it. I'm with Jimbo on this. Sorry, *Chico*."

Brett sighed and looked out the rear window again, this time with a sullen look on his face. "Fine. Whatever."

Maybe the demon will kill us all along the way and "Cheryl" will get what she wants anyway.

The nasty thought made his stomach churn. Without another word, he pulled out <u>Ghosts</u> to do some more research.

Jimbo took the phone off of hold and spoke to his girlfriend. "Frannie? Okay, I'll meet you at midnight, or shortly after. Meet me… hang on, I gotta ask Gonz." He looked at Gonzo for help.

Gonzo grumbled, "Meet her at the corner of Bourbon and St. Ann in the French Quarter. It's pretty well lit and busy even late at night, and should be safe enough."

"Did you hear that, Fran? And if you get there early though, stay in a bar nearby, it'll be safer than just standing around at night."

"Oh Jimmy! Thank you so much, this means everything to me," breathed Fran. "You don't have to forgive me, but I really feel I need to apologize in person, and... well, anything after that will happen. Either way, I need to do this, and I'm glad you're willing."

Jimbo said, "Well, we'll see. I'll be there, or I'll call if I'm going to be late. Don't drive like a maniac, I'll wait for you if I need to. I promise. Bye, Fran." He hung up the phone and put it back on the dash. "Sorry, I just need to do this, especially if it means all this is going to be over."

In the back seat, Liz put a hand on Brett's knee. He looked up from the book, eyes still hard as he met her gaze. She made a silly pouty face at him, tilting her head so she could look up at him like a puppy. He fought it, but he had to smile. "I still think this is a terrible idea."

She sighed and leaned over to put her head on his shoulder. She spoke in a low voice just to him. "Maybe you're right, but I really think this is our best shot, and it really is kind of up to Jimbo after all. We're along for the ride, but she's his demon to deal with. It's scary, since who knows what she'll do even if she's telling the truth about not being angry and the danger being over? That's why I think we need to stick together. You know?"

Brett found it hard to stay upset with Liz snuggled up to him. He didn't think she would do this as a tactic to make him change his mind, but it kind of irked him all the same. He sighed, and murmured in her ear, "Look, I'm not going to ditch everyone now, and I'm clearly overruled on this, I just feel like we've had plenty of warning on this trip, it just gets worse the further we go. For all our sakes, I hope this is the right thing to do."

Chapter 18 - Back Roads

Gonzo drove on in silence down the highway. He passed other cars regularly, his eyes fixed forward. It was dark now, *Soccer Mom*'s headlights flew along the pavement ahead, creeping up the back of each vehicle as they would approach, but just as the back of the driver's head would be fully illuminated, Gonzo would shift lanes and slide on past. The night promised to be dark, as dense cloud cover loomed in with the twilight winds.

The four friends were all lost in their own thoughts. Brett considered the others in turn. He was sure, looking at Gonzo, that he was still brooding, dwelling on his irritation at the trip not going as he'd planned, with further interruptions an almost certainty. Brett couldn't see Jimbo's face but the way he fidgeted, Brett could imagine him playing and replaying possible conversations with Fran, trying to think of the best thing to say, or even what he wanted to do. Liz was more of a mystery to him. What was she thinking? Was she like him, was she reliving the abduction? Was she afraid, thinking of what might have happened if the truck had not been stopped by the sheriff, or worse, if Gonzo hadn't found a way to defeat the possessed trucker?

He realized that this was really the first time he'd had any time to stop and think the whole trip. His eyes were drawn to the side window, with the dim countryside flying past, he had the sensation of being pulled inexorably along, a leaf in the current of some dark, swift river. Where he would be carried was a certainty now, New Orleans might as well have a palpable gravitational pull. Would it be, as Lizzie said, a final end to the troubles they'd had since the beginning of the trip?

He watched as they passed yet another large SUV, an oversized pickup truck. In the window he saw a tiny woman driving; she had a too-uniform tan from a tanning booth, he was sure. The SUV driver's hair was cut to a razor's edge of a bob, framing her face, glossy black and shining in the streetlights on the side of the highway. As he watched, she turned her head to look him in the eye. She smiled at him, showing intensely white, probably whitened, perfect teeth, made whiter by the wine-dark lipstick she wore.

Brett only saw her for a moment, but in that moment, her tanned face and precision haircut seemed to be engulfed in shadow, and her eyes seemed to glow out of the dark, the white grin curving into a more sinister leer. Then they were past her, and the SUV disappeared behind them, swallowed up into the dark except for its headlights.

Brett hesitated to say anything, but after a moment, he spoke quietly. "Either I'm seeing things, or we are still being followed."

"What?" said Liz, sitting up abruptly. Brett could feel the air cooling his shoulder where her head had been nestled for the past half hour. "You're joking. Please tell me you're joking, *Chico*!"

Jimbo turned his head to look at Brett. "No way. Even if she's wrong about it being gone, she's not mad now. There'd be no reason for it to still be out there hounding us on her behalf."

Gonzo didn't reply at all, but he pushed the aging Caravan to go a little faster still.

Brett shrugged. "I swear I just saw it again, it took over a woman's face as she looked at me. Maybe it was a trick of the light. Maybe not. She looked right at me and then went all dark and freaky, like the trucker."

Liz put a hand over her lips for a moment, studying Brett. "I don't doubt what you saw, love, but we have to keep thinking positively. For instance, if it was the demon in another body, wouldn't we have felt the cold this close?"

Brett thought about this a moment. "Well, there is that. Maybe I am just twitchy, jumping at..." He reconsidered his words to avoid a badly timed pun. "Well, maybe I'm just jumpy. Still, being positive wasn't enough to keep it at bay before. I'm going to keep alert in case I did see what I think I saw."

Liz shook her head. "I don't think we should blindly assume everything's okay, but listen to yourself, Brett, you're literally looking for trouble! Maybe Gonzo could slow down so Jimbo or I could get a look at this woman, see if we see the same thing."

Gonzo growled, "Sorry. I've got to stop for gas in a bit, but I'm not slowing down. Every delay has just made things worse, and the closer we get to NOLA, the happier I'll be. Whether or not Junior is hallucinating back there, going forward is the best policy right now."

"I can't believe I'm saying this, but I'm hungry," said Jimbo. "When we stop, I need to get something to eat."

"Yeah, okay," said Gonzo, "we can do that. I don't want to take too long, but we can sit down someplace. Get some coffee in me. I'm still exhausted from earlier."

They drove on, and the night darkened and deepened. They started to see signs for the town of Natchez, and along with it, advertisements for various places to gas up and get something to eat. Many of the suggestions were of chains, but Gonzo dismissed those as "stuff you could get anywhere" and insisted on looking for an authentic truck stop or diner. They pulled off the highway and Gonzo found a filling station to refuel *Soccer Mom* for the last leg of the trip.

"He doesn't want delays," Brett griped, "but you know he's going to hunt around for the 'perfect' place with local color. If you want to get there before midnight, we can't afford a wild goose chase."

"Well, we'll just have to help convince him then," said Liz, peering out the windows. "I think I see a sign down the ways there for someplace named 'Mom's.' How much more homey and local could you want than 'Mom's'?"

So after the tank was full, the three passengers convinced Gonzo that Mom's would be the best place to stop for a quick bite. Gonzo had to scan the other choices in the area for something more like he imagined the perfect rural meal might be found, but he agreed surprisingly quickly that Mom's was the best they could do in a hurry.

Mom's was fairly empty, since it was Sunday night. Paper pumpkins grinned from all over the place, hanging from paperclips pushed into the ceiling tiles. They hung low enough that Gonzo had to try to dodge around them, and ended up batting one away from him in frustration as they were led to a booth by an elderly waitress. The waitress wore a red gingham apron over faded denim jeans and a matching faded denim shirt, both adorned in tassels and embroidery that appeared to be done by hand. Her nametag said "Anita." The table was vintage Formica and aluminum, which seemed to please Gonzo for some reason. Brett scooted into the booth, and found that the cracked, red vinyl cushion was not attached, and he had to push it back to make it flush with the back. Liz followed him in, and took his hand under the table. Jimbo looked like he felt out of place, though Brett wasn't sure whether it was the rural location or being waited on that made his friend uncomfortable.

Gonzo also smiled as the waitress automatically produced a carafe of coffee from somewhere and poured them each a steaming hot mug without even being asked. Brett thought about refusing the coffee since he was quite anxious enough already without adding caffeine, but decided he might want some to stay alert anyway. "Anita" also filled their glasses from a plastic pitcher of ice water, and pulled straws for each of them from a pocket in her apron.

They peered at the laminated menus, which appeared to have been created on an actual typewriter. The waitress politely left them to mull over their options, then swung back by. They all decided to have some form of breakfast... Gonzo wanted steak and eggs, while Jimbo asked for biscuits and gravy. Liz was torn between blueberry pancakes and chocolate chip waffles. After some encouraging by Brett and Jimbo, she settled on the pancakes, though she held onto the menu a long time before giving it up and finalizing her order. Brett wasn't sure he was actually hungry, but he ordered the chocolate chip waffles just so Liz could try some. Liz was delighted and bounced up and down happily on the seat. Brett grabbed onto the table in case the cushion slipped off. Gonzo and Jimbo grabbed up their coffee mugs to prevent them sloshing, but grinned at Liz over the brims as they each took a sip.

"I'm not sure you actually need any coffee, Lizzie," remarked Brett as the waitress left with their menus.

Liz stuck her tongue out at him. "I might not need it, but I sure want it." Pretending to be defiant, she took up her mug and took a gulp. Brett winced on her behalf, since he knew if Gonzo had to sip it, it was near scalding. Liz sucked in some air to cool her mouth, then blew on the surface of the coffee, then reached past Brett to take the glass-and-steel sugar shaker, pouring in a disturbingly large amount of sugar. She stirred this and looked around cheerfully. "This place makes me wonder if *Soccer Mom* is fitted with a Flux Capacitor. I know Gonzo was going fast enough that this could actually be 1955." She slapped the top of her head with a hand and did her best Christopher Lloyd, "Great Scott! Do you know what this means? If Brett doesn't get Jimbo and Frannie to kiss, he'll never be born!"

Brett had to laugh. Jimbo unwrapped part of his straw and blew the remaining part at Liz like a little paper rocket. He looked like he was trying not to laugh. Gonzo cackled and remarked, "Better think twice about it, Jimbo, do you really want a kid that's this ugly?" Brett rolled his eyes and pretended to ignore Gonzo by tipping the little metal pitcher of cream to lighten and cool his coffee a little.

"Sooo, Jimbo," began Liz with a little smile, looking into her coffee cup as she added some cream, stirring with a spoon thoughtfully. "Just for a moment, let's say *Soccer Mom* really does have a flux capacitor. Would you go back in time? Would you change anything, maybe give an earlier self advice?" She looked up at him without tilting her head, just peering with her eyes.

Gonzo cut off Jimbo's reply, "I don't know what he'd do, but I'd make sure to talk him out of getting into World of Warcraft so he'd maybe have graduated and certainly wouldn't have met that Looney Tunes psychic psycho." His eyes showed he was kidding. Mostly kidding. Probably.

Jimbo shook his head. "Well, other than the obvious, I don't have regrets with Fran. She has her faults, but she's not really a psycho. I think I want to believe her that she's not been herself the past couple of days. I don't know, I doubt even Past Jimbo would believe me if I told him his girlfriend could raise demons when she gets jealous.

Maybe I'd go back and warn Fran what she's capable of, maybe she could get some help... but who do you turn to for that kind of thing? I can just picture support groups for that kind of thing... They'd be called... uh..."

"Psychic friends network?" added Gonzo, grinning some more. Jimbo took off his cap and smacked the bigger man's shoulder.

"No, no! Well, can't you just picture these nervous-looking people sitting around a room, confessing their problems? Hi! I'm Misty and I levitate when I sleep! Hi Misty! I'm Francine, I unleash lethal demons when I'm angry. Don't make me angry. Uh, hi Francine..."

Liz giggled, but reached a hand across to pat Jimbo's. "I know it's weird. Maybe she can get help still? It's not like this kind of thing has ever happened before, you know? I can't believe she's never been jealous before. And come on. Jealousy over something real is one thing, but she was having a paranoid delusion."

"She has control issues," said Gonzo, pouring more coffee from the carafe to warm his mug. "I couldn't live with that."

"Well, no one is asking you to," shot back Jimbo, testily. "I'm not really sure I can either, even if the freaky paranormal stuff is over and done with, she's really got to get a grip. It's just a fact that living eight hundred miles apart, we're going to be doing different things on our own. I have to pry myself out from behind the computer once in a while and have time to get out and do things. She's been jealous before, maybe a little nutty, and it gets on my nerves, but this honestly isn't like her, it's a whole other level... nuttiness on steroids. Godzilla nuttiness. I just keep thinking it over, going through everything that led up to the trip, and I know I'm missing something, something that set it all off."

Brett frowned, then his face lit up. "Hey! Wait a minute. What if... what if she didn't conjure up the demon? What if Frannie was possessed by the demon? She really wasn't herself, and it really did leave her when it took over the trucker!"

Liz clapped her hands together, looking excited and relieved. Even Gonzo looked up from his coffee curiously.

Jimbo shook his head back and forth. "No, it doesn't add up. Like I said, she's always had a freaky edge to her, she says it goes way back. I've seen weird coincidences before, books have flown off of shelves when she's been pissed, my computer has come on spontaneously when she was mad at me for going to bed before she managed to get online. What are the odds of being telekinetic or unlucky or whatever you want to call it and *also* getting possessed? It'd be like getting hit by lightning followed by being killed by a meteor, wouldn't it?"

"Well, I know a fella who was hit by lighting, sugar," said Anita the waitress, making them all jump. She had arrived with a platter full of food, and she started to set the orders in front of each of them. "He still runs out to get a fistful of lottery tickets on the anniversary every single year. Hasn't won more than twenty dollars yet, and we all kid him about lightning not striking twice. Figures the universes owes him for the lightning and losing his hair, figures he's due for something as good happening to him as bad. I figure he lived to tell the story, that's all the good he needs." She finished laying out the plates and silverware and syrups and placed the platter under her arm and turned to go. Over her shoulder she said, "Me, I'd still be watching out for that meteor. Universe has a funny sense of humor that way."

The friends looked at each other in surprise as Anita walked away. Then they burst out laughing all at once.

"Come on, let's drop this bullshit for a few minutes and eat," said Gonzo. They all dug into their late night breakfasts, their hunger had long since caught up to them. Liz reached over to steal a sizable bite of Brett's waffles, ooohing and aaahhing over the speckling of chocolate chips melted into the batter before she ate it.

The portions were enormous, and hungry though they were, no one came closer than halfway to finishing, except for Gonzo, who finally had to admit defeat just shy of finishing. He stared mournfully at the last bits of steak, eggs and the remainder of the chunky hash brown potatoes, then he pushed the plate away from him, letting loose a championship-class belch.

"Here's your check, honey," said Anita, appearing with the check. She ignored Gonzo's indiscretion like a professional. "I divided it up for you in case you're paying separately." She left the slip of paper on the table and left them to check it over.

Brett felt much better after having eaten, and having come upon a better theory about Frannie and the demon. Maybe going to New Orleans wouldn't be such a bad thing after all. Maybe Frannie really was a victim in all this after all, just as they had been. He looked up, and his eyes went wide, he ducked down and scooted over toward Liz.

"What's wrong, love?" said Liz, putting an arm around him, looking confused and concerned.

"It's her," said Brett. "From the road? The shadow woman, the one I mentioned!"

Chapter 19 - Mistaken Identities

The little woman leaned on the counter with one elbow, perched on a round chrome barstool. She wore an expensive-looking cream skirt suit, exposing her pantyhosed legs and tightly fitting boots. Her spiky heels hooked over the footrest ring of the stool. Her hair was still hair-conditioner-ad perfectly cut, though in the warm lights of Mom's, her hair was revealed to be a deep brassy red, rather than black. She sipped at a mug and gazed at their table thoughtfully.

Liz peered over where Brett had been looking and a hand flew to her mouth as her eyes met with the woman's. Liz thought she noticed recognition in the other's eyes, and the woman swiveled slightly on the stool to face more in Liz's direction. Liz scooted to one side so that Gonzo's head and shoulders eclipsed her, breaking the disturbing eye contact.

Gonzo looked over his shoulder. "What? What?"

"Don't look! It's her! The demon lady!" hissed Brett. "Let's go!"

"What, the aging yuppie on a stool next to the register? Looks like a model for Cosmo after Forty? That's not a demon, Junior, that's Botox possessing her face. Get up. But if she really is a demon, I doubt hiding under the table will stop her." Gonzo sounded irritated that the break had been interrupted. "Do we have to jump at every shadow and freak out over every little thing? I'm trying to enjoy myself. Just relax, we'll be in NOLA soon, and once Jimbo settles things with Too-Much-Caffeine Girl, we can all soak up the local color. And some tasty adult beverages. And some Creole cooking."

"Besides," said Jimbo, putting on his hat, "you're gonna draw more attention doing that anyway. Let's just pay our bill and get out of here, okay?"

He reached for his wallet and drew out some cash and placed it next to the bill.

Brett slid back up in his seat, carefully keeping Jimbo between him and where he'd seen the possibly-possessed SUV driver. He followed Jimbo's suggestion and fumbled for cash in his wallet as well.

Liz's hair tickled his face as it swung his way while she leaned over to rummage through her denim purse. Gonzo acted as banker, working out the transactions in rough but fair approximations, attempting to work it so they would not need to wait for change or a credit card transaction.

"Honestly, this is stupid. I'll go take this up to the register," said Gonzo, scooping up the bill and wad of cash from the table as he stood. Jimbo scooted across the booth to follow him. Liz and Brett looked at each other and started to follow after the other two.

"I knew it was you," purred the stranger's voice, "as soon as I saw you. You're the one who stole my husband. Babette. We meet at last." It was the woman, who slid into the booth just seconds after Jimbo had followed after Gonzo. Brett felt trapped. What would they do? The demon was in the booth with them and Gonzo and Jimbo hadn't even noticed yet. Liz took his hand under the table and squeezed.

"What did you just call me?" asked Liz with a note of surprise in her voice that made Brett tear his eyes away from the demon to look at her. She appeared to be shocked.

"Babette," repeated the woman, brushing her perfect, artificial-looking hair back behind one ear with one finger. "Don't think I don't know that face. I think I'd know it after seeing it day and night, watching you work, seeing you talk on the phone, even watching you eat. While you sleep, I could see your face move with your dreams. Babette, a.k.a 'Miss Led,' the woman of my husband's dreams, and my new best friend."

Brett looked back at the woman and coughed into his hand once before saying, "Lady, you've got the wrong person, her name isn't Babette, it's..." He was cut off by a rather strong squeeze of his hand under the table by Liz.

"No, she's right, dear, she knows who I am," said Liz, to Brett's bewilderment. "You're talking about my webcam, aren't you, Mrs... Oh I'm sorry, I didn't catch your name?" Liz's expression was an empty smile, but Brett could read anger rising in his girlfriend since her ears were turning a redder shade of pink.

The woman laughed. "Hmm, fair is fair, you should have something to call me, but I don't want you blogging about this. Your dozens of nerdy fans would be all over me, wouldn't they? Just call me... Lucy. Look, I'm not really angry with you, I doubt you ever knew my husband. At least not the real man, he had several elaborate personas online." She laughed, a cold and bitter laugh that gave Brett chills. Was it colder in here?

He saw, over Lucy's shoulder, that Gonzo was motioning impatiently at the door and mouthing "Come on!" from across the room. Jimbo was already on his way out. Brett nodded at him slightly. Gonzo threw his hands in the air and stalked out after him.

Brett slid out of the booth and stood up. Liz scooted over to sit directly in front of Lucy, not letting go of his hand, but not getting up yet, either. "Lucy... Look, if you watch my 'cam, you'll know that I'm not an exhibitionist in the sexual sense of the word. I change clothes in another room, I've never exposed any more skin than I am right now. I'm private in all ways outside of my blog, and I don't correspond directly with my viewers. I'm just there to keep other people company, and the cam is there to make me feel just a little less isolated in a strange city. I don't even charge money for watching. I don't even accept donations, I've turned down e-pays in the past. I can't have 'stolen' your husband, and you're right, I can't have known him."

Brett frowned. He didn't really like the webcam. He'd told Liz this before, but she really did seem to be comforted by it, and he did get the side benefit of having her up in a window most of the time. They had both moved away, but he'd been able to keep her with him in some small way.

Lucy replied, "Oh, well... no, you didn't intend to steal him. Neither did the others. He had so many camgirls he kept on that laptop. I found them all when he got careless, and I got to keep it in the divorce. You were the tamest of his virtual girlfriends, the sweet young things that distracted him from me, kept him happy as our marriage fell apart. Do you know he wrote about you in his blog?"

When Liz shook her head no, Lucy continued. "'Oh Babette, he'd write, you haunt me from your little window on my screen. I wish I was who you were talking to on the phone, you light up so bright when he calls.' Better yet, he wrote, 'I wish I was that little green cell phone so I could be held in your dainty little fingertips, under that glossy raven hair and up to those perfectly pouty little pink lips. I want you to lick the cell phone so I can imagine you licking my...'"

"Stop!" said Liz abruptly. "I don't want to know what the pervs on the Internet think about me. I know they're out there, but they can't all be like that, especially since I run such a boring cam. I don't do stunts and I don't get naked. I'm just me. Like The Truman Show, you know?"

Brett looked uncomfortably around. This woman wasn't the demon, she was just obsessed and bitter. Still, he wanted to be anywhere but here. "Lady, I'm sorry you lost your husband to porn addiction, but we've got to get moving, we're meeting with a friend in... in a few hours, so we have to get on the road." He pulled gently at Liz's hand, but Liz stubbornly sat where she was, looking at the woman with fascination and outrage.

Lucy chuckled, glancing up at Brett for a moment, dismissing him. She smirked at Liz, "Well, I don't actually blame you, Babette. You're right, you're far from the worst of them. In fact, you're the only one I kept after cleaning the slime off of that laptop's hard drive. You were actually interesting. I turned on your cam one day just to yell at you for being more attractive to him than me. I did it because I missed him, and I needed someone else to blame. I was angry. You were laughing, and I saw what he meant about your face lighting up. I wished I could be that happy. I wished I made someone laugh like that. I decided to keep you up in a corner of my screen, to watch you, maybe even get an idea of who you were. To my surprise, I got to like you over time. I read your blog, I ate dinner when you'd eat, and I watched the same shows you did when you watched them. It was like having a friend there with me. I even had you on my nightstand so I could look over and see you sleeping when I went to bed."

"Sounds creepy," blurted Brett, despite himself. "I mean, no offense, but you sound a lot like a stalker. What a coincidence, running into..." The tip of Brett's tongue touched the roof of his mouth to form the L in his girlfriend's name, but he stopped himself. "...running into Babette here, in the middle of nowhere. I think you need to back off and leave her alone. She's not your friend, she's just who she is."

Lucy turned her head and narrowed her eyes angrily at Brett. "Shut up," she snapped.

Liz reached her free hand across the table to touch Lucy's arm. She started to say something soft and sympathetic, but instead just slumped over onto Brett, her hand slipping from his limply. She let out a sigh and started to shiver, eyes closed. Lucy kept her eyes on Brett, but she frowned. "Too soon," she murmured. "Much too soon."

Brett's eyes were locked with Lucy's for a long, strange moment. He could feel the cold beginning again. "You bitch," he breathed, grabbing up Liz under her arms. "What was this all about?" He jerked Liz's hand away from the demon's arm. "Why bother with the cover story when you could just as easily just take us all again?"

Liz roused groggily as Brett pulled her to her feet. "Run!" he hissed in her ear, and she stumbled away toward the door, dragging her purse along the floor behind her. Lucy made no move to follow, but looked dismayed as Liz got further from her.

Lucy spoke, and her voice was lower and more dangerous now, "The time wasn't right, my love. I grow stronger with each passing minute, each hungry feeling this pathetic shell expends on lost causes. I was letting her feel the anger and resentment, feeding on it. I'm already strong enough to control her and to draw life from others. Your girlfriend's life force is delicious, by the way. You will be mine as well, Brett. You know it from your dreams. You can run away, but I'll always come back, and you'll have to make that choice over and over again. One moment of doubt and you'll come to me, and I'll take you in my arms..."

Brett interrupted this speech by grabbing up the carafe of coffee and hurling the remaining hot liquid in the unnaturally beautiful face. Lucy howled, and as Brett started to run away, he had a terrible insight as the woman's eyes changed from a smoldering, demonic glare to a shocked, horrified visage of the woman deep inside who was losing her mind to an intruder. The eyes pleaded for help, but the moment was gone, and Brett was pushing chairs out of his way as he ran for the door. Liz was nowhere in sight, so he hoped she'd made it out already.

The demon roared in Lucy's hoarse voice, standing up so fast that the table was knocked into the opposing seat, dishes clattering as they spilled to the floor. Brett didn't look back, though he could see from the other patrons' faces that she must have been a terrible sight to behold in her rage. Even a burly trucker near the exit looked alarmed. He could hear her heels clacking on the tile floor as she ran after him. Brett pushed with both hands against the crash bar and flung the door open, little bells tinkling as the cool night air flooded into his face.

Soccer Mom was right outside, the front passenger side door hanging open. Gonzo peered from the driver's seat at him, eyes wide with surprise as Brett burst out of the diner with the screaming businesswoman hot on his heels. Brett leaped into the seat and he heard Jimbo yell, "Go! Go!" from the back seat. The door slammed as Gonzo hit the gas. The tiny possessed woman bounced off of the side of the van and ran after them, keeping up with them for a disturbingly long time. Brett could hear her nails screeching on the metal side door and a clattering at the outside sliding door handle. He looked back and saw Liz slumped against the far side of the back seat. Jimbo held onto the armrest of the sliding door to try to keep it from opening. "Gonzo, the locks! Locks! Now!"

The locks were a half second too late, the door cracked open, and Lucy's weight pulled the door backwards as she was dragged along by the accelerating minivan. Jimbo strained and yelled for Brett to help him. Brett reached back and grabbed at the sliding door, and the two of them were able to stop it opening any further, but Lucy grabbed the doorframe with inhuman strength and began to pull herself into the van. It started to get very cold and very dim inside, and Brett felt his grip weakening. The grin on Lucy's face was horrifying and he almost let go. His eyes were held by hers again, her hair whipping around her face as Gonzo skidded the tires in a tight turn. She licked her lips and he saw her grip tighten as she scrabbled a heeled boot on the running board on the edge of the door.

Suddenly there was a crash and they were all thrown around inside the van. Liz flew into the back of the driver's seat. Brett's fingers went numb as the door was ripped from his fingers, and all he could see was green outside the door. The warmth returned instantly, and he could see the cream color of the woman's skirt suit as she lay crumpled in the bushes at the side of the road.

"There," gasped Gonzo, "I scraped her off. Now shut that fucking door and let's roll!" he muttered under his breath, "That's gonna leave a mark, damn it."

Jimbo shook his head to clear it, then heaved at the door to slam it shut. Liz slumped in her seat, but Brett could see her reach for the armrest to hold on.

Brett scrambled to get his seat belt on and pulled the door once more to make sure it was shut. He was pushed back as he heard the tires squeal and spray gravel behind them and *Soccer Mom* bounced along the country road and onto the ramp for the highway. The Grand Caravan's engine whined, and the frame itself shook alarmingly as Gonzo held down the accelerator. The minivan merged onto I-61, weaving around a little hybrid car and on into the passing lane, hitting the speed limit and still increasing speed. A large green sign flashed by, it said, Baton Rouge, 90.

Chapter 20 - On the Run

"Man, oh man," breathed Jimbo as they left the town behind. "That was so close. I'm glad you thought of slicking her off on the shrubs, Gonz."

Liz groaned from her seat and Jimbo turned to look at her. She had her eyes more open now, but she was holding her head. "You okay?" he asked. Brett turned in his seat to look at her as well.

"Mmmhmm, just woozy. Smacked my head good when we whipped around, and I... I'm still recovering from touching the demon. Kids, the lesson we learn here is, 'Don't Touch Strangers.' 'Specially strangers you thought were possessed 'couple of minutes before, hmm? The more you know..." Liz forced a weak smile and sighed. "Least we escaped. That poor woman, how awful... Her body was possessed and the new owner's making a mess of it. Someone who dresses like that is not going to be happy to wake up all scratched and banged up."

"Uh, I don't think she'll mind so much," said Brett slowly.

"Huh?" said Liz and Gonzo at once.

"Well," continued Brett reluctantly, "after Liz went and touched her arm, I noticed her wrists were not so very perfect as the rest of her. She had slashes, long ones. Didn't look healed over, either, they looked... dry." He coughed a couple of times, holding back a rising urge to vomit.

"Oh my God," breathed Liz, "So that woman... Lucy, killed herself? Over the divorce?"

Brett shrugged. "Could be. Or maybe she failed to make Saleswoman of the Year? Or her marriage failed because she was bipolar and didn't get help? Any way you look at it, no one here caused it. I feel bad for her, sure, but like the trucker, she was probably possessed after dying. Maybe the suicide left her open to it. Could be that the trucker killed himself too? Hmmm, that reminds me of something..." He pulled out the weighty paranormal tome once more and began to thumb through it.

Liz nodded, but didn't look reassured. She turned to look out the window, watching oncoming cars and road signs flash past.

"I'll bet she scratched my paint job too," remarked Gonzo, dodging *Soccer Mom* around yet another slower vehicle. The old van shuddered with the added acceleration. "Man, this old thing needs some work. That shake is pretty nasty."

Jimbo looked anxiously behind them, out the back window. "Just so long as she holds together for the trip."

"I hate to mention this just now," murmured Brett distractedly as he flipped through <u>Ghosts</u>, "but I can't help noticing that the demon came back even though Fran's feeling better. I guess that doesn't help my theory that Frannie was possessed, if this thing goes after suicides. If she was back to herself, that is..." Brett stammered over his words after he realized how they must sound to Jimbo, "I mean, she's okay now, so she's not like the others."

Jimbo didn't seem fazed. "Well, maybe all it takes is an attempt? I know that when I met her, she'd been in the hospital for bipolar issues herself, and, well, she was an inpatient there because she took a bunch of pills. That was a year or so back. In fact, I was kind of writing off her bad behavior to another episode, thought maybe she went off her meds or something. That still might be it."

Brett hmmed. "Well, the thing is, she's still alive, and the other two weren't. Sort of a zombie possession, seems like. But the only reference I see in here is kind of the reverse."

Brett read from the book. "There are documented cases of possession leading to suicide among the native tribes of Africa and Australia. The victims would not display any identifying behaviors beforehand, and in fact were generally model citizens of their societies. Hunters, matrons, hard workers and even shamans and other leaders would abruptly become 'someone else.' The behavior change, often identified as demonic possession among the primitives, was usually explained away by visiting scientists and social workers as some kind of drug, disease, poison or mental defect. However, many of the cases were attributed with supernatural powers at the height of the possession. Glowing eyes, supernormal physical strength, even a vampiric touch that sapped the life from animals and other humans. In some cases, even the weather was said to have been altered by the moods of the afflicted. This supernatural ability was followed by a rapid decline before the victim took his or her own life."

"Huh. Sounds familiar, except for the order of events there," said Jimbo. "So the cure for those possessions was death of the host. In this case, it's animating corpses? How's that work? We know that a good electric shock will drive it out, or at least it did that one time. Then can it re-animate the same corpse? Or is it all used up?"

Brett shook his head. "I don't know about that, really. The book doesn't say anything on the subject, and I'm not entirely sure this is anything like what we're dealing with. Hmm, here's something else." Brett continued reading. "The Australian aboriginals have a fable about just such an event. In the story, it is said that a Mokoi, literally 'evil ghost' became hungry and began gnawing on the soul of the Wurrunna, or chief of the tribe. The Mokoi took the soul of the chief one bite every day at sunset, forcing more and more of its own will on the chief's body with each bite. By the third bite, his wife fled with their children into the desert, fearing him greatly. By the fifth bite, the tribe had met in secret to decide what was to be done about the increasingly cruel and powerful Wurrunna.

"A magician, who had kept his arts secret from the others to this point, declared he had a solution. He asked for some blood from the chief and from one that loved him. He said that with these, and the Wurrunna's true name, he could drive out the evil spirit. A young hunter, the brother of the chief's wife, went to the desert to track his missing sister, to beg for some of her blood. The young hunter vowed that he could use a finely sharpened stick to get blood from the chief without causing him permanent harm. The magician said this was good and said that they must strike before the Mokoi took any more bites from the chief's soul.

"The story continued as the brother found the chief's wife and persuaded her to return to save her husband from being devoured. She allowed herself to be cut and her blood was placed on the sharpened stick. The magician asked for an audience with the monstrous chief, and it was granted, and he brought the young warrior with him. The chief touched the magician on the arm and began to drink his soul. So strong was the Mokoi by now that his life drained quickly. The warrior hesitated just a moment, then stabbed the chief in the leg. The magician spoke the true name of the Wurrunna aloud with his last breath. The villagers all heard a thunderclap, and the young warrior emerged from the chief's tent carrying the chief. At first, the people thought he was dead, but he woke after being ministered with water and sacred oils. Alas, the magician had died, but the tribe was saved."

After Brett finished, everyone was quiet for a bit, the only sound was the road and the vibration of *Soccer Mom* protesting the strain that Gonzo was putting her to.

"We don't have her real name, and we don't have the blood of anyone who loves her," said Liz quietly.

"Not to mention, she's already dead," added Jimbo.

"Well, yeah, there's that. But what if we could drive it out of Lucy?" said Liz, her eyes far away as she thought through some possibilities.

"What? Back into Fran? Yeah, that's a great idea," Jimbo sounded irritated, sarcasm dripping from his words. "What makes you sure it's still in Lucy anyway? Maybe it gave up on her when she got scraped off the side of our van?"

Liz looked at him and smiled a little. "No, of course I wouldn't want Fran to go through that again, if that's what's going on. Though I think it's something we should prepare for. If it is the same thing as in the book, maybe she's just not been used up by the demon yet. Maybe the others were possessed before they died, like the victims in the book, driven to suicide once they were drained cold and dry. Hon, I think we'd better get to Fran before the demon does just in case it's not done with her yet."

"Well, we're making good time at least," muttered Gonzo, still very focused on the road. "This is an awful lot of guessing and storytelling, I don't really buy it all. How can we know the right answer? It might not be the same thing. It might be something like it that acts different. It might be a whole lot of insanity that's contagious. Or something normal that just isn't within science yet."

"That's the definition of paranormal though, isn't it? Something outside of what science has the ability to explain, at least so far." Brett shut the book and turned to look at Liz. "So, what are you thinking, Lizzie? Is there something we can do, got any rituals to deal with this kind of thing?"

Liz pursed her lips and shook her head slowly no. "Hmm, not exactly. The 'magician' in the story had the right idea with sympathetic magic, but again, I doubt I could do a lot without a handle on the victim herself. Some kind of connection to work with. If I had--" Liz was cut off by yell from Gonzo, followed by a loud slam. *Soccer Mom* had been rear-ended. Brett whirled around to look and saw cracks in the rear window, lit orange by the sodium streetlights along the sides of the road. He also saw, lit dimly red by the van's taillights, a large white SUV with no headlights on, following close and closing in. He watched as it smashed into the rear again. He could now make out the face of Lucy behind the wheel, mouth open in a howl of rage, eyes wild and staring right at him.

"Fucking psycho chick! Hang on!" yelled Gonzo as he changed lanes quickly and slammed on the brakes. The SUV shot past them and Gonzo took advantage of this moment to turn left onto a county road. The gravel and dust flew behind *Soccer Mom* and Brett could no longer see the big vehicle. The van shook and rattled loudly as it raced down the gravel two-lane road. Stubble of corn stalks spread out on either side of the road, the closer parts blurring as they sped past.

"Hang on tight now," said Gonzo, and he slowed the van and pulled off the road and into the corn stubble. He had to drive very slowly, and the van bumped and bounced over the ruts and furrows. The corn made crunching noises as the wheels crushed it beneath them. Brett looked out the window with worry at the dust they had kicked up, a large cloud of it drifting down the road in the direction they'd been traveling. It slowly began to settle. When they were a ways off the road and in a slight depression, Gonzo killed the engine and the lights.

It was very dark. So dark, Brett no longer saw the road. Jimbo's cell phone glowed on the dashboard, a red light blinking to indicate that it was roaming. Brett hastily opened the glove box and stuffed the phone in, slamming it shut. The noise made him wince, though he knew there was no way it could be heard from the road and no one was in sight.

Brett could hear the others breathing, and he saw Liz and Jimbo peering out the rear and side windows as he twisted in his seat to look for the SUV himself. He wasn't quite sure where the road was, now that the lights were off. Then he heard the faint popping of gravel as some vehicle moved slowly along the road, the same way they had come. A yellow/red glow soon appeared, as the running lights of the SUV illuminated the settling dust they had kicked up. The white monster of a truck crawled along, and Brett held his breath as it slowed near where they had pulled off the road. He heard Gonzo swear under his breath. He saw Liz sink lower in her seat, peering around the side of the headrest.

Brett realized he was holding his breath and made himself take a deep breath. His heartbeat pounded in his ears and he willed himself to think of other things... Liz's cats, a laptop he had been working on back home, the coffee at Mom's diner, anything at all but what was going on right now, hoping to hide even his thoughts and calm his rising panic. Should they get out of the van and run for it? Brett's hand gripped the door handle, putting pressure on it, getting ready to open the door. Gonzo hissed "Brett, don't!" at him, and the whisper sounded as loud as a bellow to Brett in the dark silence in the van.

To the friends' relief, the demon passed their turnoff point, following the dust that had wafted further down the road. Once it passed out of sight, they could hear its engine rev and they heard gravel skitter out behind it as it accelerated down the country road. He heard both Jimbo and Liz take in a deep breath and let it out in a gusty sigh. Gonzo turned the ignition and started the van crawling slowly, blindly turning back toward the road, lights still off. Brett felt the bumps in the field rocking *Soccer Mom* slowly but roughly, and he was suddenly worried they would run something over, with no spare to fall back on if they lost another tire.

Gonzo switched on the running lights and the gravel road was not far ahead, so he made the old van move faster, turning slightly to hit the road at an angle, facing back the way they had come. Once all four wheels were on the gravel, he slowly pressed down on the pedal and switched on the headlights, speeding up gradually until the corn stubble began to blur past again.

They all remained silent by some unspoken agreement while they were still on the county road. Soon I-61 could be seen ahead of them by the lights of the sparse, fast traffic traveling back and forth along it. Gonzo didn't slow down as he pulled out onto the highway. Once they had crossed the near lane of traffic, he jerked the steering wheel to the left hard. The van's rear end slewed around to the right to face them more or less the right direction to join southbound traffic. Gonzo hit the accelerator again to get *Soccer Mom* up to speed and began catching up to and passing other cars once more.

"You think that'll fool her for long?" asked Jimbo, glancing back nervously.

Gonzo shrugged. "Maybe. Who knows how smart it is? I didn't have any other ideas other than going overland through the fields 'til we hit another road, and I didn't want to chance shaking *Soccer Mom* to pieces or popping another tire. I was counting on the dust to cover our retreat... Hard to tell which way we were going when we retraced our path."

"We can't afford too much time anyway, if we don't want to keep Frannie hanging," added Liz. She was still holding her head with one hand, Brett noticed, and he hoped it was nothing more than a bump. He reached back to her and touched her hand with his, and she looked up and smiled at him.

They traveled on in the dark for a long while. The vibration in the wheels or engine that the unusual speed caused was making Brett feel a little ill. His head was starting to ache a little bit, either from stress, the shaking, or from sympathy for Liz. Gonzo looked a bit grim at the wheel, and when Brett dared glance at the speedometer, he was amazed that they hadn't been pulled over by the police. He wasn't sure that would be entirely a bad thing. It'd make them late, but at least they might have help against the demon. "At the rate Gonzo's going, we should get there in plenty of time, barring further delays."

Liz said, "Guys, don't be freaked out, but I'm going to try to put some protective spells on *Soccer Mom* to try to keep us safe."

Gonzo rolled his eyes, but didn't object, and neither did the other two. Liz rummaged in her pack and came out with a pack of crayons and she carefully selected several colors, and began to mumble words under her breath. Every so often, she selected one of the crayons and drew a symbol on one of the windows, even going so far as to crawl partway up into the front to scrawl on the inside of the front windshield in red. She smiled at Brett while she was up there, and paused her chanting to kiss him on the cheek before returning to the back to continue her ritual.

At one point, she lit a candle and placed it in a drink holder. Gonzo objected to the fire in the cabin, but she reassured him that it was in a glass votive holder and she wouldn't need it long anyway. She melted a little of each of the crayons she had used, enough that a drop of each color mingled with the clear pool of white wax in the glass votive holder. Brett could smell the crayons strongly at that point, and then wrinkled his nose when she swirled the wax around and blew out the flame, the smoke burning his nose. As if reading his thoughts, she spoke, "I know it stinks, but don't roll down the windows, we're only protected while we keep the doors and windows shut."

An hour or so or so passed, and they began to see signs for Baton Rouge. The extra lights and denser traffic made Brett's spirits lift a bit. They soon found that the van was in the midst of a pack of motorcyclists, their engines roaring on all sides. This would normally have concerned Brett, but the noise and actually seeing other people was very comforting. Liz seemed to share this feeling, as she waved to a passing motorcyclist. The burly guy glanced over and smiled and saluted Liz. Gonzo seemed to think the gesture was meant for him, so he saluted back. After awhile, as Baton Rouge exits appeared, the pack was past them, and they followed behind, still moving a decent clip past the speed limit.

"Incoming!" yelled Jimbo, who had been glancing out the back of the van quite often. "Here she comes again!"

Brett looked in the side mirror and saw headlights, on this time, rapidly approaching from behind. He thought he could even make out the white gleam of Lucy's grin, framed by her dark, glossy hair, as she gunned the engine of her massive SUV to ram their tailgate. The bigger vehicle slammed into the back of *Soccer Mom* hard enough to throw them around a little, and Brett's seat belt bit into his shoulder as it held him in place. Gonzo kept a grip on the wheel and floored it, but the van just shuddered and only accelerated slightly, closing a bit of the distance with the last of the bikers ahead of them.

Liz unbuckled and reached over Gonzo's shoulder to lean on the horn, bleating out a series of shrill beeps. Gonzo brushed her away, shouting "Don't do that, let me drive, Goddammit!" and she scrambled for her seat belt. She was too late for the next collision, however, and was thrown back against her seat and then her head hit Gonzo's headrest in front of her.

Red lights flashed ahead of them, and the bikers fell back to surround the van again. The white SUV was forced to fall back, and was soon also surrounded by the bikers. Brett could see in the mirror that Lucy tried to ram the bikers, but they were much more nimble than her truck, and were able to dodge out of the way. Brett heard a loud, sharp crack as one of the bikers fired off a warning shot from a handgun. The second shot, a few seconds later, also made a metallic plink, and he guessed that one had made a hole in the skin of the big truck. It slowed and was surrounded.

The way was cleared in front of them as the bikers all moved over for them to pass, falling back as *Soccer Mom* sped past them, making a thicker and thicker wall of motorcycles between the SUV and them. The last biker they passed was the one who had saluted them before, and he repeated the gesture now, grinning from ear to ear. The friends all returned the salute, and Liz shouted, "Thank you!" though she knew he wouldn't hear her. He read her lips, though and made a flourish with his hand like a knight on his way to vanquish a dragon.

The friends all whooped and cheered as *Soccer Mom* pulled away from the pack and the white SUV.

Chapter 21 - Big Easy

Gonzo grinned as the tray of citrus drinks arrived at the table. The waitress looked tired, but faked a smile for them anyway as she placed one in front of each at the table. Gonzo laid down a twenty and a five and had her keep the change. She moved on through the press of people to other tables. The crowd all around them was so loud and raucous that the music playing over the house speakers was impossible to make out.

Brett stared at the drink as the others drank up. "I still think it's kind of callous to order 'hurricanes' in New Orleans. You know, they're *still* fixing the city from Katrina, after all this time."

Gonzo grinned after taking a good long pull on the drink. "New Orleans has always been about celebrating, and the locals are the first to tell you that they don't want to change who they are, even over disasters. They just rebuild and get back to partying."

Brett wasn't sure Gonzo could know the minds of the locals so well, but if Pat O'Brien's was willing to sell the drinks, he supposed it wasn't completely inconsiderate to order them. He hoped he wasn't being an ugly tourist as he drank along with his friends. He eyed his watch for the fifth time since they'd arrived. They still had twenty minutes to get to their rendezvous with Frannie. She hadn't been at the meeting place as they arrived, though they'd been quite early due to Gonzo's fast driving and luck avoiding speed traps. Liz had said the protective charms she'd put on *Soccer Mom* helped with this. Gonzo had bristled a little at this, and accused her of trying to take credit for his skill. She just shrugged and said it was most likely a combination of things, and anyway, they'd gotten here ahead of schedule and hadn't seen Lucy after the bikers had come to their rescue.

Brett noticed Jimbo glancing toward the door every few minutes, and he could only imagine what must be running through his friend's mind. He was going to have to face Frannie, whether to break it off with her or to save her from the demon.

"Okay, this is what we'll do," said Liz after she'd finished half of her hurricane. She fished around in her purse and came up with a sewing kit and one of the chopsticks she sometimes used to tie up her hair. "If Fran's possessed, I'll stick Jimbo and then Frannie. You'll have to tell me her full, legal name, Jimbo, so I can call up her soul and push out the demon. I think I know what else to do. Or at least I hope so."

"You think she'll be possessed? She said she was free of the demon, Liz." Jimbo looked on in dismay as Liz used some black electrical tape she'd found in *Soccer Mom*'s toolbox to fasten a large sewing needle on the end of the black chopstick. "How will we even know? You were fooled by Lucy back in the diner."

"Oh, well, as soon as you touch her, it should become obvious, you'll feel the cold and you'll get weak again." Liz twirled her dark hair into a knot on top of her head and stuck the chopstick through, and used another to hold it in place. The needle wasn't obvious from a couple of feet away. "That's when you have to let us know. Of course, if she's not, then we've got to look out for Lucy. I can't imagine that even the bikers could keep her long. I doubt the demon's had time to cultivate another suicidal victim to use against us, so it's got to be one of the two." Brett was amazed at how matter-of-fact Liz could be about such a bizarre and frightening situation.

"Okay, Liz. Her full name is Francine Emily Ryan, if it'll help."

"Whatever," said Gonzo. "Personally, I'm sick of all this. This is where I wanted to be, not fending off a demon stalker. What's it really want anyway? How can we get rid of it?"

Brett stared into his glass. "Sounded like it wants me for something. I can't picture why. If Fran's been any part of what it wants, it makes no sense. I'm less and less sure she's behind this, at least directly. "

Liz studied his face looking into his eyes with a serious expression on her face before asking, "*Chico*, what about those dreams you've had? I know you don't want to think this, but what if it's connected to Cheryl somehow?"

Brett looked away from Liz and refused to meet the eyes of his other friends. He shook his head violently. "Cheryl died before her time, she was a victim of an accident. She wasn't the jealous type, and she really wasn't malicious like the Cheryl that's appeared in my recent dreams. You knew her. How could she be a part of this demonic thing?"

Liz put a hand on his forearm gently. "Honey, I didn't mean to upset you. I know Cheryl wasn't like that. She was always sweet and friendly to me, the times we met. Hell, if I was into girls, I could have fallen for her. I'm just brainstorming, because I don't think we're going to see the end of this until we figure out what's really going on here." She slid her hand down to his fingers and laced hers with his and squeezed. "Anyway, it's just about time to go, so let's drink up and go see if Frannie's here yet."

They all nodded. Gonzo finished his hurricane by skipping the straw, tipping back his head and pouring it straight down in one long chug. He belched and grinned. "I have no internal organs," he joked.

Jimbo left half of his hurricane untouched, and though Brett tried to finish, he had an ice cream headache before reaching the bottom. Liz had finished hers before she'd begun talking.

They wove their way through the crowd of tourists and slipped out the door into the cold night air. Liz shivered a little, hugging herself against the chill. She leaned into Brett, who put an arm around her as they followed Jimbo and Gonzo toward the pre-arranged corner.

No one was there.

"Hmm, it's only just past midnight," said Brett. "I guess we'll have to give her a few minutes in case she's had trouble getting here."

Jimbo nodded, but he paced around, looking down each of the streets both ways in case he could see Fran approaching.

His cell phone rang. He glanced at the screen, relieved. "It's her." He pressed the "talk" button and held the phone to his ear. "Hey Frannie, we're here already, where are you?"

"Jimmy, she's got me. This messed up woman has me at knifepoint in a park..." Jimbo shivered as he heard Lucy's voice in the background, prompting Fran. "She says it's Lafayette Square. Help me, Jimmy, she's crazy and I feel so cold. I can't fight her." The cell phone went dark as the connection was lost.

"Shit!" Jimmy looked around wildly to get his bearings. "Where's Lafayette Square? Lucy's got Fran."

Gonzo pointed down Bourbon. "It's a bit of a hike, maybe a mile."

Jimbo started off at a run down Bourbon. Liz and Brett looked at Gonzo who shrugged, and they all ran after him, shouting at him to wait up. They ran past the lights and sounds of Bourbon Street, past bars and strip clubs, all glaring with neon and spilling over with tourists and locals. They had to dodge lines of people that went down the sidewalks and into the streets, and they had to ignore greasy-looking men passing out flyers describing various sleazy shows that could be seen within some of the clubs they passed.

After awhile, they came upon Canal, and Gonzo had to shout at Jimbo to get him to turn left, rather than continuing on down Bourbon, after he crossed the street. It was darker and less crowded here, and while that made the going much easier, it made Brett less comfortable. He knew they were all running into a trap, and he was sure his friends all knew it too. Jimbo wouldn't let Fran suffer through his inaction however, and the rest of them wouldn't let Jimbo run off to face the demon alone.

Jimbo slowed to a fast walk when they turned onto Camp Street, holding his side and complaining of a stitch in his side. His eyes were wild and Liz tried to calm him down. "We'll be there soon, Jimbo, and we don't want to be falling down with exhaustion when we do, or Lucy will have an even bigger advantage."

"Yeah," he panted, "I have no... fucking clue... what we'll do anyway."

"I have a couple of tricks up my sleeve, now that I have some idea what we're facing," said Liz, who wasn't quite as winded. Brett was sure she was the only one of the four of them that exercised for fun, on a regular basis. He had a cramp in his calf that was making him limp a bit. He was grateful for the reduced pace, and he struggled to catch his breath as he caught up to the others. Gonzo had been cursing much of the way.

They went the final blocks and the park loomed up to their right, its darkness only highlighted by the sparse lights along the paths. Jimbo peered into the park with dismay. "Where are they? I don't see them!"

Liz frowned, then started down toward a circular paved path around a central area of trees and shrubs. The others followed behind, and as they rounded the bend, halfway around the circle, they saw Fran and Lucy, sitting on a bench. Fran was perched with her back stiff as a board, not touching the backrest of the bench. Her face was streaked with tears, and in the dim light, her eyes were showing white, open with terror. She started to get up when she saw Jimbo, letting out a cry, then sat abruptly down as Lucy held a hunting knife to her throat. Lucy turned to regard them coolly, a small smile coming to the corners of her mouth, her eyes narrowing to slits.

"Well, you certainly are hard to catch up with," said the possessed woman softly as they approached. "Of course, it's a lot easier when I know where my quarry is headed. So much easier if I can get you to come to me like this. I do hate to be impolite, but the chase has lost its charm, and I want what's mine."

Liz stood in front of the other two women, hands on her hips, feet planted firmly. "I don't care what you want. Let her go now, while you still can, Mokoi. This is over. Go back where you came from or we'll eat you alive. I mean it."

Brett stopped short in his tracks, and saw Jimbo do the same, a few feet behind and to either side of Liz. He couldn't believe the anger and strength in her tone, this wasn't the same Liz he was used to. She was filled with a rage that showed in the curl of her lip, the flush of her cheeks and in the fists her hands formed at her sides. Everything about her body language said "back off." He looked back at Lucy, who raised her eyebrows in surprise. There was a long moment where the two stared at each other. Fran whimpered as the knife bit into her throat and drew a line of blood. A drop formed and ran down her neck to her collar.

Then several things happened at once. Lucy began to laugh, a nasty, inhuman laugh of utter contempt at Liz's show of defiance. Liz began making motions with her hands and tore something small and white in half, flinging the contents at the mocking face. Brett blinked and realized it was to-go packets of salt from a fast food place. The laughter paused a moment as Liz spat words that Brett didn't recognize at the woman. The demon looked surprised and actually withdrew the knife from the cringing Fran. She pointed the knife at Liz, hissing and rising from the bench, into a crouch.

Jimbo and Gonzo moved at the same moment once the knife was away from Fran's throat. Jimbo grabbed Fran's arms and pulled her away, pushing her stumbling ahead of him, across the circular path and into the grass of the park beyond.

Gonzo pulled his right hand from a pocket as he lunged toward Lucy. At first Brett thought Gonzo was trying to punch the demon with an uppercut, and he and Liz both cried out, "Gonzo, no!" in unison, both knowing he would be drained as soon as he touched the skin of the demon-possessed corpse. It would just be a repeat of the fight with the trucker. Brett leaped to grab at Gonzo to stop him, but he was too slow.

The big man's hand connected with tiny Lucy's chin, and it was at that moment that Brett realized that he held something small, black and plastic. There was a bright flash there in the darkness, and there was heard the snapping of the arc of electricity made by a taser. Lucy and Liz both screamed at the same time.

Lucy tensed and shook in epileptic convulsions, eyes rolling and limbs flailing randomly. Gonzo yelled, "Take that, you bitch!" as the spark flooded the body's nervous system and the taser's charge was spent, discharged completely. Gonzo turned and grinned, letting out a cheer of triumph. His smile faded as he saw the look on Liz's face.

Liz was clearly upset, but her scream died before the demon's wail was even halfway done. "Damn it, Gonzo, you should have told me you were going to do that. I was halfway through a banishment. Now it's only inconvenienced, and we don't know where it's going!" She looked back at the still-twitching businesswoman's body. She wondered for a moment what her real name was. Was it really Lucy?

The demon's wail was drawn out as it had been with the trucker, but this time it sounded predatory rather than defeated. The black mist erupted from the now-inert woman, lying on the ground between the bench and Liz. The mist didn't stream away as it had before, but rather went straight for Brett. He backed up as it flowed toward him, and then he began to run. He could hear Liz and Gonzo calling after him, though they seemed very far away all of a sudden. The already dim lighting of the park darkened and time slowed down. He could hear his heartbeat slow, even though he could still feel it pound in his chest. His feet slammed into the ground one after the other, and though he knew he was traveling headlong at full tilt, it still felt like a dream. He felt as if he was waist deep in mud as he ran.

He knew he was tripping, falling, and it seemed to take minutes as he plunged toward the ground, but he could do nothing about it, his muscles failed him. His mind was following, as it got dimmer, darker, blacker...

Chapter 22 – Till My Head Falls Off

The blackness engulfed Brett, dragging him down, back into himself, to a place walled off in his memories. A dozen or more jabbering voices in his head drowned his own thoughts. The side of his face was cold as it rested on the tile floor of his college bathroom, the bathmat all bunched up in front of him. He had hoped the pills would have a more immediate effect, but he just felt logy. And nauseated. And stupid.

Worse, he heard someone calling his name. It would be embarrassing to be caught at this before it was all done.

"Brett? Brett! Oh my Goddess, you didn't! What did you do?" Liz burst into the bathroom and seemed unbelievably tall as she stood over him, bending down to look in his eyes. She was as panicked as he'd ever seen her, and her skirt billowed out as she crouched quickly to move his head. She bit her lower lip and let out a distressed moan, looking wildly around the bathroom, spying all the open, empty medicine bottles scattered around the room.

He would have smiled at her if he could, he would have answered her, if only to say he loved her one last time and to say goodbye. But he couldn't, he was numb and dumb and could only barely keep his eyes open. He wished all the voices and music and images would just leave him alone. Maybe Liz wasn't really here. That would be sad, but also a relief, since he didn't want her to find him like this.

She smacked his face. "Wake up! Brett, please wake up! I've stuck with you this far, you can't give up now. You can't give up! Don't leave me this way! Oh Goddess, please help me!"

Everything seemed wavy, as though Brett were under water. He saw Liz rippling like a reflection in the surface of a pond, a gentle gust of wind making her features hard to see. She reached toward him. He wished he could at least smile at her. He felt like he couldn't keep his eyes open. He'd have to talk to her about this later, let her know why. Tell her how bad it hurt without Cheryl. How she had been coming to him in dreams at night, calling to him, telling him it was his fault…. that he should have taken better care of her. That his promise to marry her had gotten broken.

Liz's fingers touched his lips, and he thought how sweet it was that she wanted to comfort him in his last moments. The fingers pried his mouth open roughly, and he felt her reaching into his mouth, and into his throat. The nausea, which he'd held at bay to this point, came roaring up as she stuck fingers down his throat. Then it all came rushing up, and he was horrified to realize he was vomiting all over his friend's hand and the tile floor and onto the crumpled bathmat. Oh God, what a mess, and someone would have to clean it up. He had taken pills in the first place because he didn't want to leave a mess. This was the worst thing that could have happened.

His body convulsed as it heaved up its contents over and over. His stomach hurt, even through the numbness that the pills brought, and he retched and gagged, then paused, gasping for breath, then the horrible contractions began again, bringing up only vile watery liquid this time. There was another pause, then his stomach heaved again, but nothing else came up. The dry heaves took him, and he felt Liz stand up, the whooshing of her skirts as she fled the room stirring up a wind that felt cool and pleasant on his face. He felt hot, and also cold somehow. He shivered with relief as the vomiting slowed and stopped.

He heard Liz on the phone, talking urgently to someone. She came into the room, and he saw her standing in the doorway, holding the phone to her ear. "Yes, he's breathing, but he looks really pale…. Yes, I can stay on the line until someone gets here."

She jabbered at the phone awhile, and Brett lost focus, so he just heard her worried voice, the tone but not the words. She was so beautiful standing there above him. She was his angel, she had saved him before, and now she was trying to save him from himself. He felt so awful, so embarrassed and wretched. Why had she stopped him? Now he'd have to face her every day knowing that he'd failed Cheryl and now he'd failed Liz. How could she love someone like that? How could he go on, knowing he was that worthless?

Soon, he heard sirens, and there was a knock at the door and he was fuzzily aware of being carried away on a stretcher. Before he fell asleep, he saw Liz looking down at him, sitting by his side in the dim ambulance lights. Her hair swayed prettily as the ambulance drove, and he finally managed that smile for her and croaked out, "Sorry. I'm so sorry," and he could keep his eyes open no longer.

Chapter 23 - The Nicest of the Damned

Brett awoke, back in the present, but not in control. He felt as though he watched himself from a distance, above and away, watching his body move without him. He saw himself roll on the ground below, then watched as it picked itself up into a crouch. He heard his own voice, but deeper, growling like an animal at Liz and Gonzo. Gonzo looked helplessly on, not sure what to do. Liz chanted at the possessed thing that looked like him. He wanted to call out a warning, scream for them to run away before the thing that wasn't him did terrible things to them. He knew he'd lost to the horrible blackness inside him, he knew it had escaped him.

A voice in the back of his mind laughed in triumph. *Mine at last*, it gloated, in Cheryl's voice. He knew it couldn't be Cheryl herself, but the specter of his dead fiancée that he'd conjured up in his dreams, the one that had taunted him all these years, the one that had taunted him to attempt suicide years ago. The one that he'd locked away in a dark corner of his soul for so long. The one that told him daily that he didn't deserve Liz, until he'd finally been unable to run off with her to a new place when she'd been given an opportunity. It told him he would just hold her back, he'd just be a weight around her neck, dragging her down into the dark depths that he'd sunk. Liz's love for him, and her naturally buoyant spirit, lifted him above the depths of depression.

When she'd tearfully gone on alone, he couldn't stay where they'd lived. He'd fled to the nearest place he could think of that didn't have a shared history with either of the great loves of his life. He chose Indianapolis as his new place to start over, a blank slate unmarred by his history, undecorated by memories of the women who'd loved him. He clung to those memories in secret weak moments, like special things he kept in a keepsake box, to be opened only when he felt like drinking in the bittersweet pain of their loss. He found it easy to lose himself in the new life he built around him, effectively shutting the box when he could no longer stand the pain of might-have-beens and alternate realities where he was happy and okay with himself.

The voice taunted him, and he felt the realization wash over him that the prison he'd built for the horrible dark suicidal demon at the back of his mind had been let loose at last by Fran's unique paranormal qualities. The intense power of her jealousy reached out across the miles to unlock the demon. She was the catalyst that freed the demon to a more literal existence, unleashing it upon the world just as it had been in the stories in Klaus Reisen's book, in the ancient parable.

Brett's own suicidal despair had been like roadkill to a vulture, circling to feed on his soul. Liz's love had saved him, and with borrowed strength, he had locked it away. Reunited with Liz, that blackness struggled against its bonds, reaching out to use Frannie's powers against her, making her into a weapon to attack Brett. He remembered how Liz had told him that this time of the year, the veil between the worlds was at its thinnest, so conditions were just perfect for the abomination to inflict itself upon the world.

Images of the trucker and poor Lucy flashed before him. He felt anger rise up like bile. He was angry with himself, for his weakness, for wallowing in self-pity even while he had people who loved him all around him.

Meanwhile, Liz faced down the demon wearing Brett's body. She chanted as she dodged its lunges. Each of her movements came slower than the last. He felt sick as the demon drew her energy into his body, into its spirit, which was intertwined with his own. Her life energy *did* taste sweet, and it filled him with love and nervous excitement and disgust at his reaction to her weakening. He screamed within his own mind, there still floating above the scene, he screamed for Liz to run away and leave him to his own fate. As she should have that day back in the bathroom. He hated to be the one to drag her down into this darkness, hated to think of the demon plucking off her fairy wings and crushing her beautiful spirit.

Then Liz did what he feared most. She pulled the chopsticks out of her hair and jabbed one end into her left hand. She approached his possessed body and grabbed it in an embrace. She called out his full name at the end of her chanting, "Brett Allan Nelson" and he felt the punch of the needle in his side. The pain, and the call of his name brought him back into his body with a jolt, and he was nose to nose with Liz. Her eyes were drooping and her skin was cold, and he knew she was being drained as her essence flooded through every contact with his skin. She let out a last breath, then kissed him, on the lips.

Love swelled within Brett, and he felt the demon's corrupt energy recoil. He felt Liz's life energies within the body he and the demon both inhabited, he could feel how little was left within Liz. The energy was so delicious, so warm, it was something he craved. But he fought back. No! That was the demon that craved, not him. He was Brett, he was the one Liz had called out to, and it was a drop of her blood that flowed within his veins where she'd stabbed him. That tiny bit of her blood sizzled, and he could feel the demon shriek and burn as the blood spread throughout him. He welcomed the heat and he kissed Liz back.

He visualized Liz's life energy flowing back into her body as they kissed, and despite the demon's protests, and despite his own need for her strength and love inside him, he gave it back to her, because he would rather have Liz whole than to take from her. Because she loved him, and he knew he loved her too.

The demon whispered in Cheryl's voice to him. *You're letting everyone down. You belong with me, you should have crossed the road and saved everyone all this pain and trouble. Look what you've done to her. I know you love her, but you* promised *me. And your weakness is costing your friends. You'll keep being a drain on your friends as long as you're alive. Come to me and you won't be a burden ever again. You'll just be mine, and you won't have to worry about anything anymore, my love.*

Brett was sorely tempted to just give in, to keep his friends safe. He thought of Liz fighting to save him so many times and knew that he couldn't. *No. I've been a burden in the past, but not anymore. I've lived on my own and I have done well for myself, and despite my flaws, my friends still love me. Liz still loves me, and she risked her own life to save me. The least I can do to repay her is to live. Now, get out of my mind, and get out of my body, and never bother us again!*

The blood of his lover and the spell she had worked coursed through his body, and now Liz was strong enough to open her eyes and hold him up as he slumped against her, breathing shallowly. He felt the demon inside him grow weaker and weaker, even as they had at its touch, and now he didn't have to work to keep it locked up, it dissolved, dissipating visibly. The miasma flowed outwards, thinner and lighter until it was entirely invisible and gone.

Liz held him up in her arms, gasping in a breath. Gonzo rushed over and steadied them both, helping them back over to the bench. He called out to Jimbo, and Brett was dimly aware as he and Fran returned warily.

"We did it," said Liz weakly, smiling at him. "You're alive and it's gone. Guess I am one badass shaman, huh?"

Brett's vision blurred as waves of fatigue washed over him. He smiled and said, "You know it, and you're one hell of a reason to live, Sweetie."

And then, in each other's arms, they passed out with exhaustion.

Chapter 24 - From Four 'til Late

The lights of New Orleans bounced off the patchy clouds, miles away in the distance. The friends lounged around a campfire in a nearby state park later that night.

Gonzo was lit from below, the roaring flames threatening to light stray strands of hair that escaped from his ponytail. His shadow flailed about, looming in the leaves of the trees above, projecting an amorphous black figure above them. Brett imagined that the fire brought his friend's shadow to life, animating it with independent, perhaps sinister intent.

"There. Now that is a fire! Better scoot back, Lizzie, or you'll toast your marshmallows!" Gonzo cackled, adding even more to the weird atmosphere for a moment. Brett grinned and reached forward to pull Liz away from the campfire and closer to him. She obliged by scooting her bottom back in between his legs and leaning back against him. Her hair tickled his face, and he was glad for her warmth as he slipped his arms around his waist to hug her to him tightly.

Liz and Brett sat on the ground, Brett with his back padded by a sleeping bag crammed up against a park bench. Jimbo and Fran sat next to each other on the bench. Fran was still finishing up the sandwich she'd gotten at a convenience store on the way to the campground. Jimbo watched Gonzo fan the flames with the van's cardboard sunshade. "Hey, don't make too big a bonfire there, Gonz, we set up the tents a leetle too close for comfort. Sparks. Flame. Poof. *Soccer Mom's* roomy, but she's a tight squeeze to sleep five."

Gonzo yawned and stretched and stepped back, ruining the eerie shadow effects. He nearly tripped over Liz's outstretched legs as he made his way back to the table to join the others. Gonzo stood while drinking the bottle of beer he had been working on before the fire had needed tending. Only half-lit by the firelight, Brett thought Gonzo somehow reminded him of a jovial barbarian warlord, holding court after a successful battle. Brett lifted his own bottle in toast to Gonzo, and the bigger man grinned and returned the gesture. "Good fire," Brett agreed, drinking up with his friend.

"My little Raoul has a fiery soul, does he?" teased Liz, in some semblance of a Latin accent. She toyed with Brett's hair, stared into his eyes and said, "I have learned that he has a passion for hot, wild, untamed things!"

Brett had to swallow quickly to keep from choking as he laughed at this. "Oh my yes, my love," he said, following her lead. "It is why my heart burns for you, my dear Babette. I have a passion for you that rivals my passion for... fine Corinthian leather. Ah ha ha!"

Gonzo snorted and rolled his eyes. "I thought your heartburn was from the red beans and rice we had at Popeye's."

"Hey, that stuff was too hot for me!" said Fran, finishing her sandwich. She stole a swig of Jimbo's beer to wash the last bite down, even though she had refused one of her own earlier.

"Hot? Hot? That wasn't even spicy! You're in the wrong place if you don't like it hot, sister." Gonzo lectured Fran further, "Why, you need to try some real Creole cooking. We only settled for Popeye's because nothing else was open after midnight. Well, except for the Circle K. I can't believe you came all this way, to the culinary capitol of the United States, only to have a convenience store egg salad sandwich! It's blasphemy, I say!"

Fran wrinkled her nose. "I just don't like spicy-hot things! I didn't come here for the food." She smiled a sly smile that made her squint. Her eyes slid to one side to look at Jimbo next to her. She winked at him and kissed him on the cheek.

"Oh God, suddenly it's Makeout Point and I'm the chaperone!" Gonzo waved his hands around to ward off the impending public displays of affection. He managed not to spill the beer in the process, and took another swig. "Uh uh, no way, that is not how this is going to be. I may be the only single one here, but I am not suffering through that alone!"

Frannie stuck her tongue out at Gonzo. Jimbo laughed but was cut short as Frannie put a hand behind his head and pulled him in for a big, showy kiss. Gonzo groaned and stalked off toward *Soccer Mom,* whose open tail-gate held a styrofoam cooler full of ice and beer. He fished two out and brought them back to the table. Jimbo looked embarrassed and pleased at the same time.

Gonzo smirked at him. "Do I have to get the hose?"

He offered a beer to Liz, who considered a long moment, then waved it away. "I'm beat, I shouldn't have any more or I won't sleep right. Nothing takes it out of you like an exorcism, I always say!" She yawned theatrically, covering her mouth and smiling with her eyes at Gonzo.

Gonzo shrugged and set the spare beer on the table near Brett. He fished his keys out of his pocket. The key ring had a blue aluminum opener on it, and he used this to pop open the bottle. He pocketed the keys and flipped the cap into the fire.

"Actually," said Liz, wriggling out of Brett's grasp to stand up, 'I think I'm going to be the first to hit the sack. It's been a long day, to say the least, and I don't want to poop out now and have to get all set up for bed later." She stretched, leaning backwards to arch her back and made a vain attempt at brushing the dirt off her bottom. She crouched back down to give Brett a quick kiss. "Goodnight, *my fiery Raoul!* You may stay up as long as you wish, but know that your Babette awaits!" She grinned and touched the end of his nose with her index finger and rose to walk off, moving in an exaggerated sashay. She looked over her shoulder as she crawled into their tent. "Goodnight!" Then she zipped herself in.

Brett watched her go, smiling softly. He was aware, after a few moments, that he was being watched. He looked up to see Gonzo holding the open beer out to him. He got up off of the ground and sat on the bench of the wooden picnic table before accepting it. Behind him, he heard Frannie and Jimbo on the other side of the table. Frannie was evidently tickling and teasing Jimbo. He sighed and looked up at Gonzo. Gonzo jerked his head slightly to point with his chin toward the road. Brett stared at him a moment, then got the idea and stood, carrying the beer with him as he followed Gonzo away from the campsite. Frannie and Jimbo didn't notice them leave.

Gonzo and Brett followed the curve of the gravel road that wound through the campsites of the park. They ambled along slowly, sipping at their beer as they went, idly looking into other campsites. Most were dark at this time of night, but a few had party lights strung from an RV, music, and fires to rival the one Gonzo had built.

When they'd been walking awhile, Gonzo paused, and Brett did so as well, thinking Gonzo was about to say something. Gonzo held up a finger, then let out a disturbingly long and resonant belch. Brett swore he heard an echo, and broke out laughing despite himself. "Can't take you anywhere, can we, Uncle Gonzo?"

Gonzo's grin was just visible in the night. It wasn't completely dark, the lights of New Orleans dimly illuminated the cloud cover. The faint orange glow caused everything to look strange and surreal. "You know, Junior, most of this trip has really sucked."

"Most road trips do. You just remember the good parts later," said Brett.

"Yeah. We made it here, and after a couple of days of the Big Easy, we're still going to have to go home again. What do you think you'll do now?"

"I think Memphis sounds pretty good, really. You can drop me off there, and I'll figure out how to take care of moving everything later. Might take me a bit to find a contract or a permanent job down in Memphis, but that's just details. I should've done this years ago, instead of wasting time wallowing in my own misery." Brett started walking again, and Gonzo followed.

Gonzo didn't say anything for a minute, but after another swig of beer he replied, "Eh, you weren't ready. Wallowing is stupid, but sometimes it takes being smacked around to realize what you're doing. Some things just take a long time to work through. Just, well, most people don't banish their demons quite so literally."

"Yeah, I know," said Brett, "I still don't really get why Frannie was the trigger there. I mean, we're not even really friends, we just have Jimbo in common."

Gonzo shrugged. "I don't really understand any of this, and I don't really think I want to believe it happened, you know? It's over, and I don't want to think about it anymore. We all came out in one piece, that's the important part. I was sure you and Liz were dead there for a minute."

"So did I," said Brett, feeling a chill in the air. "I feel like I've had surgery, like something's been dug out of me, leaving a hole that's got to heal. It hurts, but it's a good kind of hurt."

"If you say so. I'm not too worried about you and Liz. It's the psycho hose beast that scares me."

"Hopefully Jimbo can keep an eye on Fran like he's talking about. Guess after the holidays, she's talking about taking a month off to stay with him, and if it works out, well, maybe she'll do like I am doing."

"I still think he's crazy to stay with her," Gonzo grouched, "She's a nutcase whether or not she's possessed. And if she can make more freaky things happen..."

Brett shook his head, though he wasn't sure Gonzo could see him do it. "You heard her, she didn't send the demon after us. In her voicemail, she was talking about the bad luck that made the scrap metal fly off the back of that pickup. The trucker was possessed beforehand."

Gonzo sighed, "Yeah, maybe so, but as long as she believes a little black rain cloud of bad luck is following her, isn't it going to rain on Jimbo too?"

Brett shrugged. "Maybe. But Jimbo's always been an easygoing optimist, I think he'll have a good effect on her. Maybe she'll begin to believe things can go right for her, you know? Hell, I'm starting to think there's even hope for me."

Gonzo chuckled. "You'll be all right with Liz. I don't think you were ever really as happy with Cheryl as you remember, you two always had drama going on. With Liz, even while you were a depressing sack of shit, you were still basically happy. You just didn't want to be. Maybe now you'll be able to get over yourself and actually enjoy life. Hard not to with her around. If you hadn't gone for her on this trip, I might have." Gonzo had to duck out of the way as Brett aimed a smack at his shoulder. He cackled and gave Brett a friendly shove away from him.

"Me," he continued, "I'm thinking Chicago's losing its charm. I went up there to build my resume, and I've done more than that. I'm not sure I can take another winter. Maybe I'll take some time to travel around in *Soccer Mom* by myself before I decide where to settle. I'm sure you'll see me in Memphis. If you ask nice, I'll help you move some stuff in the old girl."

"You know," said Brett, "other than being attacked in that one club, that night on Beale was a blast. Maybe we could both look for work there."

"It's not a terrible idea. I could look up that sassy waitress at the Rum Boogie again, if you know what I mean." Brett could see Gonzo's grin even in the dark.

They returned to the campsite. The fire had died down to flickering embers, but was still popping and crackling with heat and energy. Jimbo and Frannie weren't at the table anymore, and judging by the giggles coming from their tent, they had opted for some privacy.

Brett and Gonzo each had one final beer before shutting *Soccer Mom*. Gonzo opted to sleep in the van, though he complained that he wouldn't be able to stretch out properly. Brett said goodnight, grabbed his sleeping bag and crawled into his tent. To his surprise, he found Liz still awake, reading a book with a flashlight under the cover of her sleeping bag. When he zipped them in, she emerged with the flashlight lighting her face from below. "Now I have you in my clutches, you are mine forevah!" She giggled and pulled him toward her.

Brett knew that being in her arms was the best place in the world, no matter where the roads took him. He grinned at her and said, "I'm all yours. Think you've got room in that apartment for a new roomie?" He kissed her on the tip of her nose and searched her eyes, hoping.

Liz grinned at him. "I told you the offer was an open one. Guess I'll have to give up the webcam though."

"Nah," said Brett, enjoying the heat of her body pressed against him in their shared sleeping bag. "Maybe your fans will learn something. And I'd hate to deprive the world of Babette."

She giggled, "We'll call you Raoul, love. Let them all be jealous. Maybe we'll get more viewers, watching us catch up on lost time."

"I can live with that," he said, and this time he knew he meant it

Sinking Down

This book is dedicated to all of the friends who supported me as I was writing this book: Amy, Heather, Heather, Andrea, Amanda, Craig, Renee, Phil, and Sara. Thanks for all the ideas, encouragement, feedback and faith in me.

Chapter 1 - Hunting Trip

"Oh yuck! Sweetie, did we really have to bring our own roadkill?" Liz held her nose and made a face as Brett dumped out the gruesome contents of the large cooler they'd brought out to the woods.

"Well, how else are we going to attract this *chupacabra* or whatever it turns out to be?" The dead raccoon stank, he had to admit. His stomach churned at the thick, sweet stench of decay. With the back of his wrist, he pushed aside some of his sandy hair that had fallen in front of his glasses when he'd bent down.

Liz took a couple of steps back, her face even paler than usual. "Oh ugh, it's just so nasty! Don't get it on you!"

"I'm trying not to! I hate to remind you, but this little trip was your idea, Love."

Liz put a hand on one hip and imitated a Southern belle, "Well sugah, it was mah little ol' turn to think of something for 'date night,' and ah just couldn't come up with anything more romantic to do!" She wiggled her bottom, making the roomy, black broomstick skirt swish, revealing hiking boots and the cuffs of her black jeans.

Brett laughed and snorted. "Yeah, it's really making me swoon... or maybe it's the stink?" He smirked at her mock pout. "I don't normally get into claims of cryptozoological sightings." He continued, "I'll bet a week of doing the dishes that it's just a coyote or a wild dog out scavenging."

He wouldn't have come, except there hadn't been any worthwhile ghost investigation requests lately. He hadn't been camping with Liz since he had moved to Memphis to live with her, and it sounded fun, and he needed to get away from the apartment. The winter had been gray and oppressive, and though it was starting to warm up, he had a bad case of cabin fever.

"I hope not, I hope it's something cool! Maybe even something we've never heard of before. Little green men, maybe?" Liz giggled and made antennae with her fingers on top of her head. She spoke in a nasal, tinny voice, "Take me to your leeeeader, hu-man!"

Brett laughed at the sight of his girlfriend bugging her eyes out, stretching her face out long. "My leader? I believe that would be you, Alfette. After all, you are my landlady." He grinned, shut the cooler and put it aside.

Liz dropped her act, returned Brett's grin and handed him some baby wipes. *She knows me too well.* He hated getting his hands dirty. He scrubbed at imaginary gore from the dead raccoon and tucked the wipes into the plastic trash bag in his backpack.

"Sure, though until you get a job, I'm willing to keep on taking 'alternate payment' if ya know what I mean." She gave him an exaggerated wink and wrinkled her nose at him.

Brett felt a little pang of guilt at the mention of his continuing unemployment. He hated living mostly off of Liz and his dwindling savings. Still, between her tech support job and webcam donations, they weren't hurting for money. He sighed and pulled out a camera, turned it on, and fiddled with the settings, not looking at Liz.

"Oh, I'm just teasing, *Chico*, you know that." He felt her hand on his shoulder.

He turned to glance at her, forcing a little smile. "I know. I just don't like being out of work, I don't want to be a burden to you."

He could feel Liz watching him as he strapped the camouflaged camera to a tree near the road kill. It was too loose, so he had to rip the Velcro open and pull harder. He wedged some bark behind the camera to aim the lens a bit downward, focused just a couple of feet above the smelly mess on the forest floor.

"Well, don't worry, Sweetie," said Liz, kissing him on the cheek as he stepped back. "You'll find something soon, you're too smart and experienced not to find something. It's only been a few months."

He turned to look at her, nodding. Her smile was contagious, and he felt himself warming from his momentary irritation. "I'm sure. Anyway, the camera's set, want to help me test it?"

Liz looked doubtfully at the carcass and back at him, making a yuck face. "Do I have to go near that to do it?"

Brett shook his head no. "You can be a few feet away, it should still trigger if you walk by back there." He pointed, and she hunched her back and cramped her hands into a claw-like position. She shuffled past the camera, murmuring, "Grr... arrrgh...." She giggled just as the flash went off.

Brett rolled his eyes, but smiled. "Okay, the hunting camera looks like it should work okay. Let's get back to camp and wait, it should be starting to get dark soon."

He picked up the cooler and started to reach for the backpack, but was intercepted by Liz. She caught his outstretched hand in her smaller one as she slung the pack over her own shoulder. Her fingers felt pleasantly cool to the touch as they twined with his own. They smiled at each other, and Brett let her lead him back along the trail to the tent.

They stowed the cooler under some brush near their small green dome tent, but brought the backpack inside. Liz zipped the doorway and bounced on the air mattress, making Brett bounce too.

She laughed at his wry smile and shed her boots and sat with her legs tucked under her. Liz looked like some cute little forest elf, her hair dark and spiky, skirt pooling around her petite form. He'd initially chided her for wearing the long, flowing garment when they were getting dressed for the trip out to the woods, but so far it hadn't seemed to slow her down. The trails were well-maintained, and ground foliage had yet to recover from winter.

He pulled his gaze from Liz and glanced out the mesh window of the tent, which faced down the trail from where they'd just come. "Well, Love, we should be able to see any camera flashes from here. At least I think so."

She shifted so she could rest her chin on his shoulder as she peered out with him, slipping an arm around his waist. Brett felt warm and happy and leaned his head into hers. The scent of her hair gel was floral and chemical and was becoming familiar to him.

The tent began to rustle and shake violently around them. Liz let out a little squeak and unzipped the tent and was outside before Brett, her cheery face gone fierce and angry at what she saw. "What are you doing here?"

Brett fumbled out of the tent and stood up. He scowled.

A tall man, wearing a black trench coat and a leather cowboy hat leered at Liz. His hands were jammed in his pockets, and he wore a heavy-looking satchel slung over one shoulder. Old anger stabbed through Brett's gut, and he felt a surge of adrenaline at the way the man was looking at Liz. "Larry. What the fuck? We're a hundred miles from Memphis. Are you following us or something?"

Brett hated almost no one, but Larry Fisher was on his short list. He didn't bother to conceal the contempt in his voice. He looked over at Liz, who seemed flustered and nervous, which wasn't like her at all.

"Well, hello there! I thought it might be my favorite ex and her new squeeze. Guess you saw the same posting on the Tennessee Haunts board that I did! Well, that and there's no mistaking Miss Lizzie's orange Beetle out in the state forest lot. Just thought I'd come by and see if you wanted to team up on the *chupacabra*." He chuckled. He hadn't taken his eyes off of Liz as he spoke, but finally gave Brett a brief dismissive glance.

Brett lowered his voice, hoping to sound a bit more dangerous. "We don't need your help. And we don't need you interfering, either. Lizzie told you to stay away from her --"

"No, it's fine, Brett," interrupted Liz, her voice quiet and careful. Brett's feet froze with cold anger at her words. Liz glanced at him with a weak smile, which did nothing to calm him. She added, "He hasn't bothered me since you moved in with me."

Larry snorted. "Haven't had to, with that sweet little webcam site you have, darlin'. Get to watch the both of you most anytime I feel like. I do love those new shamrock pajamas you had on the other night. Very cute."

Brett looked at Liz and saw her cheeks flush and her eyes flash with anger, but she said nothing.

Brett took a step toward Larry and raised his voice. "Go the fuck away, Larry. We don't want you here."

Larry laughed. "Well, I'll leave you two be, but I've pitched my own tent just up the trail a ways. Do drop by if you need anything." He looked directly at Liz with this last comment, winking at her. She lowered her eyes and didn't reply. He touched the rim of his leather hat and nodded, glancing at Brett only briefly before backing up and turning to walk away.

Liz looked at Brett sadly, shrugging. Brett still felt a cold pit of anger in his stomach, and his feet and hands felt like ice. He was shaking with adrenaline. He struggled with his feelings, knowing them to be irrational, knowing he was doing exactly what Larry had wanted him to do, but was helpless to do anything but boil over with rage. "Let's just get in the tent and wait, okay? I'll take the first watch. Try to get some sleep."

Liz nodded and sighed. "Please, *Chico*, don't worry. I don't even know what I ever saw in him."

Brett just touched her hand. She took it and pulled him into a hug. Brett held her a long, warm moment, then they crawled back into the tent. He zipped it up after Liz. She kissed his cheek, then slid into her sleeping bag and lay quietly. Eventually, he could hear her breathing slow to a sleeping cadence. He still churned inside from the encounter, and listened even more intently for sounds of the interloper than he would have for the creature they had come to investigate. Night fell, and his anger gradually calmed. He peered out into the darkness for a long time.

There were flashes in the dark. A shrill, forlorn scream rang out in the woods, and then there was the sound of feet pounding along the trail, right toward their tent. Brett heard a whuffing and scrabbling, and knew it would be there at any moment. He reached to wake up Liz, but knew the thing would be upon them too fast.

Chapter 2 - The Little Ghoul

Brett grabbed for his big flashlight. It was almost as long as a billy club, and with the 4 "D" cell batteries powering it, it was almost as heavy. He shook his girlfriend's shoulder, hissing a warning, "Lizzie, something's coming down the trail, fast!"

He fumbled for the zipper on the tent opening and burst out into the chill darkness. Brett didn't switch on the flashlight immediately, but tried to peer around using just his night vision. The moon was hidden, so the darkness was near complete. He thought he saw a flicker of a campfire through the trees in the direction Larry had gone.

Feet pounded toward him, rustling leaves and beating out a strange uneven gait. It didn't sound human to Brett, but it sounded bigger than the coyote he'd suggested earlier. He heard Liz struggling out of her sleeping bag, the zipper sounding like a loud shriek in the quiet of the night.

The footsteps stopped. Brett wasn't sure if he could make out a figure, or if it was his mind playing tricks on him. He heard snuffling and groaning. Brett raised his flashlight, ready to turn it on.

He hesitated. A slow breeze rustled trees further away, moving toward the thing on the trail and toward Brett. He smelled decay, like the road kill, but much older and fouler.... He smelled stale urine and old sweat and feces. He smelled death.

Brett's heart pounded in his chest and in his ears, the blood roaring in the silence. Liz was behind him, steadying herself with one hand as she stood up. Neither of them spoke.

The thing moved just enough to snap a twig. It grunted and growled, a high, unnatural sound. Not a dog, not a coyote. Maybe a bobcat? But the stench, the uneven gait. Brett felt very much out of his element. This was no ghost, no intangible spirit or haunting. Those he was used to, and didn't fear. This was something solid and big and feral. He almost wished for his enemy Larry to arrive. Larry always carried a gun. Brett's flashlight now seemed inadequate.

"Brett," whispered Liz in his ear. "What is it? Turn on the light, *Chico*." He thumbed the switch and the area was flooded with light.

Both Brett and Liz gasped. A creature, just under five feet in height, crouched on the trail ahead of them. It raised an arm to shield its eyes and let out a forlorn cry, howling as it fled into the woods.

Liz and Brett looked at each other. Liz's eyes were wide, her mouth making an "O" of complete surprise. "Was that... was that human, Brett?"

Brett wasn't sure. It had looked smaller, and the thing's skin, where it wasn't caked with mud and blood, looked ashen and grey like a corpse. He could swear he'd seen yellow, wild eyes peering at him when the light went on, but he didn't think they looked intelligent. They looked like the eyes of a hunted animal. It was only a momentary glimpse, but he did think it might have tatters of clothing clinging to its body. Long, lank, filthy hair had obscured most of the thing's face, and it stood hunched as though it walked using its hands as well as its feet.

"I... I think it might have been at one time. I hesitate to say it, but was that a zombie?" Brett felt embarrassed, despite what he'd seen, to say that out loud. Ghosts were one thing, but zombies? The Tennessee Haunts Society would laugh him off their Internet boards for suggesting such a thing really existed. Even though Brett had seen possessed corpses walk before, he wouldn't be believed in that kind of forum.

"I need your flashlight, *Chico*." Liz pulled the club-like light from his grasp before he could object. Liz took off running through the woods, in her socks, after the creature.

Brett tried to chase after her, calling her name, but tripped over a branch and fell hard, knocking the wind out of him. He crawled back to the tent to fumble around for another flashlight as he struggled to breathe.

He was wild with terror at what might happen to Liz if that thing turned on her. It was smaller than she was, and Liz had practice in a couple of martial arts, but that was against humans. The creature was feral and unpredictable and dangerous.

He peered out into the dark, eyes and ears straining. He heard a noise, heavy footsteps coming up the path, toward him.

He swung his light around and flicked on the much smaller hand-crank LED flashlight he'd found in the tent. The figure that loomed up and got caught in the light also shielded its eyes, but didn't seem taken off guard.

It was Larry Fisher. Brett scowled at the tall man. "I thought I told you to go away, Larry."

Larry pushed the brim of his cowboy hat low on his forehead to keep his eyes in shadow, blocking Brett's flashlight. Brett lowed the light to the ground. Larry looked up and murmured, "Maybe so, but you don't own these woods." He sniffed the air and continued, "And I'd say something we're both looking for was just here unless that smell is you crapping your pants in fear, Nelson. Hah." Larry's hands were once again deep in his trench coat's pockets, and his expression held no humor. "Say, where's that old girlfriend of mine? She stay in the tent while you're out here looking for trouble?"

Brett shook his head. "I don't think that's any of your concern, Larry. You're going to fuck up this investigation just by being here. And I don't appreciate the way you talk about Liz. She's not interested in you anymore."

Larry laughed. Brett felt his face flush red in the darkness. He couldn't run off after Liz with Larry here, unless he wanted to lead Larry right to them. But the urgency of finding Liz kept his heart pounding in his chest. *Why won't Larry just go away?*

"She's not here, is she? She's run off into the woods after the *chupacabra*, then? Why didn't you go too, hot shot? Letting your woman do all the dirty work while you stand here, trading pleasantries with your old buddy Larry? Hah."

Brett shook with the cold, and also, he admitted to himself, with fury at this man. Larry had it wrong of course, but the longer he stood here, the more chance Liz could be in danger. Larry wasn't showing any signs of going away.

And, Larry had the gun. It could be useful if something happened.

Brett let out a breath and tried to forget his anger for Liz's sake. "Come on, let's go look for her, she went off this way." He shined his crank light in the general direction he'd seen Liz and the creature run, and stalked off.

Brett heard Larry hesitate just for an instant, but then the man's heavy footsteps fell in behind him, sticks and leaves crunching under his boots.

The two men moved through the woods, not speaking to each other, but both calling Liz's name. Larry hollered louder, and Brett seethed at even that, knowing that the asshole saw even this rescue mission as a competition.

They trudged in the same general direction for about ten minutes when Brett spied a scrap of Liz's broomstick skirt hanging on a thorny bush off to the right. They stopped and listened for a minute. Brett turned his flashlight off to look for signs of what direction to go from there.

While they stood there in the cold darkness, Larry murmured, "Hey Brett, you know, it's not so bad teaming up like this, I reckon. We both want the same thing, recognition for finding this monster. Care to tell me what you saw?"

Brett grimaced. The creature wasn't all that they both wanted here. He knew Larry was history to Liz, but he was sure that Liz's ex wanted her back, especially if he was cyber-stalking her. His presence here might be more for her sake than for the investigation, but how could he know they'd be here? Well, maybe Larry had followed up with the woman who'd posted about it and she'd told him about Brett and Lizzie offering to check it out. Or... no, it was unthinkable that Liz had told Larry herself.

"Larry, I don't know how you happened to be here while we are, and I don't know what you think you're up to, but this isn't teaming up for the sake of the investigation, it's to make sure Liz is okay. I think the thing we saw is dangerous, and I think Liz could be in serious danger, so I need your help and maybe your gun."

Brett heard what could be a grunt of agreement from Larry, but in the dark, he couldn't see the man's expression.

He sighed. It might be better if Larry knew what he might be getting into, for safety's sake; Liz's safety. "All right, Larry. We saw what looked like a small, deformed and filth-encrusted human with grey skin that smelled like death. If it's a person, it's a feral teenager. My gut says if it was human, it isn't anymore. It seems like bad news to me, and I really wish Liz hadn't run off after it."

There was a silence, then Larry replied, "Well, shit yeah. Nelson, what were you thinking letting her go like that? Don't you know better than to split up on something like this? Even I gave you more credit than that."

Brett warred between anger at Larry's comments and his own guilt at having let Liz put herself into danger. He opted to answer with just a grunt. He glared off into the darkness.

As he looked back over his shoulder to the right, he saw light hitting the high branches from the high-powered flashlight's beam. Liz was signaling to him where she was. He turned his own flashlight back on and motioned to Larry to follow as he headed off to where the light shone.

The men rushed through the forest, tripping on roots and getting snagged on branches the whole way. The signal light in the branches disappeared after a few minutes, but Brett was pretty sure he had the right bearing.

Brett had to stop once to crank his flashlight up. Larry appeared to have no flashlight of his own with him, or at least he chose not to use it. Larry was almost silent as they made their way stumbling through the woods, other than to mutter things under his breath as he tripped, and to curse at Brett's poor care of his ex. Brett kept silent, since now was not the time for a confrontation, with Liz in possible danger.

Brett began to smell the sickly sweet stench of death on the wind, and he knew they must be getting close. He thought he heard wet, smacking, cracking and tearing sounds, off to his right, so he turned that way and shone his light around.

A bright light flashed Brett in the eyes, blinding him. He cried out in surprise and dropped his own flashlight as he jumped back. Larry was right on his heels and crashed into him, knocking both of them down. There was another flash of light.

Brett heard Liz's squeaky laughter very close by, followed by a scrabbling and a distressed animal cry. "Oh no, no, no, come back," cried Liz. Brett pulled himself up, untangling himself from Larry, and caught a glimpse of the creature scampering off into the woods.

"Oh damn, you guys scared her off! Just when we were getting to know each other." Liz sat cross-legged on the forest floor, not far from the raccoon carcass they'd left as bait. The small corpse had been shredded, and much of the meat and organs were gone.

"Huh?" said Brett, feeling stupid. "You mean we've been searching the woods for you to rescue you, and you made friends with that little monster?" Brett heard Larry grumbling as he picked himself up off the ground.

Liz nodded and sighed, a sad look coming over her elfin face. "Well, of course! The poor dear is out here all by herself, lost, confused and scared. I followed her as quietly as I could, and she eventually circled back to the food. I turned the camera to point away so it wouldn't go off and frighten her again, but it looks like we've got some good pictures of you two now at least."

Liz stood up now and patted the camera, which flashed Brett and Larry once more. He asked Liz, in as calm a tone as he could manage, to turn off the camera. It took a little while for his vision to clear, but it didn't go off again, and Liz was soon next to him, hugging herself to his side.

Larry did not look pleased, and drew a hunting knife from his pocket. He strode towards them, and Brett thought his rival had snapped, but instead of attacking them, he pushed past and cut the straps on the camera and ran off with it into the woods.

Brett started to run after Larry, but Liz's hold on him grew stronger and she held him back. "No *Chico*, it's okay, let him go!"

"He's got the camera, that's our only evidence of this! Let me go!" Brett struggled in his girlfriend's embrace. It felt good, warm and soothing, to be in her arms, even if they were keeping him from stopping Larry.

"Calm down, big boy. He hasn't got anything he really wants." Liz let go of Brett, and he almost ran anyway, but he paused as she held up a hand.

In her palm was the small SD memory card from the camera. She grinned at Brett, and he laughed and kissed her fiercely.

Chapter 3 - Encounters in the Dark

Brett peered out into the darkness, flashlight lowered to the ground. "Well, now what, Love? I'm not sure how long it'll be before ol' Larry figures out the camera's empty and comes back."

Liz smirked and chuckled. "What if he does? What's he going to say, 'Oh excuse me, I stole this three-hundred-dollar hunting camera fair and square. For that kind of effort, I expect it to come with the memory chip it came with?' Larry was stupid to do that in the first place, the glory-hog."

Brett nodded and shrugged. "I suppose you're right, but I don't like him lurking around in these woods any more than I like thinking about that creature creeping around while we sleep. I think we should break camp and head back to Memphis. We came, we saw, we smelled. And we got what we came for, evidence." He nodded in the direction of Liz's hand, which was now in the pocket of her hoodie, "Let's go home."

Liz shook her head and looked dismayed. "No, Sweetie, we can't! That 'creature' might or might not be human, but it's pretty clear it once was a little girl. Well, a tween girl, anyway. I wouldn't feel right just leaving her out here, Brett!" Liz looked up at him with imploring, sad eyes.

Brett had a feeling of dread well up from the pit of his stomach. "You're joking, right? Even if we could catch it...." Brett paused as Liz's puppy-dog eyes hardened just a touch in reproach. "Okay, even if we could catch her, how would we keep a wild thing in the Beetle for the hour-and-a-half drive home? How would we take the stink?"

Liz scowled and looked away, out into the woods. "I don't know. We'll have to think of something, *Chico*." She sighed and looked back at Brett. "Let's stay the night. We can take turns on watch like we planned, and when she shows up again, give me some more time with her. She let me sit nearby while she ate," Liz nodded to the shredded raccoon carcass, "and didn't seem very bothered so long as I kept the light out. She was even responding to me talking to her, just a little. I think she's lonely and scared. I want another chance to find out if there's a person in there before we run off. If we can't catch her by morning, we'll let the authorities know we saw a girl out here and thought she was in trouble. Deal?'

Brett didn't like it very much. Larry might come back, and though he didn't think the jerk would actually threaten them with his gun to get the memory chip, he honestly didn't know what the man was capable of doing.

As for the creature... the strange, possibly undead child? He didn't share Liz's empathy towards it. Better to let the police deal with it. However, the odds of capturing the thing were slim to none. It had eaten and been spooked twice, so he doubted it'd be back tonight.

Well, why the hell not let her have her chance? Lots of reasons, but Liz wasn't easy to sway when her heart was set on something. "Sure, it's a deal. But if we don't see it- her by eight in the morning, we're packing up to go, okay?"

Liz nodded and sighed. She looked around in the dark. "Would you be okay if I stayed here for a while by myself? The tent isn't far away, and I'll keep your 'head-bashing flashlight' with me, just in case."

Brett shook his head no. "That's not safe, Lizzie. You may see this as a little lost lamb, but it acts like an animal. It could hurt you. You might look like dessert to it,"

"Well, maybe so, but I know how to defend myself if she gets violent. You know that. Tell you what, I'll go back and get my boots so I can run better if I have to."

They both looked down at Liz's feet, green-and-black striped socks peering out from under her jeans cuffs and the tatters of her skirt. Brett had to giggle along with her at the sight.

"Well, okay, but not all night. You'd freeze. I'll even take a shift out here if it'll make you happy. I'll come get you in an hour, then you can get some sleep, and I'll wake you later so I can get my turn in."

Liz bounced up and hugged Brett, her arms up and behind his neck, pulling him in for a long, warm, soft kiss. "Thank you, *Chico*, I just have this feeling it's what we need do to!"

Brett groaned, even if he was still smiling from the kiss. "Your 'feelings' are usually trouble, my dear." He attempted to muss up her spiky hair, but it was too short to make a difference.

Brett took Liz's hand and they made their way along the trail back to their tent. He had braced himself to find the site trashed by Larry, but it seemed untouched. As for Larry's campsite, he couldn't make out the campfire he'd seen earlier, but then again, his eyes were no longer adjusted to the darkness.

Liz rummaged around in the tent and came up with her boots, which she tugged on her feet one after the other. "There, now I'm all set. You settle in for a bit and come get me in an hour!" She kissed the end of Brett's nose and smiled at him and skipped off, swinging the massive flashlight, back to where they'd last seen the girl-creature. Brett sighed as he watched her go.

Rather than get right into the tent, he decided to do a little scouting around. He shut the flashlight off and waited a bit for his eyes to adjust to the dark. Now that the moon was up, he could see through the budding tree branches that it showed half its face. The light would be dim, but as long as it stayed clear, he might be able to make his way around without the crank flashlight.

After a few minutes, he could see the outline of trees and branches around him, and patches of moonlight made an eerie carpet of the leaves on the forest floor. He started taking slow, measured steps towards Larry's campsite. He paused every few steps to listen, but he heard nothing.

The woods were very quiet. Since it was not quite spring, not many bugs were out. He heard far off scrabblings of nocturnal animals once in a while. His own careful, quiet steps seemed much too loud to him. He had to monitor his breathing, taking deeper, slower breaths to keep his nerves from giving him away.

Brett soon saw a reddish glow ahead and to the right of him, spread out in a circle, pulsing with the slight air movements in the woods. Larry's campfire, now scattered to dying coals. There was no sign of any tent, sleeping bag, or gear. *What a relief, he's gone!*

There was a noise behind him. A snuffling. A whuffing. Brett stood still and listened, crouching down to lessen his profile. He wished once again for the big club-like flashlight that Liz held.

The stink of the creature wafted towards him. It was close. Brett heard movement. It was very close. He heard it breathing, short irregular breaths, so close Brett was sure if he reached out behind him, he would touch it. He turned around.

Brett saw the figure of the girl-creature hunkered down like a small mirror of his pose. The moon revealed a silhouette, a dark mass outlined by the ghostly tree shapes behind it.

Brett struggled with panic. If this thing was dangerous, he could be dead at any moment. It was feral, that was for sure, and he might just smell like food to it. Even as he thought that, it snuffled at him again.

He thought of the flashlight, and how light had made the thing run off twice before. He debated for a few heartbeats whether it was a good idea to freak out the little monster, but at that moment, it turned and scampered off back into the forest. It made a small whimpering noise, a bit like a dog, as it fled.

Brett drew in a deep breath and let it out, not realizing until then that he'd been holding it. He made his way back to the tent, not making much effort at being quiet.

He heard faint singing, and realized that Liz must be trying to attract the thing to her. He smiled in the dark and climbed into the tent and zipped himself in. He listened to the singing for a long while as he warmed up under the sleeping bag.

Brett woke later to Liz unzipping the tent and joining him on the air mattress. She shed her boots and snuggled up close to him. She was cold in the dark, but he let her in to steal his heat.

"I'm sorry I fell asleep, Sweetie," he mumbled, still not awake. He added, "Oh, Larry's gone, I checked."

Her body shivered as she cuddled up to him. She kissed him as she began to warm up. "S'okay baby. Just keep that body heat coming!"

Brett asked, "Did... she come to you? I heard you singing."

Liz nodded, her hair tickling his nose and cheek as she nuzzled into him. "Uh huh, she came and sat with me awhile and made little cooing noises. Some other noises too, like she was trying to talk, but couldn't quite manage it."

"I saw her too, she followed me," said Brett. "That or she was checking out Larry's campsite too. She didn't stick around long, but she didn't tear my throat out, either."

They were both quiet awhile. Liz warmed up and zipped the sleeping bags together and they made love in the dark of the woods, hungry for each other after the strange events of the night. They fell asleep in each other's arms, exhausted.

Chapter 4 - Kindhearted Woman

Brett woke as it got light, feeling warm and happy in the large shared sleeping bag with Liz. She lay curled up toward him, an arm draped over him. He watched her sleep, and thought that she looked beautiful in the dawn light, which filtered through the trees and the tent. Shadows seemed alive and excited, chasing across her features as branches above waved about in the breeze. Her lips were slightly parted, and he could hear and feel her regular breathing as she slept.

He savored this moment as long as possible, gazing at her, listening to her, feeling the warmth and closeness of her smaller body, until nature's call demanded he get up. He unzipped his side of the sleeping bag and then slipped out from under her arm, hoping he could let her stay asleep. She sighed and frowned ever so slightly in her sleep, making a little unhappy noise as he drew away. Even asleep, she missed him if he wasn't there. Brett smiled, feeling very loved.

He pulled on his boots, crouching so he didn't have to sit on the edge of the air mattress and disturb her any more than he already had.

Brett unzipped the tent flap and felt the cool, dewy air of the forest. Something smelled foul. He looked around and groaned at what he saw.

The girl-creature was curled up in the fetal position on the ground near the tent. It looked like a corpse in the light, He couldn't tell if it was breathing. Its stringy, greasy hair lay over its eyes.

This is a bad sign. Brett didn't want to deal with this just now, so he inched away and relieved himself against a tree that was out of view of the tent. When he was just about finished, he heard Liz's squeaky laughter. He finished and trudged back, full of dread.

Liz was grinning and inspecting the creature. When she saw Brett, she giggled and said, "Guess we don't have to look far to find her, do we, *Chico*?'

The creature opened its eyes and reached a filthy hand out to touch Liz's foot. It seemed very lethargic, as though drugged or senseless. Liz cooed, "Oh Brett, look at that, she's adopted me! I'm a mommy!"

Brett made a face. This was not what he had wanted at all. "A mommy? No, no. We hunt ghosts, we do research, and we help people discover what goes bump in the night in their homes. We do not take home zombies as pets."

Liz stuck her tongue out at Brett. "It'll just be until we find out where she belongs. We had a deal. Looks like we didn't even have to catch her, she's kind of caught me!"

It was much too early for this, and it was more than Brett could handle. "Where will we even put it, Lizzie? How can we live with something like that?"

Liz stuck her chin out, as he knew she did when she was being stubborn. "We can clear out the second bedroom, you share my room anyway, and only Gonzo ever crashes there, and not so much since he's gotten his own place now. And she's been out in the woods... who knows how long? We'll give her a bath and see what's under all this dirt. Maybe we'll find some way to identify her."

"But Lizzie," said Brett, not liking how it came out in a whine.

"I'm not leaving her here, Brett. I'm sorry, but this is important to me. Please help me in this, I promise it won't be forever. We'll find her a proper home or find a place for her eventually. I need you to work with me, Love. Please?"

Brett had a sinking feeling, but he couldn't really argue with Liz, since it was her apartment, her car, and now, her zombie child. "But what about the webcam? What are your hundreds of fans on the Internet going to think when they see the new addition to the family? Those folks notice *everything*. I even got email when I started brushing my hair differently. Some of the women viewers wrote to say I should put it back it the way it was. We're under a microscope as it is, how can you hide this?"

Liz shrugged. "The 'cam is only on my desk in the living room. If she stays in the other side of the apartment, there's no reason she'll be seen. Remember, you wanted 'private zones' so you could walk from the room to the bathroom without having to get dressed or be presentable."

Brett looked down at the monster girl. "We don't even know what it is. Why is it so calm and dopey this morning when the slightest thing sent it running away last night?"

Liz shrugged again. "I dunno, maybe she's gotten used to us? Maybe she's nocturnal and the daytime makes her sluggish? I bet that's what it is. Look at her, she's barely staying awake even as we argue over her."

Brett shook his head. "I'm not arguing, I'm just trying to make sense of this crazy scheme. If you're right, then what happens if it goes wild at night, going berserk in your apartment?"

Liz sighed. "I don't know, okay?" Her tone said she was frustrated. "We'll figure it out when we get there. I don't think she ever meant anyone harm, though. I think she was just scared and alone. I don't know what she is, but I'm sure she used to be human. Maybe she still could be again, if we can figure out how she got this way."

Brett didn't know what to say to that. Liz had her mind made up. He had to admit that he was at least curious as to what they'd found. Maybe he could get some help from some of his online friends and the "local paranormal geeks" as Gonzo called them. Then again, even Gonzo had seen people become possessed by a demon just last October. Despite that, Gonzo *still* didn't want anything to do with "that paranormal crap," preferring to pretend it'd never happened. Hell, Brett himself had been possessed, for a moment, right in front of Gonzo. Maybe it just wasn't something Gonzo wanted in his picture of the world. At least Liz and Brett's paranormal investigations hadn't driven Gonzo away. In fact, Brett thought last year's haunted road trip had brought them all closer together, and had been the real reason Gonzo'd left Chicago for Memphis. Not the gumbo at the Rum Boogie, as Gonzo told everyone else.

"Well? Are you helping me or not, lover boy?" Liz didn't wait for an answer, but began nudging the thing on the ground, trying to wake it up. It moved very slowly into a crouch and blinked bleary eyes at Liz. She took the former child's hand and started to lead it down the path. Liz exclaimed, "Oh, your hand's like ice, little girl!'

Then, over her shoulder to Brett, she said, "Could you pack up the tent and meet us at the Beetle, Sweetie? She's slow, it's going to take us a while to get there."

Brett nodded. "Okay. But I'm going on record saying that I have a bad feeling about this, and I think we should set a time limit on how long we'll be living with this creature."

Liz nodded and sighed. "You're right. We can talk about it after we get her cleaned up and figure out a few things, okay?"

Brett felt a little better at this compromise. "Okay, Lizzie."

Liz flashed him a smile and turned away to continue down the path with the girl-creature.

Brett broke down and stowed the tent, deflated the air mattress and rolled it up into the long bag with the tent and poles. He peered around for any trash or other things left behind.

There was something small, black and square on the ground near where the tent had been.

It was the little SD memory card from his hunting camera; it must have fallen out of Liz's pocket as she got into the tent last night. He dusted it off and started to put it in his pocket. When he reached in, he encountered his cell phone. It had an SD slot, so he decided to pop the card in to look at the pictures.

He laughed out loud, since the first couple of pictures were of Liz doing her monster impression for the test run. Those pictures were hysterical!

Next was a creepy photo of the creature hunched over the road kill.

After that, the thing was staring wide eyed into the camera, mouth hanging open and bloody from its meal, gobbets of dead flesh in its clawed fingers. Brett shivered; this was a nightmare photo, suitable for <u>Fangoria</u> magazine.

Next was a picture of himself with a look of horror on his face, washed out by the flash, with Larry Fisher peering over his shoulder at the camera, looking just as dumbfounded. Brett groaned. Liz had better not see this one, or it was going up on the Internet.

The last one made him cringe even more, there were the two of them, sprawled out on the ground together after Larry had crashed into him from behind. He felt embarrassed for his future self if either of these two ever got out. He'd never live it down.

On a whim, Brett paged back to the bloody-faced zombie child and clicked the icon to send it as an email attachment. He decided Gonzo would be the best recipient, just to start his friend's day out right. He copied his own email address so he'd be sure to have a copy.

MOTION CAPTURE

He waited a minute while the image uploaded and was sent over the 'net, then put his phone back in his pocket. He slung the nylon tent duffel bag over his shoulder and started off back to the car at a trot.

Brett was amazed to find Liz already buckling the girl thing into the bright orange Beetle's back seat. She didn't seem to be having much trouble, as the sluggish creature was dozing off even as she did it.

Liz turned around at his approach and gave him a warm smile. "Let's go," she said, popping the trunk with her key remote. He loaded the camping gear in the back, slammed the trunk, and climbed in the passenger seat as Liz started the engine.

Brett rolled his window down as the car filled with the stink of the creature. "Ugh, it's worse than Gonzo's beer farts in here. And he can make the wallpaper peel!"

Liz scowled but couldn't hold a giggle in. She swatted at Brett as she pulled the car out of the state forest and onto the highway back to Memphis. It was a quiet hour-and-a-half drive, other than the roar of the wind airing out the car with all four windows rolled down. Liz turned the heat on full, but it was still chilly. Brett preferred the chill to the reek of death and decay from the backseat.

They arrived home, the hour still early, and Liz led her new tenant up the walk to the door of the apartment. The rotting tween didn't protest, and even let out a groggy coo of pleasure as they entered. Liz said, "See? She likes it here already!"

Brett unloaded the car while Liz took the creature into the bathroom and ran some water, adding citrus-scented bubble bath. He could hear her talking baby talk to the thing as she removed the ragged remnants of clothing from the girl and coaxed her into the tub. There were many growls and squeals and a warbling that could be akin to laughing that came out of the partly open door.

Brett decided to let Liz handle it, since this was her idea. He logged into his laptop and checked his email. He was disappointed to see no reply from Gonzo yet. There was an email from Larry Fisher that said, "You'll get your camera back, sorry about my behavior. - Larry." Brett snorted and deleted the message.

After the better part of an hour, Brett began to wonder what was going on in the bathroom. As he approached, the door opened and Liz came out. "Well, she's not perfect, but she smells a lot better. I need to find her some of my clothes to wear."

Liz brought an old Batman T-shirt and some black cotton shorts with her into the bathroom, and then led the still-groggy creature out for Brett to see.

Chapter 5 - Special Needs

Liz stood smiling in the doorway, the ghastly child in front of her. Gone was the disgusting grime and blood, greasy stringy hair, tattered rags of clothing. Brett saw a girl, about ten years old, looking exhausted and feeble. Liz had tied the girl's wet, dishwater blonde hair back in a ponytail. The hand-me-down clothes hung loose on the girl's slight frame.

She looked much more human and much less like an animal. Now he began to feel bad for the words he'd used. Creature. Thing. Monster. It.

She looked normal, except for her skin, which was gray as death, and her eyes, which were yellow and unfocused. Even her scratches and scrapes were just a deeper shade of gray, like permanent dirt, rather than reddish from blood.

And she stood so still, not looking around. Brett couldn't catch her breathing. And her face, like a rubber mask, with no readable expression. She didn't move to the rhythm of life.

But she no longer smelled of death and decay. She smelled of the citrus bubble bath, and perhaps just a hint of something that reminded Brett of worms on the sidewalk after a rainstorm.

She looked up at him with dull eyes, and Brett saw a flicker of awareness. Then she looked away, the dull look returning.

"Well?" Liz asked, her smile happy.

Brett considered a moment, then said, "Much better. Almost human, even."

Liz's smile faded a bit and she sighed. "Well, I'll have to give you that. I doubt she's human anymore. She might be a zombie, I'm not sure. While she soaked, I did a little grounding and centering and cast out to her to see what I could feel of who and what she is."

Brett nodded. He had been skeptical of her dabbling in Wiccan magic, so many years ago, but in recent months had come to believe in it. In fact, she had saved his life several times with her power. "So, what do you know?"

Liz shrugged. "A normal person feels like a torch, a hot, brilliant, multicolored flame. Our little Ashleigh here... well, she has some fire left, but it's like a guttering candle, flaming up at times, almost down to an ember at others. There's not much of her left, Brett."

"Ashleigh? Where'd that come from?"

"Well, she can't tell me her name, so I gave her one," said Liz, crossing her arms.

Brett shook his head. "You know if you name her, you'll just get attached."

The sad look in Liz's eyes made Brett's heart ache, so he changed the subject. "So you say she's not human? How so?"

Liz looked down at the unmoving girl, putting a hand on her shoulder. "Brett, she doesn't have a heartbeat. She's always room temperature, except now she's warmer because of the bathwater. And if she breathes, it's only to make noises."

"She eats, at least, which suggests a metabolism, right?" Brett tried to be encouraging, but everything pointed to this being an undead child, a lost soul.

Liz shook her head. "I just don't know. She's a mystery. And there's something else. I think she has some kind of guardian spirit following her around. I get the feeling of some kind of... presence... like when we're ghost hunting and I feel someone who's not there. This one sticks to her like glue." She shivered. "I feel cold just standing behind her. She's always being followed."

Brett rubbed his cheek, remembering that he hadn't shaved in a couple of days as he took this in. "So we have two new roommates, a little ghoul and her pet ghost?"

She giggled at that. "Little ghoul, I kind of like that."

Brett liked seeing Liz smile. "So... why Ashleigh?"

Liz grinned and unfolded her arms. "Okay, it's not the best name, but her gray skin made me think of ashes, and well, it was a popular girl's name sort of around the time she was born, wasn't it?"

Brett thought it might have been popular even a few years further back, but there were plenty of Ashleighs running around, so he nodded. ' Good enough. Better to have a name than to slip and call her 'little ghoul' in public somewhere." He remembered the webcam and glanced in its direction.

"Don't worry, we're still 'on vacation.' Until tomorrow, the 'cam is off, much to my... our viewers' collective dismay. I have no sympathy though, since billing is off for subscribers, and the rest get to watch us for free."

Brett didn't like the webcam much, because he didn't like his privacy invaded and he didn't like having to share Liz with all those horny net geeks. He corrected himself. Mostly horny net geeks. There were plenty who "tuned in" just to have a virtual friend to keep them company. Liz made a lot of people happy just being herself, and she banned those who sent her lewd requests or got too "friendly." So at least the little ghoul had brought a temporary reprieve from the Ever-Staring Eye.

"That's good, less chance of curious viewers reporting us for kidnapping or child abuse," Brett said, looking at Ashleigh, who was starting to sway a bit.

Liz bit her lip and looked at Brett. "Yes, they might think that. We'll have to keep her off camera, or I'll have to blog about her as a visiting relative or say we've taken in a foster child."

Brett frowned. "Be careful with the stories, Liz. A lot of people who watch you... us... do so because they have a lot of spare time and an Internet addiction. They could do research, make some calls, and...."

"And what? Child protective services would show up? What do you think they'd make of Ashleigh here? Maybe at first they'd suspect abuse, but *Chico* the poor dear has no *pulse*, no *body heat*."

Brett shrugged. "I know, I know, but I still think we need to be careful until we learn more."

At that point, Brett's cell phone rang. The ringtone was "Sally MacLennane" by the Pogues. Brett grinned, causing a puzzled look on Liz's face. "Gonz!" cried Brett as he answered. "What's up?"

"You know what's up! What the hell was that picture you sent me? Damn it, Brett, I was eating breakfast, checking my email, and I almost blew breakfast burrito all over my desk. You're a sick fucker, you know that?"

Gonzo's voice was loud enough that Brett thought Liz could hear him, but his tone sounded amiable as always, with maybe a hint of admiration for what Gonzo thought was a prank.

"I see you've seen our new 'daughter.' Guess what we found out in the woods and brought home with us?" He winked at Liz, who had a wary look on her face. She shook her head "no" once, then led Ashleigh off to the spare bedroom.

"What the fuck are you talking about? Daughter? Woods? I thought you two just went camping. What kind of shenanigans are you trying, Junior?"

"No shenanigans this time, Gonzo. This thing is real. We're not sure what she is. We think she's nocturnal and she's just about comatose during the day. At night, she's a bit wilder, and seems to have a taste for dead things."

"Are you insane? Even if... even if it's true... Brett, why would you take something as nasty as that home?"

Brett shrugged, even if Gonzo couldn't see it. "Liz feels there's just a little bit of humanity left in the little ghoul. Maybe she thinks we can save her. Maybe she just couldn't abandon a lost soul out in the woods. I can't say I'm crazy about it. Ashleigh smelled even worse than you on the trip home. Luckily she cleans up okay, even if her complexion is a bit gray and her eyes are yellow."

"Worse than -- Shit. You're making jokes while you have a -- did you call it a ghoul? What do you mean by 'ghoul'?"

Brett chuckled. "Well, like I said, we don't know what she is. She's some kind of undead. She doesn't breathe or have a pulse, but she moves around and seems to like Lizzie. We just call her the little ghoul because it beats calling her 'the creature,' I guess."

"So, what, you've got a pet monster now? I'm barely getting used to the ghost hunting, but this is going too far, Brett. You'd better be careful; you don't know what it'll want to have for a midnight snack. It might be you. Or Lizzie."

Brett sighed. "I know. Try telling Liz that. She's got a feeling that Ashleigh was just scared, that the little ghoul needs help. She wants to find out what happened to her and to maybe find who she was, maybe even who her parents are."

"Uh, sounds like a fun hobby. Listen, you're welcome to come over here tonight for a little pre-holiday training. We've got to get in shape for St. Pat's next week."

Brett laughed. "Sure, I'll make sure it's okay with Lizzie, and I'll be over later on. Training, huh?"

"You know it. Great drinkers aren't born, they're made, and it takes work to get in proper drinking form. I'd say you're pretty out of shape. It's a damn shame. A damn shame! You could have been a contender, Brett!"

"Ha. Sounds good, I'll study with the master tonight then. Later."

"Later! And don't bring the ghoul; you know I'm not fond of children." Gonzo ended the call and Brett pocketed his phone.

Liz was just coming out of the bedroom, shutting the door behind her. "She's asleep. I don't think we've got to be quiet, I doubt an earthquake would wake her up. What was that all about with Gonzo?"

"Oh, I sent him one of the photos that the hunting camera took last night. Sounds like it scared the bejesus out of him. He thinks Ashleigh is going to eat our brains while we sleep tonight." Brett smirked at this, but felt a chill even as he said it.

Liz folded her arms and leaned against the wall next to him. "Well, we do need to figure out what to feed her. I don't think we can keep getting tasty road kill for her to feast on every night. What else do little ghouls eat? She didn't attack us, so I'm thinking only dead stuff."

"A carrion-eater?" Brett frowned in thought. "Maybe 'ghoul' isn't too far off for a classification if that's true. Ghouls are said to eat only the flesh of the dead, and are supposed to be found around graveyards."

Liz made a "yuck" face. "Nasty. So they're like zombies?"

Brett shook his head. "Technically, 'real' zombies are just people whose brains have been destroyed by drugs, rituals and the power of suggestion and are enslaved that way. Alive, but dead in the head. The classic risen-from-the-grave zombies from movies are undead but eat the flesh of the living. So she's not a zombie, but a ghoul, I guess. I wouldn't have thought either was real until today, though. Except for, well, you know. Like last year. But she sure doesn't feel like a demon-possessed corpse."

He shivered and wished he hadn't mentioned the demon.

Liz looked up at him and rose to hug him. "No, she's not that, I know we'd feel it, *Chico*."

They held each other a long moment, then Liz stepped back and said, "I'm going shopping. Can you hang around awhile and make sure Ashleigh doesn't get in any trouble?"

Brett smiled and shook his head. "Now I'm babysitter to the undead."

Liz grinned and then kissed him. "Sweetie, she's comatose. More than comatose, even. She literally sleeps like the dead. She'll be no trouble. But I need to go out and get something she might eat."

Brett failed to muss up her hair once again and said, "Go ahead, but don't be too long."

She grinned, grabbed up her purse and slipped out the front door. She closed the door, then opened it as an afterthought and said, "Love you, *Chico*. Thanks for putting up with all this. It's just for a while, I promise!"

He shooed her out the door and plopped down on the couch, pulling his laptop to him to start to do some research online.

He kept an ear out for noises from the second bedroom though, just in case.

Chapter 6 - Visions and Revelations

Brett's first stop was the Memphis Haunts website. There was more discussion in the thread where he and Liz had first made contact with the woman who had sighted the *chupacabra* that turned out to be their little ghoul. Brett sighed and rolled his eyes. *Ashleigh.* The discussion had turned derisive. Jokes about Bigfoot and The X-Files and other snark had replaced speculation. Brett itched to weigh in on the subject, to post pictures to back up his story.

But not yet. They didn't know enough, and to talk too much could be disastrous while the little ghoul was living with them. People would be on his doorstep, demanding to see her. Without knowing more, it could get messy. Brett remembered Larry's greed when he stole the deer trail camera. People like Larry might do a lot to have something like Ashleigh in their possession.

Larry, in fact, was a guy who was interested in paranormal phenomena as a way to make money. He did ghost tours, along with some of his devoted followers, around the more notorious areas of the city. Brett didn't fault him for this, many ghost groups needed a fund-raiser. But Larry used it to push his book, and he also sold "ghost detectors" to people who were new to the "hobby." These were just repackaged electrical wiring sensors. He also had a for-charge service to identify whether something in a photograph was a ghost or not. Larry was a charlatan out to make a buck.

And of course, Larry had weighed in on the thread. He spun a tale of chasing the creature through the woods last night, mentioning that he had almost caught up with it, except that the monster he sighted had been scared off by "a couple of amateurs" who had also been out in the woods. If it weren't for Larry, the man went on, these newbies would have been dead, their throats torn out.

Brett was pissed. He hit "reply" and began refuting everything Larry had said, and went so far as to upload the photo from the camera's memory card. He read over the post, and hovered the mouse over the "Send" button on the web form.

Don't do it!

A whispered voice came along with a chill on Brett's right side, from his shoulder up to his ear. It was like the chill that rolled out of a freezer. If he dared breathe, he expected to see his breath. He turned to look, startled, but nothing was there.

Brett had been around ghosts before, but they almost never approached him. This invisible presence with the whispery voice and cold chill couldn't be anything else. He wasn't afraid, but he was a little rattled. Brett liked to go looking for the ghosts. He wasn't happy that one had come looking for him.

To the air, he said, "Who's there? Don't do what?" He waited for a reply, but there was none. The chill slowly subsided, and Brett sensed that he was alone again. Except... except, he felt the strangest thing. He felt a pulling sensation, a draining feeling. He felt cold and tired all of a sudden. It reminded him just a little of the chilling energy-draining power of the demon that'd possessed him, but far weaker.

Then, that too, subsided, and calm washed over Brett. His anger had drained out of him as well. He looked back at the laptop screen and clicked "Delete" instead of "Send." Posting that would be what Larry wanted. He'd been baited, and it had almost worked.

Brett heard a creak, and when he turned, the door to the second bedroom was open, and the little ghoul was peering out at him. Maybe being mostly dead, Ashleigh had felt the presence, too. She looked at him with dull eyes and bared her teeth. Brett shivered, but not from cold. Was that a threatening look, or was she trying to smile? Ashleigh grunted a few times, then retreated back in the room, and Brett heard the creak of the bedsprings as she put herself back to bed.

"That door needs a lock on the *outside*," Brett said, his voice a little more shaky than he liked. He turned back to the laptop and did some searches for "ghoul" and "zombie" and came up with fictional or mythical references.

His sudden fatigue progressed into sleepiness and he caught himself dozing off a few times. Once his laptop even started sliding off and he had to catch it, waking up at the same time. He glanced over at the second bedroom door. It was still open a few inches. No sounds came from within the room. He sighed and hoped Liz would get home soon. It was obvious to Brett that Ashleigh liked her; he wasn't sure how the ghoul felt about him.

He shut the laptop and set it on the table next to him, too tired and out of it to continue his fruitless research for now. Sleep was overtaking him, and he wasn't sure he could do much to fight it off. The ghoul was back in her room, and seemed to be as weak during the day as he felt right now.

Maybe it would be best to get a nap in while he could. It might be a long night.

Brett felt sleep pull him deeper and deeper into a sea of fog and light even as he lay back on the couch. The white fog obscured everything at first, and he felt weightless but had a feeling of sinking down. A feeling of being outside of himself. He drifted in a pleasant haze, forgetting his troubles and worries. Everything, except for the worry of the sinking feeling, which kept him just uneasy enough to not relax all the way. *Like tipping back in a chair just past the balance point. Too far to keep from falling on your back.*

He heard whispering there in the misty whiteness. Brett giggled and shouted out, "Hey! Hey you, get offa my cloud!" He laughed at his own silliness and wondered why he felt almost drunk. His head spun and he couldn't think clearly, but he wasn't worried. It was a dream, he was napping.

The whispering grew louder, and the mists revealed another form. Ashleigh. Or rather it was a human girl who looked quite a lot like the little ghoul. Except... well, it looked like how she might have looked... before whatever happened to her.

"Thank you," whispered Ashleigh. She seemed... realer than Brett. He wondered if that was even a word. Realer. Maybe it should be "more real." He should know better. But his mind was a fog, and he was in the fog, and so was this girl who looked like Ashleigh.

"Thank me? No, thank Lizzie, she's the one who saved you. Thought you were worth saving. Saw through your grime and blood and ferality. Feralness. Feralism." Brett giggled at his wordsmithing. "I am the master of making up words, especially when I don't know what I'm talking about!" Since she was in his dream, she would have to appreciate his cleverness. Cleverality. Snort.

The girl smiled sadly and nodded. "Yes, I thank her, too. I'm so lost and confused, ever since it took over. It took my body from me. I'm only barely hanging on, you know. Tell Liz thank you for me, would you, sir?"

Brett laughed. "Sir. Sir Brett! Sir Worcestershire of Sauce! I will be your knight, my damsel in distress, and I'll slay the dragon of... Oh, oh, sorry, too funny. Yes, I'll tell her. Why am I so lightheaded here?"

The girl's eyes were so serious. "It's because you're not all here. I'm not all here either, but I'm mostly here. You're only beginning to be here. Or rather, you're starting to slip away from there. That's how it starts. You spring a leak after the hole has been punctured, and this is where you leak to."

Brett snorted. "I don't have to take a leak, little girl. Little ghoul. Little bloody-mouthed thing from the woods. You're a lot prettier here than there. It's a shame. A crying shame." Brett began to weep.

The girl watched without showing emotion and sighed. "I know. My time there is almost over, I think. I'm an hourglass and my sand is running out. Yours is slower, but the sand is piling up." She looked over her shoulder. "I have to go. Someone is here to see you."

The Ashleigh look-alike waved and walked backwards until the mists enveloped her. Brett waved goodbye from where he floated and giggled to himself. "Like sands through the hourglass... all we are is dust in the wind, dude." He grinned to himself, a little sad no one was around to appreciate his wit.

Another figure resolved into existence, coming through the bright white fog, inside his personal cloud. "Hello, Love. It's good to see you're well." The woman was blonde, with a long ponytail. She had blue eyes and a sad expression as she gazed upon him. The sight of her made Brett's heart ache.

Brett groaned aloud. "No, no, you can't fool me again, demon. Taking on Cheryl's form was a dirty trick, and I'm not falling for it again. I banished you, you're history. Liz did it too, and she's fiercer and more magical. You can't do this to me again." Brett wished he could think more clearly, but it was getting harder by the minute.

Cheryl shook her head, ponytail bobbing back and forth behind her. "No, Brett, it's me. You're the ghost here, come to haunt me. Except, I've moved on, my death was a new beginning. I miss you, but I'm happy you've got someone in life to love. I just wanted to see you, since I sensed you here."

Cheryl moved closer and touched his cheek. Brett felt her hand as very solid, very real. He felt less real, insubstantial. He suspected she could pass her hand right through his face if she wanted to. She didn't, she just touched him, and then took a step back. The cool solidity of her touch stayed with him, making his cheek tingle for a long while after she was no longer touching him.

"I made my choice in October, Cheryl. I'm staying in the world. The living world. I'm not crossing the road like some chicken to be splattered by a semi. Not giving up again." Brett felt a pull, thought he heard a distant chiming or ringing that filled his mind.

"I'm not here to ask you to join me, Brett. You already have a foot in this world, while most of you remains in the other. I'm not here to tempt you, but to warn you. If you don't want to join me here, you're going to have to do something to stop it or you'll slip away whether you want to or not. It's not about choice, but about what's been done to you." She looked smaller to Brett, more distant. "You're fading back now. Take care of yourself, Brett. Get help from Liz. I love you...."

Cheryl's voice faded as the mists closed about her and the ringing got louder and the white light faded from around him. He woke up on the couch to hear his cell phone ringing and found his eyes blurry and his cheeks wet with tears. His sadness dulled as the dream drifted away from him, not forgotten, but distant and foggy now.

He lifted his groggy head, sat upright, and answered the phone. "Hello?" Again, his voice sounded shakier than he meant it to. He felt disoriented and strange, but no longer as drained. Just cold.

"Brett? Hey man, it's Jimmy. Jimbo. How've you been?" Jimbo's voice was a welcome relief. His friend still lived in Bloomington, several hours' drive from Memphis, and he missed him more than anything in Indiana. They'd been through a lot together with Gonzo and Liz in the fall.

"Hey Jimbo! Me? I'm okay... Things are weird as usual, but you know how it is. What's up?" Brett's voice sounded more normal in his own ears, and he felt warmth and strength coming back to him as he woke up.

The line was silent for a couple of heartbeats, then Jimbo spoke, like he didn't want to be overheard. "It's Frannie, Brett. She's acting strange."

Brett laughed. "How can you tell the difference? She's always got something going on." What an understatement. Frannie's moods had always caused paranormal stirs. A tantrum would send items flying off of counters across the room, doors would slam themselves. She said bad luck followed her like a little dark storm cloud. Brett hadn't been worried about it until her intense jealousy unleashed something terrible that nearly killed them all. Afterwards, she had seemed to lose the curse, and her fear of it. Maybe some of that was Jimbo's calming influence now that the couple lived together.

"Don't give me crap, Brett," said Jimbo. "You know how it can be with her. I love her, but she's acting freaky, maybe for the last month or so. She's been sleeping in the day, even took a night job since she can't stay awake. She thought she was a vampire for a couple of days, but since she wasn't bothered by garlic and didn't have a problem going to church on Sundays, she gave that idea up."

Brett considered this. "That's not too weird. Maybe it's just a sleep disorder. Maybe she's just being mental again."

Jimbo growled. "Stop it, Brett, I'm being serious. You and Gonz always have to be like this about her, don't you? Fuck you guys. No, what I mean is, when she's awake, it's like she's sleepwalking at times. And you know how she used to be a vegetarian? She's some kind of meat-a-tarian now. She won't eat anything else, like she's on Atkins. She says she just craves it, the rawer the better. Dinnertime is me with a micro-meal and her with a quarter pound of raw hamburger. It's one of the reasons she thought she was a vampire. It's freaky, Brett. Even she thinks it's freaky. That's what scares me."

Raw meat? The image of the little ghoul gobbling up road kill floated up in Brett's mind. *How could there be a connection to Fran? It's too crazy to tell Jimbo, it'll only make him worry more.*

"Sorry Jimbo, I don't mean to rag on Frannie so much. I've seen the real effects of her 'curse,' of course. I still have to be skeptical; it's a knee-jerk reaction. I know I shouldn't, I eat weird for breakfast. Especially right now. I think if I told you what's been going on here lately, you'd laugh and hang up on me."

"Well, I just called in case you knew what I should do. Any chance you could come visit soon? You don't have any work lined up yet, do you?" Brett winced at the reminder of his joblessness.

"Well, I'll see what I can find out. I'm not sure if I can afford a road trip to Indiana just now." The thought of getting away for a little bit, to burn off some cabin fever and maybe get away from the ghoul, was tempting. *And if there was a connection to Ashleigh somehow?* Brett shivered. "You know what? I'll head your way as soon as I can, Jimbo."

"Thanks, man. I know you're better at the freaky stuff than anyone I know, so I'm hoping you'll figure something out to help her."

"Yeah, sure, Jimbo. Hey listen, I hear Lizzie coming back from the store, I've got to help her bring stuff in. I'll give you a call later. Okay?" Brett stood up as the door opened and smiled at his girlfriend. Liz made kissy faces at him and walked a couple of plastic bags full of groceries to the kitchen counter, kicking the door shut behind her.

Brett said his goodbyes to Jimbo and hung up. He stared at what Liz pulled out of one of the bags. A big heaping package of graying raw hamburger, an orange sticker on it saying "Manager's Special, Today Only!"

Brett stared at Lizzie and he had that sinking feeling again.

"Liz, we've got to talk," he said.

Chapter 7 – Divination

"What's wrong, Sweetie?" Liz asked Brett, walking over to him to touch his cheek. Her eyes searched his. "You look like you're coming down with a cold, all tired and grumpy-looking."

Brett shook his head. "No, I just woke up from a nap. I had the strangest dream... and then Jimbo called, Frannie's acting strange."

Liz smirked. Brett had to smile in return. "No, I mean stranger than usual. She's gone nocturnal, and has gone from vegan to carnivore overnight." He nodded at the counter where the raw hamburger sat. "That's her favorite meal now."

Liz looked puzzled, following his gaze to the almost-expired meat. "You're kidding. Are you saying --"

Brett interrupted her, "I'm not saying anything other than there's a strange coincidence. Ashleigh said something. It's hard to remember what she said --"

Liz put a hand to her mouth and gasped. "She's speaking! Oh *Chico*, why didn't you call and tell me?" She turned to rush to the spare bedroom's door.

"No, no, wait!" Brett stood up and dodged around the couch to hurry after her, putting a hand on her elbow to stop her from pushing the door further open. "She didn't say it in real life, she said it in my dream."

Liz looked confused. "Your dream?" She turned back to look at him, head tilted to one side.

Brett nodded. "I can only remember bits and pieces, it faded pretty quickly while I was talking to Jimbo. Something about a leak, and something about me being partly 'here' and partly 'there.' She looked whole and human, and she talked to me, but it was kind of confusing. I was a bit delirious during the whole thing...." Brett wasn't sure if he should mention Cheryl, but knew it showed on his face.

"Something else?" asked Liz, taking his hand.

"Well. Don't panic... but Cheryl appeared in my dream again."

Liz let go his hand as both hands flew to cover her mouth. "No, Brett! Not again!"

He shook his head. "No, it wasn't like... the other time. She wasn't the vengeful Cheryl that my mind conjured up last year. No, this was a dream of her more as she really was, though a sadder, more serene version. Like she'd grown all this time since her death."

Liz relaxed. "What did she want?"

"She seemed to be warning me. Not a threat, she seemed genuinely concerned. She said I had one foot... wherever she was." Brett rubbed the cheek where Cheryl had touched him. Even the warmth of Liz's hand, didn't warm it, it still felt cold. Was it just his mind playing tricks on him?

Anyway, he added, "I think you're right that we brought a ghost back with us. I heard a voice warn me 'Don't do it' and felt a chill. Why don't you put that stuff away and I'll break out the ghost gear."

Liz nodded. "Brett, do you think it's following Ashleigh? Like a guardian spirit?"

Brett shrugged. "That's your department, I don't know anything. I just want to find out."

After the groceries were put away, they both poked through Brett's case of ghost hunting equipment. Brett pulled out a compass, an EMF meter, a digital voice recorder and a small slate and chalk.

Liz took out a quartz pendulum from her purse. Brett didn't put much stock in divination tools, but he trusted Liz's instincts. He knew she wouldn't influence the result on purpose.

He noticed something. The compass wouldn't settle down. It just spun and spun. Sometimes it reversed direction. He pointed it out to Liz, who asked, "Could there be interference?" She pointed at the cell phone in his shirt pocket.

Brett made a disgusted noise. "Of course. Hang on." He walked across the room and set the phone down on the counter. Liz called, "There it goes, the needle is settling down. That's north all right."

Brett walked back over and the needle began spinning again. They both blinked at each other and looked back at the compass. Liz bit her lip, then said, "Take a step away, Brett."

Brett stepped back. He could see the needle slow down, but it pointed at him. He stepped back another pace. He couldn't make out the compass as well, but he saw the needle swing ninety degrees to point away from him.

He and Liz stared at each other. "You're a ghost, *Chico*?" she asked in a hushed tone.

Brett forced a laugh, but didn't feel it. "I'm alive, I have a pulse. I have a headache, even. I'm not sure what's going on. Let's try something else."

Liz snapped on the EMF meter. Brett approached and was distracted by the compass resuming its wild spinning back and forth. The EMF meter bleeped and flashed at his approach then went dark and silent. "Hmm," he said. "Doesn't seem as responsive."

Liz shrugged. Brett took the slate and rubbed a piece of chalk sideways on it to cover a large area, then set it on the table. He laid the chalk in the middle of the slate, hoping it looked inviting. He'd seen words and drawings appear in chalk dust on one or more occasion. It was worth a try.

He also turned on the voice recorder, announcing the date, time and location, so that perhaps he could pick up any voices they couldn't hear out loud.

"Maybe something's attached to me, or following me in particular around. I did hear that voice earlier. It seemed to draw out our little ghoul as well, she was peering out of her room after I heard the voice. She went back to bed afterwards."

"This is really weird, *Chico*, even for us." Liz sat on the couch in front of the slate and dangled the pendulum in front of her. She smoothed the string to stop it swinging and held it delicately between thumb and index finger. Her face went calm and blank as she concentrated.

Brett watched as Liz asked aloud for "yes" and "no" to calibrate the responses. Yes was side to side for her, while no was back and forth. The EMF meter bleeped and flashed a moment, startling them both, but once again went dark and silent.

Liz asked, "Is there someone here?" The pendulum swung side to side. "Yes. Thank you. Welcome. Are you the spirit of the little girl sleeping in the other room?" The pendulum swung back and forth.

"No. Okay, are you here to protect the little girl, a guardian spirit?" The quartz started to swing side to side, but ended up tracing out a rough oval in midair. "Not yes and not no. Okay, thank you."

Liz looked up at Brett. "Sorry about this, but I have to ask."

"Are you Brett Nelson?" Liz asked, not looking at him.

Brett let out a laugh, but at the same moment, the compass reversed direction, the EMF meter went wild with flashing and beeping, startling him. He looked back at Liz stared at him wide-eyed. The pendulum was swinging side to side in a most emphatic "yes."

Brett snorted. "How can my ghost be talking to you if I am sitting right here? I sure don't feel dead." The EMF meter settled down again.

Liz just shook her head. "I... I'm not sure why I asked that question, it just seemed like I should. I don't know what it means. You're you, I can feel in my heart that you are. But... what did you say Cheryl said? That you've got one foot in the other world?"

Brett didn't know what to say. "I was going to say, sometimes a dream is just a dream. But it makes more sense than anything else. Maybe it's from what happened last fall?"

Liz pursed her lips in thought a moment, then shook her head. "No, we've been on a dozen investigations since then, and the equipment hasn't acted funny until now."

Brett thought about it. "Actually, that's not true. Remember a month ago when I couldn't get the compass to settle down for almost a minute, and not until I stepped away from it? It wasn't spinning like this, but it swung back and forth. Remember I made a lame joke about finally inventing a perpetual motion engine?"

Liz nodded and frowned. "So it's something that's been around a month or so and got stronger? Did you say Ashleigh called it a leak? What's leaking, Brett?"

Brett felt the sinking sensation again and the EMF meter went wild at the same time. He frowned at the electronic gadget, then looked up, finding himself looking into Liz's worried eyes.

"I'm not sure." He was starting to feel worried too, thinking of Frannie, but didn't want to show it, Liz seemed upset enough. "If it's a leak, it's a slow one, and Cheryl suggested it could be stopped, I just had to figure out how." He didn't recall her saying those words, but he felt a little exaggeration to reassure Liz wouldn't hurt. He could use a little reassuring himself.

Liz asked the air, "Brett's spirit, is there a way to stop this leak?"

The pendulum started to go back and forth but then widened into a slow circle.

Liz frowned. "You don't know either. Great. Was the dream real?"

The quartz crystal continued to spin in a circular pattern, but now it was an oval that favored side to side.

"Maybe, kinda-sorta? Was Cheryl a complete figment of your imagination?"

The oval flattened out into a straight line of forward and back.

"No? So she was Cheryl's actual spirit?"

The pendulum slowed and swung side to side. "Yes, sort of? Hmm."

She looked up at Brett. "What now, *Chico*?"

Brett reached for the voice recorder and stopped it, hitting play. They listened, the volume on the little device at full. Just as they got to the part of the recording where Liz asked Brett if the compass spinning was something that was getting stronger as time went on, a whispery voice could be heard talking over her. They had to replay it several times to make it out.

"It sounds to me like the voice said, 'Ashleigh's emptier than me.' Brett, is your spirit telling us that you're like Ashleigh somehow?" Liz touched his arm, letting the pendulum drop onto the slate with a clatter.

Brett sighed and didn't meet her eyes. "Maybe. But why? We just found her yesterday, how could we be linked? I can't have 'caught' it from her like a disease. The first sign was a month before we even met. What do we have in common?"

Liz shrugged. "And Frannie? Think she's got a case of ghoul fever too? Remember, she doesn't even know about Ashleigh, so you can't accuse her of being a hypochondriac this time."

Brett frowned. "Well, suppose she does. Lizzie, what about you?

She tilted her head to one side. "What about me, *Chico*? The compass doesn't act funny if it's just me sitting here, only when you're nearby."

"Yeah, of course. So what do Ashleigh, Frannie, and I have in common?" He drew in a deep breath and let it out. "Liz, I have to get out of here awhile. I need to think. Gonzo invited me over tonight, maybe I could see if he wants company sooner?"

Liz hugged Brett to her and he felt her nod. The EMF meter bleeped again, and as soon as she let go, he reached down and switched it off. The compass still spun. "Yes, I understand, *Chico*, that's okay. She'll sleep awhile, and I really don't think she's a danger to me anyway. I think I've been adopted as mom for now."

Brett felt a pang of guilt at leaving Liz alone with the little ghoul, but he used her confidence as justification and smiled at her. "I'll be back later. Call me if anything happens. Both of us will be right over." He cracked a grin. "Maybe I'll be here in spirit to keep you company, hmm?"

Liz gave his upper arm a playful slap, scowling at him. "Stop, I don't want to joke about it. I'm going to do some research while you're gone, maybe I can find a way to stop the leak. Maybe we can turn the hourglass back upside down so you'll have all your sand."

"Funny, that's exactly the metaphor Ashleigh used in the dream, now that you mention it." Brett sighed and kissed her.

They both turned as the door to the second bedroom swung open. Ashleigh stood there, her usual blank look on her face, making noises like she wanted to speak but couldn't.

Liz went to the ghoul and crouched down to brush the girl's hair out of her face. "It's okay, little one. We're working on figuring you out, maybe we can make you all better too."

The ghoul looked past Liz to Brett and worked her mouth and grunted, nothing intelligible coming out. She stomped and looked frustrated, then fell into Liz, flailing her arms. Liz looked startled, then put her arms around the girl, hugging her.

Brett took a breath, grabbed his coat and the compass and left, making the sign for "I love you" with one hand at his girlfriend. Liz returned the gesture, her face worried.

Chapter 8 - Come On In My Kitchen

"Hey Junior. Did you know you look like a *precious little angel* when you're napping on the couch?" Gonzo greeted Brett at the door to his apartment, with a snide but cheerful tone to his voice. He wore cut-off sweats and an ancient "I'd Rather Ball U than IU" T-shirt, its lettering cracked and thin. He was the better part of a foot taller than Brett, and while he had a heavy frame, Gonzo wasn't pudgy. He stood in the doorway tying back his long, stringy, reddish-brown hair in a ponytail with a rubber band. This was Gonzo's idea of making himself presentable. At least at home. Friends were family to Gonzo, Brett knew, and you didn't need to be formal with family.

"Huh? What are you talking about?" asked Brett.

Gonzo grinned and motioned Brett inside. "You left the 'cam on, doofus. Liz's vast fan base got to watch you drool on the sofa pillows and scratch yourself."

Brett frowned. "Liz said the webcam was off."

Gonzo nodded. "Yeah, it was, Liz put up an 'on vacation' image while you were away. But I checked this morning after I talked to you on the phone and it was up and running. Said it'd been up for six hours. I saw you do some crap with gadgets and a pendulum, then figured you were coming over here when you left." He picked up a full beer glass and led Brett into the kitchen, where he nodded at another full glass sitting on the counter. "First one's ready for you. You can get your own after this."

Brett still felt confused, but the beer seemed inviting and welcome, even in the afternoon. He realized that it was still pretty early for Gonzo, who was delivering pizzas again to make ends meet until he found a more technical job. Still, beer for breakfast was no surprise.

Six hours? Brett sipped at the coppery colored beer. "Dude, we were asleep in the woods at that time of night. It would have had to turn itself on while we were gone."

Gonzo shrugged, still just carrying his beer around untouched. Gonzo wandered into the living room, leaving Brett to follow in his wake. Gonzo paced. "Were your clocks flashing this morning when you got in?"

Brett blinked, then smacked his forehead with his free palm. "Oh crap, yeah they were. We must have lost power. That'd reset the server, I think. Shit! Where's your computer?"

Gonzo nodded toward a side room intended to be a breakfast nook. It was just big enough for a desk, a couple of bookcases and a chair. The desk was cluttered with motorcycle parts on newspaper, antique tin toys and precarious stacks of paperback books. A CRT monitor glowed, and Brett spied motion in one small window in the corner of the screen. He grabbed the mouse and maximized the window.

On the screen was Liz's apartment. The camera focused on the living room and dining area. Liz lounged on the couch, legs tucked under her. She drank from a water bottle and watched the off-camera television.

The little ghoul also lay curled up next to her. Liz stroked Ashleigh's hair. The girl still appeared gray and dead as she lay perfectly still. Ashleigh didn't breathe. He knew that, but it was still disturbing.

Brett pulled out his cell phone and called home. He watched as Liz leaned off camera and came back with a cordless phone, examining the caller ID. She smiled and answered.

"Hey Chico, miss me already?" Liz chirped, her lips on screen out of synch with her voice on the phone.

"Lizzie, the webcam's on. I think it reset when we lost power overnight. I see you and Ashleigh on screen right now." Brett tried to keep from sounding as panicky as he felt, but wasn't sure he succeeded.

Liz sat up and stared right at the camera, her mouth making a small "O" of surprise. She glanced at Ashleigh and then turned to the side. "Crap! She came out of her room and curled up next to me after you left. I thought it'd be okay! I should have noticed the green light on the 'cam, but it's normally on, so I forgot!"

Brett took a deep breath. Gonzo paced in the other room, waiting for him. "I should have checked too, especially after she peeked out of the room earlier. It's too late now. You'll just have to blog about babysitting your sick niece or something, right?"

He saw Liz nod. "Yeah, that'll work. At least I got her cleaned up and dressed out off camera. I'd better check my email and post something,

I'm sure there are comments by now." Brett watched her slide her legs out from under her and walk right up to the camera as she sat at the computer desk. Her face almost filled the window, slightly off-center. Even with a concerned expression, Brett thought she looked beautiful, and had a sudden pang of jealousy at having to share her with so many online admirers. He also felt a surge of pride that she only wanted him. She read something on her computer screen, then bit her lip.

She said into the phone, "I'd better let you go, I have a couple of dozen emails wanting to know about our guest, Sweetie."

Brett nodded, forgetting that she couldn't see him. "Okay, Love. Try to keep her off-camera as much as you can, okay? She is most definitely not ready for her close-up."

Liz laughed, her eyes lighting up. "Gotcha. You have fun with Gonzo, Babe. I'll take care of things here. Love you!"

"Love you too, Lizzie. I'll check in on you later." She made a kissy-face at him, then ended the call. On the monitor, the image of Liz began to type.

A caption appeared on the bottom of the video feed as she typed: *"Back Early. Babysitting sick niece. Happy Friday!"*

Brett went back out into the main area of Gonzo's apartment. Gonzo still had a full beer. "You gonna drink that, or just fondle it?" asked Brett, still trying to appear calmer than he felt.

Gonzo made a rude noise, eyeing Brett's almost empty pint glass. He raised the glass in a toast and tipped it back, drinking the whole thing in one long gulp. He lowered the glass, paused a moment, then let out a champion's belch. This trick never failed to amaze Brett, and he smiled.

Gonzo grinned. "I'm available for weddings and parties," he quipped. "I'll be here all week."

Brett rolled his eyes and drank more beer. It must be Bass Ale, he decided, based on what his friend stocked in his fridge. Gonzo might not have champagne tastes on a beer income, but he liked to have the best beers when he could afford them.

"So, the little monster's name is *Ashleigh*?" said Gonzo, with both curiosity and derision in his voice. He didn't wait for an answer as he wandered back toward the kitchen and opened the fridge, coming out with two more bottles.

Brett had to laugh. "Yeah, Liz named her, since she didn't have any way of knowing her real name." He accepted a bottle and waited for the bottle opener. "And she got tired of me calling her 'the creature.' It's almost like when she named the little ghoul, it magically granted a bit more humanity."

Gonzo shrugged. "I'd believe almost anything of Liz. She's a great gal, and people always seem to come more to life around her. Especially you, Junior. You were goddamn depressing when you were apart."

Brett watched Gonzo fill his pint glass. He took the bottle opener and popped open the bottle and followed suit, making a bit more foam as he did so, and he had to slurp off the excess. "Yeah, I know. I just wish I could find work so I wouldn't feel like such a leech."

Gonzo shrugged. "I bet I could get you on at King's Pizza. You used to be one of the best drivers Pepperoni's had, back in the day."

Brett nodded. "I might just have to do that. It's not good for the resume though."

Gonzo snorted. "Work is work. I felt stupid doing it again, but in a way, it's freeing. There's never a pizza emergency after hours. Second shift lets out in time for me to hit the bars on Beale, and I can catch some great bands that way."

Brett nodded. "Well, if I don't get something soon, I'll drop by and apply sometime when you're on the shift." He sipped at the beer, colder than the last.

Gonzo grinned. "Sure, but I'm going to warn them about your compulsive booger picking habit." He turned sideways to mime digging deep into one nostril.

Brett had to laugh, maybe a bit more than the crude joke deserved. "If they'd have you, Captain Flatulence, I'll bet that won't bother 'em."

Gonzo pretended to look offended. "Captain Flatulence? I'll have you know I'm a Major."

"A major something," said Brett, smiling.

Gonzo snorted and polished off the second beer all at once, like he had the first. After the obligatory window-rattling belch, he said, "Drink up, we're going out."

Brett tried to catch up, but he couldn't match Gonzo. He drank down maybe a third of the glass. "Out? I thought we were hanging out here?"

Gonzo shrugged. "I feel cooped up, I want to be at an Irish pub. The County Cork is just a few blocks away, it's within staggering distance. Like I said, we need practice for the big day."

Brett gulped more beer. "Sounds good. I could use a little something to eat, too."

After Brett finished his beer, they walked to the County Cork, a pub he'd been to with Gonzo a couple of times before. It was still early, even for dinner, so they had the place almost to themselves. They sat in a booth by the bar and ordered some dinner. Brett ordered a shepherd's pie and Gonzo corned beef and cabbage. They each had a Guinness. Brett worried a bit about money, but decided that if he was going to have a job soon, even if it would be a pizza delivery job, he could afford to spend out of his savings.

Hours passed, and he and Gonzo did some people-watching as they digested their dinner and nursed their beers and talked. They watched the dinner crowd filter into the pub, while the bar gathered some regulars and a few tourists. The waitresses were nice to watch as they flitted past, each wearing billowy white blouses and knee-length, black flouncy skirts.

Brett noticed a petite girl at the bar who sported a blonde buzz cut with dyed-blue bangs and many tattoos. He caught Gonzo looking at her too, and they grinned at each other.

"She's hot," remarked Gonzo. The girl seemed to feel their gaze and turned to look right at Brett, catching him looking. She smiled a secret little smile and stuck her tongue out at him. Brett blushed and looked down to study his almost empty beer. "Busted!" he muttered.

Gonzo chuckled. "She was looking at me, Junior."

They went back to their idle talk, watching the crowd change from couples having dinner out to groups of friends there to drink and pick at appetizers.

Their waitress appeared at their table with a tall, narrow glass, filled with a light brown liquid, ice and straw. She set it down in front of Brett, who looked up at her, confused. "Sorry, I don't think that's mine," he began.

She smiled and winked at him. "A young lady at the bar sent it over for you. It's a Long Island." Brett peered over to see the girl with the blue bangs and tattoos sipping an identical drink and looking right at him. She stood and began to walk their way. The waitress left them and Brett looked at Gonzo, who shrugged.

The girl slid into the booth next to Brett. He had to scoot over to give her room. She slid over again to touch him. "I saw you looking," she said. "I thought you and your friend could use some company. I sure could. I'm Shell."

Brett wasn't sure what to do, and Gonzo remained silent. Brett caught the slightest shake of his head from side to side. He looked at Shell and said, "I'm Brett. Uh, thanks for the drink. I didn't mean to give the wrong idea, I just thought you looked interesting."

She looked at him over the rim of her glass and sipped, the level of her own Long Island sinking as she studied him. Her lips let go of the straw and she said, "I think you're cute. You have a girlfriend?"

Brett nodded. Images of Liz came to mind, and he clung to them even as he was tempted by the closeness and directness of the very attractive woman sitting next to him. She reached up to play with a lock of his hair that had fallen out from where he'd tucked it behind an ear. It made Brett shiver. This had to be some kind of joke. Women didn't just approach him like this.

She leaned in and kissed him before he could stop her. He closed his eyes and let her, not knowing what else to do. It was a nice kiss, she had small lips that nibbled at him. She tasted sweet from the drink, and the alcohol on her tongue left little traces of heat as she licked his lips. The kiss didn't last long. She pulled back and tapped the flat of her hand on his cheek.

"Shame on you, then, letting someone like me come on to you." She slid out of the booth, leaving her empty glass behind as she stood. She looked over her shoulder, then winked at Brett and smiled at Gonzo. "Bye guys."

With that, she sauntered out of the pub without looking back.

Gonzo said, "Junior, I don't know what happened, but I've got a bad feeling about this."

Brett looked back at Gonzo, mind still reeling and heart still racing. He sipped the strong drink and was silent a long while. "Yeah. I don't get it either. What was that all about?"

Gonzo shook his head and flagged the waitress over. He ordered a couple of more beers and asked her, "Do you know what Blue Bangs was up to?"

The waitress shrugged. "Never seen her in here before. Maybe she just wanted to play with you guys. I've seen a lot, working here, but I have to say, I don't usually see anyone that forward." She looked at Brett and grinned. "Did you get her number?"

Brett shook his head. "She just kissed me and left after I told her I had a girlfriend."

The waitress giggled. "Well, your secret is safe with me, Romeo."

Brett blinked at her and said, "Thanks, I think,"

After another couple of hours, he and Gonzo made their way back to the taller man's apartment. Brett was tired and his head swam from all the alcohol he'd had, but he couldn't help peeking at the computer screen to see what Liz was up to.

A black window met his eyes. The webcam was off again. "Gone for a few days, sorry!" said the caption. Brett's heart sank. He checked his cell phone and realized he'd missed a text message from Liz.

Brett, Larry was here to return your camera. Looks like you had some fun tonight. I'm going with him, he says he knows someone who might have a cure. <3 Liz.

Attached to the text message was an image. A picture of Shell kissing Brett in the booth as Gonzo looked on in surprise.

Chapter 9 - A Kiss is Just a Kiss

Brett cried out as he read Liz's text. He was tipsy, not drunk, but he still fumbled with the cell phone and dropped it, kicking it under the desk in his frantic scuffle to retrieve it. He had to talk to Liz and straighten this out before she got too far away.

"What's your damage, Brett?" Gonzo loomed in the doorway blocking the light, leaving Brett to grope under the desk. In the bluish glow of the monitor's tube. "Don't tell me you saw another ghost?" He paused a beat, then added, "No, don't tell me, I sure as hell don't want to know if there's one living with me. Then again, I could stop blaming the terrifying noises on the 'barking spiders'...."

Brett made a strangled sort of noise as he contorted on the floor. "Gah, I can't reach! Gotta call Lizzie! She's gone! I gotta stop her, Gonz! Help me!"

Gonzo snorted. "Yeah, right. Don't get weird on me now, Junior. Liz wouldn't leave you unless you murdered someone. Maybe not even then. 'Sides, that desk is on gimbals, you can just roll it out instead of squirming around down there like you're having a seizure. Come on, move."

Brett scooted back, and he watched Gonzo roll the desk out to retrieve the phone. Brett reached for it.

Gonzo seemed to have second thoughts and snatched the phone out of his reach. "What's this all about, anyway?"

Brett swallowed a scream. He scrambled to his feet and grabbed for the phone. "Just let me call her. She's gone, Gonz!"

Gonzo studied Brett, holding the phone far above his head. "Not until you calm down, Brett. You call Lizzie like that right now, all freaking out and crazy, and you're just going to make whatever it is worse."

Brett blew out a hard breath and fought down the rising panic. She was getting further and further away. The longer he waited, the more trouble there would be.

Gonzo stood, stone-faced, waiting. Brett glared at the taller man, fear turning to anger. "Look, it's not your fight, it's between Lizzie and me."

"And if you want there to be a 'Lizzie and you,' you'll take my advice and calm down first. Take another deep breath and tell me what's going on, and then I'll give you the phone.

Brett growled, but did as he was asked, pulling in a deep breath, then exhaled in a whoosh. He felt a little of the fear leave him, just for a moment. Calm, he explained, "Look at the screen and tell me what you see."

Gonzo stepped a pace back, hit a button to light the screen, and groaned. "Shit. How'd she get this? I didn't see anyone in the bar take a picture."

"I don't know, but it was a setup!" Brett cried. "She says online that she's going to be gone a few days, and the text said Larry happened to drop by, that he told her he could find a 'cure' so she went with him. It's a bunch of crap. He watches Liz's webcam all the time. No matter how many times she bans him, he comes back with another false name. He must have put that Shell girl up to coming on to me to get that blackmail picture."

Gonzo nodded, pushed some buttons on the phone and said, "It's worse than that, even. This came in an hour ago." He looked at Brett and thought a moment. "Want me to call her for you?"

Brett shook his head. "No, I need to talk to her, Gonz." He took the phone and punched at the speed dial key on "L" for her cell phone.

The far end went to a woman's voice and at first Brett went cold inside, thinking he'd been sent to voicemail, but the voice said, "Please listen to some music. You're being connected." The music turned out to be "Who Can It Be Now?" by Men at Work. Brett rolled his eyes. Sometimes, Liz's endearing whimsy could be annoying.

Just as Brett was sure it'd go to voicemail after all, the other end picked up.

The phone screamed. It was a long, wailing, forlorn scream. A female scream of horrifying agony. A feral, animalistic scream.

Then Brett heard a gruff male voice in the background shout, *"Shut that thing up! God damn it, I can't drive with that noise!"* Larry.

"Lizzie!" shouted Brett, as though the power of his voice could reach across the line and make her hear and feel him. "Lizzie, are you there?" Digital garbling distorted the screams and voices. This wasn't a good connection.

The sound became muffled, and Brett imagined Liz putting a hand over the mic. He still heard her say, "Larry, stop, she's just scared. She doesn't know what's going on!" The muffling ended, the screams and groans of the little ghoul coming back loud and clear. Liz attempted to talk over the din and said, "Brett, I'm really angry right now, I don't think this is the best time. Why don't I call you in the morning?" The distance in her tone scared Brett.

"No, Liz," he pleaded. "That girl in the picture had to be a plant. Larry set it up to get you to go with him! You have to believe me, that girl kissed me, I didn't kiss her!"

Liz didn't say anything for a long moment. Brett felt weak, like he was losing everything, in that silence. After a long pause, she said, "I don't know what to think about that. I didn't go with him because of the picture, Brett, even if it pissed me off. I went because Ashleigh has a ghost too. After you left, I tried out the EMF meter on her, and it went crazy. I popped the bubble compass off of my car's windshield and brought it near her and it spun wilder than it did near you."

Brett started to reply, but she cut him off. "No Brett!" she snapped, "I'm not done, and my battery's low. I think her ghost is draining it, and I don't have a charger with me, I left in too much of a hurry. That proved my suspicion, whatever she is, you are, Brett. Whatever happened to her is going to happen to you. You're so tired in the daytime lately, aren't you? Hungry for meat yet? You will be."

"But..." began Brett.

"No! Listen to me! I called Jimbo and had him bring a compass near Frannie. Brett, she's the same, except further along than you. We've got to find out what you all have in common and stop it before I lose you." Brett's heart filled with hope. She wasn't leaving him!

He heard Larry mutter something. Liz covered the mic and hissed something back. Then, to Brett she said, "Look, we're on our way to Bloomington to see Frannie and Jimbo. I need you to sober up and do some research and I'll call you when --" and the line went dead.

Brett stared at the display. The call had lasted 5 minutes and 22 seconds. "Her battery died," he explained numbly to Gonzo. "They're on their way to Bloomington to pay Jimbo and Frannie a visit. She says Frannie and I've got what the ghoul's got, and Larry's got the cure."

Gonzo frowned and thought a moment. "Let's go," he said, walking off to fetch his keys off of a hook near the door.

Brett rushed after him, "You okay to drive, Gonz?" He grabbed up his jacket. He still felt a little tipsy himself.

Gonzo nodded. "Yeah, I nursed the last beer at the Cork for over an hour. Thought I'd have cheaper stuff before bed when we got back here. Guess that'll have to wait. You're right. I don't trust Larry Fisher any further than I could throw his pompous ass. Liz, I trust her, but he's up to something."

Brett stared at Gonzo as he opened the door. "You know Larry?"

Gonzo shrugged. "Liz and I are friends too. Before you moved here, she'd confide in me about the guy because you didn't want to hear about her boyfriends. She knew why too, and was always looking for flaws in the guys she saw because they weren't you. Anyway, he's bad news. He 'borrowed' money from her lots of times and conveniently never had it when she asked to be paid back. He talked shit behind her back, and she found out about it and dumped him. He was a stalker in the purest sense of the word for weeks after that. Part of why she wanted to come along with us to Nawlins was to get a break from Larry."

Brett seethed at the thought. "And yet she goes with him now? She's smarter than that, Gonz."

They stepped outside, and Gonzo locked the door. Gonzo said, "Yeah, she is, but she's crazy about you, and her heart's gone out to this little monster. If she's got no other options, it wouldn't take much to get her to follow on just that hope. Larry figures you'd interfere, so all he needed was to make Liz mad enough to leave without talking to you first. So he asks a friend, Shell, and probably an accomplice with a camera phone, to help him out."

As they got to the cars, Brett used his remote to open the lock on his old Saturn. Gonzo objected, "No way, Junior, you're not driving."

Brett shook his head. "Nope, you are, and we're taking *Soccer Mom*. I just gotta get my charger out of the car so I can do some Internet searches and whatnot on the road without worrying about my battery. Looks like my ghost has already got the charge down to one bar."

Gonzo looked confused. "Uh. Your ghost? You carry one with you? Are you drunker than I thought?"

Brett laughed. "I'll explain on the way."

Gonzo glanced at his beat up old minivan. "*Soccer Mom*? Maybe we should take the Z. It's faster and easier on the wallet. Gas is crazy. I've even been delivering 'za in the Z lately."

"Nope, it's got to be *Soccer Mom*. The Z has only two seats and a hatch. I don't think even Liz wants to ride in the hatch with the ghoul."

Gonzo sighed. "Shit. I don't want to ride with that thing in the same vehicle as me."

"Gonz, I'm not going to be able to drive for a couple of hours at least, and we're losing time. I need your help. Please?"

Gonzo thought a moment, stalling by retying his long ponytail. 'Okay. Let's roll." He didn't look happy, but he unlocked the passenger side door and crawled across to the driver's seat, mumbling, "The lock's frozen on the driver's side."

Brett hopped in, and had just gotten the door shut when Gonzo brought *Soccer Mom* to life, its engine hesitating and complaining. After the engine died once, Gonzo got the elderly minivan running and threw it into reverse as Brett scrabbled for the seatbelt.

Gonzo backed *Soccer Mom* out of the parking spot, revved the engine, then pulled out onto the road and headed for the Interstate.

Chapter 10 - Terraplane Blues

The Interstate stretched out before them, the minivan's headlights illuminating the white dashes that divided the lanes. Few cars came over the hills to shine their lights from across the grassy median. Time seemed to stand still as they raced to catch up on Larry's long lead.

Brett's face reflected in the window, lit from below by the soft glow of his cell phone. He pecked at the screen, making little synthesized clicking noises. Tethered to the cigarette lighter power source by the coiled wire of the charger, he had to fight with the tension of the too short coil. It threatened to pull out of the power socket on the phone.

Internet access by cell tower was spotty and slow, out here in the middle of nowhere. Even between dead spots, response was glacial, making his research tedious. Impatient and irritable, he had taken to looking out the windows or over at Gonzo between "click" and screen refresh.

Gonzo looked tired, and had spoken only a half dozen words for the couple of hours they'd been on the road. They revived some when they made a pit stop at a rest area a half hour before, but Gonzo was beginning to fade again.

Brett broke their weary silence. "Want me to take a turn driving, Gonz?"

Gonzo grunted. "Nah. I'm okay. Find anything?"

Brett peered at the cell phone's web browser. He sighed. "It's all crap. We're only calling Ashleigh a ghoul because her behavior fits the mythical profile. I can't really find anything using that word, ghoul, that isn't fictional."

Gonzo grunted again in reply. After a long pause, he asked, "Jonesing for some steak tartare yet?" Brett caught the tiny hint of a smile on Gonzo's face, but he was too tired to be annoyed.

"No, and fuck you. It's not funny. If Lizzie's right and I've got Ghoul Syndrome, I'm gonna end up like the photo I sent you this morning. Animalistic, brutal, and lifeless. Frannie too, and it sounds like she's on the fast track there."

Gonzo scowled. "Until we know what we can do about it, don't be like that, Brett. Lizzie saved you when you got taken over by the demon, she can help with this. She might be angry, but she's doing what she can for you." He stabbed the button on the CD player and the music of The Clash blared out of the speakers. The speaker beside Brett vibrated, either loose in the door or on its way to being blown. Gonzo drummed his hands on the wheel to the beat.

Brett sighed. His insides ached. His stomach muscles hurt from worry. Liz was out in the dark far ahead, angry with him. The picture of himself being kissed by Shell, her hand around the back of his neck looped in his brain. He barely recalled the actual kiss, but the grainy digital image Liz sent him was burned into his memory.

She was angry with him, and she'd gone off with her ex, the asshole Larry Fisher. He tried to tell himself she wouldn't be interested in the jerk, but his imagination was far too good at conjuring up images of Liz in Larry's arms, kissing like Shell had kissed him. Of them finding a hotel room somewhere off on a side road, maybe sharing a bed so that neither of them would have to sleep next to the little ghoul.

Brett felt the cell phone's plastic frame creak as he gripped it. He fought to push down his anger and fears. Failing, a growling, moaning sort of noise escaped him.

Gonzo glanced at him sideways. Brett looked up, straight forward, not at Gonzo, but at the road.

His eyes focused on his own reflection in the window. He saw the anger highlighted by the phone's light from below. The image repulsed him, and his vision dimmed as a haze of exhaustion washed over him. Being angry took a lot of energy, and he didn't have much left at four in the morning. He hit the off button on the phone to kill the light so he didn't have to look at himself.

Brett slumped against the passenger side door. He felt the cold of the outside through the glass as his head rested against the window. The road sped by, almost unnoticed by him. He knew the <u>London Calling</u> album by heart, so even its raucous noise didn't keep him from drifting off to sleep.

*   *   *

Brett ran across a field with something heavy slowing him down. He struggled against the resistance, but the more he struggled, the slower he went. He ran among a dead stubble of corn stalks, the lines of the rows converging to a point in the distance.

Far, far ahead was Liz. She skipped and laughed and did cartwheels in the field, playing with a little girl that looked like Ashleigh, only alive and well. Ashleigh trailed a large green-and-white striped balloon, string held in one hand. He called out to the two, but they didn't look, didn't seem to see him at all. They kept moving free, but he was held back.

Larry joined them. He took Liz's hand and led her even further away from Brett, the little ex-ghoul dancing in their wake. They looked like a family. Brett shouted louder, but couldn't catch up.

He glanced over his shoulder and saw that he was tethered to a parade balloon. An *angry* version of him, fifty feet long, was bobbing in the wind. One fist held out an accusing finger, pointing wildly about in different directions as the wind made it wag this way and that.

He tried to find what held him fast, and it was a single silvery rope. He couldn't reach to where it attached to him. The wind picked up and thrust the balloon backwards, dragging Brett with it.

He looked around and saw no trace of Larry, Liz and Ashleigh, but now the striped balloon she had carried flew free and floated higher and higher, faster and faster, becoming just a small dot high in the clear, pale blue sky.

Brett's balloon jerked upward and he bounced like a marionette on strings, thumping hard against the ground, feeling his head loll, a pain flaring in his shoulders and neck.

A flash of green blurred by and his head banged along against something hard and cold and flat. Confused for an instant, he then turned to see Gonzo nodding off at the wheel. *Soccer Mom* still raced along at highway speed, veering off into the grassy median, rattling the old vehicle's frame.

"Gonzo!" Brett shouted, grabbing onto the steering wheel, missing by inches a guard rail and a ravine.

Gonzo snapped awake and gripped the wheel, slamming on the brakes, throwing Brett into his seatbelt. Pain shot through his stiff shoulder and nearly knocked the wind out of him.

Soccer Mom fishtailed, her back end slewed left and right before Gonzo got her back under control. He brought the minivan to rest at the side of the Interstate, and killed the engine. "Fuck! What are you trying to do, Brett, get us killed? First you mumble and whine in your sleep and now you're grabbing the wheel? What the fuck!"

Brett shook his head. "You were asleep, Gonz. So was I, but I woke up when you went into the grass."

Gonzo looked wildly around, but there were no other cars on the road. The green digits on the dashboard clock glowed 6:43. "Shit. I'm getting too old for this crap. Used to be able to drive twenty hours straight through to Houston. I'm not even sure where we are. I think we might be on 70."

Brett rubbed his face, trying to clear his head. "They might be to Bloomington by now. Should I try calling Jimbo?"

Gonzo started the van's engine and pulled back out onto the Interstate, his hands trembling. "No, I think they'll call you when they get there. It's too early to wake them up, Jimbo's got that daytime programming job, and they're probably still asleep."

"Frannie might be up, she's nocturnal these days..." said Brett. A pang of fear struck him. What she was going through would happen to him, too.

Gonzo shook his head. "Just wait for the call, okay? I know you're Captain Neurosis over there, but if Lizzie's mad, it's better for you to let her cool off and come to you."

Brett powered on the screen of his phone as they got back up to speed. No messages had come in while he slept. He paged down through his contacts, pausing at Liz's number. He pushed the "Call" button, ignoring Gonzo's advice. It rang once, then he heard Liz's voice, cheerful and chirping from the speaker, but his hopes sank as he realized it was just her voicemail greeting. He pushed "End." He paged down further to Jimbo's number, but sighed and didn't call. He shut the phone off.

After a long silent while, the sky began to get light. The colors went from gray to rosy as Brett watched, circular thoughts and anxiety chasing each other around in his head and his heart. He felt hungry and tired, but no longer sleepy.

After another hour or so of watching the brightening landscape sliding by, he began to recognize the hills around Bloomington. Warmth crept into him, thawing out the icy fear, as though the place had a protective field around it, a whispered promise that everything would be all right. It wasn't home anymore, but it had been once, and he'd been happy here.

They pulled into the lot of Jimbo and Frannie's apartment complex. Brett didn't see Larry's truck anywhere. He shoved his cell phone into his pocket, and as soon as Gonzo parked *Soccer Mom*, he jumped out of the van, jogged to the building and knocked on Jimbo and Frannie's apartment door.

After a second round of pounding, Gonzo came up behind him and started to say something irritable, but they heard the bolt slide back and Jimbo peered out at them through bleary eyes.

"Have they been here?" asked Brett, feeling a little light-headed with anticipation.

Jimbo blinked at him a second. "Brett? Gonzo? Has who been here? What are you doing here?"

"Lizzie said she and Larry were coming here, dude. They left a long while ahead of us, they have to be here by now. She said she'd call me in the morning." Brett felt panic start to creep in. Gonzo put a hand on his shoulder, but he pulled away, waiting for Jimbo to reply.

Jimbo shook his head. "She didn't say anything to me about coming here. Said she'd call me back too, said you were on the other line, but she never did. Why don't you guys come in and have some coffee or something. You look like hell."

Chapter 11 - See Me, Touch Me, Feel Me

Jimbo turned out to be a decent cook, even hungover. Brett and Gonzo brought him up to date on the little ghoul, Liz and Larry. She hadn't mentioned the photo of Brett being kissed to Jimbo, and he laughed and whistled. Brett didn't care for this, but kept his mouth shut. Worry, lack of sleep, and hunger had him on edge

Oh, the hunger. The frying bacon smelled so very good. He wished Jimbo would hurry up with it. He'd been hungry before they arrived, but the aromas made his stomach ache.

Jimbo served up bacon, eggs, and buttered wheat toast. Brett and Gonzo dug in, Jimbo joining them after setting out some orange juice in plastic Pepperoni's stadium cups.

The bacon was amazing at first, but the more Brett ate, the more it tasted like ashes to him. Too hungry to care, he washed each salty, ashen bite down with orange juice. The juice tasted watery and bland, too. Brett wondered if Jimbo had been shopping at discount grocery stores, getting generic expired goods. He had seen the juice carton, though. It had looked like a brand name. The bacon looked and smelled normal too.

He dug into the eggs, and though they felt odd in his mouth, they hit the spot. The sound of his chewing was loud in the now silent room.

Gonzo and Jimbo stared at him. He'd almost cleared his plate, and it looked like they'd maybe had a bite or three. "What?" he said, mouth full of eggs. He could feel the color creeping into his face, and he put his fork down.

Jimbo shook his head. "Man, that's how Frannie started out... wolfing down her food like that." Gonzo looked away and then resumed eating, but avoided looking at Brett.

The sinking feeling pulled at Brett. Something slipped away from him, the pull reminding him of... he couldn't remember. Something recent? Yesterday?

He decided to change the subject. "Where is Frannie anyway?" He looked around, as though she could be hiding somewhere in the kitchen area.

Jimbo sighed. "She took off sometime before I got up. She left me a note that she was going up to Indy, that she wanted to visit a big cemetery up there. Hill something. I'll have to get the note."

Gonzo swallowed half of his orange juice in one gulp and asked, "Why would she want to do that? She know someone buried there?"

Jimbo shrugged. "Nah, ever since the possession, she's been into cemeteries. She's been out with a couple of ghost groups, here and in Indy. She gets weirder each time she goes, I think. At first, I thought her second shift sleep schedule and bizarre diet were due to influence from those folks. I remember how Brett here's told me about the kooks that get into his hobby, but nothing like this level of weird."

"So she went ghost hunting up there?" asked Brett.

Jimbo shook his head. "No, she's gotten less into the ghost hunting and more into the cemeteries themselves. She says she feels calmer in quiet places. After what Lizzie said though, I'm beginning to put some pieces together."

Brett and Gonzo just listened. Jimbo took the cue and continued. "Well, I figure there's got to be some connection between the three of you, Brett, Frannie and... What did she call the monster?"

"Ashleigh," supplied Brett. The word 'monster' gave him a pang. *I'm turning into a monster.*

"Yeah, her. You're all leaking your souls out. I've been worrying about Fran so long that I guess I worked some of it out on my own, but didn't want to voice it, since it sounded crazy. But with the compass spinning around her and you and the ghoul, and the other symptoms...." He nodded at Brett's plate, which only had toast left on it.

Brett blinked at his plate. The toast just didn't appeal to him, even though he still felt hungry. He tried a bite, but it was dust and ashes in his mouth. He almost spat it out, but opted to drink some juice instead.

Jimbo nodded. "Thought so. Anyway, like I said, you're leaking. Ashleigh has leaked so much that she's practically standing outside herself. Frannie's about half gone." His voice went a bit hoarse as he said the last word. He paused a second and then continued, quieter, "She's about half gone, while you, Brett, you're like your dream said. One foot in the grave."

Brett pressed his lips together hard.

Gonzo said, "Well, this could all be bullshit. You're pulling it all out of your ass, Jimbo. Maybe it's just some kind of disease they all have."

Brett murmured, "Ashleigh doesn't *breathe*, Gonzo. No pulse."

Gonzo folded his arms. "Well, I haven't seen it for myself. Maybe she just breathes shallowly."

Jimbo sighed and looked at the table. "Frannie's been getting cold too. I took her temperature last night because she said it felt hot in here, and she was at eighty-one. That's not possible for someone still walking around, is it?"

Brett and Gonzo shrugged.

"Anyway, it's real, Gonzo, and it's not natural. What I think is, it has to do with the possession. Both Brett and Frannie were possessed. Maybe the ghoul was too."

Brett shook his head, a little too hard. "No, that can't be it. If it was, wouldn't I be more or less exactly as far gone as Frannie? It was about the same time, it was the same demon...."

Jimbo nodded. "Yeah, I thought about that too. How long were you possessed, maybe five minutes? Frannie was ridden by that thing for a day or so. Maybe a lot longer, I'm not sure. Maybe it tore a hole in her and she's leaking out."

"Well, sitting around here rambling on about oogie boogie shit isn't getting us anywhere. Lizzie's still missing with that fuckup Larry somewhere and we don't even know where." Gonzo mopped up the last of his egg with the last of his toast, and washed it down with his remaining orange juice.

All of a sudden, a heavy weight settled on Brett's shoulders. "Yeah, and Lizzie lied to me about where she was headed."

Gonzo glared at him. "Maybe plans changed. Maybe they had another stop first. Maybe they're smarter than we are and stopped somewhere."

Visions of Larry and Liz in the same hotel bed tore a painful path from his gut to his mind. He pinched his lips together hard to keep any paranoid blurtings inside. Gonzo gave him an odd look, but didn't say anything.

"She still said she'd call me," Brett whined, hating the sound. "Now what do we do? We can't go to sleep, they could be getting further away!"

Gonzo stretched. "I can't keep going at this pace, and we don't even know which way they went. We may have passed them. I think that's the most likely thing. We could just wait here. Might want to move *Soccer Mom*, though. She's a bit obvious."

"I got a nap in, a couple of hours, right? You could sleep on the way up to Indy," suggested Brett. "Jimbo can stay here and wait in case they show up. It's only an hour away."

Gonzo looked confused. "Why Indy? Frannie got herself up there, she'll come back on her own." Jimbo nodded in agreement with Gonzo.

Brett looked from Gonzo to Jimbo and back again. "I've got to talk to Frannie. See how she is. If I'm going to be like her...."

Jimbo nodded. "Yeah. I got it. I just thought of something else. Know who else was possessed? That crazy Lucy woman. Maybe we can track her down and find out what happened to her, too."

"That's what she told us to call her. We never knew her real name. How would we track her down?" Brett asked.

Jimbo shrugged. "Maybe Liz's server has records of who was a subscriber last year, maybe she can figure it out."

Gonzo hopped up. "Thanks for the breakfast, Jimbo. Brett, if we're going to go, let's go." He walked out the front door, leaving Brett and Jimbo at the table.

Brett shrugged and followed, waving goodbye to Jimbo. "Call if you hear anything, okay?"

Jimbo nodded.

Brett woke up a bit as he digested his breakfast and drove *Soccer Mom* to Indianapolis, another of his former homes. He knew Jimbo must mean Crown Hill Cemetery. It was the city's largest, and one of the largest cemeteries in the world.

The traffic was sparse this early on a Saturday morning. Gonzo had reclined his seat as they set out and snored like a chainsaw all the way there. Brett exited the highway in the older neighborhood closest to Crown Hill, and drove a few more miles to get to the entrance, three giant stone arches with massive wrought iron gates, which stood open. They pulled inside and found Frannie's little red Ford Focus parked at the visitor's center, driver's side door still open, headlights still on. Frannie wasn't inside.

Brett parked next to Frannie's car and woke up Gonzo. Gonzo looked disoriented, but got out of the van and stretched in the sunlight, his black leather motorcycle jacket creaking along with his joints. He fixed his ponytail and wandered over to the open Focus. Brett watched Gonzo, failed to get out of the driver side door, and followed, sliding out the passenger door, muttering to himself about *Soccer Mom*'s shortcomings.

Gonzo switched off the car's headlights, grabbed the keys, and locked the car. He looked around. "This place is huge. Where the hell do we even start looking?"

Brett pointed at a white line painted on the pavement. "I think I know where I'd go if I were her." He followed the line, and Gonzo fell in beside him.

They walked for ten or fifteen minutes and came upon a hill. The monuments here, larger and more expensive-looking, grew more so as they climbed the steep paved road that wound its way up toward the summit. Both he and Gonzo were short of breath before they got two-thirds of the way up. They passed some beautiful, expensive marble mausoleums. He didn't see flowers or other memorials laid at any of them.

The summit of the hill came into view. A stone gazebo crouched atop a mound on the hill, stairs leading up to it.

James Whitcomb Riley's tomb. Unlike some of the lower monuments, the Hoosier Poet's grave was a place people visited. The tomb stood at the city's highest point; Brett had been there before to look out at Indy's skyline. It helped put things in perspective for him sometimes.

It was also a powerful place. The tomb had been built by coins left by children on Riley's original grave. People still left coins, as at a wishing well, from long tradition, and he'd seen flowers and ribbons and small toys left here.

Frannie sat slumped at the top of one set of stairs, her eyes staring back at them, looking through them and back at the city.

Brett walked up and waved a hand in front of her eyes. The short, plump girl took a moment to track his hand, pulling herself out of some faraway place and focusing in from infinity to his hand. She looked up at him, her face as expressionless as any of the tombstones below.

Brett realized that Frannie had lost a lot of weight. Her clothes hung loose on her, and so did her skin. Still heavy, she had the look of someone on a starvation diet. She had deep, dark circles under her eyes and looked pasty and colorless, rather than her usual florid complexion.

"Frannie? Do you see me here?"

Frannie nodded and grunted. "Brett. Hey." She looked past him at the skyline again.

Brett moved over to get in her line of sight. She looked at him, and he saw that the irises of her eyes had gone from brown to a disturbing khaki-yellow color. "Frannie, what are you doing here?"

"Dunno. I wanted to be alone. It's nice here. I feel at home."

This wasn't the Frannie he knew. She was always high energy, whether she was chattering on about whatever crisis had befallen her at the time, raging at someone for a perceived wrong done to her, or gushing about her latest interest, or about Jimbo. That passion was gone, and what sat before Brett was a guttering candle stub, not the fiery torch of a nutcase that his friend loved.

"Come on, Jimbo's worried about you, you should get back." He reached out and took her hand in his. Everything dimmed around them. A hush came upon the already quiet cemetery, sounds becoming distant and muffled. He looked around to see what blocked the sun, but Gonzo was still standing back on the road at the base of the mound.

The sun itself was dimmer, like an eclipse. The sky was dim. Spread out below, the mausoleums, tombs, and fields of tombstones *glowed*. As the light dimmed further, it reminded Brett of a nighttime cityscape, warmly glowing windows replaced by coldly glowing graves. He felt warmer, and he turned back to Frannie... Frannies. Another, glowing Frannie was superimposed on her, looking more like herself than the dull version that sat on the steps.

She gave him a weak smile. "You see too? So it's not just me."

Brett opened his mouth, but at just that moment, his phone rang.

Startled, he let go of Frannie's hand. Light and sound returned in a rush, overwhelming his senses, and he lost his balance, sitting down. He dug his phone out of his pocket. The number was unfamiliar to him. It was an area code in Indiana, up north.

Liz's voice was frantic on the other end of the line. "Brett, I'm stranded! Larry tricked me. I feel so *stupid*. He didn't go to Bloomington; he let me sleep a long time. When I protested, he said we'd just get out for a bathroom break and then head back. He took off with Ashleigh and left me at the station."

Brett asked, "Where? Where'd he leave you?" Gonzo had begun climbing the stairs as the conversation began, but Brett waved for him to be quiet.

"Lafayette, I think. I'm at a payphone. I know someone up here. I could give her a call and see if she can help me go after Larry."

"Lizzie, we're in Indy. Gonzo and Frannie and me, that is. We'll be up there in about an hour. Call me back when you know where to tell me to go, we're on our way."

Chapter 12 - Sabotage

Brett fought the urge to leave Frannie behind, since she could not be coaxed to walk faster than a slow stroll. He thought about touching her hand again so that he could talk to her more direct, since she responded to their urgings with dull assurances that she was already hurrying. But he'd been more than a little scared by the other world that touch had revealed.

Brett thought about the vision as they walked. He'd never touched the little ghoul. He wondered what he would have seen if he had. Maybe it would be like the cloud-like place in his dream? The place here he'd seen Ashleigh as she used to be. Where he'd encountered Cheryl's ghost.

Where I was a ghost. Brett shivered at the thought. His reverie broke when Gonzo shouted next to him.

"Hey! Get the FUCK away from my van!" Gonzo took off at a run. Brett saw a skinny teenager with blue-black hair hanging over his eyes. He wore all black, and had numerous large metal piercings on his face. The kid looked up from where he crouched near the rear driver's side tire.

Brett heard a loud hissing even at this distance, and watched the van sink. The front tire was already flat. The kid looked terrified as the 6'4, 250 pound Gonzo pounded toward him.

The goth kid bolted, disappearing around *Soccer Mom*'s bulk. The stone arches of the Crown Hill entrance gates loomed up behind.

Brett took off after Gonzo and the kid. As he rounded the minivan, the kid passed through the arches, Gonzo right on his heels, shouting and cursing.

As Brett passed through the gates, he took a hasty glance over his shoulder. Frannie was stopped, slumping in the road where he'd left her, looking around her at the trees and stonework. He yelled for her to go to the cars and kept running after Gonzo, though he was losing ground.

The kid ran down the road they'd come in on, one of the borders of the huge cemetery. Brett panted as he ran down the sidewalk along the wrought iron fences and brick pillars that made up the perimeter of Crown

Hill. The kid tore open the door of a small, rusty, white pickup truck, hurled himself inside and slammed the door behind him.

Gonzo grabbed at the door handle an instant too late. The kid locked the door just in time. It didn't stop the big guy from yanking on the handle and pounding on the window, red-faced with anger. Brett saw the kid in the truck's side mirror, round-eyed, face gone ghost-white, terrified. The engine of the little truck tried a couple of times, then started up. Gonzo let go the handle as the truck started to move. The thing lurched, and Brett guessed it must still have the parking brake on.

Gonzo took this opportunity to leap into the bed of the truck. Brett had almost caught up by this point, and just about fell down as Gonzo threw something at him.

"Go get Liz, I'll catch up with you later!" cried Gonzo as the goth kid's truck started forward again. Gonzo crouched in the back, gripping the side of the truck bed. He still looked furious, but offered Brett a salute and a grin before the truck's tires squealed and it pulled away too fast for Brett to follow.

On the ground, he found a set of keys with a Ford emblem and plastic beads on a string that spelled out FRAN. He scooped them up, panting hard. He called out, much too late, "Damn it, Gonzo!"

Brett walked back to the entrance, finding Frannie sitting on the ground between *Soccer Mom* and her little red Focus. She took a second or two, but looked up at him and sighed.

Brett looked at the flat tires on the other side of the minivan. The valve stems had been sliced off. Brett shook his head, went around and opened the passenger door, fished out his phone and car charger and stuffed them in a pocket.

He cursed under his breath, realizing that Gonzo didn't own a cell phone. He said he didn't believe in them, that he didn't want to be reachable all the time. Brett wondered how the hell Gonzo would catch up with them later. Maybe a payphone?

He took a deep breath and reached out a hand to Frannie to pull her up. As he did, he was back in that hushed twilight world, facing the double-exposure of Frannie. Her ghost's weak smile returned, superimposed on the dopey look on her sagging living face. It was both creepy and reassuring at the same time.

Brett had never been close with Fran, and the two had been at odds many times in the past, over her possessiveness of his friend's time, and her undisguised jealousy of Liz. Things had gotten a lot better between them now that she lived with Jimbo.

"Now what?" asked her ghost, her body's lips twitching just a little along with the words.

Brett said, "Well, Gonzo's not going to be back for a while, and the van's not going anywhere for a few hours at the very least. Liz is stranded an hour from here. Can we use your car to go get her, Frannie?"

Frannie's ghost nodded. "Of course. Do you think she can do anything to help us?"

Brett shook his head. "I don't know yet. If anyone can, it's her. We just have to figure this out. She's waiting, let's go, okay? Can you steer your body over to the passenger side and get in."

Both Frannie's body and the superimposed image nodded at the same time. She broke the contact, and sound and light washed back over Brett. He took in a deep gasping breath and felt his heart pound double time. It was like... well... had his heart and breathing stopped while he had that conversation?

Brett shuddered. He realized he'd dropped the keys while talking to Frannie. He stooped, picked them up and unlocked the car. He opened the door and unlocked the other side with the switch inside the door. Frannie was still shuffling around to that side, and opened the door as he sat down and pulled on the seatbelt.

Once Frannie was in, he had to put her seatbelt on, avoiding contact with her skin. Her breathing was so slow it was as though she was already asleep with her eyes open, though she watched what he did with the vaguest of interest.

Brett pulled out of the cemetery and drove the way the pickup truck had gone. But he didn't know where it'd turned at the intersection, much less where it'd gone after that. He paused, looking each way, torn with indecision. He realized the light was green when the car behind him reminded him with a long blast on its horn. He felt an ache of regret at leaving Gonzo, as he turned left, back toward the Interstate.

*　　*　　*

The hour to Lafayette was very quiet. Fran just stared out her window at the fields and towns passing by. Brett couldn't stand the screaming death metal music Frannie had in her CD player, and didn't want to stop to rummage around for other music, so he tuned it to a local classic rock station to keep him company and keep him awake. He sang along with Kansas as "Carry On Wayward Son" played.

He'd gotten most of the way to Lafayette when he realized Liz hadn't called to tell him where to pick her up. He dug into his pocket to fish out the phone and charger.

The phone was dead. He pushed at the buttons to wake it up, but its battery was drained. He'd had it on the charger all the way up from Memphis. He guessed that the same forces that drained Liz's phone were doubly at work with Frannie... and himself, he supposed.

He plugged the phone in, and after it powered on, he heard the chime that told him he had voicemail. He put it on speakerphone and punched the button to play the messages.

"Brett, this is Liz. My friend Caroline, strangely enough, was just down the road from where Larry dumped me. She's here, but is in the middle of something at Springvale Cemetery. Take the 25 exit and it's there on the right as you get off the highway. There's a bunch of people there, you won't be able to miss us. See you then." The message ended. He noticed that she didn't end on "I love you!" like he was used to. Ice stabbed through his stomach at the words' absence.

He started to call back, but remembered that her phone was dead, so she must have been calling from a land line at the gas station. He'd have to find her at the cemetery. What was it with cemeteries today?

Trying not to dwell on the missing endearment, he forced a positive tone as he spoke to Frannie's now-comatose form. "Hey Fran, you'll be glad to know we're going to another afterlife assisted living facility." Frannie made no reply.

The classic rock station began to fade out, so he let it scan for a local station. The Eagles advised him to "Take It Easy" on the first station he found. He muttered to the radio, "Easy for you to say," but kept it on the station, turning the volume down so he could watch for the right exit.

After ten minutes, he pulled off the Interstate and thought he'd made a wrong turn until he saw the tombstones on both sides of the highway. Frannie woke and sat up, blinking at the cemetery.

Even from the road, Brett saw many people wearing black sweatshirts with cartoon ghosts on them, walking around the cemetery, picking up sticks and plastic flowers and wreaths that had been blown around by the wind. He pulled in behind the other cars in Springvale. The gold Saturn ahead of him had a bumper sticker that read, "I Brake for Cemeteries!" and a Barry Manilow license plate holder. Brett blinked at this, then got out of Fran's car. Frannie didn't need to be prompted to get out, leaving the door open behind her as she wandered out into the cemetery, gravitating toward a small stone gazebo nearby.

Brett decided to leave her be while he looked for Liz.

The group was one Brett knew from when he lived in Indiana, but this particular chapter of the Ghost Trackers seemed very industrious, being directed by a cheery, pleasantly plump woman. Her face was framed by medium length, straight brown hair with bangs. She seemed to know what she was doing, helping out even as she ran the show. Brett saw that Liz was tagging along with the woman, smiling as she helped pick up sticks.

Brett walked up to the two women, and Liz's friend chirped a bright "Hello!" She stuck out a hand and Brett shook it. "You must be Brett. We're out here cleaning up a bit, to keep good relations with Springvale. I'm Caroline."

Despite the cold, Caroline wore a T-shirt and jeans. The black T-shirt had simple white lettering that asked, "Ever wonder why your mother named you Mandy?"

Liz's smile seemed forced, and she stayed at Caroline's side. "Hi Brett. Thanks for coming."

Brett wanted to hug her, kiss her, but Liz's body language said that would not be a good idea. He sighed and put a smile on for her, even as he felt coldness grow at his center, pulling at him again. He felt so tired.

He looked back to Caroline and said, "It's lucky you were nearby to help out Liz. Thanks for helping out. This has been a crazy couple of days."

Caroline shrugged. "So I've heard!" Her eyes fixed Brett's, sizing him up. Though the warm smile never left her lips, it didn't quite reach her eyes. Maybe Liz had shown her the picture.

"Looks like you've got a good group here," said Brett to Caroline, "to be out here on a Saturday. That's dedication."

Caroline's smile warmed. "We just like to give back, and this is a great place, one of my favorites."

He nodded and the conversation stopped. Caroline seemed content to wait for him to talk, and Liz looked divided, uncomfortable. He looked at her and said, "So she's gone?"

Liz's fragile smile crumbled and she looked at the ground, nodding. "Yeah. Larry hates her. I don't know why he took her and left me behind. I don't know why he tricked me."

Brett wanted to take her into his arms, but Liz's arms were folded, eyes cast down, which said to him that she was hurt and didn't want to be touched. Caroline stood just a little in front of Liz, protective, saying she would stand between them until she decided what she thought of Brett. Brett was annoyed, but it was what he'd do. If a friend had come to him upset, he'd make sure they were okay before getting out of the way.

"So you don't know where he took her?" asked Brett.

Liz shook her head. "I honestly thought we were going to Bloomington. He said he knew people there. He was on the phone while I slept, I think. He hung up quickly when I woke up, which should have been my first clue."

Caroline offered, "Well, I could post something, asking around if he's been seen around the state. Dunno if an Amber Alert is a good idea, due to her, hmmm, condition. And we don't know her name or anything." She pulled out a pink-cased iPhone and began poking at it.

Brett nodded. "Thanks. I think we've got to think like Larry here. What would he want with a living dead girl?"

Liz shrugged.

Brett said, "If I was the kind of guy Larry is, I'd want to see how I could make money off her. She's unique, or at least as far as he knows."

Liz shook her head. "He knows about Frannie. And you. Sorry."

Brett sighed. "Well, Ashleigh's more obviously... different. She'd be awfully interesting to just about any doctor. But how could he make a quick bundle off of her?"

Caroline frowned and tapped her lips with a finger, rolling her eyes up to the sky in thought. "Well, there's the ParaPrize, I suppose."

Brett blinked at her. "Huh?"

Caroline smiled, still poking away at the phone's touch screen. "The ParaPrize! That million-dollar prize offered by the Knights of Skepticism. The leader of the KoS, what's his name...."

Recognition dawned on Brett. "Ellis Richter. Righteous Richter. The guy who says everything we do is hooey."

"Yep! That's him. He's got that standing offer of a million dollars for any hard proof of the paranormal. I can't think of anything better than your little friend, walking around at room temperature, making compasses spin...." A funny look came in her eye. "Do you mind if I...." She pulled a compass out of her purse and looked at him with a question.

Brett laughed, letting out a bit of tension. "Sure, go ahead."

Caroline held out the compass and it spun. She took a step back, and it stopped. She took a step forward and it spun. She grinned and said, "That's spiffy! Thanks!" She glanced at Liz, who nodded. "I'll leave you two alone now. I've got to wrap up this party."

With that, Caroline turned and stepped away at a brisk pace, calling out to her group. Brett didn't pay attention to what she was saying, as he found himself looking into Liz's eyes.

"I'm sorry," she said. She looked so sad and small just now. He hated to see her lose her spark over this mess.

Brett shook his head. "No, you don't have to be sorry. I was stupid to let that girl near me. I should have known it was a trick, too."

She looked away when he mentioned the girl, then sighed and looked back at him. "Brett, I understand and I forgive you, but I'm still mad, okay?"

Brett felt a glimmer of hope at this, but still felt the distance between them. He didn't feel he could take her in his arms and comfort her like he wanted. He just nodded instead. "Okay. Want to go back to Bloomington?"

Liz scowled. "No! We have to find her, Brett! Where's Ellis live, anyway?"

Brett blinked. "Uh. California somewhere?"

Liz ran a hand through her spiky hair and let out a frustrated little noise. "Why would he come this way if he was going west eventually?"

Caroline appeared from behind Brett and chimed in. "Hello! Sorry to interrupt, but I just found something out."

Brett and Liz turned to look at her. Caroline held up the pink phone and showed its screen to them. It showed a banner that said, "Chicago Ghost Convention!" When she saw that they'd seen that, she used a finger to scroll down, then zoomed in to show the words, "Special guest, Righteous Richter, will debate the audience."

Chapter 13 – Haunted

Brett fumed as he drove along the Interstate, heading north towards Chicago. It had been an hour now, and he was still angry. He glanced in his rear-view mirror, despite knowing it'd just get under his skin. They were back there, laughing. Brett drove Frannie's car, while Liz rode with Caroline, following Brett in her gold Saturn. They'd been carrying on, laughing and smiling and talking, as though nothing was wrong. He kept on looking behind him anyway.

When he looked this time, they had their mouths open, heads tilted back, eyes half-closed. They opened and closed their mouths in unison, and he realized that they were singing. Brett guessed they sang along with a song playing on Caroline's car stereo. He could just guess who it might be. Brett knew he was overreacting, but it consumed him anyway.

Back at Springvale, Brett had brought the two women up to speed on what had happened at Crown Hill Cemetery, with *Soccer* Mom, Gonzo, and what happened when he'd touched Frannie. After some discussion, Caroline had announced that she was curious about the Chicago Ghost Convention and wanted to come along to help search for Ashleigh. She'd spoken with a few of the other Ghost Trackers, who were wrapping up the cleanup efforts, made a phone call, and took charge of the expedition. She suggested Brett fetch Frannie from the stone gazebo where she'd been sitting, and he found himself cooperating. Frannie didn't want to follow him right away, but was coaxed into it after a few minutes.

Brett hadn't protested until he discovered that Caroline planned to drive her own car, and she steered Liz into the passenger seat. He walked up to tap on Liz's window, and she just shrugged at him, deferring to her charismatic friend.

He spoke with Caroline, trying to keep his upset from showing too much. Her bright smile and brisk reply said that he'd failed. She said that another car would be needed for the return trip with Ashleigh. When he protested, clarifying that he wanted to talk to Liz, she explained that she and Liz had some catching up to do, they hadn't seen each other in at least a year. That seemed to settle things as far as Caroline was concerned. Brett looked at Liz, and she agreed with a nod.

Brett wasn't pleased. He wanted to settle things with Liz, talk things out. He knew it'd just make matters worse for him to stew over it, but he was upset, and he needed her. He wished Caroline had just minded her own business.

Frannie dozed in the passenger seat next to him. Sometimes she woke enough to look around at her surroundings, murmured some kind of acknowledgment to Brett, and then dozed off again. He spoke to her every so often, not caring if she heard and understood him or not, just to vent and keep himself company.

"It's not fair, Frannie. Liz knows it was nothing. If anything, she should ask me for forgiveness for running off with Larry. For believing I'd ever cheat on her. For riding with Caroline, leaving me to hang for another couple of hours. They both know I've got the same problem you do, that I'm losing my soul slowly. Shouldn't we be together, brainstorming a cure, now that we know Larry lied about having one? Instead, just look at her back there, having fun, singing, forgetting about me."

Frannie roused a moment, peered at Brett and snorted. "You, you, you. Selfish." Then her eyelids drooped and her head lolled as she fell back asleep.

Brett pursed his lips and gripped the wheel, angrier still. "Selfish," he muttered. As he reached this new height of anger, he felt a touch of vertigo. It felt like the bed spins, a dizzy spell, something like that. It ended as abruptly as it had begun, but he felt weaker when it was done. A strange sense of surreality was added to the drive, like it was a dream or a memory, not something that he was experiencing himself right then.

He came upon a wooded stretch of the median which he'd passed many times on his trips to visit Gonzo when his friend had lived in Chicago. It was a mile or two long, and as far as he could tell, the median was fifty or a hundred feet wide. When he had first started passing the area, he'd noticed it was filled with blackened, dead skeletal trees among the living ones. He thought there must have been a fire there years ago, but other things had grown up out of the ashes. The black tree trunks stood taller than the budding trees surrounding them; reaching out crooked limbs in what he'd always thought was a creepy and foreboding manner. He'd called it the "Haunted Forest" as a joke for so long that the name had stuck among his other friends who'd traveled that way. Gonzo had claimed that it was even mentioned in a short story about intelligent bears, and had gone on at length about how he could tell it was that same spot.

The odd thing was, he thought he saw movement among the trees far ahead, some kind of glowing, like... he couldn't place what it reminded him of. At that moment, Frannie woke up and stared where he was looking and cried out, pointing. She reached over and gripped his arm as she did so.

The sky went dark. The Interstate was a blur of light, a tunnel of colorless streaks moving north, an airborne river-rapid following the path of the millions of people that had passed that way before. Brett wasn't sure what he was seeing, but there hadn't been many other cars on the road around him. It was dazzling, confusing, and he struggled to get his arm away from Frannie's touch. He felt numb and cold, and his efforts didn't seem to do much good. Frannie's ghost was pointing too. "Stop here!" she cried.

He saw the figure whiz past him as she pointed, then contact was broken as Frannie's hand was bumped from his arm by the car leaving the highway into the grass, toward the trees.

Brett found his arms in his lap, his feet off of the pedals. The car was veering and slowing down, but not enough. He heard brakes squealing, and saw the gold Saturn flash past on his right, too close. He found he could move, so he grabbed the wheel and slammed on the brake.

The car fishtailed in the overgrown roadside grass, and he heard rocks hitting the underside, kicked up by the skidding tires. The tires bounced off of some large rocks, jerking the car this way and that. The trees were still coming toward him much too fast. The car didn't have ABS, so he had to pump the brake, and by turning the wheel into the slide, he got steering control back.

The car came to an abrupt stop in a low ditch that was hidden by the wild grass. The engine died. Brett and Frannie were thrown forward into their seatbelts, but the air bags didn't deploy. His left shoulder hurt, as did a diagonal band across his chest where the seatbelt had bitten into him. Frannie let out a whimper and peered out the window, but she seemed unharmed. Brett remembered to breathe, and he took in great gasps of air and felt his heart restart, pounding in his chest.

He hopped out to survey the damage, walking around the car, wading in the grass. His foot splashed in muddy water in the ditch. The car looked pretty much okay, except that the driver's side front tire was down in the mud of the ditch, and a corner of the nose of the car was buried in the mud as well. The hood was bent up just a bit on that side.

The road was obscured by some of the taller grass and brush, so he walked back toward it, following the path the Focus had taken, since it was easiest.

Once he reached the cleared grass along the shoulder, he saw Liz running toward him, with Caroline following further away. He stopped and waited for her, feeling numb and exhausted, and a bit relieved to see concern on her face.

She rushed up and hugged him tight, burying her face in his shoulder. She was crying. "Are you all right, *Chico*?" It felt good, not just to be held by Liz, but to hear her personal endearment once again.

He nodded, knowing she could feel it. He didn't feel much like speaking at the moment. He put his arms around her and just held onto her for a long moment until Caroline arrived,

"Wow, that was scary!" exclaimed Caroline. "What happened, did you fall asleep? It's a dull piece of highway, it happens to the best of us."

Brett shook his head, and let Liz go. He still didn't want to speak, in particular not to Caroline. He thought he might like the woman under other circumstances, but right now he wanted to just be alone with Liz. "No. I saw something in the Haunted Forest, a misty white figure. Frannie saw it too and grabbed my arm." He told this to both of them, but looked into Liz's concerned eyes. She wiped at her tears and regained her composure.

Liz asked, "Did it happen again, then? The otherworldly visions, the dark sky and all that?"

Brett nodded, happy that she understood. Caroline folded her hands in front of her, standing to one side of the other two, listening now. Brett said, "It was like a stream of light, like a time-lapse movie of superfast comets of light along the highway. I couldn't see to drive, and I couldn't move enough to steer. I think... I mean, I was...."

"Dead?" asked Caroline, making both Liz and Brett turn to look at her, startled. Her cheeks colored. "Sorry. But I thought you said last time, your heart stopped and your breathing stopped."

Brett wasn't sure how he liked that image, but he thought she might be right. "Well, even Frannie's not dead, not like Ashleigh. She breathes. Her heart beats. Just very, very slowly. But something like that."

Caroline nodded, and then asked, "You look unhurt, how is she?"

"She sounded unhappy, but she didn't look hurt. The car might be stuck"

Liz smiled the faintest of smiles. "I'm getting *deja vu* here." To Caroline, she added, "If someone stops to help, run."

Caroline looked puzzled, and this made Brett laugh. He laughed far too loud and too long, the little callback to being accosted by the roadside last year wasn't funny, except in the way Liz had said it. It was a release Brett needed, to let out some of the pent-up frustration, anger and shock he'd had simmering at a low boil for too long now.

Caroline smiled, a bit warmer this time, and Liz did too. "Let's see about the car," said Caroline as Brett wound down laughing. Brett nodded and took a deep breath. He hugged Liz with one arm first, and he was happy to find that she didn't resist.

Brett led the two women down the new path plowed by Frannie's car, where they found it, passenger side door open. Frannie was gone.

"Shit," said Brett. "She was so languid all day, I didn't figure she could go anywhere while I took a look around. I didn't think she would. What's here to draw her away?"

Liz looked at him and arched an eyebrow. "Didn't you say you both saw a figure, and that's why she grabbed you and caused the accident in the first place?"

Brett just groaned and nodded in response.

Caroline was already searching the nearby area. "Where did you see it? Did you pass it?"

Brett pointed back the way the cars had come. "Yeah, we passed the figure just before she grabbed me. I think she was urging me to pull over, though I don't think she meant it to happen like this."

The sound of traffic on the highway seemed loud in the pause in conversation. Caroline began hiking off in the direction Brett had pointed.

Liz frowned, following in Caroline's wake. "What's she after? Why's she so driven after being so logy?"

Brett, glancing back at the car before following, answered, "Well, if it was a ghost, maybe she wanted to make friends?"

Liz shot him a look that made him rephrase what he said. "I don't mean to be flip, but you don't just see ghosts in broad daylight along the highway. Maybe the Haunted Forest really is haunted, and since she's half ghost already, maybe she knows something more somehow?"

Brett kept from saying his next thought out loud. *Maybe I saw it because I'm becoming more of a ghost all the time myself.* Liz nodded at what he said, but bit her lip at what he didn't say, and he was sure she must have had a similar thought. He could never hide anything from Liz.

Without a word, she took his hand and they walked along behind Caroline in silence awhile. After a few minutes, Caroline called out, "Frannie! Where are you, Frannie?"

Liz and Brett took turns calling out to their missing friend. Brett thought over that word, friend, and though Frannie was irritating and not someone he'd been close with, they'd been through a lot together, and here he was, looking after her. And like it or not, their destinies were now intertwined once again. If he and his other friends couldn't save Frannie, he didn't have much more hope himself.

Unbidden, the photo he'd sent Gonzo of Ashleigh, bloody-faced and feral, came to him in his mind. He didn't want to end up like that.

Chapter 14 - Echoes of the Past

The three trudged along through the wild grasses, weeds and shrubs between the Interstate and the Haunted Forest. The craggy black tree corpses loomed over them in the late afternoon light. They kept on calling Frannie's name as they went but got no reply. Brett peered off into the woods to their right, and found he couldn't see very far in, despite knowing that it wasn't all that far to the other side of the Interstate. No sound or glimpse of cars could be seen from the other side.

"Okay, I've lost her trail," announced Caroline, putting her fists on her hips, pivoting at her waist to look from side to side. "The grass was trampled up until this point, but now it's gotten rocky, and I don't see her trail resume over there." She pointed at a continuation of the grass on the other side of a gravel-covered area. It might have once been pavement that had been abandoned; perhaps the highway had been rerouted. The grass had just taken over everywhere else but this strip, which was broken and still supported some hardy low weeds.

"Maybe we should go back to the highway and look, since we can't see over the grass so well?" suggested Liz.

Caroline shrugged. "I suppose. What attraction would the highway have for her?"

Brett paused a moment, then said in a low voice, "Roadkill. Maybe she's hungry."

Liz touched her lips with her fingers, staring at Brett a moment with sad eyes. "Oh, Brett. Don't talk that way."

"He's right," said Caroline, "You said that the little ghoul wanted dead meat, and we know Frannie's been eating only raw hamburger for a while now." Caroline's eyes met his a long, meaningful moment and she pressed her lips together into a tight line.

Brett broke eye contact with Caroline when he noticed Liz's hand tremble, just a little, in his. Her eyes glistened and her cheeks were turned red. Brett took a deep breath and squeezed her hand tight. "Come on, let's find her," he said in a calmer tone than he felt. "We'll figure other stuff out later."

They looked up and down the shoulder of the highway. Other than the blinking hazard lights of the Saturn and the skid marks left by the Focus back the way they'd come, they didn't see anything interesting at first.

Then Liz pointed and pulled Brett along behind her. "Look! A marker!" she cried, and now Brett did see a small, plain white wooden cross, planted in the grass ahead of them a few dozen feet away. The three jogged over to it, though there was no sign of Frannie nearby.

"Josh Carpenter," read Liz as she caught her breath when they came up to the cross, "Killed by drunk driving."

Caroline was already on the other side of the makeshift marker. "There's more over here." She read, "Now he rests near his brother."

Brett had seen far too many of these roadside memorials, and had even griped about the elaborate displays some people had put up, saying that the distraction might cause other accidents. But at this moment, second-hand grief welled up inside him, imagining someone losing two sons. He spotted an old, weathered photograph on the ground nearby; he picked it up and looked at it.

It was faded to yellows and browns for the most part, but the picture was of a family of five in front of a Christmas tree. The mother and father stood behind two boys of maybe ten and thirteen years in age, and a toddler in a holiday dress, sitting on the floor in front of them.

The girl had an uncanny resemblance to Ashleigh, though quite a bit younger. He showed Liz, and without saying a thing to her, she cried, "Ashleigh! Oh goddess, it's her!"

Caroline frowned and walked over to take the picture from her friend and examined it. "That's pretty unlikely, isn't it? I mean she's about ten, and if the oldest was Josh, and he died six years ago... well, maybe. But what are the chances of us coming upon her brother's roadside marker like this?"

Liz took the picture back to stare at it some more as she said, "Maybe her brother called out to Frannie? Or her other brother, who 'rests near' here?"

They started to look around for another marker, but nothing presented itself. Liz frowned and asked Brett, "Can I borrow your cell phone?"

Brett handed it over, but she made a frustrated noise and handed it back. "It's dead, like mine."

Brett frowned. "Well, it's been on the charger in the car, but once I'm away from the car, it drains fast."

Caroline shooed at Brett. At first, he was irritated. Was she trying to separate him from Liz again? What was her problem, anyway?

His irritation must have showed, since Caroline explained, "I'm giving her my phone, but you'll have to step away so it'll hold a charge, Brett!" She flashed him an amused smile that he decided to take as friendly, rather than condescending. She hadn't given him reason to think she had anything personal against him, it was just his irrational feelings that made him upset with her earlier. He stepped back and let go of Lizzie's hand.

Liz shrugged and smiled, walking a short distance away to talk in semi-private. On the phone, she laughed and giggled and then became more serious, talking away.

Brett looked at Caroline and she shrugged. "Hello!" she said with a bright smile.

He let out a little laugh and gave her a half-hearted wave.

She said, "She's crazy about you, you know?"

Brett felt color come to his cheeks. "Oh, I know. That's why it's hard when we're apart, or when she's mad at me. Which is just about never."

Caroline nodded. "You're lucky that way. My husband and I have been together for too long, and we hardly do anything together. He just scoffs at my ghost hunting, and I have no interest in what he does. I'd give a lot to have what you and Liz have."

Brett sighed. "I hope she realizes that kiss was a setup," said Brett. "I've never wanted anyone but her since we got together. Not even when we were apart for a few years."

Caroline nodded. "It's not my business, really, but she wasn't hurt by the kiss. She was hurt that she found out from Larry, not you."

Oh!

Before Brett could reply, Liz returned. "I called Jimbo," she said. "I told him that Frannie's with us and that she's okay, more or less. I asked him to check around about Josh and his family."

Caroline took her phone back from Liz and started poking at the screen. "I can do better than that. I can look him up on Find A Grave and see if he's there."

Liz explained to Brett, "Caroline's also a 'graver.' She volunteers to submit photos of tombstones for this online database of the deceased."

Brett nodded, remembering something about this. "I saw that. Kind of like Facebook for dead people."

Caroline looked up to give him an evil eye, but she let him see a small smile afterwards. "It's not that, but close enough. You'd be surprised at how much an online memorial can mean to the family of the deceased. It's very rewarding. But you can get obits and biographical information from the site as well."

After a minute or so of waiting on Caroline to navigate around the site, they heard a howling, hoarse, human shout come from the Haunted Forest. Caroline pocketed her phone and they all moved in the direction they'd heard the shout.

They waded through the grass, moving as fast as they could without tripping on weeds or rocky debris. Brett managed to trip anyway, being kept from landing hard on the ground by Liz's strong grip on his hand. She pulled him upright and they kept moving.

Once they reached the trees, the going went slower. It was dark a short ways in and among the forest, but Caroline surprised him by producing a small flashlight from a pocket. When he remarked on it, she smiled and said, "I'm always prepared."

Brett felt like a bad ghost hunter all of a sudden, but a squeeze from Liz's hand reminded him this wasn't an ordinary circumstance.

Ghost hunter. What did that make him think of? *Compass!* He fished around in his pocket and pulled it out. The needle spun as wild as before. He showed it to Caroline. "I've got an idea. Maybe if you two moved away from me a bit, you might be able to use compasses to find Frannie?"

Liz took his compass from his hand and gave him a brilliant smile. "That's a great idea!"

Caroline nodded in appreciation and pulled her own compass out. "You're going to have to get further away. Presumably, she'll have a stronger effect on the compass than you, but if you're closer, you'll just interfere. No offense, Brett."

Brett shrugged. "I'd turn it off if I could, but I can't, so I'll hang back a bit." Once again, he hated to let go of Liz's hand now that they were together again, but he was feeling a bit better overall about the situation between them.

The two women studied him and then looked down at their compasses. Caroline swung hers in a slow, careful arc. "It twitched in this direction," she said, pointing slightly to the left.

Liz nodded. "Mine too, but it doesn't stay that way, just twitches when I pass that point."

Brett waited a dozen paces back from them, and hesitated for a few moments after they started to step away from him. He heard them speaking in low voices, pointing in different directions.

Then he saw something, a soft light visible through the surprising gloom of the narrow woods. He walked faster, pushing branches out of his way and trying not to trip, and caught up with the women.

"Hey! You're messing up the compasses!" said Caroline, her eyes narrowing in a glare, though the corners of her eyes told him she wasn't serious.

Liz stopped walking a second and studied him walking past. "You see something, don't you, *Chico?*"

Brett nodded. "Don't need a compass, something's up there. Guess I should have known you couldn't see it, too." He led the way now, the others putting away their compasses and crunching through the brush behind him.

They were reaching the dead heart of the median. Brett thought now that it must be wider than he first thought, as a hush fell and the dark of the woods went from twilight to night. Caroline's dimming flashlight beam played around his feet, helping him make his way through the denser and denser woods. He motioned for her to back off a step, so he didn't kill the flashlight's batteries. Living trees became fewer, while Brett began encountering more and more looming, skeletal trees. The black branches reached downwards, foreboding and sinister. He had to duck under some or clamber over others that had fallen in his path.

Then, he reached a small clearing. *Soccer Mom* would have filled most of the space. But no trees, alive or dead stood here, no vegetation of any sort. Just bare earth and some scattered stones in the shadowy space. Bowling ball sized fieldstones piled in a knee-high pyramid, right in the center. *A cairn?* It appeared lit as if by moonlight, even though Brett knew it was still late afternoon outside of the dim Haunted Forest.

He stood still a moment, and was joined by Caroline and Liz. They started to speak, but he held up a finger to his lips, and they fell silent.

Frannie crept out of the woods, and she held one hand aloft, seeming to pull a misty glowing figure with her. She held hands with a ghost. Brett noticed a faint milky aura around her. A shiver went through him. Why could he see her ghost, and this other one? It'd taken Frannie's touch to see otherworldly things before.

Frannie led the ghost to the cairn. It let go her hand and sat atop the stones. It was a thin figure, blurred and shifting so that Brett could not make out any features. Sometimes he thought he saw an eye, or movement of misty hair, but the figure was too faint.

Brett looked at Liz. She and Caroline looked at each other, not the figure on the rocks. Caroline glanced once at the cairn, seeming to follow Fran's gaze.

Brett turned back toward the ghost and drew breath to speak. "Hello?" he said, feeling awkward. This was not a threatening figure, but what do you say to a lost soul like this? He'd had practice doing sessions with a voice recorder, and he'd heard answers recorded, but that was hours or days later. This entity was right in front of him.

A thready, whispery, response wafted to his ears, like wind in the branches, and the figure gestured.

"I can't hear you, please speak louder?" asked Brett. The whispering continued and Brett felt frustrated.

He looked back at Liz, and she dug through her purse. She looked at him and held up her index finger to ask him to wait a moment. He did, and she came out with a hairbrush.

"Brett, here, take this," she murmured, pulling a strand of hair off of the brush and offering it to him. "I brushed Ashleigh's hair with it. If you're seeing the ghost of her brother, maybe you can make a better connection with something of hers in your possession."

He took the hair and looked at the ghost. It did look clearer. On an impulse, he made a loop of the hair and peered through the middle. The ghost came into focus, and he could make out the features of the older boy in the photograph.

"You must let go!" he heard the ghost cry. The voice was still faint and whispery, but clearer.

"Did it work?" asked Liz, but out of the corner of his eye, Brett saw Caroline put a hand on her arm to quiet her. Brett swallowed, his mouth dry. "Let go? Let go of what?"

"Let go! You must let go! Before! Let go before! You, she, and her! Let... go!" The whisper sounded like a faraway scream, and the figure gestured, pushing his hands toward Brett over and over in warning or banishment.

Brett shook his head, confused. "I don't understand. Let go of what? Before what? Let go how?"

"Let go before it's too late! Before she is lost. Find her, tell her, and warn her." The spirit's voice was pleading, and grew thinner and more distant, even as the glow began to fade. The loop of Ashleigh's hair didn't help anymore; the ghost's features dissolved into formless mist once more, sinking into the stones.

Frannie waved goodbye, then looked up at Brett. "I felt his presence a long way off. His brother too. His brother flagged us down. So lonely, it breaks my heart. He knew you'd been around his sister."

Everyone looked at Frannie. Caroline spoke. "Frannie, what did he want? What was he trying to tell Brett about letting go?"

Frannie shook her head in a slow sad arc from side to side, and Brett was surprised to find he missed her usual annoying, passionate babbling.

"He's been here too long, there's not much left of him. All he says is to let go and to warn her to let go too."

"Before it's too late," added Brett. Liz and Caroline looked at him. "He said that too. It wasn't a very helpful conversation."

Liz looked at Brett, and then hugged him to her fiercely. She felt very warm to the touch. Feverish. "I'm not letting go, Brett. We'll find a way to hold on."

He kissed her hot forehead and she shuddered. "What?" he asked.

"It's just, well...." Liz wouldn't meet his eyes.

"Cooling off?" offered Caroline, her voice gentle.

Liz did meet Brett's eyes now, and she nodded. It was dim here, but he could see the glimmer of a tear beginning. "Your lips are cold, *Chico*. I'm sorry."

Brett broke the embrace and stepped back. "Let's go. I don't want to be here anymore." He turned from Liz to look at Frannie, "Are you done here?"

Frannie looked back at the stones for a moment, then turned back and nodded. "Yeah. Sorry, Brett."

Brett saw Caroline study him and the others in turn, then she turned and led the way back towards the Interstate. Brett let everyone go ahead of him, following Frannie so she wouldn't wander off again.

They made their way back to the highway, and then followed it back toward where Brett and Fran had slid off the road. They followed the trail down to the Focus and Brett got inside and started it up. He put it in reverse and tried to back up. He saw the girls scatter out of the way in the rear view mirror, but the car didn't budge. He pressed down more and more on the accelerator, revving the engine. He heard the wheels spin without purchase. He saw a spray of mud come from the front wheels, splattering the weeds and brush in front of him.

"Stop, stop!" came Caroline's voice, rapping at the car window. Brett let off the pedal and the engine just idled. He rolled down the window and waited, looking at Liz's cheerful, bossy friend. "You're not getting anywhere, and it'll take more than us to get it out of that ditch. Let's just take my car. We'll think of something when we catch up with Ashleigh."

Brett sighed and nodded, not wanting to give up. Maybe being all in the same car would be better anyway. The accident and the ghost's warnings had him more shaken up than he wanted to let on. He grabbed his stuff out of the Focus, and helped Frannie find things she wanted to take with her as well, and they all trudged back up to the Interstate shoulder where the Saturn waited, hazard lights flashing at them.

Chapter 15 - Baby Don't You Wanna Go?

Back on the road, Brett found himself in the back seat to the left of Frannie. Liz sat up front chattering at Caroline, who was driving. He suspected Caroline of separating him from Liz for whatever reason she might have. The anger that'd cooled off after Liz had softened toward him flared back up inside him. He was sure it must show in his face, though he tried to keep it bottled up for the sake of keeping the peace.

Brett seethed in silence.

He stared out the window, watching the farmlands slide past, and he felt more and more like time was slowing down. The sun was bloody now, low in the west, coloring everything a furious shade of scarlet. It fit his mood.

He turned when he heard his name called. The smile Liz gave him was low wattage compared to her usual brilliance. He couldn't even fake a smile for her. She tilted her head to one side and mouthed "What?" He shook his head, but jutted his chin at her and then looked at Frannie, then back at her.

Her puzzled look was replaced by a sad smile, and she reached back toward him with a hand. He took it, feeling confused. Her hand was hot.

Liz glanced at the dozing Frannie, and whispered as low as she could to Brett, "Sweetie, we don't want to have an accident. And well...." She glanced at Frannie again.

Brett calmed a bit. Frannie was the problem, not him. Liz didn't want to avoid him because he was cold and seeing ghosts, and she didn't seem angry about the kiss in the bar. It wasn't about him. He let go of some of the anger, and found he'd hunched his shoulders with tension. He took a breath and let it out along with some of the ugly feelings.

"Sorry," he mouthed back at her.

"It's a small car, you two, and if you're going to whisper, I'm going to have to turn up the music!" Caroline chuckled at her own joke.

Liz's cheeks colored, but she laughed. "Just straightening out the seating chart for my man!"

"And we can hear Barry just fine already," muttered Brett, wondering if the song playing, "Can't Smile Without You," had anything to do with his previous mood.

He saw Caroline's evil eye in the rearview. "Hey!" she snapped. "Don't you say anything about my Barry! I can stop this car!" He had to grin at her. She stuck her tongue out at him and looked back at the road.

Brett was left to his thoughts for a while. He wondered what they'd find when they got to Chicago. Would Larry have already gotten to Richter? What would happen to Ashleigh? What could they do about it?

"I hope Gonzo's okay," said Liz to both Caroline and Brett. Brett felt like a selfish jerk, he hadn't even thought about Gonzo in all the confusion!

"Damn, I wish he had a cell phone. At least if he did, it wouldn't drain while he doesn't have one of us ghouls hanging around." Brett tried to keep his tone light, but the words sounded bitter to his ears.

Liz shot him a sharp look and snapped, "Don't say that! You're not there yet, Love."

Brett shrugged and glanced at sleeping Frannie and back to Liz. "Getting there. Hate to say it, but I could go for a really rare steak right about now."

Liz bit her lip and looked forward again, away from him. His heart sank. "Liz...,"

Liz didn't look back at him. Her voice shook a bit as she said, "Stop, Brett, just stop. This is hard enough. We've got to stay positive, we *will* find a cure!" She glanced at him over her shoulder, eyes damp, a shining tear track running down the cheek he could see. "We beat that demon, we can beat this. We have to."

"I'm sorry, Lizzie. I have to joke or I'll fall apart."

She nodded and sniffed, wiping at her cheeks with her sleeve. "I know."

Caroline's eyes fixed on him through the rearview, then looked over at Lizzie, and then she went back to singing along with Barry.

Brett jumped as the sudden loud sound of the Imperial March played from somewhere around his feet. After the initial startle, he recognized the "unknown caller" ringtone of his cell phone. It was tethered at the limits of his charger to the power plug in the front seat, lying on the floor.

He held the phone in his hand and answered, putting it on speaker. "Hello?"

"Do you have Prince Albert in the can?" Relief flooded through Brett as he heard Gonzo's voice.

"No, but my refrigerator is running," offered Brett in return.

Gonzo cackled over the phone. *"Goddamn, that was fun! That little goth fucker drove me all over the 'hood. Guys on the sidewalk were cheering me like I was Teen Wolf, surfing in the back of the pickup. I didn't even have to pound on his window or scream at him. I knew he couldn't just drive around with me standing up in back without getting pulled over eventually. And after vandalizing my van, there's no fucking way he could afford to talk to the cops."*

Brett had put Gonzo on speaker so that the others could hear. Liz clapped her hands, grinning with glee as she heard their missing friend's voice. "Gonz, Liz, Frannie and a friend are here, we're passing... Merrillville? I think. Where are you now?"

"Slow down, Junior, I'm getting there! So the kid pulls over and opens the sliding window between us. I crouched down and faced him and let him know he was in a lot of trouble, messing with Soccer Mom, and that I took it awfully personal. I might have used some more colorful words in there, and I might have suggested some things that might happen if he didn't cooperate. It was a standoff, he was stuck in the cab until we reached some kind of understanding, and without my own wheels, I had pretty much all the time in the world to wait him out."

"Oh Unca Gonzo, you didn't hurt the poor wittle goffic boy, did you? Goffic boys can be so pwetty!" Liz couldn't stop herself from giggling.

Over the phone, Brett heard Gonzo snort. *"Naw, I didn't have to. Goth Boy was already peeing his pants up there. He spilled like the Exxon Valdez, told me anything I wanted to know. Evidently our pal Larry made a call at some point before leaving Memphis, offering Goth Boy a reward if he could track us down in Bloomington and stop or at least delay us following him. He lied to Lizzie so she'd send us off on a tangent. The kid didn't get to Soccer Mom before we left, so he followed us all the way up to Crown Hill and flattened my tires. Fucker."*

"So, what happened, where are you, Gonz?"

"I'm getting to that! After I made him understand just how angry I was, and after finding out just how much Larry'd promised him to do the job, I suggested he could afford to fix his mistake. So here we are at Pop's Tire on 38th while my stems get replaced. Soccer Mom is up on jacks, and my new friend's going to help me replace the tires when we get back to Crown Hill with the wheels. He's paying, and in return, he gets to keep all his piercings. Probably."

Brett had to laugh in relief. "Damn, Gonzo, I was worried, but I guess you're okay, that's cool."

"Hey Gonzo!" cried Liz from up front. "Did you hear scientists are working on goth grass?"

"Yeah, yeah, I know that one, so it'll cut itself, very funny. Good to hear you. Come to your senses about that Larry character?"

"I knew he was a jerk when I went with him, Unca Gonzo." She didn't look at Brett then. "The picture pissed me off, but I went because I wanted to believe he knew someone who could help. Larry's an ass, but he's well connected."

"I gotta vouch for Brett, he was like a deer in headlights when that blue-bang girl slid up next to and kissed him. Shoulda known it was a setup, but we'd had a couple of beers, you know."

Liz snorted. "What's a 'few beers,' in Gonzo-speak, hmm? It's a wonder you guys found your apartment afterward."

"Hey, it was a few over a lot of hours!" Gonzo protested. His voice began to have a hiss of static rising louder and louder. *"I think I'm losing you guys. This kid's phone is pretty cheap."*

Brett shook his head, "No Gonz, it's probably interference from me and Frannie, like I was talking about earlier. We got a couple of clues. Also, we had a strange warning." Brett worried that the phone might cut out at any moment. "You wouldn't believe the source. But we're told to 'let go' and we have to tell Ashleigh that too. If you think of anything, get back in touch, okay?"

"Roger that. Hopefully I'll have the van back on the road soon enough, but I'll use up some more of Goth Boy's minutes and tell Jimbo what you said. Gotta go for now, looks like Pop is done with my wheels!"

"Hey wait a sec, Gonz. Where are you going when you get *Soccer Mom* back up and running? We know where the little ghoul is going to be, up at a conference at the Embassy Suites by the lake. Larry's got her still and we're pretty sure his plan all along was to cash in on her."

"You guys are headed to Chicago? I'll be damned if I drive all this way without having some ribs at The Boneyard up in Chi-town! I'll catch up with you tonight sometime. I'll find you. Later!" Gonzo hung up.

Brett hung up his end. The phone was down to one bar of battery, even plugged into the charger. He shook his head, wondering what they'd do for a phone away from the car if it drained that fast near Frannie and himself. He leaned down and put it on the floor, as far from him as he could reach.

When he looked up, Caroline steered the car onto an exit to a different Interstate, heading toward the deep red sun. He had to shift in his seat so her seat shaded him.

Liz peered back at him, "How are you, *Chico*?"

He hated to see the concern on her face. He needed her to be herself, bouncy and carefree, not worrying about him. "I'm okay, Sweetie. We need to put our heads together though. What did the ghost mean by 'let go'? Is he talking about letting go of the material world and passing on? Or is it something else?"

Liz bit her lip and looked away a second. He knew he'd said the wrong thing again. But he could feel time slipping past and as time went on, he knew he was moving further toward being like Frannie, as Frannie became more like Ashleigh. He couldn't ignore the problem and hope it'd go away, and he needed her help. Even if it wasn't comfortable.

She looked back at him. "I just don't know, *Chico*. If that's what he means, it means I'm going to lose you, so I have to think it must mean something else. We have to believe that and hold on."

"But holding on... that's just what he's saying not to do, Lizzie. Not like I know how to 'let go' even if I wanted to."

Caroline chimed in, "Maybe it's something more specific than letting go of life, of your body, maybe it's something else."

"Like what?" asked Liz, turning toward her friend.

Brett could see Caroline's hair move as she shook her head, red light spilling through as she did it. "That's just what we have to find out. I bet Ashleigh might know more of what her brother means. That's just a guess, but I trust my hunches."

Brett caught her studying him in the rearview mirror, and he met her gaze and nodded. They exchanged a brief smile. Caroline's confidence was contagious, and it made him feel more optimistic.

The sun touched the horizon ahead of them, and at that moment, Frannie woke up. She turned and seemed confused as she looked at Brett. But then she looked around her and took a breath and sighed.

"Where are we? Where's my car?" asked Fran.

"You don't remember going off the road? You wandered into the Haunted Forest in the median? The ghost you led by the hand to talk to me?"

Frannie blinked. "Oh. I thought that was a dream. It didn't seem real.... So my car's still back there?"

Brett nodded. "Yeah, sorry, it was stuck. We'll go back for it later, but it'll probably take a tow truck to pull it out of the ditch where we ended up."

Frannie nodded. She seemed more coherent to Brett than she had all day. Maybe sleep had done her good?

Maybe it's because night's coming. I'm feeling more energetic, too. "Anyway," said Brett, "we're not too far from Chicago now. We're after Ashleigh."

"Ashleigh?" asked Frannie. He realized he'd never filled her in, since she'd been so lethargic all day.

"Yeah. She's like you. And me. She's losing herself. Only she's lost a lot more than you or me, she's gone feral and wild."

Frannie's face scrunched up and she wiped at the tears that came to her. "What's she... what's she become, Brett?"

Brett thought once more of the image on the memory card in his phone, but knew better than to show it to Frannie. He tried to think of what to say that wouldn't panic the younger woman.

"She's still human, Frannie," said Liz, turning around in her seat again. "She's just a lot further along than you and... and Brett. She's in there somewhere. Or rather, like you and Brett, some of her is outside of her body. Most of her is outside of her body. Her body keeps on, but...." Liz trailed off, looking at Brett.

Still human?

Brett didn't agree with Liz. Ashleigh's humanity lived outside her body. A flash of the two Frannies came to mind. He filled his lungs with air and let it out in a gust, just to feel alive.

"But we need to help her before it's too late, so we can help you and Brett," said Caroline in a firm tone that wasn't open for debate.

Frannie looked from one person to another, then made long, uncomfortable eye contact with him. "What do we need to do?"

Brett answered before Caroline could. "Well, the first step is finding Ashleigh." He tried to sound as decisive and confident as Caroline, and he thought he did a good job, since Frannie nodded and relaxed, and when he looked at Liz, she smiled at him.

He wished he felt as confident as he sounded.

Chapter 16 - The Hunger

The Chicago skyline loomed up before them, set against incandescent shades of orange, red, and on into mysterious purple. Something inside Brett was grateful they'd arrived in the city before dark. The Richter talk started at 8, so they only had a couple more hours to catch Larry.

The Saturn wove in and out of traffic, as Caroline took opportunities to get ahead of the already bewildering traffic heading into Chicago. Brett was surprised at the sheer volume of cars at this time of the evening. He would have said something about her aggressive driving, since it wasn't helping the anxiety he was already trying to hold down, but he also felt the pressure to hurry.

After some more twists and turns on the highway, he recognized that they'd ended up on Lake Shore Drive. Lake Michigan appeared to be on fire, as the spectacular sunset glinted off of the rippling waves, stretching out toward the horizon. Liz pulled out a camera and made delighted noises from the front seat as she snapped pictures of the scene. Brett smiled and watched her, happy to see her being herself again for a moment.

Caroline pulled the Saturn into the underground parking lot for the Embassy Suites. Brett saw a sign that said, "Parking Validation Available for Chicago Ghost Convention parking at Ballroom Entry." Caroline rolled down her window and took a ticket from a machine. Looking at the rates, he couldn't imagine what the entry fee must be in order to cover the outrageous parking.

Caroline pulled the car into a spot after circling around awhile. Brett spied many obvious convention-goer vehicles, Ghostbusters emblems and "Got Ghosts?" bumper stickers along with large magnetic paranormal club logos on car doors. He'd heard of the convention before, but had never attended. Brett preferred to work as an independent of the paranormal clubs and didn't often go to gatherings like this.

Larry, on the other hand, had connections in all the organizations that he could. Since his motivation was profit, it made sense for Larry to make a lot of contacts. Socializing made Brett uncomfortable, and he was more interested in the scientific aspects of the paranormal world than the social side of things.

It occurred to him that this place was Larry's turf. He'd be pretty well known here, while Brett would be virtually unknown, except for those who had seen his posts on Internet ghost forums.

Brett would be at a disadvantage. Except... "Caroline, have you ever been to Chicago Ghost Convention before?" He was pretty sure she'd said otherwise, but there was always the chance.

"Nope! But my group's hosted a convention down in Indy once or twice. I was the organizer for the last one. Wow, it was a lot of work, but meeting people from all around sure made it worth it. It was great publicity, and we had some amazing guests. I don't think we would have had Richter though... He charges too much, I hear. And we like skeptics to a point, but people like Richter are only out to discredit us, not work with us to find the truth. We ready?" Caroline opened her door without waiting for an answer and hopped out of the car.

The rest followed suit, though Frannie was still a bit slower than anyone else. Brett watched her as he shut his door. She seemed much more energetic, but still unfocused and distant. Liz slipped behind him and put her arms around his middle, feeling so very warm and strong to him as she did. Caroline led them away as she locked the car with her key remote, not glancing back.

They found an escalator and rode it up into the hotel. The place was huge. Brett saw a large central court, surrounded on all four sides by hotel open corridors; dozens of floors stretched far above them to a skylight roof. Glass elevators crawled up and down, filled with people wearing jeans and black T-shirts.

This was a bigger convention than he'd pictured. There must have been many hundreds of attendees, several times what he'd seen elsewhere. It was no wonder they could afford Richter. If Larry and Ashleigh were anywhere, that's where they'd be.

But where?

The four friends walked across the vast court area, weaving around tables full of paranormal enthusiasts. Brett saw that they were eating fast food or boxed meals from the hotel. The smell made Brett's stomach cry out for *meat.*

"I'm hungry," announced Frannie. Brett felt it too. The scent of burgers, chicken tenders, and even pulled pork barbecue made his mouth water.

Frannie started to grab at a sandwich in a woman's hand, but Caroline caught her. Frannie whined like a thwarted child. The woman glared at Frannie, but didn't say anything.

"You know," said Liz, getting on the other side of Frannie as her younger friend's eyes hunted for other nearby meat within reach, "I'm a little hungry too. We don't have our bearings yet, so maybe we should sit down a moment."

Brett warred within him. On the one hand, he felt the urgency of finding Larry and Ashleigh as a matter of survival. On the other, he was going out of his mind with hunger, and worried he might not be able to stop himself from grabbing up and gobbling handfuls of the bourbon chicken on a plate that was unattended for a moment, just a few feet away. It was an overwhelming feeling. Not just hunger, but also lust.

Liz took his hand in one of hers, and pulled his chin toward her so that he looked at her. She studied him. "Yeah, let's get something to eat."

"Gotcha. Let's go." Caroline steered Frannie toward one of the few empty tables. It still had some trays and cups on it. Frannie grabbed at a sandwich wrapper that looked like it'd held a sloppy joe or barbecue on a bun and licked it greedily.

"Oh dear," said Caroline, looking around. "You all sit here and I'll get us something to eat right away." Without waiting for a reply, she made a beeline for the row of fast food places along one wall beyond the overhang of upper floors of the hotel.

Brett was embarrassed, but jealous, as Frannie moved on to picking shreds of meat from a half-eaten sub sandwich. The urgency of his need to eat overwhelmed him, and he couldn't think of anything else.

"So, uh, I guess we all missed lunch?" said Liz. He looked up at her and nodded. "Yeah. Gotta eat. Sorry." Brett winced at how rough and curt his reply was. He just had to focus and not let this hunger overwhelm him.

Out of scraps, Frannie looked around, her eyes wild, her mouth open, sniffing at the air. She stood up, and Brett forgot and grabbed her by the wrist to stop her.

The murmuring roar of a hundred tables of people talking among themselves muted to near silence, only nearby sounds reaching him unmuffled. The artificial lights in the room went from bright fluorescent to dim flickering candlelight. The vast space seemed to close in on him and his two friends.

A luminous version of Frannie stood beside herself, hands clasped in front of her, sad eyes fixed on her more solid form. She glanced up at Brett, and he found he was not quite where he had been, standing behind someone. Standing behind a chair that held his body, which was hanging onto Frannie. He saw Liz move in what seemed like slow motion, as she rose from her seat and reached out to both of the others at the table.

Brett saw a bright, pulsing, silvery cord that connected his neck to his body's neck, reminding him of an umbilical cord. He peered around into the gloom and thought he caught glimpses of other misty figures. Except it seemed to him that the misty figures were more solid and real than the shadowy bodies sitting at the tables near him.

Far off, he heard a scream. It was Ashleigh, and she sounded frightened and lost. He could almost make out where....

Liz broke the contact between Brett and Frannie. Brett cried out as the light and noise of the hotel flooded his senses. Frannie cringed as well, and toppled back into her chair, dazed.

"Don't do that, *Chico*. Don't touch her. I don't know what you see when you do, but I know you're not in there anymore and it scares the shit out of me. Okay?"

Brett broke out of his gaze enough to see the look on Liz's face and he was sure he'd never seen her that dead serious before in all the time he'd known her. He remembered to breathe, and his heart thumped in his ears, and he closed his eyes for a long moment.

He nodded to her. "Believe me, I won't, not on purpose."

"Chicken!" Caroline plunked a big bucket of fried chicken on the table and handed another bag to Liz and stepped back.

It was all Brett could do to keep from diving for the bucket. He still reached out and plucked a crispy, meaty breast from the bucket as Fran snatched it from the middle of the table and feasted on the chicken.

Brett was sure fast food chicken had never tasted this good. He tried not to wolf the meat down, in an attempt to exercise control over himself. Something primal in him wanted to grab the bucket from Frannie so he could take more meat. More for him. She ate and ate, bones cracking and breading falling all around her, grease making her hands and face shiny.

He took another piece of chicken. Frannie *growled* at him. Inside, he felt anger rise again, but he pushed it down, Frannie's display giving him more than enough reason to fear letting his emotions take over.

After the chicken was gone, he looked up to see Liz and Caroline halfway through chicken sandwiches and waffle fries, eating in silence and watching the feasting in front of them. Caroline seemed withdrawn and distant. Liz failed to disguise a look of horror on her face.

Brett realized he'd eaten more chicken than he would have thought possible. The bones were picked clean in front of him. He reached for some napkins and began cleaning himself up.

Frannie cried into her hands next to him. Liz stood and helped her clean up the grease all over her face and hands and shirt. She said soothing things, and Liz seemed to shift from frightened to pitying as she helped.

Just then, Brett spied a leather cowboy hat bobbing through the crowd. He sat up and moved his head from side to side to see around people.

It was Larry.

Brett stood up and stalked across the court toward him. Larry had a smirk on his face as he talked to someone Brett didn't see. Fury rose up inside him. The closer he got to the man, the hotter the anger burned inside him. Larry didn't see him, so to get his attention… Brett knocked the hat off of the jerk's head.

Larry whirled. The snarl on his face fled as he met Brett's eyes. Larry backed up, hands held up in front of him. Some small part of Brett cheered. He'd never scared anyone like this before, especially not someone as tall and cocky as Larry Fisher. He kind of liked the feeling. Somewhere deep down, he wondered what Larry saw when he looked at him, though.

"Larry, you asshole! Where is she?" Brett felt the blood pounding through his body, every nerve burning with hot anger. He was on fire, and he wanted Larry to burn to a cinder before him. He realized he had his hands clenched into tight fists at his sides.

Larry didn't speak, but instead he turned and ran, crashing into a busboy as he did, knocking trays and trash everywhere. Brett howled and pounded after him, not able to think of anything, just seeing red and trying not to fall on the debris scattered in his path.

He thought he heard noises behind him, voices he should recognize, calling his name. He stumbled and ran, dodged and screamed as he pursued Larry through the crowded court. He had him on the run and it made him feel good. He'd feel better when he caught up and made Larry pay for kidnapping Ashleigh. For fooling Liz. For pissing him off.

A wall rushed up from one side and slammed into him, hard. Brett hit the floor and saw flashes of light in his eyes and his ears rang. He found himself flailing on the marble tiles of the court, scrabbling to get up, but was pinned down by a much larger man.

"Security!" he heard a man yell in his ear. He had an impression of a buzz cut and a blue blazer and tie with a gold name badge. "Stop where you are!" As if he could have gone anywhere with a uniformed gorilla sitting on him.

Brett saw Larry disappear into the crowd, lost to him.

Chapter 17 - Friends in Low Places

"He's not himself right now. Officer. Er. Sir." Liz pleaded with the burly hotel security goon as he dragged Brett to his feet. The big guy's face had no expression as he grabbed Brett's elbow and put his face inches from his own.

"Listen to me. I don't care if you're not yourself, I don't care who you normally are. You both have to leave this hotel and not come back. Do you understand me?" The lack of emotion in his voice snapped Brett back from rage to a touch of fear. This guy was a professional who maybe didn't see a lot of the kind of action he signed on for. Brett didn't want to be today's entertainment. He nodded. He glanced in the direction that Larry had gone, but sighed and let the man lead him to the lobby, and show him the door. Liz followed along, looking back over her shoulder.

Out in the entryway, cars lined up, blinkers flashing away as luggage was loaded or unloaded and people departed or arrived. There were uniformed porters with gold piping on their blue blazers, caps on their heads and a shine on their shoes. The security tough went up to the porters and pointed at Brett and Liz. Brett guessed they porters were being told not to let them back into the hotel They were sunk. There was no way they'd get in to confront Larry at Richter's talk in less than an hour.

Then he noticed the vampires.

Brett could tell they were vampires by the way they dressed. Top hats on men and women, anachronistic formal wear, torn black clothing, and lots of dyed black hair and silver jewelry. These were live action roleplayers, also known as LARPers. They pretended to be vampires as part of an ongoing game, where they stayed in character for hours or days at a time.

Liz shivered, wearing only jeans and deep-green tunic cable-knit sweater in the early March evening air. It had to be below freezing, but he didn't feel it at all. It felt good, he felt a sort of relief from the hot stuffy air inside the hotel. *I'm cooling down.*

He took off the sweatshirt he wore and handed it to Liz.

She stared at him, standing there in his green Jameson T-shirt and black jeans. "Aren't you cold?" she asked.

He just shook his head, not wanting to talk about it. She pulled the sweatshirt over her sweater and hugged herself against the chill.

"What happened to Frannie and Caroline?" Brett asked Liz.

She raised her hands, palms up. "Caroline told me to go after you, and said she'd take care of Frannie, and that we'd catch up later."

Brett started to answer, but was interrupted. "Babette!" came a cry from across the entryway. Both Brett and Liz looked over to the group of vampires, where one short, pudgy guy in a cape and a vest grinned and waved like a muppet. A tall, skinny girl on his arm hid her face with one hand, looking like she would rather be anywhere else right now.

Brett groaned. Not another webcam fan. This happened more often than he liked. Liz returned the guy's grin and waved the same silly wave back at him.

The vampire dragged his embarrassed girlfriend over to them. He stumbled once and Brett could smell bourbon on his breath. "Hey! You're Raoul, aren't you?"

Brett sighed, nodded and forced a smile.

Liz shook his hand and gave him a half hug. "Hello!" Liz had never met a stranger. "Who are you two?" she asked.

The pudgy guy actually blushed and scuffed his feet. His girlfriend looked up, swaying into him and said, "He's Stuart, I'm Skye." She still seemed to want to be elsewhere, but Liz's warm charm could be hard to resist.

"Skye? What a great name! How do you spell it? With an e?"

Skye nodded. "Right. Not two y's like the vodka." She giggled.

Liz laughed.

Brett had to keep his eyes from rolling, and said, "Are you two here for the Con?"

Skye shook her head, making her long, brownish hair fall from behind her ears and into her face. "No. Well, Stu is, but I'm not. I'm just into the vampire stuff going on around here, you know?" She slurred her words just enough that Brett thought the extra y might be more appropriate.

Liz grinned. "That's awesome! So, what's going on, is there a live action roleplaying event being run parallel with the Con?"

Stuart found his voice. "Yeah, some of us are attendees, so the local club decided to run an adventure in and around the hotel." He glanced over at the porters. "The hotel's not too thrilled with us, we keep getting told to leave if we don't have a room key."

"But it's totally not a requirement to have a room to attend ChicaGhoCon," said Skye, raising a finger to make a point. "Anyone can be here, and you only have to pay admission to get into the ballroom. We can wander the main floor as much as we want!"

Liz nodded as Skye talked. "That makes sense. So you're viewers?"

Skye made a face. "He watches you, I don't. I mean, like, not like I have anything personally against you. Either of you. It's just kind of, I don't know, weird."

Stuart glared at his girlfriend.

Liz smiled and laughed. "It's totally weird," she said. "I let people watch a piece of my life. I mean, how is that normal?"

Skye lowered her eyes and nodded. "Yeah, I know what it's like to be outside of normal. I mean, why would I be dressing up like a vampire on a Saturday night out on a beach?"

"Beach?" asked Brett despite himself. He kind of wanted these two to go away so they could figure out how to get back into the hotel and stop Larry from making Ashleigh into a spectacle. If that happened, they might not find out what her brother meant by letting go and he'd continue to lose himself.

"Yeah, like, the game moves from here to some park that borders on a beach on the lake in about an hour. There's supposed to be a bonfire and stuff," Skye explained.

Liz nodded, listening, then replied, "We just got kicked out too, and we really need to see the Richter talk."

Stuart snorted. "Righteous Richter? What a fraud! That guy wouldn't believe the sky is blue if someone showed it to him. He's got the big prize for proof, but the rules are set so that only he can determine the criteria for proof. If it was my money, I wouldn't believe anything, either, you know?"

Brett nodded. He was a skeptical sort, but Richter gave skeptics a bad name in the same kind of way that Larry Fisher gave paranormal enthusiasts a bad name. The guy was in it for the fame and the money, not to determine what was real and what was fake.

"Hey! You two were kicked out? I know someone who can help you get back in." Stuart swayed as he said this, and Brett had his doubts.

Liz seemed interested. "Oh, we really do need to get back in, but security's going to be looking for us."

Stuart and Skye looked at each other and smiled. "Leslie!" they both said at once. Skye's smile transformed her from mousy to pretty. It was fleeting, and she faded back to unremarkable as soon as the smile was gone. She needed to smile more.

Stuart motioned for them to follow him, and led his girlfriend down the sidewalk, away from the hotel. Brett looked at Liz, following her lead. She shrugged and took his hand and followed her new friends, lacking any better options.

They made their way to a parking lot, which was lit by a dimly stuttering sodium lamppost. Brett had serious doubts about this, and was about to say so when the side of a van slid open and Stuart and Skye cried in unison, "Leslie!"

Leslie turned out to be one of the biggest, hairiest men Brett had ever seen. He had a thick curly beard and tangled hair that fell to the middle of his broad back. Liz leaned over and whispered in his ear, "Oh my goddess, it's Hagrid!" Brett had to agree with her.

Leslie sat at a small table inside the van, which was lit by a dome light. He appeared to be painting Vulcan eyebrows on a pale college-aged girl who was wearing a flowing black lace dress.

The van was full of costumes and masks and props of all sorts.

This was clearly a man who knew theater. He himself wore a leather biker jacket that made Brett think of Gonzo. He had about half a dozen silver earrings lining his left ear, and a tattoo of the comedy/tragedy masks of theater on his neck.

Leslie turned and looked at Stuart. "More noobs?" he asked in a rumbling voice full of gravel.

Stuart nodded. "They need to have the full treatment. They want to really look like new people."

Leslie looked them over and nodded. "Moment." He finished painting the eyebrows on the young lady. She looked in a mirror and pouted a bit. He supplied a tube of lipstick, and she applied it. It was a shade Liz had referred to as "slut red," and Brett had to admit that the color was a nice contrast to the black monochrome of the rest of her outfit. She smiled and hugged Leslie and swept off into the night without even a glance at the others.

Liz let go of Brett's hand and stepped up. Leslie looked her over with a critical eye and rummaged around in the van until he came up with a few articles of clothing. He handed her black fingerless gloves, a tattered black shawl and a long, tight-curled blond wig. She put these on, and he opened a fishing tackle box and began applying makeup to her.

When Leslie was done, Liz had the face of a china doll, the palest white with vivid red lipstick and blush, arched eyebrows and a false beauty spot on one side of her chin. Brett thought this would be good enough to get her past security.

Liz beckoned to him, and Brett hesitated only a moment. He didn't want to be made up to look ridiculous, but he had to get back into the hotel soon. He stepped into the van and sat across from Leslie.

The hairy man studied him a long, uncomfortable moment. He grabbed a plastic cone, similar to what dogs wore after surgery, and had Brett put it on his head. Skye giggled somewhere in the darkness outside of the van. Leslie stood and shook a can, and Brett heard him spray painting his hair within the cone. Leslie had him take off the cone and wiped at his hairline with a towel to get rid of extra paint. Brett glanced in the mirror and saw that his hair was now raven black, at least on the surface. Leslie put on gloves and rubbed the temporary color into his hair, making him feel even more uncomfortable.

Leslie then pulled out what looked like paisley pantyhose, and had Brett put his arms through the opening on one end of each of two filmy nylon tubes. They turned out to be false sleeve tattoos, intricate patterns now covering his arms from his wrists up into the sleeves of his T-shirt.

At last, Leslie pulled out another tube of lipstick and started dabbing it onto Brett's lips. Brett became more uncomfortable by the minute with this whole thing. When he looked in the mirror, he saw black lipstick, dramatic enough with the black hair color and tattoo sleeves that he didn't recognize himself. Leslie clipped on a few earrings on one ear and grunted to declare him done. "Bring the stuff back after the bonfire or give it to Stu to give to me next month, okay?"

Brett nodded, impressed by the rapid transformation. He stood up and stepped out of the van. Liz clapped her hands and hugged him. "Oh, my Raoul, if I'd known you looked this good as an emo boy, I'd have put you in lipstick years ago!"

Brett rolled his eyes. "Thanks, you guys. Hopefully this will get us back inside for the talk."

"Why do you want to hear that crap anyway?" asked Stuart.

Brett looked at Liz, unsure of what to say. She answered Stuart for him, "Someone we know has some pretty damned good proof of the paranormal being real, and we've got to be there when he unveils it. You could say we have a lot riding on it."

Skye put a hand on Liz's shoulder, a warm smile touching her lips. "Good luck, Babette. You're pretty awesome, I'm sorry I was a bitch before."

Liz smiled a cheery smile at Skye and patted her hand. "It's okay. Like I said, the webcam thing is pretty weird, but I meet some of the coolest people because of it." Skye lowered her eyes, and even in the darkness, Brett could tell she was blushing.

They left Stuart and Skye, and made their way back to the Embassy Suites. Liz slipped her arm inside of his, and he felt a bit warmer inside. As they walked up that way, he noticed that the other vampires were no longer clustered around the entrance.

The porters didn't give them a second look as they walked past and into the hotel. They took an escalator up, following signs to the Ballroom. Brett saw that there was a crowd gathering around the entrance, filing in one at a time. It was getting close to the Richter talk.

They came up to the ticket table, and the tired volunteers just glanced at them and waved them on. It was so close to the end of the convention, this being the last scheduled event of the night, that Brett guessed that they were no longer selling tickets and were more interested in a big turnout and closing down afterwards.

There wasn't an empty seat to be seen, and all the people entering the ballroom just lined the walls, standing up. They'd gotten there none too soon, as he heard people protesting as the line was cut off, and he overheard something being said about fire codes.

There had to be at least five hundred paranormal enthusiasts in the room, maybe more. Some wore black T-shirts, others wore gowns and ties and other formal wear. There were a handful of the vampire LARPers there and there.

Up at the front sat Richter, all by himself. Brett recognized the balding, hawk-nosed man from the book jackets he'd seen in stores, and from television talk shows. He had his arms crossed in front of him, a defiant and confident look on his face. He wore a black silk shirt and a brilliant red tie.

An MC introduced Richter and the room was filled with scattered applause, cheers, and boos. Richter was a controversial figure. He thanked the crowd, despite the booing, and invited members of the audience to step up to a standing microphone and challenge him.

Several did, bringing photographic evidence and audio recordings of various sorts. Richter always explained the evidence away as false positives, electronic malfunctions or outright fakes. One man was so upset with Richter's response that he had to be escorted away by a security guard. Brett was relieved that it was not the same guard that had shown him the door earlier.

Then the doors at the back of the room burst open and Larry wheeled something in. It looked like a luggage cart with a clothing rack with a bedspread draped over it. A woman with blue bangs aided him. Shell. Brett was surprised to see her here.

They wheeled the cart up near the microphone and Liz started toward him, but Brett held her back. He had a funny feeling about this.

"Richter, prepare to be amazed!" proclaimed Larry. "I bring you the undead, a living dead girl!"

He motioned for Shell to pull off the bedspread. The whole room held their breath, watching as the cart was revealed. Even Richter looked interested, for the first time that night.

It was empty, except for tatters of duct tape around the brass poles of the cart.

Ashleigh was gone.

Chapter 18 - Dust My Broom

The crowd erupted in jeers and laughter, some taking to their feet. Larry turned bright red and glared at Shell. The girl with the blue bangs showed the palms of her hands and replied with something Brett couldn't hear over the noise.

At the front of the room, Righteous Richter stood up, peering at the empty luggage cart mildly. He started to speak and the crowd quieted down so they could hear. "...congratulate you, Mr. Fisher, on your capture of an invisible person at long last! Or is it perhaps an invisible Bigfoot?" He allowed himself a dry laugh, then his face hardened. "Why do you waste my time... *everyone's* time like this?"

Larry sputtered. "I had the ghoul here, out in the hall, but it escaped." He looked at Shell once more and she still just looked baffled.

The crowd murmured, some still laughing, some peering at the exits. Brett couldn't help but feel some glee at Larry's embarrassment, and he was thrilled that Ashleigh had gotten away. He turned to grin at Liz, but she too was gone.

He stood up and looked around for her, and spotted her curly blonde wig bobbing up the aisle between seats, marching right up to Larry, unnoticed so far. He started after her, hoping to stop her before she did anything rash.

Liz didn't approach Larry after all. She walked right up to Shell and slapped her face. Shell's eyes grew wide, and she fled the room through the door where she'd brought the cart. Liz turned on her heel, and Brett saw dark lines of her makeup running. She was crying, and from her expression, they were tears of anger.

The room burst into chaos. People were on their feet, going for exits or rushing up towards Larry and Richter or just standing and shouting to be heard over the din. Liz reached Brett and grabbed his hand and towed him toward the door, ahead of the crowd.

Her hot hand gripped his, steering him. They made it out into the hall as other people started flooding around them. Liz pulled him along, not looking back, not looking at him, down the hall to the escalator. They were swept down toward the main floor, where they were greeted by shouts and screams. Liz pulled him on, running down the steps to hurry their progress.

Several blue-blazered security personnel flashed past the bottom of the escalator as they reached bottom, and they almost collided with the same goon that had ejected them earlier. He didn't even look at them.

Liz pulled Brett along in the guards' wake, and he couldn't see what was ahead, but he hoped it was Ashleigh. He didn't see how they'd catch up with her before the guards. Liz made a serious effort, however, and her fingernails bit into the back of his hand as she tightened her grip and urged him forward.

The doors burst open ahead of them and the bluecoats stopped right outside, blocking that exit. Liz dodged around them, shoved the revolving door, pulled Brett in with her, and the door turned on its axis to let them outside.

Brett couldn't see Ashleigh anywhere. The blue blazers chattered among themselves, with amazement on their faces. Brett overheard one say, "Damn, did you see that thing eat? It was disgusting!" Liz let go of Brett's hand and walked right up to them, demanding, "Where did she go?" Her tone was shrill.

The goon from before looked at her and frowned, but pointed toward Lake Shore Drive. "What's it to you, lady? Are you the mom?"

Liz didn't waste any more time on him, but pounded off down the sidewalk, boots making a rapid tattoo of clacking as she did. Brett had to take off at a run to try to catch up with her. They pelted down the sidewalk and reached an intersection.

Liz stopped and looked both ways and looked back at him in despair. "Can you do anything? We're losing her, Brett, and she's going to get hurt or caught if we don't find her!"

Brett's stomach knotted in fear, mind whirling with confusion. *Let go*, came the voice of the ghost of the Haunted Forest, surprising Brett enough that he looked around to see where it came from. Liz looked at him, bouncing up and down in place in panic, eyes fixed on him.

Then an idea came to him. He wished Frannie were here, since that would have been easier. But he closed his eyes, took a deep breath, and said to Liz, "Catch me if I fall, Sweetie?"

He reached out with his feelings to find the part of him that was outside of his body. Nothing happened at first. He just felt more and more rage at the whole situation. At Larry's greed. At the unfairness of losing himself like this. He felt the fear he'd felt when he thought he was losing Liz.

He felt dizzy and disoriented, losing his grip on his material self. Falling, falling.... He started to try to hang on, but he remembered at the last to let go.

The world changed around him. His eyes were still closed, but he could see. The lights from the buildings dimmed and blurred together. The roads became solid tubes of light and crackled with energy. It was otherwise dark.

He saw Liz holding up his body next to him. She was crying his name, but the sound was distorted and distant, and he felt as though he was watching videotape, rather than something happening in front of him, happening to him.

He spread his fingers and arms out wide and reached out with his senses. It was difficult over the roar of the street energies, but he picked out the terror and hunger of Ashleigh, like a flicker of light and sound at the edge of his perception, and he noted the direction. She was already over a block away from where they stood, crossing under Lake Shore Drive.

He reached back toward his body, and for a panicked moment, he thought he couldn't go back. But he grabbed ahold of the silver cord and pulled and felt a tug. He pulled harder and merged with his body with a wrenching sensation.

He gasped for air, and found himself supported by Liz, though she was wobbling a bit. She was crying and saying his name. "Brett, come back to me, come back!"

He kissed her cheek, leaving a black impression where his painted lips touched the white makeup on her face. She turned her head and kissed him with a fierce, urgent intensity. He felt strength flooding back into him and he gained his feet on his own. He didn't break the kiss until she was hung on him instead of the other way around.

When they parted, she came down off of her toes and he gasped for breath. He pointed. "That way. Under the highway."

They dashed under the overpass and Brett lagged as he struggled to regain feeling in all his limbs. His heart and lungs struggled to catch up.

"Don't make me carry you!" cried Liz, but she panted even as she said it, and they had to slow down in the dark under the highway.

A pair of shadowy figures jumped up in the dark ahead of them, arms out to grab onto them. Liz shrieked, unable to stop, and she and Brett crashed into the other figures. Arms closed around him, and Brett stumbled as he and his assailant crashed to the broken sidewalk below. He heard another muffled thump nearby.

"Ow, ow, ow, stop, it's me, cut it out!" It was Stuart's voice, punctuated by what sounded like meaty thumps.... Liz punched and kicked him as they lay tangled on the ground. Meanwhile, Brett realized the skinny form of Skye was clutching him hard. She smelled of gin as she giggled in his ear. He tried to free himself, but found the wind knocked out of him. She nibbled on his earlobe and breathed, "Looks like I've caught me a vampire victim. I'm like, the vampire, and you're gonna be my thrall now. That'll be delicious, won't it?" Brett felt chills, and a thrill of pleasure, from her drunken pass at him. But the girl could barely be twenty-one, making him half again her age.

Brett gasped, wondering if he'd ever breathe right again. Liz wouldn't be pleased at yet another woman making advances on him. He wasn't sure if it was for his sake or Skye's, but he struggled harder to free himself from the girl. He managed to squirm out of her embrace, but she clung to his leg as he pushed himself up. She made a sad, whiny noise, but slid a warm, long-fingered hand up along his leg to grab his bottom. Giggling, she squeezed and Brett jumped, trying to shake her off.

Meanwhile, Liz stopped her pummeling of Stuart and was murmuring apologies, and he could see their outlines rise, helping each other up. "What are you two doing here?" he asked, reaching a hand down to pull Skye off of the ground. She clung to his arm, pulling the sheer, false tattoo sleeve off of him as she did. She needed the support, swaying on her feet. She readjusted her stance, and Brett let out a yelp as a spiked heel stabbed into the top of his sneaker. Skye pulled away and landed on her rear on the ground with a squeak. Brett considered leaving her there this time.

Stuart stepped over and lifted Skye off the ground and set her on her feet, holding her by both shoulders. She giggled.

Stuart said, "We could ask you the same thing. We were heading to the beach for the bonfire. We were just about run over by a wild dog or something a couple of minutes ago, and now you two." He laughed a bit more than his joke was worth.

"We're sorry, but we have to run after that.... It'd take too long to explain. We'll look for you at the beach," said Brett, taking Liz's hand and starting off again.

He heard Skye giggle and say, "I'll get you yet my little thrall, you can't escape!" and he heard Stuart shushing her. He called after them, "See you later!"

Brett and Liz ran on, and a large, tree-filled park appeared ahead on one side. Paths cut through it, with signs indicating the beach. They looked at each other, and picked a likely path into the park.

"Where do you think she's going?" asked Liz.

"I'm really not sure. She's probably just running away, scared by the guards and noise in the hotel."

"Not to mention," Liz added, "being duct taped to that rack, held prisoner. Larry's such a bastard!" They moved into a darker part of the park, the path lit by small mushroom lights at their feet.

They stopped at a Y in the path and Liz looked at Brett. "Can you feel her, Brett? I don't really want you to do go dead on me again.... I died a little myself when you stopped breathing."

Brett wasn't sure he wanted to do that again himself. He shook his head and shrugged. "I can try."

He closed his eyes and tried to see or hear from within. It was quieter here away from the roads, and the direction they traveled was quieter still. He felt presences moving around in the woods around them, some alive, some like drifting faint spirit essences. Though unsure of how he knew, he listened to his gut.

A flickering spark of cold fire burned and bobbed and tumbled ahead and to their left. It was far off, radiating fear. Brett opened his eyes and pointed, and Liz smiled at him, pulling him along again. "You're kinda handy to have around, *Chico*."

Brett laughed. "I suppose being half ghost has its advantages at times."

She squeezed his hand a few times as they jogged along. "If it weren't for... well, for the consequences, I'd say it's kinda hot. You know how I love ghosts." He looked over and she favored him with a sad smile and a wink.

They came through the woods after another five minutes or so and a vast sandy beach opened up before them. Brett couldn't see the water in the dark from where they were.

He did see the bonfire. It was a hundred feet away from them, but Brett imagined he could feel the heat where they stood. Flames leapt twenty feet into the night sky, and shadowy figures danced and wandered before the blaze.

They drew up to the fire, and industrial music pounded out of a boom box. Dozens of vampire wannabes cavorted and clumped into groups, drinking from red plastic cups or from many kinds of bottles.

They stopped short and Brett said, "I'm going to try to find her again." Liz nodded and slipped an arm around his waist. He closed his eyes and reached out again.

Brett's senses were assaulted by chaos and confusion, a burst of mental static that overwhelmed him. The world spun like he was drunk. Except it was the collective drunkenness, angst and excitement of the assembled vampire LARPers on the beach. It was blinding and deafening, and Brett clutched his head and groaned in pain. Liz held onto him and said, "What's wrong, *Chico*? Brett? Stop now, come back to me, please!"

Brett opened his eyes and the world swam and he landed on the sand, off balance. He heaved and vomited, moaning in misery and embarrassment. When he was done, Liz touched his back and a circle of vampires surrounded him, looking at him with mixed sympathy and disgust.

Brett's head ached. It wasn't fair, he hadn't had anything to drink, but now he felt hungover. Twisting shapes of energy played in his peripheral vision, and he knew he wasn't going to dare to try that trick again soon.

Chapter 19 - Hellhound on My Trail

Brett felt the world spin around him, the strange, made-up faces of the vampire roleplayers surrounding him. Liz clutched his hand and he saw her worried face swimming near him. She felt so warm. He met her eyes and the spinning receded away from her, she was his one fixed point to hang onto, the center of the painful, nauseating world around him.

"Brett? What happened? Oh *Chico*, talk to me!" Brett hated to hear the fear in her voice. He wanted to comfort her. He tried to sit up and failed. "Too... too much," he croaked out, throat burning from stomach acid still. "Thirsty," he managed.

Liz nodded, and asked the nearby gamers to get some water or juice. A couple of the vamps offered their cups, but Liz specified it be non-alcoholic, and they withdrew.

"Heads up!" came a cry from the bonfire. Brett saw Liz catch something. It was, of all things, a juice box. She waved her thanks and put the straw in and brought it to his mouth. "Drink this," she said, face full of concern.

Brett sipped at the straw and though it tasted awful to him, after he emptied the box, he felt some warmth and strength flow through him. The spinning slowed and he sat up. The crowd around him had thinned, going back to the warmth of the bonfire, but a few concerned people still crouched near him in the sand.

"I'm okay.... I'm just overwhelmed. I've got a migraine, and I feel dizzy, but I'll be okay." Someone handed him a bottle of water, and he accepted with gratitude. He rinsed his mouth and spat, and then drank down some of the water.

The vampires saw that he wasn't going to die right there in front of them, so they gave their well-wishes and went back to their party. He drank while Liz watched him, her eyes owlish in the flickering light of the fire.

Now that they were alone, he said, "Remind me to never try reaching out with my senses in a crowd again. I was looking for a candle flame in the distance, but got the mental equivalent of that fire over there. Ow. I don't think I can risk doing that again."

Liz listened and nodded. "So we'll just have to find Ashleigh another way."

Brett sighed. "Yeah, but she could be anywhere, maybe getting further away all the time. What can we do?"

"Can you stand?" she asked. He wasn't sure, but he nodded. She stood, still holding his hand and helped him up. He felt unsteady, but she put his arm around her shoulders and let him lean on her.

Stuart and Skye arrived. Skye looked as unsteady as Brett felt, and Stuart grinned, his cheeks rosy. "Hey there you guys are!" Stuart called. Skye made a face at the mess on the ground and kicked sand over it.

Brett tried to smile, but was pretty sure it came out more like a grimace. Liz greeted them with more warmth. "Hey! Nice bumping into you again, er, without actually knocking anyone down, that is."

Stuart guffawed. Skye gave Brett an exaggerated stage wink. Her clumsy attempt at being sly just made Brett more uncomfortable. She reached up to brush some of her wind-mussed hair behind an ear and her sleeve fell down, baring her wrist for just an instant.

In that instant, he saw that Skye had lines on her wrist. Scars. To him, the scars glowed with a cold white fire, and he felt sympathy for the gawky young drunk. He'd been there himself, down in that dark place. He felt a pang of guilt, knowing that this was how everything started, at least for himself and Frannie. His suicide attempt left him open to possession by a demon that fed on his insecurities and fears until it was strong enough to leap to other hosts.

"Say, could you guys help us out again?" asked Liz, bringing Brett out of his dark thoughts. "We're out here looking for my ten-year-old niece Ashleigh. She's run away, and is out here on the beach somewhere. She's... well, she's special needs, and she hasn't had her medicine. We're really worried about her."

Skye and Stuart looked at each other and shrugged. "Sure," said Stuart. "I'll ask around the party and see if we can get some help." He led Skye toward the bonfire and she gave a sloppy grin over her shoulder at Brett as they went.

Liz asked, "Can we go with them? Or is it still too much?"

Brett smiled. "It's okay, as long as I don't try to reach outside my pounding head, it shouldn't bother me."

They plodded back toward the fire, Brett still leaning on Liz while he regained his strength and balance. Walking on sand didn't help matters much, but he felt a bit more confident as they went.

They arrived to find Stuart proclaiming nonsense. "There is a human child lost in the wilderness nearby! Those of you who would think of eating her need to know that she is off limits as prey. She is under my protection as Baron of the Court. These visitors seek her, and if she is not found, or if something should happen to her, our Court could lose honor among the vampire Courts and Clans in the region. She is under our protection. We cannot afford to let the Fangs of Kenosha gain a foothold in our area. They have already challenged our authority enough. Lake Shore Court, I command you, go forth onto the sands and into the woods and find this girl."

Stuart turned to Liz and Brett with a smile. "The visitors will now describe the child."

Liz laughed out loud, and couldn't stop laughing. She wasn't used to roleplaying. Brett wasn't into live action games, but he knew where Stuart was headed with this. It was lucky for them that Stuart was a bigwig in-game. The other vampires would be eager to help, since whoever found Ashleigh would gain favor in the Court.

Liz laughing didn't help, however. He squeezed her and shushed her before speaking. "Let it out, let out the hysteria we feel," Brett said, his performance wooden, unused to acting. "She's lost and confused, our ghoulish little charge. She's mute and frightened and may flee you, but call the name Ashleigh and she will come to you. She's under five feet tall and has light hair and a grayish complexion."

The vampires looked excited. When he said "ghoulish" and mentioned her complexion, many of them grinned. Brett hoped the context would just lead them to believe she was in costume and playing a role. Liz had quit laughing and was staring at him with a surprised expression.

The vampires proclaimed melodramatic oaths that the Baron's command would be carried out, and they slunk off out of the circle of light and into the darkness. Only as they rose from the sand and wandered away did Brett realize just how many people were there. There had to be at least two or three dozen going out to search. A handful of them remained behind, tending the fire, or too drunk to play the game.

Brett's hopes rose as the vampires fanned out. He managed to stand on his own and took a step toward Stuart, shaking the vampire Baron's hand. "Thanks, we really owe you one. Two now, for the costumes...."

Stuart shook his head. "Naw. You're good people, and I figure it's the least I could do for my favorite web celebs."

As he stepped away from Liz, her cell phone rang, playing the tune of "Jimmy Crack Corn." She fumbled in her purse to find the phone. "Jimbo!" she cried into it as she answered. "It's so good to hear from you! What's up?"

Brett wanted to lean in close, but he felt it was lucky he hadn't drained her phone's battery already. Liz nodded as she talked to Jimbo, and seemed to have the same thought, glancing at the screen of her phone. She bit her lip.

"Uh, Jimmy, could you give me the Reader's Digest condensed version? I'm down to no bars and falling here."

He watched Liz's face, trying to divine the other side of the conversation. She looked amazed, then concerned, then said, "You are lying, Jimmy! Really? No shit?" Brett was more curious than ever. Even Stuart turned to look at Liz, though he'd drifted a few more feet away to be polite.

"What? What?" asked Brett, feeling impatient and anxious at her reactions. She shook her head once and held up a finger. "Jimmy? Jimbo? Hello?" She looked at the phone and sighed, snapping it shut. "That's that, no more battery."

She put it away and looked up at him. "Jimbo says that a few minutes after you and Gonzo left his place, he started to feel cold and sick. He says he couldn't stay awake, and just passed out on the floor for like three hours or more. He didn't say anything before because he thought it was a stomach bug at first. Now he's starting to think it's connected with everything else that's been happening."

"Cold? Sick? What are you saying?"

Liz wet her lips before she continued. "He said he had a nightmare about the time the demon came after us, wearing that poor trucker's dead body. It just kept coming at him and he couldn't move to stop it. He had it over and over, *Chico*.

"When he finally woke up, he found he had a message from Gonzo telling him what we'd said. Jimbo's been hitting the net, and found out some things from the Find A Grave site. Brett, that possessed woman, Lucy? She's in the family photos for Ashleigh's brothers' online memorials. It was her, she's Ashleigh's mom. Only her name is really Britney. Ashleigh, I mean. Lucy really *was* named Lucy, it wasn't a pseudonym. Or rather, she *is* named Lucy."

Brett felt ice stab through his stomach. "What do you mean, *is*? We left her in New Orleans when the demon jumped from her to me."

Liz nodded. "And where'd it go from you? Back into Lucy, it seems. Jimbo found out that Lucy, Ashleigh and the brothers used to live up in Crown Point, Indiana. He had to hit the Wayback Machine Internet archive… It seems her brother kept a blog. He wrote about how his teenage brother acted more and more depressed, that he was scaring little Britney.

"Josh said his parents took Michael to a psych ward. He grew wilder and angrier until he escaped. Josh's last entry was strange, he said that Michael was gone, buried in secret, and Josh was going to live the rest of his life like Michael would."

Brett wasn't sure what to think about all this. "So something bad happened in her family, several bad things did. You said Lucy's still not listed as dead?"

Liz shook her head. "No, according to records they found, that's right around when Josh was said to have gotten drunk and crashed his car, right near the Haunted Forest on 65 where he had buried his brother. It wasn't long before their parents and sister moved away, down to Mississippi. I lost Jimbo at that point, but we know most of the rest."

Brett closed his eyes and felt his head throb and saw lights flashing from the pain. "Yeah, they grew apart, the husband got addicted to porn and found your webcam, and then they divorced and Lucy became suicidal. She was a perfect host to use to come after us on our trip."

Liz paused a moment, and even with his eyes closed, he could just picture her biting her lower lip in thought. "Brett, he also said she moved from Mississippi to Memphis just a month ago. I think the demon fed off of that whole family, and Ashleigh escaped, but was all used up and leaking her soul out, becoming... what she is now."

"Who knows how many lives this demon's ruined. Britney's whole family. That poor dead trucker. Then on to Frannie and me. Or... God, what if it was me who raised the demon, back when I was ready to give it all up?"

"*No* chico! Absolutely no way you did this. You just don't have that kind of mojo. Fran might have, but it's clear the demon was feeding off the Carpenters a few years before it came after you and Fran last year."

Brett met her eyes. "Not enough mojo? How do you know I don't? The timing of my," he took a breath, "you know, my *attempt* was years ago too. Maybe I got its attention and then when you saved me, it found other victims?"

She took his hand in hers again. Her warmth made some of the gloom retreat, his mood lifted from the cold depths where it'd been sinking. "Brett, I'm the expert on mojo between us, right? Now think like a ghost hunter here. Your depression, was it natural or paranormal in nature?"

Brett pushed aside some nasty memories and ignored the blackness in his gut they churned up. "I suppose there wasn't anything paranormal about it, not until all the stuff that happened last year, when I had dreams about Cheryl's death."

It felt good to be using reasoning, it slowed the sinking, made him feel more in control.

Her smile warmed him even more. "Attaboy! So the Carpenters came first, and you were just a juicy target, a meal on wheels, passing through."

Brett shook his head, making it throb some more. He closed his eyes again. "No, but what about it possessing Frannie, hundreds of miles away?"

"You've got me there," Liz said. "If I had to guess, I'd say it's because she herself has paranormal powers. If her problems came before the Carpenters, I might believe she was the summoner, but that still doesn't work here. I guess it can jump from host to host, through personal connections. Lucy was connected to me through her husband watching me online, Frannie was connected to us through Jimbo..."

Brett opened his eyes and saw Liz outlined in the now calmer bonfire's flames. "None of that matters. We still don't have a cure, and we still don't know where she is."

Liz stood up straighter, looking determined. "We will, *Chico*. We have to. The vampires are out looking for her, and maybe she will know what to make of her brother's message to 'let go.'"

Her determination made Brett feel a bit better. He pushed away some nagging, negative thoughts and focused on what he could handle. "Let's join the search. I'm still feeling a little weak, but I don't want to just stand around and wait."

Liz took his arm, but before they got more than a couple of steps, Stuart grabbed Liz's elbow and asked, "Hey, if you see Skye out there, would you make sure she makes it back here okay? She wandered off when I wasn't looking. I guess she went off to search too."

Brett and Liz agreed, then walked away from the fire and out toward Lake Michigan. He smelled rotting vegetation in that direction. Once they were far enough from the fire, he saw the lake itself, moonlight glinting off its waves. They were still a few minutes' walk from the shore.

In several directions, he heard the gamers crying out Ashleigh's name. He made out a few figures, paired up for the most part, but a few lone vampires stalked the sands in the search.

They came across a body lying in the sand. It was Skye, her eyes closed, fallen in an awkward pose. Liz let go of his hand and crouched down to her. "Skye? Are you okay?"

The vampire girl half opened her eyes and groaned. "It was so cold," she said, shivering as she straightened herself out a little. She didn't rise, and her movements were very slow. "She was so cold."

Brett asked, "Who, Skye? Was it Ashleigh?"

Skye looked up at him. Her eyes were distant and dreamy, and not in a drunken sort of way. "No, not a kid. She was this crazy lady in a dirty white skirt suit and heels, out here on the sand. I asked her if she'd seen Ashleigh, but she just smacked me. Her hand was like ice, and I fell, and felt cold... cold inside too, as I blacked out."

Brett and Liz looked at each other at the same time. He knew his expression was a mirror of hers.... Terror and panic came over him, numbing his hands and feet, stealing his breath. The demon Lucy was out there, very near them somewhere, and she'd come for her daughter.

Chapter 20 - Letting Go

"Skye," said Liz, "we need you to tell us which way the cold woman went, it's really important. Life or death important."

Brett watched as Skye fought to stay conscious, eyes closing, head coming to rest in the sand, then snapping awake, eyes coming open with an effort, head raising just enough to look at Brett and Liz. "So tired."

"Which way, Skye?" Liz took the woman's hand in her own. Liz reached down into her sweater to pull out a black silk cord, a silver pentacle dangling from it. The moonlight reflected off of its face, and he saw that it was the one with the Celtic design he'd given her as a present years ago, when they'd parted ways. Seeing it brought him a measure of comfort, remembering the affection they'd had for each other even when they'd stopped being lovers for a time.

Liz pulled the cord from around her neck and dangled it like she had the pendulum just the other day. Brett felt amazed that he wasn't even more tired, since he'd only gotten a few cat naps worth of sleep since he woke up yesterday morning. He looked at Liz as she concentrated on the swinging pentacle. She looked exhausted, her eyes tired, her shoulders slumped. Still, he watched as she concentrated and he was surprised to *see* energy flowing over her. A soft light, the color of robin's eggs, spread from the hand that held the pentacle. The light went down the string to the silver medallion, and up her arm and across her breastbone and down the other arm.

Soon a soft glow suffused both women, and as Liz seemed more tired, Skye seemed to become more alert. The young vampire LARPer stared at the swinging pendulum, and its swing changed from left to right to a circular motion. With each back-and-forth, the circle flattened out, and the arc of the swing widened and pointed out toward the lake, and a bit to the right.

Liz opened her eyes and followed the direction, then muttered something and the blue glow stopped. She let go of Skye's hand and stuffed the pentacle in the back pocket of her jeans.

Brett was surprised when Skye sat up, groaning. He had to help Liz up from her crouch. He was glad he was feeling more himself, or at least whatever passed for that lately, or she might have pulled him over as she climbed to her feet.

"Stuart is looking for you, Skye," Brett said, pointing toward the bright spark of light of the waning bonfire in the distance. "He asked us to make sure you made it back to him. Thanks for your help."

Skye nodded sleepily and stumbled off toward the fire. Liz hung on Brett's arm, fighting exhaustion. "Wow, *Chico*, I'm out of shape, metaphysically speaking. That shouldn't have taken so much out of me."

Brett shrugged. "When was the last time you slept?" He regretted saying it right away. She scowled at him. "Sometime between the Indiana border and Lafayette. If I hadn't...."

Brett hugged her to him, still marveling at how very warm she felt to him. That would happen as he approached ambient temperature. "Shhh. Don't be like that. That's very un-Lizzie of you. Where's my unsinkable Babette?"

She let out a weary chuckle. "I think she got a contact buzz off of our friend Skye just now. Guess I have a taste of what happened to you earlier. Just up close and personal."

Brett smiled at her, wishing he could boost her spirits the way she always did with him. She reached up and kissed him. Even just that little peck was like hot cocoa after shoveling snow.

"Oh brrrr! I'm sorry, *Chico*, but you're like ice!" Liz squeezed him tight, then stood on her own, taking his hand. "Come on, let's go. Who knows how long it's been since she knocked Skye out?"

They started off in the direction the pendulum had pointed, and soon came across other fallen vampires in the sand. This matched couple clutched each other in a tangle, and at first Brett had thought they were interrupting something. Except they didn't move, so Liz checked their breathing and pulse and declared them alive but unconscious.

"Brett, should we?"

He cut her off. "No. If Lucy's out there knocking out vampires, we'll never catch up if we stop to take care of them. They're okay for now. We'll come back for them or send others after them."

Liz nodded, rising reluctantly.

He led her further along the beach, drawing ever closer to Lake Michigan. Brett still heard the faint calls of the vampires looking for Ashleigh off in other directions. It was quiet in this direction. The moon slid behind some clouds and it became darker too. Off in the further distance, he could see the headlights and taillights of Lake Shore Drive, curving around the beach and disappearing behind the park behind them. Far out on the lake, he saw the dim, distant lights of boats and ships winking like stars.

They found another fallen vampire gamer, this one sprawled spread-eagle on his back. He too was unconscious but breathing normally. Liz pulled his cape over him to keep him warmer. Brett urged her to hurry.

They moved with greater speed now, feeling surer of their direction. Brett felt heaviness in the pit of his stomach, dread growing inside him like a malignant tumor. He hated to say it out loud, but he said to Liz in a low voice, "Sweetie, what are we going to do when we find Lucy? We haven't got anything to use against her, we're just going to end up unconscious like the vampires. Or worse."

"We haven't got any choice, *Chico*. We'll have to think of something. We've got to remember everything we have that she doesn't. Love, *Chico*, and friends, and reasons to live on. Like in New Orleans, remember? It was love that defeated her before."

Brett nodded. Lizzie's words gave him warmth, and a second wind. His mind worked on the problem of what the little ghoul's ghost brother had meant and how that could be used against the demon. They walked on at a better pace.

Liz paused at the next unconscious vampire, a shapely woman who seemed to have put a lot of money and time into her Victorian dress and hairdo. Liz pulled the pentacle out again and confirmed the direction.... It pointed toward a boardwalk that led to a small pier. The moon came out from behind the clouds at that moment, and Brett could see two figures standing on the far end, tiny with distance.

Liz wrapped the cord many times around her hand so that the pentacle lay in her palm. Brett grabbed her other hand and pulled her after him. He pointed at the pier and Liz nodded.

Their shoes banged on the planks of the boardwalk, and rocks and shells skittered in their wake as they ran toward the pier. It was easier going now that they were out of the sand. The figures at the end of the pier had to hear them. If they did, Brett couldn't see any reaction.

They pounded down the pier, the breeze even cooler out on the water. No one was nearby and no boat lights bobbed anywhere close either. Brett saw the white-clad figure of Lucy, her back to them, clutching another figure in front of her. Lucy whirled around as they approached, dragging Ashleigh with her.

Ashleigh's face was a mask of animal fright, mouth covered by one of Lucy's hands. The girl bit at her mother's hand and drew blood, but this didn't seem to bother Lucy at all.

"You," breathed Lucy. "What are you doing here? Haven't you done enough to me and my daughter?" The words were spoken in a hiss that brought Brett and Liz up short. It was as if they'd hit a wall twenty feet away from the woman. Her words sounded human enough, but Brett's senses told him another story.

Where Liz had emitted light as she cast her divination and healing spells earlier, this creature seemed to ooze darkness. No, not darkness. Some kind of... anti-light? It hurt his eyes. Inky black smoky tendrils flowed from the woman's fingertips, and it leaked out of her eye sockets. Ashleigh seemed to be wrapped in the anti-light glow, her form becoming dim and hard to see.

Brett was sure both Liz's glow and this anti-glow weren't visible to normal people. It was a sign that he was slipping further out of the world of the living, as Frannie had before him. As Ashleigh had lived for... how long now?

"Let her go, Lucy," warned Liz, no sign of fear in her voice, though he could feel her hand tremble in his. They let go, standing far enough apart to cover the pier to keep Lucy from getting past with her daughter. Ashleigh didn't move in Lucy's grasp, but she did appear to be standing on her own.

"How dare you! My own daughter, aided in running away by you two." She said to Liz, "You corrupted my husband online, and then both of you caused me to become involved in your little problems." All Brett could imagine she meant was her "involvement" as she chased them in her SUV most of the way through Mississippi and into Louisiana before they had been saved by a friendly motorcycle gang.

And then later, when she held Frannie hostage to lure them to her, attempting to consume them. Only a ritual Brett had found in a book, performed by Liz at risk to her own life, had driven the demon out.

They had no such spell prepared now. Brett hoped Lucy didn't know that. "No one asked you to attack us, Lucy Carpenter."

The black tendrils jerked back toward Lucy, shock showing on her face. "I see you know more than you let on. Listen to him, little Britney, he's the one who killed your brothers and ruined our lives."

"That's bullshit and you know it!" cried Liz. "It wasn't any human agent that did this to you, or to Brett, for that matter. You're a life-sucking demon, nothing but a disgusting parasite! You jump from host to host, destroying lives and whole families. If the real Lucy Carpenter is still in there, I beg you to fight this evil that possesses you!" She raised her hand, revealing the pentacle, which was now pulsing with a bright blue light. Lucy took a step backwards and raised a hand against the light.

Ashleigh struggled free and screamed a hoarse, terrified scream, stumbling and falling between her mother and the two friends. She panted hard and curled up into the fetal position, rocking back and forth.

Liz stepped forward, her other hand reaching for Ashleigh, not looking at Lucy a moment as she watched the little ghoul with concern. Brett could see the girl's ghost standing nearby, looking on with a worried expression. He also saw the silvery cord, connecting ghost to ghoul-body. It was thin, like spider web, compared to the thumb-thick cord he'd had tethering his own spirit.

He looked back at Lucy, and now he saw two of her, one darker than dark, wreathed in the anti-light, and the other a faint luminous white. The fainter spirit struggled and wrestled to free itself, and he heard her screams, though they were unreal and distant.

The dark half struggled to maintain control, impossible ultra-black tendrils reaching towards the ghost to pull it back in. "Lizzie," Brett said in a low voice, "she's fighting, keep it up!"

Liz repeated Lucy's name and called to her to fight. The light brightened, and the smoky tendrils burned off, becoming lighter and less substantial, like fog in the full morning sunshine. Meanwhile, Liz had crept almost to Ashleigh.

Brett didn't know what to do. He didn't dare approach the conflict between the demon and Lucy's ghost, and he had no idea what he could do if he did. The spirit howled in pain and anguish as the demon growled and fought to maintain domination of the body and soul of Lucy Carpenter.

The demon had enough. It gave up holding Lucy back, using this energy to send a blast of the anti-light in a wave at Liz and him, washing over them. Brett felt the cold and drain of the demon's power, and both of them fell to their knees as the night became darker and darker around them. He felt his head becoming light. Liz's light went out and she fell to the ground, weeping.

Brett did the only thing he could think of. He gathered his will and stepped out of his body even as it hit the boards of the pier. He looked down for a moment at his weakened body and then looked up at the scene.

He couldn't make out the pier itself, and he couldn't see the lake. He could just make out Ashleigh's huddled body only a few yards in front of him. It was like a layer of reality had been removed, blotted out by the darkness of the demon. He wondered a moment why he didn't feel the drain so much now, just a sucking cold where the silver cord came from his body. He felt emboldened and stepped toward the dark and light forms ahead of him as the shimmering spirit of Ashleigh looked on to one side.

The demon took a step back. He moved closer, laughing, but he felt anger well up to fuel him. Rage and fury burned inside his spectral form. He'd scared the monster somehow! He strode forward with his new furious confidence.

Brett stopped in his tracks. He could move no further. He looked back to see what was holding him, half expecting a parachute or a balloon. The silver cord, taut, was at its limit, and he'd only made it halfway to the demon and Lucy.

The demon laughed and began to pull Lucy back in. Lucy screamed, no longer distant. She seemed solid and real as she shouted, "Help me, oh God, help me!"

Brett turned and saw Ashleigh's spirit wringing her hands. It came to him, what he'd come here to do in the first place. "Ashleigh... Britney...." The ghost of the girl looked at him, fear abating for just a moment, despite the horror of her mother being consumed by the demon. "Britney, your brother

Michael sends his love and a message: Let go, Britney. He says to let go. He said you'd know what to do."

Her eyes widened and she froze for a long moment, then she nodded. "I know." The ghost pulled on the silvery spider web and re-entered her body.

Brett was astonished as the body glowed and stood, radiating pure white light that drove back the preternatural anti-glow like roaches fleeing a kitchen light.

"Mom!" she called out in both worlds, "let go! Fight it! I'm coming!" The body stood and took a step, then another, then broke into a run, head down, glow brightening with each stride.

Brett turned to look where she ran. Lucy took strength from her daughter's words and her light. She pulled free just as Ashleigh's body collided with hers, standing safely to one side.

Ashleigh's body wasn't massive, but the collision caught the demon off guard, still reeling from the unexpected spirit light and distracted by Lucy breaking free. The girl was moving fast when she butted her head into the stomach of her mother's former body.

Both of them fell away from Brett and were lost to sight over the end of the pier as they tumbled into the water with a splash. There was no sound from below after that.

He swore he heard a twanging sound, and he saw the end of a glowing, silvery thread lash around on the now visible pier. The other end was attached to Ashleigh's ghost, clutching at her mother's spirit. The two cried on each other, letting out years of anguish and despair as they embraced, even as their physical bodies drowned.

Brett felt the pull of his own cord, dragging him back toward his unconscious form. He tried to stop, but he was unable to resist and all was dark as his body and spirit merged and he slept there on the pier.

Chapter 21 - Sinking Down

Brett awoke to the sound of his name being called. It sounded far away, and he didn't grasp that the calling was for him. Maybe it was for some other Brett. His head spun and he felt like a sumo wrestler was sitting on his chest. He tried opening his eyes.

Liz's tear-streaked face was inches from his. His own face felt wet, and he felt one of her tears hit his cheek. "Oh Brett, you're okay?" He felt himself lifted into an embrace, though his limp arms hung at his sides. He tried lifting them to wrap them around Liz's body. He was rewarded for his effort by the sensation of thousands of pins and needles as feeling began to creep back into his limbs.

Liz cried on him as she held him up. "I thought I'd lost you. You weren't b-breathing, and I couldn't find a p-pulse, and you're so cold...."

Brett tried to come up with something funny to say to calm her, but thinking hurt. "I'm still with you, Love."

"Ashleigh and Lucy must have gone after we got knocked out," said Liz as she cried. "I don't know how we'll catch up to them now. It's been almost a half hour since we got here."

With an effort, Brett held her with more strength and scooted so that he was sitting up rather than making her hold him up. "Lizzie, Ashleigh's gone."

She drew in a breath mid-sob. "Yes, Brett, that's what I'm telling you, she's not here." Liz sounded apprehensive. He could see a change in her expression, sadness turning to fear.

He shook his head, rubbing against her damp, hot cheek. "I'm sorry, Liz. Ashleigh let go, and she pushed Lucy off the pier and they both went into the water. They both let go, I saw their ghosts holding onto each other as I passed out."

Liz put her hands on his shoulders and pushed him back enough to look in his eyes. Hers were round with horror. "She's *dead?* We couldn't save her, Brett, even after all this?"

Brett lowered his eyes. "It's what had to happen, her brother knew it, and when I told her what he said, she knew it too, and she sacrificed her body to save her mother's soul. Her own soul, too."

She tilted her head to the side and down, into his lowered gaze to catch his eyes. "Do you believe that? There was no other way?"

Brett tilted his head up just a bit and nodded. "The demon was too powerful and had too great a hold on her mother. Ashleigh's plea to her was what allowed her to escape long enough for Ashleigh to make one last effort and let go."

Liz sniffed and just stared into his eyes awhile. Then she said, "Brett, what about you? How do we make you whole and alive again? What about Frannie?"

Brett sighed and shrugged. "I don't know. We'll have to think of something. We could research spells, maybe... or see if a doctor could help? Hell, I don't know, maybe we can duct tape my ghost in my body and hope for the best!"

Liz let out a short laugh and he felt himself smile and warm just a bit. He summoned more strength than he thought he had and hauled himself to his feet. Liz followed suit, arms still around him, squeezing him almost painfully tight. "You're right, *Chico*, there's got to be a way, we just have to find it."

Brett led Liz to the end of the pier and looked out into the water and down. There was no sign of either body. He shuddered, not sure whether he had hoped to see them, or if he could have handled it if they'd still been floating there.

The skies were clearer now, and the gibbous moon shone her cold light down on them. Liz shivered next to him, and he knew she had to feel the cold of the night. He hardly noticed unless he thought about it.

"Let's go see if the vampires are okay," said Brett, taking Liz's hand in his. She nodded, and they headed back up the pier and toward the low flicker of orange that marked the distant bonfire.

They found no passed-out vampires along the way, or any other signs of the search still going on. As they approached the fire, they saw that about half of the original number of partying vampires remained around the dying bonfire. They huddled close, in pairs or in groups for warmth and comfort. A gamer detached himself from one such cluster and met them on the edge of the light. Stuart no longer displayed his trademark grin.

"Good to see you guy. Have you seen Skye?" asked Stuart.

"Sure, we found her collapsed on the sand maybe halfway to the lake," said Brett. Liz elbowed him and finished for him. "She was okay, she'd just had too much to drink, I think. We woke her up and sent her back to you. We saw her walk back this way. She didn't come back?"

Stuart's face hardened a bit and he shook his head. "No. I don't know where else she would go. She's been acting funny all night. Goofy and giggly one moment, then dark and brooding the next. Kinda hyper bipolar, you know?"

Brett nodded. "We'll look for her on our way back. Maybe she headed back to the hotel instead of the fire?"

Stuart shrugged. "Yeah, maybe that's it. If she was sleeping on the sand, she was probably thinking about bed." He paused, then asked, "So you didn't find your 'special' niece? Everyone here gave up a while ago, a lot of people got too drunk and passed out tonight it seems. Even," he said in a hushed tone, "people who I didn't see drinking earlier. You two know anything about that?"

Liz answered before Brett did. "Stuart, I don't know if you'd believe me if I told you."

"Try me."

"There was this demon who was after my niece. She's not really my niece; I've just been taking care of her. She wasn't really human anymore, I guess. She sacrificed herself to save us and free herself. And to stop the demon." Liz and Stuart stared at each other in a long silence after this.

Stuart said, "You're right, that's really beyond belief, even for a guy like me that pretends to be a vampire. But I believe that you believe it. You both look like hell, come on over and join the cuddle puddle and warm up."

Brett shook his head. "It's cool of you to invite us, but we've got friends to find back at the hotel. Besides, I feel like we need to look for Skye now. We owe you a few times over."

Stuart shrugged. "Whatever. Be safe."

Liz detached herself from Brett for just a moment. She hugged Stuart tight and kissed his cheek. "You too." Stuart blushed.

Liz took Brett's arm again and they were sent off with a chorus of lethargic goodbyes from the huddled vampires. Brett felt something nagging at the back of his mind, something about Skye. Something important. It was on the tip of his tongue, but he couldn't place what it was.

He and Liz walked across the sand to the wooded park in silence. The rush of cars along Lake Shore Drive in the distance beckoned to them, and Brett was surprised to be cheered by the sounds and lights of the city ahead.

As they wound their way along the curving pathways of the park, Brett felt uneasy. "Lizzie, do you…."

"Shh. Yes, I know, it's creepy, like we're being watched."

Brett saw fleeting, shadowy movement out of the corners of his eyes, just outside the pools of light provided by the occasional mushroom lights along the trail. The one time he stopped and looked, nothing was there.

"Skye!" shouted Liz, looking in the opposite direction, down a different path. He turned his head just in time to get an impression of skinny legs running away from them.

"Come on, I'm sure it was her!" cried Liz, grabbing his hand and running.

Brett's stiff muscles protested, and he struggled to keep up with his girlfriend as they pursued the strange girl.

Liz called out after her. "Skye! Wait! Stuart's worried about you! Come back!"

Skye didn't come back, and though he could hear her running up ahead, she didn't answer. Why would she run? Had she seen something on the beach? Had the encounter with Lucy spooked her to the point of panic?

Skye ran down the trail, which led to a grassy picnic area and a large parking lot. Skye's strides were awkward but long, outdistancing them in this open area.

There were a few cars in the parking lot. Brett thought they must belong to some of the vampire LARPers out on the beach. They parked in a staggered, gap-toothed pattern that suggested that many had left for the night. Skye dodged behind a beat-up minivan that was parked right up front, its headlights on and engine running.

Brett felt a bit exposed as they ran into the beams of the headlights of the van. The lights shut off. It seemed much darker since their eyes were dazzled by the headlights.

It was *Soccer Mom*! "Liz look, Gonzo's here, he found us! Hey Gonz!" he shouted, coming to a stop at the edge of the lot, waiting for his friend to emerge from the passenger door. He peered into the windshield, eyes still dazzled from the headlights' glare. Greenish spots still swam in his vision, and as they faded, he only saw Frannie in the front seat. Something was odd about her mouth. He made out... duct tape?

"Brett, I don't think Gonzo's in there," said Liz, taking a step back. He looked at her, then turned back to look at *Soccer Mom* as the side door slid open.

Out of the dark interior of the van stepped Larry, his leather hat back on his head. He leered, orange light glinting off of his teeth as he stepped toward them. He had his pistol out in one hand, pointed at Liz. "I wouldn't do anything funny if I was either of you. Now, tell me, where's the little monster?"

"Ashleigh's dead, Larry," said Brett. "She threw herself in the water and is probably at the bottom of Lake Michigan, or floating off to the Upper Peninsula by now."

Larry growled, looking from one of them to the other. "If that's so, I'm going to need me another circus freak to show off. Maybe two. Got one in the car already," he said, jerking his head toward Frannie without looking away from Brett. Frannie was peering out at them wide-eyed inside *Soccer Mom*, struggling against the tape, and likely other bonds Brett couldn't see from where he stood.

"Oh, and for a little insurance, I've brought along another little friend. Come on out, darlin', thanks for leading them to me."

Skye stepped out from behind the van and moved to Larry's side. Her eyes were dark, hooded, and she stood with haughty confidence, one hand on her hip.

Brett's heart sank. Now he remembered the scars he'd seen on her wrists. Even without reaching outside of himself, he saw inky darkness leaking out of her eyes like smoke.

Chapter 22 - Steady Rollin' Man

"You can't be back so soon," said Brett to the demon inside of Skye. "I saw you go over inside of Lucy's body!"

Liz took in a sharp breath, squeezed his hand next to him and fumbled around in her pocket. Maybe she could hold off the demon with her pentacle again.

"Hold it right there, unless you want Larry to blow your head off!" screeched Skye, her voice like a warped vinyl record album.

Something's wrong. Maybe the possession hadn't taken complete hold yet, or maybe Skye fought for control of her own mouth and body. No way to know, but Brett hoped it meant the demon was weakened.

Liz froze as Larry made a show of displaying the gun, raising it up at arm's length to point right at Liz's head. His leer melted into a hard-eyed smirk. Larry meant business.

Brett stalled for time. "Lucy, I asked you a question. How did you survive being pushed off of the pier?" He had to think of some way to get the gun from Larry and free Skye from her possession for all their sakes. Perhaps even Larry's. Did the asshole even understand what he was in league with?

Skye shrugged and smiled a lazy, quirky smile. "What can I say? One meat suit or another, it doesn't really matter. I miss wearing you most of all, I think. Mmmm, what a fine mind to explore, what a delicious soul. I still dream about it at bedtime, Brett. I remember what your girlfriend's soul tastes like too, don't I, Lizzie? Oh, she's not open to me now, but she will be, after she sees you beg me for mercy."

Brett suppressed the panic rising in him. "And how would you do that? We threw you out once before, and I'm pretty sure that protection's still there or you would have tried something again before now."

Larry rolled his eyes. "Hey! I haven't got all night. Richter's taking a red eye flight back to California. I gotta get you freaks back to the hotel to show him. I'd been counting on the living dead girl, but hell, two room temperature stiffs, even if they're well preserved, should still make for a million dollar show. Probably make me a big name. National, even."

Liz laughed. "You're nuts, Larry! How do you think you can just show off Brett and Frannie like animals? You can't hold them against their consent."

Larry chuckled. "I think my young chickie here can help with that. If Brett here sees you all sucked dry of your will to live by the cold mojo of this hellion, he'll pretty much do anything I say to save you. Won't you, Brett?"

Skye grinned and stepped forward and raised her arms. Brett saw the waves of anti-light curl from her fingertips, reaching tendrils out toward Liz and him. The light around them dimmed, and Brett's body seemed weighted down by what felt like a dozen sandbags piled on his back and arms. Out of the corner of his eye, he saw Liz struggling to stay standing as well, her teeth clamped together and lips curled back with the effort of fighting the draining energies. He felt faint. A million sparks swam in his vision. His ears roared and pounded with his weakening pulse. Liz fell to her knees next to him and let out a frustrated sob.

Then it was over. Skye let them go, lowered her arms and took deep gulping breaths. "Just... a... sample...." Light returned, the soft whush of the cars on the highway replacing the roaring in his ears. He found strength and stood. He reached down and helped Liz up.

Why was Skye breathing so hard? Why stop before they were unconscious? Brett began to get a glimmer of hope that Ashleigh's sacrifice had weakened the demon. It wasn't an idea yet, but he felt like time was on their side.

"You c-can't use me that way, cowboy. Your hell bitch might have some scary mojo, but it'll be too much work to watch the three of us night and day," said Liz. Brett was pleased to hear her voice strengthen from shaken to clear and sweet and defiant. "Fuck you, Larry, and fuck your demon too. You know she's not doing anything for you; she'll turn on you as soon as it's convenient."

"Ah, thanks for the offer, darlin', but that ship's sailed," drawled Larry. "You're just jealous because I found someone who can satisfy me in ways you can't." Larry laughed at his own joke.

The sound of cloth ripping came from the open side of the van. Larry glanced back, and Brett looked up. Frannie's eyes were wide, sitting there watching from the front seat. She sat still for a moment, then started struggling to free herself again.

"Damn," said Larry, looking back at them. "Thought maybe the other one was getting loose."

"Gonzo's in there?" asked Brett, still stalling for time.

"Naw," said Larry. "Couldn't take the chance. We left him taped up back at the hotel. Your friend in the Mandy T-shirt's back there, sleeping in the back seat. All three of 'em went down nice and easy earlier, when my friend here wore another body. I gotta say, that one was a lot more my speed, darlin'."

Skye snorted. "That one was used up, I would've had to find a new vessel soon enough. Enough of this banter. It's time to go, if you wish to see that Richter fool and part him from his money."

Larry shrugged. "Up to you. Do that voodoo you do so well."

Brett saw Caroline appear in the open side doorway of the van, holding a finger to her lips. She didn't look any worse for wear, though perhaps a bit tired. He shook his head ever so slightly in warning, not wanting her to get hurt too.

Skye raised her arms once more and ultra-black ooze smoked forth with greater force, bringing Brett and Liz to their knees with a metaphysical shove. All the world around them dimmed and muted as Brett felt his body's energies draining out to feed that awful power that pulled at them.

Somewhere, far away, Brett heard a motorcycle's engine roar.

Brett heard a whispery voice in his ear. *Let go, Brett.* The voice was Ashleigh's, urging him as he'd urged her earlier. Was it a trick from the demon? He heard the voice plead with him again, using the same words: *Let go now!*

Brett let his body fall to the ground and stood up, feeling once again a distance between the cold numbness of the demon's tendrils and himself, felt only through his silver cord. The cord itself seemed thinner this time somehow, he noted.

He looked around him. The world was far away, and seemed to slow down. Skye still stood with her arms up, and he could see the anti-light of the energies she used, stretching from her fingertips to the two motionless bodies, crouched on the ground next to him. His own body looked pathetic, curled up against the cold that way.

Larry still stood, holding his gun raised and pointed at Liz, looking amused at the scene.

Caroline crept out of the van without a sound, wielding a tire iron in one hand. She raised it behind her head, then turned to look to one side, surprised. Brett followed her gaze.

A motorcycle, all shiny chrome and black paint, roared up on one wheel, gravel of the parking lot spraying out behind it. The front wheel came down and Brett thought for a moment that he saw a leather-clad knight, wielding a lance, galloping into battle.

Gonzo, in full leathers and goggles, astride the motorcycle, swung a wooden baseball bat over his head. Gonzo screamed at the top of his lungs, "Booooger!"

Larry and Skye turned in surprise as Brett's best friend bore down on them. Gonzo swung the bat at Larry, whacking the man's arm with full force, sending the pistol skittering across the lot. Larry howled in pain.

The demon's energies stopped as it was distracted, watching Gonzo skid the bike, laying it down as he leaped away from it to roll into the nearby grass.

Brett felt stronger and more solid in ghost-form. He had to use the moment somehow before the demon could take them all.

Ahead of him, Liz raised her hand and displayed her silver pentacle in the palm. She gritted her teeth, scowling as she concentrated her will on the demon. Skye's body turned back, holding up her arms to try to shield itself from the Liz's intense blue energies hurled at it.

Caroline hurled the tire tool like an enormous four-pointed, wrought iron throwing star. It glanced off of Skye's shoulder, making her stumble and whirl around to face Caroline.

Gonzo ran up without the bat in his hand while Larry backed up into *Soccer Mom*'s bumper. As Brett watched, Gonzo tackled Larry and slammed him against the hail-chipped paint of the minivan's hood.

The demon recovered, and the darkness flowed out to battle with Liz's blue power, shadow against light. Liz began to falter. Skye reached out with one hand, standing like a traffic cop, aiming dark energies at her other attacker. Caroline began to sway and had to hold onto the van's door to remain standing. It was time for Brett to act. He lunged toward Skye, but was pulled up short by his silver cord.

Let go!

He didn't see Ashleigh anywhere, but neither was he under the influence of the demon's energies.

His thoughts whirled as his friends struggled and the demon began to win. He could think of only one solution. He had to truly let go.

He reached for his silver cord, holding it up in one hand to examine it. It was perhaps as thick as his index finger, and felt slick to the touch. He tugged hard on it, but it wouldn't give, his body wouldn't move. He sighed… It was now or never.

He held the cord up in front of his face, gripped by a fist on either side. He saw Liz's energy fall back. Caroline slumped to the ground, eyes closed.

Brett bit down on the cord with all his might. It was the worst pain he'd ever experienced. He felt an electrical shock spreading up his spine and out into every nerve in his spectral body. He saw his physical body go into spasms, a seizure of some sort. The cord resisted, but he bit harder still, putting all his anger and pain into it.

The cord severed. Dizziness threatened to overwhelm him, but he discovered he could draw energy from the ground, the air, and from within himself. His anger roared inside him like a furnace, rage made him stronger and more powerful than he'd ever imagined. Electricity crawled all over his ghostly form crackling with raw power.

He rushed Skye's form, reaching *through* her throat to grapple the Shadow itself. He jerked the vile blackness out of the poor girl's body and squeezed, trapping it with one arm and choking it with the other.

The demon squirmed in Brett's grasp like a wildcat, lashing about with its energies, trying to get purchase on him. But he was on a level field with the demon now. Spirit to spirit. Having been evicted from Lucy as her body drowned, the demon had used up too much energy draining Liz and Brett. It struggled and bucked and tried to get free. Searing pain wracked Brett with every strike and lash from the demon, but he used his fury to hold firm. Now beyond life and its pains, he'd let go of his body to save the people he loved.

Brett burned with all the anger and hate and ugly jealousy he'd pushed out through the cord, every time he felt himself slipping away. He unleashed his ugly darkness on the demon, willing it to be destroyed.

The demon screamed. It withered and shrank in his grasp, burning with cold violet flames. He screamed as the fire consumed him, and the world fell away from him.

Someone smacked his face. "Damn it, Brett, wake up, you asshole." His eyes popped open to see Gonzo and Liz looking at him from above. He blinked. "Didn't I die?"

Liz threw herself on top of him and kissed him. Her tears ran onto his face and he tasted their salt on her lips.

"Hey now, break it up," growled Gonzo. "The cops will be here soon, and you don't want to get arrested for public indecency, do you?"

Brett realized that Liz didn't feel feverishly hot as they continued to kiss. He shivered, wearing a T-shirt in the chilly spring night air, lying on the pavement. His heart hammered in his ears, not the dull, slow thud of before, but a rapid beat. His body also responded in other, rather human, ways to Liz's body on top of him as they kissed.

When she came up for breath, he said, "I don't get it. I bit through my cord. I let go. I was a ghost, Liz. I think I was burned up as I squeezed the demon into nothing. Why am I here? Why do I feel better than I've felt all year?"

Liz grinned and wiggled around on top of him before getting up and helping him up with a hand. He shivered in the cold. She hugged him tight to her, helping keep him warm. "I don't know, *Chico*. All I know is, the demon beat me down, then suddenly it was gone and you went into some kind of seizure."

"That sounds like a load of shit to me," interjected Gonzo.

Brett looked Gonzo's way and saw the unconscious form of Larry lying across the hood of *Soccer Mom* like a game animal. Trussed up with duct tape, he looked like he was out cold. The minivan had a few new dents in its hood.

Skye huddled scared and cold inside Gonzo's leather jacket, sitting on the ground against one of the *Soccer Mom's* tires. Her eyes stared off into space, vacant. He felt for her.

"Maybe it sounds like a load of shit," said Brett. "But it's the truth, Gonz. Lizzie, what if… what if Ashleigh leaked almost all the way outside her body, and I was only maybe half gone. Maybe I just lost the part that had leaked out?"

Liz squinted at Brett. "*Chico*, something *is* different. Your flame, your soul, it's brighter than it's been to me all day, but it's not a full flame."

Brett said, "Have you got a compass?"

Liz dug in her pockets and came up with one. They peered at the needle, which swung back and forth a few times before settling in on magnetic north.

"Yeah, what I saw, that was a last memory from my missing other half, the part of my soul that lived outside of me. I gave up the ghost." He grinned at the others.

Gonzo snorted. "So you're the boy with half a soul now?"

"Maybe. But I don't think you can have *half* a soul. I think if you slice it in two, you have less than you started, but still a soul. Maybe it'll grow back, like when you donate bone marrow?"

"*Chico*, is the demon gone for good this time?"

Brett nodded. "Yeah, I feel like it's finally over. It's hard to describe. When I tried to off myself years ago, if that selfish, stupid attempt is what drew the demon to me…"

Liz finished for him. "Then 'letting go' to sacrifice yourself for all of us was something it couldn't deal with. An unselfish act of love, *Chico*."

Brett let out a sigh, feeling lighter and calmer than he had in years. "Yeah. This time, it's destroyed, not just driven off. I *felt* it die."

Gonzo groaned. "I repeat. Load… of… shit!"

Caroline walked up and hugged both Brett and Liz at once. She smiled sweetly at him. "Glad you're okay. Frannie's exhausted though. Maybe you should tell her your secret when she wakes up?"

"Yeah, yeah," said Gonzo. "Let's get this over with. The cops are coming. Once they take our statements, we've got a date with The Boneyard tonight. I'm starved!"

Chapter 23 - The Rest of the Story

The Boneyard turned out to be a short taxi ride away from the hotel. Liz and Brett arrived to find Gonzo already holding court at a large round table with Caroline, Stuart and Skye listening with amusement.

"...so the cop was so shaken up by being blindsided by a possessed zombie trucker, he just let us go." He held up a finger as he polished off the beer in his glass and let out a monstrous belch, then continued. "On top of that, the guy let me keep his taser, 'just in case!'"

"At least this time, you're not telling people how you wrestled the trucker to the ground with your bare hands after he took out a half-dozen cops!" added Liz, giggling as they came up behind Gonzo.

Gonzo turned and put a hand to his heart, looking wounded. "Lizzie, I would *never* exaggerate like that! How could you even *suggest* such a thing?" He allowed a sly grin to creep across his face. "Least, not until I've had a bit of the Irish."

Brett sat next to Gonzo, and Liz sat between him and Caroline. Liz and Caroline clinked beer mugs and shared a grin.

Gonzo elbowed Brett in the ribs. "So, Junior, where's the Franster? Did you help her, or is she out stalking the night, looking for braaaains?"

Brett rolled his eyes. "Lizzie and I helped her out. She wasn't keen on the idea of biting through her cord. It was the hardest thing I've ever done, and I only did it in desperation."

Liz continued his story. "We tried something else. Since we knew she had to cut the cord or continue leaking away until she was just a ghoul, I realized I had my athame with me." She patted her purse. "It's a special knife I use in my rituals. Brett says he can see its aura now, even after cutting his ghost loose."

Brett nodded, not looking at Gonzo, knowing his skeptical friend wouldn't believe what he said. "Yeah, I see a lot more than I used to. Can't step out of my body, thankfully, but having been out there, I seem to have a connection with another sense now."

Skye nodded at this, directly across the table from him. "Me too. I... well, this sounds crazy, but I think I've seen some ghosts, or fairies or something. Freaky stuff."

He nodded. "Out of the corner of my eyes mostly, but yeah, I see them too."

"Anyway, you were saying about Frannie," prompted Caroline in a quiet, curious tone. Brett glanced over at her and she gave him a winning smile and sipped at her beer. Gonzo slid empty glasses from near the pitcher in front of both Brett and Liz and filled them with beer while Brett continued.

"Well, since I could still see Frannie's ghost and her cord, I offered to help. I borrowed Lizzie's athame, which she sort of powered up beforehand. Think of it looking like a dagger-sized lightsaber."

Gonzo, Stuart and Caroline all laughed at the image. Gonzo put a hand over his mouth and made heavy breathing noises. He lowered his voice and said, "Brett, I am your father! Come to the dark side!"

Brett stuck his tongue out at Gonzo and grinned. "Anyway, with Fran's permission, I used the little lightsaber to sever the cord. She didn't seem to feel the pain like I did, at least her ghost didn't do more than wince, but her body fell unconscious right away."

Liz put down her glass, having drunk half in one long gulp. She burped, and continued for Brett while he drank from his own beer. "I thought for a minute that we'd killed her, but she fell into a natural sleep. There's even less of Frannie left in there, so it's going to take more time for her to get back to normal."

Brett belched, though it wasn't much, and Gonzo gave him a thumbs-down. He snickered and shrugged. "Anyway, Frannie's ghost stuck around long enough to thank us for helping her. Said she wouldn't haunt us too much, whatever she meant by that. We left Frannie's sleeping body in Larry's hotel room, since we know he won't be back, and it's paid for."

Caroline piped up, "Yeah, the cops said they even had witnesses from the hotel who saw him leaving with Fran and me, duct tape on our mouths. It wasn't any trouble for them to believe Larry kidnapped Frannie and me and held the rest of us at gunpoint until Gonzo arrived. Dunno if he'll get off, but I'm sure he'll be waiting in jail at least a few days."

Liz looked at her and tilted her head to one side. "Why didn't anyone stop Larry at the hotel, if you were obviously held against your will?"

Caroline took another sip of beer before answering. "Lucy. Anyone who approached them, she'd drain them enough to slow them down or stop them. She left a pile of security guys and bellhops at the front entrance before he led us out to the van."

"You know, I don't even know how Larry knew where to find *Soccer Mom* like that." mused Gonzo.

"I'm guessing Lucy again," answered Liz. "She'd seen it before, Gonzo. She got scraped off the side of it last fall when she was after us. I'm sure she hadn't forgotten."

Gonzo nodded. "Yeah. Still, you think that fucker's gonna come after any of us someday?"

Brett said, "No, I think he's gonna want to forget this week ever happened. I hate to say it, but I think Larry was deluded the whole time about who was pulling the strings. He thought he was using the demon to get what he wanted, but she had him doing *her* bidding. Larry's an asshole, but I can't picture him as a kidnapper or willingly throwing in with a demon, not for just money anyway."

Gonzo rolled his eyes. "So, the devil made him do it?"

"More or less," said Brett.

"If that's so," said Gonzo, "Why didn't the demon just possess him?"

"We think it can only possess those who attempt suicide, it opens a door. The demon had to threaten or persuade or delude Larry." Wanting to change the subject, Brett said, "So, Gonz, how'd you get caught anyway?"

"It was stupid. I rode into town, found the hotel and parked in a nearby lot. I saw bunch of Goth types there, and I thought back to being taken off guard by that kid back in Indy. So I took out the Louisville Slugger I keep in the back of *Soccer Mom* and stuck it most of the way into my backpack. I thought maybe I could get it into the hotel as a piece of sports equipment, and not have it noticed as personal defense.

"So I make my way to the hotel and find that it's in an uproar. Ghost geeks are freaking out all over the place, talking about a real ghoul being sighted running amok in the courtyard, feasting on fast food, and then escaping out the front doors with security in hot pursuit.

"I look around a bit, hoping to find signs of you guys, and then I see Frannie sitting in the main lobby next to Caroline here. I introduce myself and she fills me in on what she's heard."

Caroline nodded. "Yep. I didn't know where you guys went, and my iPhone was dead in my purse, so I thought I'd wait and see if Liz and Brett would happen by. I was kind of worried, really, but I couldn't go far. Frannie ran off not long after Lizzie had to go after Brett. I had to hunt around the hotel and completely missed the Richter talk. Funny enough, it was the uproar as Ashleigh made her escape that helped me find Frannie. Poor dear was rooting through a garbage can, and I had to get her calmed down and cleaned up before I ended up in the lobby with her."

Gonzo picked up where he left off. "So while we're introducing ourselves, Larry walks by with Shell. I get the idea to be careful, so we followed. When they got into the glass elevator, we watched from the court to see where it went. We can see them get off the elevator, thanks to his hat and her blue hair, a few floors up, and since the corridors are open, I see which room they go in."

"We take the elevator up, I get out my Louisville Slugger and knock on the door. Lucy answers, and before I can so much as get a hit in, all three of us blacked out, crashed on the floor.

"When I wake up, everyone's gone except for Shell. She's pacing the room, talking on her cell phone to someone, begging them to come get her, saying Larry's gone crazy and she needs to get away."

"That bitch," growled Liz.

Gonzo held up a finger to indicate he wasn't done. "So, I'm bound with duct tape pretty firmly, so all I can do is make noises through my nose at her and give her the puppy dog eyes."

Caroline and Skye giggled.

"She starts to look worried, so she hangs up and starts talking to me. Confessing that she only helped Larry because he seemed like someone who knew what he was doing, like he was on to something big. But the more she was in on it, the worse it all felt, and she said when she got slapped, I can only assume by our Lizzie," he paused as Liz grinned affirmation, "she realized she wasn't on the right side of things. She tried to get away, but while she was still packing her stuff to go, Larry came in with Lucy and she was too scared to do anything but go along with what he asked."

Brett asked, "So what happened to her?"

"I was getting to that, Junior. After pouring her blue-banged heart out to me, she takes pity on me and rips the tape off my mouth. After that, I tell her that this is her only chance to get away, and that if she leaves me behind, she'll be an accessory to murder if Larry decides to finish me off with that gun of his, or if the demon sucks the life out of me."

"So, she loosens the tape to where I can struggle free, but takes off before I do, asking for a head start. I didn't much care where she went, but I knew I had to try to get to you guys before Larry did."

"How *did* you get that motorcycle, Gonz?" Brett remembered to ask.

Gonzo grinned. "Funniest thing. I was headed out to get in *Soccer Mom* and was cussing up a storm when I found her stolen, when this big hairy guy comes up and tells me he saw someone in a cowboy hat take off with my van and which way they went. He says he figures they're headed for that park by the lake, since there's a big vampire gamer party going on. I tell him about my missing friends, and he remembers you two, and says he wants to help. Turns out, he had a restored Norton Commando along, and he said as long as I took care of it and brought it back, I could borrow it. He said to watch out for Stuart and Skye here while I was at it, since they're friends."

"Leslie's a great guy. Seems to have an instinct for who he can trust, and a generous heart," said Stuart with a sleepy smile. Skye nodded her agreement.

"Wait," asked Brett, "Leslie had a van and a motorcycle there?"

Stuart shook his head. "That's not his van, it's mine. As Baron, I keep all of the Court's stuff with me. He just works out of it to do his costuming and makeup for people. Leslie goes everywhere on that motorcycle. Loves to make an entrance with it after everyone's all set."

Brett and Liz went "Ohhhh!" at the same time. Caroline giggled.

At this point, several of the wait staff arrived with platters of ribs, sandwiches, fries and a few salads. These were distributed around the table, along with another pitcher of beer. Brett and Liz thanked Gonzo for putting in an order for them.

Brett stared at the huge beef ribs, thinking they resembled something Fred Flintstone might eat. A smoky, spicy aroma steamed off of the plate. Now that the meat was here, Brett wasn't quite as sure he wanted it. He was pleased to find he no longer had an overwhelming craving for raw meat. He was hungry though, so he grabbed some fries to start with.

"So, instead," Liz said, after everyone had eaten a bit, "Gonzo got to make the grand entrance as the knight errant coming to our rescue! That was absolutely fantastic!"

Gonzo grinned around his pulled pork sandwich, which he held in one hand. With the other, he made a flourish and nodded in a sort of sitting bow.

"I have to thank you guys," said Skye in a soft tone, sipping from the water glass in front of her. "For saving my life. I was sure I'd be eaten alive by that shadow demon thing. It kept me shoved way back inside, and I could only watch as I did those terrible things."

Liz reached across the table in front of Caroline to pat Skye's hand. "No, it wasn't you, hon. You were taken over. You're safe now though, we took care of that."

Skye blushed and lowered her eyes to the table in front of her. "Thanks for that too. I hope your spell keeps me from leaking out like the others did, and keeps the demon out."

Liz pulled her hand back and picked up a mozzarella stick. Before eating it, she said, "You had to want it to work for it to work."

Brett added, "I saw it work, that's how I got the idea to use the same athame to help Frannie."

"We'd better let Jimbo know what's going on," said Brett, realizing it had been hours since they'd talked to him.

Caroline held up a finger and washed down some of her salad with a swig from her beer. "Done. I went back to the car and put the iPhone on the car charger. Gonzo asked me to take care of it while you two were still helping Frannie. I'll call him again when we get back and know more about how she's doing."

"I'm sure she'll be fine, if my *Chico* here bounced back, I doubt anything will keep Frannie down for long. She's got a lot of spirit."

Gonzo snorted. "Too much, sometimes."

Brett grinned at him. "So what's the plan, Gonz?"

"Well, after we eat and have a couple more beers, I guess we taxi back to the hotel and all crash in Larry's room for the night. We can head back when we get up in the morning."

"I'm driving home tonight," said Caroline. Liz pouted at her. "Sorry. My husband's going to be annoyed with me as it is. I've been out on ghost hunts until morning before; I can make it a few hours back to Lafayette on my own. I'll switch to Diet Coke after this beer's gone."

"We'll have to backtrack a little on our way. We have to see if we can get Frannie's car out of the ditch next to the Haunted Forest on 65," said Brett.

Gonzo cracked his knuckles with his fingers laced and palms out. "Shouldn't be a problem."

Brett smiled, and then looked at Liz. "While we're there, I think I want to stop and pay my respects to the Carpenter brothers, maybe let them know that their sister and mother are free now."

Liz gave him a sad smile and nodded at him. "That's a good idea. I want to go with you. I'm still really torn up about what happened."

Brett shook his head. "It was just too late for Ashleigh, Lizzie. She was only hanging on by a thread, and if that was cut, I don't know if there was anything left to grow back, and her body was so ruined after all this time.... I think it was a mercy. She ended by saving her mom, and helped me make sure the demon couldn't do it again."

Gonzo raised his glass. "Let's have a toast."

"To friends and love," said Brett, clinking his glass to Gonzo's.

Gonzo scowled. "That's my toast, Junior. Get your own."

"Okay," he said, and thought a moment. "To life, and to the friends who help us hang onto it."

They all clinked their glasses and drank up. "Not bad, but too wordy," muttered Gonzo.

Brett looked at Gonzo, about to retort, when he saw a faint, glowing figure drift across the room behind Gonzo. The female form sat upon the empty chair to Gonzo's left. Ashleigh smiled at him, miming an empty-handed toast in his direction and nodding at Liz as well. No one else, not even Skye, seemed to notice.

Brett decided to keep this bit to himself, but smiled and said, "Okay, then, how about to friends gone, but not lost?"

"Not bad. I'll drink to that," said Gonzo.

Me and the Devil

This book is dedicated to all of my friends, especially those who encouraged and supported me along the way: Amy, Amanda, Dawn, Phil, Heather, Heather, Craig, Sara, Renee, and Sarah. Oh yes, and the wise and patient INklers too. I could not have done it without your belief in me. Thank you all.

The quotation used at the end of Chapter 27 is from "Ikey and Mikey" by Benny Bell Samberg. Used with written permission from his son, Charles Samberg.

Chapter 1 - Going Mobile

"Got it," said Gonzo, before hanging up his cell phone. He looked up at the others. "We're live in sixty seconds, Junior," he said to Brett as he adjusted the zoom on the camera.

Brett nodded and took a deep breath and let it out, trying to will his nerves to calm. He snuck a glance at Liz, who was perched near him on a low stone wall. She crossed her eyes and stuck her tongue out at him, twiddling fingers under her chin.

"No, no, stop!" Brett whispered, fighting to keep from bursting out in laughter. The grin that spread across his face was mirrored in his girlfriend's eyes as she let out a squeaky giggle at his reaction.

"Sweetie, it'll be fine. We're on camera all the time at home. This isn't any different, except for the sound being on." She gave him a playful wink.

Gonzo snorted, watching his friends through the camera's screen. "Shoulda taken that swig of Irish I offered. You wouldn't want your nerves to disappoint your tens of Internet viewers, would you? Jimbo says we're up to forty-five already. Might have to refund the no dollars they paid for this."

Before Brett could respond, Gonzo looked at his watch and put a finger to his lips. Video rolling, they were streaming live.

Brett straightened and forced a smile for the camera. "Hello, and welcome to our first broadcast. I'm Brett and this is Liz," he said, trying not to stumble over his words. "We're in Ohio at historic Loveland Castle tonight, broadcasting to you live for the next few hours."

Liz waved and hopped off the wall, her hiking boots making crunching noises in the gravel. She smoothed her green knit sweater-dress, sliding it back down from her lap to just below her knees as it clung a bit to her black leggings. She waved again and grinned at the camera, "Hi, Mom!"

Brett blinked at her and continued without comment. "This is the first of three broadcasts, leading up to our Halloween ghost hunt on Friday. Tonight, we'll explore this hand-built Norman castle."

Liz interrupted him. "It's a really cool place, built by one man. It took him over fifty years to finish!" She pointed, and Gonzo panned the camera to take in the exterior of the castle, which had one main tower and a side wing. It was lit with the reddish-orange light of the fading sunset. Individual stones were highlighted with deepening shadows, and all of the windows Brett could see were dark.

He wasn't sure what he wanted to add to that. He decided action was better than being wordy, so after a little more back and forth about the castle, he turned and walked toward the entrance.

The massive wood and iron door was already open as they approached. Just inside, one of the Knights of the Golden Trail that maintained the place greeted them, glancing from Brett to Liz to the camera, looking uncertain.

The Knight wore torn muddy jeans and a flannel shirt. He set a gnarled, carved wooden walking stick on the glass counter just inside the door. Liz favored him with a warm, winning smile and shook his hand. The Knight grinned and relaxed as he launched into the history of the castle and its builder, Sir Harry Andrews.

Liz interrupted in the middle of the spiel, curiosity overcoming her. "What do you mean he was legally dead during World War One?"

The Knight looked startled and was silent a moment, looking at the camera again, then back to Liz. "Sorry, I'm used to going through the whole speech all at once. Sometimes I have to start over from the beginning if I'm stopped."

Liz's hand flew to cover her mouth. "Oh! Sorry, Mister Knight. I didn't know. Please go on."

The Knight just stared at the camera for a long, awkward moment. His lips moved without any sound, finding his place. "It's all right. Uh, Harry was declared dead, and he lay in the morgue, thought to be dead from spinal meningitis for three days. Just as the mortician was cutting into him to do an autopsy, Harry twitched, and to everyone's amazement, turned out to be alive after all. They kept him in quarantine for a month, but by the time he was declared 'undead,' six months later, his fiancée had married another."

Liz looked sad about this, but didn't say anything, letting the Knight go on with his story.

Brett could feel her sadness. He thought that he ought to be sad too, but somehow it didn't come to him. It was like touching something he expected to burn him, but instead finding it to be room temperature.

Liz was nudging him with an elbow. "Brett," she whispered. He blinked and realized he'd gotten lost in thought and hadn't noticed when the Knight finished speaking.

"Oh. Um, thank you for sharing that with our viewers. So," he said, covering with information he'd gotten off the castle's website, "the Knights inherited Loveland Castle and have cared for it since Harry's death?"

The Knight nodded. "We're a small but dedicated order. The castle, Chateau LaRoche, is a haven for us. Those of us who knew Harry, we see him in every stone and mortise of this place. This castle was his labor of love, and we intend to keep it in his memory."

"When you say you see him..." began Brett, but he was cut off by the Knight.

"No. We don't see his ghost. Sure, like any castle, we have our ghost stories, but I've spent weeks here by myself, and I've never seen or heard anything unusual. I've always said, if you believe in ghosts, you'll find them here. If you don't, you won't. I don't." The Knight's tone was light, his eyes amused, but Brett thought there might be more he wasn't telling. But this wasn't the time or place to press the point; they were lucky to have gotten permission to broadcast their tour in the first place.

"Let's leave the man be, Brett, and go look around," Liz said, tugging at his sleeve. He smiled and let her lead him. They passed an ornate wooden throne where dozens more of the carved walking sticks leaned, each with a price tag attached.

Liz turned to address the camera at the base of some stone stairs leading up. "I want to check out the tower. The stairs go up in a spiral, so our cameraman will need to be extra careful." Gonzo made a face at her, sticking his tongue out. Liz giggled and gestured to let Brett lead the way.

Brett could hardly see the tight spiral of stairs ahead of him in the castle's gloom. They plodded up the stairs, grateful for the iron railing bolted to the wall. They emerged into a room that led out into a hall filled by a great table. Another archway led off into the other wing. A set of stairs spiraled higher.

Brett decided to continue on upwards. He heard Liz and Gonzo following behind him. Knowing Gonzo, their audience was being treated to a view of Liz's bottom as she climbed the stairs. He smiled a little at the thought. He knew that despite his new abilities and years of experience with the paranormal, Liz was the real reason they had an audience.

After all, her webcam had earned her quite a following. All she had to do was be herself. Her sunny charisma and pixie-like features earned her quite an online following of viewers. Brett didn't blame them a bit, and he knew he'd become the envy of hundreds since he'd moved back in with her. That was fine with him.

This was different, though. It was a webcast with a purpose. Liz might be the draw, but to keep the audience, and to go somewhere with the show, they'd have to do more, make it interesting.

He emerged onto the roof to find the sunset had faded to a much dimmer twilight. Gonzo would have to flip on the infrared night vision on the IP camera. He hoped the broadcast was going well. He reassured himself with the thought that Jimbo hadn't called yet, so he must be getting it fine.

Liz hopped up the last few stairs and hugged him, feeling warm and good against his body. He snuck a quick kiss from her as Gonzo caught up. His large friend was breathing a bit hard, his face red with the effort. Gonzo gave him a look of annoyance, then his eyes went wide, focusing on something behind Brett and Liz. He pointed.

Liz detached herself from Brett as they both turned to look.

Brett drew in a hissing breath as a luminous figure came into view. It glowed with its own light, a short, roundish spectre approached them with a pair of shadows following.

"What do you see, sweetie?" asked Liz.

Brett squinted, still not at home with his new ability to see into the shadowy spirit world. His heart beat faster, wishing he could show the others what he saw.

"I'm not sure," murmured Brett. He forgot about Gonzo, the camera, and their audience for the moment. "Something... Maybe a ghost?"

They stood still, not daring to breathe. The figures stopped a few feet away, and the glowing figure merged into one of the shadows. They stepped into the light of the doorway.

"Oh no! No, no, uh-uh. I'm not going to be on camera. Turn that thing away right now." Brett relaxed, since he recognized the dry, matter-of-fact voice that matched this face. Caroline, Liz's friend from Indiana, scowled at him. She looked thinner than he remembered, and instead of the Ghost Trackers sweatshirt he'd seen her in earlier this year, she wore another black hoodie, zippered with the word MANILOW in block letters across her chest.

Despite her tone, Caroline smiled as Liz squealed and hugged her tight. Behind the two women, Brett saw another come into view, Jimbo's quirky girlfriend Frannie. He thought Fran looked a lot more together than the last couple of times he'd seen her. More present, he thought, not lost and hollow like she'd been for months.

"Hi, Liz," said Caroline, smiling as she escaped the hug. "Seriously though, no cameras, I don't want to be broadcast. Nope, uh uh."

Liz ignored her friend's protests and moved on to embrace Frannie. Frannie smiled and said, "Hi guys. We didn't think you'd come up here first."

Brett was forced to move out of the way as Caroline squeezed past him to get to the stairs and out of the view of the camera. Gonzo smirked at her and she rolled her eyes at him.

"The Knight didn't mention you arriving, and we didn't see your car. How'd you even get here?" Brett asked.

Frannie shrugged, watching Caroline disappear down the stairs. "She didn't want to take her Saturn down that hill to get here, so we parked and walked down instead. The Knight must have thought you knew we'd be here. Sorry."

Brett realized he could see a faint glow about Frannie. So, perhaps her soul still showed through after being leaked in March? *Interesting.*

"What?" asked Frannie as she caught Brett staring at her. "Do I have pizza on my shirt or something?" She started pulling her shirt out to look at it.

Brett shook his head. "No, nothing like that. I'll tell you later. Do you want to join us on the ghost hunt? We're here for a couple of hours."

Fran smiled and nodded. "Oh yeah. We drove down when we heard about the show. Caroline just wanted to socialize and do some investigating on her own, but I'd be glad to be part of things."

Liz grinned. "Great! Maybe we can chase Caroline around and around the castle as she avoids the camera." Her squeaky giggle was contagious.

Brett turned to the camera and said, "For our viewers' benefit, this is Frannie, she's a ghost-hunting friend who will be joining us. Pay no mind to the other person, she's not really here. Nope."

Off camera, Caroline stuck her tongue out at both Brett and Liz.

They poked around the crenelated tower top, taking the camera to look out onto the river and surrounding grounds. Frannie broke the unspoken rule and talked to Gonzo a few times, and answered text messages on her phone, annoying Brett more than a little. Liz seemed unconcerned, but he supposed that this wasn't meant to be scripted, so he tried to relax and let it slide for now.

Looking down from the edge of the tower top, he could see the parking lot, lit by a bright, halogen dusk-to-dawn light. Gonzo's ancient minivan, *Soccer Mom*, in her rusty, peeling glory, sat in the lot. He thought he saw movement near the van. He stared a bit longer, waiting for a repeat, but was pulled away by Liz, who wanted to move on. He followed her toward the stairs, giving a last look over the ramparts. He didn't see any more movement, so he shrugged and went on downstairs.

After exploring the large hall with the table, they settled in and got out equipment. Brett set out a compass with a red LED light in the center of the table. Liz wandered around with an EMF meter, reporting that the levels were very low.

Frannie poked at the suits of armor and heraldry on the walls. Caroline, as expected, was nowhere to be seen.

After establishing some baselines for electromagnetics, Brett led the three in an EVP session. He asked questions to the open air, as though another person sat with them at the table, while a couple of digital voice recorders listened for the unheard responses that were called Electronic Voice Phenomena.

Since they had lots of time, Brett and Liz agreed that it might be good to play back the recording for the camera. Brett was pretty sure they wouldn't get anything, since he hadn't seen any sign of activity other than the odd otherworldly glow that only he saw surrounding Frannie. He'd made her sit a bit away from the recorders and instruments, just in case.

They listened, though, just in case. The recorder played back their questions.

He heard himself ask, "Is there anyone here?" To his shock, a loud, deep voice answered,

"YES." This was not a faint, whispery reply, and it sounded a little familiar. There was a faint crackle of static just before and after the voice. He and Liz exchanged wide-eyed looks of surprise. Gonzo coughed behind him, startled. Frannie swore.

His voice on the recorder continued, having not heard the voice in real time. "What is your name?" The reply came, again with static before and after.

"NONE OF YOUR BUSINESS, FREAK." Liz's laugh didn't reach her eyes. She looked worried, peering around the room.

This time, Gonzo swore. "That's fucked up, Junior!"

Brett's recorded voice went on, asking, "Do you have any messages for us?" The voice answered in a hiss this time.

"YEAH. BRETT NELSON IS A FAKE!"

Chapter 2 - What Condition My Condition Is In

Brett stood up out of his chair so fast it fell over behind him. "What? Someone's messing with us!"

Brett cast his gaze around the room in a panic, searching for clues.

Brett watched as Gonzo propped the camera on its tripod, then pulled his phone from a back pocket. Gonzo frowned at the screen, then looked up to catch Brett's eye, head tilted in an unspoken question. The big guy then cut his finger across his throat and pointed at the camera.

Brett shook his head no. He looked over at Liz, who scrambled around the room looking under things and out windows. Frannie bit her lower lip, focused on her phone as she typed away.

Brett said to the camera, "Not cool. Let's figure this out." He felt calmer than he thought he should, almost like it was happening to someone else. He and Liz searched the room.

"Where was this recorder, exactly?" he asked.

Liz leaned back in from the balcony on the far end of the room to point. "My side of the table, by that second chair."

Brett walked to that chair, pulled it out and peered under the table. He didn't see anything at first. He pulled out his flashlight and then he saw it: something duct-taped to the underside of the table.

Brett ripped the tape off and came up with a handful of electronic devices. "Look! Someone taped a two-way radio under here... and it's plugged into some kind of battery-powered amplifier... which is plugged into..." He tore at the tape more to reveal a small cylinder, wrapped in thin copper wire. The ends were soldered to a jack that plugged into the amp.

"A subwoofer speaker coil," Gonzo finished for him. "Guess someone's fucking with you, Junior. A signal sent to that radio from another, amplified, would induce current in your mic. There's your EMF."

Brett looked at Gonzo and the camera, holding the parts up to be seen. "Yeah, a strong alternating field would be picked up by the recorder's mic without being heard by us. Shit."

Liz appeared by Brett's side, her arm slipping around his waist, peering at the device. "Guess they knew we were coming. Maybe they're still out there?" She reached over and unplugged the radio and ripped it off the duct tape.

Liz pressed a button on the side and spoke into it, her tone bright and artificial. "Welcome K-Mart shoppers! Today, we have a Blue Light Special on whoopass! Come on up and get yours today!"

There was a short burst of static and they all waited a few moments for a reply. Liz set the radio down and it burst to life. The speaker filled the room with a deep belly laugh.

I should be angry about this. Brett felt very much like some part of him must be furious. In fact, as he watched, he saw himself fly into a rage. He howled and threw ghost hunting gadgets across the room. Frannie jerked as an EMF meter shattered on the wall behind her. She dropped her cell phone and let out a little shriek of surprise.

Brett, still watched, stunned, as he saw himself stalk from the room. Like a tethered balloon, he bobbed along behind his body as it stomped down the stairs and pushed past Caroline. He could only follow along as he passed by the Knight and out the castle door.

It's like watching myself on video. A howling scream escaped his mouth. Obscenities roared forth in a childish display of temper. He thought he should do something about it, but could only look on in dismay.

Soccer Mom and the Knight's primer red pickup truck sat side by side in the long gravel parking lot. Brett trailed behind as his body ran down the path that skirted the castle. There was an impressive rock garden, including a long concrete sculpture of the Loch Ness Monster, which appeared to break the surface of the ground in several places.

He passed under the balcony at a run, and he heard Liz call out his name from above. His head didn't even look up. He really hoped his body calmed down soon. It was screaming and yelling incoherent curses as he passed more stonework and gardens. He stopped at a wicker gazebo at the end of the path, his body panting for breath.

He looked around, but there was no sign of whoever was on the other end of the radio. Brett looked on at his furious self standing there in the moonlight, breath slightly visible in the chill air, fists in tight balls by his sides. He stood there a long while and stared into the woods.

Brett saw himself whirl at the crunch of gravel on the path behind him. It was Liz, looking worried. He wanted to comfort her, but she looked past him, to where his body scowled.

"Brett? It's not that bad, honest! Jimbo told Fran that the broadcast is going wild. We've gone from tens of viewers to hundreds, and it's still climbing. He's not sure the server can keep up. This is a good thing."

"God damn it!" He heard himself say. "Someone's trying to make us look like idiots, and now we have a huge audience to witness it!"

Liz smiled. "Sweetie... we'd look like idiots if we bought into the 'EVP' they left. You found them out, and that shows we know what we're doing. Now, storming out and screaming like that, well... maybe that's not as cool, but Jimbo thinks that might have bumped our numbers even further."

Liz had been walking closer to his body, step by cautious step. "But come back in. I've got poor Fran wandering around with a meter to try to see if there are any more of those things around. She's not going to hold the net's attention very long. We've got to jump back in.

Okay?" She leaned into him, arms around his waist, chin up to hold his gaze. Brett longed to feel that.

And as sudden as it had started, it was over. Liz pressed her warm, solid, *real* body against him. Muscles from his forehead to his shoulders were strung tight, like hot wires. He drew in the cool night air and let it out, his tension melting away as he came back to himself. His heart pounded in his chest and the knots in his stomach loosened.

He put his arms around Liz. "I... I'm not sure what happened there. Lizzie, that wasn't me. Well, at least if it was, I wasn't doing it."

Liz frowned, and her eyes searched his. "What? Like... Oh God, Brett, like possession again?"

Brett paused a moment, thinking, then shook his head. "Noooo... not exactly like that. Like watching me on TV. I was in third person for a while."

"An out-of-body experience? Brett, I know it was upsetting, but..."

He shook his head and pulled out of her embrace. He took her hand to walk back to the castle entrance. "Well, that's the thing, I never really *felt* upset. I just watched as I blew up."

Liz let out a nervous little laugh, not looking at him. "The Devil made you do it?"

He chuckled. "Something like that? Too bad I didn't find the guy; maybe the rage would have been put to good use, delivering your Blue Light Special."

Liz giggled like a squeaky cartoon character. "Well, it's probably best we don't broadcast you assaulting someone over the Internet."

They encountered Caroline down in the entryway. Her eyes sparkled with amusement. "Feel better?"

Brett scowled. "No, not really. I wasn't myself for a bit."

Caroline nodded, concern dimming the sparkle. "Gonna be okay?"

Liz squeezed his hand and smiled at him. "He's fine."

Brett nodded. "Yeah, just this is really important, and someone's gone to a lot of trouble to try to screw it up. I thought I saw someone lurking around the van when we were up on the roof earlier. Guess I should have looked into it then."

Caroline nodded and shrugged. "I'll keep a lookout just in case they come back." She glanced at the Knight, who nodded and picked up his walking stick and smacked it into his other hand. He grinned.

Brett smiled. "Thanks. Let's get back up there before we lose our viewers."

They returned to find Frannie babbling into the camera about how unethical it was to interfere with a paranormal investigation, holding up the evidence. Gonzo looked relieved as they arrived, glancing from them to Fran, rolling his eyes.

Brett moved the investigation into the newer wing of the castle, where many mementos, more armor, and American flags were on display. Many rocks that made up the wall bore etchings of names of the places where they originated.

They searched the room for more electronics. Also, Brett made sure the radio he'd found was turned off and stowed it in his equipment case.

Liz danced around the room, picking things up, peering under them, and waving a CellSensor around. When she stopped and saw Fran and Brett staring at her, she dissolved into giggles. "Hey, I believe it's in my job description to make this look fun!"

Fran gave Liz a raspberry. Brett laughed and declared the room free of snoops, bugs and traps. Liz celebrated with a little jig, then plopped onto the floor, sitting cross-legged.

Brett took this as a cue to do the same. Fran sat on a bench, next to a looming suit of armor. Gonzo found the light switch, and the room plunged into darkness. Brett heard the snick of Gonzo switching the camera to night vision.

Brett could see Gonzo's face, lit from below by the camera's preview screen. He could see a red LED light on the meter Liz held. He pulled out a compass and placed it on the rug in the middle of the stone-walled room. He then put a small flashlight that cast only a dim red light on top of the compass. That way, it could be seen in the dark without spoiling their night vision. He aligned it with care, until the needle pointed at N.

He and Fran placed their voice recorders on the floor, recording. He peered into the heavy darkness, eyes straining to make out the forms of things in the room. He sensed Liz's eyes on him, and as his eyes adjusted further, he could see the glint of the compass light in them.

Frannie no longer glowed in the dark. There had always been something strange about the girl, and much had happened to change her since they'd met. At least she seemed a lot calmer and more stable these days. The glow could be a few things, none of which Brett cared to think about just now, and its absence was a relief.

Brett let himself relax and let his senses extend out from him, taking in the minute sounds, smells and feel of the room. There was an old, dry smell to this place, a little like a used bookstore, he thought. He heard his friends breathing. He felt a faint air current moving through the room.

Liz spoke, breaking the thick silence. "We're here to talk to whoever might be here. My name's Liz, what's yours?"

There was no answer, so they waited a couple of dozen heartbeats and she continued. "This is an amazing place. I can see why you might be drawn to it. What do you think of all the visitors that come here?"

Again, she paused, the silence settling like a heavy blanket on them in between questions.

Brett began to be aware of a presence in the far doorway. He couldn't see or hear anything. The perception of someone standing there came as a combination of things: a change in air pressure, sounds from beyond the doorway muffled. He'd expected to see *something*, since his senses had been tuned into the spirit world for months now. It'd started after his soul had leaked halfway out of him months ago. Not seeing anything disturbed him more than any apparition.

Well, maybe it wasn't a spirit, but something physical? Was someone in the room with them, standing right there in the darkened doorway, watching and listening? He glanced down at the red-lit compass on the floor. Its needle twitched, swung back and forth a few degrees, and then swung to point east, toward the doorway.

Brett reached into his pocket, as quiet as he could manage, and pulled out his flashlight. It had a built-in laser pointer. He covered the end with a hand and slid the switch to turn the laser on. He removed his hand and pointed it at the doorway.

The beam made a red dot on the stone on one side of the door. He heard Fran move as the light appeared. He moved the light to aim into the doorway, and saw it travel down the wall in the hallway beyond.

Then it just disappeared. The light was still on, but the red dot just didn't appear. It was being eaten up by the shadow in the doorway. He could see occasional flecks of dust sparkling along the line of the laser. The shadow, and the feeling of a presence, came closer.

"Sweetie, what is it?" asked Liz in a low voice. He heard Fran let out a groan as she shifted around where she sat.

Brett didn't answer, but stood and stepped toward the approaching shadow. "Hello?" he called out quietly. The laser light disappeared only a foot away from him now. He felt a chill ahead of him. *A cold spot.*

He felt an icy touch on his cheek. Anger flooded through him, though he didn't know why. He was shaking with it. He raged inside, angry at this intrusion, at the room, even at his friends.

Brett felt a growl deep in his throat, growing louder as the anger burned brighter in his chest. He felt like he might burst into flames, that he might explode if it went on even a few seconds longer.

He felt another touch. It was Liz, reaching up from the floor to take his hand, tangling her fingers with his in the dark. Her cool touch soothed him. "Brett, what *is* it?" she repeated louder this time as a demand, not a question.

Brett took a step backwards and plopped onto the floor next to Liz. As he did so, the icy touch withdrew, the anger going with it. The feeling of a presence withdrew as well. He felt the shadow slip from the room, the draft from the doorway caressed his face once more. He saw only a red light on the far wall, and he realized that the laser was now unobstructed.

"Tell me you got all that on camera, Gonz?"

"Yeah. Couldn't see a damned thing past you for a little bit there."

Frannie spoke up. "I saw something. I mean, I didn't. When you were standing up, there was something between me and you, and for a second, I didn't even see the compass."

They were silent for a while. Gonzo cleared his throat and Brett remembered they were still broadcasting. "That was... unsettling," he said. "Everyone watching, I don't know what you saw, but there was something in the room with us, it touched me, even. Some kind of 'shadow person,' maybe?"

"Battery's low, make it quick, Junior."

This was sooner than Brett expected. Perhaps the shadow had drained the camera's battery? "We're going to have to sign off now. Any final thoughts? Fran? Lizzie?"

Liz sprang to her feet, close to the camera, shining a flashlight under her face, grinning from ear to ear. "Yeah! That was *cool!* See you tomorrow night at Hell's Gate everyone!"

Chapter 3 - Ghost of a Smile

"BACON!!!"

Brett and Gonzo both winced when Liz and Caroline cheered the arrival of their favorite breakfast meat. The waiter who brought their midnight breakfast almost dropped the tray. Tears streamed down Fran's face as she fought to breathe and laugh at the same time.

Caroline giggled and said, "Sorry!" to the college-aged server as he backed away from the table in confusion. "We're crazy, but we tip well." She and Liz grinned at each other. Each picked up a piece of bacon and pretended to swordfight, then each bit off a crunchy bit of the end.

Brett put his face in his hands. "I can't take you two anywhere," he moaned.

He felt Liz nudge him with an elbow. When he looked up, he had a strip of bacon hovering an inch from his mouth. "I smell bacon!" she cried. He took a bite to humor her. It was much saltier than he expected, and was thick, making it a bit like crunchy jerky. He chewed and Liz kissed him with bacony lips.

Brett circled his ear with a finger while looking from her to Caroline. Caroline pulled her plate away from him as though he might try to take some of her bacon.

"I thought we were done with demonic possession. You psycho girls scare me more than that... whatever it was back there," Gonzo said as he rubbed his hands together and dug into his chocolate chip waffles.

Caroline sipped at her heavily doctored coffee and stuck her tongue out at Gonzo. "Hey. I'm off the diet for 'Grease Feast,' so I gotta have the good stuff!"

Fran wiped at the tears on her cheeks, "Ugh, I haven't wanted meat since... well, *since*. I'm back to vegetarian again." She poured ketchup on a pile of fried potato cubes and speared a few with her fork.

"Bacon *is* a vegetable!" cheered Liz, crumbling one of her bacon strips onto the omelet on her plate.

Brett poked at his scrambled eggs and toast. Breakfast in the wee hours was a time-honored ghost hunting tradition, but he found he didn't have much of an appetite. He started to make a joke about bacon trees, but was saved by his cell phone ringing.

It was Jimbo, so he put the phone on speaker. "Hey Brett, doesn't anyone have their phone on? I've been texting for a half hour and no one replies!"

Liz laughed around a mouthful of breakfast, "Om nom nom. Blue Wizard needs food. Badly. Green Archer shot the food!"

Jimbo talked louder than necessary when he realized he was talking to everyone. "Uh oh. Grease feast, huh? Well, you guys are gonna crap your pants at the numbers we got. We broke the server, it had to turn people away! I read that people were out there rebroadcasting our stream once the limit got hit. Guess the poker guys got their money's worth out of tonight!"

Brett had been skeptical about taking a gambling sponsorship, but PokerZombie paid enough to cover gas, food and a payment on the IP camera. "Good. That means whoever tried to screw with us just ended up helping us."

Gonzo mumbled around a mouthful of waffles. "It's just like any of the stupid reality shows out there." He washed his food down with some coffee and said, "You got a train wreck? Idiots everywhere want to watch."

"Gonzo!" cried Liz. "How could you? We've worked hard on lining this show up. Aren't you having fun behind the camera? Would you rather be in the limelight too?" She batted her eyelashes and made kissy faces at Gonzo.

Gonzo made a rude noise. "Pppht. Nah, no one wants to see that. I'm fine with the show, it's been fun. Just saying, idiots want things to go off the rails. Maybe a hundred of those want to see ghosts, but more want to see Brett lose his shit on camera."

Brett glared hot death at Gonzo.

Gonzo held up a hand. "Hey, I'm just sayin'! PBS makes wonderful TV, but it doesn't draw like 'Who Wants to Father Britney's Two-Headed Love Child?' or 'My Husband the Oversexed Drag Queen'.... Crap outsells science, man. You couldn't have planned this, but it worked. Maybe this leave of absence from King's Pizza can go on indefinitely, hmm? Enid's gonna be pissed."

"She'll get over it. You did put her in charge while you're gone, after all. And that's the idea, Gonz. I just didn't want to get my hopes up about this taking off so quickly."

"No shit, we planned for like a *fifth* of these numbers," said Jimbo. "After my guild meeting, I'm gonna hit up some of the advertisers who turned us down. They might be in for tomorrow or the Halloween show."

"You're so sexy when you sound like you know what you're talking about," said Fran in a drawl.

"Aw, Fran, shut up! Bad enough you went without me, and I'm stuck at home with web monkey duties, you don't gotta rub it in!"

Fran chuckled. "Miss you, my little web monkey!"

Liz made "Oook ook eeek!" noises while Caroline made loud, wet, kissing noises.

"Okay, that's it, I'm hanging up on you freaks now. I just called to give the good news. The cell feed for that IP camera went better than I expected. I'll call you tomorrow afternoon to get set up again, okay, Gonz?"

"Yep. I should be in advanced stages of hangover by then."

"Love you, baby!" cried Fran just before Jimbo hung up.

"Hangover, Gonz? Did you bring that much Irish?" asked Liz.

Gonzo looked at her and grinned. "Don't be stupid. I'm not gonna use it all up in one night. Nah, my buddy Ralph lives around here. He's the guy I said we could crash with. It's always a party at his place."

Liz shook her head. "No, no. I've heard about Ralph. Half of the stories involving him end with his name meaning something else. We've got to be awake for the show tomorrow night!"

"Oh, sweetie, it'll be fine. We'll go over, have a few drinks, then crash 'til afternoon," pleaded Brett, though he could tell from her exaggerated pout that she wasn't going to budge on this.

"You can stay with us," offered Caroline. "I booked a room for Fran and me before I took off. There are two king beds, you can bunk with me. It'll be a slumber party!" She flashed Liz a cheesy grin.

Liz clapped her hands together. "Oooh, that sounds perfect... I even brought my Powerpuff Girls PJs!"

"Mind if I set up the camera in the room, ladies? Just for security purposes, of course." said Gonzo, waggling his eyebrows at Caroline.

She swatted him with her cloth napkin, glaring. "Down boy. Heel!" She favored him with an evil look. "As much as my husband would like that footage, what happens at Best Western stays at Best Western." She gave Liz a big wink.

"What?" Brett felt his face flush a little. "You're ditching me to take off with her?"

Liz leaned over and kissed Brett's cheek. "Don't worry, handsome, she's all talk. She'll never see what's under Bubbles. Buttercup, maybe. But not Bubbles. And only you know what secrets Blossom holds...."

Brett looked to Gonzo for help. The big guy grinned. "Aw come on, let 'em have a girl's night. We'll hang out at Ralph's place."

He raised his orange juice glass and looked upward as if toasting the gods. "Manly man stuff, drunken fun!" Gonzo cackled.

"I have a bad feeling about this. Can I just join the slumber party instead?" Brett asked Liz without much hope.

She put a hand on each cheek and drew him in for a warm, luscious kiss that made him forget where he was for a moment. "I'm sorry, sweetie. Girl time. Brett not girl. Brett get girl back tomorrow. Ug!"

Brett scowled and said nothing. Liz took her hands off his cheeks and kissed the end of his nose, then looked at Caroline with a shrug.

"Don't look at me, I left mine at home. If yours isn't paper trained, you can go take care of him instead." Caroline turned her attention to her breakfast.

Brett tried to say, "I'll be okay, you go ahead," but instead felt a great shove and found he was watching himself and his friends from above the table.

What he heard himself say instead was, "Bitch!"

Liz and Frannie turned to look at Brett in shock. Gonzo coughed into his napkin to cover a laugh.

Caroline's head jerked up from her breakfast, eyes narrowed and focused on Brett from under her bangs. "Hmm. You say that like it's a bad thing. Liz, can you put a leash on yours?" Brett noticed, looking at the top of her head, that her hairband was covered in little grinning skulls.

"Brett, this isn't you talking, is it?" said Lizzie.

"Of *course* it's me. Who else would put up with this crap?"

Brett watched as his body stood up, pulled out a couple of twenties and threw them on the table, then stalked off. Again, he was pulled along behind. It was strange to see the back of his head. He thought maybe his hair could use a trim.

He heard Gonzo and Liz get up and argue in a loud whisper as his body pushed open the door to the restaurant with too much force, its tinkling bells jangling in alarm.

Once outside, his body stomped up and down, not having keys to either of the cars. He watched as he tried each of the doors to *Soccer Mom*.

The bells of the door jingled, and he saw Liz come out, wet streaks glinting orange on her cheeks in the sodium lights of the parking lot. She ran to Brett and grabbed his shoulders. "Brett! Come back! This isn't you!" She pulled her silver pentacle out of her blouse and peered through it at Brett. "Sweetie, you're warded against any further possession, but you sure aren't yourself. But, I don't see signs of the demon, just something odd with your aura."

"I'm as much me as I ever have been," came out of his mouth. "Caroline never liked me. She liked it better when we were split up."

Liz dropped her pentacle and held onto his shoulders. She tried to make eye contact, but he could see his eyes were looking anywhere else but at hers. She blinked and more tears flowed. "Oh, sweetie, that's not true. She's my friend, she knows how I was when we were apart, how I missed you. You need to calm down and come back to me, love. I don't want my friend and my boyfriend fighting. She didn't mean anything. She just teases like that. Trust me, sweetie, she wouldn't do that if she didn't like you."

Brett watched as he pulled away from Liz. He didn't like seeing Liz cry, and he didn't like the sob she let out when his body walked away from her. He thought maybe he should try to be in control.

At the thought, he was drawn back toward his body. He felt cold hands shoving at him as he approached, but with an effort, he shoved back, still feeling calm and distant.

There was a disorienting spin to the world, and after wrestling with the unseen coldness a while, he found himself sitting down hard on the cold pavement. He yelped at the sudden pain and tried to get up, but fell on his side, dizzy.

Liz's hands were warm to the touch this time as she helped sit him up. He had a glimpse of Gonzo in the doorway, looking at him. He felt embarrassed.

Looking at Liz, his head swam. He said, "Oh Liz, it happened again. I was only watching... I can't explain...."

Liz wiped her cheeks with a sleeve of her sweater dress. Confusion showed in her eyes, and she bit her lower lip. "Brett, I'm not sure what's happening to you, but there's no demon this time. I'm sure of it. These angry outbursts, they're not like you, but at the same time, when I touch you, it's not a monster touching me back. It's *you*, I can feel you in there. Angry, pissy, unpleasant, for sure, but not *demonic or evil.* I know my *Chico,* and I love him, moody or not. Maybe it's a side effect of your soul leaking out, maybe it's growing pains while you recover? Fran's never been the same since the same thing happened with her. You just have to try harder to control it."

Brett hugged her tight to him. "Lizzie, can't you ward me with a spell, like you did against the demon?"

Her head shook from side to side. "No. I can't ward you against this because it's not something external. It's something going on with *you*, don't you see?"

"Not really," Brett said. "I don't know how to stop it, and it feels like someone else, it's not in my control."

"Brett, I think you should apologize to Caroline. Even if it wasn't you, she's really pissed."

He nodded to Liz. "I don't understand what's happening. I wasn't happy about splitting up tonight, but whatever took me over overreacted."

Liz let out a little humorless laugh. "You think?" She studied his face a moment, then hugged him. "I'm still going with Caroline, okay?"

Brett nodded. "Yeah. I'm sorry. It's okay."

Liz kissed him, then dragged him back to the doorway by one hand. Gonzo had come outside, leaning on *Soccer Mom*, pretending not to overhear.

Just inside, Brett could see Fran and Caroline talking. Caroline's face was still cold and she shook her head at something Fran said.

He opened the door, and the two women stepped outside. "Look, Caroline, I'm..."

"No. It's okay. Really." She wouldn't look at Brett. "We should get going." She pulled keys from her purse and yellow hazard lights flashed once on her car as it unlocked.

Brett looked to Liz for help. She shrugged. "I'll try to explain later, love."

He sighed and nodded. Liz gave him one more hug and kiss and the three women got into Caroline's car. Brett was disappointed that she didn't look at him as they drove off.

"Eh, don't sweat it, Junior. She was being a bitch. Got a chip on her shoulder. Besides," Gonzo affected a stage whisper, cupping a hand alongside his mouth, "Ralph doesn't stock the piss water beer she likes anyway."

Brett snorted out a short laugh. "Gonz, this is Ralph we're talking about. He drinks worse stuff than that. He still misses generic beer. He thinks Hamm's is stylin'."

Gonzo grinned and landed a light punch on Brett's shoulder. "Come on, he's probably a couple of sheets to the wind by now. Texted me earlier to tell me Tod the Rod, Jenny and The L.T. are over there already."

"Oh, shit, this is going to be worse than I thought,"

Gonzo grinned. He opened the driver's door with the key, got inside and reached over to open the passenger door. Brett climbed in and said, "Remember, I can't get hungover and I've got to get some sleep before tomorrow."

"Relax. I'll get you back to Liz and your adoring public in one piece. Probably."

I hope that's the worst I'll have to worry about. He gripped the armrest of the van as though it could hold him in place in his body.

Chapter 4 - Carry on My Wayward Son

Brett and Gonzo found Ralph and The L.T. were singing as they arrived. Gonzo's friends sat on the short wall bordering the porch of Ralph's rented house. A bug light was the only illumination outside, so they were seen in silhouette.

"I wanna be a pervert!" sang Ralph.

"And you can be my butt plug!" The L.T. replied, his words slurring.

They repeated this verse a couple more times. Since neither had an idea of how to complete the parody, Ralph greeted Gonzo and Brett with a toast. He raised the quart-sized Big Gulp cup up high. "Gentlemen, welcome! Join us!"

The L.T. followed suit, sloshing the contents of his cup a bit with his enthusiasm. He had a wad of gauze taped to his forehead. His head was shaved, with just a hint of stubble showing. He grinned and pushed the cup under Brett's nose. "Hey! We're drinkin' *Raid!*"

The dark, fizzy beverage did smell quite a lot like insecticide. Brett turned his head away. "Ugh, what the hell's in there?"

Ralph looked pleased at the reaction, beaming at Brett. He pushed a greasy lock of hair out from behind his thick-lensed glasses. "Uh, Captain Morgan and Dr Pepper."

"Gin," added The L.T.

"Yeah, probably some gin in there too," said Ralph. "Gonz! Good to see you, you big fucker. What's Memphis got that you can't get here?" He pointed at a small table, and The L.T. nodded, mixing up a couple more of the noxious drinks.

"Morals, principals and a sense of dignity, that's what it's got. Why the fuck do you think I had to come visit you assholes?"

Gonzo grinned and bumped fists with The L.T., who handed one of the large cups to him. The big guy took a sniff and made a face. "God damn, you bastards sure know how to ruin a drink," he said. He put his head back, poured about a third of the cup down his throat and let out a spectacular belch.

Brett took the large drink from The L.T., eyeing it with suspicion before tasting it. It turned out to smell much worse than it tasted, so he drank quite a lot so he could avoid inhaling any more vapors. It was warm and fizzy, and the bubbles and alcohol burned all the way down. A warm glow spread outward from his stomach.

"Guh!" said Brett, coming up for air. "What's wrong with you guys? Were they out of turpentine?"

Ralph's laugh was loud and honking, but his lazy smile was genuine. "Eh, you know Jenny. Too good for turpentine, so I had to get the good stuff while she and Tod visit."

"Where are they, anyway?"

"Oh, they're inside listening to Pink Floyd and staring at each other. Typical 'depression session,' ya know?"

The L.T. tried to get back up on the wall and failed, more Raid spilling from his cup with each attempt.

"What happened to your forehead, dude?" said Gonzo as he watched The L.T.'s struggle.

Ralph honked again.

The L.T. scowled at him. "Knocked on a door with my forehead."

"It had a nail in it," said Ralph.

"It was dark and I had a beer in each hand, you fucker."

Brett took another long drink of Raid to keep from laughing at The L.T.

Ralph stood up and waved overhand toward the door. "Come on, let's crank some tunes."

Brett had to help The L.T. from falling off the porch steps. The L.T. shook him off, looking irritated.

They went inside, finding a couple sitting in the living room. Tod's black, stringy hair framed his face, his tattered tie-dye T-shirt several sizes too big for his scarecrow frame. He sat cross-legged facing Jenny, whose clothes mirrored his, though her shirt clung to her curves more interestingly. Her dishwater blonde hair was held up in a bun with disposable wooden chopsticks.

They faced each other, knees touching, eyes locked, hands flat against each others', making small circles as they listened to the closing track of *The Dark Side of the Moon*. The room was lit by a single, bare, black light bulb. They didn't seem to notice anyone else come in.

Ralph stepped around them to the turntable. Ralph owned the largest collection of vinyl LP records Brett had ever seen. Ralph picked up the needle and put the album lovingly back into its sleeve.

"Hey!" cried Tod and Jenny in unison, breaking hand contact.

"Sorry folks, it's not that kind of night." Ralph riffled through his albums and came up with one. He put it on the turntable, then let the automatic mechanism place the needle at the start. Pops and static from dust came from the speakers as the music of Devo filled the room.

"Aw, not that crap," said Gonzo, making a sour face.

Ralph folded his arms and threw back his head. "Ah ha ha ha ha! Oh *yes*, this crap! I've gone mad with power, you see. *Mad*, I tell you!"

Gonzo snorted and took another long swallow of his Raid.

Tod and Jenny stood up, looking irritated. "Ralph, come on," said Tod.

"Yeah, Ralph," said Jenny.

The L.T. began to do a jerky dance around the room, a confused mix of Moonwalking, "the robot" and stumbling.

"There's one vote for Devo," said Brett, grinning. "I can take it, too."

Ralph clapped Brett on the back, honking. "See, some people have taste." He reached over to the volume knob and turned it up a quarter turn.

Brett was sure the house would come down around them from the vibration.

"Jesus H., Ralph! What the hell is that, God's Stereo?" Gonzo tried to cover both ears but failed, since he hadn't put down his drink.

Brett felt waves of sound coming from what he'd taken to be matching cabinets, each as tall as him.

"Damn it, you have this awesome machine?" said Gonzo. "What, are you taking from the till at that shithole of a pizza place again?"

Ralph adjusted his glasses and stood straighter. "That's *my* shithole of a pizza place, I'll have you know. The chain decided to drop it and I got a loan, and it's Ralph's Pizza To Go as of last month."

Gonzo whistled. "Movin' on up, dude. I'm impressed. So, you used part of the loan for the stereo?"

Ralph shook his head. "Nah, that's from the rent-to-own place. I'm about halfway there."

The L.T. danced too close to the turntable and the needle skipped, landing in the middle of "Speed Racer." He cheered and sang along. "I drive real fast, I'm gonna last!"

Brett was still sipping at his Raid, listening to the half-shouted conversation through the pulsing waves of the monster speakers. He watched Tod and Jenny take turns talking into each others' ears. Tod announced with a yell that he and Jenny were leaving.

Ralph dialed God's Stereo's volume to non-seismic levels. "Hey, don't go, the party's just starting!"

Tod and Jenny exchanged sulky glances.

"I got it," said Gonzo, flipping through the record collection. "Brett, you have to see this, it's fantastic. Come on, Tod, it's time." He set down his empty cup and slid out a 45 rpm record. He spun it around a finger through the large hole in the center. Ralph, taking his cue, replaced the Devo album in its dust jacket.

Ralph then placed the needle in its proper groove on the new record. An eerie voice yodeled, unaccompanied. Tod's face lit up. Ralph grinned. Gonzo cackled. The three lined up, side by side, and they swayed together more or less in time to the drums.

Jenny covered her face with her hands and groaned, "Oh no! Not this again."

The L.T. cheered. Brett wasn't sure what was going on until the "wimowehs" started and the trio bobbed their heads up and down.

Tod the Rod held an invisible microphone in front of him and began to lip-synch, "In the jungle, the mighty jungle..."

Brett laughed, set down his Raid and clapped in time with The L.T. When the song came to the second round of "wimowehs," all three cupped their crotch with a hand. To get the higher notes, Brett guessed. The trio spun and capered as the song went on.

Jenny remained embarrassed throughout the performance, but did part her fingers enough to watch.

The three lined back up in formation for the final, fading yodels of the song. As it ended, they grinned and bowed in unison. Brett and The L.T. applauded with tipsy enthusiasm.

"See, now it's a party!" said Gonzo. "Beer," he announced, and went to the kitchen to find more drinks. Brett and Ralph followed along.

Gonzo rummaged in the fridge and came out with three bottles of beer, which he passed around. Brett had only a third of his Raid left, so he downed it in several long gulps and belched.

"That's only a worth a four, Junior, and I'm being generous."

"I'm trying!"

"No. Do not try. Do. There is no try."

Ralph looked up at Gonzo. "Aren't you a little tall to be Yoda?"

Gonzo affected a wounded expression. "Judge me by my size, do you?"

Ralph had no reply, so he just laughed.

"And well you should not! For the farts are my ally, and a powerful ally they are! Pull my finger." Brett and Ralph backed away, hands up in surrender. Gonzo squinched his face and let loose.

All three fled the room, bumping into The L.T. coming the other say. Ralph grabbed The L.T. and said, "Sorry, man, the EPA's closed that room for the duration."

"Duration?" asked The L.T.

Brett said, "It'd be safer to make yourself more Raid for now."

The L.T. thought this was a great idea and went out to concoct more of the nasty libation.

After selecting some Creedence to play on God's Stereo, everyone went out to sit on the yellow-lit porch. "So, what brings you up this way again, Gonz?" asked Ralph.

Gonzo shrugged. "Ah, Brett and Liz needed help with their ghost busting."

"Not ghost *busting*, ghost *hunting*. We did a webcast from Loveland Castle."

Ralph and the others looked at Brett. "Ghost hunting webcast? Sounds cool, man! I didn't know that place was haunted."

Brett shrugged. "It's not notoriously haunted, but they have their ghost stories. We're going down to Hell's Gate at Bobby Mackey's tomorrow night."

Ralph shivered. "I wouldn't go near that place. Too many rednecks."

Brett laughed. "No, the bar's going to be closed early that night. They've got a private party that only goes 'til eleven. We get the run of the place for a few hours after that."

Ralph nodded. He was silent a while, a faraway look in his eye. 'Hmm, you know this place is haunted too, right?"

Brett looked at Gonzo, who shrugged.

"I've had weird stuff going on here since I moved in a few years ago. Tod and Jenny lived here last summer, they can tell you."

Jenny nodded. "I was having an argument with Tod one time--I think it was over paying the gas bill..."

Tod interrupted. "Aw, don't bring that up again!"

She shook her head. "Let me finish! We were arguing in the kitchen, and the phone *flew* off the wall and hit the cabinets. By itself!"

Brett wished he hadn't finished his Raid so quickly. His head was swimming, and he wanted to remember the stories. "Wow. What else?"

"Well," began Ralph, looking uncomfortable, "around that time, I started having nightmares. At first, it was just of darkness and feeling trapped. Later dreams, I was a little girl, clinging to my sister in the dark as a monster loomed up at the top of a staircase, the only light coming from behind it."

Everyone was quiet as Ralph talked. He paused to finish his beer. God's Stereo could be heard inside playing "Bad Moon Rising." He adjusted his glasses and continued. "Well, anyway, everyone joked about those dreams. I wanted to pull out the nails shutting the basement door to look for evidence they might be true, but these two didn't like the idea. One day, we started having sewer problems, and I *had* to go down there. It was a mess, ankle deep in water, TP and unidentified floating objects, for the most part. But the floor sloped upward toward a crawl space, so it was dry over there."

Ralph looked like he didn't want to go further. The L.T. offered his cup of Raid to him. Ralph shook his head and continued.

"Up in the crawl space, I found two doll heads."

After a long silence, Brett heard The L.T. curse. He turned to look at Tod and Jenny and they were nodding to back up Ralph's story.

"You're so full of shit, Ralph," said Gonzo.

Ralph shrugged and smiled. "Hey, believe what you like, but I know what happened."

Brett was amazed at Gonzo's continued disbelief concerning anything paranormal after all they'd been through together. Ghosts, demonic possession and ghouls... The big guy knew firsthand that at least some of it was real, he just didn't like to admit it.

"Whatever," said Gonzo, mixing another super suicide combo drink from the assembled bottles. He handed it to Brett and started one for himself. Brett sniffed. It wasn't Raid, but he guessed it was at least as strong. *Tomorrow's gonna suck.* He drank deep.

Ralph stood up and raised his cup high. "Gentlemen--oh and lady... and you too, Gonz... We have a mission."

"Huh?" asked The L.T.

Ralph used his free hand to wipe hair out of his eyes again. He said, "Yeah. Some people talk about ghosts, but guys like Brett and me? We find them. Let's go."

Big plastic cup in hand, Ralph marched off the porch, not looking back. Gonzo cursed, looked at the others and said, "Okay, come on, we'd better keep him out of trouble."

Chapter 5 - Stand By Me

They followed Ralph and Gonzo down the street, each still carrying their drinks. Tod had to run back to the house to lock up, to preserve God's Stereo if nothing else. Brett could still hear Creedence playing half a block away. He hadn't heard that Ralph was a ghost hunter. If so, this broke some important rules about sobriety... Who'd believe any ghost stories that involved alcohol? Whatever the mission, though, this wasn't anything official, he told himself. They went to the end of the street and ducked under some branches and climbed a small hill. Brett tripped on a railroad tie, and almost spilled his drink. The tracks led off into the darkness in both directions.

Gonzo looked up and down the railway. "Hey, Ralph, these tracks are abandoned, yeah?" Ralph didn't answer, but started off down the tracks to the left. Trees formed a corridor as far as Brett could see. In the moonlight, at least, he could see the ties ahead of him.

"Ten or fifteen years ago," Ralph said from up ahead, "there was this school, kind of an old one-room schoolhouse that was set up again for gifted kids. A magnet school. But it was really old, from settlers' days. Anyway, the school was restored and kids were bused in from all over the area. It showed up on the news now and again, if it was a slow news day. There were maybe thirty students, so it was more of a showcase than anything.

"Anyway, they called it the Mounds School, because it was on land that used to belong to the Mound Builder Indians. You know, they made these huge earthworks, no one's sure what for, or even how they managed it. They lined up with the stars and the Sun like Stonehenge and shit like that. The place had been a park forever, and still was, except for the school."

Brett thought the story sounded familiar somehow. He thought maybe he'd heard it in Indiana, or maybe even Tennessee. Maybe this was one of the urban legend type ghost stories, he thought. Like every county in Indiana has its very own "screaming bridge" from which lovers had leaped, mothers had dropped their babies, or someone had been struck by a car late at night.

Still, the Mound Builders had spanned a large area. Brett had also heard that in addition to astronomical correlations, the locations of the earthworks fell along other lines. The supposed lines of power called "ley lines," along which metaphysical energy was supposed to flow. He and Liz had visited Mounds State Park up near Anderson so she could experience the lines. He remembered watching her dangling crystal pendulums at various points in the park until she found just the right spot. She'd sat there for the better part of an hour, meditating. He remembered being glad he'd brought a book with him.

The trees parted to reveal a tributary river, maybe a hundred feet across. The tracks continued on over the river, carried by an iron suspension bridge. Ralph continued walking, stepping from one tie to another as he talked.

Brett saw Gonzo hesitate. He looked back at the others behind him and swore. He drank deeply from his cup and started across, staring at his feet as he stepped less certainly onto the bridge.

Brett was next. He could see between the ties, down the steep embankment. He could hear the water rushing and splashing on the rocks on the bank thirty feet below. He took a step onto the first tie, then to the next, hoping to get a rhythm going so he wouldn't have to think about it.

He heard The L.T. and Tod arguing behind them. He heard Jenny say out loud, "No fucking way, Tod. Ralph's nuts, let's go."

Brett glanced back to see Jenny towing Tod the Rod back the way they'd come. The L.T. gave him a little salute with his big cup and came after. Brett turned ahead again. His head spun enough to make him lose his bearings for a moment. With everything doing a slow orbit around him, Brett had only a guess at which way was forward.

Brett's right foot stepped out onto air. He started to pitch forward. His foot found nothing to stand on and he began to fall. He was already too far off balance to throw himself back, and Gonzo was a few ties ahead, so he had nothing to push off of in that direction.

He was sure he was going to end up falling into the river below when he heard a yell, and his belt pulled hard into his gut.

Enough to steady his balance and get both feet on the same tie. He thrashed and threw his weight backward. His cup sloshed and the drink splashed. His back bumped into The L.T.'s head. The L.T. let go his belt, letting out a whooping yell.

Brett stood up with great care, ignoring the spinning. He saw Gonzo and Ralph turn around at The L.T.'s yell. When he saw the looks on their faces, Brett could feel the foolish grin spread across his face. "Hey, thanks--"

"Dude. Don't turn around. Thank me later," said The L.T. from behind him. "Let's go."

Brett took a swig of what was left in his cup, drew in a deep breath and stepped to the next tie.

"Thought I might be dead there for a moment," said Brett as he reached the middle of the bridge. He was very aware of a cool wind coming down the river's course. He saw traces of mist chasing along with it. It made him feel like he was walking on a diagonal. He had to concentrate on Gonzo's back to right himself.

"S'okay. Ever think about dying?" said The L.T.

"Huh? Yeah, just then, that's what I meant."

"Naw, not just then. I mean, what if a train came along now, like in that movie with River Phoenix? Except we're drunk, and trains don't go that slow." The L.T.'s voice held a nervous edge that Brett didn't like.

"Uh. Yeah. Why, do you hear something?" Brett started counting ties to keep his focus. One. Two. Three. Four.

"Maybe. Don't look back, but what if there was a light in the distance, heading our way? Would you be okay if that was it? I think I would. I've had a good life, you know?"

Brett almost turned around to see if The L.T. was serious. Now he imagined a light behind them, gaining on them fast. He couldn't help breathing faster, felt his heart beat harder. He had to keep counting. Twelve. Thirteen. Fourteen. Was that a train whistle?

"Um, actually, I'm hoping my best years are ahead of me, man," said Brett. Sixteen. Seventeen. Eighteen. He glanced up and cried out in surprise as Gonzo was right in front of him.

The big guy grabbed his shoulders, grinning into his face and pulled him off the track to one side onto solid ground. Brett cheered and made a show of getting down on the ground to kiss the dirt. It wasn't as good an idea as it seemed, and he wiped the dirt on his sleeve.

He looked up in time to see The L.T. stumble on the rail close to him. Brett had to move his hand to keep The L.T. from stomping it with his boot. He looked up and they traded grins and laughed.

"Had you going, didn't I?" said The L.T.

Brett pulled himself up and dusted off his knees. He looked back across the bridge. It was dark as far as he could see. "Maybe. Hey you know what?"

"What?"

"Looks like we all still have our beverages!" Brett raised his in a sloshing toast. Gonzo looked at the cup as though it was a wondrous discovery and joined Brett and The L.T. in the toast. They each drank down what was left in the big cups. Gonzo made a show of hiding his cup in some bushes near the end of the bridge. Brett and The L.T. followed his example. They could pick them up on the way back.

Ralph walked back to where they were and pushed his thick glasses back up his nose with the back of his hand. "Hey, come on, it's not much further."

They fell back into single file and walked in silence a while. Brett tried walking from tie to tie again at first, but his slip made him move with extreme caution.

After a few minutes, Gonzo asked, "So what's the big deal about this school anyway, why's it supposed to be haunted?"

Ralph stopped and held up a finger as they came to a clearing. A hill rose up on one side of the tracks. He pointed up the hill, which was black against the sky. Black, ragged clouds flowed across the face of the Moon like lost souls grasping at its cold light. A small building stood silhouetted against the sky.

"There it is. Let's go up and I'll finish."

The L.T. was the first up the hill, climbing it in a scramble that reminded Brett of Gollum. Ralph picked a slower, more deliberate way up. Brett and Gonzo had a worse time of it, losing their footing and falling on their hands and knees a few times as they climbed. Gonzo was breathing hard and cursing steadily as he got to the top. Brett was last, feeling disoriented and lost as he followed along.

They huddled in a little circle as Ralph spoke. "Okay, so the school went on like that, gathering two or three dozen gifted and talented kids each year, for a few years. The buses brought them up here each day, then came and took them home again.

"Then one day, the buses came and no one came out of the school. On the news, the police said they found the lights still on, books still open on desks. Lunch boxes still had lunches in them. But no kids, no teacher, they were all gone."

"Someone kill them all?" asked The L.T. "Some kind of psycho?"

Ralph shook his head. "No, man. None of those kids or the teacher were ever seen again. It's been ten years, and the parents still hold memorials up here for the twenty-nine kids lost. They even interviewed this teenager one time, I guess she called in sick that day or something and was the only one of the class left."

Brett shivered and looked at the school. The sign was small and carved out of a plank of wood. It said "Mounds School." He saw that they were near a window, and he took a step towards it, seeing a pale light within.

He listened with only half an ear as Gonzo debated the story with Ralph behind him while he peered in the dirty glass pane. Old fashioned wooden desks were lined up, facing away from him. There was a chalkboard, but he couldn't make anything out on it.

Brett went to the door and tried the knob. It spun in place, but didn't release the catch, it just rattled.

Ralph joined him. "If it was that easy, kids all around here would have broken in long ago. I guess some have anyway, the windows get broken every few years on Halloween. But I guess no one stays too long. It's creepy here. But I come prepared." He searched around in his pants pocket and came up with a jangling handful of keys.

He picked through them until he came up with a long iron key. "I figured, it's an old place, maybe a skeleton key would get me in. I went on eBay and bought a box of them and came down here one night and tried them, one after another. I thought I'd be here all night, I had a couple hundred old keys in that box. But it opened after maybe a couple dozen or so tries."

Ralph fit his key in the lock and turned. The bolt slid back with a screech, and the door swung open. There was weak applause from Brett and the others at this feat. Ralph twisted the key again to free it and put the key ring back in his pocket. He took a little bow and motioned inward with an arm.

Brett was first in the door, and his ghost hunting habits made him do so with great care, so as not to stir up dust and ruin ghost photography. He realized no one had a camera, shrugged, and walked right up to the chalkboard.

The board appeared to have been wiped clean, though he imagined he could see faint letter- and number-shaped variations in the chalk dust on it. A sudden wave of dizziness washed over him, and he had to catch himself on the chalk tray.

The room grew brighter around him, like a gray fog lit by headlights. He spun around to see a room full of foggy students sitting at their desks, facing him with expectant looks on their faces. He heard no sound, and the kids were very, very still.

The vision disappeared, gone in a blink, and he was facing the dark chalkboard again. There were words there now, written in large, shaky block letters:

YOU ARE GOING DOWN, SOON.

Brett gasped. "Guys, look! This wasn't here before!"

He turned to see the others giving him a look like he'd just told a bad joke. "What?"

Gonzo sighed. He said, "Look, we're not stupid, Junior, just drunk."

"Yeah, drunk," said The L.T.

Brett blinked at them, then looked at Ralph.

Ralph smiled his small, lopsided smile. "Come on, Brett. We saw you write it yourself, just now."

"Loud and screechy," added The L.T.

"But, I was just looking at it, then I saw... and...."

"Brett, you're still holding the goddamn chalk," said Gonzo.

Brett looked at his hand, feeling stupid. But there it was, a small piece of chalk, still held between his fingers.

Brett set the chalk down and stared at the words. "W-well," he said, "what's it mean? Who's going down?"

Aa Bb Cc D
YOU AR
GOIN
DOWN

"Depends on how much sucking up you have to do with Liz, I'm guessing," said Gonzo, cackling.

Brett looked up at him. "I'm serious, I didn't write this. Or if I did, I blacked out. Is it a message for me?"

"What do you mean, for you?" asked Ralph. "If you wrote it, why would it be for you?

Brett started to explain, but Gonzo cut him off. "Brett hasn't been himself lately. He's been losing his temper and doing things he regrets later. Probably just the stress of this webcast project."

"Uh, that's not quite-"

"You need to relax, Junior. Enjoy yourself. I mean here you are in your element, a creepy old place, with friends. Live a little."

"Yeah, live it up, party on, dude!" added The L.T.

Ralph studied Brett a moment, then nodded. "Well, if you're writing messages to yourself, I'd guess Gonz is right. And if that IS for you, it doesn't sound like you like yourself very much."

Beams of light shined in the windows and made bright spots that swam around on the walls. Brett hit the floor, acting on reflex. "Shit!" whispered Gonzo, whose face was inches from Brett's. The lights went out and Brett heard voices.

Brett saw Ralph slither along the floor, under the window. Ralph raised himself up on his arms inch by inch until he could peer out. "Girls!" he whispered toward them. "A bunch of 'em. Let's keep down."

Brett watched the doorway. Skinny figures crowded around, lit by the moon. They wore pink and black hoodies. They looked like teenage girls, huddling together, tiny sticks of some sort poking out of their mouths. At that age, it could be either cigarettes or lollipops, he thought. The hoodies looked funny though, something poking up on top of their heads. It dawned on him, these were anime fans, the kind that wore cat ear headbands. *Catgirls.* It was only a couple of nights until Halloween, so he guessed they were only up there for a thrill. It hit him that that's why he and the guys were up there, too; drunk and telling ghost stories.

Gonzo held a finger to his lips and caught Brett's eye. Brett could tell by the wicked smile on his friend's face that he was up to something.

"Hungry. So hungry, mommy," whispered Gonzo in a hoarse voice. "Mommy...."

The catgirls froze in the doorway, clutching at each other and shrieked.

He started to rise up off the floor in the dark and moaned, continuing the hoarse whisper. "Mommy, take me home. Mommy? Is that you, Mommy?"

As the girls screamed and ran away, they tripped over each other and their flashlight beams flailed around in the darkness. Gonzo cackled and the others laughed in relief, standing up.

Brett smacked his head on the underside of a small, heavy, wooden desk and saw stars. His body fell away from him and he was swept out the door, unable to call for help from the others.

Chapter 6 - When You Got a Good Friend

Brett kicked with his feet and clawed with his hands. He thrashed around in the night air above the schoolhouse, but he couldn't pull or push himself at all. He was suspended in the moonlight. From up there, Brett could see the catgirls tumble over each other to get away from the schoolhouse. He heard their screeching cries, though more muffled and distant than he would have expected.

Ralph appeared outside the door of the schoolhouse, looking after the girls. He bent down to pick up one of the sticks the girls had been holding in their mouths. Brett could barely hear Ralph say, "Ha. It's Pocky!"

From inside, he heard Gonzo call his name. "Brett! Yo Brett, you okay?"

Without willing it to happen, Brett drifted back down toward the doorway. He was pulled back, he thought, when Gonzo called to him. He let it happen, though he seemed to have little choice in the matter.

On his way through the doorway, he passed *through* Ralph. For a confusing instant, the world reversed direction and he saw through Ralph's thick glasses. He felt Ralph shiver. The chatter of Ralph's thoughts filled his mind, though they sped by too fast for him to pick out more than impressions and flickering images.

The instant ended as he passed on into the room. The students at the desks were much more solid now. They all turned to watch him drift through, waiting and watching in expressionless silence.

A shadow moved among them, slithering like a snake made of inky darkness. As Brett watched, it wrapped in tight oily coils around a little girl ghost. The last part of her to disappear was her face, mouth open in a silent scream.

Brett's body lay sprawled out on the floor, a trickle of blood running from his hairline across his closed eyes. Gonzo hunched over the inert form and slapped his face. "Hey, wake up, we can't carry your ass back across that bridge."

The black shadow snake crept up on another ghost child. Brett was pulled inexorably by the connection with his body on the floor. He tried to cry out to warn the child while he remained in the spirit world. Before he could utter a sound, he saw his own eyes snap open.

The force that drew him inward stopped abruptly. The eyes fixed on him and narrowed. He heard his voice say, "No. Go away. It's my turn now." His body sat up and raised an arm and swatted at him. Brett felt the flat of his hand hit him with a searing cold that sent him tumbling through the air, back the way he had come. He swam in the air ineffectually, watching Gonzo and The L.T. and his own body recede rapidly. The students in their desks looked on, heads turning in unison to track his flight. He could no longer see the shadow snake.

Gonzo reached down to help his body up. He saw himself punch Gonzo in the jaw and heard his friend howl. Brett fell ever outward, out the door and into the night again. He heard shouts and a scuffle from inside, but everything became foggy and gray, brighter than the night, more and more uniform in all directions. Brett didn't feel cold, and he didn't feel warm. He wasn't standing on anything, but didn't have a sense of which way was up anyway.

He was lost and alone, in this... well, it was the spirit world, he supposed. Like in the dreams when he'd been out of his body. When his soul had been leaking out. But back then, he'd been tethered to his body by his silver cord. To end the leak, he'd had to sever that cord. He'd come back to himself when that happened, no longer half in and half out. Now he was out of his body with no tether, no frame of reference. Nothing to hold him to the material world. What was in his body? It didn't seem like the demon he'd banished twice before. This thing was angry, that was clear. But it didn't feel evil, even if it was hateful.

The words on the chalkboard had said, "You are going down, soon," Brett recalled. So, it had been a message from this other entity to him after all. He'd been ousted. Brett couldn't seem to get angry about this. It was unfair, and he was feeling more than a little afraid in this nowhere place.

And what the hell was that shadow snake thing? Something that eats *ghosts? Is it a demon?* Brett shuddered at the thought, but rejected it. The demon felt different. It had feasted on the suffering of living souls, and he suspected these dead ones, they'd be the wrong sort of nourishment. *What's it got to do with what's possessing my body? Is it part of the same thing? Or something else?*

There must be a way out, a way back. Possession may be nine-tenths of the law, but he'd forced the thing out of him once before, back in the parking lot. He could still see the tears shining on Liz's face. Thinking of Liz, the warmth of her embrace came to him, an almost tangible memory. He longed for her, wished for her to tell him he'd be all right. He could hear her voice calling him.

"Brett... Brett where are you?" came her whispered, distant words.

He felt a pull, and had the sensation of movement again. Despite the uniformity of the gray misty realm where he floated, he felt an unseen landscape moving faster and faster around him. He felt the pressure of passing through trees and buildings like cobwebs on his skin.

The gray mist began to recede, and a room began to resolve itself out of the formlessness. It was a hotel room. There was just one light on, over one of two beds.

Caroline sat up in the lit bed, wearing only a long olive T-shirt, legs crossed at the ankles, attention focused on the notebook computer in her lap. She chewed her lower lip in concentration, reading something on the screen, typing now and then.

On the other bed, Frannie was curled into a ball under the covers, a thumb in her mouth. Her mouth opened around the thumb to let out occasional soft snores.

Between the beds, Liz sat on the floor, cross-legged. She still wore her black tights from earlier, but now had one of Brett's faded old Star Wars T-shirts on as a nightshirt. She had a black square spread out in front of her, a sort of bandanna cloth. It was embroidered in silver thread with a circle and compass points and symbols and words. Liz held her hand out over the center of the cloth, dangling a silver ring from a black cord. It orbited the center in a small, slow circle. The ring, he realized, was his, the old silver Celtic knot ring he had given her as a token of his devotion when they had first fallen in love. She had never given it back, not even when they had parted ways for a few years. She had said she liked to hold onto it because she could still feel his energy on it. She said it was a comfort. Liz had taken to wearing it on a cord around her neck again when they resumed their relationship the previous year.

Brett's attention focused on the circling ring. The circle became an ellipse, longer and narrower, until it swung in a straight line back and forth between two symbols.

"Brett, what are you trying to tell me?" murmured Liz, brow furrowed in frustrated concentration.

"He's telling you to let him dig himself out of his own messes. He says, 'go to sleeeep, Lizzieee, go to sleeeep!'" said Caroline, who didn't look up, face lit by the glare of her screen.

"Shh. The pendulum says he's lost, but nearby."

"I doubt that, even if he got a ride. Gonzo just called a few minutes ago, he can't have gone far."

"Well, maybe I'm not interpreting the pendulum right. I swear, I can almost feel him." Brett watched as a stray wisp of Liz's hair slipped from behind her ear to curl on her cheek. He reached out to touch it, to brush it back. He couldn't move the hair, though he felt a tickling pressure as his fingers passed through her cheek. Startled, he pulled his hand back away.

"What you're feeling is the sandman," said Caroline. "He's trying to tell you it's bedtime."

The ring began to swing in circles again, and Liz sighed and put it down on the cloth. She looked up at Caroline. "Brett's out there, lost and alone. I just feel so helpless."

Caroline glanced up from the screen to meet Liz's eyes for a second, then went back to typing. She said, "Well, he's not answering his phone, and Gonzo said he was throwing punches before he ran off. My guess is, he's drunk and sleeping it off somewhere. He's a big boy, he can take care of himself, Liz."

"I'm telling you, something's wrong. We both saw him change yesterday... He wasn't himself. You know he's not like that, Caroline."

Caroline glanced at Liz again. "Sure. We all have our bad days. It's fine, I'll get over it."

Liz curled her legs under her, folded her arms on the edge of the bed and rested her chin on them as she looked at her friend. "No, I mean, he really wasn't himself. It was someone else in there."

Caroline bit her lower lip and shut the laptop with a snap. She put it on the nightstand next to her and rolled over on her side to face Liz, propping herself up on an elbow.

Gonzo would give a lot to have this invisible vantage in the girls' hotel room. Being in Liz's presence cheered Brett, and he appreciated the view of Caroline in her nightclothes, but he was still only a ghost, impotent and intangible.

Caroline said, "Look, Lizzie, how serious are you about this? You love him lots, it's easy for anyone to see that. But love can cloud your view of people, you know? Think about it. Wouldn't you feel it if he was possessed by a demon again? Wouldn't he be more than just bitchy and shitty?"

Liz shook her head. "No, it's not a demon. I have him all kinds of protected from possession, and he cut off his vulnerability to that when he severed the cord last year. And yeah, I *would* feel it if he was possessed somehow anyway. It's not a demon, but it's... someone else, I'm sure of it."

Caroline sighed and said, "You feel that, and I believe that you believe that, but you can't really *know* it. I don't think he's a jerk, deep down, but I think he's lashing out after bottling things up for months."

Liz frowned. "Well, yeah, you have a point. I did tell you that he's been cooler, more distant, since all that stuff happened with the little ghoul. Ashleigh. He lost something there, and I always just thought he just needed to grow back the part of his soul he lost when he bit through the silver cord."

Brett felt uneasy hearing this. He was eavesdropping, even if it wasn't under his control. He wasn't sure he liked hearing what Liz was saying about him. Had he been that distant since March? He recalled her approaching the subject a few times, offering to do a ritual to help him heal. He hadn't felt diminished or wounded, just calmer. He'd been happier, in fact, without the anger and jealousy he'd felt when Larry had come between them briefly.

Caroline patted the bed next to her. "Come on. Just leave your cell phone on, and get some sleep. Hopefully he'll call you or Gonzo soon enough. Meanwhile, there's no reason everyone has to be exhausted tomorrow. Assuming the webcast is still happening, that is."

Liz buried her head in her arms and sighed heavily. Brett hated seeing her like this. He reached out to touch the back of her head, taking care not to pass his hand through her, and stroked her hair. He felt her warmth, and something akin to static cling. He wished he could smell her scent right now.

As helpless as he felt, he wanted even more to comfort Liz. He tried to call out her name. "Lizzie! I'll find my way back," he cried. "It'll be okay, I promise!"

Liz's head popped up and she looked around. "Did you hear something?" she asked Caroline.

Caroline shook her head. "Nope. Uh uh." She patted the covers again. "I want to sleep."

Liz looked around her. Brett had a moment of excitement as she seemed to lock eyes with him. But she kept on sweeping her gaze around the room, not seeing him. She slumped her shoulders and sighed. She reached over to gather up the cloth and ring, which she placed on the bureau between the beds. Liz gathered herself and pushed up to stand over the bed. She smiled at Caroline and leaned over and kissed her, just a soft peck on the lips.

Caroline's eyes widened. "What was that for?"

Liz slipped under the covers next to her friend, giggling. ' Nothing like Gonzo might like to imagine. Just a thank you for staying up with me while I worry about my wayward boyfriend."

Caroline's cheeks turned pink and she allowed herself a smile. ' Sure. You'd do the same for me, I'm sure." She reached over and patted Liz on the top of her head. "Nite nite." She turned away to lay on her other side.

Liz lay on her back, staring up at the ceiling a moment, then reached over to the lamp on the desk and switched out the light. In the dark, Brett could see a dim glow around all three of the women, a warm, living light.

He thought she might be asleep, but after a couple of minutes, she reached over to the bureau and touched his ring. "Goodnight, Brett," she whispered to him. "Come back to me, please?"

Brett floated free again, the room dissolving into gray mist once more, the warm light of the women was the last to fade. He felt a pang of loneliness now, lost and alone. He had to find his way back to the world, for Liz, for himself. But how?

Chapter 7 - Some Are Born to Sing the Blues

The gray space extended as far as Brett could see. He had no frame of reference, so that could be feet or miles of nothing in all directions. He felt like he was floating at the center of an empty world.

He thought back to his lucid dreams from the previous year. He'd dreamt of his dead college fiancée. In that dreamworld, he had almost unlimited control over the environment just by imagining it.

Brett tried to imagine a floor to sit on. Nothing happened. Maybe that was too much. How about a chair to sit in? He closed his eyes and concentrated.

He pictured the chair in as much detail as he could imagine, focusing his thoughts on it. He thought of one of the big chairs from the Student Union back in college. Made from dark old wood, they were almost too heavy to scoot around without help. The chair was covered in deep brownish-red leather, a faint patina worn into its seat by half a century of student bodies settling into it for hours at a time. The stuffed leather was held firmly to the frame by metal studs, placed end to end all along the seams. The cushions were stuffed to bursting. It had a high back and wide, welcoming arms. He'd studied and slept in many chairs just like it.

He had the image firmly in mind, nothing but the chair before him. He knew that when he opened his eyes, it'd be there in front of him, and he could just slide into its soft embrace.

Brett opened his eyes. He saw nothing but grayness.

"Hello?" he said, experimentally. "Can anyone hear me? Help! Someone help me!"

As he began to panic, he put more force into the words. He could feel the tingle of contact from far, far away. Something was on the way to him.

A black speck approached rapidly. It wasn't easy to tell what it was. It grew in size until he could make out features.

Hideous features. Covered in days' old dried blood, hair greasy and stringy. Its eyes were sunken into sleepless, nearly lifeless hollows. Its clawed hands grasped open and closed repeatedly. It made grunting, snorting noises as it approached, smelling at him. Brett smelled rot, decay and old feces.

"Hey Ashleigh," Brett said to the feral creature, smiling. "It's good to see you."

The creature made a horrible gurgling and wheezing sound that racked the smallish body over and over. It sprayed Brett with vile bodily fluids and corruption.

He realized that the little ghoul was laughing.

"Mmmmph. Bwitnah. Britnahh," said the ghoul with a growling voice.

"Oh sorry," said Brett. "Britney. Ashleigh was what Liz called you when we didn't know better."

The gurgling and wheezing shook the small form again with wet heaves.

Brett rolled his eyes. "I'm pretty sure you don't have to appear that way. What's up with you?"

The monster stuck its black, swollen tongue out at him and began to change form. The gobbets of rotting gore faded, and the corpse-like preteen girl became cleaner and not as fragrant. Brett waited and watched as color returned to the dead child's gray cheeks. The eyes brightened and twinkled with amusement, focused on him.

In a few moments, the little ghoul had reversed the process of decay to appear living and whole once more. Britney raised her smooth, pink hands and grasped her fingers to mimic claws, pretending to menace him. She said, "Raar!"

Brett had to laugh. "See? You clean up nice, kiddo."

Britney hugged her knees to her chest, floating a couple of feet away from him. She shrugged and tossed her glossy dishwater blonde hair, her expression haughty for a second before she burst into giggles. "You're in a much better mood," she said.

Brett wasn't sure what she meant by this. "Well, I shouldn't be. I'm trapped in this place, separated from my body, wherever it's gone, and I have no idea how to get back. Can you help me, Ash... er, Britney?"

Britney smiled and reached out to pat his shoulder in reassurance. "It's okay, everyone has trouble at first. You'll get used to it. How'd it happen anyway, if you're ready to talk about it?"

Brett shrugged. "I'm really not sure. I've been having these short out-of-body experiences. Seems like I just slip out and watch my body go into a rage each time. When I'm not in there, whoever's running things is a real jerk."

Britney frowned and shook her head. "No, no, I meant how did you *die*, Brett?"

Brett blinked at her in surprise. "What? I didn't die. I was drunk, stood up too quickly and banged my head on a desk, then I flew out of my body, watched things from above."

Britney nodded. "Your body's still alive? Huh. You probably got a concussion or caved in your skull or something."

Brett shook his head. His voice sounded higher and squeakier than he liked as he protested. "No! I didn't die. I watched myself wake up. I saw 'me' punch Gonzo in the nose before I got shoved into the gray mist. I heard Liz telling Caroline how no one knew where I was, so my body must have run off. I'm not dead, Britney."

Britney stared at him a long moment. "But you're not anchored. No cord, no body... you're a ghost, Brett. You're dead."

Brett felt a shock at these words. He'd 'hunted' ghosts for years, and now a dead spirit was telling him he was one. "But my body lives on, and someone's in there and it's not me." He hated how that came out in a whine, like he was pleading with the dead tween.

Britney's pitying look made his heart sink further. "I'm sorry, Brett," she said. She pursed her lips in thought, stared at her hands and avoided his eyes.

"Isn't there anything I can do? I shoved it out before! All I have to do is get back to my body and I can evict it again and live again."

Britney looked up at him, eyes showing surprise. "You did? Well, okay. That's a good sign. And yeah, if you have a living body to go back to, there's some hope. Not sure how you'll stay anchored without a silver cord though."

Brett felt the cold lump in the pit of his stomach warm and start to thaw. "How do I get there? I don't even know where I am!"

Britney looked around her and swept the surrounding nothing with an arm. "This place isn't anywhere. It's the clay of space and time, waiting to be worked by a soul."

Brett frowned. "I can't make it do anything. So far, I've just been towed around when someone says my name. I can't swim or kick to move, and I can't make things or places out of my imagination like I can in dreams."

Britney smiled. "Well, as far as I can tell, reality on this side is formed by feelings. You have to really *want* it, Brett. You have to put some of yourself into it. You can't just picture things you want, you have to feel them, inside and out. To move, you have to long for someone or someplace. You have to ache, maybe even cry. Or rage and scream at the unfairness that you're stuck here. Gather your joy, love, hate, your *passion*, Brett, and you can draw yourself to what you desire in the land of the living. It's how you called me... you put feeling into reaching out."

She took a breath and shook a finger at him. "But it's a lot of trouble, and it does take something out of you. Some souls burn brightly and have power enough to materialize as apparitions. Some barely have the power to visit those they've left behind. Expending emotion is like using yourself for fuel. Once it's gone... well, as far as I can tell, the soul evaporates."

Brett listened to this, trying to fit it to paranormal phenomena he'd observed on the other side. He thought it explained a few things, but raised too many questions he didn't have time for. "Well, if I can get back to my body that might not matter. Can you show me?"

Britney nodded. "Sure. Just be careful, Brett. You're a good guy. You and Liz helped me when you had no reason to. I owe you, really."

She held out a hand.

Brett looked at the hand for a moment, looked into Britney's eyes and saw an invitation. He reached his hand out to take her smaller one in his. Her skin was soft and cool to the touch. She squeezed his hand in hers and smiled.

"Come on, I'll take you," said Britney, scrunching up her face in concentration. Brett's skin prickled with tiny sparks of static electricity. The mist around them started resolving into night sky, trees, the Moon, a river and train tracks.

Brett's body came into focus, stomping from one rail tie to another. The river was far below, but he looked straight ahead, eyes flat and hard below low, angry brows. His face was smeared with blood, inky dark in the moonlight. Brett watched the rhythm and confidence of his body's steps as he crossed the railroad bridge at a normal walking pace.

"You sure look pissed," said Britney, trailing along with him in the air behind himself.

Brett laughed, "Yeah, that's me whenever I'm not there, I think. That asshole has a temper, that's for sure." He reflexively reached up and covered his mouth. "Oh. Sorry, kiddo, I should watch my language."

Britney laughed at him. "Brett, I'm *dead*, how can bad words corrupt me over here? I swear, not only am I never going to grow up, but no one's going to let me do it, either."

Her laughter was contagious, and Brett laughed too. His body paused on the tracks, nearly to the other side now, standing with both feet on one tie. His head turned in a slow arc to face Brett and Britney. His eyes narrowed. He raised his hands, Brett's body's hands, and made a pushing motion.

Brett was pushed, losing his hold on Britney's hand. He was thrown a hundred feet upriver and the world tumbled around him, making him dizzy. Everything started to fade into grayness.

The former ghoul shot after him and grabbed onto his hand again. The world came back into focus. Britney's face bobbed in front of his. "Hold it together, Brett, okay? Whatever's in there is strong and full of powerful emotions. And it's burning them in a big bonfire to fuel that power you felt. How did you win against it before?"

Brett thought back to the parking lot. He saw the tears on Liz's face. He remembered feeling weight behind the push he made to get back in himself. "I just *needed* to take over. He was hurting Liz and her friend."

Britney nodded. "Yeah, that's the stuff. What else makes you want to go back? Why do you *need* it, Brett?"

"Well, it's f... fudging up my life," he said.

Britney frowned. "Fudging?"

Brett sighed and let himself loosen up. "Okay, he's *fucking* up my life. He's punched Gonzo, he's made Liz cry, he's pissed off Caroline, and he's acting like a god damned asshole. All while wearing *my* body!"

Britney grinned. "So, whatcha gonna do about it, chump? Just sit there and take it?"

Brett felt a hot ball of something where the cold lump had been before. "No. I'm taking it back. Thanks, Britney."

She waved, smiled, and vanished. All there was in the world was the railway where his body stomped along, back toward Ralph's place. Stealing his life and trashing it. Brett felt hot, feverish even.

He moved. The trees came closer, he floated lower to the ground. He moved faster and faster, his stolen body the focus of the outrage he'd summoned. He fell feet-first toward his body, burning like a meteor entering the atmosphere.

Brett saw his own head whip around to look at him in fear. Too late. His feet smacked into that face going a mile a minute, ejecting the other with the force of a runaway car.

Brett hurt. His stomach was a boiling cauldron of grease feast, Raid, beer and battery acid. He felt a dozen bruises on his legs, arms and back. Worst of all, the top of his head felt like it might come off if he moved too quickly.

He also felt drunk again. He thought it might take some effort to keep from vomiting. The world did a slow spin around his head, and he had to concentrate to see straight. He was cold, sweat drying on his skin as a breeze streamed past him.

The other was gone for now, he was sure of it. He was back on the railway. He laughed, a touch too shrill, he thought.

He had to get back. He had to let Liz know he was okay. He felt around his pockets. He had keys, wallet, but no cell phone. He nearly tripped as he started to run down the tracks.

Soon, he came to where the trees thinned out into bushes, and he could see the dead end of Ralph's street. He scratched his face and fell down as he fought his way through the brush. He scrambled to his feet in the yellowish pool of streetlight and took off at a limping run down the block.

Ralph's house loomed up, dark and peeling, on his right. He climbed the porch steps and pounded on the front door through the screenless screen door. "We hear you knockin', but you can't come in!" sang a sloppy duet inside the house.

"It's me, Brett, come on, open up!"

The chorus repeated. "We hear you knockin', but you can't come in!" Brett was sure Tod and The L.T sang the song.

"Look, I'm sorry... I wasn't myself. Blame the Raid, or chalk it up to a bad day, but if I did anything to piss you off... well, I don't even remember it. Is Gonzo in there?"

"Gonzo's out looking for you, dickweed!" came The L.T.'s voice. "You might not wanna be here when he gets here, neither."

Brett felt more chilled than he could blame on the outside temperature. "Yeah, I know. I got some 'splainin' to do. I fucked up big time."

Tod and The L.T. laughed sloppy laughs inside.

"Brett, you fucker!" Gonzo's voice came from behind him. He turned to see the big guy stalking up the walk toward him. His eyes were flat and angry. "Where've you been, we just about called the cops, and believe me, you didn't need the cops finding your publicly intoxicated, bloody-faced, belligerent ass out there before we did."

"Gonz, I-"

Gonzo smacked him on one side of his head with the flat of his hand hard enough to make Brett's ears ring. He fell off balance enough to have to catch himself on the porch railing.

Guffaws came from within the house.

Brett held up his hands. "Gonz, I'm sorry! You won't believe me, but it wasn't me. Something took me over back at the schoolhouse when I hit my head. I only just got back in control."

Gonzo's hand balled into a fist, and he drew it back. Their eyes locked for a terrifying moment. Brett saw Gonzo's eyes soften before he dropped both his gaze and his fist. Gonzo turned around and walked a few feet away. "Fucker."

"Sorry, I'm so sorry. I think I've got it beat, I kicked it out, Gonz, I took my life back."

Gonzo didn't look at him, but slumped down on the porch step. After quite a few heartbeats, he replied, "Yeah. Sure. The Devil made you do it. It's always something paranormal with you, isn't it? Sure is easy to do whatever the fuck you feel like and then blame it on ghosts, ghouls or god damned fucking demons, huh Brett?"

Brett wiped at his eyes with a sleeve. "No, it's not like that, dude. Look, it wasn't me, but I'm taking responsibility for it. I really am sorry. I'm gonna do everything in my power to keep it from happening again. I'm gonna ask Liz to help, too."

Gonzo didn't answer, just waved a hand behind him dismissing what Brett had said. He stood and went to the door, turning so he wouldn't have to face Brett. His face was shrouded in shadow as he reached into a pocket and pulled out his keys, which he hurled at Brett.

The door opened to let Gonzo in. Brett started to follow, but the door slammed in his face. Tod and The L.T.'s laughs were hyena-like.

"See you in the morning, Junior," came Gonzo's voice, receding into the house.

Brett looked out at the street where *Soccer Mom* sat on the curb. He sighed and slouched off to the van, hoping to get some sleep. Maybe things would look better in the morning.

He doubted it.

Chapter 8 – Take Me to the River

Brett swam in an oily black sea under a charcoal sky. The shredded clouds rushed by, lit on the edges by a moon they never revealed. The cries of crows filled the air from nowhere Brett could see. The head of his body fought a losing battle against the endless, patient cold of the waters. His limbs ached with tired and deep-soaked chill, and his breath came in gasps as his face surfaced with each kick of his legs.

He dared stop for a long breathless moment to pull off his sneakers and let them fall away into the deep darkness. He made better progress now, but still the cold sapped his already waning strength. He thought he heard a splash off in the distance. He peered out over the water each time his eyes cleared the surface.

Ripples made a V, pointing at him, as the wake of something moved toward him.

"Hello!" he called out with one breath.

The ripples grew sharper as the subsurface thing came at him faster. Two points of yellow light glowed under the waves, eyes focused on him. Hope turned to panic, and Brett took deep breath and threw his body to one side.

A slimy but solid impact sent Brett tumbling in the water. The sense of some large creature streaking past like a fleshy torpedo came as the thing's wake knocked him around. His head rang with the blow and he lost all sense of up or down, his eyes saw light and stars in all directions. His lungs ached for breath, but he could not find the way to the surface.

The eyes reappeared as the leviathan whipped around to come at him again. A skewer of fear pierced Brett and in animal panic, he flailed arms and legs to get away from the eyes.

His left hand made a splash as it touched air and sank back under water. He scrabbled that way, and his face touched the cool night air. Breath exploded from his burning lungs and he pulled in a new breath.

A dozen bright points of pain broke out as great jaws bit sharp teeth into the flesh of his right calf. Brett glanced down and aimed a hard kick at one of the glowing yellow eyes. The creature jerked and Brett cried out in pain as the teeth bit deeper, then released. A small thrill of victory rushed through Brett as he saw that one eye had dimmed.

He swam as hard as he could, though his injured leg moved more feebly than it had before.

"Help, help!" Brett cried, though the unseen crows might be the only ones to hear.

A voice came to him, speaking in his head. *Give up, Brett. I have all the time in the world to let you bleed, to freeze, to die. I bite at you for sport.*

The thing bit and held onto his other leg and shook him. It pulled him just under the surface of the water, and though he could see the distorted light of the tattered moonlit clouds rushing by, he could not swim hard enough to reach the surface his fingertips brushed with each stroke.

Brett looked down and could not see either of the yellow eyes, but he kicked at the beast with everything in him. He connected, but the jaws did not let go this time. The teeth sank in deeper, and Brett lost some of the precious air in his lungs as he cried out in pain.

Then came the crows. They shot into the water like dozens of black darts, leaving contrails of bubbles as they shot down toward the bulk of the monster below. The teeth clamped and Brett lost more air. Somehow, the water or the connection with the beast conducted the oddest rhythmic pulsing, popping, tapping. Not quite a sound, but the suggestion of the sound of pecking. The creature thrashed and writhed and thrashed Brett from side to side. Brett kicked hard once, twice, then the monster's jaws released him, and he broke the surface.

And then Brett woke.

Chapter 9 - Captain Kelly's Kitchen

Tap. Tap. Tap-tap-tap. Someone was tapping, and each tap was like a quick, painful flash of lightning behind Brett's eyes. He preferred oblivion, so he tried to stay asleep, because somewhere up there on the surface was an ocean of pain.

Tap! Someone was going to break the glass. It really wasn't his problem. He needed sleep, he clung to the shreds of sweet unconsciousness. Someone was shouting his name. Everything started rocking. His bed, well, it wasn't a bed, was it? The place he lay, hiding from the pain, it was being rocked from the outside. The van. *Soccer Mom. Crap*, he thought. *Now that I've pictured where I am, there's no going back.*

His head was in a cruel vise and his mouth was dry. The world was rocking and someone... Gonzo... was still shouting his name. He tried to reply, but it came out muffled, so he flopped a hand around to try to show he was awake and getting around to whatever it was that Gonzo wanted.

Oh, yeah. The keys. He'd locked himself in, since Ralph's neighborhood made Brett nervous. He needed the keys. He pried his eyes open and regretted it as the light of day slammed against his retinas to burn a path to the back of his head and out the other side.

"Brett, wake up, you fucker!" Gonzo was very insistent.

Brett groaned and looked back and forth around him. He was lying across the back seat of the Grand Caravan, a tattered green plastic tarp pulled over him for a blanket. It crinkled with a horrible noise as he twisted to sit up and look out the window.

Gonzo's face scowled back at him from the other side of the window. He couldn't figure why Gonzo was so fuzzy at first, then he wiped at the glass with a sleeve. It was foggy on the inside with condensation from his breathing while he'd slept.

Gonzo tapped on the window again. "Open up, we've gotta roll!"

Rolling did not sound good to Brett. His stomach felt better than when he'd passed out in the last night, but his head could not take anything remotely resembling rolling. He realized he'd drifted off into a haze when Gonzo passed a hand back and forth between them to get his attention.

Brett fought with the loud tarp, the crinkling a cacophony in the van. He wadded it up with a wince and stuffed it into the next row of seats behind him. There was a sudden terrible, metallic jangling. Church bells could not be louder than this. The noise stopped as it hit the floor. He peered down by his feet. The keys had fallen out of the tarp.

Brett picked up the key ring as though it might explode, to keep the keys from making noise. He dropped the keys once, sighed, and tried again and lifted them up to show Gonzo.

"Very good!" came Gonzo's sarcastic voice. "Now open up."

Brett looked for the car key on the ring. One said Dodge, so that must be it. He took just that key and went for the door. He couldn't find a place to put the key in.

"Un. Lock. The. Door," said Gonzo.

Brett didn't think this was very helpful, but noticed the nub of the door lock and realized his mistake. He popped the door lock up and Gonzo opened the door. Brett realized he'd been leaning on the door, and started to tumble out. Gonzo caught him.

"Uhnnngh..." said Brett. The cool, fresh outside air felt really good on his face and in his lungs. Gonzo helped him out of the van. He leaned heavily against the vehicle's side.

Gonzo looked him up and down. "You're a hell of a sight. Ralph and them aren't up yet, so you can sneak in and get a shower and we'll go meet Liz. Just don't wake anyone up. You're not exactly Mr. Popular in there."

Brett squinted at Gonzo and didn't have a response he could articulate. Gonzo popped open the hatch and handed Brett his backpack. Brett took this and slung it over a shoulder. He shuffled toward the house, then stopped.

After a couple of false starts while he worked up enough moisture in his mouth to speak, he asked Gonzo, "You call Liz? She was worried."

Gonzo nodded. "Yeah, I did. Damn right she was."

Brett felt a little better and made his way into the house and into the bathroom, where he peeled off his slept-in, partially bloody clothes. He worshiped the hot water that came out of the rusty nozzle in the little glass booth of a shower.

After getting dressed, he drank about a half gallon of water straight from the tap in the bathroom sink. Brett held out hope that he might survive. He found some ibuprofen in Ralph's cabinet and swallowed four like a junkie getting an overdue fix.

He pulled on clean black jeans and an elderly gray T-shirt with Indiana in red letters across the chest. He balled up his dirty clothes under one arm, grabbed his bag and walked out of the bathroom.

Ralph stood in the hall. He didn't look happy. Brett started to apologize, but Ralph cut him off.

"Brett, don't. You were an asshole last night, but I know what was going on. Gonzo tried to cover for you, said you were having a bad time of it, under stress. I know better. You're fighting with yourself. You're split down the middle. You're trying to be someone everyone else wants you to be, but deep down, you're someone else."

"But..."

Ralph waved a hand at him and continued talking. "Now, I looked you up online this morning, and I guess they say you've got some kind of second sight, a gift, maybe even one foot in the other world. It's really cool and all that, but I can tell you're in deep shit. You gotta hang on and decide who you are, Brett, and when you do, you're welcome back in my house. The L.T., Tod and Jenny have short memories, they'll forgive and forget soon enough, but before you come back, I want your head on straight, okay?"

Brett wasn't at all sure what Ralph was talking about, but it beat getting whacked on one side of his head again. "Okay, Ralph. I'm still sorry, and I'm hoping to get it together soon."

Ralph nodded, shook his hand and slapped him on the back. "Hey, take this, would you?" Ralph handed him a coin. It was an old silver dollar.

"It's sort of a good luck charm of mine. Keep it in your pocket and hang onto that silver when there's nothing else to hang onto, you got me?" Ralph seemed solemn and serious.

Brett flipped the heavy coin over and over in the palm of his hand, then looked up at Ralph and smiled. "Thanks, I will."

Brett joined Gonzo, who already had *Soccer Mom* started and music playing on the stereo. The hard driving beat of the Ramones made his head sing with bright, high-frequency pain. They pulled away from Ralph's place and out onto the city streets.

"I called Liz and she and the girls are meeting us at Captain's Chili for lunch," said Gonzo. He tapped the digital clock on the dash. It was three in the afternoon, Brett saw.

Then he processed what Gonzo had said. "What? Chili? Lunch? Oh Gonz, there's no fucking way."

Gonzo cackled. "Buck up, son. There's nothing better for a hangover than some good ol' greasy Cincy chili. Five- or six-way for me!"

"Normally, I'd be more concerned about what that'd do to *you*, dude, but after you locked me out of the house last night, I left the contents of my stomach in Ralph's bushes. I don't think tempting my stomach with chili is such a good thing."

Gonzo made a rude noise. "Those bushes have seen worse, believe me. It'll just add to the charm of Ralph's place. Anyway, you have to show your stomach you're in charge. Gonna be a long night, and we might not get another chance to eat 'til late."

Brett grunted, knowing it was pointless to argue once Gonzo was set on a personal mission. He'd talked about Cincinnati chili all the way up from Memphis, and there would be no denying him.

They drove on without talking much more until they got to the chili place.

Liz tackled Brett when he got out of the van. She covered his face in little kisses and squeezed him in wonderful, painful embrace. "Oh, *Chico*, I'm so glad you're okay!" she cried. Then she pushed him back and looked at him critically.

"I'm glad to see you too, Liz, and yeah, it's me in here," he said. He smiled at her as she studied him. He added, "Thanks for thinking of me last night, Lizzie. I think you helped me get back to myself, in a way." He winked at her. "Are you going to share?"

Liz looked puzzled. "What?"

"Caroline. Do I get to kiss her too?" Brett's smile became a big grin and he made kissy faces at Liz.

"How do you know about that!" she cried.

Caroline appeared nearby. "Know about what? Did I hear my name?" She looked at Liz, but not at Brett. Her tone was dry, her eyes tired.

Liz's mouth made a small "o" as she looked back and forth between Brett and Caroline. "It's nothing, really...."

Brett laughed and took Liz by one hand and squeezed. "I know, I heard. Let's go in before Gonzo comes to carry us in one by one."

"I'd like to see him try," said Caroline, raising her eyebrows. One corner of her mouth turned up in a half smile and she glanced at Brett for the smallest fraction of a second. They collected Frannie, forcing her off a phone call with Jimbo to bring her inside with them.

They went through the line, which turned out to be a make-your-own chili buffet. Various types of chili were in big pots in a steam table, along with pasta, shredded cheese, diced onions, green peppers and other fixings.

Brett, while still skeptical about how well it would stay down, found the aromas in the place convincing enough that he felt hungry. He filled a bowl with some chili with cheese over spaghetti noodles.

They all sat at a table and ate in near silence for a while. Liz glanced up at him a few times, eyes filled with questions. He ate his chili, and had to admit Gonzo was right. The combination of meat, spice and carbohydrates brought him back to life, with only a token protest from his abused stomach.

After they'd all had a chance to eat a good amount, Caroline spoke up. "So, we've got a problem," she said, looking at Brett for a full second, then back to Liz. "Your boyfriend can't guarantee his behavior, and we've got a show to do tonight."

Brett felt hot embarrassment spread across his face. He started to respond, but was cut off by Gonzo.

"Yeah? What's this 'we' stuff, sister? I don't remember you being part of this. You're just along for the ride, a roadie at best."

Caroline gazed at him with cool eyes. "Liz asked me to help organize things. Looks like you could use the help."

Brett broke in, "Look, that's fine, you're right, we can use all the help we can get. And yeah, I have had a problem, I'm sorry, and I'm trying to keep it from happening again."

Caroline glanced at him and nodded. "Well. Yes. Thanks. But we're going to have to have someone keep an eye on you. Gonzo, would you be so kind as to try to watch Brett and sit on him the next time he goes nuts? Fran can take the camera."

Gonzo ate another big bite of chili before answering. "Sure, whatever. Since you ask so nicely."

Liz sighed. "It was a long night and we're all tired. There's more going on here than meets the eye, isn't there, Brett?"

Brett wasn't sure what to say, but he nodded. "Yes. Believe me or don't, something's trying to kick me out of my own body. He... the thing... is a real jerk, and it's tough for me to get control back once I'm kicked out. I've got some more idea of how now, though."

"What helps, *Chico*?" asked Liz.

Brett saw that she was toying with his ring on its cord around her neck. He pointed to what she was doing and said, "That helped bring me to you last night when I was lost." He looked at Gonzo. "Saying my name helped pull me in too."

"What the fuck are you talking about, Junior?"

Brett sighed. "Well, it's hard to explain, it's really weird, and I don't blame you if you don't get it. But if you want to help, remember that saying my name might snap me out of it."

Gonzo ate some more chili and grumbled.

Caroline said, "Well, I'm not sure what to think, but we have to compensate for the behavior, whatever the cause. I mean, sure, you might get more viewers if you go off like that, but do you really want to be known for that, or do you want to be known for your abilities, both scientific and paranormal?"

Brett was reassured that Caroline was talking more directly to him. He said, "You know the answer to that. Of course I don't want to be lumped with the sensationalist shows out there. I want us to be taken seriously. I just need to get a better handle on this thing. Unfortunately, it seems to be a side effect of how I got the ability to see more than most people see."

Liz's fingers brushed his shoulder. He looked over at her. She reached behind his neck to pull him in for a kiss. Her lips were warm and soft, and the kiss ended much too soon for his liking. She held his eyes with hers and said, "We'll help you."

Gonzo grunted affirmative.

Caroline just said, "Yup."

Frannie said nothing. She'd finished her vegetarian chili three-way and now focused on texting. She had a gleam in her eye and a twisted smile. Brett thought there were many ways of not being in your own head. Fran at least seemed anchored.

"Fran," he said. She blinked and looked up.

"What? What? Sure, yeah, I can do camera while Gonzo sits on you."

Liz burst into squeaky giggles and fell over to drape herself on Brett.

He suppressed a grin and said, "Fran, you went through what I did. Worse, even. Have you had to fight like this, do you have problems hanging onto yourself?"

Gonzo cackled. "That's a little personal to ask over chili in public, don't you think?"

Fran blushed and sent another text message before putting her phone away. She said, "No… No, not really. After Liz stopped the soul leak, everything just sort of came back to me. I never see into the other world like I used to, and I don't crave rotting meat anymore."

Caroline put down her spoon and pushed away the rest of her chili. She coughed.

Brett shrugged. "Well, I was done with the bad meat after I cut off the leak. I just kept the sort of second sight, though it's much fainter and less reliable than when I could step outside of myself. Though now, I guess I can do that part again, kind of."

Frannie shrugged. "So, it's different for each of us. It was different for Ashleigh too. She was almost gone when she died."

Brett felt Liz shift in her seat next to him. She leaned her head onto his shoulder. Her hair tickled his cheek. She felt warm and good. It was very reassuring.

"I should tell you, Frannie, back at Loveland, I saw... well, a glow around you. Just for a bit, when we ran into you, not later. I'm not sure what to make of it. I just wondered if there was a connection to what's going on with me."

Fran looked at him with a peculiar expression. "Uh. That's freaky. I can't explain that. Maybe you were seeing things?"

"Maybe. It was a pretty strange night."

"Anyway," said Caroline, "now that we're full of chili and we've got some ground rules, do you want to tell them what we found out, Liz?"

Liz sat up and everyone's eyes were on her. "Well, Jimbo said our site got a comment from Righteous Richter."

"Oh really?" Brett wasn't happy to hear this.

"Uh huh. It's just a link to a YouTube video," she said, poking at her phone's screen.

Richter was the guy with the million dollar paranormal challenge. He claimed that reports of paranormal happenings were delusions, misinterpretation of evidence, or blatant fakery. In reality, anyone who took his challenge had to submit to terms that let Richter be the final judge of the evidence. Needless to say, no one had satisfied the man with the money, and he used this as counter-evidence in his public appearances.

Liz smirked. "Ooh, looks like our little webcast caught his attention, the video is titled, 'Brett and Liz's Bogus Adventure'." She held up her phone, which started playing the video. The friends leaned in to peer at the little screen.

A middle-aged man with a prominent, curved nose and a shiny bald head sat in a director's chair against a rough brick wall. His vanilla suit and apricot tie clashed with the sketchy alleyway, his easygoing posture conflicting with the sour look on his face. "Good evening. I am Ellis Richter. I appear to you tonight from a reputedly haunted location some of you may recognize." He gestured at part of the wall made of fresh bricks in the shape of an archway.

"Biograph!" said Caroline.

Gonzo laughed. "What?"

"Shhh," said Liz.

"Haunted theater in Chicago," said Brett.

Richter's speech continued. "…warn my viewers against yet another group of charlatans, led by Brett Nelson and Liz McEnzie."

Everyone at the table cheered.

"What's his angle?" said Gonzo. "That's free publicity for you."

"Shhh," said Liz.

Richter said, "…antics on the airwaves of the Internet cater to the most base and banal viewers, thrill-seekers. Not truth-seekers."

Gonzo said, "What's with that funky tie clip?"

Brett squinted at the screen, leaning in at the same time as Caroline. Brett said, "Is that a golden bear head?"

"Bear or a fat dog," said Caroline.

Liz pulled the phone in for a close glance, "With yellow eyes?"

"Shhh!" said Gonzo.

Liz stuck her tongue out at the big guy and showed them her phone again.

"…invite the miscreants to submit to my Million Dollar Paranormal Challenge. Contact me through the usual means, and we shall see what can be arranged. Until then, I shall debunk each and every one of your laughable investigations, with help from my Righteous Revolutionaries."

"His what?" asked Gonzo.

Caroline said, "Richter's Righteous Revolutionaries are his minions, people who pick apart paranormal claims for fun and Richter's favor."

Richter stood up. "…will see you tonight, loyal viewers. We shall expose the chicanery of Nelson and McEnzie for all the world to see, as we have done with all the other spectral snake oil salesmen in the past. Good day."

Chapter 10 - Hell's Ditch

Caroline smiled and slurped her drink in the silence that followed the announcement. "So, what do we think? We know Brett's the real deal, the trouble's proving it. If we win, that's a crapload of money you can finance something more with, and if not... well, like Brett says, it's publicity, even if it does add to Richter's massively smug ego."

Brett hesitated. He looked over at Gonzo. Gonzo held his hands palms upwards and shrugged.

Frannie was back texting again. She must have felt the others looking at her, and she put the phone down, blushing again. "Well, why not? What's the downside?"

"The downside is if he makes us look like idiots and gets his skeptics' brigade working on smearing our credibility. Worse, if I go..." Brett searched for the right word.

"Apeshit," suggested Gonzo.

"Yeah, if I do that again, that's not going to go well for us, they'll jump all over it."

Frannie poked at her phone and said, "Hey! Jimbo says that PokerZombie's going to spring for the extra server power and network if we're oversubscribed tonight, since our ratings were so high last night!"

Liz hugged Brett and he held her close to him. She was bouncing up and down in the seat in excitement. "Yipee! Now we can conquer the galaxy with this *fully operational* webcast! Muahahaha!"

"So, I say we take Richter up on it," said Caroline.

Brett wasn't so sure. "I've never heard of Richter approaching anyone for a challenge. He usually mocks people through his website and broadcasts until they have to challenge *him*. There's got to be a catch."

Caroline nodded. "There kind of is. He wants to be on site for our webcast on Halloween. He's up in Chicago again, appearing as a guest on Jerry Springer. He wants to know where our show will be ahead of time so he can get there when we do, to observe."

Brett shook his head. "I haven't told any of you where that is yet, because it's a surprise. Liz knows, but that's all. It's within a few hours' drive of here, and it's at least as scary a place as Hell's Gate."

Liz nodded rapidly and showed her teeth in a wicked grin. "Oh man. You are just gonna love it, Caroline. I *wish* I could tell you...."

Caroline pursed her lips and nodded. "Ah well. Fran, could you have Jimbo write back to Richter and say it's no deal?"

Fran started to thumb the keys on her phone. Brett held up a hand.

"Wait. Tell him we'll let him know twelve hours ahead of time. No, wait, tell him to be ready at four on Friday afternoon to drive up to six hours from Chicago to meet us at the site. We'll tell him then where it'll be. That way, he can't rig the site ahead of time."

Fran looked at Liz, then Caroline. Caroline nodded. "Sure, okay." Fran keyed in the message and said that Jimbo was on it.

"One thing's for sure," said Gonzo, "if someone went to the trouble to plant that radio and coil to fuck with us back at the castle, we're gonna have to be double careful to cover our asses with money riding on it."

"Good point," said Brett.

Caroline and Liz nodded agreement. Frannie nodded belatedly and said she'd tell Jimbo.

Liz said, "So what's with that bear thing on Richter?"

Caroline shrugged. "Not sure. It looks awful familiar. Maybe it's a trophy from one of his past challenges?"

"Yeah, it does look familiar," said Brett, something nagging at the back of his mind. "I'm sure I've seen it before in one of my books. I don't know if it matters, but if I get a chance, I'll do some digging."

The five friends finished up their meal and went over the directions to get to Hell's Gate. The site was a building that dated back over a hundred years, along a river and a railroad track on the Kentucky side of the Ohio River. Brett laughed when he noticed it wasn't far from Ralph's place. The building had been a slaughterhouse and had in the past been the site of Satanic rituals and sacrifices, including a grisly murder. The victim's head had never been found, and was thought to have been buried in a well in the basement. The well was what was referred to as Hell's Gate, and it was said to be a very haunted site. Some even said it was a 'portal,' a gateway to another dimension or plane of existence... possibly even to Hell itself.

Brett wasn't sure it was that, but he had always heard it was a spectacular place to investigate. When he'd called to arrange the webcast, the folks who ran the place were friendly and used to paranormal groups coming in to look around.

Caroline's own group had been there a few times, though she herself had not yet been there. She had offered her connections to give them a good reference, however, which is one reason Brett didn't want to rock the boat when Caroline had taken charge of things. They might not always get along, but Brett had to admit she was a charismatic and confident organizer and leader.

Also, her help freed him up a bit to just concentrate on the broadcast and investigation. It was also a way for him to show Caroline that he hoped there were no hard feelings from the previous night. While she wasn't very warm to him, she had stopped only referring to him in the third person at any rate. *Now, if only I can stop from watching myself from a third person point of view....*

They took both cars over to Bobby Mackey's so they could take a look in the daylight. It was a long building that had entrances on two levels. On the street, there was a door for the bar patrons to enter. Below, there was a large gravel parking lot, and one end of the building had a large hinged door, closed with a padlock.

There were a dozen or more cars and trucks in the lot when they arrived, and music could be heard from within. They were met at the door by the manager, a friendly middle-aged woman whose voice sounded like decades of cigarettes had made it rough and come-hither husky.

"Well, y'all are early! You're gonna have to wait 'til ten or eleven for the wedding party to clear out upstairs, but Dan can let you in downstairs to look around when he's done helpin' the band set up on the stage."

"Okay!" said Liz, "We can wait downstairs."

"Won't catch me down there," said the manager. "Been down there just once. Never again. Something touched me in the dark. Nearly peed myself, and I knocked Dan down on my way out. If you ask me, y'all are crazy, but hey, we'll take your money." The woman rubbed her hands on her tight jeans as though to warm her thighs.

Built into a hillside near the river, the building met the road in front, but the entrance to the half-buried lower level was down stairs where they'd parked cars in the gravel lot. Train tracks ran between Bobby Mackey's and the water. Brett tried to picture the place as a slaughterhouse in the 1800s, and his mind turned to the well they called Hell's Gate, somewhere behind the barn-style doors they stood before.

Dan turned out to be a short, stocky, bearded man of few words and many tools. He clanked as he walked, adjustable wrenches and screwdrivers on his belt clattering together as he met them at the padlocked door. He produced a key from his pocket and unlocked the door, ushered them in, but didn't follow.

Brett led the quick tour through the basement. Though he'd never been there before, he'd read up on the place, and had seen a couple of paranormal shows cover it. The place was full of junk, from an old truck in the back, to a refrigerator hanging open, to Christmas and other props for the stage. The floor might have been concrete layered in a hundred years of dried mud or just hard packed dirt. There were bare incandescent light bulbs hanging at intervals, but this wasn't enough to keep the deep gloom from pooling in the corners and behind things.

Brett found his ears ringing in the place, whether from remnants of his hangover or from some energies there, he wasn't sure. There was thumping and shouting and country music coming from the ceiling above. The wedding party must've been in full swing. He frowned to himself, thinking of all the dust and smoke that'd be in the air up there, making reliable ghost photography unlikely later.

Liz skipped along behind him, excited to be there. Gonzo ducked around the hanging bulbs and brushed off imaginary cobwebs as he followed. Caroline looked around her critically, sizing the place up. Frannie trailed, still texting and smiling to herself.

"Over here," Brett pointed to the right, "is the room with the well, the place Pearl Bryan's head was said to be lost. That's Hell's Gate, supposed to be a demonic portal. We'll want to cover that place for sure." He pointed as they moved along. "There's a room in there that's just called 'The Room of Faces' which will make good TV... er webcasting. And down there are some old dressing rooms, I'm not sure whether those will be interesting."

"Hey! Who's there?" shouted Gonzo from behind him. Brett turned to look at him, but Gonzo was already pushing past to dodge around the junk ahead of them.

"Gonz, there can't be anyone..." Brett stopped when he saw a shadow detach from the side of a dirty old hulk of a truck on the far end. He followed Gonzo as quickly as he could. Brett tripped and recovered before he fell. Unfortunately, one side of his foot came down on a two-by-four, and his foot turned sideways with a nasty, painful crunch.

Sheet metal banged, and there came a tortured metallic screech. Two long slits of windows rose above the clutter as the far wall revealed itself to be an old overhead garage door. It raised maybe two feet and stopped. Brett heard Gonzo shout. Brett hobbled and winced along behind, his sprained ankle shooting fire up his calf. He could stand on it, but running didn't seem to be an option.

As he gained on Gonzo, he saw a dark figure roll under the opening, pulling it down behind him. Gonzo grabbed at the door to heave it upwards, but there was a clank as the bolt was shot in place from the outside. Gonzo fumbled around for a release mechanism.

Brett turned to hop and limp his way back to the way they'd come in. Liz had already slipped out the door, despite warnings from Caroline to stay inside. Frannie looked at Brett in confusion as he made his way after Liz.

Gonzo caught up with him in the doorway, and they passed through together. "Come on!" shouted the big guy, and he didn't look back to see if Brett kept up. He soon rounded the corner of the building.

Brett hobbled after Gonzo, pain shooting up his leg with every step.

Gonzo ran down the side of the building and picked up speed as he pounded along the grassy gravel. He shouted at someone Brett couldn't see. Brett couldn't hope to catch up in time, so he moved to one side as far as he could before having to climb the hill to the railway. He heard an engine start up, followed by a grinding squeal of tires spitting gravel as a car or truck accelerated out of the lot on the other side of the building.

Brett reached the far end after a long painful walk, finding Gonzo doubled over, cursed and gasped for breath.

"Fucker got away," Gonzo breathed. "Ten bucks says he's the same guy that planted that trick under the table."

Brett leaned his weight on the building, pulling his right knee up to take pressure off his ankle. "You think? I guess we did post the first two places we planned to go online. But really, do people really have that much free time to mess with my little project?"

Gonzo looked at him. "Don't be stupid, Junior. If it's worth fucking with you one place, why not go across the river the next night to do the same? We gotta go over that place and look for surprises."

They walked around the corner to see the outside of the garage door. There was a handle in the middle of the door with a keyhole in it. Battered and bent, recent scrapes on the keyhole showed fresh, shiny metal under layers of paint.

Gonzo looked over the door and lock closely. "Looks like this is how he got in here. It's less obvious from the street, and from the looks of the paint on the seams of the door, it's been shut for a really long time 'til now.

Brett peered out at the highway that passed by the bar as though he could peer hard enough to make out the long-gone lurker's car. "Who the hell has it in for me enough...."

He looked at Gonzo and found him staring wide-eyed back at him. His friend's eyes held the same realization in his eyes that Brett had just felt in his gut.

"Larry!" they said together.

Gonzo grabbed Brett's shoulder. "We're gonna have to be more careful, Junior, if that psycho's sneaking around here."

Chapter 11 - Another First Kiss

"But it *can't* be Larry, *Chico*," said Liz, her voice edged with a whine, willing it not to be true. "I mean, yeah, he got out on bail, and then got his parole, but that means he can't leave Tennessee, right?"

"Basically," said Gonzo. "He'd have to tell his parole officer, and he'd better hope he stayed out of trouble, not so much as a speeding ticket. I sat in on the hearing. Judge Judy sure didn't want to let Larry go, but he was too slick and somehow afforded a damn good lawyer. And really, he had no previous convictions, so it made for a pretty good argument."

Brett nodded. "Yeah, and none of us wanted to drag it out and go bankrupt."

Frannie and Caroline looked at each other. Caroline said, "Yeah, and well, I didn't need to give my husband more reasons to hate my interest in the paranormal, so I kept it quiet."

Frannie patted her arm. "It's okay. I was just too scared and weak at the time to do anything."

Liz stomped one foot. Brett couldn't help but think this was cute, but he didn't say anything. She said, "Well, dammit, so now we have him after us again? Is he crazy? I mean, yeah, last time he had an excuse, the demon controlled him. But now?"

Gonzo said, "Yeah, uh huh. It was the demon. Right. Larry's got more than a few screws loose, and he's dangerous."

"Well, we don't know it's him for sure," warned Caroline.

"Aw come on. Who else'd have it in for Brett and Liz enough to make a hobby of following 'em to screw with this little production? He burned a lot of bridges in March and he's had to lay low since he got back to Memphis."

"Enough to risk breaking parole?" Caroline asked, holding Gonzo's eyes with hers for a couple of seconds. "Maybe going to jail after all?"

Gonzo shrugged. "The man's a lunatic. First he kidnapped Liz and the stinky little monster, stole my van, then duct-taped you and Fran in the back. Or have you forgotten? Need more reasons why he'd be rash enough to break parole?"

Brett said, "And he would have let the demon have its way with all of us, too. He's psychotic."

Caroline shrugged and lowered her gaze.

"Sure," said Liz. "A motive, a goal would be nice, to explain it. Remember, I know him better than any of you," Liz said, glancing a sheepish, apologetic look at Brett, "and I'm sorry, that man doesn't do anything just out of spite or meanness. He's got to have a profit too. Which wouldn't do him a lot of good in jail. So, I wonder, what could possibly be in it for him?"

Brett bit his lip, then said, "If not Larry, then who?"

Liz shrugged. "I dunno. You could be right, it could be him. Could be anyone. What about one of Richter's rabid fans? All he has to do is say the word and eager beaver skeptics would jump at the chance to discredit people like us."

Brett shrugged and glanced at Gonzo. Gonzo shook his head and mouthed "Larry." Brett smiled.

"Well, whoever it was, they shouldn't have been in here, and there could be tampering to interfere with our investigation," said Caroline.

Brett said, "She's right. Let's search around for anything out of place."

Brett and Liz started searching the dressing rooms at the far end. Caroline and Frannie started in the well room, since Caroline insisted, eager to see the most haunted parts of the place first. Gonzo stood guard, pacing up and down the length of the basement area.

Liz helped Brett up a step into the farthest dressing room. Inside, a ragged, old orange couch took up most of one wall. There were dirty, whitewashed counters and a frame where a mirror had once been.

Brett saw that they were not alone in the room.

A gauzy white figure of a woman stood in front of the counter, peering into the mirror-less frame. She wore a long dress that covered her arms and the lower half of her body, touching the floor. Her feet were not visible. On her head, she wore a rounded wedge of a hat with an enormous plume adding almost a foot to her height.

The woman flickered, colorless, and made no noise, as though taken from a silent film.

Brett stopped Liz on the threshold, holding a finger to his lips. She looked at him in confusion, so he pointed to his eyes and then at the dressing counter. Liz mouthed a silent "oh!" and squinted at the spot, frowning.

The female spirit didn't seem to notice them as she touched her face here and there, going through the motions of applying makeup. Brett saw her smile at the wall as though she saw herself reflected where the mirror had been. The ghost primped at her hair, tucking smoky wisps of it under her hat. Her motions were hurried and she kept glancing at the doorway, looking right through Brett and Liz. She turned, hiked up her gossamer skirts, and dashed for the door.

"Hang on," Brett whispered to Liz. "Here she comes!" Liz's eyes were wide as she turned to face the room. Though he was sure she couldn't see what he saw, he thought she might feel something.

He was right. As the flickering, misty woman dashed from the room, Brett felt his whole body shudder as she ran *through* the two of them. For just an instant, he thought he heard the bawdy peals of a cabaret piano player. He felt the urgency of being *late* for something, felt the faintest swish of her skirts enveloping his legs. Liz grabbed his hand, held tight and let out a little squeak.

They whirled to see what might be behind them, but not even Brett saw anything.

"Oh. My. Goddess! That was fantastic, *Chico*! What did you see?" Liz hopped up and down, smooshing their noses together a little hard as she kissed him.

Brett described the woman's ghost as best he could. Liz produced a notepad from her purse and scribbled down notes as he talked. They decided it wasn't an intelligent spirit at all, but a repeating, recording-like phenomenon called a residual haunting.

They waited a while for more activity, but nothing happened. Liz suggested they come back and cover the room during the webcast, and he agreed. Brett went to work searching for anything left behind by the intruder.

Liz plopped down on the couch and watched Brett bend over to look under the counter for any more electronic tricks.

Brett felt a pinch on his bottom. "Hey!" he said. Liz giggled and stuck her tongue out at him, laying back on the couch.

Her smile was lazy but her eyes were sly. Liz wore a purple Moon Faerie T-shirt whose collar had been cut much wider. Brett loved how one side of the neck slid down over one shoulder, revealing a black bra strap. Her legs crossed at the knee, one denim-clad leg bounced a slow beat, the tip of her pointy boot bobbing, drawing Brett's eye.

"Want something, love?" said Liz with an exaggerated drawl.

Brett found that he did, very much. It came over him like a sudden fever. He knelt on the floor next to the couch, feeling like a servant attending a pixie queen.

Liz's eyes searched his, sparkling with mischief. She leaned in and kissed his nose and giggled again. "Come and get it, hot stuff."

Brett felt the tug of duty fall away from him as Liz filled his senses. He felt the wet from her kiss on the tip of his nose. He felt the heat of her breath as she laughed at his expression. He smelled her subtle soapy, earthy scent. He saw the very real dare in her eyes.

He felt heat rise in him and he drew her lips to his, one hand on the nape of her neck. He wanted to devour her, be consumed by her. His desire was out of place and irrational, in this dirty old haunted place, but it was also irresistible. He didn't know where the sudden intensity came from, but he went with it with enthusiasm.

Liz seemed at least as surprised as he, but they both struggled to pull off each others' clothing. They fumbled at zippers and buttons, moaning each time they had to break the kiss for even a moment.

They froze for a couple of heart-pounding seconds as they heard Gonzo's boots plod past the doorway. When the footsteps receded, Brett and Liz resumed their hasty, hungry explorations of each other.

Brett had the oddest sensation that he wasn't in control of his own actions, which was confirmed when he found, to his horror, that he could see the back of his own head. He saw the heels of Liz's bare feet crossed in the small of his back as she pulled him into her.

He watched in amazement as his body brought Liz to climax once, twice, then it shuddered and his back arched as he joined her in ecstasy. Brett was too stunned to do anything but watch, detached, for a moment.

He burned with outrage. He'd been pushed out at the worst possible time. Was he angry? He decided he should be. He directed the spinning energies of interrupted passion toward his body, which now lay entangled and panting with a very happy-looking Liz. His Lizzie.

He snapped back and felt something leave as he saw out of his own eyes again. Was that a whispery laugh he heard?

He saw that Liz was staring at him with a question in her eyes. He murmured that he thought he heard something, then studied her.

He didn't dare tell her about this. Would she feel violated? He knew with a sudden shame that he did. It was a demonstration by the usurper; he'd been caught off guard.

How much had been his own passion, anyway? Had the other crept in and taken over without him realizing?

"What is it, love?" repeated Liz.

He shook his head and kissed her. They heard Gonzo's heavy footsteps returning, so they scrambled to get dressed. The moment disappeared as quickly as it'd come. Brett felt cheated. The secret smile Liz gave him warmed him some, but he felt a pang of loss, wondering how much of that glee belonged to him, and how much was owed to the other.

Gonzo's steps ended at the door, and Brett forced a smile for his friend. Gonzo rolled his eyes.

"What?" asked Brett.

"Shirt's untucked, you slob." he said, poker-faced.

Liz giggled, still fighting one of her boots back onto a foot. "We have to be really thorough searching, don't we, Gonz?

Gonzo sighed and clumped away. "Searching, yeah," he said as he paced toward the other end again.

They did resume searching, but both had reason to have trouble concentrating on the task. Liz kept catching his eye to wink at him or touched him in passing. Brett's mind was whirling with confusion, both appreciating Liz flirting with him and feeling a cold distance because of what had happened.

There was a shriek from the direction of the well room. Liz and Brett looked at each other and took off in that direction. Brett forgot, for a moment, that he'd sprained his ankle, and took a tumble coming down the step from the dressing room. Liz helped him up and nudged her shoulder under his arm to help support him as they did an awkward stagger together across the basement.

Gonzo had already disappeared into the well room, and when Brett and Liz arrived, they found Frannie backed into a corner, eyes closed and hands flailing out in front of her.

"Spider," explained Caroline.

"Spider!" shrieked Frannie. "Get it off, get it off!"

Liz laughed and used a finger to detach a strand of spider silk with an enormous spider dangling from the bottom. It scrambled toward her fingers, but she wiped the web off on a wooden railing in the room. The spider climbed up on the rail, over the top and to the other side, where it went out of view.

It took a few minutes for Liz and Caroline to convince Frannie that it was safe to open her eyes and be led from the room. While all this went on, Brett got a good look at the well. It was a hole in the ground, the railing keeping them from approaching closer than a few feet. It seemed to be filled with broken concrete nearly to the rim. He somehow still got a feeling of depth from the well all the same. That, and a thick, electric feeling in the air around it that made Brett's instincts tell him to go elsewhere. This was not as friendly a place as the dressing room.

It was intriguing, though. He felt drawn to it, his eyes unable to move away from it without great effort. He leaned over the railing to get a better look. It was darker now, he thought, or maybe his eyes were tired. In his mind's eye, he could see past the broken concrete filling it, its former dark depths superimposed like a daydream over what his eyes saw. It went down and down, the cool damp depths calling to him....

Big hands grabbed his shoulders from behind and yanked him back. "Hey! Brett, what are you trying to do, fall in there?"

Brett still stared into the black depths. If anything, it pulled at him stronger, and he didn't feel the hands or railing holding him back at all now. The mouth of the well known as Hell's Gate seemed to widen and deepen, and he felt he'd be swallowed up. He wondered what it'd feel like, would it be the dark oblivion he craved this morning before he woke? Sleeping forever in the cool depths of the well....

Something pushed Brett, hard, and he fell into the well, head spinning.

"Look at his eyes!" said Caroline from somewhere far away.

Gonzo's voice was lower, quieter, distant now as he said, "Shit. Is that some kind of seizure?"

"Brett! Brett!" came the faint cries. He thought they sounded familiar to him. There wasn't much but chill, inky darkness surrounding him, and he let out a relieved breath as he left feeling, light and warmth somewhere above and his thoughts dissolved.

Chapter 12 - Honky Tonk Woman

"Brett, you asshole," said a voice in the darkness, very near him. The voice sounded familiar, male but not deep. He wasn't sure where he'd heard it before. Was it someone from television, maybe?

Brett felt sleepy, oh so sleepy. Why was he being bothered? "Don't wanna go to school today, Mom," he said, swatting at the dark around him. Well, that's what he thought he was doing. He was numb enough that he wasn't sure he even had arms, even ghostly ones.

"I'm not your Mom. I'm not anyone you want to know," said the voice.

"Mmmhmm. You're badass and scary. Now lemme sleep," said Brett.

"Fuck you. Pull yourself together you analytical wimp. Guys like me get all the blame for bad stuff happening, but you take the cake, giving in so easily. And it's not the first time, is it? Easier just to let go and give up than fight your way through life, isn't it, you pansy?"

Brett decided he didn't like the voice much, and it wasn't just being kept awake. "Yeah, whatever, sure. I'm a quitter. Tell me about it in the morning, sporto."

There was a lash of cold fire across Brett's numb face. He still saw nothing distinct, but there seemed to be a somewhat lighter patch of darkness near him, roughly his size and shape.

"You better not be that fucking demon again," murmured Brett. "I owned that thing's ass."

"You think so? All by yourself? Or did your girlfriend do it for you? Or was it the little dead girl who saved you? What do you really do for yourself, Brett? Think you can sail through life just by having your friends live your life for you?"

Brett really didn't like this guy. He shoved out in the direction of the shadow. "Are you still here? What do you care, anyway? You hate me so much, just let me sleep, mmmkay?"

"Sure, 'sporto,' whatever you like. Guess I get Liz all to myself then. She's a real wildcat in the sack, isn't she?"

Brett had just about tuned out the voice, but now he opened his eyes, looking out at the lighter patch of dark in front of him. He tried to kick at the shape, at the hated voice, but it seemed too far away now. He tried scrambling his arms and legs to swim that way, but nothing happened.

He thought of what Britney had said about this. He had to want it. He thought of watching his own body take Liz right in front of him, right out from under him.

The image stung. He felt heat rise in him, pushing the cool out of his bones. He focused on the shape, narrowing his eyes, and he felt himself begin to move.

So did the shadow. Up and up it went; Brett followed behind. He felt like he'd been underwater too long, suddenly frantic to get to the surface where this monster was headed. He wanted to choke the life out of that smug voice. That usurper of his body.

The shadow vanished as the dim circle of light grew above him.

But now he felt weighted down, something pulled at him again. He needed to get away, but the weight was so heavy, even his rage didn't seem sustainable enough to let him go high enough to grab an edge.

Brett needed something to hold onto.

Liz's voice was just a whisper. "Brett!" He tried to answer, but his mouth made no sound, and he couldn't draw breath to try again. He felt even more like he might be drowning, though it wasn't water that suffocated him.

"Oh Brett, come to me, please?" Liz was pleading now. He could never say no to her, and her voice drew him to her more powerfully than his anger had pulled him up.

A hand, icy cold, reached down into the pit and hauled him out. He wasn't sure how he could feel such pain in his shoulder muscles if he was a ghost. He held onto the hand and onto Liz's desperate call to him.

Light burst around him, brighter than the sunlight had been to his hung-over self earlier. With it came pain, aches and pains all through his body. Especially painful was the palm of his right hand.

The cold hand was gone now and he felt himself supported on one side by Liz and on the other by Gonzo. He opened his eyes to see his friends. Frannie hovered nearby, staring at him with big round eyes. Even Caroline looked on with a concerned expression.

A reddish-orange light illuminated everyone. The Sun was setting. He was outside, he realized. Liz and Gonzo set him down on a grassy patch at the edge of the parking lot, against the wall of the building. He looked up at them and smiled.

Liz saw this and crouched in front of him, her face filling his vision. He wanted to reach up and tuck a little stray lock of her midnight hair behind her ear. He couldn't though, he was so cold and tired just now. "Oh *Chico*, you scared me! Don't ever do that again, okay?"

Brett managed to murmur, "Didn't try. Got pulled in. You saved me. Again."

Gonzo nudged him with a foot. "Saved from being a dumbass."

Caroline appeared to one side of Liz's face in Brett's view, blocking the light of the sunset. "I'm starting to think we should just cancel. This is just a webcast, we can't risk anyone getting hurt."

Brett shook his head. "No, it's okay. This is important, I'll be more careful."

"*Chico*, maybe she's right-"

"No!

I don't *want* to cancel," he said, meeting the eyes of each of his friends in turn. "This is important to me. This web show, I mean. I've got a shot here at maybe turning a dream into something bigger. I know it's dangerous, but if I run away now, I'll be throwing that dream away. I want to push on. If anyone doesn't want to risk it, go ahead and sit it out, but I'm going on."

Caroline pursed her lips and shook her head. "No. I'm staying."

Gonzo snorted. "As if."

Frannie bit her lip, then said, "I'm not leaving."

Liz's eyes held his for a long moment, then she sighed. "I understand. I'm just scared." She glanced down at his hand. His fingers were still balled into a fist so hard that his they ached. She reached with both of her hands and lifted it up. She asked him, "What are you holding onto?"

His hand shook as he released his grip, and Liz helped uncurl his fingers. Angry red half-moons marked his palm where his nails had bit into his flesh. Cradled in his palm was the silver dollar coin Ralph had given him.

He and Liz exchanged a glance. Brett said, "I don't remember taking that out of my pocket. Ralph said to hold onto it, so I guess I was?"

"Silver," said Caroline, peering over Liz's shoulder. "Protection against ghosts, usually. Lots of ghost hunters wear silver rings, earrings, bracelets, belt buckles... as sort of ghost repellent."

Gonzo snorted. "That's stupid. Why carry something to ward off what you're hunting? Why not give a deer hunter pots and pans to tie on himself to clank together as he walks. You know, just in case a deer happens by?"

Caroline glanced at Gonzo, then back at Brett. "Well, it isn't anything so dramatic, it's to keep them from following you home. We like to observe ghosts in the wild, not take them home as trophies... or guests."

"Sounds like New Age crap to me," Gonzo said. Liz turned to stick her tongue out at him, and he sighed. "Yeah, okay, it's not all crap, but if loose change is all it takes, then ghosts aren't anything to be scared of."

Caroline touched her nose with her index finger. "Now you're getting it, big guy. Ghosts aren't dangerous the way that demon was. They're not harmful, just scary to some people. Not us. We've got more to fear from the living than the dead."

Brett shrugged, pleased that he could, even if it made him wince. Feeling was coming back now, in hot pins and needles. "Well, what happened at the well wasn't like any ghost I've encountered. I'm a special case, there's something odd going on with me."

"Sweetie, maybe Caroline's right. I don't know what happened, but you passed out when Gonzo pulled you back from the well. This is called 'Hell's Gate,' it might not just be ghosts here."

Brett sighed. He was tired from overdoing it the night before, bad sleep, and his struggle to keep hold of himself. "Look, we're here, we have the equipment, and I know not to go so close to the well. Let's get through tonight, and if it's too rough, we'll call off tomorrow night, okay?"

His friends looked around at each other.

Caroline shrugged. "If you're up to it. If it's too much, get away and take a break. We don't want something like that to happen again."

Brett recovered his strength soon after that. He got up and limped up and down the parking lot, gravel crunching underfoot. Liz helped him at first, but he let her know he was okay, that he just wanted to warm up a bit. She still looked at him with concern.

Caroline, Frannie and Gonzo went back into the basement of the bar to continue looking for evidence of tampering. Liz stayed with Brett, watching him pace.

"Sweetie, we've got a few hours yet before the webcast. Maybe you should lay down in the back of *Soccer Mom* and get some rest?"

He nodded and let her lead him to the battered old minivan. She rummaged around in the far back of the vehicle and came up with her sleeping bag, which was pink and black striped. She unzipped it and shook it out. She covered Brett and guided him to recline on the long back seat, partly lying on top of him. She smiled and kissed him.

Brett felt a stirring inside him at the warm pressure of his girlfriend atop him. At the same time he felt a sharp pang at the memory of the dressing room. She studied his face a moment, then kissed him again and slipped off and stood up.

She wadded up a sweatshirt from her bag as a pillow. She leaned on him once more to reach to place it under his head. "I'll get you up an hour before the show, love," she said, favoring him with a tender gaze for a few moments before sliding the van's door shut. He heard her voice – was she singing? He lifted his head to peer out the window and saw Liz holding up her pentacle, eyes closed, speaking rhythmic words he could not hear. *A protection ritual, maybe?* She met his eyes and shook a finger at him. They exchanged smiles, and he watched her turn and walk back toward the building. Brett settled back down and closed his eyes.

Brett's thoughts were turbulent and chaotic and he groaned aloud, fearing that he'd be unable to sleep. Soon though, exhaustion took over and he drifted off.

He dreamed of drifting in that misty grayness. He saw faces. Liz, sticking out her tongue at him, eyes smiling. Frannie chattering at someone he couldn't see. Cheryl, his long-dead college fiancée, winking at him. Ashleigh the little ghoul... no, it was Britney, the lost little girl. Larry, laughing under his cowboy hat, eyes hidden.

Faces and scenes swirled around him and made him dizzy and confused. He tried to block it out, but his eyes wouldn't close.

"Stop!" Brett shouted, and there was just the gray mist.

And a shadowy figure, off in the distance. Thinking of the dressing room, of Liz's face, angelic in ecstasy, Brett wanted to punch the figure in the face. With that thought, he accelerated toward it.

"Well, well, well. As in, you made it out of--" began the shadow as Brett approached.

Brett socked the shadow, hard. He felt his fist connect this time, and felt a wild glee as it reeled back, tumbling. So, it might be a ghost or something else insubstantial in the waking world, but here in dreams, it was as solid and vulnerable as himself.

The figure straightened and clenched its fists and came at him in a snarling fury. Brett felt a shock of fear and then he found himself knocked to the unseen misty ground, which felt like the gravel of the parking lot.

The shadow scrambled on top of him and blows rained down on Brett's face, head and shoulders. Each one didn't so much hurt as it disoriented him, dispersed him. He felt like he was made of liquid and each punch made his form ripple and splatter, made his thoughts harder to hold onto.

He flailed without effect at the icy cold, heavy, angry spirit, and he found it harder and harder to breathe.

The shadow screamed words at Brett as it continued to pummel him. "I hate you, you weak, stupid, pliable yes man. You just do whatever anyone asks, you make everyone happy, whatever the cost. Everyone else, that is. And I ask myself, what's in it for you? You want something in return, but what do you do if you're denied, if you're taken for granted? You shove it all down inside, don't you, wimp?"

"What... what... stop it, you crazy fuck!" said Brett, trying to pull together to fight off the monster. "What's it to you? Who am I to you?"

With an effort, Brett pushed on one side of the thing and rolled its weight off of him so he could scramble away. It came at him again and he shoved it away. "You think you can just come in and mess with my life, just when I'm getting it back together?"

The shadow swung at him, and Brett couldn't get out of the way quickly enough, so the blow landed on his shoulder instead of his head. He took a half second to glance where he'd been hit and saw a hole where his shoulder had been, plus a smoky trail where the shadow had passed through. Even in that quick glance, however, he saw the smoke gather inward and his shoulder start to come back together.

"You're wasting your life, living in the shadows of your friends." The thing aimed a kick at him.

Brett jumped out of the way and aimed an angry punch for the middle of the thing's face, "Maybe at one time, but not anymore!"

The shadow's head exploded in smoke, and its body crumpled to the ground. The head started to reform, so Brett kicked at the faint substance to re-disperse it.

"Don't mess with my life!" He kicked again, shouting curses.

And again. The thing twitched and the head started to coalesce once more.

Again, harder, with a scream of rage.

The shadow's whole body exploded into smoke which swirled around and around him, as the faces had earlier. Brett held up his hands to block the sight, but the dizziness came again.

Then it stopped, it was calm and quiet. He put down his hands and found himself standing outside of *Soccer Mom*. He heard the distant beat of some familiar song. No one was in sight, so he walked over to the door to the basement. There was a note on the door.

Liz's loopy but precise handwriting was on the paper in purple ink: "Brett, Teena invited us to her wedding party! Come on up when you wake up. Love and smoochies! <3 <3 <3 Lizzie"

Below this was scrawled, in hasty black block lettering, "P.S. Save me, Elvis! Gag, ack barf!"

That had to be Gonzo. He smiled and started the climb up the stairs to street level. As he approached, he realized what was playing. It was "You Shook Me All Night Long," except not by AC/DC this time. It was sung by a female lead, and the tempo was much faster. It sounded like she was backed by more than one banjo. Maybe an electric banjo?

He came to the door of the bar. There was a large bald man sitting on a barstool there, looking bored. Brett introduced himself as being part of the paranormal group, saying that the bride had invited him. The guard ignored him, messing with his cell phone instead.

Brett shrugged and slipped on into the open door. He had to grin at the famous yellow sign with black handwritten lettering:

Warning to Our Patrons:

This Establishment Is Proported

To Be Haunted. Management

Is Not Responsible And Cannot

Be Held Liable For Any Actions

Of Any Ghosts/Spirits On This Premises

Chapter 13 - All Night Long

The party inside was in full swing. Brett hadn't seen a wedding like it before. Frankenstein danced with a zombie nurse, Doctor Horrible danced with Janet Jackson. In the eye of the roiling party storm, a tall woman held court. She wore impossibly tall stiletto heels, making her easily taller than Gonzo. Her slinky white dress clung to her curves, slit up one side to mid-thigh. She had bone white powder on her face and blood red lipstick on her languidly smiling lips. Her eyeliner was dark and sharp. Her hair, or wig, was long, black and uneven as it fell on her improbably ample bosom, one strand falling to be lost in her bottomless cleavage. Brett recognized her as Elvira, Mistress of the Dark: a luscious vision in white.

Next to her were Liz and Caroline. Both women had to tilt their heads back uncomfortably far in order to talk with their hostess. They laughed at something the woman said.

Brett couldn't recall making his way through the crowd. He was now up next to Liz, and could just barely hear her over the odd rockabilly band.

"This is fantastic, Teena, a haunted wedding at Hell's Gate, the day before Halloween!" Liz's voice rang shrill as she struggled to be heard over the noise.

The bride, Teena/Elvira, smiled, and showed brilliant, perfect teeth. She said, "Yes, it is, isn't it? We tried for Halloween, but Mackey's wanted far too much to close down on a weekend night. They tried to talk us into Sunday or Monday night, but I thought Devil's Night was good enough if Halloween was out of the question."

Liz giggled at this, but Caroline looked puzzled. "Devil's Night?"

"The night before Halloween," explained Liz. "Some people call it 'mischief night.' I guess they have a lot of problems up in Detroit, kids took the 'trick' part of 'trick or treat' to extremes. There was arson back in the '90s, even. It's not as bad these days, but it's still got a reputation for TP-ing, flaming bags of poo on doorsteps, and vandalism."

The groom, a rather short Edward Scissorhands, slipped an arm around his new wife's slender waist, which was at chest height on him. His 'scissorhands' were some kind of silver painted foam, much shorter than the movie versions. Brett still wondered how the man would go to the bathroom.

The groom twirled Teena around and buried his face in her boobs, which were at a convenient height for him. He made happy blubbery noises. She sighed and endured this with grace for a long moment, then gently pushed him a few inches back.

"You will excuse me for a moment?" she asked Caroline and Liz. The two smirked and nodded, waving her away in unison. The bride and groom waded into the crowd to dance. He beamed a tipsy smile up at her cool, amused face.

Brett found himself next to Liz, who did not seem to notice him. He thought he saw Caroline glance his way once, but no recognition showed in her eyes. He didn't think this strange at the moment, he was still fuzzy from sleep and the fight with the shadow.

"So, you seem a lot peppier," said Caroline, elbowing Liz. "Is it a relief having Dr. Jekyll down for a nap?"

Liz laughed, which made Brett feel a heavy lump in his stomach. "No, no, not that. It's kinda the opposite...." She bit her lip and looked up at the ceiling to avoid Caroline's eyes.

Caroline poked Liz. "Come on. Spill. What's going on?"

Liz's lips spread into a wide grin and she lowered her gaze all the way to the floor. "Oh, nothing right now, but earlier... yum."

Caroline looked astonished. "What? Here?"

Liz looked up at her friend and nodded. "I know, right? It was crazy! I just turned on a little 'come hither' on Brett and suddenly he was all Pepe Le Pew on me. It was *amazing*, Caroline!"

Caroline snorted and rolled her eyes. "Where? In a dirty old dressing room? What a romantic."

Liz reached up and rested her fingertips on Caroline's arm. "Oh but it was! Brett's not been spontaneous like that since... well, months and months at least. And passionate? He wanted me more than any time I can remember, ever. I like the change."

Caroline nodded. "You did say he'd lost a lot of his fire last year. I wondered if he'd gotten it back or if things were just settling into routine."

Liz nodded. "Yes, I thought maybe it was living together, breathing each others' air, you know? But Brett's been through a lot too, so I was waiting for him to recover a bit. Hoping. I mean, I love him, and I'd stay with him either way, but wow, I didn't know how much I missed being wanted that much until we were tearing off each others' clothes!"

Brett listened, heart sinking as he knew she was talking not about him, but about the usurper. She preferred him to her.

Caroline held up a hand to stop her. "Okay, TMI, dear. You can't kiss a girl and then tell about your other romantic conquests."

They both laughed, and Liz hugged Caroline and kissed her cheek. "You know you're my girl," she said. "And if it weren't for that husband of yours, I'd come steal you away."

Caroline made a face. "Yeah, you, Brett, my kids and me, all crammed into your little apartment. We'd be a hell of a reality show on your webcam."

Brett felt sullen and left out. Why did they talk as though he wasn't here?

Liz laughed her high, squeaky cartoon character laugh, attracting the attention of people around her for a moment.

Brett saw the bride and groom swinging a wide path around them as they cavorted to a bluegrass rendition of "Hey Bartender." Liz and Caroline jumped back out of the way, but Brett didn't move in time.

Edward Scissorhands swung Elvira in a clumsy arc and her fine pointed heels skittered on the dance floor. He braced for the impact, but she passed *through* him. For an instant, he felt what she felt... heels losing traction on the floor, dress straining at parts that Brett didn't have, heart pounding and thrilling to the dance, gazing into her husband's eyes....

Then contact broke and Brett saw the bride begin to fall. Her husband caught her around the waist, turning the fall into a dramatic dip. She smiled her thanks at him.

Brett felt himself begin to fade and the room lost definition and color. He felt a snap and his eyes flew open to see the roof of *Soccer Mom*, still covered by Liz's sleeping bag. Night had begun to fall. He heard rockabilly music in the distance.

He threw off the covers and fumbled for the door, letting in a blast of cold air as he stumbled out into the lot, his ankle stiff and painful. He found the same note taped to the basement door and felt a cold lump in his stomach. So, it wasn't just a dream, after all.

He considered going up to the party and confronting Liz. He pictured himself shouting at her, making a scene at someone else's party. The cold lump heated up and his stomach burned with the beginnings of anger. There was an unexpected thrill of glee somewhere in the back of his mind.

But then he imagined Liz's face falling, remembering the tears back at the Grease Feast. He couldn't do that. He couldn't tell her it wasn't him that'd made her feel that way, either.

He swung open the basement door and walked in to find Gonzo sitting, reading a thick, ragged-looking paperback book. Gonzo put the book down as Brett entered and watched him limp toward him. Brett felt quite a bit cheered to be noticed, glad that this wasn't just another dream.

"So is it Brett or psycho Brett?" asked Gonzo with a slight smile.

"What's the difference?" Brett laughed. "I'll fuck things up either way."

Gonzo punched him in the shoulder. "Don't be stupid. You're a lot more fun when you're psycho."

Brett winced. "You too? I'm starting to think whatever's taking me over would be more popular than me."

Gonzo's smirk turned serious. "Hey. Don't be so touchy. I'm kidding. Maybe you could use some loosening up, but no one wants to see you go apeshit."

Brett wasn't so sure, and he didn't say anything in return.

Gonzo studied him a moment. "Look, I don't know what's going on with you. Maybe you're having problems, and after all you've been through over the past year, who could blame you if you lose it a little now and again? But you can't let this thing rule you, you have to know who you are, who you want to be, and make a stand. You know?"

Brett thought about that and nodded. "Wish it was that simple, Gonz. It's just... one minute I'm myself, then the next I'm watching someone else fuck up my life."

Gonzo leaned to one side and let out a disgusting noise. He grinned, pleased. "That'll ward off some evil spirits for you." When Brett didn't share his crude sense of humor, Gonzo sighed and said, "Look. Brett. You're always in control. You've seen me lose it before, right? I'm not called Gonzo just because I idolize Hunter S. Thompson. I just have to deal with the consequences and move on. If things get too much, and you lose that control, well, maybe it needed to happen."

Brett didn't want to talk about this anymore, as Gonzo wasn't buying the out-of-body experiences he'd been having. He didn't get that it really wasn't him throwing fits, but some... other.

"So where are the girls?" asked Brett.

"Your girlfriend and The Queen are upstairs with the wedding party. Frannie went to nap in the Saturn. I didn't feel like partying or sleeping, and someone needed to keep an eye on the place in case Larry comes back. It's spooky down here, but I haven't seen any boogeymen."

Brett chuckled. "Well, maybe I'd better check in upstairs."

Gonzo grunted and went back to his book.

Brett had a funny sense of *déjà vu* as he climbed the stairs and came to the bouncer at the door. The man glanced up and nodded as Brett let himself in. The same sign stared at him. It was a challenge to weave through the costumed crowd.

He didn't see Liz immediately, and since he felt the need, he went into the men's room, using the long steel trough provided for that purpose.

Back out in the bar, the band launched into a twangy rendition of "I Would Walk 500 Miles." Brett wasn't a fan of country music, but he liked this band. They dressed as mummies and zombies. The lead singer was a sultry vampiress with fangs and a trail of fake blood dribbling from one corner of her ruby lips to her chin.

Someone grabbed his hand and he was pulled firmly out onto the dance floor. To his surprise, it was Caroline, who had Liz on her other hand. Liz giggled and grinned and swung around to take his other hand, forming the three of them into a little circle. She leaned in to kiss him with her warm, sweet lips.

Brett felt the cold anger he'd felt at being an outsider melt away as the two women spun him around in their circle. Caroline's warm smile seemed genuine, and he couldn't help but smile back at her.

Liz made it difficult to maintain the circle as she started to do a jig, bouncing up and down. Brett and Caroline laughed along with Liz and they broke apart into three, but still faced inward as they danced.

He found himself staring at Liz, wondering what to think about what he'd heard and what had happened in the dressing room below. Liz's eyes met his, and she leaned over to whisper to Caroline. Her friend nodded and excused herself to go to the ladies' room.

Liz towed him over to the bar and looked him in the eyes, serious. "What is it, sweetie?"

Brett looked down at his hands for a moment, then looked back at Liz. He couldn't keep anything from Liz after all. "I'm scared, Lizzie. I have to admit something."

She looked at him with concern and waited, listening.

"After we got hot and heavy in the dressing room, just at... um, the important part, I wasn't me, I was watching from outside."

Liz's face was blank as she processed this, then a smile came to her lips and she took his hand. "Sweetie, if there's one thing a woman knows, it's what her lover feels like. *Chico,* I don't know what you saw or felt, but that was *you* with me down there."

Brett blinked and shook his head. "That's not possible."

Liz nodded and reached her other hand to press his hand between both of hers. "Yes, sweetie, it is. I think I know what's going on with you now."

It was Brett's turn to wait silently, listening.

"Brett, what happened in March?"

"You know what happened... I started to leak out. My soul did."

She nodded. "I remember you describing it later. Every time you got angry or jealous or violent, you felt a little bit of yourself slip away."

A light went on somewhere in Brett's head, and a cold bit of fear accompanied the illumination. "So... when I bit through my silver cord to cut off the leak...."

Liz nodded, her face serious and gentle now. "Yes, Brett. You cut off that part of your soul. The anger, the hurt, the jealousy... and that's the part of you that finally beat the demon."

Brett wasn't sure what to say.

"And that part of you was shut out all these months, which is why you've not been a whole Brett. Oh, you've healed and made progress to being who you were before, but I think the other half of you is back now, and wants back into your life."

Brett frowned. "If you're right, it seems more like he wants my life with me not in it."

Brett felt a cool, slender hand on his shoulder, and he turned to find himself looking into the eyes of the bride, her scarlet lips just inches from his. She touched his chin to turn his head so she could whisper in his ear. Liz still held his hands, looking up at Teena in surprise.

The woman's breath was warm in his ear. "I saw you, I felt you. Beware, dear, or you could become a permanent resident here."

And with that, she slid her hand down his arm to touch Liz's hands. "Hold onto your man," she murmured, still staring at Brett, "or he may slip away."

Elvira the bride withdrew, swallowed up by the crowd, back to playing the lovely hostess to her well-wishers.

Chapter 14 - In the Midnight Hour

Liz's hands held onto Brett's hand tighter as she watched the bride fade into the crowd. Caroline returned from the restroom, and Liz filled her in on what had just happened.

"So, what was that all about?" asked Brett.

Caroline said, "Before you came up, she was telling us how she picked this place for the wedding because she's a sensitive. Says she's made friends with some of the spirits here. She also implied she had flashes of precognition. So she probably thinks something's going on with you."

Liz let out a nervous laugh and looked at her friend. "You think? She was pretty dead on if she meant Brett's other half wrestling for control of his body." She didn't let up her grip on his hand, taking the bride's advice a little too literally, in Brett's opinion.

"His what now?" asked Caroline.

Liz related her theory about the shadow.

"That fits," Caroline said with a nod. "Question is, what now? Are you going to play tug of war for the rest of your life, maybe get diagnosed with multiple personalities and mood disorders? Could drugs even help with this situation?"

Brett wasn't sure he liked the idea of being medicated to solve this. "I don't know, and we can't answer that easily. Maybe I can have a more civil discussion with the thing and come to an agreement?"

Liz laughed. "What, like time-sharing?"

Caroline smiled. "Sure, I could write up a calendar and you could propose a compromise. Maybe you'd alternate weekends and have certain hours of the day...."

Brett frowned. "But then I'd spend life as a part-time ghost, during which times my life's out of my control, being ruled by an overly-emotional maniac version of myself."

"Could be fun to watch, at least," offered Caroline.

Liz sighed. "I don't know, *Chico*. We'll just have to see what happens. Gonzo did say he'd sit on you if you went out of control again. Maybe we can try to reason with Terb then."

Brett and Caroline spoke in unison, "Terb?"

Liz grinned, sat up straight and did her best imitation of the cartoon mouse, Pinky, using her squeaky voice to good effect. "Narf! It's Brett in the mirror! Terb!!!"

Brett groaned. "Now you've done it. You've given it a name, and now you're just going to want to keep it."

Liz grinned at Caroline. "I've always wanted my very own pet ghost!" She looked at Brett with a wicked gleam in her eye. Her voice teased, "Ooooh, and you get to be my pet ghost sometimes too. Could be fun, parading around you naked when you can't do a thing about it, hmmm?"

Brett felt a hot flush come to his face. He couldn't look at Caroline, but he heard the woman try and fail to suppress a snicker. He didn't say anything, but freed his hand from Liz's hold.

She touched his face. "Oh Brett, my little prude. Seriously, we'll figure something out, love. I'll do what it takes for my part to make it work, okay?"

Brett still didn't trust himself to speak, since he was embarrassed and a little put off by the 'prude' comment. After all, his other half had shown it wasn't shy the way he could be.

Then again, it *was* he who'd responded to Liz's seduction, wasn't it? It was he who pulled her clothes off, he thought. It wasn't until the critical moment he'd been outside. If all his passionate emotions were in his other self, how had that happened?

They waited out the party so they could set up their webcast afterwards. Servers offered them drinks many times. They refused anything with alcohol, since they wanted to be taken seriously by those watching the investigation. Brett left to relieve Gonzo on watch. Fran, who came in yawning and stretching, joined him in the basement.

"Saturns are not made for sleeping," she observed.

Brett smiled. "Yeah, I wouldn't think so. Feel any better?"

Frannie held up a finger while she yawned again. "Yeah... I just need so much sleep anymore."

Brett studied her a moment. "You know, Frannie, we went through the same thing last year, we both lost a lot of ourselves. As I understand it, you lost even more than I did."

Frannie sat on a folding chair near him. She nodded. "Sure, but I'm better than I was before."

Brett nodded. "Do you... well, have you ever felt anything odd because of that?"

Frannie gave him a blank look. "Huh?"

Brett paused and thought a moment before continuing, "Liz thinks these outbursts of mine, the out-of-body experiences... well, she thinks it's the part of me that got cut off trying to rejoin me. Or push me out."

Frannie shrugged. "It's weird. I have times where I don't remember doing things people tell me they saw me do, but nothing wild or violent like you. It's just been sort of sleepwalking kind of, I thought. And it's not a total blackout, really, it's just stuff I forgot I did and can't explain why I did it. Memory lapses. But it's rare. Also, I've felt guided at times, like I'm being watched over by a guardian angel. I saw a psychic who said she saw a second aura around me, said it was my spirit guide. I believe it, that fits so well. It's comforting."

Brett nodded. "So I wonder what the difference is? Is it just how much we each lost?"

Frannie shrugged, glancing down at her buzzing cell phone. She poked at the keys to send a text reply to someone before answering. "Hmm, dunno, Didn't you also lose yours when it fought the demon off? Maybe that's done something bad to your shadow."

My shadow, thought Brett. He recalled a story, a fairy tale maybe, of a boy who had lost his shadow and had to have it sewn back on. Was it Peter Pan? He couldn't recall. But the idea of having this angry, jealous, violent shadow attached to him didn't appeal much. How could a nasty thing like that be his guardian angel?

A guardian devil was more like it.

Brett went into a brooding silence for a while. He picked up the ragged science fiction paperback Gonzo had left behind and started reading it, to help pass the time.

He and Frannie didn't speak for at least another hour as he read. The sounds of music, dancing and cheering came from upstairs. An ice machine made startling crashing noises once or twice an hour. A constant buzzing hum came from a transformer in one of the dark alcoves. Frannie clicked away on her phone, buzzing coming with replies every few minutes.

Then the door to the basement flew open, hitting the outside of the building with a bang. Brett and Fran looked up to see the short Edward Scissorhands groom standing in the doorway.

"Boo!" he cried, giggling at his own joke.

Brett put on a smile for the man. "Hey. What's up?"

The groom shrugged. "Teena won't come down here, but I thought I'd see what it was all about before we say our goodnights." He took careful steps into the basement, looking more than a little tipsy.

Brett stood up to join the man and to help guide him around. "Well, there's not a lot to see at first glance. Waiting around for ghosts isn't nearly as exciting as you'd think."

The groom grinned. "Yeah, I know, that's what Teena says. Says you're haunted yourself, followed around by your own personal ghost. Must make ghost hunting easy if you bring your own, huh?"

Brett let the polite smile fade a bit. "Well, I suppose that's one way to look at it, but funny enough, I wasn't aware of it myself until very recently."

Frannie was standing up now, looking the groom over, smiling. "Great costume! I love Edward!"

The groom menaced her with his foam scissors. "Thanks! She has a thing for Johnny Depp, and *everyone's* done Captain Jack Sparrow, so this was what I came up with."

"She's a really fantastic Elvira in white, herself," said Brett.

The groom grinned. "Oh yeah, and she's all mine, now!" He winked.

"So she sees a lot about me, is this common for her?"

The groom nodded. "Oh yeah, all the time. I thought she was bullshitting at first, but it was charming, so I just went with it. But more and more, I'm seeing she's for real, and she's right most of the time, especially when she's not personally involved. Guess being too close to someone makes it harder to see."

Brett nodded. He'd heard other psychics, both real and fake, say something like this before. Maybe it was a matter of losing objectivity and seeing what you hoped to see, rather than what was really there.

He and Fran showed the groom around the basement. Brett saw the dressing room haunt go through its recorded routine again as they passed. Neither Frannie nor the groom showed any indication of seeing the ghost, though Frannie did shiver when the spectral image of the woman passed through her. Brett thought he saw an odd glow flash around Frannie as that happened, reminding him of a Star Trek force field being hit.

Brett stayed in the doorway of the well room this time, and though the groom went right up to the railing by the pit, he seemed unfazed by the pull that Brett could feel even from where he stood. Brett was relieved to leave the room.

The groom thanked them for the little tour and said that the party was already being wrapped up, that they should all be out by midnight. "I'd like to say we'd like to stick around for the show, and maybe Teena would if I left it all up to her, but it's our wedding night, so we have other plans." The groom waggled his eyebrows. Fran chuckled.

Brett put on a smile for the guy. "I don't blame you."

As he showed the groom out, Brett was met at the open door by Gonzo, who was carrying the video camera, tripod, and the laptop bag. Liz and Caroline weren't too far behind, and they chattered to each other.

"Equipment check," announced Gonzo. Fran nodded and relayed this to Jimbo with rapid thumb typing.

Gonzo set the stuff down on a battered old table and found an extension cord and outlet. He set up a power strip and plugged in the camera to top off its battery. He flipped open the laptop, and established a cellular Internet connection. Brett made sure the IP camera synched up with the laptop, and they tested light levels around the basement. Gonzo peered at the video window on the laptop as Brett walked from room to room.

"This should be a better quality broadcast than over Bluetooth and cellphone," said Brett. "At least it has a hard disk to spool up video if we lose connection, so it can be recorded and resumed later."

"Are we starting down here, *Chico*?" asked Liz, who was going through the case of ghost hunting equipment, testing batteries.

Brett shook his head. "No, I think if we start upstairs, once the party clears out, it'll be a great place to establish some history and color, leaving the well and Room of Faces for last."

Caroline nodded her approval. "Good plan. Now, you and Liz are the talent. I'm thinking Fran can run the camera. Gonzo can be security and can stand by in case Brett needs restraining. Sorry, Brett."

Brett sighed. "Guess that makes sense. What'll you be doing?"

Caroline mimed putting a crown on her own head. "Me? I'm the Queen, of course," she stuck out her tongue and smiled. "I'll be supervising and floating around as needed." She frowned and sighed. "I ll even appear on camera if need be, but I'm not wild about the idea."

"Sounds like a plan, your worshipfulness," said Gonzo. "Since nothing turned up in our search, I'll bet Larry's still around somewhere."

"You know, I half expected him to crash the party upstairs," said Liz. "But we were up there a couple of hours and didn't see him."

"Well, he doesn't seem to be much for a direct confrontation," said Brett. "He used a remote at the castle, and he's run away twice."

"You guys just don't get that Larry's dangerous, do you?" said Gonzo. "He's taking a giant risk to do a few stupid pranks. There's more behind this, and we know he's capable of some pretty fucked up stuff. We shouldn't leave Brett alone. None of us should be, especially during the webcast."

"He can't afford to get caught," said Caroline. "He'd be breaking parole. Anyway, you get to keep an eye out, Gonzo. The party's breaking up, we should be able to start soon."

They watched as the costumed guests wandered out into the parking lot and drove away in their cars. Teena and her new husband lingered, thanking their guests. The Elvira in white saw Brett and Liz standing in the basement doorway and beckoned to them, so they joined the couple in the parking lot.

The groom, whose name turned out to actually *be* Edward, greeted them with tipsy cheer, hugging both Liz and Brett. Teena favored each of them with an embrace that included a full kiss on the lips. Liz giggled and Brett blushed. The bride smiled a wicked smile and said, "You've got to kiss the bride, it's tradition!" Edward grinned, shrugged, and kissed her as well. It was deep and went on long enough to make Brett and Liz look away after a moment.

They were alone in the lot, just the four of them and a few cars. Brett noted that even at a country bar out on the edge of a small town, *Soccer Mom* managed to stand out.

As the bride and groom said their goodbyes, he felt Teena's stare. He returned her gaze, and found it hard to hold eye contact with her. Her eyes held him despite his discomfort, and for just a moment, there was no sound, no movement around him. Just those deep, dark, intense eyes. "Hold on, Brett, and stand up for what's important to you, no matter the cost."

He nodded and then she and Edward were gone and Liz was leading him by the hand.

Chapter 15 - Get Rhythm

The others were already making their way upstairs, Gonzo carrying the bulk of the equipment.

Once upstairs, they let themselves in. The staff had begun cleaning up after the party. Brett heard the roar of big exhaust fans somewhere above, but the air still seemed stale and smoky.

The lights were dim along the bar and its adjoining rooms. The stage and dance floor area were dark. Brett saw another room full of tables and a large cleared area that was dominated by an actual mechanical bull.

They set up the laptop on a table near the bar and tested the video equipment and cellular network uplink again. Fran was on the phone with Jimbo, confirming that everything was a go on both ends.

Brett paced around the place. There were poolrooms that didn't seem to have any feeling of paranormal activity. There was a room with an enormous metal safe, which Brett thought must date back at least a hundred years.

He thought he caught wispy glimpses of faint figures out of the corners of his eyes in the bull room. Wandering into the stage and dance floor area, he had an even stronger impression of ghosts, but none as solid as the one he'd seen in the dressing room below, and nothing as malevolent as what he'd encountered in the well room.

"Jimmy says we already have almost a hundred viewers, and those are just watching the countdown to broadcast," called Frannie from where she and Caroline sat at the laptop.

Brett felt nervous. He looked around for Gonzo, but his big friend wasn't nearby. He guessed he must have gone outside to patrol. He looked around for Liz, and after a moment, found her astride the mechanical bull.

"Yee haw! Look at me, I'm a cowgirl, Brett!" She slapped her thigh and kicked her heels into the leather sides of the "bull." She threw a hand into the air and waved it around, acting out a struggle to keep from being thrown.

"Rodeo clown, maybe," muttered Gonzo, who appeared from behind the bull. He didn't pause, but showed a big leering grin at both Liz and Brett. Liz stuck her tongue out at him, but dissolved into a fit of giggles and let herself down off of the bull.

Brett had to laugh at the scene. "Having fun?" he asked, glad for the distraction from his nerves.

Her arms circled his waist and she kissed him, but Brett found he had to help keep her standing up as she burst out laughing again. "Oh Brett, we've got to get us one of these!"

"Uh yeah, sure, we'll put it in the living room after we win Richter's million."

Liz's hand flew to her mouth. "Oh! I forgot to mention, while you were sleeping, Jimbo texted me to tell me that Richter's reluctantly agreed to the terms, though he reserves the right to send a proxy if the location isn't someplace he wants to go. By the way, when are you going to tell *us* where we're going, *Chico*?"

Brett smiled as she kissed the end of his nose. "Well, maybe I'd better--"

Caroline's yell interrupted him. "Five minutes until airtime!"

Brett walked arm in arm with Liz back to the laptop table. Frannie was playing with the camera and Caroline was sitting with headphones on. She turned and gave them a brief smile.

"Brett was just about to tell us where we're going next!" teased Liz.

"Not on camera, I'm not!" he protested.

"We're not on the air just yet." said Caroline. "I'd kind of like to know where you're going so I can see if I can help or not."

"Well, okay," said Brett. He didn't really want to reveal the secret so soon, but he'd put his friends through so much lately, they deserved to know. "I got a contact at Central State, the old abandoned insane asylum in Indianapolis."

Liz jumped up and clapped, arm still tangled in Brett's. He had to grab a nearby railing to steady himself. Caroline blinked at him and just said, "Wow!" Fran lowered the camera and shook her head. "You're kidding! No one gets in there, at least not with permission!"

Brett grinned. "They're tearing it all down to make condos and stuff like that soon anyway, so my contact, who works at one of the remaining buildings, got us permission."

Caroline was about to say something else, but she put a hand to one side of her head, listening to the headphones. Brett could see a postage stamp-sized window on the laptop screen with Jimbo's face in it, talking.

"Okay, okay, one minute, guys," said Caroline, all business once more.

Brett and Liz looked at each other. Liz dashed for the bar and sat on one of the stools, spinning back and forth once. She patted the stool next to her.

Brett joined her at the bar, and Frannie followed them with the camera. When Caroline gave the signal, Liz began to talk.

"Welcome back ghosties and ghoul-friends! We're at the famously haunted Bobby Mackey's Music World in Wilder, Kentucky! Brett and I are gonna take you on a tour, and hopefully capture some activity on camera."

Brett smiled and didn't know what to say for a couple of terrifying heartbeats. "Lizzie and I have already been around the place, and let me tell you, there's more spirits here than just liquor, beer and wine." Brett saw Gonzo lurking in the poolroom behind Frannie, rolling his eyes.

After some more introductory chatter, they gave some of the history of the place; its century as a slaughterhouse, a speakeasy, and several incarnations as a bar.

Brett decided to start the investigation in the bull room, so they wandered about that space, letting Frannie give the viewers a good look around. Brett saw Liz looking at the bull again and could just about feel her thinking about playing with it again. He put a hand on her arm and shook his head. She moved so that Brett was between her and the camera. She stuck her tongue out at him and smiled. He winked at her.

They found a corner where Brett had seen some of the wispy figures and sat down on the floor. They put a compass, an EMF meter, and a voice recorder out in front of them.

Liz and Brett introduced themselves and asked questions to the air. They asked the spirits to talk into the recorder or to make the needle of the compass move to show their presence.

Brett again saw the faintest wisps of light, like illuminated jets of steam, which flickered into view for instants before vanishing once more. But there were many of them, so the air seemed to him to be alive with the flickers and flashes.

"Do you see them?" he asked Liz.

She shook her head. "What do you see?"

He described the flickering spirits, feeling self-conscious, since he knew that if Liz couldn't see them, then neither could the audience. He knew that if he'd seen such a thing on TV or a webcast even a year ago, he would have been very skeptical. After all, there was no hard evidence of the spirits, and only he was seeing them.

"Lizzie, these spirits may be here because it brings back memories for them, it might have been a focal point in their lives. They came here to be social and to be entertained. Could you sing something for them?"

Liz looked at him a moment, frowning. "If I do that, we'll lose the web audience."

Brett laughed. "Come on, just a little. Maybe the spirits can show their approval by moving something if they like it?"

"You're gonna get it for this," threatened Liz, smiling even as she shook a finger at him. "Okay...." Liz drew breath and sang like a kindergarten teacher. "Well, she'll be comin' round the mountain when she comes! She'll be a-comin' round the mountain, she'll be comin' round the mountain...."

Brett saw the spirits flicker faster, lingering longer, more like twinkling white Christmas tree lights. There were brief flickers on the lights of the K-II EMF meter. He pointed toward the compass so that Fran could zoom in on it.

The needle twitched. It swung in a short jerky arc. It moved back and forth, and then spun in a circle. As Liz finished singing, the needle came back to rest at north, and the EMF meter settled back to a single green light.

Liz clapped her hands with glee. "It worked, Brett! Hey, I have another idea!"

She hopped up, leaving Brett to gather up the equipment. Frannie followed her with the camera. Brett trailed along behind.

Liz passed the command center where Caroline monitored the broadcast on the laptop. She went on out onto the dark dance floor and hopped up onto the stage. Brett followed, stepping up the side stairs to sit down beside her.

Liz dug through her pockets and came out with another digital voice recorder. "I put this recording on here when I was doing research about this place. Bobby Mackey doesn't believe his own place is haunted, but he did do a song about one of the stories told about the place. He wrote this song... and I bought the MP3 to listen to on the trip up."

She placed the recorder between them, selected a track and pressed play. It was faint and tinny, so she upped the volume.

The voice of the country singer spun the sad musical tale of a long-ago resident of the bar, the daughter of the owner who fell in love with the wrong man. Her father had him killed, and she followed him to the grave, taking her own life.

"Johanna! Johanna, where are you now?" cried out the chorus. "Is it true that you're still here somehow?"

Brett felt chills just listening to the song play from the little speaker on the recorder.

Then he saw *her*.

Her long black hair was tied back and she wore a long gown. Either a veil covered her face, or she was just insubstantial enough not to show features. He felt cold, and he felt the sadness that poured from this sad soul.

"She's here," murmured Brett, indicating the direction with a jut of his chin. Liz squinted in that direction and Frannie swung the camera, but if either saw what he did, they didn't say.

The song drew to a close, and Johanna paused and became fainter. Liz pressed play again, and the song started over. Johanna became more solid again and moved with slow purpose toward the two of them, hands clutching her head. Brett could see a mouth now on the ghost. It was open wide in a silent scream.

He started to ask Liz to stop, but before he could, Johanna lunged at Liz. He gasped and Liz turned to look at him. The ghost missed her and swiped at the recorder instead, and knocked it off the stage to the floor below with a clatter.

The music stopped playing and Johanna burst into mist and faded from Brett's view. "Guess she doesn't like that song so much," said Brett. Liz hopped down and picked up the recorder and examined it.

"Looks like the battery's dead, *Chico*. She knocked it off and drained it." She showed the device to Frannie and their audience. "Isn't that cool?"

Much of the rest of the investigation on that level was quieter after, and even Brett only caught fleeting glimpses of spirits now and again. Caroline let them know, by holding up messages written in thick black marker, that they were beginning to lose viewers.

Brett announced that they'd take a short break and when they came back, they'd move downstairs to visit the spirits in the Room of Faces and the infamous Hell's Gate.

The transmission cut out, and they gathered equipment, moved out of the room and made their way down to the basement entrance.

Gonzo was waiting for them there, having borrowed the key to the padlock from Dan. He undid the lock and let them inside.

"Haven't seen anyone out here, though I've seen a few cars drive by awful slow," said Gonzo. "Maybe they're fans and maybe they're not. I don't think anyone could get in here without me knowing though."

They all filed into the basement. The lights had been turned off for the webcast, and they saw only by their flashlights. The camera would see more clearly than they would, with its infrared floodlight and night vision. Gonzo shut the door behind him, sitting in a chair to watch both the main entrance, and to keep an eye on the far garage door, just in case.

Brett thought Frannie's face looked eerie, lit by the greenish light of the preview screen on the camera as she took in the main room. He could see the faint foxfire aura of her "guardian angel" and wondered what it must be like for her to live like that.

Brett realized that Liz had been talking to the camera, describing the darker history of the place while he'd been lost in thought. It was where the Satanic cult had made their sacrifices and held their eldritch, malevolent rituals over a hundred years before.

The place was also where Pearl Bryan's missing head was supposed to rest, somewhere in the well. The head that had been "cleanly" severed from her pregnant body when two dental students, Alonzo Walling and her boyfriend, Scott Jackson, murdered her. The men were said to be cultists, and went to the grave with the secret of the location of Pearl's head.

Hearing Liz talk about it sounded unnatural to Brett's ears. She was a creature of light and whimsy, of passionate living fire. Hearing her speak of such dark things seemed like defilement to him.

Caroline joined them on the investigation this time, though she kept off camera as much as she could. Brett was glad to have her calm presence with them as they entered the well room again. She grabbed Brett's sleeve without a word, holding him back. He looked at her and she glanced at the well, then back at him and shook her head. He nodded.

He hung back and used an EMF meter while Caroline and Liz dared to go closer to the railing in front of the well. It made him anxious, thinking about that sucking coldness, with his love and her friend so close to it.

They cut the flashlights off and put out a voice recorder and a compass while Brett held the K-II EMF meter. He noted aloud that the copper pipes near the ceiling had high levels of EMF, but the meter didn't register in the direction of the well itself.

The darkness was near total, lit only by tiny LED lights on the devices they'd brought. The glow-in-the-dark paint on the needle and face of the compass was difficult to see, but there was no motion.

Caroline startled him by speaking in a loud, clear voice. "We're here to speak to anyone who might have a message for us. I'm Caroline. Why are you so scared?"

The dead wouldn't stick around in the room by choice. And if they did, the pull Brett felt even then would be hard to resist.

He found Liz standing toe to toe with him, hands on his chest. "Stop, Brett!" He realized he'd walked a few paces closer to the railing without thinking about it. *This must be what a sleepwalker feels like if woken.*

Shaken, he said, "I need to get out of here. Now."

Chapter 16 - Hell's Bells

Liz and Caroline turned on flashlights, scooped up the equipment. They formed a two-woman wall and led him from behind, out of the well room. Frannie and the camera's eye watched them leave. He felt relieved, but embarrassed.

He took a break in the main room, and sat next to Gonzo for a few minutes while Liz and Caroline toured the dressing rooms. He saw their flashlights flick from place to place on the other end of the main room. Frannie followed behind with the camera.

When they were alone, Gonzo murmured, "You okay, Junior?"

Brett nodded, and then realized it was too dark for his gesture to be seen. "Yeah. Just shaken up. I don't like that room. It sucks."

"Ha. Can't be too bad off if you're making lousy puns."

Brett chuckled. "Yeah. Hear or see anything out here?"

"Nah, not really. I see lights from the road hit the garage door windows once in a while, but nothing much else. Maybe we scared him off. He's got a lot to lose if he thinks we identified him when he took off."

Brett sighed. "Well, we didn't, did we? It might not have been Larry, you know?"

Gonzo grunted. "You believe that? Who else has it in for you?"

Brett had no answer for that. They sat for long minutes in near silence while Brett recovered.

After maybe a half hour, the girls came back their way. Brett stood up and turned on his flashlight and walked to meet them. Liz flashed him a grin and took his hand for a moment.

He told the camera he was feeling better and that their next stop was the Room of Faces and then he led the way back there.

The long narrow room was a more claustrophobic sort of place than the others they'd been in, Brett thought. It felt more like a prison cell than the storage room it was used as now. There were boxes and stacked chairs in there. Three of the walls were blank gray concrete, reinforcing the prison feeling he got. The wall they faced as they entered, one of the long walls, was covered in markings. They were smudgy, and it looked like some effort had gone into cleaning them off. But they remained, overlapping indistinct patterns, looking like sooty fires had painted them.

And if he looked at the patterns for more than a few seconds, faces leaped out of the wall, leering and howling. Not all of them were even completely human faces, though it was hard to say, since they were so stretched and distorted. They seemed like lost souls, trapped forever, straining to be free.

"Do you see them too?" he asked.

The girls both nodded, faces serious. Liz and Caroline were quieter in this room, visibly nervous as they set up for another EVP session. Lights went out. Brett could still feel the faces staring out at him, begging for release he couldn't grant. He and the girls asked questions of the air as usual, but there was an unusual urgency, shorter pauses between their questions. None of them wanted to stay there long.

Brett noticed white lights zipping around the ceiling, so faint that he thought he might be imagining them.

"Brett, do you see that?" asked Liz from much closer to him than he'd thought.

"Yeah, I wasn't sure until you said something. Caroline?"

"Yep, uh huh. They've been swimming around up there like phosphorescent spermies for a few minutes now."

Brett had to let out a nervous laugh. "'Spermies'! Well, that's what I thought they looked like too, but wasn't gonna say it."

Liz giggled, but it seemed muted, and she took his arm there in the dark. The contact was very much welcome.

Then it happened.

An image superimposed on the scene, and it seemed to him as though the room was suddenly brightly lit.

In his mind's eye, all of them threw back their heads and screamed at the top of their lungs.

His heart pounded in his chest and he almost panted as he fought down the panic he felt.

"Brett, what did you see?" Caroline's shaky, hoarse whisper told him she'd seem something too.

He related what he'd seen.

"Let's get out of here, I saw something too, but I can't say it here. Outside. Really outside, I mean."

They all hurried out of the room, leaving the equipment this time. The hair on the back of Brett's neck stood up and chills raced all over his body. He felt the darkness slam closed behind them, and he felt pursued. He had to fight his instinct to flee, knowing that not only would running headlong away be dangerous, but it'd look awfully unprofessional. *Some predators attack when their prey panics.*

It was all he could do to stay at a quick walk toward the door where he knew Gonzo sat. The big guy turned on the light switch and the basement flooded with light. He saw Brett and the three women's faces and he threw open the door to let them out into the night.

Caroline led the way, Liz and Brett following right behind, Frannie trailed somewhat, camera still running. Brett felt much better out in the cold night air, but a knot of fear remained in his stomach.

You're gonna need me, Brett, let me take the wheel.

———

Brett looked around for the source of the voice, but saw nothing. He didn't answer but shook his head. *Not yet. You might be right, but not yet.*

Caroline stopped and turned to face them. She took in a deep breath and let it out. She repeated this a couple of times, calming down. Liz touched her shoulder and looked into her face. "Are you okay? What did you see, what's wrong?"

Caroline didn't answer, but shook her head and looked at the camera, then at Liz. Liz got the hint and turned to talk brightly to the camera. "Break time folks! We'll be back after these messages!"

Fran lowered the camera and shut it down. She looked uneasily at the others, taking a few steps past them into the parking lot to make a phone call to Jimbo while they were off the air. She stayed within eyeshot.

Brett and Liz stood near Caroline, watching her. After a minute or so, she spoke. "So, Brett, at exactly the same moment you said you saw us screaming... I saw a face."

"What kind of face?" asked Brett, the knot of dread freezing solid in his belly.

Caroline didn't seem Queenly at the moment, a hint of fear showed in her eyes. "Well, I didn't want this on camera, because it'll sound dramatic, but I saw an angry, screaming man's face. He had big horns coming out of its forehead, and its skin was red." She shivered, rubbing her arms with her hands and hugging herself.

"The *Devil*, Caroline?" Liz asked, her voice high and squeaky.

Caroline shrugged. "See, I told you it sounded crazy. I don't know, if there were Satanic rituals done here, it might not be that, but maybe the image of something that happened here. Someone in costume, maybe. But I didn't like it, and I had to get out."

Headlights played slowly across them from the highway. Frannie returned from her call, standing nearby, peering at Caroline with curiosity.

Brett nodded and patted her shoulder once. "I don't blame you. I think it's time to call it a night."

Liz nodded her agreement.

Caroline shook her head. "No, I just needed to get myself back together. Let's--" She stopped mid-sentence and looked up at the road, her face fully lit by the headlights.

Headlights that drove straight at them. The truck's engine revved and its tires roared as it accelerated through the gravel of the parking lot. Brett pushed Liz and Frannie one way, while Caroline threw herself the other way.

The truck's brakes slammed on before it came within ten feet of them, making the back end fishtail around.

An arm clad in brown leather reached out of the open driver's side window. The hand held an oversized gun of some kind. The gun fired, pop, pop, pop!

Brett felt something whiz past him. He threw himself to the ground, the sharp gravel cutting into the palms of his hands.

Frannie's scream of agony tore the night air, then trailed off into a forlorn wail.

Brett looked up as the truck continued its slide, turning a half circle to aim back toward the exit. He saw Frannie fall and Liz scramble over to check her.

Brett watched Frannie's protective spirit dissipate like morning fog.

The cold knot caught fire inside his gut. Again came the voice. *Now, Brett! You know you need me for this! Let go and let me get that bastard!*

Brett hesitated only for a second. Letting his other side take over was dangerous, but in this case, some rage and fury was necessary. *Okay, let's do this, it's your turn.*

Brett let the fire consume him. He heard his own scream of anger and watched his body pound across the lot to where *Soccer Mom* was parked. He could only stare in fascination as he ripped open the door, started the engine, and tore out of the parking lot after the pickup truck. He could hear the old van's tires squealing as it picked up speed down the highway to catch up.

He willed himself to follow his own body, and had the thrilling feeling of flying along the road. He sped just a few feet over the surface, faster and faster, the world blurring to misty gray in his peripheral vision.

Brett rounded a curve and saw the taillights of *Soccer Mom* weaving from lane to lane. He heard a loud bang and metallic clatter, and the van lurched as it slowed. Brett gained ground now, and he saw a crunched bumper tumble out from under the backside of *Soccer Mom*.

His alter ego... Lizzie called him Terb... was ramming the pickup truck.

He heard another loud crunch of impact and the squeal of tires. He managed to float just above the roof of the swerving minivan. It helped to think of it like water skiing, being pulled along by his desire to be reunited with his own body.

Brett saw the pickup truck speed up further to get away from the van. The chase went on, following the two-lane highway's hills and curves.

Brett closed his eyes and plunged through the roof of the van, down into the passenger seat. It was disconcerting, since there was no pressure from the seat to hold him in place. If he lost concentration, he was flung around the cabin, even finding himself outside at one point.

"Stop! Stop, you fucking idiot! You're gonna get me killed, and you'll wreck Gonzo's van!" Brett shouted at 'Terb.'

Terb just laughed, a cackle that reminded Brett of Gonzo, though it held a wilder edge. "I'm gonna get that asshole!"

They careened around a curve, and the truck came into view again. Terb hunched over the wheel and stomped on the accelerator. The van lurched forward, making a disturbing, tearing squeal.

The truck rushed up close, and Terb jerked the wheel to one side just as he hit the back end of the pickup. The truck lost traction and spun. *Soccer Mom* slammed into the side of the bed of the truck, making it roll. Both vehicles left the highway and tore great wounds in the grassy hillside as they did.

Brett was terrified to see the river looming before them. Steam and smoke belched from under the crumpled hood of *Soccer Mom*. The truck completed its roll just before the riverbank, but didn't stop in time, its front end going into the water.

Brett saw a figure struggling to get out of the vehicle. Terb stomped on the accelerator again and again, but the van no longer responded, and came to rest just behind the truck.

Terb pushed open the door and leaped out, running down toward the figure laying on the riverbank. Brett followed as close as he could.

As expected, he found Larry lying on the ground, his trademark leather cowboy hat on the ground next to his head. He had a bloody cut on his upper lip. Terb loomed over the bigger man. He made a fist and began to pound Larry's face.

Brett watched in shock. He didn't realize he had that kind of strength or hatred in him.

Larry groaned and tried to fend off the attacks, but blow after blow landed, further bloodying the man's face. Larry scrabbled around on the ground with one arm. He came up with the gun.

Brett tried to cry a warning to Terb, but it was too late. He heard the gun pop several times, aimed point blank at his body. He saw Terb jerk and screech, but he kept on pounding until Larry was unconscious.

Then Terb stood, his fists shaking with effort and adrenaline. He faced Brett. There were shiny silver splats all over his body and he leered and laughed.

"So what are you going to do now, you lunatic?" Brett wanted to keep Terb upset so he could launch himself at the body and take it back. His body.

Terb grinned, reached into a pocket and held up a coin. Ralph's silver dollar.

"Nope, my turn's not over yet. I *like* being alive and whole again!" His fingers closed over the silver dollar, making a fist.

Before Brett could say a word, the fist smashed into him and he knew nothing more but gray mist, fading to darkness.

Chapter 17 - Ain't Got Nobody

Brett wasn't. He had no awareness, his essence diffuse and scattered. He was the gray mist that his world was made of, no more substantial than a cloud.

The cloud of memories, thoughts and feelings that added up to Brett began to condense bit by bit, like stardust falling inward in a primordial solar system. When enough of him had collected, it ignited like a newborn sun and Brett dreamed.

Each memory that came back to him sparked and flashed, tiny explosions of experience. Here was the birthday when he fell and chipped a tooth. There was his awkward prom photo being taken. Now he was his first kiss with Cheryl. Then her funeral, and all the pitying looks from her friends and family. Gonzo toasting in New Orleans. Frannie standing alone in the cemetery. The little ghoul, gore dripping from the roadkill she held in one hand.

Lizzie in butterfly wings, dancing with him.

Brett's essence became more solid by the moment, but he was still lost in the mists of the other world. What should he do now? He couldn't go back to his body. Terb had the silver coin and was using it to block him.

Silver kept out ghosts. Ghost repellent, as Caroline had described it. She was right.

And he was a ghost. Now, more than ever.

He felt panic rise in him. What *could* he do? He was insubstantial and lost, and even if he returned to his friends, as a ghost, they wouldn't know he was even there.

He thought about poor Frannie. He couldn't believe Larry had shot her. Those shots were meant for him. Larry might be a jerk and a backstabber, but no matter how much Brett had hated him, the guy just wasn't a killer.

Or was he?

But then he'd seen Larry shoot Terb at extremely short range, the muzzle of the gun practically touched his body. And Terb had stood up with just shiny splats on him. How had he managed that? His other half couldn't be bulletproof just by force of will.

"None of this makes sense," Brett said out loud.

"Does it have to?"

Brett turned to see Ashleigh/Britney floating nearby. She gave him a sad little smile and pushed strands of hair out of her face. She wore jeans, a Homestar Runner T-shirt and flip-flops. All her colors were washed out and muted, sort of sepia-toned. She was blurry too, and Brett couldn't decide if his vision was recovering, or if she wasn't all there with him.

Brett warmed at the sight of her anyway. "Hey! Do you ever knock?"

She shrugged and smiled. "I wouldn't be here if you didn't want me here."

Brett grinned. "You got me there, though I didn't specifically think of you."

She reached over and patted his hand, her touch impossibly light but warm. "You could use a friend right about now, I'd say."

Brett nodded. "I could use more than that, but you'll do."

She tilted her head to one side. "Oh? What could you want more than a friend? When you come right down to it, friends are what makes life worth living, a reason to go on. Once upon a time, you and Liz befriended a monster in the woods. You didn't have to. She smelled bad, she was barely human, even. But in doing that, you saved her soul. My soul."

Brett sighed. "Yeah, I know you're right. But Britney, I've just had my body, my life, stolen from me."

"So you're out in the big gray nowhere feeling sorry for yourself," she said, nodding with sympathy in her eyes, along with another emotion with a harder edge.

Brett looked away from her. "Sorry. I know you lost your body too. You sacrificed the little bit of life you had left to save others. But I'm not done living yet. I hate the thought of that jerk screwing up my life while I cool my heels in this afterlife."

Britney laughed. "Oh, this isn't the afterlife. This is just in between. Shadow. You wouldn't be here if you were done living, trust me."

Brett stared at her a moment before asking, "You have more living to do?"

She shook her head. "Nah, I'm dead. I'm just not able to walk away from life yet. I feel just like you do, cheated, robbed of my life. I don't have any chance of going back, just watching and waiting until I'm ready to move on."

"What do you think of my chances?"

"I'd say they're pretty good if you can say you have reason to live with a straight face. Aren't you the guy who got possessed once because he'd tried to die? On purpose?"

Brett had to look away again. "Okay, yeah, I know. So maybe I don't deserve to live?"

Britney grabbed his arm, and he felt her fingers this time. He looked at her, startled.

"No! Don't say that! I didn't mean that at *all*. I'm saying that you gave up on life, but friends... Lizzie... dragged you back to life. And now you're a ghost and that gift of hers, that borrowed will to live, it's still with you. If death is what you wanted, you could stay here or move on. But Brett, you want back in the game. You want to *live*."

Brett couldn't break eye contact with the girl. He felt a deep conviction that she was right. He'd rejected death consciously when he and Liz had expelled the demon from him. And again when he'd bit through his silver cord to stop his soul from leaking out.

And now. He wanted his life back.

He had the feeling of motion, the impression of shapes darting by, far off in the mist. "Where are you taking me now?"

She giggled. "I'm not doing it, you are. You want something, so you're headed there. I'm just hanging on for the ride."

Brett saw a large rectangular area, lit from a yellow-orange light atop a pole. There were cars and people. One of the people was laying on the ground while others crouched or stood nearby.

It was the parking lot at Bobby Mackey's. His friends were clustered around Frannie's inert body. He got closer and things came into more solid focus. He hovered near Liz. The sight of her was comforting, even if she looked distressed.

"Where could he be? Did he follow Larry all the way back to Memphis?" She was angry with him? With Frannie lying dead on the ground?

He floated down near Frannie's body. Silver splats were on her zippered hoodie jacket, just like on his body. Her chest moved up and down and he could see her breath in the cold air.

Caroline sat on the ground, stroking Frannie's hair, looking at her face with calm concern.

"I swear he needs to be tied down."

Gonzo paced up and down the lot between the women and the spot where his van used to be. "Damn it, I shouldn't have given him the keys to get stuff out of *Soccer Mom*. I should know better."

Liz turned and shouted at Gonzo. "Well, wouldn't *you* have gone after Larry?"

Gonzo stopped in his tracks, shocked. "Huh? Hell no! The guy had a real gun, as far as I knew! Not a fucking paintball gun."

Paintball? Brett heard giggling from Britney. He looked at her. She just shook her head. "That's funny, a paintball gun!"

Liz stomped up to Gonzo, looking nearly straight up to stare at him. "Brett thought... we *all* thought that Larry had just shot Frannie dead. She's not actually doing very well, if you hadn't noticed! Brett went after him because he was angry, Gonzo. Because someone hurt one of us."

Caroline appeared between them, a hand on either's shoulder. "Hold on now. Calm down."

"You calm down, sister. It's not your car that's being used for a high speed chase somewhere out there, driven by Brett the crackhead."

"He is *not* a crackhead!"

"I'm just sayin'...."

Brett regretted letting Terb have his way even more than before.

"Stop." Caroline didn't shout, but the others went quiet and sullen.

There was a moan from Frannie and she sat up.

Caroline glared ice at her friends and went to crouch next to Frannie. "Are you okay? Talk to me, Fran."

Frannie looked at Caroline and at the others. Her eyes blinked with recognition, but when she tried to speak, they had to strain to hear her words.

"I'm gone. Gone." Frannie's voice was a whisper and a wail at the same time.

"Nonsense, you're right here." There was no arguing with Caroline's firm tone.

Frannie shook head. "No, not me, but the rest of me."

Liz was nearby now. "Your 'guardian spirit,' honey?"

Frannie looked up at Liz and nodded. Tears glistened on her cheeks, bright streaks lit by the streetlight. "Gone."

"So let me get this straight," growled Gonzo. "Larry shoots her with paintballs and she's lost her soul? The shit gets deeper and deeper around here."

Liz scowled at the big guy.

Caroline looked up at Gonzo. "Yeah, I think Larry knew what he was doing." She took a finger and wiped some of the paint off of Frannie. She held it up to the light. "Silver paint, actually. Metal flakes of silver in a gel, looks like. He wasn't trying to kill a person, he was trying to harm a ghost. Question is, was it meant for Brett?"

Liz turned and shook her head. "No, there's no way he could know that'd work."

"Why not," said Gonzo, a tinge of sarcasm in his voice. "He practically advertised that he had one foot in the grave after St. Pat's."

Liz protested, "But even *we* didn't know he wasn't firmly anchored to his body, or that the other half of him even existed, until yesterday."

No one had an answer for that. They decided that Frannie's physical body was all right; calling an ambulance wouldn't help things.

"What about the police?" asked Gonzo.

"No, Gonzo! With Brett in the state he's in, he'd probably get arrested."

"And we'll bail him out, and I'll think about not pressing charges for running off with my van."

"Look," said Caroline, "Let's wait a bit, make sure Frannie's okay, then we can go looking if Brett's not back soon."

No one was happy waiting, but Caroline got them moving, helping her get Frannie to the Saturn, propping her up in the front passenger seat, reclined back.

Once Fran was settled, Caroline grabbed Gonzo's hand, surprising him. "Okay big guy, you and me are going back in there to get the equipment. Liz, look after Fran for a bit, will you?"

Gonzo let himself be led. Brett watched them go, not wanting to go back near the well or the Room of Faces as a bare spirit himself. Teena the bride's warning came back to him. He had no desire to be trapped in that place.

He looked around for Britney, but the tween spirit was gone. He moved close to Liz, trying to touch her, but his hand passed through her. He shouted at her, trying to get her attention.

Liz just sat in the driver's seat, staring out the window, up the hill at the road. Her eyes were tired and sad. Brett could not seem to make her hear, see or feel him. He felt helpless and panicked, just staring into her face.

He leaned back and felt something cold brush his neck. Brett turned his head and saw a clear quartz pendant hanging from Caroline's rear-view mirror.

It swung ever so slightly back and forth from the contact.

Brett swatted at the light-catching prism and was rewarded by its swing widening just a little. He swatted again and again, putting hope into the strikes. Soon he got the rhythm going, like pushing a swing on a playground to go higher and higher.

The crystal was swinging in a respectable arc forward and back. Liz, staring ahead, didn't notice right away. She glanced at the crystal and reached up to still it.

Brett was frustrated. He took it out on the crystal, smacking it sideways this time. He had even better success than before, the pendulum building up a healthy swing with only a few tries.

Liz sat up in her seat. She breathed the words, "Brett? Is that you? Make the crystal swing forward and back if it is you." She stared at the makeshift pendulum.

Brett found this to be more difficult, he had to slow the swing first, then start it swinging again in the other orientation. Liz clapped her hands in glee and said, "I thought I felt your presence! Okay, now what? You're here, you're a ghost. My poor ghostly sweetie! We've got to do something so I can talk to you better, and so you don't get lost again."

She rummaged around in her purse and came out with the black embroidered bandanna. She used a pocket knife and cut it into strips. She took the chain with his ring from around her neck.

Liz tied the cloth strips with deft motions of her fingers, and threaded some through the ring. Soon, she had a small figure in her hand made of knots and his ring. She concentrated and spoke a rhyme:

"Brett my love, come to me,

into this poppet for to be,

for a time held in place,

not my prisoner, but my embrace."

Brett could see a blue aura surround her hand and the crude doll. He felt a tug toward her hand, and for an instant, he had the sensation of being held by a giant Liz.

"Lizzie, help!" he called to her.

She heard him, eyes becoming round in wonder.

But it didn't last, the form didn't fit right, he couldn't hold on.

"Brett? Are you there, Brett?" Liz tried for a few minutes to talk to the poppet, but sighed.

Caroline and Gonzo soon returned with the equipment cases. They both looked a little edgy, peering over their shoulders at the now closed basement door as though something might follow them. Brett was happy to see that nothing had.

Gonzo said, "I locked up and left the keys with Dan. We're done here."

After they put the cases in the trunk, Caroline shooed Liz out of the driver's seat. As she stood, Caroline noticed the poppet and asked about it. Liz explained that she'd had contact from Brett, and that she'd tried to conjure him into the poppet so she could talk with him better, but it hadn't worked for more than a moment.

"What do you think the problem was?" Caroline asked.

Liz shrugged. "Well, I'm tired, and my magickal skills are a bit rusty these days. But if I had to guess, I'd say I can't make a human-enough figure out of cloth."

Caroline stood up and opened one of the doors to the back seat area. She rummaged around, reaching under a seat. She came up with something, grinning. "The girls leave their things in the car all the time. Will this do?" Brett groaned when he saw it.

Liz giggled and took the thing from Caroline, tying Brett's ring onto an arm. She spoke her spell again. The blue was much stronger this time, and he felt it surround him and pull him in. And though he resisted on principal, he was pulled into the little plastic body.

Liz laughed long and hard when she heard the words that came only to her ears. "Oh Liz, how could you!" he cried from within the Barbie doll that she held in her hand.

Chapter 18 - Rag Doll

Three huge faces peered down at Brett. Liz laughed so hard that tears glinted in her eyes. Caroline covered her mouth with one hand, eyes crinkling in amusement. Gonzo blinked at him, looking confused.

Brett's embarrassment was beyond bearing. Maybe Liz thought it was a good idea, but it was humiliating. He tried to escape the little plastic body, but Liz's spell trapped him in place. It wasn't painful, and not all of him was *in* the doll. It was more like wearing a mask that he couldn't take off.

Still, he felt part of him fill the doll like a glove, and it was his only physical interface with the world. He felt the breeze stir his long, brassy, synthetic hair. He felt his bottom supported by Liz's warm palm. He could see his impossibly long and skinny legs stretching out to bare pink feet in front of him. He felt his arms pointing straight down at his sides.

He felt his mouth frozen in a permanent smile.

Since he couldn't leave, he tried to move, feeling a powerful desire to hide from the faces of his friends. He couldn't move at all, the body was just a vessel that was almost the right shape for a human, despite its exaggerated features and proportions.

Gonzo said, "A doll? You're trying to tell me Brett's in a Barbie? Okay, that's it, Liz. Don't get me wrong, I love you, you're one of my favorite people. But I've gone along with a lot of unbelievable shit you've said before without complaint--"

"You *always* complain, Gonz!" gasped Liz as she struggled to stop laughing.

"Oh Lizzie, please let me go," Brett said, feeling wretched and pitiful. She wiped at her tears with her free hand, then held it up to stop Gonzo's tirade, shushing him. "Brett's talking, hold on."

Then she made things worse. She picked up the doll that imprisoned his spirit and kissed it on top of its head. She held him very close to her face. "Brett, sweetie, this is just for now, we have to know what happened. And it's safer with you anchored in place than floating around out there."

"Safer? Lizzie, I've never felt so helpless in my life!"

Liz pursed her lips, holding back new giggles as he spoke. "I'm sorry," she whispered, "but you're just so *cute* in doll form, *Chico*."

Brett needed to get out of the little body. "Stop, please, just stop. I don't like this at all. If I tell you where to find Larry and me, will you let me loose?"

"What's he saying?" asked Caroline. Gonzo threw his hands in the air and stalked off to pace the parking lot. It was clear he was past his limits.

Liz looked up from Brett and turned him a little, posing him so he could see both of them. He felt even worse as Caroline peered at him with curiosity.

"Let's try something. You take him." Liz held the doll out to Caroline. She looked unsure, but reached out toward him. He wanted to flee, but still could not move. Her fingers curled around him and she held him around his waist. She pulled him up close, inches from her face. Caroline filled his world and he wanted to be anywhere else.

"I don't see anything different, it's just a doll," said the woman holding him.

"Brett, please say something to Caroline?" Liz asked, no trace of laughter in her voice now.

"Hi," said Brett, not really wanting to do this.

Startled, Caroline's hand flew open to drop him, but one stiff doll arm hooked on her fingers and she grabbed at him to keep him from falling. "Oh my," she said with wonder. "He really is in there."

As embarrassing as it had been to be held by his girlfriend, this was worse. He liked Caroline, but he didn't like being a toy in her hand. He felt afraid, trapped and out of control. "Yes, it's me. I don't want to be here."

Caroline looked at Liz. "I thought you couldn't, or wouldn't, do spells that were against someone's will?"

"Well, no, not really," Liz bit her lower lip in thought. "But it's ultimately to help him, even if he's uncomfortable. What if Larry blasts his ghost with the paintball gun like he did to Frannie?"

Brett hadn't thought of that. As a ghost, he was vulnerable. Bound to a ... vessel, he wasn't quite as exposed. "Let's just get on with it," he said to Caroline, who straightened his plastic legs to a standing position and brushed back wild wisps of his hair. He wished she'd stop; her touch all over his vessel was very disconcerting and distracting.

Caroline looked at him again. "Okay. What now, then?"

Brett spoke to get her attention back to him and not the body he wore. "Terb... my alter ego, chased Larry down the highway a few miles. He forced him off the road and both trucks are off to the right side, on the bank of the Licking River."

Caroline repeated this to Liz, who asked, "Are you okay? Your body, that is?"

Brett tried to shrug but could not. "Well enough to beat Larry unconscious and punch me into the other world."

Caroline relayed this, then offered Brett back to Liz. Liz shook her head and instead circled her hand around the doll's thighs so that both of them held him.

Brett got the idea. "Can you both hear me?"

Liz smiled and nodded. Caroline said, "Yep. Uh-huh."

"We should get going quickly, I was knocked out for a while, and I can't force my way back into my body. Terb's using a silver dollar to keep me out. As long as he holds onto that, I'm stuck as a ghost. Or like *this*." His tone was sour, and he regretted it, as Liz reached with her other hand to stroke his face with a finger. Her attempt to be soothing was having the opposite effect on Brett.

"Don't worry, sweetie," she said. "This isn't for long. We'll think of something. Maybe I can calm Terb down and he'll let you back in. He can't control himself, he's all raw emotion. Maybe I can appeal to that."

"Why would he let me back in?"

"Well, even he's got to see that you need each other, he can't manage by himself unchecked."

Maybe we have to figure out how to work together, to end the tug of war. "I hope you're right. Promise me this though, Lizzie. You'll let me go when I ask to be let go? I don't like feeling trapped."

Caroline exchanged a glance with Liz. Liz looked down at the doll in their hands. "I want to keep you safe, *Chico*, but like Caroline pointed out, I don't believe in doing anything against your will. Please don't ask me to release you for a while? I feel better being able to talk to you, knowing where you are."

"Fine. Just please, no more laughing. I didn't ask for this. It's not funny."

"Well," said Caroline, "it really *is* kind of funny, but we'll try." She glanced at Liz, who nodded, smiling.

Caroline let go of Brett and went to collect Gonzo. Brett could see her trying to explain what was going on. Gonzo stood with folded arms, not very receptive to any of this.

Liz held him up to her face. "I'm really sorry for laughing, sweetie. Hey, at least this doll has *pants* on, not a dress!"

He grumbled, "It's okay, Liz. But the pants are Capri's, I feel like I'm wearing flood pants."

She giggled and kissed his face, her lips huge and warm. "It'll be okay, I promise!"

Caroline talked Gonzo into the car, opening the other rear door for him to get in next to Liz. She had to help Fran straighten the passenger seat so Gonzo's knees would fit. She got in the driver's seat and pulled the Saturn out onto the highway.

Liz clutched the doll in the crook of one arm, hugging Brett to her. With no one looking at him, Brett felt comforted, but he was very disoriented. He still wanted his own body back, or at least some freedom to move on his own.

Liz's cell phone started making "waca waca waca" noises as it rang. "It's Jimbo!" she explained, fishing for the phone in her purse. Brett was jostled a bit as she did that.

She found the phone and talked with him a while. At first she listened, and then she explained what had happened with Frannie. She reassured him over and over that she wasn't harmed, she just wasn't herself for now. Mercifully, Liz left out details on Brett's current condition.

The car swerved and Liz was pushed against the door. She held Brett tight. Caroline cursed and muttered about a bumper in the road.

"Hey, you may need to hold me up so I can tell you where we went off the road," said Brett, interrupting. She nodded and scooted the doll up to her head's height, holding him by his stiff legs. Liz told Jimbo she'd have to call him back.

He recognized the curves of the road, and he was sure they were getting close. He shouted "There!" as they reached the curve. Liz told Caroline, but the car was already slowing, as Caroline explained that she'd seen the tire skids on the pavement.

Caroline pulled the car off the road into the grass. She left the engine running and turned to talk to Liz and Gonzo. "I'll keep an eye on Fran, you two... you three go look and see what's going on. Be careful, Larry might be around."

Gonzo got out and walked ahead of Liz. Brett found his lower half tucked into Liz's sweatshirt pocket, her hand still curling around him within the pocket.

"Well, there's *Soccer Mom*. Where's Larry's truck?" Liz asked Gonzo.

Gonzo was too busy cursing as he saw the damage to the van's front end to answer her. He didn't even have to pull the release for the hood. As crumpled as it was, he was able to just lift it up. He had to hold it up himself, as the hood prop bar was missing.

"Fuck. I don't think she'll run again, at least not without a lot more work than she's worth. She's not going anywhere without a tow truck tonight."

Liz prowled around the area, peering at the ground. She followed the tire marks left by the truck into the river. There was another set though.

She called out to Gonzo, "It looks like the truck's front tires went in the river, but someone managed to back it out and drove back up onto the highway."

Brett stayed quiet, agreeing with her assessment.

Gonzo opened up the side door and tossed out their bags, blankets and other supplies. "Fucking Brett. Now *Soccer Mom* will probably end her life as a flop for homeless people down by the river. Better get out anything useful now. I doubt it'll be here when we get back to it."

Liz helped him carry the stuff back to the Saturn. Caroline popped the trunk, and they loaded it full, taking several trips back to the van.

Last of all, Gonzo pulled out his Louisville Slugger. He hefted the bat in his hand, smacking it into the palm of the other. He looked menacing, and Brett hoped he didn't get any ideas about the doll in Liz's pocket.

"I don't know who I'm more pissed at," he said as he opened the car door.

"Should be Larry," said Caroline from within the car. "If it weren't for him hurting Frannie, Brett wouldn't have gone off. Well, Terb, not really Brett, I guess."

"You guess? Look, Brett's got problems, whether they're oogie boogie ones or mental issues, that's clear. But if he can't control himself, he's still responsible for his actions. He can't just say 'not me!' and make it all okay. He's made you cry, he's wrecked my van, and now he's run off. How is that all okay?"

Brett couldn't defend himself, and he wasn't sure Gonzo was entirely wrong. And in this case, he had allowed it to happen, even if he didn't know what Terb would do once he handed over control.

In fact, though it was an overreaction and much more violent than he imagined himself to be, Brett approved on some level of his double's actions. He regretted that the van had been wrecked, but it had felt so good to watch himself beat the snot out of Larry.

They all sat in the car a few minutes while Gonzo ranted about the van and Brett and Larry. Brett felt Liz stroke his hair in reassurance when the big guy badmouthed him. Her touch was pleasant, but it didn't make him feel it was all right. He was still distressed that he'd upset his best friend so much, and that he couldn't even apologize directly.

The only way he could talk to Gonzo would be to be held by him. This was a disturbing image. Chills overwhelmed him, thinking of the violent things that could be done to a little plastic doll by his friend's strong hands. Bound to this anchor by Liz's spell, he wasn't sure what that would do to him, but it could be very bad. Fortunately, he doubted Gonzo could be coaxed into trying to talk to a doll. He hoped Liz didn't think of it.

After Gonzo wound down and went quiet for a minute, Caroline asked, "Well, where to now?"

"Well, where would you go, if you were an angry Brett who's pounded the crap out of Larry?" asked Gonzo.

Liz looked down at Brett's doll face to see if he had an answer.

"Me?" he asked her. "Well, I don't know. I guess I'd go back to Mackey's or I'd go on to Indy to confront Richter. Think he took Larry's truck? No one's here."

Liz asked his questions to the others. He was happy she didn't mention the source. Maybe she realized that he didn't want attention drawn to him out of embarrassment, or maybe she had the same thought about Gonzo pulling the arms and legs off the Barbie that Brett inhabited.

"Yeah, I guess we don't know if one of them is on foot," said Caroline, pulling out onto the highway, going the direction of the tires, away from Mackey's. "I'm guessing they both left together, since Larry's probably unconscious and had to have been moved. The truck's gone, so Terb must have taken it. Guess Larry can't call the cops, since he's breaking his probation by being out of state."

"Well, then they could be going anywhere," complained Gonzo. "This highway leads to Cincy, and there are several Interstates that go in and out of there."

"Anyone tried calling him?" asked Caroline.

Liz reached for her phone, but stopped before putting her hand in her purse. "Well, we can't. It's probably in the woods or in the river near Ralph's place. It was lost last night."

"During his last hissy fit," said Gonzo.

"Well, what about Larry?" asked Caroline.

Liz reached for her purse again and snapped open her phone with one hand, scrolling through the listings. "Good idea, I have him in here."

"You do?" Brett hated the tinge of jealousy in his voice. Hadn't all that gone away with Terb?

Liz looked down at him and squeezed his body with the hand that held him, glancing between him and the phone she manipulated with her other hand. "Oh sweetie, don't be like that. I only keep his number in my phone so I'll know it's him calling to screen him out. He was history to me *before* he sicced a demon on us for fun and profit."

"Who are you talking... oh yeah, your imaginary boyfriend, never mind." Gonzo sounded disgusted.

"He's *not* imaginary!" shot back Liz, but then she turned her attention to the phone as she clicked on Larry's name to make the call. Gonzo sneered and started to retort, but she held up a finger and said, 'Shhh! It's ringing!"

Brett felt very exposed as Liz raised him up so he could listen too. Gonzo rolled his eyes and turned to look out the window, watching the road slide by.

The other end picked up. Brett heard his voice, which was cold with anger. "So, Lizzie, now you're calling Larry? I've gone 'apeshit' so you're calling your old boyfriend for help? Just like when he tricked you with that staged picture of Shell kissing me? Fuck you, Lizzie!"

Chapter 19 - All of Me

Liz held the phone and Brett away from her face and stared. Her face was lit by the phone's display and he could see the hurt in her eyes.

"Don't listen to him, Lizzie," Brett said, trying to be reassuring. He wished he could reach and touch her. He wished he could make his alter ego shut up.

"Brett," Liz said into the phone, holding back tears, "I'm not calling Larry, I'm calling you. I thought you might be with him, seeing as I know you caught him."

"I suppose *he* told you that. Goody goody for him, he's got it all, doesn't he? He can't fight me, so he runs crying to you. Well, let me tell you something, I'm sick of taking a second seat. It's his turn to live on the outside, looking in."

Liz closed her eyes and took a breath before answering.

"Are you there?" came the shout from the phone. "Are you going to give me the silent treatment now?"

"No, Brett. This is hard. I love you. I love you when you're calm and I love you when you're passionate. I just hate to see you do this to yourself."

Brett wasn't sure how he felt about that. Again, he felt a slight pang of jealousy, only now it was over Terb. How could he be jealous of himself? Then he thought back to the dressing room and realized that he could. Suppose they did timeshare the body, assuming Terb would agree to and honor such an arrangement. What then, would he be the "just friends" side, while Terb was her lover? It didn't seem fair.

"He's a jerk, Lizzie," Brett said, feeling as small as the doll to which he was bound.

Liz looked at him there in her hand. "I'm sorry. It's true, I want you *whole*, Brett, not just half at a time."

Gonzo made a rude noise next to her and she jammed an elbow into his ribs.

There was no sound on the other end of the line other than breathing.

"Brett, where are you? Let me come to you and we'll try to heal you. Okay?"

The connection went dead.

"Oh, he hung up," said Liz.

Brett was relieved, in a way. He didn't want Liz to become close with Terb. It sounded like she had sympathy for him at least, and he didn't really want to share her with someone else, even if it was *him*.

But on the other hand, he couldn't see much future to their relationship with him as an insubstantial ghost or a doll-bound spirit. He needed a body, his own body. But Terb had him locked out.

Liz was his best hope for regaining his life, but he didn't like any of the options he saw for that. Even if he got control again, he'd have to stay on guard to keep Terb out.

"Lizzie, can you think of a way to evict Terb and keep him out?" he asked.

Liz shrugged. "Maybe. But evicting him would be breaking those rules about acting against someone else's will, as would keeping him out. Sweetie, what if… what if you could *merge* with him again? Be whole, like I said. Be yourself again."

"What, like Wimpy Kirk and Evil Kirk in that old Star Trek episode?"

"Yes, *Chico*! Exactly like that!"

"In case you hadn't noticed, we don't have a transporter to merge the halves of me together again."

"There's got to be something we can do!"

Gonzo spoke up. "I hate to interrupt your angsty conversation with yourself, Liz, but where are we going?"

"I wouldn't put it that way, exactly, but I do need a destination," said Caroline. She guided the car onto the Interstate. They crossed the bridge into Ohio, the lights of Cincinnati ahead of them.

"I don't know for sure," said Liz. "We know he's got Larry, or at least his phone. Since he didn't come back and he didn't tell me where he is, we're back to guessing. What possible goal could he have?"

"You mean other than trashing my life?" said Brett. He felt despair and panic wash over him.

"You're not gonna like this, but I think we should just go back to that hotel and crash for a few hours," said Caroline. "It was a long night last night, and we don't have any idea where to go yet. Maybe something will come up while we rest."

"No," said Frannie. She had appeared to be asleep, chin on her chest, and she didn't look up or open her eyes as she said it.

"Hey, she can talk," said Gonzo, his voice soaked in sarcasm. "Maybe we can teach her other words, like 'Brains'?"

"Shut up, Gonzo," snapped Liz. "You're not helping things any."

"Yeah? Well, neither is calling your crazy boyfriend or talking to dollies."

Caroline slapped Gonzo on his bicep. "Listen here, bud. You're being a huge dick right now. We're all sorry about *Soccer Mom*, but if you give a crap about Brett and Frannie at all, you need to stop being so negative and think about someone besides yourself for a minute."

The air in the van froze as Gonzo's eyes locked with Caroline's for a long moment.

Gonzo let out a gusty sigh and swore under his breath. "Yeah, okay fine. You're right. I'm sorry."

Brett forgot everything for a moment. In all the years they'd been friends, Gonzo had never once said he was sorry for anything. He'd made up for it in other ways later, swept arguments under a rug, but never apologized. A knot of icy anger thawed a bit inside of Brett.

Liz broke the awkward moment that followed. "Maybe we do need to stop and see if we can help her."

"Well, all of us seem to want to stop, except Frannie," said Caroline.

"I don't want to stop," said Brett, heard only by Liz. She didn't relay this or speak to him, which made him feel even more trapped. Instead, she spoke to Frannie. "Why not?"

"Gone. Gone. Keep going," was all she said, sounding like she was talking in her sleep.

"I'm sorry, Frannie, but I think you're outvoted," said Caroline.

"Guess I am too," said Brett bitterly.

Liz turned toward the window and held him up to her lips and whispered, "I know, I know. Gonzo's just been so pissy, and we're all tired. If you have any other ideas, I'll tell the others."

"So, because Gonzo's pissy, you have to pretend I'm not here at all?"

She kissed his plastic face again, a strand of the doll's hair sticking to her lips for a moment as she pulled away. It was beyond bearing, being so close, being held, but being unable to move to return the kiss. Even if he could... well, he felt ridiculous.

"Let me go, Lizzie." he said.

"No, Brett, it's not safe!" her pleading whisper and sad eyes pulled at Brett's heart. Part of him wanted to make her happy and stay with her. But he couldn't keep it up. At least as a ghost, he had some control and at least he had his own form, insubstantial or not.

"You said you would if I asked. If you're so worried about acting against *his* will, won't you listen to me and let me take my own chances?"

The terror of being trapped rose within Brett as Liz didn't answer right away. *She has to think about it, even though she'd promised?*

"Or do you really want a Barbie doll for a boyfriend, forever? Keeping me trapped here might be safer, but it's not what I want, Lizzie."

She sighed and closed her eyes and hugged the doll to her for a long moment. Brett was entirely surrounded by Liz. It was warm and safe. It was a very pleasant prison, but he still needed out.

"Okay, Brett," she sighed, holding him up to whisper to him, eyes searching the smiling but expressionless face. "But you have to come back to me. You'll find a way to let me know you're here?"

"Of course. I'll be back, and I'll even submit to this form again to talk to you if I have to. But I need to be free. Maybe I can find something out from Terb. We haven't got any other way to find out, do we?"

She shook her head. "No, he's not telling, and we can't get into his head...." She bit her lip. "Sorry, I didn't mean--"

"It's okay, I know what you meant."

She stroked the doll's hair one more time, then repeated, "Come back to me, Brett." She untied the ring from the doll's arm and made some gestures over him. "You're free."

Brett felt his essence slide out of the doll shape. It felt so much better to be free! He looked down to see Liz still holding the doll to her as though he were still in it. It was sweet, and he longed to comfort her.

He leaned in and kissed her. His lips passed through hers. He thought about the pendulum experiment, how more feeling gave his actions more force. He closed his eyes and thought of kissing Liz, of making love with her, of how wonderful she felt. Of how much he'd like to kiss her right then.

He felt the lightest of warm touches, a tingle, on his lips, and he heard Liz draw in breath, holding a hand to her lips. She had felt it!

Brett felt a thrill at this success, the first bit of hope he'd felt since he'd given Terb control. He let go of his hold on Liz and the others and floated up and away, the small car leaving him behind. As he did this, the world faded and he was in the misty, featureless other world once more.

It was quiet there, and peaceful. His panic at being trapped faded. It was a lonely place, but his thoughts cleared there. He let his mind wander, trying not to actively think of anything, to see what came to him.

More dreamlike images floated by, just like they had when he'd pulled together after being struck by Terb's silver-clutching fist. He watched memories and faces, experienced feelings and places, like a jumbled up photo album.

When he was calm and centered, he thought of himself. He felt a little tug toward his physical self, but wasn't ready to go there just yet. He felt he needed to be better prepared. He thought about poor Frannie, her external spirit having been dispersed. Was she really gone, as her zombie-like physical body had said?

Could a simple paintball gun with silver-infused paint pellets really destroy a soul? His instinct told him it couldn't be that simple. But he'd *seen* the aura around Frannie fly apart when she'd been shot.

Maybe he should try to find her.

He thought about Frannie, pictured what she looked like, how she moved, what it was like to be around her. She was a friend, even if she could be irritating sometimes.

Brett felt himself being drawn back to the car, with the physical Frannie inside. That wasn't what he wanted. He changed his tactic. He thought of the times he'd seen her outside of herself. That time in Crown Hill, his first view of the other world, the luminous, sad Frannie standing over her mostly hollow physical self.

That image came to him strong enough that he felt himself drawn in another direction. Somehow, he felt he was moving further from the physical world, though he couldn't describe the direction. It was a little like slipping into a dream, he thought.

The faint outline of Crown Hill Cemetery appeared around him, as though sketched onto the mist with light pencil strokes. He was in the same spot he'd pictured, up on the high hill, at Riley's tomb. He saw that the sketchy trees moved in a wind he didn't feel.

He was alone, but he felt a pull, like the one he felt when someone called his name. Except he was already in place. Something was coming to him instead, he felt.

A sketchy outline of a short, round woman appeared, sitting on the steps of the tomb. Frannie's image rippled and disappeared, then snapped into more solid focus. Brett was reminded of a flaky digital satellite signal.

Frannie's signal was acquired, though she looked as flat as a TV image, her colors muted like Britney's had been. She looked unhappily at him. "Hello, Brett."

"Frannie! What happened to you?"

She shrugged. "Larry shot me."

"Well, yeah, I know that. Your body's as lifeless as it was when we had the ghoul syndrome. Gonzo's already making zombie jokes. Can't you return?"

Frannie's ghost shrugged again, flickering once. "I'm not really sure there's a point, Brett."

"What kind of way is that to talk? What about Jimbo, do you think he wants a nearly comatose girlfriend?"

She looked up at him. Her eyes were dark and troubled. "He might not want me either way," she said with a sigh.

"Yeah? Why not? Don't go all angsty on me, Fran. You know he's nuts for you. He stuck with you when you were possessed and even when you became a rotten meat-eating creature of the night. What could put him off of you after all that, honestly?"

She allowed herself a bitter little smile, lowering her eyes. "You'd be surprised."

"Look, whatever it is, I'm sure it'll be fine. I'm sorry, Frannie."

"For what?"

"Well, for you getting shot instead of me, for starters."

She blinked. "You think... Oh, Brett... I don't know how to say this, but Larry was after me."

Brett was confused. He shook his head at her. "No, there's no way he'd be after you, he hates me. He's been following us to wreck this webcast. You heard that faked EVP, he said my name."

She smiled again. "Always about you, is it? Well, there are things you don't know, Brett. I think you'd better figure them out before you go much further."

"Uh, why can't you just tell me and save me the trouble?"

She chuckled. "Well, that would be telling. And well..." she looked out over the cemetery, anywhere but at him. "Telling would be telling on me, and I can't face up to some things yet."

Fran's image became sketchier, transparent, and more distant.

"Wait! Don't go! You need to get back to yourself, Frannie. You can't just leave things like this."

"You like my life so much, Brett? Why don't you take it. Go ahead. Be me for a while. If my body needs a guardian spirit, you be it." She laughed. "That'd be funny to watch. Let me know if you do it."

Brett considered that for a moment and shook his head. "No, I want my own life back. Nothing against you, but I doubt Lizzie would be happy with me in your body, and Jimbo... well, he's not my type."

"Goodbye, Brett. I can't tell you more, but I'll give you a hint. If you can't trust yourself, who needs enemies? Hint. You do." Frannie wiggled her fingers in a little wave and faded from the scene.

The wind seemed to be picking up in the pencil-drawn cemetery; the trees were waving back and forth, seeming distressed and foreboding. The shadows seemed to be more solid than the tombstones and monuments that cast them. A black moon hovered in the colorless sky.

Brett felt the place suited his mood. Perhaps that was why ghost hunters went to cemeteries like this one. Maybe other melancholy spirits needed a place to brood. He started walking, following the outline of the road that wound up the hillside. It was surreal, but comforting. He felt more real there than in Liz's world.

The trees waved overhead and the solid-seeming shadows lengthened. They were inky shapes cast by stones like ice sculptures. He admired the brilliance of the crystalline angels that watched over the place. They looked at him with stern eyes, as though they didn't approve of him being here.

What did Frannie mean? Why did she have to be cryptic, was it some kind of unwritten rule among ghosts? He chuckled at the idea. He thought at least he was pretty straightforward, so maybe he wasn't in on the rules yet.

He sighed, feeling the angels' stare, feeling that it was time for him to move on. He wanted to confront Terb and try to get his life back, but Frannie's words made him hesitate. How else could he approach it? He needed to know where his body was headed so that he could tell his friends. He didn't much like the idea of watching Liz interact with Terb while he was a mere ghost, and he sure didn't want to do so while trapped in the doll again.

His enemies. Larry was with Terb. Maybe unconscious, but maybe that might make things easier in his spirit form. Hadn't he had contact with spirits in his own dreams before?

As much as he hated the idea, he thought of Larry. He saw the tall man looming in the woods, smirking and cocky. He saw him holding him at gunpoint. He thought of the bastard dating Liz while they'd been apart.

The cemetery faded, replaced by the forest where they'd found Britney. Larry sat at his campsite, roasting a couple of hot dogs over a dying fire. He wore that cowboy hat of his, and didn't seem to see Brett at first.

Brett stepped into the firelight. "Okay Larry, let's talk."

Chapter 20 - Boss of Me

Larry jerked his head up, startled by Brett's presence. He clambered to get up, fumbling in his long coat's pockets hastily.

"Hey, hey, calm down there. I'm here under a flag of truce," said Brett, holding his hands out to show he wasn't armed.

Larry's hand came out of his pocket with a gun. It looked like a real one this time, the big pistol Brett had seen on him before. Brett wondered why he never had a gun to use in his own bad dreams.

"Yeah, a truce, sure. Easy to say when you've got me knocked unconscious and taped up in my own truck, asswipe," Larry's gun barrel wobbled, but kept Brett covered. "This is my idea of a truce, you with your hands up, me blowing you away if you say anything I don't like."

"Look, Larry, you're dreaming, I doubt that'll do anything to me," said Brett, though he raised his hands just in case.

Larry nodded his head, pointing with his hat at Brett's hands. "Sure, of course this is a dream. And I reckon even if it doesn't kill you in real life, it'll sure feel good here."

Brett put his hands down slowly. "Maybe you think this is funny. Like how funny you looked when your paint gun didn't work on me and I messed up your face, huh?"

Larry's eyes narrowed, but he didn't lower the gun. "If you're really here, I'm guessing something bad's happened to you too." Larry glanced around the campsite, searching the darkness surrounding them, worry lines wrinkling his forehead. His eyes focused on Brett again. "Unless you're the pansy. You know, you talk tough, but I bet that's who you are. No way you'd have come after me like that. Had to be the other one."

Brett attempted a poker face. "I don't know what you're talking about. The demon's been gone since before you got hauled off by the cops."

Larry lowered the gun slightly and fired at the ground at Brett's feet. The report was louder than Brett thought it should be, and he couldn't help but jump back a step.

Larry laughed. "Not so tough now, huh? Yeah, you've gotta be the wuss. I know your secret. A little bird told me you're a two-for-one special. One of you has all the guts, the other might as well wear a dress. I figure I pissed off the nasty side of you. You wouldn't have the balls to fight me, not before, and not now."

"Easy to say from behind a gun, isn't it?"

"Nice, way to dodge the issue. Don't you wanna know who the little bird is?"

"Probably a bug somewhere, like the one you planted at the castle," said Brett, mind racing for other answers when Larry's smile told him this wasn't the right one.

"Guess again. And I didn't plant that."

"Bullshit," said Brett. "It was your voice on the recorder, idiot."

Larry let a slow grin cross his face. "Didn't say it wasn't. Just said I didn't plant it. I had help. Never set foot into the castle." He raised a hand and gave the two-fingered salute. "Scout's honor!"

If Larry was telling the truth, who else could have planted the device? The only person other than his friends in there was the caretaker Knight. "How much did you have to pay the guy?"

Larry pushed his hat back with his other hand and grinned. "You really don't have a clue, do you? Well, I guess two heads aren't better than one. Or is that the problem? Two's a crowd?"

"Larry, I didn't come here to play stupid guessing games. If you're going to tell me, just spit it out."

Larry raised the gun and aimed at Brett's face, sighting down the barrel with one eye. "Not sure I care why you're here, freak. You've got hell to pay when I wake up, maybe sooner, depending on where you're taking me. Or rather where your macho self is off to. And I've had *enough* of being harassed in my dreams lately." Larry raised the gun only slightly as he pulled the trigger.

Bang. Brett ducked, but knew that if he could hear the sound of the gun, it was too late. His head failed to explode, much to his relief. What *would* happen if Larry killed him, a ghost, here in a dream?

Larry laughed long and loud. "Oh man, you should have seen your face! Did you piss yourself there, wuss?"

"Give me the gun and let's see how brave you are being shot at. I'm still standing here, talking to you, aren't I?"

"That don't make you brave, that makes you stupid. Can't you take a hint? I've tried to be reasonable with you, but you crossed a line, Nelson."

"Yeah, like you crossed the Tennessee state line, hmm?"

The gun aimed at Brett's head again. "Yeah. Just like that. And that, my friend, is the only thing that kept me from fighting back effectively. Too much at risk. Once this job's done, I'm heading home. You're not worth it."

"Job? Who are you working for, Larry? I thought this was all you, out to get petty revenge."

Larry chuckled, but he shifted his stance, looking nervous. "Never you mind. Let's just say messing with you was a lot more pleasure than business up 'til tonight. Though things could still look up."

"Larry, I didn't have to come here to talk to you. Tell me about the job, who you're working for, and maybe we can both walk away from this fight and call it even."

Larry snorted. "Even? Sure, I inconvenienced you, you knocked me out and kidnapped me. Sounds even to me."

"You're forgetting Frannie. You really damaged her in your crazy paintball drive-by. She's back to being almost a vegetable because of that little stunt."

"Heh, yeah, I didn't really believe that'd work myself," said Larry, with a nervous laugh.

Brett smiled. "Sure, and while the police might not believe that silver dust in a paintball could do that to a person, they might believe that thinking she was shot might cause mental trauma. With four witnesses who could identify you, that'd be a really interesting case. You'd be a two-time offender, Larry, and this time, I doubt you'd be able to charm your way out of going to jail."

"Shut up! You wouldn't dare, you wuss."

"Believe what you want about what I'm capable of, Larry, but do you think Liz would back down from that fight? No, I think you'd better do some quick thinking and give us a damn good offer not to turn you in."

"Go to Hell," said Larry as he pulled the trigger.

Brett didn't even hear the bang this time. Everything went black. Instead of dispersing, he kept a painful awareness, like a whole body migraine. Pain made it impossible to think or concentrate. All he could do was pull inside himself and curl up into a ball.

He felt something try to uncurl him, using panicked force. He was aware of a reddish glow, and he realized it was light filtering through eyelids. He heard a car horn blare. He felt himself shaken from side to side with sickening swerves.

Eyelids, he thought. He tried to open his eyes.

The road rushed at him and a crazy angle, and at first he couldn't make sense of the lines on the road. There were street lights flashing by, the concrete highway quite well lit. It was still night.

His hands gripped the wheel. He realized he was driving Larry's truck. The truck seemed to be trying hard to cross several lanes of traffic, headed for the left retaining wall. It was a bridge or ramp of some sort.

He pulled on the wheel to the right, and the truck straightened out. He felt resistance from his own left hand. The truck banged into the left wall and scraped and sparked and screeched for a moment until he wrestled the wheel to point back into the far left lane.

He saw that the truck speed along at over ninety. He let up his tense right foot off the accelerator. The truck gradually slowed back down to a saner rate of speed.

He still had to wrestle with his other arm, which did not seem to be under his control. He looked around the cab. Larry was propped up in the passenger seat, belted in. Larry's hands were under a blanket, and his hat was pulled down over his eyes. Brett caught a glimpse of something shiny over the man's mouth. Duct tape, he supposed.

He had the road to himself. The dashboard clock said 3:17. The steering wheel had a Post-it note stuck to it. It said, "Richter 7am CS adm bldg."

Interstate signs loomed up ahead, and as they came into view, he recognized that he was in Indianapolis. Soon after, the skyline of the city appeared in the distance.

"Get out!" Brett felt his mouth move, making the growled warning. He decided to bite his own tongue. It hurt, he tasted blood. A yelp came from his throat at the pain, though it wasn't from him, since he'd expected it.

"No, I'm not going anywhere," said Brett. "You're the intruder, and you're fucking everything up. You're proving you can't be the one who runs my life, Terb."

"Terb? Who the fuck is Terb?"

"That's what Lizzie calls you. It's Brett backwards. Shows you're not really Brett, you're something else that doesn't belong in here."

"She called me 'Brett' over the phone. She recognizes my right to be here. You're weak and limp, she misses my passion."

"But you're a maniac, Terb. You have no self-control. You're Mister Furious, all full of rage. If it was just you in charge, you'd get arrested or committed real soon. Not to mention pissing off all my friends and ending up alone. Gonzo's furious about *Soccer Mom*."

There was a pause, then a low growl. "Fuck Gonzo. Who needs that guy, if his old shitbox van means more than me. Or Frannie."

"Yeah, this is all about poor Frannie. Did you really care about her, or did you just use her to get me to let you take over?"

"Doesn't fucking matter. I got in control, and I kept you out for hours. Not sure how you got back in, but I'll throw you out again yet. Emotion is power, I'm sure you've noticed. But by pushing out all your emotions, you made me stronger and stronger and yourself weaker and weaker."

Brett realized Terb had a point. It'd taken a lot to get much of a reaction out of him, and he'd only kicked Terb out through short outbursts of feeling, and through surprise.

He was as surprised as his alter ego to be back in his body, but he guessed it was the shock, terror and pain of being shot in Larry's dream that had sent him fleeing into himself, and he'd caught Terb off-guard.

"So maybe you're right," said Brett. "Suppose you can evict me and go on with your rampage with your buddy Larry here. Where are you going, and what do you hope to prove? We're just going to keep knocking each other out, back and forth, the rest of our lives? Can you avoid Lizzie forever? I know you're running from her because you know she can work a spell to put me back in the driver's seat." Just for emphasis, he revved the gas pedal.

"What options are there?" asked Terb, avoiding the subject of Liz. "Wanna live like this, like a split-brain freak, walking around like a three-legged race? Or maybe we'd take turns like joint custody? I know who Lizzie will like better in the sack at least."

"Shut up," snapped Brett. "I don't like it any better than you. It's clear we need each other and we've got to work something out. Turn around and I'll tell you where Liz and the others are staying. She'll know what to do."

"Sure, leave it up to Lizzie to solve your problems again. Or maybe you'll just figure a way to banish me entirely? No, I'll take my chances and stay in control."

Brett's left foot stomped on the brake and threw him forward, banging his head on the steering wheel. Before Brett could protest, his left hand stopped pulling against his right, his left foot stepped on the gas pedal, and the truck swerved hard toward the wall.

Brett panicked, and in that instant, he heard laughter in his head and he found himself ejected again, watching Larry's crumpled pickup truck fishtail to avoid the wall and speed on into the night away from him.

Chapter 21 - Birdhouse in Your Soul

As the gray mist closed around Brett, he shrieked out his frustration in a long wail. He just didn't know what to do. Terb really was stronger in many ways. And if Brett tried to directly take over, he could be effortlessly blocked by silver, if Terb was ready for him.

So, what now? He knew some things he didn't know before from his conversations with Larry and Terb. Things that his friends would need to know if he wanted help from them.

He concentrated on Liz. *Oh Lizzie, I need you.* The pull was weak, like pulling on cobwebs. He thought of Lizzie taking care of him after Cheryl died. He thought of her finding him after his overdose, saving his life. Lizzie, who sliced a shadow demon with her katana, dressed in black pajamas. Lizzie who fought for his life many times. Lizzie who believed in him.

As the pull became stronger, Brett had a cold realization that he did need her, she'd always rescued him. That's why she'd wanted to keep him "safe" in the doll body. She could protect him that way.

He loved her for it, but he didn't like how that made him feel about himself. Couldn't he fight his own battles? Couldn't she depend on him the same way he'd depended on her?

A hotel room came into vague focus. It was dark, the only illumination coming from the digital alarm clock, and a stripe of moonlight that fell across the beds from a parting in the window curtains. Gonzo slept on the floor, cocooned in a puffy sleeping bag. He shook the room with his inhuman snoring. Frannie lay flat on her back on one bed, her eyes open, blank and staring at the ceiling. Liz and Caroline faced away from one another, sleeping on the other bed. Caroline had a pillow and an arm over one side of her head.

Brett moved very close to Liz. The moonlight fell across her face. She looked beautiful and otherworldly, peaceful and happy in sleep. She clutched the Barbie doll to her chest. His ring lay on the pillow next to her, back on the cord she wore around her neck.

He floated closer still, adoring his love, and aching for her touch, fear of losing her one way or another welling up inside him. He thought of kissing her again, wanting nothing else so much as to feel her lips on his right now. He felt the tingle and warm feather touch of her kiss. He felt drawn into the kiss, almost as though she could breathe him in as she slept.

Even as he ached for Liz, he began to feel her surround him, intertwine with him. It felt like it had when she held him in the doll in her hand, as though she reached out in her sleep to pull him in.

The room began to recede and fade. Liz's face loomed large, oh so large, beyond edges of his vision. She was a planet and he was her moon, locked in her orbit, always facing her. She was a lush, green, living world. A world-being, a Goddess. He felt his orbit spiral closer and closer, and he feared he'd crash and destroy that beauty in the impact.

But he wasn't a moon anymore. He flew through Liz's atmosphere, gentle clouds of thought, howling winds of emotion whipped past him. He felt the rain of her tears, the buffeting winds of her laughter, the lightning strikes of her anger.

Now he descended further, slower, into a deep rainforest. The tangled deck of jungle trees parted before him as he came down into a swampy area, felt the warm damp water soak him up to the waist as he landed with barely a ripple.

Brett wasn't sure what was happening. He called out, "Lizzie? Hello? Where am I?"

"Found someone, you have, hee hee hee!" came the squeaky voice. A short, green figure in tattered robes sat on the shore, toying with a gnarled stick. It was Yoda. No, he could recognize Liz's face in between those pointed ears.

Brett waded onto shore, and he saw he was now dressed in an orange flight suit. He looked back, half expecting to see a sinking spaceship or the periscope of a sunken robot. He saw only scummy water, vines and flapping creatures.

"Okay, so this is what you dream of? You're Yoda and I'm Luke?"

Lizzie-Yoda giggled. "Like you not this place? My home it is!"

Brett put his hands on his hips and looked down at his diminutive girlfriend. "Well, I would have hoped for Leia or Amidala after kissing you like that."

"Hmm, a point you have," she said, and grew rapidly to her normal height, looking very much like herself, except in white Princess Leia robes, her black hair rolled into earmuffs on either side of her head.

Brett found himself wearing a white shirt, black trousers and vest, a blaster at his side. "Ah, okay, so we're not related. This is a good sign. I wouldn't want to have to settle for sisterly love from you, dear."

Liz put her arms on his shoulders and clasped her hands behind his head, pulling him in for a much more solid kiss. His heart raced, his body responding to her enthusiasm and hunger.

Just as he was losing himself in her a second time, she pushed him gently to arm's length. "Does that feel like a sisterly kiss, hmm?" She winked at him and her eyes traveled downward. "I'm guessing not!"

Brett grinned. "Glad you can see me as the scoundrel in your life, despite--"

She put a finger to his lips to stop him, "Shush. It's not a choice between you, Brett. He's you. You were just split. Remember that, okay, *Chico*?"

Brett shook his head. "We *were* one, now we are two. Now it's either a competition or I have to share you, and I hate it, Lizzie."

She broke her embrace with him and walked a few squishy paces to lean on a tree, facing him. "It's going to be a problem only as long as you look at it that way, Brett. Do I love you? Yes, as much as ever. Do I love 'Terb'? Yes, he's a part of you. Yes, I missed that part of you, even the bad stuff. I love you without him, but I'll admit, I had been hoping you'd regrow that side of you before I knew that part was still in existence."

Brett felt stupid for being jealous of his other half, but he was. Something occurred to him. "Lizzie, I'm not passionless. Look at me tearing myself up with jealousy and anger.... If all of that went to Terb, why am I feeling this way?"

She smiled and shrugged. "Maybe you did grow some of that back. Or maybe being around him has intermixed you. You *have* been more emotional since he's returned, and well, he's starting to act slightly more rational, isn't he?"

Brett hadn't thought of that. "But that just means we're becoming individuals, either way. Either growing into two separate, whole souls or needing each other less and less."

Liz shook her head. "No, Brett. You're still always going to be halves of a whole, no matter how good you each get at coping with the loss."

"So far, we've just bumped each other out, there's nothing holding us together. I don't know *how* and he's not exactly Mr. Cooperative."

She beckoned to him. He slogged toward her. She took his hand in hers and looked in his eyes. "We'll make it work somehow, *Chico*. I'm willing to stick with you no matter what. Just trust me and give me the same, okay?"

He swallowed and wet his lips and nodded once. "I'll try, Lizzie."

"There is no 'try,'" she said in Yoda-voice, a playful smile lighting her face.

He kissed her again, and it was more sweet than hungry this time.

"But that's not why you're here, is it?" she giggled. "Unless you're planning on trying to take up residence with the other voices in my pretty little head?"

He smiled and shook his head. "No, I've come to tell you something before I go back to fight with Terb again. I know where he's headed."

Liz tilted her head to one side, waiting.

"Larry was heading to Indianapolis, to Central State, to meet up with Richter at seven in the morning at the admin building," he said.

"What? How would they know that's where our next webcast was?"

"That's a good question. I talked to Larry too, though he wasn't thrilled to see me. He was hinting that he's got an accomplice and a way to spy on us. He knew about me being split too. Said a little bird told him."

"Well, that's creepy.... I wonder what he thinks it gains him to arrive so early? It didn't do him a lot of good at the other two locations," said Liz, who was fluffing her hair danishes as she stared off into space, thinking.

Brett shrugged. "Probably wants to make sure *we* don't have anything set up ahead of time. Richter will do anything to keep from losing that prize money. And his livelihood as a professional skeptic."

"Yeah, like hiring Larry, maybe?"

Brett nodded. "Sure looks like it. Get Larry to do his dirty work. If Larry gets caught, no one looks further, because he's got reason to hate me."

"Except he's got too much to risk. I can't see Larry doing any of this with a good chance of ending up in the slammer. He's been quiet for months, why blow it now?"

"Yeah, it doesn't add up. Also, what was with his drive-by? That was the riskiest thing he's done. It was a desperate move. He even told me he didn't think the silver paint gun would really work. It didn't work on Terb, so I guess if he'd hit me in the first place, nothing much would have happened. I wish he had, then Frannie wouldn't be all Night of the Living Dead right now."

Liz let out a gusty sad sigh. "Oh Brett, I don't know what to do about her. I tried doing a short calling spell to pull her spirit back, but there was no answer. Could she really be gone like she says?"

Brett shook his head slowly. "No, she's out there. I spoke with her, actually."

Liz looked up at him, startled. "You did? Oh *Chico*, that's great news! What's going on with her?"

Brett shrugged. "She was really pretty cryptic, kept saying she couldn't go back and face us, like she thought she'd done something unforgivable. Other than being glued to her phone every waking moment, I can't think of anything she's done that's even been annoying this trip, much less something that bad."

"Maybe she sees some bigger picture thing on the other side that we're not seeing," said Liz. She stood up away from the tree and took a step to him, curling an arm around his waist. She continued, "Some action of hers that led to... well, I can't think of what she'd be ashamed of."

An idea came to Brett. "Lizzie. I don't mean to make an accusation, but do you suppose *Frannie* is the mole? All that time she spent on the phone or texting... what if it wasn't Jimbo she was talking to?"

Liz shook her head, dislodging one soft black spiral of hair. "No, there's no way Frannie would willingly spy for Larry, or Richter for that matter. She's flaky sometimes, but she's a good friend."

Brett nodded. "No, not willingly," he agreed. "But it makes sense... she could have been the one who planted the EVP faking device, and she's one of a very few who knew about my 'condition.' I only told you, Gonzo, Caroline and Frannie that Central State was our next destination."

Liz bit her lip and lowered her eyes. "I don't want to think that about a friend. We'll let her tell her side of things when she comes back to herself."

Liz felt very warm and soft as she hugged him. Conflicting feelings warred within him. On one hand, he wanted Liz. He wanted also to prove that he could be passionate without Terb. On the other hand, he felt time slipping away from them.

He lifted her chin and began a soft, warm kiss with her. She responded with eagerness as she nibbled on his lip and held on. She met his eyes and made a growling noise.

He murmured around the kiss, "Sweetie, you need to wake up and come to Indy. But you feel so good...."

The swamp faded and they were in the hotel room, alone. She pulled him to her bed without breaking the kiss, hands clasped at the nape of his neck again. "Know what'll help me wake up, love?" She giggled.

He had a pretty good idea.

She let him part the gauzy white dress as she pulled his shirt and vest off him. They kissed and fondled each other, and as she began to breathe harder, the rest of their clothing was gone.

Brett knew he was in her dream, but everything about her felt very real. The urgency with which they wanted each other became more and more feverish, and they joined, moving together like they inhabited a single body together.

In a distracted moment, Brett realized they did, in fact.

The climax, when it came for them both, tore at the reality they shared and Brett found himself in the real hotel room, others still as they were. Liz sat up in bed and gasped, a hand flew to cover her mouth. She glanced over at Caroline's still sleeping form and relaxed.

She looked upward and said to the air, "I love you, Brett. Now go find yourself."

He caressed her face, and then did as she asked.

Chapter 22 - Basket Case

Brett sped through the mists once more. He smiled, feeling confident and more in control. He pictured his body. His. He couldn't let Terb win, something had to give.

And Brett held onto the certainty it wouldn't be he who gave. After all, Terb was a creature of rage and temper, how hard would it be to manipulate him? As sketchy outlines of buildings and power lines began to resolve and fly past him, he felt unstoppable.

The world gained structure and solidity. It was very dark, the only light coming from distant houses. He was floating over a grassy area with old brick and stone buildings, their windows boarded or broken.

He found himself. Terb stalked around the grounds of Central State, breathing hard. There was a look of determination on his face that puzzled Brett. What could he be up to? He'd clearly bested Larry. Brett had no way of telling time, but the seven o'clock meeting between Larry and Richter must still be a ways off.

Brett tried the direct approach. He focused his desire to be in his own body and threw all his mental weight at Terb.

Brett slammed into a solid wall, inches from his body.

Terb stopped in his tracks and turned to grin at him. He held up his left hand and peeled his fingers open one by one to reveal Ralph's silver dollar coin. "Doesn't work like that, not while I'm focused on keeping you out."

Brett glared at his alter ego. "You can't keep me out forever. You have to sleep sometime."

Terb nodded. "Yeah, I know. We've been through this. I can keep throwing you out and blocking you as long as I need to."

"And I can keep haunting you, wearing you down," replied Brett.

Terb sighed. "So, are they on their way?"

Brett was surprised. "What?"

"Well, no one knows you better than me, so I figure when I threw you out, you zipped back to Lizzie to tell her where I was. I figure they aren't likely to get here by seven, though."

"What's going on at seven?"

Terb smiled. "Dunno, but I know Richter thinks Larry will be there. It'll be me instead, and I'm going to give him something to think about."

"So, where's Larry? If you left him duct taped up in the truck, the police will happen upon him soon enough."

Terb barked a short laugh. "Ha. You really don't give me much credit, do you? You know those pits with grates on them they have here?"

Brett did, of course, since they shared memories. "Yeah, so the inmates could get some fresh air, they had these underground pit areas with metal grating. The guards could bring the more unruly patients outside and put them down there, they could see the sky and sun a while, and the guards wouldn't have to keep constant watch on them."

Terb nodded. "Seemed like a perfect place to stow a loonie like Larry."

Brett said, "Sure, for now. But what about--"

Terb interrupted him. "Anyway, I've got some things to do, so why don't you go scamper off and do ghostly things somewhere else."

Brett shook his head. "Not a chance. If you're not letting me in, I'm haunting you until you do, or until you fall asleep."

"Suit yourself," said Terb as he stalked off toward a large building that Brett recognized as the abandoned asylum's administration building. Brett followed along, watching for Richter or other signs of life.

He watched as Terb found the main door secured with heavy chains. Terb started pacing the perimeter, trying various side doors. After some searching, he found a broken window nailed shut with plywood. It was loose, and came off with only a few minutes' struggle. There was a crash as the plywood fell to the ground, but Terb seemed unconcerned. They were alone out there.

Terb swept broken glass off the windowsill with his sleeve and felt around for a good place to grab. He hoisted himself up and into the building. Brett floated along in his wake.

Terb looked around the dark room. It turned out to be a room full of battered old metal filing cabinets. There were stacks of papers on the floor here and there, and some of the drawers were open.

Terb crept toward the single door in the room. He reached to turn the knob.

"Yeeearrrgh!" Brett screamed, inches from Terb's ear.

Terb cried out and whirled, and barely missed Brett with his silver-clutching fist. "You fucker! Don't do that!"

Brett hovered out of reach. "If I'm going to be made to be a ghost, I'm going to play the part. I'll help out if we can be partners."

Terb glared at him and took another swipe with his coin hand. Brett was ready and dodged out of reach in another direction.

"What have you got to lose?" asked Brett, appealing to Terb's ego. "You kicked me out before, after all."

Terb stared at him a long while. Then he slid his hand into his pocket, coming back out with it open and empty. "Fine. But I'm in charge, and when Richter gets here, you're out, okay?"

Brett wasn't too sure about the terms, but he nodded anyway. It was a start.

Terb reached the hand out and Brett took it and was pulled in. It felt amazing to be back to himself. He wiggled the fingers of his right hand and stretched the arm out.

Terb started to walk toward the door, but since Brett was still reveling in being corporeal once more, they fell to the floor.

"Goddamnit, this isn't gonna work!" said Terb, pushing up to a crouch. Brett cooperated as they stood up.

"Sorry, it's going to take some coordination," said Brett.

Terb grumbled. "Door's easier right-handed."

Brett reached out and turned the knob and pulled the door inward. Then, they lurched out into the hallway.

"This is stupid," complained Terb.

"It'll be okay, I promise." Brett sounded more confident than he felt at that moment. Terb had a point, it was creepy to feel his left side moving on its own, and having to match movements. It was still such a thrill to feel his heart beat and to draw breath into his lungs. Even if the air was stale and smelled of mildew.

There was still electricity there, evidenced by the dim light cast by exit signs at either end of the hallway. Doors lined the hall, many left standing open.

Brett kept catching movement in the edge of his vision, but when he'd turn to look, much to Terb's annoyance, there was nothing to be seen. Terb did admit he'd seen something here and there, but replied, "That's why you were coming here, dummy, it's *haunted*."

"So what are we here for?" asked Brett after they'd poked through a few offices, storage rooms, and a bathroom that looked and smelled like it was now home to a family of raccoons.

"Eh, I'm just looking around, killing time, looking for anything that might be useful."

Other than old records, they didn't find much of use, so they settled down in a massive wooden office chair, which they rolled out into the main hallway, waiting for signs of Richter.

Just as they started to doze off, there came a rattling of the chains on the other side of the door. Terb urged Brett to stand with him, and they started to lurch off toward the office with the open window.

The chain slid loose and the double doors opened wide. In the doorway stood Ellis "Righteous" Richter. Moonlight gleamed on his teeth and shone on his balding head as he spied Brett.

"Hmm, not who I expected, but this saves some time." The hawk-nosed man strode into the building as though he owned it.

Brett and Terb froze, holding the large rolling chair between them and Richter. "Hey there, double-R, it's amazing the people you run into out here in the asylum." Brett realized with a shock that he couldn't tell whether Terb or he had formed those words. *Maybe we can make this work after all?*

"Hmm, yes, quite true. Given your recent antics on your little web program, I'd say it's a fitting place to meet you."

Brett used his internal monologue to warn Terb, "Be careful, he hasn't hung onto his prize money by being a fool."

Terb ignored him and said aloud, "That's a funny thing, isn't it? Never know what's going to happen in this field. Paranormal stuff, it surprises you. Like your challenge. Why would you challenge me when you know I'm the real thing, Richter?"

Richter waved a hand, entering the room, circling around Brett. 'Camera tricks, histrionics, fabricated evidence and lies, all of it. Very entertaining, to be sure, but shame on you for playing on gullible people out there, tsk tsk."

Brett and Terb turned to keep facing Richter. They could see his face more clearly up close, and his eyes narrowed as he got closer to them. Brett thought it strange that the man wore a gray suit and tie in a place like this. Stranger still, a pendant hung around his neck, the cord so long that it reached the bottom of his tie. The pendant had a face of a bear on it. The bear's eyes gleamed yellow.

Strangest of all, an inky black aura surrounded Richter's head like a wreath.

Brett spoke up at the same time as Terb, and stumbled over his words. Terb let him speak. "Richter, if you thought that, why would you come here personally? My web show isn't popular enough yet that a cameo will gain you much publicity. You know I've got something. You knew about the little ghoul. I'm betting its escape at the convention in March was at least partly your doing. You're not just in the debunking business, you're also trying to actively suppress it."

Richter didn't even smile. "You think that, do you? I thank you for the compliment.... How Machiavellian and terrifying I must seem to you. How threatening to your operation as well. This is a make-or-break show for you, isn't it? If you can somehow produce evidence of the so-called paranormal, with me in attendance, that'd be a major coup, wouldn't it? But if you fail, you lose face and credibility, like all the other charlatans and hucksters I've exposed over the years. This isn't an urgent matter for me. It's *fun*, don't you see?"

Terb took over their side of the conversation again. "Sure, loads of fun for everyone, while you hire someone you've humiliated before to hound a new threat to your prize. Where do you suppose Larry Fisher is, anyway? It'd be such a shame if something happened and you got connected to him. It'd look really bad for you and your spotless reputation, wouldn't it, asshole?"

Richter's eyes hardened and he straightened and held up his hands. "There's no reason for that kind of language. We are just businessmen, aren't we?"

Brett's thoughts mingled with Terb's rage, and they pressed the point with one voice. "You sit on your high horse, the King of

Smugness, going on TV talking crap about every fringe thing that comes along. Yeah, sure, lots of the paranormal community are delusional weirdos who 'want to believe,' and yeah, a lot of them lack critical thinking skills. But not too many I've met are total frauds. Larry's one of those, he's a jerk who just wants to make a buck off of rubes. But notice though, he came running to get your prize when he had something tangible to show you... a living corpse... and you made it disappear. How are you any less of a fraud for making money off of people who want to feel superior and join in your smugness?"

"Mr. Nelson," said Richter, putting his hands on his hips, "I regret to inform you that it's very early on Friday morning, not Sunday. I didn't come here to listen to a sermon. I came here to do business. Now, would you take a lesser sum, perhaps $10,000, to just go away? Drop out of this business. I don't ask that you denounce what you've said and done so far, but give up broadcasting. That includes Internet postings. What do you say?"

Brett surprised himself, and he could tell Terb felt it too, as he shouted at Richter. "Fuck you! I don't even *care* about the prize, or your money. I'm not selling out. I'm bringing you down my own way, you crook."

Richter chuckled. "Well, that was the easy way." In a louder voice, he called out, "Gentlemen, it's time for the hard way."

Brett heard heavy footsteps in the doorway behind him. Two big men in dark clothing and ski masks blocked the dim light of the false dawn, filling the doorway. They had short clubs, and they advanced on him without a word.

Brett tried to run, but Terb tried to run in the other direction, so they fell on the floor. Brett heard Richter laughing. Hard blows began to fall on Brett's shoulders and back. He looked up to see Richter, whose aura stretched further out from him. One of the men gave Brett's head a solid whack.

Brett collapsed and saw stars, his vision narrowing to a tunnel. As he faded, Brett saw a ghostly image of Richter. Indistinct figures hovered around him. He thought he saw a nurse in an old-fashioned, white dress uniform looking sadly down at Brett from behind Richter. Then the world faded to gray and he slept.

Chapter 23 – If I Had Possession over Judgment Day

Brett sat at the bar in the County Cork Pub. A waitress in a short, black dress slid a beer up to him. He smiled, but when he looked up, she had no face.

He pushed away from the bar with such force that his barstool toppled and he landed in a heap on the barroom floor.

Familiar nasty laughter and a slow clap serenaded him as he scrabbled to his feet.

His twin sat on a barstool next to him.

"Terb?"

"I hate that name, you know."

"Lizzie made it up for you," said Brett, standing his stool back in place. He sat down, facing the other version of himself.

Terb shrugged and took a sip of his beer. Brett saw that it was a black stout with a white cap. *Guinness, if I know me.*

Brett raised his own golden beer, in a toast to his rival. "Cheers."

Terb snorted, but clinked his glass against Brett's. Both drank deep, watching each other. Brett's beer tasted like Harp.

"So why are we here?" asked Brett.

"Good question. Guess we're knocked out again. Seems to happen a lot."

Brett nodded. "We can't go on like this, Terb."

Terb glared at Brett. "I can keep it up as long as you can. Longer."

"You need me. You're too reckless without me to curb your impulses. All rage, no finesse."

"And without me, you're a passionless wimp."

"If you 'win,' you'll end up in jail or worse, you'll hurt someone."

"And if I lose, what's life worth living for if you can't do it with feeling?"

They stared at each other and drank in silence a long while.

Brett took another long drink of his beer and studied Terb a moment. "Look, this is nice and all, sitting down to talk over beer at the pub, but in reality there's just one body to go back to, and it's unconscious on the floor at Central State, exacting revenge on Richter by drooling on his shoes if we're very lucky."

"Guess who'd be the better choice to take over to beat the snot out of that guy?

"And his goons too?"

"I could take them."

"No. You couldn't. You didn't."

"I had you tripping me up, zigging when I wanted to zag. You're worse than dead weight, Wimpy McWimperson."

Brett put his mug down and stood up and held up his fists. "You want to have it out? Let's have it out, tough guy."

Terb drank down the rest of his Guinness and stood, knocking down his barstool and the one next to it. His hands curled into white-knuckled fists. His eyes narrowed. "Yeah, let's."

Though they had to be the same size, Brett had a feeling as though Terb loomed over him.

Use your head. He can't be stronger, we are the same. We are one. Brett held up his hands before him and took a step backward.

Terb advanced, a grin creeping across his face.

Step, one, two, three, *now!* Brett grabbed up his wooden barstool and smashed the legs into Terb's shoulder.

It bounced off.

Terb laughed. "You forget, wimpy boy, it's all about emotion here in dreamland. You gotta *want* it. You have to *feel* it. And I'm all that bad stuff you pushed down and out, all those unpresentable feelings, like anger and jealousy. You've got nothing, you're all talk."

Terb slapped Brett's face hard enough to make him see double.

His head rang with pain and flashes of light. He glanced around him for more weapons. "May-- maybe back when we split, that was true. But I'm more than that. I grew back some of what I lost. And so have you! You're more rational now than you were even a couple of days ago, aren't you?"

"Yeah. Which means, I don't need you, doesn't it?" Terb kicked Brett in the shin then knocked him to the floor with a punch to the stomach.

Brett wasn't sure how he could have the wind knocked out of him when he had no body, but he gasped like a fish in a net there on the floor. *What would Terb do?* He grabbed at his double's legs and bit into a shin as hard as he could. The image of biting through his own silver cord, back when he'd separated from Terb came to mind. The memory of that terrible pain helped fuel his attack, and he heard Terb howl in pain, and blows rained down on Brett's back

Brett got his feet under him, angled a shoulder into Terb's knees and shoved. Unbalanced, Terb fell over his shoulder and hit the floor with a crack.

Brett stood over his double's body and let out a whoop of victory. "Who doesn't need who now? I got you, jerkface."

Terb remained motionless on the floor.

Brett leaned down and shook Terb, but the only reaction was his head flopping to one side, at an angle that worried Brett. *Could he really be dead?*

"Terb. Hey Terb! Get up!" Brett kneeled next to the prone body on the floor and shook with both hands.

Iron bands snapped into place around Brett's throat as Terb lunged to choke him. Brett pulled at Terb's arms, tugging and scratching, but his windpipe closed, and the room dimmed and filled with static. Brett's vision narrowed, only showing him red-faced Terb, teeth bared in a feral snarl.

What happens if I pass out when I'm already unconscious? Brett kicked at Terb, but couldn't connect with a solid blow.

Even as he faded, a new thought came to Brett. *Let go.* It was what the little ghoul had told him, it was what led to this split, and it was the only option he had left. He willed his body to become limp, he stopped resisting. Terb was him, and he was Terb. There was no way to win except not to play at all, as the old movie said. *Oh God, please don't let my last thought be about Wargames....*

He closed his eyes and waited for the end, whatever it might be. Terb's grip loosened. No, not quite that. For a strange moment, he was both the strangler and the strangled, attacker and defender, looking up at himself, and looking down.

Die!

No, I want to live.

You can't stop me!

No, but you can't kill me. I am you.

Don't you understand? I have to win!

You will. And so will I.

We can't both win!

Yes, we can, and we'll be stronger than before we were when we split.

But--

Join me, Terb. We'll be Brett together again.

Brett couldn't explain what happened, he had no idea what an observer in the room might have seen. But he had the sudden image of two bubbles colliding, spinning around each other, watching and waiting to see which of the two popped first. Except only the part between the bubbles popped, and they merged into a single, bigger bubble.

And though they had fallen down together, Brett and Terb stood up as one.

Brett let out a primal scream and felt whole for the first time in a year or more. Every thought, every motion had a tiny echo of lag. Decision and action. Emotion and reason.

No more arguing, let's go.

Brett's anger rose in him. Anger felt *good*, and it felt better to be able to control it, channel it into action. He strode toward the door of the pub, back toward the waking world and his body. And Liz.

Chapter 24 - Me and the Devil Blues

Brett's world was dark, cold, and full of pain. The shuffling sound of boots crunching on gritty concrete came from near his head. The sound was the only way he could tell his head was still attached to his body. *Maybe being corporeal isn't all it was cracked up to be.* He opened his eyes, afraid of what he might see.

It was worse than he thought.

"Haw. So you're alive. At least that's one thing they can't pin on me," said Larry. The tall man leaned against the far wall of the underground enclosure, his hat pulled down low enough to shadow his eyes. Gray light filtered in from above.

Brett groaned. He tried to sit up, but was punished by dizziness and dazzling detonations of pain from all over his body. He settled for trying to inspect the lump he knew would be on the side of his head, raising a hand to probe the knot with the lightest of touches. His hair was wet and sticky in that area. The bump felt hot to the touch. It throbbed at even the light exploration, so he pulled his hand back, resolving not to do that again soon.

"Yep, Richter's boys sure did a number on you. I wonder if he'd have done the same to me if I'd made it to that meeting," said Larry. His tone turned sarcastic. "Lucky I've got you to keep me safe, eh Brett?"

Brett trembled with the chill that had soaked in while he'd been laying there on the concrete, for who knew how long. He wondered what had happened to Terb. He called out inside his head, and got only a surly, incoherent response. Brett seemed to have full control of his body for now, other than the painful repercussions of the beating he'd endured.

"Ungh," said Brett, trying to speak, his mouth too dry and pasty to manage anything.

Larry approached him, and from his vantage on the floor, Brett could see the pointy cowboy boots his rival wore. He braced himself for another beating, since he knew Larry was the kind of guy who always found a way to get revenge. What could be easier than for Larry to kick Brett when he was down?

To his surprise, Larry crouched down, pulling a metal flask out of his jacket pocket. "Here, have some, you'll need your strength," said Larry, unscrewing the top and holding it to Brett's mouth.

Brett's mouth filled with sweet, burning liquid fire. He took a couple of swallows and held up a weak hand to tell Larry to stop. He got a bit more before Larry took the flask away. Brett swirled the liquor around his mouth to clear it out a bit and swallowed.

A warm feeling spread throughout his body, and gradually, the aches and pains receded a bit as well. It took him a while, but he managed to sit up. The room swam around in his vision for a minute. Then he said, "Thanks, Larry. What's your angle?"

Larry held out his hands, palms up. "Just tryin' to help, is all."

Brett went to shake his head, but thought better of it. "Yeah, well, if you say so, Larry. Last time we talked, you weren't so friendly. Maybe you're a different kind of guy when you have a gun."

Larry snorted. "Yeah, if you'd left me that or my cell phone, we could be outta here by now."

Brett felt around in his pockets, but found only his small LED flashlight. Even Ralph's silver coin was gone. Larry shook his head. "Already checked. Richter's not an idiot."

"So what do we do now," asked Brett.

Larry shrugged. "I'd hoped you'd have an idea. Maybe you can pull your ghost trick and fetch us help?"

Brett was reluctant to leave his body now that he'd returned, but he closed his eyes and concentrated. Nothing happened. He thought of Lizzie. He felt strong, full of powerful emotions, his love fueling his desire to go to his girlfriend. Perhaps Terb was assisting?

He felt hot lines coiling around his arms, around his ankles and around his neck. It felt like they cut into him like searing razor wire. He had to stop, so horrible was the sensation.

He pulled up the sleeve of his jacket to look at his forearm. A silver spiral traced around his forearm, going around twice and ending in a thin, drawn-on bracelet ringing his wrist. His other arm matched, as did each ankle. He'd been dyed with silver ink while he was unconscious!

"Shit!" said Brett.

"I take it that wasn't there before?" asked Larry. "Doesn't seem to be your style, really."

Brett felt trapped now, and he had a sinking feeling they were going to be trapped there for a while. "Can I have some more of that bourbon?"

"Just a sip," said Larry, offering the flask again.

Brett took another swallow and handed it back. He sighed and pulled himself to his feet. His head throbbed and a dozen bruises shrieked complaints. The world wobbled a bit as he stood, and he had to steady himself on the rusty iron ladder on the wall.

"I've seen this pattern before," said Brett, once he'd gotten his balance. "It's some kind of spirit binding, part of a ritual usually done on corpses. To keep the ghosts of troublesome people from escaping to bother the living. Looks like I can't get out to go get help. I'm stuck."

Larry glanced up the ladder at the edge where the grate was bolted shut. "Well, shit, what good are you, then? I'd say we could start screaming for help, but you may understand my reluctance to be seen here by the police."

So, that's why Larry's being so civil. He's still afraid of the consequences of breaking his parole. Brett shrugged, then winced. "Larry, I'm not dying down here to keep you from going to jail."

"Yeah, but you let out a peep, and I'm gonna whup you upside your head, right on that bump, and you'll be back out. So, think again, how do we get out of here?"

Brett felt cold anger freeze his insides. He thought it might be a mute contribution from Terb. "Okay, any idea what time it is?"

Larry shrugged. "You were gone a couple of hours after dumping me here. Then Richter and his goons showed up and tossed you in with me, saying he had business to attend to. Maybe an hour after that, he came back and threw this in, said you'd know what it meant when you woke up. Maybe an hour or so ago."

Larry pulled a Barbie doll from his jacket pocket and tossed it to Brett. The same doll from Caroline's car that he'd been bound to earlier. The one Lizzie had slept with just hours ago.

Brett felt a chill shudder through him. "Did... did Richter say anything else?"

Larry nodded. "Yeah. He said you wouldn't see your three friends again until you agreed to the terms he'd discussed with you. Oh yeah, and he fired me. I shoulda known it wouldn't be worth it, but he didn't leave me much choice."

"Huh? What do you mean?"

"You think I'd stick my neck out this far just to be paid to screw with you? Naw, Richter helped me with my legal fees. That's how I got off in March. He threatened to bring forward new evidence or disrupt my parole in some other way if I didn't help him. I figured I didn't have a choice. He blackmailed me into it." Larry looked away as he said, "Not to mention the nightmares."

"Nightmares?" said Brett, thinking of the snake-leviathan attack. He thought about the thing he's seen in the schoolhouse that had *eaten* a ghost whole.

"Don't want to talk about it, but yeah, he's got somethin' that lets him into people's heads."

"Yellow eyes," said Brett.

Larry whirled. "You seen 'em too? It's like your damn soul is his chew toy. For awhile there, I never wanted to sleep again."

Brett nodded. "Yeah, it's all making more sense to me now," he said. Then something came to him. "Wait. He said *three* friends? You're sure of that?"

"Yeah, that's what he said."

"Of course!" cried Brett, feeling his pulse quicken and hope rise in his chest. "Frannie's not able to move around on her own without her protective spirit. Liz, Gonzo and Caroline would have had to leave her somewhere if they were coming to help me."

"So? Big deal, if Richter's captured the others, how's your vegetable friend gonna help?"

Brett considered that for a few minutes. "Well, if they left her behind, maybe they left instructions with Jimbo to call for help if he didn't hear from them in some time. He could be on the way already, or the police."

Larry frowned. "I sure hope it's not the police."

Brett held up a finger. "Hang on, I have another idea. Maybe I can get her to help."

"I thought you were trapped by the tats?"

Brett shrugged and shook his head. "Not tats. Well, they don't hurt like tattoos, but I'm stuck anyway. But maybe I can bring her to me."

Larry shut up and leaned back against the wall, waiting. Brett closed his eyes and thought about Frannie. Her pleasant round face, her chattiness. He felt a pull, but the hot wires of the silver dye held him in place. He pictured Frannie's ghost in the sketchy Crown Hill Cemetery he'd met her in the last time. He called her name out loud. "Fran. Frannie! Come to me, I need your help."

"Hello, Brett," came Fran's sad voice from above him. He looked up and saw her misty, shimmering form peering down at him through the grate.

"Frannie, we're in a mess. The others are kidnapped somewhere by Richter, and Larry and I are trapped down here. I know what you did, and I know why. Yellow eyes, Fran, am I right?"

Her mouth formed an O of surprise, and she nodded.

Brett waved his hand in the air as if to erase all guilt. "That doesn't matter now. If you can help us, all will be forgiven, I promise."

Larry looked at Brett, then up where Frannie's face appeared and said, "Okay, you'd better not be shitting me here, Nelson. Or just letting the crazy leak out. She really here?"

Brett just nodded to Larry.

Frannie thought a moment, then said, "Brett, I betrayed all of you, I gave updates to Richter about what was going on. He gave me nightmares, he invaded my dreams like Freddie Krueger, Brett. Every time I dozed off, there he was, torturing me with… I can't go there. Just trust me, it was horrible. Those eyes, those terrible yellow eyes! I didn't even know it was him to start with. Then he started whispering to me, telling me what I had to do to get him to stop. As long as I did as he said, he left me in peace. He promised not to hurt anyone, he just wanted to ruin your webcast and keep his reputation as the ultimate skeptic."

Hot anger welled up in Brett, but he held it back. Frannie might be weak, but hadn't he been manipulated in other ways? *Richter is much more than he seems to be.* He thought of the bear pendant and the black aura around the man. He thought of the eyes in the pendant and the eyes of the black shadow snake at the school. He thought of what Richter had made Frannie do, and what he'd manipulated Larry into doing.

Brett drew in a deep breath and let it out, calming the fury he felt at Frannie and refocusing it on Richter, the one who'd been pulling all the strings all along.

"Yeah, that's shitty of you. But Frannie, I promise, if you can go back to your body and come up here to let us out, I'll stand up for you to the others if they have any issues with you. I'm betting that something I know now will keep Richter from ever bothering you, or anyone else, again."

Frannie's eyes widened and her form frayed around the edges, losing focus. "Brett, if you can do that- -I'll do what I can. I still owe you big time. I owe everyone."

With that, Frannie's ghost vanished like morning dew in the sunlight that peeked through the clouds above. The sun felt good on his skin.

"So what'd she say, assuming you're not jerking my leg?" said Larry.

Brett told Larry how the other half of the conversation had gone. He was relieved that it had worked. It meant he hadn't completely lost all paranormal abilities, even having merged with Terb and being trapped by Richter's silver paint.

He had to admit, he felt more alive and full of energy than he'd felt in almost a year. A rush of warmth inside him let him know that the part of him that had been Terb agreed.

He smiled.

Brett and Larry waited for Frannie, the time seeming to crawl by. Neither had much more to say to each other at the moment. Brett thought Larry was probably working on ways to keep out of trouble once they were freed. Brett found himself toying with the Barbie doll, marveling that he'd been in that little plastic body. Larry caught him doing this and grinned at him. Brett stuffed the doll in his pocket, embarrassed.

Within an hour, they heard huffing and puffing as Frannie arrived, this time in the flesh. "Okay, there's a big bar out here, I'll slide it open. But Larry, you gotta leave me alone if I do."

"I got no problem with you, sweetheart. I was just under orders. Glad you're okay."

Brett said, "She's right, Larry. Mind your manners and help us out, and no one's going to the cops. Any funny stuff, and you'll wish you never left Tennessee."

Larry made an X across his chest and held fingers in the air. "Want me to pinky swear on it, Nelson?"

Brett ignored him and climbed to the top of the ladder. Fran slid the bolt back and struggled to lift the grate. She couldn't swing it all the way back, so she lifted it just enough for Brett to wiggle out. He helped her hold it up while Larry crawled out.

"Thanks, Frannie," said Brett, squeezed in an embrace from his plump friend. He made a mock protest, but he was still chilled and grateful for her warmth.

Larry started to walk off. Brett called after him, "Not so fast there, man. We'll need your help finding and freeing Lizzie, Gonzo and Caroline."

Larry looked unhappy, but nodded. "Okay, but after that, I'm out of here and we forget any of this ever happened, right?"

"It's a deal," said Brett, still held tight by Frannie.

"But where can they be?" asked Larry.

Brett didn't have an answer for that.

Chapter 25 - Black Friday Rule

Brett untangled himself from clingy Frannie. "Fran, do you have your phone?"

She nodded. "Not much power left, but yeah."

"Can you try calling Lizzie or Caroline?"

She shook her head. "I tried that on the way from the car, neither of them answers. I did get ahold of Jimbo, though." Her smile was shy, thawing out her sullen demeanor. "He was glad to hear from me. Anyway, he said Lizzie texted him to say you had sent her a message saying to meet at the stairs outside the dormitory building nearest the entrance. They told Jimbo they'd check back in an hour, and it'd been just about that long. He was trying to decide whether to call the cops, but I told him to wait until we could see what we could do first."

"I sent them a message? Crap. Richter must have used Larry's phone to impersonate me." Brett turned to face the entrance. He spotted the dormitory Richter must have meant. There was no sign of anyone near there.

Still, he waved the others in that direction and they crossed the grounds of the former asylum. Brett felt exposed, since there wasn't much cover. He looked around for signs of Richter and his men, but there was no one around that he could see.

They had to go halfway around the large building before they found a stairway leading downward. At the bottom was a painted steel door. The paint was scraped away in places to form graffiti. A rusty, broken padlock lay on the ground, looking like it'd been snapped with bolt cutters.

There was a shiny new padlock on the door.

"Look! It's Gonzo's baseball bat!" called Frannie from a few yards away. She picked the Louisville Slugger up out of the grass.

Larry frowned at this. "That's not good. Looks like Richter wasn't bluffing, and if they took your bruiser friend down, I'm not sure what good we'll be against them. Also, if I'm right, that door goes to the tunnels, and there're miles of those under Central State."

"I'm not even sure how we'll get in there," said Brett, feeling very tired and sore.

"Reckon I can help with that, 'long as it's okay if I split afterward," said Larry, adjusting his hat. "Can you tell me where my truck is? I'll need to get something."

Brett thought about it. Terb let him know that the truck was just outside the gates, across the street. Deep down, he didn't trust Larry, but he knew the man was in a tight spot, and Brett held the power to send him to jail.

"All right, Larry," said Brett. He pointed and told him where to find the truck. "But don't take long. I don't like them being down there any longer than they have to be."

Larry tipped his hat and started off at a jog toward the entrance.

"Hey Larry!" Brett found himself calling. Terb asserting himself, maybe. *Oh well, let him.*

Larry stopped and looked back.

"I've got your license number, do you understand me?"

Larry nodded, eyes flat. "Crystal clear, dude," he said, and then he was off again.

Frannie and Brett waited at the stair, not saying much to each other. Time crawled by and Brett worried that he'd placed too much faith in his rival's fear of being turned in.

Pop! Splat!

Brett jumped as silver paint splattered on the brick wall next to him. Frannie hit the ground with a heavy thump.

"Haw, you're funny when you're freaked out, know that, Nelson?" Larry swaggered up to them, lowering the paintball gun. Frannie looked up from where she lay and let out an exasperated noise.

"Damn it, Larry, what are you fucking around for?" Brett was furious, but was relieved that Frannie wasn't harmed this time.

Larry turned the gun around and handed it to Brett butt-first. "Just keeping you on your toes. I figure you might get some use out of this, what with all the ghosts running around here. Never know who you can trust, eh Fran?"

Frannie stood up, brushing grass and leaves off of her clothes. "You bastard."

Brett took the paintball gun from Larry. It had a clip on one side, so he hung it from his belt. He felt a little silly. "That's your help?"

"Naw, this is more what I had in mind," said Larry, producing the revolver Brett had seen on him before. Brett flinched at the sight of it, though he hated showing a reaction in front of Larry. Frannie let out a shriek.

"Hey now, I'm a lot of things, but I'm not a killer," said Larry, making a show of pointing the gun away from them. He descended the stairs and shot at the lock. The report was so loud that Brett was sure it could be heard miles away. He seemed to have missed the lock, and Brett was worried he'd have to shoot again, but Larry pulled the latch back on its hinge.

"Shooting the lock wouldn't have worked," said Larry. "Saw it on Mythbusters. So, I shot the bracket it's attached to. Thinner metal, popped it right off there. This way, you don't have to worry about someone coming along and locking you in later."

Larry swung the door open and jumped back, but no one was in the doorway. He turned and looked back up at Brett and Frannie. "Okay, kids, this is where I get off. Have fun storming the tunnels, and I'll see you in Memphis."

Larry climbed the stairs and clapped Brett on the shoulder with his free hand.

Brett nodded, making brief eye contact with his rival. The word, "Thanks," escaped his mouth before he could stop it.

Larry grinned and touched his hat's brim and stalked off again.

"We'd better get down there before the cops come," said Frannie, worried.

Brett shrugged. "Larry's the only one who needs to worry about the cops. I've got my contact that got us permission to be here. Kitty will stick up for us if there's trouble."

They descended the stairs and passed through the doorway into darkness. Brett fished out his flashlight and shone it around. The tunnel was low enough that Larry or Gonzo would have to stoop to keep from hitting their heads on the ceiling. The walls were lined with dusty pipes and conduits of all sizes. He could see some that were marked, telling him they once carried steam or chilled water. He saw cloth-insulated wire strung along the wall, light bulbs and empty sockets spaced every fifteen feet. The lights weren't lit, and broken glass littered the floor where old bulbs had been just dropped or stepped on.

The tunnel went on a long, long ways straight ahead. Brett could see many dark recesses that he thought must be side passages. He stepped forward and felt something crunch under his foot.

He shined the light down and lifted his foot. It was a souvenir button with a black background and the words "Her name was Lola..." printed in white on its shiny surface.

Brett picked up the damaged button and showed Frannie. "Well, it looks like Caroline was here. She left us a calling card."

Frannie nodded. "Well, we kinda knew that, but it's good to confirm that we're going the right way."

Brett led the way slowly down the long hallway, Frannie walking a bit too closely behind him. Once the light from the doorway was far enough behind, Brett started catching wispy movement anywhere he wasn't looking directly.

Then they came to the first side passage. It was even narrower, and the darkness looked almost solid. "Which way?" Brett wondered out loud.

He and Frannie tried to find any evidence on the ground down each way, hoping for tracks or more trinkets left behind, but nothing obvious presented itself. They stared at each other, surrounded by the dark and silence around their little pool of light.

"Maybe we should ask someone for directions," said Frannie, allowing herself a faint smile.

Brett blinked. "Yeah, I guess we could!" He shut off the flashlight and let the dark wash over them. Only the slightest glint of light reached them from the doorway now, and if he stared that direction, it seemed to flicker and disappear like a mirage.

"Um, hello?" he called to the darkness, feeling like he was conducting an EVP question session. "We have friends who are lost down here, can you help us?"

There was no answer.

"We really need your help," called Frannie, facing down the side passage. "I'm Frannie, who are you?"

There was a slight breeze of cool dusty air from the long tunnel, and a soft whispery moan came with it.

"We can't quite hear you," said Brett, straining his eyes to peer into the dark of the tunnel.

A figure appeared, faint and transparent, sitting up against one of the walls. The figure held its arms over its head and hung its head as though supported at the wrists.

"Turn back," it whispered without raising its head. "Turn back while you can. This place is death."

Brett stayed where he was, hardly daring to move. "Please, we can't leave our friends down here, we have to help them. Can you tell us which way they went?"

The figure struggled and raised its head, peering through stringy, dirty hair. Brett could not tell if the ghost had been male or female. Its eyes were glazed over. They looked in his general direction, but not quite at him. "They go as no one knows, they go seeking life in this place where the dead roam. They go in the dark and may not return."

"Please," asked Frannie, "we need your help."

The ghost coughed and pulled at intangible chains that held it to the wall. "They do not waver from their path, but go straight on to the source, where the power was, where the pipes end. Find the way up, though it may be blocked by lost hopes. You shall flee into his grasp, but the hopeless may help you, by and by."

Brett started to ask for clarification, but the figure burst into laughter and hauled itself to its feet. Brett heard the clanging ring of broken chains. The figure stretched and advanced on them, laughing and screaming. Brett put his hand on the paintball gun and prepared to see if it was any use, but the figure exploded into shreds of misty light before reaching him. Its laughter rang in the corridor for a while after the shreds faded.

"Well, that was fun and unhelpful," said Frannie.

Brett shrugged, clicking his light back on. "Sounds to me that we don't take any turns, and we follow the pipes back to the power house on the other end of the campus. Not sure what the rest means, but maybe it'll make more sense when we get there."

They made their slow way down the long corridor, spending only a little time looking for clues at each side passage. Brett had a feeling that the ghost was telling the truth, that if Liz had been trapped in this place, she'd want to find another way out, far from where they'd been imprisoned. So it only made sense that they'd head to the power house.

Once, they came upon a place where Brett's flashlight showed a rusty metal hatch in the ceiling, but there was no obvious way to open it. Brett shoved at it, but wasn't tall enough to put much power behind his efforts. There was always the way back, he thought, but he didn't like the idea of traversing all that way twice.

Besides, he couldn't shake the feeling they were being followed. Brett kept looking behind him, shining the flashlight into the darkness the way they'd come. Each time though, no one was there. He imagined the ghosts of the patients that'd been punished by being put down there watching them as they made their way down the tunnel.

After another long interval of shuffling along in the dark, the passage came to a T-intersection.

"Now what?" A whine crept into her voice.

Brett looked each way down the hall. To the left, the corridor seemed to go on forever. To the right, it bent again to the left within fifty feet or so.

"Let's go to the right," he said. "It's kind of a dog-leg, but it continues on in the same direction."

Frannie shrugged and let him lead the way once more. They were just about to the bend when a nurse appeared, an almost solid apparition in their path.

"What are you doing up?" demanded the nurse. She wore a stiff white dress that swept the floor. There were faint pink smears on her sleeves and where her thighs should be under the skirts of the dress. Handprint-shaped smears. Hands on her hips, she had black holes instead of eyes.

Brett stammered, "What? I don't belong here, ma'am, we're just looking for some friends."

The nurse hissed and lectured him. Brett was reminded of a particularly temperamental first grade teacher he'd had. "No one belongs here, no one does. Do you think I belong here? Do you think I like this place? There's no room for the likes of you roaming about free. If you're down here, you have to stay *put*!" She started to stalk toward them.

Once again, Brett's hand went to the paintball gun. He wasn't sure how well it would work. It would need to hit something solid to spray the silver flecks around. The nurse was out in the middle of the hall. Would it pass right through her, or would the pellet itself be enough to disrupt the angry spirit?

"No, really, ma'am," said Frannie suddenly, "It's not we who should be here. We're visitors, locked in by the man with the amulet. It has yellow eyes and he invades your dreams," she said with a touch of fear in her voice.

The nurse stopped in her tracks. "The man with the bear," she said, one hand flying to her mouth. "He is here? I felt him, heard the patients crying out in pain. He tortures them, devours them sometimes. He's a monster."

Frannie nodded. "Yes, we know. I know. He's come to me and twisted my purpose, made me betray my friends. I hate him. He's locked our friends down here, and we're trying to help them. We'll leave you in peace once we're away from here. When we're away from him."

The nurse stood still, the dark holes staring into them a long while. Then, she vanished without another word, leaving the way clear.

"Wow, that was great, Frannie!" said Brett.

Frannie nodded. "Yeah, great, thanks. It's true, you know. That's how he got to me. Night after night." She shivered.

Brett put his arm around Frannie and gave her a quick hug. "I'm sorry. We'll be done with him soon, I hope."

Brett and Frannie held hands as they made their way in the dark tunnels, helping one another over steam pipes at intersections.

Brett caught a glimpse of a light down one side corridor.

They rushed toward the light. Brett tripped over something large and heavy in the path, and was saved from a fall by Frannie. He thanked her, then turned the flashlight downward to see Gonzo sprawled across the tunnel floor, his mouth working in a silent scream.

"Oh my gosh," said Frannie.

Brett found the light came from a glow stick that hung from Caroline's neck. She lay near Gonzo, legs kicking and face contorted in pain.

He scanned the area with the flashlight, whose light seemed dimmer to Brett now.

The light revealed Liz, curled into a fetal ball, rocking back and forth. A whimper escaped her.

"We have to wake them up," said Frannie. "I think Richter's got hold of all of them in their dreams."

Chapter 26 - If I Ever Leave This World Alive

Brett slapped at Gonzo's face and shouted at his friend. "Wake up!"

Gonzo showed no signs of hearing him.

"Maybe they're drugged," said Frannie.

Brett stood in panic a long moment. If he couldn't wake his friends, what could he do? He imagined the giant, yellow-eyed shadow snake eating his friends one at a time.

A long moan escaped Liz's mouth and her body shook.

Hot anger roared like a furnace in Brett's belly. Terb's voice came to him. *Don't just stand there, dumbass,* do *something!*

Brett took in a deep breath and said aloud, "Okay, we need to go in after them."

Frannie shook her head and backed up a step. "No. You have no idea, Brett. You can't ask me…"

"Actually, I do. He attacked me in my dreams, though I didn't know it was him. I can't make you, but you did say you owe all of us, and I need your help."

"I… I'm sorry, Brett, but I just can't."

Brett had to fight his Terb nature from lashing out at Frannie. He counted to three, then said, "Okay. I guess we need someone awake in case something happens in the real world.

Fran bit her lip and held his eyes a long moment. "I'm sorry, Brett. It's more real to me especially, since most of me lives there."

"I know, Frannie. I guess you can stand guard anyway," he said, handing her the paintball gun. "Got any ideas how to go to sleep quickly?"

She shrugged. "Count sheep?"

Brett stepped over Gonzo and Caroline, and sat next to Liz. He stroked her cheek with the back of his hand and it came away wet with tears.

"Damn it!" he hissed. *There has to be some way to help them!*

He hugged Liz to him. A faint chemical smell, like acetone and rubbing alcohol, mixed with Liz's own scent in his nose. He looked around and found a damp rag on the cellar floor. He picked it up and sniffed and his head spun.

"He knocked them out with chloroform! I'm going in, Fran. Be careful!"

As he covered his face with the rag and breathed deep, the room spun faster and faster and his vision dimmed.

Too late, Frannie called out a warning, and he heard her footsteps running away, down the hallway.

Brett forced his eyes open, and the last thing he saw was Richter and his two goons rush around a corner toward him. The eyes on Richter's pendant glowed an intense yellow that made Brett's woozy mind think of evil Jawas. Richter grinned as Brett fell into a deep, black sleep.

*　　*　　*

Brett stood in a clearing of a forest. Blackened trees were being overtaken by new growth, though everything seemed twisted and distorted by some kind of cruel sickness. It reminded him of a place....

In the center of the clearing was a pile of stones and a cross made of sticks and twine.

He knew the place. They'd called it the Haunted Forest as a joke, because the dead trees from some fire in the past made the woods in a long, wide median of Interstate 65 seem foreboding. They'd found this clearing inside, and the magic of the place was such that the woods seemed much vaster than it could possibly be. The cairn was the final resting place of Ashleigh's brother Michael, a victim of the demon that had destroyed their family. The demon that had plagued Brett and Frannie and had caused their souls to leak out through possession.

The dream had all the senses. He felt his skin prickle with fear at the thought of the demon. *No. It's gone, I destroyed it.* Terb's memories of strangling the supernatural creature until it dissolved came to him like a forgotten dream. His anger flared and Brett felt strength come to him.

A mist formed from the stones, and Brett waited, expecting to see the Carpenter boy's ghost.

Instead, it was Gonzo, withered and vaporous, his mouth set in the same howl he'd seen on the big guy's sleeping form. Sound came faint, then louder, a scream like none he'd heard from Gonzo in waking life.

"Gonz! It's me, Brett! You have to wake up, this isn't real!"

Yellow eyes appeared in the stones, and a shadow cobra unfolded its hood as it rose up to strike at Gonzo's ghost. Gonzo screamed and writhed in agony. The tenuous mists that made up his form tore in ragged slashes where the cobra's teeth entered him.

Brett struck out at the snake, intending to grab and rend it.

The yellow-eyed Richter snake darted and sank its fangs into Brett's hand and held on. Icy venom from the bite burned its way up his arm and caused him to cry out and jerk back. The Richter snake grew in size with every beat of Brett's heart, feasting on his essence.

Panic bloomed again inside Brett. *What can we do?*

You're the brains, I'm the passion. What can we do together?

Terb had a point, and it gave Brett an idea.

It's feeding on our fear! Let's poison the milk. You strangled a demon to death! How silly is a little snake by comparison?

The tide turned within Brett, and icy fear blazed into anger that pushed back the snake's poison. The shadow cobra withered, and its eyes dimmed. It hung limp from Brett's arm and fell off as its jaws went slack.

Brett faced Gonzo's ghost. "See? Just a dream!"

Gonzo's words echoed and warbled as he spoke. "Brett, you fucker, you got me into this!"

"Yeah, I did, Gonz, and I'm sorry. I'm getting you out of it. I'm getting us all out of it, I promise."

As the two spoke, Gonzo's form became more solid, his voice clearer. "You'd better. I'm still pissed about *Soccer Mom* too, Junior."

Brett had to smile. Maybe all wasn't lost if Gonz was calling him "Junior" again. Brett said, "You know I'm sorry about that. Maybe it was Terb, but Terb is me. You were right all along to hold me responsible for his actions. My actions."

Gonzo scowled, no longer transparent. "That's too bad, because I wanted to kick his ass."

Brett tapped Gonzo's shoulder with his fist. "Well, he and I are one again, so you can still do it, if you want, but wait until I save everyone else. I think you're good to wake up now?"

Gonzo clapped a hand on Brett's shoulder and grinned. "Yeah, we'll see about that. I think there's someone else who needs an ass kicking more than you."

Brett couldn't help but notice that Gonzo's hand passed through him, now more solid than Brett himself in this place. "Fran's got your baseball bat."

Gonzo cracked his knuckles, his grin widening. "Roger that. I think I can open my eyes now."

And in a blink, Brett found himself alone in the clearing.

The bright moonlight revealed a path behind the cairn. Brett followed it, eyeing the blackened trees that bent down as if to reach toward him as he made his way through the forest. The path narrowed and leaves and branches brushed and scratched his arms as he walked.

A woman's voice cried out for help in the distance, so he doubled his pace along the path, the forest picking at his clothes and skin. Blackened twiggy branches of dead trees clawed at his face, and he had to raise an arm to protect his eyes.

He burst into a vast clearing, still moonlit, covered in orderly stones of varying sizes. A cemetery.

Something big hung from a tree in the middle of the cemetery. Shaped like a cocoon, it writhed and swung to and fro. The cries he'd heard came from the cocoon and he saw a glimpse of a face at the top.

Caroline's face was as he'd never seen her before. She always projected cool confidence. Not now. Liz's friend sobbed and cried out in fear as a spider as big as a pit bull touched her face with a spiny appendage.

The massive spider had many eyes, but two of them glowed yellow.

Brett dodged headstones as he ran through the cemetery. Caroline's feet, clad in low-heeled boots, were all that he could see of her from below. He grabbed onto the boots and pulled. The branch above them groaned, and he heard the twang of the thick spider silk going taught with his added weight.

Brett heard himself cry, "You can't have her! She's *my* friend!" He felt Terb's wrath grow within him, and this time, he let it flow, embracing the torrent of emotion as his own. It was a heady, delicious feeling, and he found he could direct it. The newfound power gave him an idea. *This is just a dream. What if it were a* lucid *dream, and I had control over it, like I have before?*

Brett pictured himself growing larger and denser. Maybe some kind of being made of stone, a living statue. Caroline groaned at the added weight and the branch cracked like a gunshot.

Stone giant Brett stood up, at least 8 feet tall, cradling the now smaller and lighter Caroline in his arms. The spider hissed and leaped for his face. Caroline screamed and begged him to kill it.

For the moment, his stone skin protected him, so Brett had enough time to set Caroline down on the cemetery grass.

He swatted at the spider, which scuttled around his shoulders and failed to pierce him with its fangs. Brett said, "I'm not afraid of you, and you can't hurt her anymore, Richter."

The shadow spider melted, and Brett found himself covered in a black ooze. Everywhere it touched him, his stone skin smoked and burned with preternatural acid, soaking into him, dissolving him. Brett scraped at the goo, but his massive stone fingers burned and slipped right through the gelatinous mass without effect.

Then Brett remembered the silver lines that had been drawn on him to imprison him in his own body. He visualized them becoming veins of pure, solid silver, all up and down his limbs. He grabbed at the Richter blob with his forearms and heard the sizzle and scream as the designs touched the goopy creature. The acidic burning stopped as the monster evaporated into the night air.

Brett reverted to human form and proportions and dreamed up a silver pocket knife, which he used to cut the wiry, silken cords binding Caroline. Each one twanged like a broken guitar string, and some lashed his fingers as they snapped.

Caroline struggled free of the last few cords and they both stood. She hugged him, shaking. "Thank you, Brett. I... have a thing about spiders. They freak me out. Little ones, too."

Brett held her a long moment, then stepped back and said, "I'm sorry I called you a bitch, and I'm sorry for my jealous behavior, Caroline."

Caroline wrinkled her nose and said, "It's okay. You weren't yourself."

"No, I kind of *was* myself. Just not all at once."

"Whatever, Brett. You're fine. I don't hold onto grudges. Thanks for coming to my rescue from that… that…."

"Richter. He's behind the yellow eyes. He's feeding on ghosts and on us in our dreams."

Caroline's eyes narrowed. "Okay, yeah. Things make more sense now."

Brett nodded.

Caroline took on a greater solidity, as Gonzo had before he'd disappeared. She seemed to be more and more intensely Caroline, more real than her surroundings, more real than Brett.

"Brett, why are you fading, what's happening?"

"You're waking up, Caroline."

"But I wanted to help go after Richter!"

"Thanks, but this one's my fight. Wake up, Caroline, and see what you can do there."

"Yeah, got it."

Caroline favored him with a tight smile and a twinkle in her eyes before she popped out of the dream world.

Brett searched the graveyard and could find no pathways out of it, not even the one he'd come by from the Haunted Forest.

He scanned the area for anything resembling a portal, a way out.

His gaze came to rest on the one mausoleum in the cemetery, a small stone structure with a heavy steel door. Above the door, etched in stone, was the name "McEnzie." Liz's last name.

As Brett approached the mausoleum, he heard a humming, like an electrical transformer. His skin prickled with anticipation as he reached for the door handle, expecting a massive electric shock.

Instead, only the chill of the metal door met the skin of his hand. He pulled, and the door opened, revealing an empty chamber. Brett stepped inside. There were two stone sarcophaguses in the small room. As he moved further into the room to peer into one, the door shut behind him.

To say the chamber was dark would be an understatement. No light reached Brett's eyes. He could find no indication of direction other than the buzzing sound, which he used as a guide. He inched his way along the floor, past where the wall had to have been, then further still. All the while, the humming grew louder and louder.

He reached hands out and touched walls. Not stone walls, but something slippery and metallic. Soon the walls widened to where he had to pick a wall to follow. Something bounced off his face, and he swatted at it. Something stung his neck, and he cursed and flailed around him.

Then he saw the eyes. Tiny yellow pinpricks of eyes, hovering before his face, right before they rushed him and a sharp sting in his nose made him cry out again.

Then the deep dark swarmed with pairs of yellow eyes, all around him, hundreds of them, all in constant darting motion.

And somewhere in the middle of the swarm, he heard Liz whimper and then cry out in pain.

Brett hit the floor and crawled toward where he'd heard Liz. His hands found her, all curled up like she had been in the tunnel. His hands found her face, damp and sticky and bumpy. He kissed her and she groaned. "Oh Brett, get out of here, save yourself. They're *everywhere!*"

The invisible insects converged on Brett and stung him over and over, which made him angry, but frustrated efforts to concentrate while under attack. Each sting was like a searing hot needle followed by a cold numbness that soaked deep into his skin. He felt his energy sapping away with every strike. He tried to shoo them away, using his silver lines as weapons. But they were too many, and they were too quick, and he weakened minute by minute.

His heart throbbed with a dull ache as he knew he'd be beaten down by thousands of tiny attacks he couldn't stop. He rallied by thinking of Lizzie and how she'd saved him in the past with her magic and unstoppable enthusiasm. He hated to think of her beaten this way by Richter, using his evil magic to sting them both to death, adding to his supernatural powers in the process.

We have to save Liz, came the thought from Terb. He agreed. He had sacrificed himself once before to save her, and he'd do it again. He covered her body with his, and ignored the pain with this last driving need to protect his love. He felt as though he had on a thick cloak that he wrapped the two of them in, covered like a dome. The stings hurt less and less as he thought more of his love for Lizzie and how they'd survived the demon's many attempts on their lives. Now Richter tried, and he would not succeed at least in getting Lizzie.

A blue glow grew around them, like foxfire at first, then blazing forth as an incandescent light, illuminating the interior of the metal room, stacked with boxes, and filled with nasty, little black wasps with yellow eyes.

The light drove the wasps back and away from them. Brett did not rise, but remained as Lizzie's cloak and force field against Richter's soul-devouring evil.

Brett knew where they were now. Inside the back of a moving semi truck. The one the possessed trucker had imprisoned them in a year before.

We escaped that prison, we will escape this one.

The blue glow grew so bright Brett had to close his eyes. He felt Lizzie move around under him, rolling to be face to face with him.

She smiled and cried and laughed. He kissed her with a passion that came from both Terb and himself as a single person. The wasps popped like fireworks all around them, and they kissed for a moment that could have been any amount of time, as lost as Brett was in the joy of surviving, of Lizzie living on with him.

They came up for air and sat facing each other. The truck hit a bump and Liz giggled and Brett laughed along with her.

"I knew you'd come for me," she said. The stings on her face faded away even as he watched.

"Well, you'd do the same for me. You have before."

She squinted at him. "You're really *you* again, aren't you?"

Brett shrugged. "Depends on which of me you mean."

She swatted his arm. "Don't be a tease. And that gives you away you know."

"What?"

She nodded with sage wisdom, her lips curling in a playful smile. "Oh yes. Brett the Brain didn't have it in him to tease, that'd be too persnickety."

"What? Hey!"

She held a finger to his lips. "And Terb the rage machine didn't have the subtlety to toy with me that way. So you are peanut butter and chocolate, reunited at last to be my lovey dovey peanut butter cup."

Before he could object to her silliness, she kissed him again.

Brett forgot any objections he might have had to being compared to a peanut butter cup.

They opened their eyes and smiled at each other. "I'm glad you're whole again, *Chico*. Truth to tell, I didn't want to choose, and I didn't want to settle for half of you."

Brett smiled. "I'm glad to be back. It just took being forced to cooperate, and here we are.

Liz glanced around them. "We are in a truck?"

Brett shrugged. "It's a dream, or wherever dreams take place. I've gotten kind of familiar with this shadow world. I'll be glad to wake up."

"So let's wake up!"

Brett watched her become more solid. "You are about to. I have one more thing to do before I can. I have to stop Richter."

"Richter?"

He nodded. "The yellow eyes match his bear amulet, and he's been haunting dreams and eating ghosts to power up. Once you're safe, I'm going after him to make sure he can't do this anymore."

"But *Chico*…" said Lizzie, just before she disappeared into the waking world.

Brett crawled to the back of the semi and tried the door. It opened into a small bathroom. His college bathroom. He tried to stand up, but could not, still weak from the wasp stings and cobra bites. So he crawled.

On the floor lay a shadow shaped like himself, a spilled bottle of pills by its head.

The shadow Brett had yellow eyes. The room swam just as though he'd just taken all those pills, like he had so long ago. The shadow Brett sat up and faced him.

Richter's voice came from the shadow. "So, here we are at last, Mr. Nelson. Your nightmare."

"I'd have tidied the place up, but I didn't know I'd have company," said Brett with as much bravado as he could fake.

The shadow laughed. "I should have known it'd be like this. No monster scares you like you do yourself, hmmm?"

"So what, you're going to *talk* me to death, is that it?"

"Come now. You know I can be anything I need to be to squash you like a bug. Perhaps I should become your dead fiancé? Or perhaps dear sweet Lizzie?"

"You live on fear, Richter, I get that now. I'm not afraid to die, I've done it before. You can't harm me. Even if you consume me now, I've got enough control of this dreamworld that I can become a poison or a disease to eat you from the inside out and destroy you."

The yellow eyes narrowed. "You think so, do you? Perhaps I shall not devour you then. You've done *quite* a job leading me to fresh spectral energy to devour. The children's ghosts in the abandoned schoolhouse alone have proved an abundant feeding ground. And Central State? Why this place is a smorgasbord of delightfully insane spirits. I shall grow and grow in power, and I shall live forever. I need to thank you, Brett. Really. It's been an honor."

"You're *not* letting me go, Richter. We're having this out, and only one of us leaves."

Brett's ears rang as Richter's laugh echoed off the bathroom tile. "Oh, you misunderstand me. I shall not *eat* you, but I will still tear your spirit into shreds too small to stitch together. Goodbye, Mr. Nelson."

The shadow Brett grew in size and sprouted claws that glinted in the fluorescent lights over the sink. Brett braced himself against the tub, turning his skin to stone.

The claws tore through the stone as easily as flesh, and Brett screamed in agony.

And then there came a scrabbling at the bathroom door. The lights flickered.

Richter stopped. He whirled around. "That's impossible. There are just the two of us here."

Brett caught his breath and called out for help.

"No! I'll finish this. Now!" Richter slashed at Brett again.

Brett focused his will and brought himself back to the day of his attempted suicide. He'd have died, laying on the bathroom floor like this, if Liz hadn't found him and convinced him to throw up the contents of his stomach and gave him reasons to live.

He focused on that love, on thoughts of Lizzie and the blue glow of the force field snapped back into existence. Richter snarled and hurled his body against the shell of energy. Brett felt and heard a crack and the force field collapsed, and Richter's weight lay on top of him. Claws and teeth ripped at his unprotected flesh and Brett sank into himself, out of ideas.

The scrabbling at the door became the crunching sound of wood being pulled apart. Hands grabbed the edges of the doorway, and it too was pulled apart, as was the wall.

Richter shouted, "No! I'm not done yet!"

Dozens of forms stood in the space where the bathroom wall had been. More hands pulled at the other walls, and soon the bathroom was reduced to rubble. The light came only from the luminous forms of people all around them, glaring at the shadow that crouched on top of Brett's prone form.

A spectral nurse stepped forward, the one that Brett had seen before. "No more," she said, and reached for Richter's shadow creature.

He threw her off, but two more took her place. Then a dozen hands pulled at the shadow. Then a hundred, all grabbing and pulling at his shadow stuff, bits of him coming away with each grab.

Richter screamed and fought and clawed. Still the massed army of Central State spirits came, wave after wave. Richter got off Brett and fled down the corridor, harried and pursued by ghosts as he went.

And then Brett saw her. Frannie's ghost stood behind them all, the slightest hint of a smile on her face. She looked right at Brett and shrugged. "I brought some friends."

Brett found the strength to pull himself together and stood. He watched as the yellow-eyed shadow was buried under a pile of ghosts.

When the pile dispersed, nothing remained.

The nurse faced Brett and said, "Leave this place, and leave us in peace. Do not take the amulet, it should not be wielded by the living. We will hide it."

Brett nodded and said, "Thank you." He could see the ghosts and the walls and Frannie fade and become less and less solid by the second.

*   *   *

He woke up on the floor where he'd knocked himself out. Everyone else stood around him.

"Welcome back, Junior, you had me worried there for a minute."

Brett found his glasses on the floor near his head and put them on as he sat up. "Gonz!"

Liz pulled him to his feet and hugged him tight. Her body heat felt almost as hot and good as it did when he'd been turning into a ghoul. Lying on the concrete floor had him shivering with cold.

Gonzo said, "Yeah, after you woke me up, I found Richter and his thugs standing guard over us. Fran left me my Louisville Slugger and I took 'em by surprise and kneecapped the goons. Richter was in a daze, so all he could do was run away."

"What happened to them?" asked Brett.

Caroline approached and said, "After I woke up, Gonz and I told them you and Fran had called the cops. They weren't being paid enough to go to jail, so they ditched Richter and disappeared up a hatch down the hall. Gonzo made sure they didn't lock us in, and watched them leave. Richter showed his face once, and collapsed for just a moment when Lizzie woke up, but then ran back down the hall. That amulet around his neck had those two glowing yellow eyes, so we were able to follow him."

Liz let go Brett and said, "So he kind of curled up in a corner and babbled out loud awhile."

"I got some amusing video of him telling an invisible person how he was eating ghosts to gain supernatural powers and that he'd live forever?" Caroline laughed.

"You did? That's great!"

"It's probably best we did, *Chico*," said Liz. She wet her lips and looked at the others. "He, uh, isn't doing so great."

"What do you mean?"

"He's gone fucking nuts," said Gonzo.

Brett nodded. "Frannie came to my rescue, with a few hundred Central State patients and staff as the cavalry. They didn't care for what Richter's been doing, and she must have rallied them to rise up against him before he ate more of them. Where *is* Frannie?"

Liz pointed to where Frannie leaned against a wall. Her smile was weak but she waved and said, "Guess I'm not completely useless?"

Brett returned her smile and said, "I'd say that goes a long way to evening the score, Franster."

She saluted and closed her eyes and heaved a big sigh.

He turned to Liz and said, "We have to get out of here, all of us. Right away."

"Why, *Chico*? We still have a webcast to do."

"Are you shittng me?" said Gonzo. "Let's get out of here. We can webcast all you want, but I want out of here."

"Are you saying you believe in ghosts now, Gonz?" said Liz.

Gonzo met Liz's eyes and said, "It's not a matter of belief. You know I've seen stuff with you weirdos that can't be explained away. Ghosts, demons, ghouls and what have you. But that doesn't mean I *want* them to be real. Doesn't mean I'm going to accept every strange thing as a spook, spectre, or walking dead creature. What I do know is this place is dangerous, and I've had my fill."

"Besides, I promised the residents that we'd leave. And we have to leave Richter's amulet behind. In fact, I'd suggest we do anything we can to take it off him without touching it."

Looks were exchanged among all of them, but they all agreed to Brett's suggestions.

Caroline led Brett and the others to where Richter's body lay. His chest rose and fell with breath. "What do we do with him?"

Brett said, "We need to find a phone that works and call an ambulance. If he ever wakes up again, I doubt he'll have any sanity left."

Chapter 27 – Within a Mile of Home

In the wee hours of the following morning, they all sat around a table together, along with Jimbo, who'd driven up from Bloomington to join them. Brett thought it was a bit strange to be drinking beer with his plate of eggs, sausage and toast, but as Gonzo had promised, it was oddly satisfying.

"Yay, grease feast!" cheered Caroline and Liz together. Each bit into a strip of bacon. They grinned at each other, lips shining with bacon fat.

Jimbo grinned like the cat who ate the canary as Frannie smothered him with affection. Her mood had improved greatly since he'd arrived. He said, "You wouldn't believe the traffic we had when I broadcast the stuff you sent me. I'm just glad PokerZombie said they'd pay for more bandwidth. And they let me know they're *very* happy with the exposure they got from tonight and the last couple of nights."

"Huh. They'd better be. Are they happy enough to buy me a new van?" said Gonzo, refilling his beer mug from the pitcher. He topped Brett off while he was at it.

"One way or another, Gonz, I'll find a way to pay to fix or replace *Soccer Mom*," said Brett, "I'm still sorry about that."

"Hmm, you weren't yourself, I guess." Gonzo pretended to be more interested in the steak and eggs on his plate for the moment. Brett thought he'd probably been forgiven, but the big guy wasn't much for coming out and saying things like that. Gonzo continued, "If we could get ahold of Richter's prize money, we could all buy fleets of *Soccer Mom*s."

Caroline shrugged. "Nope. Uh uh. The terms are pretty clear, only Richter can declare something as definitive evidence in order for someone to claim the prize, and he's not gonna have the marbles left to do that. Not that he ever would have. If it's any comfort, we did show that he believed in the paranormal."

"You know, none of that matters. We're all here and in one piece," said Brett.

"You're right, *Chico*," said Liz, sipping her own beer. "And we got that call from the ParaTV cable channel with an offer to pay for us to make a few episodes to run on their network, and if the pilot works out, they'll buy more and we'll have a series!"

Brett grinned. "Yeah, it's more than we hoped for when we started this project. I mean, I hate to have to give up pizza delivery..."

"Fuck pizza," said Gonzo. "If this doesn't work out, King's Pizza will hire us back anytime. That or we can take the money we get paid and open our own place. Maybe a beer and barbecue joint."

"In Memphis?" asked Liz. "You think anyone would go for that?"

Gonzo shrugged. "Hey, there's always room for one more down there."

Brett looked at Jimbo and Frannie, who were engaged in a tickle fight. "What about you guys, are you on board?"

"Well," said Jimbo, grabbing both of Frannie's hands to stop her from tickling him, "I'm still in school for another semester, so I can't really travel much. But I can still do the 'net side of things like I've been doing."

Frannie stuck her tongue out at Jimbo and said, "I might be able to help sometimes, when I'm on break."

Brett turned to Caroline. "How about you?"

"Me? Oh I don't know. On weekends, maybe, but I've got my hands full at home, and there's only so much my husband will put up with. He still thinks this is all a bunch of crap. He texted me asking if I got Richter's autograph," said Caroline, rolling her eyes.

Liz giggled at Caroline. "Well, you've *got* to come along when you can, I need you for a proper grease feast."

Caroline smiled and nodded. "Sure thing, Liz. I'll squeeze you guys in whenever I can."

Frannie poked Brett. "Hey. Let me see that ink again."

Brett pulled up his sleeve, feeling a bit self-conscious showing the silver spiral that had been dyed into his skin.

"It's actually kind of sexy," said Liz. "I bet we could work on doing something like that for you, Frannie. Richter seems to have done Brett a big favor in trying to imprison him in his body."

Brett nodded, covering his arm again. "Yeah, it might seem like fun to get to be a ghost now and again, but it was a complete loss of control. Terb and I *had* to come to terms again, and in doing so, we're mostly merged. Just don't make me angry. You wouldn't like me when I'm angry." He raised his arms and made a monstrous face.

Liz's giggles were uncontrollable. "Oh my, Mister Hulk, your big green muscles are ever so hot!" Caroline and Frannie laughed with her.

"I think we need a pitcher of ice water to cool her off," grumbled Gonzo.

Liz turned toward Frannie as her giggles subsided, "We might need to try something more permanent for you. I know a tattoo artist here in Indy who does tribal art and is into the paranormal, I'm pretty sure he'd work with us."

Frannie gave Liz a sad smile. "Thanks, but I don't deserve it. I'm really sorry--"

"We've been over that," interrupted Brett. "All is forgiven. You were under Richter's influence. We all felt the power he had in dreams, and most of you is over on that side. Besides, I'd be dead or insane if you hadn't saved the day."

Frannie met Brett's eyes for a long moment, then nodded. "Well, I did have a choice, he just made it seem like I didn't. I'm glad I could help make up for it."

Gonzo started to retort, but Brett talked over him. "And without your help, we'd all still be locked up, cold and hungry, at Central State." Brett looked at Gonzo as he made this point.

Gonzo sighed and nodded his agreement. "Yeah, I guess we're even, Fran."

"Just come to me next time, dear," said Liz. She reached across Brett to touch Frannie's hand. "I'm the one with mojo in our group. I could have tried to help you."

Frannie nodded and squeezed Liz's hand.

"We need a toast," said Brett. Everyone nodded. Glasses around the table were topped off with beer, coffee or orange juice.

Everyone looked expectantly at Gonzo. "What? My turn again? Okay, give me a minute."

Gonzo raised his glass and looked toward the ceiling, his face solemn. "The immortal Benny Bell once sang:

"The morning sun may kiss the grass,

the clock may kiss the hours that pass,

the flowing wine may kiss the glass,

But you my friends -- drink hearty!"

Glasses clinked and all drank deeply. Frannie looked troubled. "But that doesn't rhyme!"

Everyone else laughed.

Spectral Delivery

"Call off sick, Enid. Trust me, you don't want to get stuck in a car all night training with that freak, Brett. I hear he's a Devil worshipper!" My friend Viola, working the phones, covered the mic of her headset as she whispered this warning to me. "I mean, he and that creepy Goth girl hang around in cemeteries at night. I saw them once, they were just sitting there, like, on someone's grave, with flashlights and junk."

"So?" I said, drawing my ponytail through the back of my King's Pizza Delivery hat. "He seems nice enough, what do I care what hobbies he has? So long as he drives fast and gets me out of here by 11 tonight for my late Valentine's date, he could be on the Devil's bowling team for all I care." I adjusted the curve of the bill of the hat, hoping I didn't look as dorky as I felt.

Viola reached over and tucked some stray hair up under my hat for me. She shrugged and said, "Just keep your phone on you. Text me if anything funny happens. Or better yet, text Jeff, he can be your knight in shining armor!" She fluttered her eyelids and cast her gaze dreamily at the ceiling.

I swatted at her. "As if. He's ticked at me already for having to work on Valentine's Day as it is. And with him, it'd be wool armor, bundled up in one of his sexy lawyer suits."

She laughed. "Pre-Law, you mean."

I felt a pang of failure at the mention of my former major. Lack of funds had kept me from getting past my second year. Oh well, maybe someday. Meanwhile, I could live vicariously through Jeff. "Whatever. I'm not calling off sick to avoid Brett. You stuck your neck out to get me this driver job, so I'm gonna be a good girl and do as I'm told. Besides, I don't think I want to tick off the boss."

"Enid! Order up! Brett's waiting!" As if on cue, my shift manager "Uncle Gonzo" growled from the other end of the counter. I don't know his real name, the big guy's name tag even has that nickname on it. He slid the pizza into its box, partitioning it with four strokes of his deadly-looking rocker blade. "And ladies, cut the gossip, the phones are ringing, okay?" He favored me with a squinty glare, but his lips curved upward just a twitch as he slid the box my way.

I grabbed an insulated pizza delivery bag off the shelf and slid the box into it, noting the address.

Viola grinned at me. "Say hi to the 'Hey Dudes' for me, hmm?"

"The 'Hey Dudes'?"

I heard Gonzo cackle behind her, but when I looked, his back was to me.

Great.

"Uh Gonzo, is there any chance I could be out of here by 11?"

"Not at the rate you're going. Scoot!"

I picked up the bag and sighed, shooting a glare back at Viola as I hustled out the door and into the cool dark night.

Brett's car, an elderly black Saturn, idled right out front. I pulled open the back door on the passenger side, popped the pizza bag in next to the one Brett had taken out a minute before me. I slammed that door and hopped in the front seat next to him. He wore the same red t-shirt and ball cap uniform as me, and I felt a silly kinship as he grinned at me. Something about him made me think of a cheerful beagle.

"Welcome aboard, Enid. Where are we going?"

I rattled off the address.

Brett groaned. "Oh. Not the 'Hey Dudes' again."

"That's what Viola said, too. What's up with that?"

Brett pulled the car out of the lot and out onto the city streets. "You'll see!"

My cell phone vibrated in my pants pocket. I slipped it out and glanced at the glowing screen. Jeff's words spelled out, "Where R U?". I'd never upgraded to anything smarter, so I was able to type out my reply without having to look, using the numeric keypad. "Working. Try 2 get off early."

His reply made me bite my lip to hold back an exasperated sigh. "It's late already. This sucks."

I sent back, "Sorry. Need the job. On a run gtg"

I waited for a reply, but after a minute of silence, I guessed that my honey was too irritated to say anything back. What could he say? I *did* need the job.

If Brett cared that I was texting as he drove us around, he didn't let on, eyes still on the road.

"Aren't we going to your pie's address first?" I asked, as he dodged around slower-moving vehicles along our route.

"Nope! The 'Hey Dudes' are closer, and the other pie is a special delivery. Has to be there at a certain time."

"Speaking of time, how long do you think this run will take?" I asked, trying to sound casual.

Brett just shrugged and didn't look at me. "I dunno. Not too long. It's just two pies."

"I was just kind of hoping, since it's Valentine's Day night, and…"

"Yeah I know. My girlfriend keeps texting me what she's not wearing, I want to get done as early as we can, believe me!"

Relief flooded through me. Brett had a reason to hurry, too. And he not only had a girlfriend, he mentioned her in my presence, so the guy wasn't about to hit on me, either. Not that I'd mind so much, Brett's not half bad for someone ten years older than me. But it could be awkward, especially if he's really as creepy as Viola says, despite appearances.

Maybe Viola's just pulling my leg about Brett.

We pulled up to a large, two-story house in a neighborhood a couple of blocks from campus. A neon beer ad glowed in the front window next to the front door. I grabbed up the pizza bag and followed Brett up the walk. I couldn't see inside as we stepped up onto the porch, all the windows I could see had blinds pulled.

Brett gestured at the door, and I looked at him a moment before I realized he wanted me to knock.

So I did.

The door swung open and four shaggy-haired guys in Hawaiian shirts cried out in a chorus, "Hey, Dudes!"

Hence the name…

I felt a stupid grin take over my face and I replied, "Hey! Pizza's here."

"Well all right! Come on in!" cried one dude, who wore a friendly wolfish grin on his face. He pushed open the screen door and gestured a grand invitation.

"I don't think…" I started.

"Don't worry, these guys are okay," said Brett, taking the door and waiting for me to go in.

I looked from Brett's calm face to the wolfish Hey Dude and my gut said this was okay. "Sure, but we have to get rolling, right?"

Brett nodded. "Right!"

Wolf Dude stepped aside as I got the pizza out of the bag and walked to a messy kitchen table in the room inside. Another Hey Dude, who seemed more fox-like than wolfish, swept empty beer cans, an ashtray and various snack wrappers aside, making enough room for the pizza box. I set it down and turned to find Brett talking with Wolf Dude.

"So yeah, like I told you, it started last week," the Dude said to Brett. "Pots and pans, banging in the middle of the night, crazy faces in the bathroom mirror in the wee hours…"

"You said 'wee', dude!" said Fox Dude, snickering.

"Shut up, I'm talking to the ghost dude, okay? Maybe he can help."

I blinked. "Ghost dude?"

Brett reddened a little. "It's just a hobby of mine."

"Dude's a ghost buster!" said Fox Dude.

"I prefer 'paranormal investigator'," said Brett, lowering his eyes to stare at Wolf Dude's shoes. "But my trainee and I have to run…"

"Aww, dude, can't you just, I don't know, have a look around?" begged Wolf Dude. "I'll make it worth your while." He pulled out cash to pay for the pizza and added a ten dollar bill. I don't know what kind of tips Brett normally got, but the fifty-percent tip got his attention.

He looked at me, waiting for me to decide for him.

I sighed. "I guess. Let's get it over with."

Brett took something palm-sized out of his pocket. A compass. As he paced around the front rooms, he held the compass far out in front of him as though balancing a glass of water.

The Hey Dudes followed him around in single file, weaving around furniture and trash bags behind him. They whispered jokes and swatted at each other. This procession made me think of ducklings flapping and waddling after their mama. I followed when they left the dining area.

Buried under pizza boxes, well-loved but under-washed clothing, video game controllers, DVD cases, and occasional abused books, the floor and furniture of the living room showed primarily by outline. All except a threadbare armchair and ottoman, their scratchy-looking orange cloth exposed to view.

Brett sat cross-legged on the floor of the living room. He stared down at the compass and his smartphone on the ottoman. The phone displayed a classic microphone graphic, and a red dot in the corner made me realize he was recording with some kind of app.

"Is there anyone here?" he asked the air in front of him. He seemed to wait for a reply for a long moment.

Fox Dude broke the silence. "What's ghost dude doing?"

"Shut up, he's on the phone with the dead," explained Wolf Dude.

Brett scowled at them both, but continued talking to the air. "If you speak, I *will* hear you." He paused. "Try to make this compass spin so we know you're here, okay?"

So help me God, the needle of the compass twitched. I felt the little hairs on the back of my neck stand up.

The Hey Dudes whooped and high-fived each other.

Brett went on, "Thank you! So please, tell me, what has you upset?"

The Hey Dudes hushed each other, straining to listen for a reply.

My cellphone buzzed. I peeked. Jeff asked, "Done yet?"

I just sent back, "No. I think we're having a séance."

His return text said, "You're shitting me."

I smiled and sent back, "Tell you later."

After a few more questions, Brett stopped the recording and said, "Okay, I'm going to play this back. I think we'll hear replies between the questions if we are very quiet, okay?"

The Hey Dudes nodded and Wolf Dude pretended to lock his lips and threw away the imaginary key. The other guys followed suit.

I just sat on my hands and tried not to think of time slipping away from me, my Valentines Day with my honey running out. But despite my anxiety, I still listened in silence, wondering what we'd hear.

"Is there anyone here?" said Brett's recorded voice. After Fox Dude's joke repeated, there was a voice.

"Yessss…" It was a long, drawn out hiss of a whisper, so faint I thought maybe one of the guys in the room had shushed another.

They all looked at each other with wide eyes. They hadn't.

I shivered.

The recording went on, and we heard Brett ask for the compass to move. I thought I heard a grunt after that request. The Hey Dudes made faces at each other, pointing at the compass, which twitched again. Brett held up a hand to keep them quiet, eyes still focused on his phone.

Next on the playback came Brett's question, "…please, tell me, what has you upset?"

The voice came like a screamed whisper. "*Filthy!* Tidy up!"

We all traded silent, wide-eyed glances. I think I gasped. Brett's recording went on, playing Brett's questions, but there were no more replies from the voice.

During this, Brett scooted a foot further from the ottoman. His eyes didn't meet our glances, he stared at a point about three feet above the tattered piece of furniture.

"Like, what's it mean?" asked Fox Dude.

Brett cleared his throat and stood up, collecting his phone and compass. "It means, your ghost is pissed. She thinks you need to clean up around the place."

"She?" said the Hey Dudes in unison.

I asked, "How can you tell?"

Brett caught my eye, glanced at the door, and jerked his chin. "It... just sounded like a woman's whisper. Like someone's cranky grandma who likes everything in its place." He walked to the table and picked up the insulated pizza bag.

I made my way to the door, checking my cell phone again.

Jeff had sent, "Did you raise any spirits? I've got wine."

I replied with, "Very funny. Kinda creepy stuff here."

Wolf Dude beat me to the door, blocking Brett and me from opening it to leave. He held out his hands, palms up, in front of him. "Tell me, what do we do?"

Brett and I exchanged a look and I told the Hey Dudes, "I'd say you should do what the lady asks and tidy up around here."

"Will she stop bugging us if we do?"

Brett looked past Wolf Dude to a spot above the ottoman. He nodded, then looked at the shaggy guy and said, "Yeah, I think that's the deal."

"Aw man," I heard Fox Dude complain, "It's like having my *mom* live here!"

Wolf Dude sighed, relaxed his shoulders to a more natural slump, and smiled. "Thanks, Dude," he said, then added, "Dudes," and favored me with a bright smile. He stepped away from the door and held it open for us. Brett slipped out first.

"Uh, nice to meet you," I said. "Oh! Viola back at the store says to say hi. Hi!"

"Dude! Tell Viola to rock on!" He grinned at me and took a couple steps to the table. "Give her this for me, would you?" Wolf Dude took the receipt from the pizza box, scribbled something, and folded it up. He walked back to me, quite close, and placed the note in my hand. I liked the comforting warmth of his hand closing around mine. I expected him to smell of pot or patchouli, but instead, I smelled something like gingerbread.

I said, "Sure thing... Dude." I felt dumb for adding that, but it earned me a brighter smile from him.

"Don't open it, it's for Viola!"

"Of course I won't. I'm a *professional* delivery girl!"

My phone buzzed in my pocket at the same time Brett called from outside, urging me to get going.

Now who's in a hurry?

I left the Hey Dudes and trotted down their walk after Brett. "That freaky stuff back there, that's normal to you, isn't it?"

He nodded, getting in the car.

I got in the other side and barely had time to buckle up before Brett launched his Saturn down the street. I said, "You know more than you're saying, aren't you?"

He shrugged, looking at the road. "I told them the truth."

"What did you see over that ottoman?"

He glanced at me, then back at the road. "Noticed that, did you? Yeah, I saw the former owner of the ottoman, a prim little housewife dressed in 50s fashion, perched there after the compass moved. She had her arms folded in front of her, and a disgusted sneer on her face."

I thought a moment. "So why just the past week? I'd bet a lot those guys didn't just start living like pigs."

He laughed and shook his head. "You're a bright girl, Enid. No, I'd bet my tips for the night that they just got that ottoman at Goodwill a week or two ago, and that housewife came along with it."

"What? Why would she haunt furniture?"

"Who knows why any ghost haunts anything? Maybe it's the last piece of a set of furniture that was in her house, and even that's gone now. Maybe it had sentimental value,"

I checked my phone. "Is that guy you're training with being a creep?" I sent back a reply, "Strange. Not creepy. One more run and I can go, I think."

Something occurred to me. "So, if the Hey Dudes just got rid of that ottoman, wouldn't that take care of their problem?"

Brett snorted. "You got it."

"Then why didn't you tell them that?"

He shrugged. "I figured that place could use a woman's touch."

We both laughed at that one.

*   *   *

Brett pulled his car up in front of a little brick house on a dark street. There was a porch light on.

I recognized it. This was the witch's house.

No, not like Wiccan Earth Mother types, lighting candles to celebrate the full moon or whatever. I know some Wiccan, they're cool. They throw the best parties.

No, this was the old lady everyone talked about on this side of town. She lived alone, she seemed like was like a hundred years old when I was a little girl, and no one dared set foot in her yard. Not for wayward frisbees, not to sell Girl Scout cookies, and *not* for trick-or-treating.

She scared the hell out of kids.

Now we walked up to her door. On this cool spring night, I got a chill as a dew of sweat evaporated off the back of my neck.

Brett nodded at the door.

I shook my head. "I... I uh, got the last one."

Brett hefted the pizza bag and frowned at me.

My stomach knotted. "Aw, Brett..."

I was saved from having to knock by the door opening. Inside, in a dark entryway, stood a stooped old woman. She wore a white frilly dress that matched the thinning curls that framed her long, lined face. She seemed to chew as she spoke. "Do you have it? Just as I ordered?" Her voice sounded rich and strong despite her appearance. Her eyes shone with an intensity I didn't expect.

Brett said, "Yes, the special delivery you ordered, ma'am."

She huffed a breath. "Don't you 'ma'am' me, boy. It's got to be just right, you know. Hold on a moment, hold on, I'll be right back."

The door shut, and I heard her shoes clicking on the hardwood floor as she walked away from us inside.

"What?" I said, looking at Brett.

He just smiled. "Customer's prerogative."

I started a reply, but my phone buzzed.

My honey texted me, "Almost done yet? You should have some of this wine."

"Not yet. Special delivery to THE witch." Jeff grew up in this neighborhood, too, he'd know who I meant.

"Huh? What kind of pizza place is this? Are the Addams Family next?"

I shut my phone.

I heard her clicking shoes coming back, so I put away my phone and stood up straighter.

The door swung back and the old woman got in my face. "Let's see it." Her breath smelled like lavender mint.

Pretty sure I squeaked when I took a step back, and I almost stumbled into the grass.

Brett pulled out the pizza and opened the box. I could see and smell that it was an EBA - Everything But Anchovies. A "garbage pie" that had to weigh as much as a gallon of milk with all those layers of toppings. Usually a favorite of guys like the Hey Dudes or prank callers that sent expensive deliveries to random addresses.

She raised a spidery old hand and shook it over the pie, muttering something I couldn't hear. Flakes of something fluttered down, and I realized she had some kind of spice shaker.

Why add seasonings here at the door? Could it be a spell? Is it poison?

She took a deep breath of the steam that rose from the thick pizza and made a face I could only guess was a smile. I worried something might break off of her.

"Is that what you want delivered?" Brett asked.

She nodded and patted his arm. "There's a good boy." She glanced at me and her smile disappeared. "What are *you* looking at, girlie?"

"I... nothing, ma'am." I glanced back toward the car, the instinct to flee rising in me.

"Let's go, or we'll be late," said Brett, sliding the pizza back in the hot bag. He held it up with one hand and took my elbow with the other and turned me to march back to the car.

I looked back once as I got in.

She stared with those laser-beam eyes. Right at me.

I couldn't find my breath for a second, like I'd forgotten how.

Brett got in on his side and plopped the heavy pizza bag in my lap. I just stared at it while Brett buckled his seatbelt. *I didn't sign on for this! What pizza has a layover stop?*

The car started, and Brett pulled us away from that house, drove one block down, and stopped.

"What the hell, Brett?" I asked. My mind whirled. *Should I go along with this? What if the old lady had just poisoned the pizza before sending it to someone else? What does he know that he's not saying?*

He turned to me and said, "As I said, this is a *special* delivery. Follow my lead, okay? We're going on foot from here."

*   *   *

Let me tell you, it's rough carrying a heavy bagful of garbage pie, texting an irate boyfriend, and following a deranged pizza delivery ghost hunter around the darkened streets of Memphis, but somehow I managed it. I should get an award, maybe a scholarship, don't you think?

Brett shushed me. "For the last time, no, this isn't illegal, but we don't want anyone to see us doing it, okay?"

"But why are we walking?" I hated whining, but my honey had run out of patience. And the pizza weighed a ton.

"Like I said, people would notice us pulling up, and we'd look suspicious." Brett's voice dropped to a whisper. "Okay, down this alley. Can't risk a flashlight, so be quiet and watch your step!"

The old bag had better have tipped even better than the Hey Dudes for all this crap I'm going through.

The alley turned out to be paved in bricks, showing the age of the neighborhood. Fences and detached garages lined the alley, decorated with trash cans here and there.

Something the size of a small dog, with a naked rat's tail, scuttled across the alley in front of Brett. It stopped, and its beady eyes glowed *pink* as it turned its pointy nose in our direction and sniffed.

I didn't scream, the noise I let out sounded more like a leaky tea kettle at a low boil. My gut said to throw the garbage pie at the giant rat and run.

Brett grabbed a plastic garbage can lid, held it up like a shield in front of him, and charged the creature. It *hissed* and scurried into someone's yard.

"Oh my God," I whispered.

"Calm down, it's just a possum," he said, replacing the can lid.

"Really? I guess I've never seen one that's not dead on the side of the road before."

We walked past another couple of garages and heard giggling.

Brett held up a hand to stop. My phone buzzed, but I left it in my pants pocket.

I crept close to him and asked, "What's wrong?"

"Kids," he whispered. "Can't have kids seeing us go to the house."

I handed him the pizza bag. "I'll take care of this."

Before he could object, I marched toward the giggling and clapped my hands three times and said, "Hey!"

The giggling stopped. I waited. No sounds.

"I said, hey! Get out of there!"

I heard Brett groan behind me.

After a hushed conference, several teenaged girls slouched out into the alley. Their eyes darted around, anywhere but at me.

"What were you kids doing?" I said in my best babysitter voice. I put my hands on my hips and frowned at them.

"Well, we were just, I mean..." said one mousy girl, hair falling to conceal her eyes.

"It's not like anyone lives there..." said a strawberry blonde girl, who reminded me of an orange tabby cat my mom used to have.

"She dared me, it's not my fault!" crowed a third, dressed like a junior Goth wannabe, complete with a Jack Skellington T-shirt, black lipstick and too much eyeliner.

"You'd better go," I said. "You could get in trouble, trespassing like this."

Mouse tugged at Crow, who started to inch away, but Tabby stood her ground. "Says, who, a couple of pizza delivery dorks?"

I took a step toward the teen Goth chick. "Says a pizza delivery dork with a cell phone. One who knows you're out after curfew."

"You'd call the cops on us? Why, you think you'll get a better tip?"

"One," I said, quietly.

"Come on, let's go," said Mouse.

Crow glared at me. "Oh, like counting like my mom's gonna scare me."

"Two," I continued, narrowing my eyes.

Mouse grabbed Tabby's hand and dragged her down the alley at a jog.

Crow tried to stare me down, but glanced back as her friends bolted.

"Three," I said, taking my cell phone out of my pocket.

"Bitch," spat Crow as she took off down the alley after her friends.

I turned and curtseyed to Brett.

He favored me with that beagle grin of his and took the lead. "Nicely done. Just for that, I'll carry the pie."

I followed and snuck a look at my phone. More complaining from my honey. I tried to appease him by suggesting that I was working up a sweat with this delivery, so they'd *have* to let me off after this. I even threw in some sexual innuendo. He reminded me of the time again, so I just shut my phone and put it away.

I hate Valentine's Day.

Brett led me into the gap in the fence where the girls had come from. Tall weeds snagged on my jeans as we followed stepping stones around the garage and up to the back door.

He pulled out a key, unlocked the door, and opened it. He took a step in and looked back at me.

I stood there, shaking my head. "You're crazy. Why are we going in without knocking?"

"Like the teen girl squad said, no one lives here."

"Then why are we delivering pizza here? Why do you have a key?"

"Just trust me, okay?"

I sighed, looked around to see if anyone was nearby, hoisted up the lump of ice in my stomach, and slipped inside.

Brett used the flashlight on his cell phone to light the floor in front of us. Dust, dead flies, leaves, and other debris littered the floor. Bits of glass crunched underfoot. The smell of mildew permeated the air.

What a lovely place…

The back door had opened into a small kitchen. Brett led us down a hallway into a larger room, a round table with two chairs the focus of the room. Unlike the floors, walls, and other things in the house, the table and chairs appeared to be spotless, dust-free, and well-cared-for. I thought maybe there was the scent of lemon furniture polish to relieve my nose from the moldier odors of the house.

Brett set the bag down on a chair. He pulled something smallish, wrapped in paper, out of his back pocket. Tearing it open, he revealed five black candles in little chromed holders, which he set on the table at equal points around the table. He adjusted the chairs, positioned them between candles, one space apart. He ignored my questions about what he was up to.

Then, he pulled the pizza box out of the insulated bag, opened the box, and folded the lid underneath. The fragrance of the EBA pizza lost its charm amid the lemon and mold scents, and my stomach churned a bit, thinking of the dead flies littering the place.

Brett set the pizza in the center of the table and started lighting candles.

"Isn't that... isn't that a fire hazard?" I said, stomach continuing to rebel with nausea and a touch of fear.

Brett didn't answer me, muttering to the air. Or to himself.

I took two steps back and pulled out my phone and texted Jeff. "Creepy here. Candle pentagon around the pizza."

Jeff texted back, "Get out now!"

I shut the phone and backed up another step. The phone buzzed in my hand. I kept my eyes on Brett.

"Hang on, Enid. You'll want to see this," said Brett, his voice husky, eyes hidden in flickering shadows cast by the candles.

I paused. If I ran out now, I could call a cab and find another job. If I played along, maybe he'd just let me go on a promise not to tell anyone.

Too late for that.

"What's going on?" I asked.

"Just hang on. What time is it?"

I flipped open my phone. I had a text from my wireless carrier, saying my Phone Finder had been activated, my GPS coordinates had been sent to Jeff. I felt a tiny bit safer. "Uh, the time is ten fifty-eight. Why?"

"Just about time. Just stand back and watch." He turned his back to me to look at the table.

Run now!

But I didn't. I stared at the table with Brett. I thought I'd kept my eyes open too long, as a mist appeared before me, blanketing the room. I blinked a few times, but the mist remained, swirling around the perimeter of the candles and the table, wreathing one of the chairs.

"Holy crap," I whispered, as the mist condensed into an indistinct figure, sitting in one of the chairs. It looked like a guy in an old-fashioned suit of some kind, wearing a fedora. As the mist became more and more solid, I got the impression he was a young guy, no older than Jeff or me, maybe even younger, his sad eyes contrasted with a confident presence in a way that conjured up the image of a rooster in my mind.

The candle flames dimmed in his presence, guttering and wobbling like Beale Street drunks at last call. I felt a chill, though not so much in the air as deep down in my gut. The air thickened around me, leaving a metallic tang on my tongue as I drew in breath.

"Who... who is he?" My voice came out in a hoarse whisper, sounding like a stranger to my ears.

Brett looked away from the seated misty figure and met my eyes with his. "So, you *can* see him too?"

I nodded. "Yeah. Hello there, Bing."

He smiled and looked back at the spectral figure. "Naw, nobody that famous, but you're in the right ballpark."

The man made of fog paid us no mind whatsoever. He took his eyes from the circular feast laid out before him and gazed toward the front door. The longing on his face nearly broke my heart.

This is a guy who's been waiting on a date for decades.

Just a hunch, maybe influenced by the table setting for one, but I knew that had to be it.

Tall blue and red rectangles of lights flickered across the wall adjacent to the front door. These widened as they flowed rapidly across the wall to our side and behind us. The lights dazzled my dark-adjusted eyes, and I put a hand up to block them.

Brett and I said, "Shit!" at the same time. I looked at him and saw indecision in his eyes.

My mind raced. Had someone seen the candle light from the street? Had my honey used my phone's GPS and called the police?

"Let's run out the back," I suggested.

He shook his head. "Worse to get caught fleeing like we don't belong here."

"But we *don't*..."

There came a pounding on the door. "Police!"

I glanced at cocky, sad, fog boy. He disappeared with every flash of the light. I walked up to the door and opened it.

"Good evening, officer, happy Valentine's..." I began.

"Put your hands where I can see them, ma'am," said the dark, hunky, uniformed policeman. I put my hands out, palms up, and tried to smile.

I felt Brett's presence as he stepped up behind me. He said, "I can explain..."

The officer took a step inside. His car's spotlight, aimed at the door, flooded the room. I had a hunch that he wouldn't see our insubstantial dinner guest.

"Don't you need a warrant?" said Brett.

I shook my head. "Abandoned property." See? Pre-law was worth something after all.

The cop talked into the radio on his shoulder. Said he was apprehending trespassers.

My heart sank. Now, I stood a good chance of having this as a blot on my record. Not good for my chances of going back to law school. My cell phone buzzed in my pocket. I wanted to throw it to the floor and stomp it into tiny pieces.

Something blocked the light bathing us from the doorway. A black silhouette of a stooped figure, draped in a translucent, billowing aura. I felt the blood drain from my face. I tried to cry out, but my throat closed with fear.

The figure raised an arm, a long finger pointing at us. At me.

The silhouette spoke in a rich, commanding, feminine voice. "Get out of my house! All of you!"

I think no one would have blamed me if I'd peed myself right then and there.

She took a couple of slow clicking steps into the room and her features could be seen once she left the doorway. Our client, the old lady who ordered the EBA. She wore not just any white dress, but a wedding dress.

The cop let out a gust of breath next to me. "This is your house, ma'am?"

Her fierce eyes pinned the much larger man. "Yes! I don't live here, but I have the deed, if you care to check at the court house. Margaret Giordano, look it up. And how *dare* you interrupt my Valentine's ritual."

"Ritual?" asked the cop, glancing at the pentagon of candles surrounding the thick pizza.

"Yes! Every year, my Harry and I share a pizza on Valentine's Day. He's been gone since the war, but I keep up the ritual in his memory."

The cop looked at each of our faces, at Brett's hat and mine, at the pizza bag on the other chair and relaxed. "My apologies, ma'am. Enjoy your dinner."

Without another word to us, the policeman left. He shut off the spotlight and party lights when he reached his car. After a couple of long minutes, he drove off.

As the dark settled back in the room, the woman's Harry flickered back into existence, his gaze longing for his Margaret. She met his stare and tears melted away from her face, eyes bright now in the candlelight.

"I said, get out of my house," said Margaret, her tone softer than her words.

I wanted to hug her.

"Let's go, Enid," said Brett.

"One second," I said, holding up a finger. "Margaret, what was that you put on the pizza?"

She had eyes only for Harry as she crossed the room. "Basil. My Harry always has to have his basil on his pizza."

Brett took my arm and led me out. Before he shut the door, I saw Margaret sit and reach out a hand, met by Harry's, both of them looking beautiful in the candlelight.

*　　*　　*

Brett drove us back to the store. I'd let Jeff know how furious I was that he'd called the cops. He said he was worried about my safety. Maybe so, but I told him I didn't want to see him tonight after all. I shut the phone all the way off so I wouldn't be tempted to get into a nastier argument with him.

As we walked inside, Viola ran to me and touched my arm. "Enid! I heard you got in trouble with the cops!"

Bad news travels fast.

I shrugged. "Nothing came of it."

"I was so worried. I mean, out with Brett and then the police... I was right, wasn't I?"

I shook my head. "Not at all. I like Brett. Tonight was more fun than any Valentine's date."

Her eyes widened. "So you... and Brett..."

I laughed and pushed her hand off my arm. "Nothing like that at all. But I did get a note for you from one of the Hey Dudes." I reached into my pocket and produced the receipt.

She took it from me, face full of confusion. She unfolded it and smiled, handing it back to me.

The note said: "Viola, please give your friend Enid my number. I think she's cute. - Lowell" It included his digits.

My face warmed up and Viola grinned at me. She sang, "Enid likes a Hey Dude..."

I swatted at her. "Shut up. Well, he was kind of nice..."

Gonzo loomed over us. "Ladies, we'll start closing early tonight. We're dead, and I know Enid wants to get out of here."

Viola scurried off to start putting away toppings.

I shrugged. "My date's off, I'm on my own tonight. No rush."

He made a low growl and squinted at me. "Huh. Sorry. Didn't realize it was that urgent."

I smiled. "It's okay. I need this job more than I need... Well, never mind."

He nodded. "Hey, if you're at loose ends, I know a guy who's got an anti-Valentine's party going on. He's in food too, so it doesn't start until after midnight. I was thinking of going. I'd drag Brett along, but he's got plans."

Brett stuck his tongue out at Gonzo.

Gonzo made kissy faces at Brett. It was disturbing.

"Sure, why not? Beats sitting around, feeling sorry for myself. I'll pick up some beer to contribute on the way."

Gonzo clapped a paw-like hand on my shoulder. "That's the spirit!"

I thought of the candlelit couple, separated by time, felt the receipt in my pocket, and said, "I dunno about that. Maybe I'll invite a new friend along, too."

The Adventure Continues with The Tipsy Fairy Tales!

Here ends the Road Ghosts trilogy, but the characters and world live on in the Tipsy Fairy Tales! This was Brett's story, but Skye's has only begun. We met her in Sinking Down, caught up in the struggle, and now she is the star of her own epic. The Tipsy Fairy Tales takes place after Skye leaves Chicago with Stuart, having moved to Indianapolis. Much like Frannie and Brett find themselves changed by their experiences with the supernatural, Skye, too has changed, one foot forever in another spirit realm. Except Skye doesn't live partly in Shadow. She has a bit of her soul in what we'd call the world of fairies.

More specifically, the detached bit of Skye's soul has become her own little person, a spirit world sibling Skye calls Minnie. And though their connection never breaks, it is stronger when Skye's been drinking, since it puts her closer to the state she was in when she changed. In such a state, Skye sees the true forms of fairy folk who walk among us, seeing past their glamours and a bit into that other world.

She sees enough to know that there's danger all around her, even as she and her live action roleplaying friends pretend to be vampires. Skye is torn between the imaginary vampire world, the fairy realm, and her real life, living with her fiancé Stuart, working her day job as a barista.

The Tipsy Fairy Tales includes many crossovers with the. Road Ghosts, including some familiar faces, especially as the series progresses.

I am happy to present both series, set in the same world, to you, and if you enjoyed the Road Ghosts, I think you'll love the Tipsy Fairy Tales as well!

Oh, and if you should bump into the Transit King sometime, say hi for me, but be careful what you promise him.

About the Author

E. Chris Garrison writes fantasy and science fiction novels and short stories.

Her urban fantasies feature ghosts, demonic possession, and sinister fairy folk delivered with a "lightly dark" side of humor.

Her latest series is Trans-Continental, a steampunk adventure with a transgender woman protagonist. The series is set in one of the worlds in Chris's dimension-hopping science fiction adventure, Reality Check, also published through Silly Hat Books. Reality Check reached #1 in Science Fiction on Amazon.com in 2013. Silly Hat Books released Alien Beer and Other Stories, a collection of her short stories, in 2017.

Chrissy lives in Indianapolis, Indiana, with her wife, step-daughter and many cats. She also enjoys gaming, home brewing beer, and finding innovative uses for duct tape. Keep up on the latest news and releases from Chris at https://sillyhatbooks.com/

Photo Credit: (c) Ellie Sophia Photography

www.elliesophia.com